James Joyce's
DUBLINERS

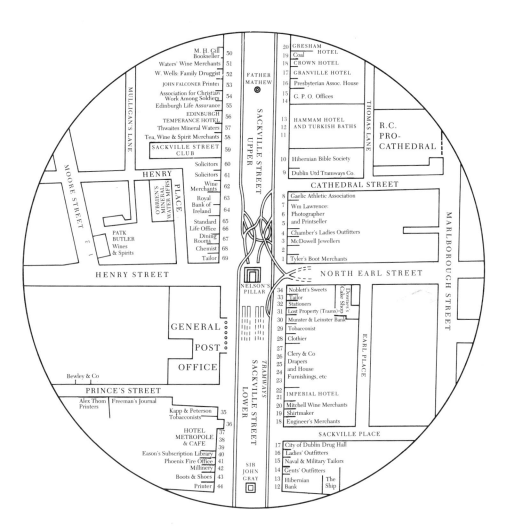

James Joyce's
DUBLINERS

AN ILLUSTRATED EDITION
With Annotations

JOHN WYSE JACKSON & BERNARD McGINLEY

St Martin's Press

Library of Congress Cataloging-in-Publication Data

Joyce, James.
    The Dubliners / James Joyce: edited by John Wyse Jackson and
Bernard McGinley. – An illustrated ed. (with annotations)
       p. cm.
    ISBN 0-312-09790-5
      1. City and town life–Ireland–Dublin–Fiction.   2. Dublin
(Ireland)–Fiction. I. Jackson, John Wyse. II. McGinley,
Bernard. III. Title.
  PR6019.09D8 1993c
  823'.912—dc20   93-17426
                                            CIP

First published in Great Britain 1993
by Sinclair-Stevenson
an imprint of Reed Consumer Books Ltd

Book design by Dorothy Moir and John Holmes

Maps drawn by
Leslie Robinson

Printed and bound in Great Britain by
BPCC Hazell Books Ltd
Member of BPCC Ltd

First U.S. Edition October 1993

10 9 8 7 6 5 4 3 2 1

Contents

Map: North central Dublin   vi
Introduction   vii
Map: South central Dublin   xvii

Childhood   1

THE SISTERS   2
Irish Homestead version of 'The Sisters'   10
AN ENCOUNTER   12
ARABY   21

Young Adulthood   28

EVELINE   29
AFTER THE RACE   35
TWO GALLANTS   42
THE BOARDING HOUSE   53

Mature Life   61

A LITTLE CLOUD   62
COUNTERPARTS   76
CLAY   88
A PAINFUL CASE   95

Public Life   105

IVY DAY IN THE COMMITTEE ROOM   106
A MOTHER   122
GRACE   135

'The Dead'   157

THE DEAD   158

Acknowledgements   200

North central Dublin

INTRODUCTION

James Joyce has been described, almost mean-inglessly, as one of the greatest writers the world has ever produced. In the years that are to come, it seems likely that he will be seen to dominate the literature of the twentieth century as William Shakespeare dominates that of the seventeenth. Today, however, to the so-called 'general reader', who is often deterred by Joyce's reputation, his writing is less familiar than Shakespeare's. His works are accused of being impenetrably obscure, or hopelessly Irish, or – only marginally better – utterly obscene. This general reader has heard that entire books have been devoted to extracting some degree of meaning from Joyce's ramblings, and every summer the more cynical Dubliner observes scholars from Japan and America risking their health and their cameras in pursuit of their obsession through the seedier areas of the Irish capital. As early as 1949, Myles na Gopaleen, a brilliant writer who chafed more than most under Joyce's shadow, was telling his readership in the *Irish Times* that Joyce had 'reduced the entire literary world into a state of chronic and helpless exegesis'. Joyce himself is said to have commented, rubbing his hands together, that *Finnegans Wake* would keep the professors busy for centuries.

However, what may be true about *Finnegans Wake* should not affect our appreciation of Joyce's earlier work. *Dubliners* was written to be profitably read at face value. A fine film was made by John Huston, which does no disservices of omission or commission to the work upon which it is based, 'The Dead'. Joyce intended the stories in this book to be as immediately accessible as the stories of Chekhov and de Maupassant. What then is the point of this annotated and illustrated edition?

At the end of 'The Dead', the snow, which is 'general all over Ireland', falls, in the famous phrase, 'upon all the living and the dead'. Every-one knows what snow is: cold, white accretions of frozen water, associated with Christmas, traffic problems and children's games. That is all you really need to know. However, if you examine a snowflake under the microscope, you will learn that each one is composed of crystals, that each crystal has a complex and regular pattern, and that no two are identical. So too with the stories in *Dubliners*. The pictures and notes of this book take a microscope to Joyce's first great work. It is hoped that the process will help to lay bare at least some of the half-hidden complexities, the local, historical and bio-graphical details, the forgotten jokes and the ill-remembered social habits of Dublin almost a century ago. Readers are assured that, unlike snowflakes, the stories of *Dubliners* will not melt away during the examination. They are of more durable stuff than snow.

Much more so than most, Joyce was an intensely autobiographical writer (often extend-ing the habit to include real people – a cause of embarrassment for some Dubliners in the 1920s and 30s). He stated specifically in a letter to his brother Stanislaus that the first three stories of *Dubliners* were 'stories of my childhood'. He might have gone on to say what Stanislaus already knew, that the other stories were also lightly adapted from elements of his own life. The process whereby Joyce transmuted the mundane elements around him into his clear, hard, engaging fiction can be clearly observed only when that reality itself is known. T. S. Eliot, in his preface to Stanislaus' memoir, *My Brother's Keeper*, agreed:

> In the case of James Joyce we have a series of books, two of which at least are so auto-biographical in appearance that further study of the man and his background seems not only suggested by our own inquisitiveness, but almost expected of us by the author himself.

We want to know who are the originals of his characters, and what were the origins of his episodes, so that we may unravel the web of memory and invention and discover how far and in what ways the crude material has been transformed. Our interest extends, therefore, inevitably and justifiably, to Joyce's family, to his friends, and to every other detail of the topography and the life of Dublin, the Dublin of his childhood, adolescence and young manhood.

While inquiry into family details can be carried too far, especially if it focuses on generations living long after the writer, the task of recreating the background of *Dubliners* is a useful one. As well as uncovering something of the lives of those who inadvertently contributed to the stories, this book attempts to convey a feeling of what it might have been like to live in Dublin between 1894 and 1905, the period of the stories. Taken largely from the contemporary newspapers and magazines that Joyce knew, read and appeared in, illustrations, quotations and advertisements have been juxtaposed with Joyce's text. It is hoped that this effort to reproduce visually some of the texture of Joyce's Dublin, as the stories do verbally, will be found both useful and entertaining.

One aspect of life in the Dublin – and the Ireland – of Joyce's time that is difficult to represent visually is the dominance of the Roman Catholic Church over its flock, which made up a large percentage of the country's population. Joyce was a child of the Jesuits, and although he was to reject Catholicism as a religion, he never entirely ceased to be influenced by their values and methods. This is not to say that he approved of their activities; merely that he had been to a great extent formed by them. Clongowes Wood College and Belvedere College, which taught Joyce almost all he did not teach himself up to university level, were both Jesuit establishments, as was University College itself. At Clongowes, Joyce had served at the altar during Mass, and at Belvedere, presumably because of his outward piety, he was for two years Prefect of the school Sodality, (which in effect made him head boy).

The various vicissitudes of the religious faith of Stephen Dedalus can be followed in *A Portrait of the Artist as a Young Man*, and run parallel to Joyce's own.

The results of spending his youth and adolescence steeped in this religious atmosphere can be clearly seen in *Dubliners*, where, as in Joyce's later work, the Church does not get a particularly good press. Although Joyce's artistic honesty would also lead him to record the benignity of Father John Conmee SJ (very much a 'real person') in *A Portrait* and the first section of 'Wandering Rocks' in *Ulysses*, sometimes Joyce seems to blame the priests for all the miseries of the people of Ireland, miseries which are amply portrayed in this book. In *Stephen Hero*, Ireland is described as

an island the inhabitants of which entrust their wills and minds to others that they may ensure for themselves a life of spiritual paralysis

– this spiritual paralysis, connived at by the priesthood, being one of the main themes of *Dubliners*.

Herbert Gorman, Joyce's first biographer, who worked under the dim but fastidious eye of Joyce himself, quotes one of Joyce's notes for *Stephen Hero/A Portrait*, which reads:

Spiritual and temporal power
Priests and police in Ireland

The implication is obvious and uncontroversial, and is explored in 'Grace', the opening of 'The Boarding House' and elsewhere, but the second phrase of the note contains an echo that says a great deal. *Priests and People in Ireland* (1902) was a widely read and reprinted book by Michael McCarthy, a Roman Catholic graduate of Trinity College, Dublin. Perhaps influenced by continental traditions, the book attacked what McCarthy saw as the crippling grasp that the Catholic priests had on the minds and pockets of their flock. Though it is unrecorded that Joyce read it, Stanislaus certainly did (he mentions it in *My Brother's Keeper*); it is furthermore equally unrecorded that Stanislaus ever read a book without Jim having done so first. McCarthy's work, which was either reportage or propaganda depending on what one thought of it, publicly dared to expose the Church from the inside, and in example after documented example the book accused the priesthood of what Joyce would certainly have considered institutional simony. As a source for Joyce's point of view when writing the first fourteen stories of *Dubliners*, it is impeccable.

The influence on Joyce of religion and its ritual was, however, not altogether a negative one. In a letter to his friend Con Curran written one rainy Friday in 1904, while Joyce was planning the collection that was to become *Dubliners*, he referred to 'The Sisters' as the first of his planned 'epicleti' – a word which he adapted from the ritual of the Orthodox Church, and meaning 'a prayer to invoke the Holy Ghost to transmute bread and wine into the body and blood of Christ'. Symbolism, so important in the Catholic Church, was to play an equally prominent part in all Joyce's writings, and not least in *Dubliners*.

A Companion to the Catechism, published in Dublin in 1886 and widely used in Irish schools, quotes the following:

> The altar, which is approached by steps, represents Mount Calvary. The crucifix placed at the top of the altar shows us Jesus Christ dying on His cross. The lighted tapers are symbolical of the faith and devotion with which the faithful ought to assist at the holy sacrifice. The sacred vestments, marked with the sign of the cross, indicate that the priest is the minister and visible image of Jesus Christ crucified, who is the principal and invisible High-priest. The inclinations and genuflections are acts of adoration and signs of respect. The multiplied signs of the cross, made by the priest over the Host and the chalice, tell us repeatedly that we are offering to the Heavenly Father the Divine Victim of the cross, and that we must unite ourselves to it by the love of the cross, of patience, and of Christian penance.

In short, while everything is entirely itself, at the same time everything has another, more significant meaning.

This is also the case in those 'naturalistic' stories, *Dubliners*. Surrounded for all his formative years by the elaborate and puissant symbolism of the Church, Joyce imported something like it into his fiction. Though it is not essential, if a member of a church's congregation knows the meanings of the 'different ceremonies', that knowledge will augment for him or her the potency of the holy Mass. For similar advantageous reasons, readers may, if they wish, keep an eye on Joyce's use of symbolism: the notes in this book make some suggestions as to where to look.

When he began the first of the stories that were to form *Dubliners*, James Joyce had written little and published less. In an influential London magazine there had appeared a perceptive critique of Ibsen's *When We Dead Awaken*, written when Joyce was seventeen. There were some essays, an unpublished play (Ibsenesque, and now lost), some translations and a good deal of poetry with a rather precious, turn-of-the-century air. Even in Dublin, Joyce was primarily known, if at all, as the author of an article, 'The Day of the Rabblement'. Published in pamphlet form, the article accused Yeats' Irish Literary Theatre of courting popular success instead of pursuing its original high artistic ideals – specifically its commitment to stage the modern plays from the continent that Joyce wanted to see, by writers such as Hauptmann, Ibsen, Strindberg and Maeterlinck, writers who formed an *avant-garde* in the best sense.

Joyce had also written his Epiphanies, literary equivalents of the Surrealists' *objets trouvés*. As Joyce conceived it, the 'epiphany' (from the Greek, 'a showing forth') was a fragmentary 'moment' invested with significance. The Stephen of *Stephen Hero* defined it as

> a sudden spiritual manifestation, whether in the vulgarity of speech or of gesture or in a memorable phase of the mind itself.

While not in themselves works of great merit, the epiphanies were the earliest positive indications that Joyce was to be much more than the sort of poetaster whose attitudes he would ridicule in 'A Little Cloud'. He was to incorporate several epiphanies into his later work, and their combination of the lyrical and the mundane was repeatedly echoed in the short stories. In the detail is the revelation and, like the epiphanies, the stories have a double purpose, being designed both as 'slices of life' and as bearers of a higher significance, where neither reading negates the other.

Because of the epiphanies or the poems (both of which Joyce carried round with him and showed to anyone who cared to look), or perhaps because of the 'Rabblement' attack, by the time Joyce met the leaders of the Irish Revival, Yeats, Lady Gregory and AE (George Russell), he was taken seriously enough.

AE controlled the *Irish Homestead*, a journal of 'agriculture and co-operation' (which Joyce blithely referred to as 'the Pigs' Paper'). The first story of *Dubliners*, 'The Sisters', was Joyce's response to AE's request for some writing with 'simple, rural, livemaking pathos' which would not shock the readers of the magazine. The nominal editor H. F. Norman paid Joyce one sovereign. 'Easy earned money ...', AE said, 'if you don't mind playing to the common understanding and liking once in a way.' Joyce (in a letter written in November 1916) said that after two stories Norman had told him that the readers had complained, and though three were finally published in the 1904 *Homestead* (under the name 'Stephen Dædalus'), it would be a long time before other complaints about *Dubliners* would stop.

Joyce by now had a book in mind. Even before he left Dublin with Nora Barnacle in the autumn of 1904, he had told Curran of his plans for a series of ten stories. In the following year, 1905, though busy also with Nora by the Adriatic, he wrote a number of other stories — 'The Clay', 'A Painful Case', 'The Boarding House', 'Counterparts' and 'Ivy Day in the Committee Room'. He also revised – to differing degrees – the published ones.

Despite Dublin's condition as a backwater (which it had been for a century, since the Union), and despite the hardiness of the pastoral myth – stronger in the Ireland of the Gaelic Revival than even in industrial England – urban

ideas could still percolate. Books from England were widely read. Though Joyce was later (in a letter to Grant Richards, October 1905) to point out that the word 'Dubliner' had some meaning – in contrast with 'Londoner' or 'Parisian', which he doubted had any – it may have been the following novel which gave him the idea for the title of the collection:

The Londoners

An Absurdity

By
Robert Hichens

Author of
' Flames,' ' An Imaginative Man,'
' The Green Carnation,'
etc., etc.

London
William Heinemann
1898

In September 1905 Joyce wrote to Stanislaus about *Dubliners*, by which time the structure of the collection had the now familiar four aspects (each containing a group of three stories): Childhood, Young Adulthood, Mature Life and Public Life. During that same month he wrote 'An Encounter' and 'A Mother', and in November he wrote 'Araby' and 'Grace'.

His twelve stories were now complete, but Joyce was not finished. 'Two Gallants' was conceived and written in January 1906, and 'A Little Cloud' brought the total up to fourteen by the following April. During an unhappy sojourn in Rome, where he was working as a bank clerk, Joyce continued to think of additional stories to write: 'Ulysses' was to be one, and among the others were 'The Last Supper', 'The Street', 'Vengeance', 'At Bay' and 'The Dead'. Joyce explained to Stanislaus in February 1907 that he could write them 'if circumstances were favourable'.

Though circumstances, and inspiration, were such as to allow only 'The Dead' to be written over the summer of 1907 (changing significantly the tone of *Dubliners* as a whole), Joyce's publication difficulties were already well under way. At first, apart from the discouraging attitude of the *Irish Homestead*, things had seemed to go well. In October 1905, the manuscript so far was sent to Grant Richards in London (whom Joyce before leaving Dublin had already unsuccessfully tried to interest in publishing *Chamber Music*). Richard liked the short stories and Joyce accepted his terms: the publisher proposed a plainly bound book costing five shillings, 'in a rather slim crown octavo volume, carefully printed in heavyish type on a rather yellow paper'. By March 1906 a contract was signed and publication was envisaged for September – or perhaps even as soon as May.

A month later, however, Richards sent Joyce back some of his material, asking him (at the printers' instigation) to suppress or modify 'The Two Gallants', and also objecting to passages in 'Counterparts' and to the use of 'bloody' in 'Grace'. Joyce was icily contemptuous of the worth of the printers' opinion. In the vigorous correspondence which followed, both men argued their positions well: Joyce knew the precision with which he had chosen his words and achieved his effects, and he stood by his work, which had been written in accordance, he said, with 'the classical traditions of my art'. Richards, however, who had followed closely recent literary brouhahas such as the scandal surrounding George Moore's *Esther Waters*, and who had not long previously gone bankrupt, could not afford to fail again. Furthermore, the printers were legally responsible for what they set, and regardless of what one thought of their judgement, they represented the market in microcosm – a commercial verdict it would be foolish to ignore. (Mysteriously, the printers began setting 'Two Gallants' first – two frag-

ments survive from this episode, one eloquently annotated 'we cannot print this'.)

Joyce defended the descriptive element in his writing – printers were setting sordid details every day in the newspaper reports from the divorce courts. While the printer denounced 'Two Gallants' and 'Counterparts', a Dubliner, said Joyce, would denounce 'Ivy Day in the Committee Room'. As for the 'enormity' of 'An Encounter', which 'the more subtle inquisitor' would denounce, the printer, being 'a plain blunt man', could not even see it. Richards wrote back, agreeing that *Dubliners* was 'what you wanted it to be – a chapter of the moral history of your country', but he felt unable to give way and still sought a rewriting of the numerous 'bloody' passages. (He later agreed that wherever it was used 'bloody' was 'the right word; on the other hand a publisher has to be influenced by other considerations'.) Joyce offered some concessions, but with jejunely Jesuitical logic had relentlessly asked again why the theme of 'An Encounter' – and, for good measure, that of 'The Boarding House' – were not objected to. As a result, 'An Encounter' joined the list of contentious aspects of the book, and its omission was requested (along with 'Two Gallants'), though Richards was prepared to accept (despite its salaciousness) the expression 'two establishments to keep up' in 'Counterparts'.

Soon the situation was a civil stand-off. Richards sent the balance of the manuscript back to Joyce in June, in the hope of various emendations. Joyce made it clear that he felt put-upon, but he duly resubmitted the book in July, having removed a number of 'bloodies' and having rewritten a 'Counterparts' passage (concerning the provocative behaviour of a young woman in Mulligan's of Poolbeg Street). He wrote to Richards at about this time:

> These are operations which I dislike from the bottom of my heart ... I will not conceal from you that I think I have injured these stories by these deletions but I sincerely trust you will recognize that I have tried to meet your wishes and scruples fairly.

Joyce insisted that he had 'written nothing whatever indecent in *Dubliners*'. At the same time, however, he unwisely said that he did not greatly care whether he had or not. After further futile exchanges with Grant Richards the manuscript was rereturned to Trieste in October.

Joyce was forced to begin again, and his postal expenses were soon mounting. In December 1906 he sent *Dubliners* to John Long, but this firm too declined to publish it. It went off to a number of other publishers: Hutchinson advised that it was pointless sending it to them. By 1908, Alston Rivers had also rejected it unseen. Arthur Symons tried it on the literary agent A. P. Watt, but that achieved nothing. Edward Arnold said no; Greening & Co said no; Archibald Constable said no; Sisley Ltd said yes, but only if Joyce substantially subsided it – which was almost worse than if they had said no in the first place.

The London publisher Elkin Mathews had in 1907 brought out *Chamber Music*, Joyce's first appearance in book form. Mathews had already suggested an approach to Maunsel & Co of Dublin (where Joyce already knew from the old days the occasional poet George Roberts, now its Managing Director), but it was not until 1909 that Joyce submitted *Dubliners* to the Irish publisher. By August of 1909 he had a contract for the book to appear within fifty-four weeks. At last, things seemed to be looking up, and an announcement even appeared.

DUBLINERS. By J. Joyce. Crown 8vo,
cloth. 3s. 6d. net   (*24th Nov.*)

A book of studies of Dublin life, which, although detached, is by no means a mere collection of sketches, but has a very distinct unity. Never before has this side of Dublin life been presented in quite so real a manner. The author's style at once removes the book from the category of ordinary fiction and makes it the piece of literature that will no doubt win the same recognition from discerning critics as did his book of poems published a few years ago, of which Mr. Arthur Symons wrote: " . . . so singularly good, so fine and delicate, and yet so full of music and suggestion, that I can hardly choose among them . . . to do such tiny evanescent things . . . is to evoke, not only roses in mid-winter, but the very dew on the roses. Sometimes we are reminded of Elizabethan, more often of Jacobean lyrics."

MAUNSEL & CO., LIMITED
96 Middle Abbey Street, Dublin.

The book soon ran into difficulties over the deemed offensiveness of 'Ivy Day'. One factor was the possibility of offending certain authorities (notably Dublin Castle and the Catholic hierarchy), the vernacular observations on Edward VII being found particularly objectionable – although the king's death in May 1910 ought to have eased that situation.

The delay in the publication of *Dubliners* affected the progress of Joyce's other writing and added to the already considerable domestic friction back in Trieste. (Significance might be found in the detail that the two men of his play *Exiles* bear the singularised names of both much-written-to potential publishers of *Dubliners*, Richards and Roberts.) Two years after his contract had been signed and stamped, in August 1911 the book still had not been published by Maunsel. Joyce, exhausted and exasperated, wrote to a multitude of newspaper editors (and also to Grant Richards) with a chronicle of his discontents, though only two printed his letter (one in Dublin, one in Belfast). What is particularly interesting about this statement is its public capitulation: it shows Joyce at the end of his tether. Reffering to 'Ivy Day', he wrote:

> I hereby give Messrs Maunsel publicly permission to publish this story with what changes or deletions they may please to make and shall hope that what they may publish may resemble that to the writing of which I gave thought and time.

Joyce's wrangles with George Roberts (who had refused to be shamed into submission) continued. Though the book had been set in 1910, and proofs printed, one postponement was followed by another. Joyce later had Herbert Gorman, his first biographer, hint darkly that 'influence was exerted' by a person no longer alive – meaning his old friend Thomas Kettle. In July 1912 Joyce travelled back to Dublin from Trieste in the hope of resolving these problems. He got a legal opinion confirming the harmlessness of 'Ivy Day' and 'An Encounter', but Roberts refused to accept it. Joyce then capitulated again and in August wrote to Messrs Maunsel that 'An Encounter' could be omitted providing that this was made known in a foreword, and that the incomplete *Dubliners* be published by 6 October 1912 (Ivy Day). Roberts promptly made new difficulties and sought impossible indemnities. He asserted that the opening of 'Grace' was offensive, as well as three paragraphs of 'Ivy Day' and part of 'The Boarding House', and he asserted that the use of real names – e.g. of pubs or railway companies – was unacceptable in the stories. (Joyce plaintively argued that nothing happened in the public houses: people drank.)

Still in Dublin, Joyce emulated Farrington of 'Counterparts' and pawned his watch in an attempt to keep the project alive. By early September he had agreed with Roberts to take over the thousand unbound sets of sheets himself: his plan was to publish his book in Dublin with the help of his brother Charles, under the imprint of the Jervis Press. Roberts typically reneged on this and so Joyce decided to bring out the book in Trieste – this time with the help of Stanislaus, under the imprint of the Liffey Press. But now Roberts' printer, John Falconer, raised his own objections to *Dubliners* and refused to release the sheets to Joyce. (The diatribe 'Gas from a Burner' was at one stage titled 'Falconer Addresses the Vigilance Committee', but eventually Joyce decided that his little local *Dunciad* should not deign to so dignify such a knave.) Fortunately, Joyce had already obtained through a subterfuge a full set of proofs, but the mounting adversity was quite enough for him: on the day in September 1912 when the entire edition of sheets of *Dubliners* was destroyed, he left the city. Roberts, until his death in 1953, never again wished to speak of Joyce. Joyce, for his part, never returned to Dublin.

Martin Secker then said no to the book. Elkin Mathews and also John Long said no, again. Mills and Boon said no. However, in late 1913, during the Dublin Lockout and with the Home Rule crisis rapidly deepening, Joyce got back in touch with Grant Richards, and soon was writing about the possibility of resuming their arrangement:

In view of the very strange history of the book – its acceptance and refusal by two houses, my letter to the present king [whom Joyce had vainly lobbied], his reply, my letter to the press, my negotiations with the second publisher – negotiations which ended in malicious burning of the whole first edition – and furthermore in view of the fact that Dublin, of which the book treats so uncompromisingly, is at present the centre of general interest, I think that perhaps the time has come for my luckless book to appear.

Richards received the set of Maunsel proofs, as well as Joyce's proposed preface, 'A Curious History' (which was in fact published by Ezra Pound in *The Egoist* in January 1914). Here Joyce documented in detail his difficulties, one in particular of which was impossible to overcome:

...Then Messrs. Maunsel asked me to pay into their bank as security £1,000 or to find two sureties of £500 each ...

Although Richards did not know how much the manuscript had changed since the wrangles of eight years previously, he indicated his willingness to publish *Dubliners*, subject to certain clarifications – e.g. on the likelihood of libel, about which Joyce assured him there was none. Joyce also agreed to the suggestion that 'A Curious History' be replaced by someone else's introduction.

Progress was rapid, and *Dubliners* finally appeared (without an introduction) on 15 June 1914, the eve of the tenth anniversary of Bloomsday. 1,250 copies were published (of which Joyce was obliged to take 120). The 379 copies sold by the end of that year scarcely compensated for the fact that ten summers had passed since 'The Sisters' had first appeared in the *Irish Homestead*.

The basic text of *Dubliners* in these pages is this 1914 first edition, the last version to which Joyce made any substantial revisions. However, the long and frustrating process of battling with publishers, the prospect of at last seeing his book in print, and the fact that he optimistically and mistakenly thought he would get one final opportunity for a revision, meant that Joyce failed to achieve some of his preferences on various matters of style. After all, his book *was* coming out, he was exhausted by the struggle and he was now busy with other writing. Some alterations have therefore been made in this edition to accord with Joyce's expressed – but ignored – wishes.

The most immediately noticeable change is that the punctuation dashes have been restored in accordance with Joyce's then preferred style. In a letter of March 1914 to Grant Richards, he repeated his consistent opinion of inverted commas that they gave 'an impression of un-reality' and were

> an eyesore. I think the page reads better with the dialogue between dashes ...

Although Joyce's original manuscripts had dashes wherever inverted commas would con-ventionally have been, and in other places as well, this device proved ungainly – especially in the case of asides and parentheses. In his own revision, such as the second fair copy of 'Ivy Day', Joyce himself arrived at the style which has been adopted in this volume. The same elegant and readable style can be seen in the first edition of *Stephen Hero* (London, 1944).

Additionally, Joyce's sparing use of the comma – often reflecting speech patterns rather than grammar – has had to be attended to, as each successive copy-editor and print-setter of the stories added another speckling of them (and sometimes lost a few as well). This corrective process involves editorial judgement on con-textual grounds, as in many cases Joyce's alter-ations are indistinguishable from those of others. The original informality of style has also been restored in such words as 'the pope', 'the mass', 'the park' etc.

Furthermore, for various reasons, some of Joyce's revisions failed to appear in the first edition. These have now been included. In several other cases, his revisions of the 1910 proofs show Joyce returning to words and phrases from an earlier version of the manu-script: for example, Maria in 'Clay' has a 'rain-cloak' in the 1910 Maunsel proofs but a 'waterproof' in the manuscript, in the 1914 Richards proofs and in the first edition. In this edition, the question has been decided – as it

surely was by Joyce – in favour of the latter. Many other textual variants are recorded in the notes.

Because of the contradictions (which are minor) between the Roberts and Richards ver-sions and the 'Corrected Text' of 1967, and given also the incomplete *stemma* of Joyce's manuscripts, proofs and published versions, each differing from the other, the curious history of *Dubliners* makes a definitive text impossible to achieve. Inevitably, any text of *Dubliners* must be based on aesthetic as well as historical con-siderations. But Joyce's preferences, as far as they can be established, are a target towards which this edition aims.

Joyce himself was never to forget his first book of prose. His Paris friend Robert McAlmon reported that Joyce wondered in the mid-1920s whether it might not have been better to have developed his writing in the 'Dubliners' style 'rather than going into words too entirely'. Joyce elsewhere said that *Ulysses* was a continuation of *Dubliners*, and it is true that many of the characters and concerns of the stories appear in the novel. In the same way, the logorrhoeal maze that is *Finnegans Wake* may be seen as a continuation of *Ulysses*. Personages from *Dubliners* survive to attend the universal *Wake*, and what is more, on pages 186–7 of that book there are hidden in a single paragraph the titles of all the stories. The *Wake* bears glorious witness to Joyce's continued determination (expressed in *Stephen Hero*) to do battle against possible banishment

> to what he now regarded as the hell of hells – the region, otherwise expressed, wherin everything is found to be obvious ...

There is a difference, however, between what is not obvious and what is obscure. While the difficulty of Joyce's last book cannot be denied, for too long the academic James Joyce industry has given the impression that all Joyce's works share in the *Wake*'s obscurity. In his writing Joyce practised precision, and one of the great joys of *Dubliners* is its readability: the first twenty-three words of 'The Sisters', for example, are monosyllables. Each story tells it straight, and the puzzles are mostly to be found elsewhere than in its language.

Still, the accessibility of *Dubliners* is also somewhat lessened by a factor over which even Joyce had no control: the passage of time. Things have altered in almost a century of the most rapid change since the disappearance of the dinosaurs. Furthermore, Edwardian Dublin was in every sense another country. Politically it was part of the United Kingdom and for many Irish Nationalists it was a Crown-dominated urban carbuncle on the face of Gaelic Ireland: having been within the Pale, it would never be truly Irish. Except for an almost entirely Church of Ireland (Protestant) élite, socially it was backward. Religiously it went to Mass. Dublin's housing and public health were a slow scandal. It was a city that we cannot now know at first hand.

In combination with the specifically local setting of the stories, the time-gap has given rise to certain confusions and misunderstandings. The 'barrels of pigs' cheeks' mentioned by the narrator in 'Araby', for example, were assumed by at least one reader to be barrels of beer, whereas pigs' cheek was (and is) a cheap cut of bacon eaten in Ireland. Even in 1914 the *Times Literary Supplement*'s review of *Dubliners* considered it helpful to point out what a 'curate' was in the context of a Dublin pub. There are many other half-forgotten details of Joyce's world that inform his writing, including old street-names and old street furniture, political, religious and literary ideas, newspapers and the stories in them, social and municipal institutions and customs, ephemeral slang terms, the local politicians and other personalities of the city, and Joyce's own family and its circle of acquaintances. Sometimes even the decade that elapsed between Joyce's embarking on *Dubliners* and its publication was long enough to obscure an illuminating nuance. An increased knowledge of some of these details can only increase the reader's appreciation of the causes and effects of the collection, and of the writer's skill in controlling them.

From the evidence of his books alone, Joyce was obviously extremely well-read. *Dubliners* contains many echoes of works by other writers, a few of which are acknowledged in the stories – Caroline Norton's poem in 'Araby', for example, or Byron's in 'A Little Cloud'. The Dantean structure of 'Grace' was testified to by Stanislaus in *My Brother's Keeper*, and is incontrovertible. There is also a large number of unacknowledged quotations, from sources such as Shakespeare, Jonson, Milton, Dickens, Pope, Shelley, as well as from the classics and the Bible. These (or rather, many of these) have been identified in the notes, but it should be borne in mind that such identification does not necessarily imply that Joyce always consciously borrowed the phrase or idea in question: it is sometimes more profitable to view such echoes as fruit stemming from Joyce's cultivation of the rich soil of past literature. In a similar spirit, the notes also indicate occasional areas where the later Joyce – and also several other writers after him – used *Dubliners* for inspiration or allusion.

The indisputable test of a written work of art is generally acknowledged to be that of time. *Dubliners* is approaching its centenary, and will be read long beyond that. There is also a more personal test which involves time. How long can a reader profitably and with continued enjoyment spend reading and re-reading a book? As editors and annotators of this book, we have carried out this secondary test, having spent many hours, days, weeks and months reading, thinking about and discussing *Dubliners*. We are glad to report that as time went by the stories became richer and more rewarding. Joyce's sardonic wit, not always immediately evident in this book, came closer to the surface. His astringency bit. The precision of his imagery showed itself in wordplay, in documentary detail, in the interrelationship of parts. Joyce's other works, *Ulysses* in particular, also gained an added lustre. And yet it became clear that a great deal was going to have to be left unsaid. All great works of art are, finally, unknowable.

However, as we read, annotated, re-read and re-annotated, one common element slowly emerged as the basic motive behind the book. Although Joyce's art, like Wilde's, avoids an explicit moral stance, the stories read like modern parables, whose characters – incomplete, lonely, paralysed, spiritually and physically impoverished, betrayed and betraying – have been damaged by dishonesty, be it their own or that of others. The stance from which Joyce was writing is one that the rejected Christianity of his youth shared with the abandoned socialism of his young manhood. It is applicable both to victim and perpetrator: dishonesty leads to misery. It is a lesson worth learning.

John Wyse Jackson
Bernard McGinley

London and Dublin
15 June 1992

A NOTE ON THE ANNOTATIONS: Those who do not know *Dubliners* are advised to read each story before coming to the notes: there is no initial substitute for one's own personal reaction. This book is one version of ours. The notes do not claim to tell the reader what to think, but are an attempt to suggest how some of the byways of Joyce's fictional city may be explored.

References in the notes to other books are self-explanatory, with a few exceptions. Stanislaus Joyce's memoir *My Brother's Keeper* is *MBK*. *Stephen Hero* is simply noted as *SH* (as even the chapter numbers vary from edition to edition). There are too many editions of *A Portrait of the Artist as a Young Man* and *Ulysses* for page numbers to be useful (though *Finnegans Wake* is still standard in this respect): instead, references are to chapters and (where applicable) sections. This will involve some enthusiastic riffling, itself no bad thing.

xvi

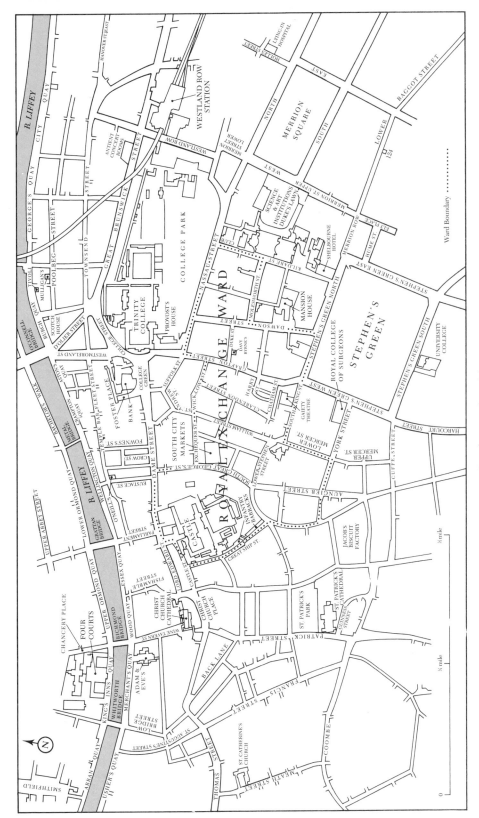

South central Dublin

Childhood

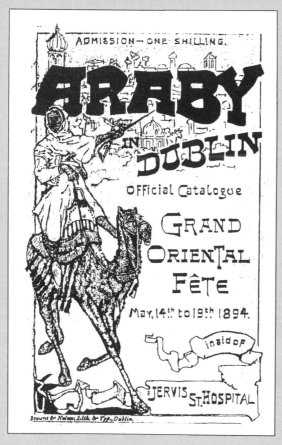

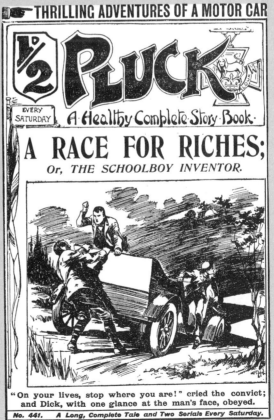

Clockwise from top left:

★ *Dante with Vergil: 'Abandon hope ye who enter . . .' (2b).*
★ *Title page (21f), with a prayer from the book.*
★ *Dublin in the 1890s.*
★ *Cover of Pluck (12d).*
★ *Advertisement for the Union Jack (12c).*
★ *An artist's impression of the 'Araby' catalogue.*

NOW ON SALE!

Look out for HERBERT MAXWELL'S latest and best Long, Complete Novel, entitled:

THE SLAVES OF SANTA FÉ;

Or, THE ROMANCE OF A COALMINE.

This powerful story is certain to win a lot of new readers for the

UNION JACK

A COMPLETE NOVEL for
ONE HALFPENNY.

"Come, do as I tell you; push back the stone!" Very sullenly and reluctantly the man obeyed. (*The above is a thrilling incident in this week's UNION JACK.*)

THRILLING ADVENTURES OF A MOTOR CAR

½ **Pluck** ⅞

EVERY SATURDAY

A Healthy Complete Story Book.

A RACE FOR RICHES;

Or, THE SCHOOLBOY INVENTOR.

"On your lives, stop where you are!" cried the convict; and Dick, with one glance at the man's face, obeyed.

No. 441.   A Long, Complete Tale and Two Serials Every Saturday.

a) THE SISTERS: The title is discussed in the Afterword.

b) *There was no hope*: The opening phrase serves as a welcome to the reader and recalls Dante's well-known warning: 'Abandon hope ye who enter ...' (*Inferno* III.9). The first sentence is composed entirely of monosyllables, like the first line of Joyce's first book and the last line of his last.

c) *the third stroke*: Not, as might be thought, of a clock. A third stroke is popularly supposed to be fatal.

d) *lighted square of window*: Light and dark are abiding images in *D*. The boy stands in the dark and looks at the light, as will many characters in the book. The windows in Great Britain Street were not actually square, but oblong, except on the top floors.

e) *two candles must be set at the head of the corpse*: Candles are to appear several times, and this early mention suggests that they can be interpreted as a sign of death in *D*.

f) *I said softly to myself the word*: Joyce was always interested in the relationship between the sound and meaning of words, and with the very strangeness of naming things at all, as discussed in *P* (V. 1) with 'home', 'Christ', 'ale' and 'master'.

g) paralysis: Paradoxically, the Greek root means 'to be loosened'. Like 'gnomon' and 'simony', the word indicates a theme of the collection. Joyce wrote in 1904 that the book was called *D* 'to betray the soul of that hemiplegia or paralysis which many consider a city'. (Hemiplegia is a paralysing stroke, usually caused by a lesion or clot in the brain.)

h) *the word* gnomon *in the Euclid and the word* simony: The word 'gnomon', which is linked with gnosticism, has several related meanings. It is an interpreter or indicator (particularly of a sundial), a t-square as used by masons and carpenters, and jocularly, 'the nose'. Gnomons are also the (large, yellow) teeth of a horse, used to tell its age. In geometry, a gnomon is the part of a parallelogram (or any rectangle) which remains after a similar parallelogram is taken away from one of its corners. (The idea is therefore analagous to a community or family after the death of one of its members.)

Joyce knew *The Elements of Euclid, For the Use of Schools and Colleges* (1862), edited by I. Todhunter, MA FRS, and mentioned ('toadhauntered') in *FW* (293). Joyce also later had a copy of H. S. Hall and F. H. Stevens, *A Text-Book of Euclid's Elements* (1900), stamped 'J.J.' The Catechism of 1877 from the German of the Jesuit, the Rev. Joseph Deharbe, quotes the first Commandment: 'I am the Lord thy God. Thou shalt not have strange gods before me; thou shalt not make to thyself any graven image, to adore it'. The Catechism then asks:

> May we sin in any other way against the first Commandment?
> Yes; we can sin also against the first Commandment by idolatry, superstition, witchcraft, sacrilege, and simony.

Deharbe continues:

> Who is guilty of simony?
> He who buys or sells spiritual things, preferments and the like, for money or money's worth; as Simon, the magician, intended to do.

This is Simon (Magus) of Samaria, the sorcerer who offered money to the Apostles for his spiritual advancement. *Inferno* Canto XIX begins (uniquely) with an address to Simon Magus. Joyce's use of the name for Stephen's father in *P*, *SH* and *U* is hardly an accident. The boy's three words are examined in the Afterword.

i) *Old Cotter was sitting at the fire, smoking*: This second paragraph begins *in medias res*, and bears no relation to the previous 'now'. There were several Cotters known to the Joyces: Patrick Cotter, grocer, tea wine and spirit merchant on Lower Drumcondra Road; William Cotter, Commercial Traveller, of 2 St Peter's Terrace, Cabra in 1902, when the Joyces lived at No 7; and the most likely model for Old Cotter, E. G. Cotter, with whom John Joyce had worked in the Collector General's office. Joyce might also have heard his father speak of Patrick Cotter O'Brien (c. 1761–1806), a circus giant said to have been over eight and a half feet tall, from County Cork, or, indeed, of property which Joyce *père* owned in Cotter Street, Cork. In English, the noun

THE SISTERS

THERE WAS NO hope for him this time: it was the third stroke. Night after night I had passed the house (it was vacation time) and studied the lighted square of window: and night after night I had found it lighted in the same way, faintly and evenly. If he was dead, I thought, I would see the reflection of candles on the darkened blind, for I knew that two candles must be set at the head of the corpse. He had often said to me: *I am not long for this world*, and I had thought his words idle. Now I knew they were true. Every night as I gazed up at the window I said softly to myself the word *paralysis*. It had always sounded strangely in my ears, like the word *gnomon* in the Euclid and the word *simony* in the Catechism. But now it sounded to me like the name of some maleficent and sinful being. It filled me with fear, and yet I longed to be nearer to it and to look upon its deadly work.

Old Cotter was sitting at the fire, smoking, when I came downstairs to supper. While my aunt was ladling out my stirabout he said, as if returning to some former remark of his:

—No, I wouldn't say he was exactly . . . but there was something queer . . . there was something uncanny about him. I'll tell you my opinion . . .—

He began to puff at his pipe, no doubt arranging his opinion in his mind. Tiresome old fool! When we knew him first he used to be rather interesting, talking of faints and worms; but I soon grew tired of him and his endless stories about the distillery.

—I have my own theory about it, he said. I think it was one of those . . . peculiar cases . . . But it's hard to say . . .—

He began to puff again at his pipe without giving us his theory. My uncle saw me staring and said to me:

—Well, so your old friend is gone, you'll be sorry to hear—

—Who? said I—

—Father Flynn—

—Is he dead?—

—Mr Cotter here has just told us. He was passing by the house—

means: 1) cottager, 2) bolt, locking-pin, 3) entanglement, trouble. The verb 'to cotter' means to coagulate or clot (as of blood), thus providing a link with Fr Flynn's stroke.

j) *stirabout*: Porridge. Stirabout rather than potatoes was the staple diet in parts of Gaelic Ireland.

k) *faints and worms*: In the first version of the story the words seem to apply to the 'batch of prize setters' kept by Old Cotter, but in fact they are from the distillery trade: a worm is a long spiral tube in which the vapour from the still is condensed, whereas faints are impure spirits produced early and late during distillation. Purity of spirit at the beginning as well as at the end of life is a concern of 'The Sisters'. Joyce's father had been Secretary of the Dublin & Chapelizod Distillery Company (95e).

l) *my own theory*: Cotter's 'theory' is never stated. Drink, some homosexual misdemeanour, simony, and even syphilis have all been unprovably suggested.

m) *My uncle*: The boy is living with his uncle and aunt: his parents are presumably dead. The uncle is a clear portrait, however, of Joyce's father. Flann O'Brien later used similar uncle/father figures in his novels.

n) *Who?*: This, with 'Is he dead?' is the only direct speech from the boy.

Vergil and Dante examine the simoniacs (2h)

a) *I knew . . . me*: The boy at once the perpetrator and the victim of dissembling.

b) *a great wish for him*: An idiomatic phrase from the Irish: *Bhí meas mór aige air*, 'he had a high opinion of him', 'he esteemed him greatly'.

c) *like that*: Like what? We never actually learn – one of many examples of what Phillip Herring has called 'Joyce's Uncertainty Principle'.

d) *Am I right, Jack?*: In the earlier version 'John' (10).

e) *Let him learn to box his corner*: To stand up for himself. In carpentry it means to make an angle by joining planks with a tenon and mortise joint. A box in a corner could resemble the diagram of a gnomon.

f) *rosicrucian*: The Rosicrucians were a society or order which was supposedly founded by a 'magus', one Christian Rosenkreuz in 1484. During his 'Golden Dawn' period, W. B. Yeats became involved with Rosicrucianism. Shelley, when he was nineteen, published a Gothic novel, *St Irvyne, or The Rosicrucian*. Here, however, the word is simply used derisively: a dreamer, a young Stephen Dedalus.

g) *a cold bath*: This has been seen as an echo of the baptism ceremony, but is a traditional bromide.

h) *Education is all very fine and large . . .*: A dismissive attitude which will be shared with Mr Kernan in 'Grace' (149k).

i) *the safe*: Meat was stored away from flies in a meatsafe, usually kept outside or in a cool scullery.

j) *their minds are so impressionable*: The Jesuits famously turned such a situation to their advantage.

k) *rednosed*: The beacon of the drinker. In *U*, 'Proteus', Stephen ruefully recalls: 'You prayed to the Blessed Virgin that you might not have a red nose'.

l) *paralytic*: The word is still a slang term for being helplessly (and culpably) drunk.

m) *Christmas*: Birth, as opposed to death. Conventional pictures of the Christmas Story show shepherds and others with 'blankets' over their heads. Christmas is returned to in 'The Dead'.

n) *the grey face still followed me*: After his mother's death, Joyce was similarly visited at night by a skull.

o) *I understood that it desired to confess something*: In his dream, the boy puts himself into the position of a priest. While at Belvedere, where he was for two years Prefect of the Sodality of Our Lady, Joyce was asked to consider taking Holy Orders. His connection with church sodalities continued into his early years at University – which is not the impression given in *P*. To some extent this story can be seen as an exploration of the author's youthful experiences of the Catholic Church. In *SH* the

I knew that I was under observation so I continued eating as if the news had not interested me. My uncle explained to old Cotter:

—The youngster and he were great friends. The old chap taught him a great deal, mind you; and they say he had a great wish for him—

—God have mercy on his soul, said my aunt piously—

Old Cotter looked at me for a while. I felt that his little beady black eyes were examining me but I would not satisfy him by looking up from my plate. He returned to his pipe and finally spat rudely into the grate.

—I wouldn't like children of mine, he said, to have too much to say to a man like that—

—How do you mean, Mr Cotter? asked my aunt—

—What I mean is, said old Cotter, it's bad for children. My idea is: let a young lad run about and play with young lads of his own age and not be ... Am I right, Jack?—

—That's my principle too, said my uncle. Let him learn to box his corner. That's what I'm always saying to that rosicrucian there: take exercise. Why, when I was a nipper every morning of my life I had a cold bath, winter and summer. And that's what stands to me now. Education is all very fine and large ... Mr Cotter might take a pick of that leg of mutton, he added to my aunt—

—No, no, not for me, said old Cotter—

My aunt brought the dish from the safe and laid it on the table.

—But why do you think it's not good for children, Mr Cotter? she asked—

—It's bad for children, said old Cotter, because their minds are so impressionable. When children see things like that, you know, it has an effect ...—

I crammed my mouth with stirabout for fear I might give utterance to my anger. Tiresome old rednosed imbecile!

It was late when I fell asleep. Though I was angry with old Cotter for alluding to me as a child, I puzzled my head to extract meaning from his unfinished sentences. In the dark of my room I imagined that I saw again the heavy grey face of the paralytic. I drew the blankets over my head and tried to think of Christmas. But the grey face still followed me. It murmured; and I understood that it desired to confess some-

relationship has somewhat deteriorated: for Stephen, the Church is beset by weakness and 'nervous tremblings'; it fears or distrusts 'day and joy' and 'man and life'. This is 'hemiplegia of the will' in the body of the Church, which is 'burdened and disaffected' by the priests, 'black tyrannous lice'.

A contributor to red noses, from Thom's Directory

a) *pleasant and vicious region*: An allusion to the East (5s). As always, Joyce chooses his words carefully; there is a hint that the boy is making an incursion into the region of solitary and pleasurable vice.

b) *paralysis . . . simoniac*: These two strange ideas are coupled again in the boy's brain. There is no indication, however, that Fr Flynn is technically guilty of simony.

c) *Great Britain Street*: Named after Great Britain, the street was then a busy, though not particularly prosperous shopping street, crossing both sides of the top of Sackville (O'Connell) Street. It is now Parnell Street.

d) Drapery: Various draperies came and went here over the years. Mrs Dignam, silk mercer, linen draper, hosier and haberdasher, had been at No 149 in 1850, when Mrs Alicia Donovan, cap and umbrella maker, was at No 40, and Eleanor Wyer, draper, was at No 117. By the mid-1890s all these shops had gone, and among the drapers in the street were the Misses O'Leary, the Misses Monaghan, and William and Maria O'Connell, draper, outfitter and boot warehouse at No 79. This is one contender for the model of the house in this story, as John Joyce was related to the family, which had a silenced priest in its past. However, it is difficult to be certain: the Monaghans seem equally likely, and Flynn was the maiden name of the aunts upon whom the sisters of 'The Dead' were based. For Joyce, there was no shortage of material in those draperies.

e) Umbrellas Recovered: The concept of recovery casts a shadow over this story: Fr Flynn wants to recover his Irishtown past, and his sisters bury him in his vestments in an attempt to recover his full priesthood.

f) *crape bouquet*: Now usually 'crêpe'; probably, in fact, Irish poplin, which was widely used for funeral purposes in Dublin at this time.

g) *July 1st, 1895 [etc]*: The date was a Monday, half way through the year, the Feast of Christ's Holy Blood, and technically the anniversary of the Battle of the Boyne. But 1895 could be seen as the start of a new technological era: Marconi's wireless telegraph was beginning, the cinematograph first saw the light, and during that year Röntgen first demonstrated his X-Rays. Fr Flynn was of another age, born in 1829 or 1830, and coming to adulthood during the famine. In the first published version of the story the date was printed as 'July 2nd, 189–', but in the later manuscript Joyce wrote the year as 1890.

The Rev. James Flynn: It seems likely that Joyce based Fr Flynn on a real priest, perhaps a Rev. O'Malley who lived in North William Street c. 1893–5 or one of his O'Connell relations who had his parish taken from him. In the book, only Jimmy Doyle, of 'After the Race', also shares Joyce's Christian name.

S. Catherine's Church, Meath Street: Dedicated to St Catherine (of Alexandria), Virgin and Martyr (d.307), whose day is 25 November. It was built in 1852–8 in the old part of the city, the parochial headquarters having previously moved from the fugitive church in Dirty Lane which was used during the penal times. This church and parish should not be confused with the Church of Ireland St Catherine's around the corner in Thomas Street.

h) *High Toast*: A light-coloured snuff, manufactured in Ireland by Grants and by Gallahers. It could be bought from Patrick O'Keeffe, tobacconist, at No 199 Great Britain Street. The words 'High Toast' seem to combine most economically the liquid, solid and spiritual elements of the Mass, and the scene parodies a priest and an altarboy using incense during a service.

i) *his hands trembled . . .*: As Florence Walzl has pointed out, Fr Flynn's symptoms are closer to those of Parkinson's Disease than to those of a series of strokes, which very often affect speech. However, in the case of palsy, cognate with paralysis, loss of sensation and movement can be coupled with trembling.

j) *little clouds*: Clouds have an important presence throughout *D*, as in the later story, 'A Little Cloud'. The images used here in Joyce's treatment of dry snuff are uncommonly liquid: clouds; dribbled; showers; green.

k) *red handkerchief*: A necessary part of a snuff-user's equipment, as the colour hides the inevitable brown stains.

l) *inefficacious*: Here, as often in these first three stories, the young narrator seems to be using words to impress. He may have got the word from the theological concept of Efficacious Grace: God always offers the sinner Sufficient Grace, but only contrition determines its efficacy.

m) *I walked away slowly*: The reaction is similar to that of Master Patrick Aloysius Dignam (*U*, 'Wandering Rocks' 18) as he goes windowshopping after his father's funeral.

4

thing. I felt my soul receding into some pleasant and vicious region; and there again I found it waiting for me. It began to confess to me in a murmuring voice and I wondered why it smiled continually and why the lips were so moist with spittle. But then I remembered that it had died of paralysis and I felt that I too was smiling feebly, as if to absolve the simoniac of his sin.

The next morning after breakfast I went down to look at the little house in Great Britain Street. It was an unassuming shop, registered under the vague name of *Drapery*. The drapery consisted mainly of children's bootees and umbrellas; and on ordinary days a notice used to hang in the window, saying: *Umbrellas Recovered*. No notice was visible now, for the shutters were up. A crape bouquet was tied to the door-knocker with ribbon. Two poor women and a telegram boy were reading the card pinned on the crape. I also approached and read:

> July 1st, 1895
> The Rev. James Flynn (formerly of S. Catherine's Church, Meath Street), aged sixty-five years.
> *R.I.P.*

The reading of the card persuaded me that he was dead and I was disturbed to find myself at check. Had he not been dead I would have gone into the little dark room behind the shop to find him sitting in his arm-chair by the fire, nearly smothered in his greatcoat. Perhaps my aunt would have given me a packet of High Toast for him and this present would have roused him from his stupefied doze. It was always I who emptied the packet into his black snuff-box, for his hands trembled too much to allow him to do this without spilling half the snuff about the floor. Even as he raised his large trembling hand to his nose little clouds of smoke dribbled through his fingers over the front of his coat. It may have been these constant showers of snuff which gave his ancient priestly garments their green faded look, for the red handkerchief, blackened, as it always was, with the snuff-stains of a week, with which he tried to brush away the fallen grains, was quite inefficacious.

I wished to go in and look at him but I had not the courage to knock. I walked away slowly along the sunny side of the

(e)

4

(d)

(l)

(f)

a) *the Irish college in Rome*: Founded in 1628, it was, and still is, a respected training centre for Irish priests. Although Fr Flynn came from a poor background, it is clear that he once showed enough promise to be sent there.

b) *pronounce Latin properly*: There was a three-way dispute at this time as to how to pronounce Latin – Joyce originally wrote 'speak Latin in the Italian way'. Later, Evelyn Waugh met the controversy in his youth, and mentioned it briefly in *A Little Learning*.

c) *the catacombs*: The subterranean cemeteries of Rome where the early Christians secretly worshipped, and were buried, and where the bodies of SS Peter and Paul are said to lie.

d) *Napoleon Bonaparte*: The (apocryphal) story always told (as in *P* (I.3)) to First Communion classes ends with Napoleon saying 'Gentlemen, the happiest day of my life was the day on which I made my first holy communion'. It is unlikely that Fr Flynn told the boy how in 1798 Bonaparte closed down the Irish college in Rome. It did not reopen until 1826.

e) *the different ceremonies of the mass*: The phrase is found in *A Companion to the Catechism*, Dublin, 1886, by the Christian Brothers, which instructs that 'they serve to show two things; namely, the Passion of our Saviour and the dispositions with which we ought to assist at Mass', and goes on to explain the symbolism of the altar, crucifix, candles, vestments, inclinations, genuflections and signs of the cross.

f) *the different vestments*: Various symbolic clothes were worn by the priest (e.g. on the wrist and neck). Each day of the year had a designated colour, including white, green, red, purple and rose. Black was mandatory for Good Friday and for the Liturgy of the Dead.

g) *mortal or venial or only imperfections*: Mortal sin is a 'grievous offence' against God, made with full knowledge and full consent. Without both of these, the sin may be venial. An imperfection is not culpable.

h) *complex and mysterious*: Stephen in *P* (III.1) considers some of these questions. Of the seven Sacraments of the Roman Catholic Church (Baptism, Confirmation, Eucharist, Penance, Extreme Unction, Holy Orders and Matrimony), it can be argued that only Matrimony is not touched upon in this story.

i) *the Eucharist*: From the *Maynooth Catechism* (1883): 'The Blessed Eucharist is the sacrament of the body and blood, soul and divinity of Jesus Christ, under the appearances of bread and wine.'

street, reading all the theatrical advertisements in the shop-windows as I went. I found it strange that neither I nor the day seemed in a mourning mood, and I felt even annoyed at discovering in myself a sensation of freedom, as if I had been freed from something by his death. I wondered at this for, as my uncle had said the night before, he had taught me a great deal. He had studied in the Irish college in Rome and he had taught me to pronounce Latin properly. He had told me stories about the catacombs and about Napoleon Bonaparte, and he had explained to me the meaning of the different ceremonies of the mass and of the different vestments worn by the priest. Sometimes he had amused himself by putting difficult questions to me, asking me what one should do in certain circumstances or whether such and such sins were mortal or venial or only imperfections. His questions showed me how complex and mysterious were certain institutions of the Church which I had always regarded as the simplest acts. The duties of the priest towards the Eucharist and towards the secrecy of the confessional seemed so grave to me that I wondered how anybody had ever found in himself the courage to undertake them; and I was not surprised when he told me that the fathers of the Church had written books as thick as the *Post Office Directory* and as closely printed as the law notices in the newspaper, elucidating all these intricate questions. Often when I thought of this I could make no answer or only a very foolish and halting one, upon which he used to smile and nod his head twice or thrice. Sometimes he used to put me through the responses of the mass, which he had made me learn by heart; and, as I pattered, he used to smile pensively and nod his head, now and then pushing huge pinches of snuff up each nostril alternately. When he smiled he used to uncover his big discoloured teeth and let his tongue lie upon his lower lip – a habit which had made me feel uneasy in the beginning of our acquaintance before I knew him well.

As I walked along in the sun I remembered old Cotter's words and tried to remember what had happened afterwards in the dream. I remembered that I had noticed long velvet curtains and a swinging lamp of antique fashion. I felt that I had been very far away, in some land where the customs were strange – in Persia, I thought ... But I could not remember the end of the dream.

j) *the courage*: See 9c.

k) Post Office Directory: Almost three inches thick.

l) *the law notices in the newspaper*: A sample (actual size) is opposite.

m) *halting*: A degree of paralysis is perhaps already affecting the boy.

n) *responses of the mass*: Answers made by the altarboy to the priest in the liturgy of the Mass. Buck Mulligan mockingly intones 'Introibo ad altare Dei' on the first page of *U*, and Stephen's perverse response comes in 'Circe': '*Ad deam qui laetificat juventutem meum*'.

o) *pattered*: The verb 'to patter' is from 'Paternoster', the Lord's Prayer, and means to repeat prayers, especially in a rapid, mechanical and indistinct fashion.

p) *his big discoloured teeth*: In February 1907 Joyce complained that his mouth was 'full of decayed teeth' and his 'soul of decayed ambitions' (17a).

q) *his tongue*: It is in the position adopted for the acceptance of the Communion wafer. The sense of unease here is similar to Stephen's memory of his First Communion in *P* (I.4).

r) *long velvet curtains ...*: Imagery from the East, which is also reminiscent of Roman Catholic ritual, as in 'Araby'.

s) *Persia*: Long notorious as a hotbed of heresy, being home for Simonites, Zoroastrians and other sects, and the object of great romantic interest at the time. In these early stories the idea of the exotic Orient is frequently contrasted with the mundane reality of Dublin.

From a late-Victorian poetry book

Fr Flynn was not the only instructor of youth in Dublin

a) *the window-panes of the houses that looked to the west reflected ...*: An evocation of the first and last paragraphs of *D*.

b) *the tawny gold of a great bank of clouds*: The sun keeps on bursting in to this story, and the misty, Celtic-twilight image of clouds is recurrent.

c) *Nannie*: Nan, Nanny: Christian name, from Anne, and also children's slang for grandmother.

d) *unseemly to have shouted*: She is deaf.

e) *The old woman pointed*: Although she is in the title, she will not say a word in the story.

f) *dead-room*: A room in which a dead body lay.

g) *I pretended to pray but I could not ...*: The narrator is forced to dissemble again. Inability to pray is a common complaint:

> But wherefore could not I pronounce 'Amen'?
> I had most need of blessing, and 'Amen'
> Stuck in my throat.

(*Macbeth* II.ii.)

> My words fly up, my thoughts remain below:
> Words without thoughts never to heaven go.

(*Hamlet* III.iii.)

> I looked to heaven, and tried to pray;
> But, or ever a prayer had gushed,
> A wicked whisper came, and made
> My heart as dry as dust.

(Coleridge, 'The Ancient Mariner'.)

h) *I noticed ...*: One of many pointers to the sisters' (genteel) poverty; she is literally 'down at heel'.

i) *fancy*: From the same source as 'fantasy'. (In *U*, 'Eumaeus', there is a parody from *The Merchant of Venice*: 'O tell me where is fancy bread? At Rourke's the baker's, it is said'.)

j) *There he lay ...*: Mrs Purefoy, in *U*, 'Circe', has the same pose, though for the opposite reason: she's about to give birth.

k) *copious*: Large, full of matter. An echo of (though technically unrelated to) 'cope' – a priest's long vestment.

l) *vested as for the altar*: Joyce wrote to his brother in December 1905 asking if a priest could be buried in a habit. Stanislaus answered that a priest was buried in a habit if he belonged to an order which wore a habit: otherwise, like Fr O'Malley, who had his parish taken away from him, he would be buried in his vestments (4g).

m) *a chalice ...*: In each of the versions of the story, Fr Flynn holds something different: a rosary, a cross, and finally a chalice.

n) *– the flowers*: The dash indicates the boy's rapid

In the evening my aunt took me with her to visit the house of mourning. It was after sunset; but the window-panes of the houses that looked to the west reflected the tawny gold of a great bank of clouds. Nannie received us in the hall; and, as it would have been unseemly to have shouted at her, my aunt shook hands with her for all. The old woman pointed upwards interrogatively and, on my aunt's nodding, proceeded to toil up the narrow staircase before us, her bowed head being scarcely above the level of the banister-rail. At the first landing she stopped and beckoned us forward encouragingly towards the open door of the dead-room. My aunt went in and the old woman, seeing that I hesitated to enter, began to beckon to me again repeatedly with her hand.

I went in on tiptoe. The room through the lace end of the blind was suffused with dusky golden light amid which the candles looked like pale thin flames. He had been coffined. Nannie gave the lead and we three knelt down at the foot of the bed. I pretended to pray but I could not gather my thoughts because the old woman's mutterings distracted me. I noticed how clumsily her skirt was hooked at the back and how the heels of her cloth boots were trodden down all to one side. The fancy came to me that the old priest was smiling as he lay there in his coffin.

But no. When we rose and went up to the head of the bed I saw that he was not smiling. There he lay, solemn and copious, vested as for the altar, his large hands loosely retaining a chalice. His face was very truculent, grey and massive, with black cavernous nostrils and circled by a scanty white fur. There was a heavy odour in the room – the flowers.

We crossed ourselves and came away. In the little room downstairs we found Eliza seated in his armchair in state. I groped my way towards my usual chair in the corner while Nannie went to the sideboard and brought out a decanter of sherry and some wine glasses. She set these on the table and invited us to take a little glass of wine. Then, at her sister's bidding, she filled out the sherry into the glasses and passed them to us. She pressed me to take some cream crackers also, but I declined because I thought I would make too much noise eating them. She seemed to be somewhat disappointed at my refusal and went over quietly to the sofa, where she sat down behind her sister. No one spoke: we all gazed at the empty fireplace.

dismissal of other possible sources of the odour. Fr Flynn's nostrils will smell no more.

o) *We crossed ourselves ...*: This entire paragraph is an echo of the Mass: the room is dark and silent; the sherry is served from the (Holy) table. The boy will not take the wafer, and hesitates to take the wine.

p) *in state*: The boy notices wryly that Eliza has assumed the status (and the armchair) of the head of the household.

q) *cream crackers*: Invented by the firm of William B. Jacob, who moved to Dublin from Waterford in the 1850s. (In *U*, 'Circe', the '*Dominus vobiscum*' of the Mass is parodied as 'Jacobs vobiscuits'.)

r) *too much noise*: This silent scene prepares for the awkward conversation which is to follow.

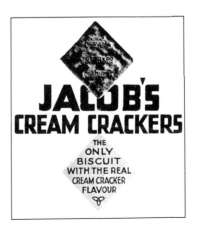

The West door of St Catherine's, Meath Street (4g)

(k)

a) *Did he . . . peacefully?*: The boy's aunt, more 'respectable' than the sisters, will not use the words 'die' or 'death'.

b) *ma'am*: Another indication of the difference in social standing between the sisters and the boy's aunt.

c) *a beautiful death*: Although it sounds odd, this, like 'a beautiful corpse' below, is a common phrase in Ireland.

d) *And everything . . . ?*: She is asking if Father Flynn died in a state of grace, and whether the sacrament of Extreme Unction had been administered.

e) *a Tuesday*: On Tuesday, six days before his death – plenty of notice, but a long time to wait in an anointed state.

f) *He looks quite resigned*: The boy has described him as looking 'very truculent'. Note, however, from the *Maynooth Catechism*:

> Q. How should we prepare ourselves for Extreme Unction?
> A. We should be prepared for Extreme Unction by a good confession, and we should be truly sorry for all our sins, and resigned to the will of God, when we are receiving the last sacrament.

g) *in it*: Literal colloquiality from the Irish *ann*, 'there', 'in existence'.

h) *Nannie . . . about to fall asleep*: A pre-echo of Gretta in 'The Dead'.

i) *the woman to wash him*: This task was performed by professional women who assisted one's exit from (as midwives assisted one's entry to) this world.

j) *the chapel*: The traditional distinction between a chapel and a church in Ireland (the former Roman Catholic, the latter usually Church of Ireland) was being eroded by the massive church-building programme from c.1870, and by the many pulpit injunctions to a proper pride in Roman Catholic churches. Even still the distinction lingers. The usage is seen again in 'Counterparts'.

k) *Freeman's General*: Miss Flynn makes a malapropism for *Freeman's Journal*, the major Irish newspaper of the day. It professed a Nationalist stance, though was justly accused of kowtowing to British rule. A facsimile of the Bloomsday issue of the *Freeman* was published in 1988.

l) *the cemetery*: This would probably have been Glasnevin in north Dublin, whose offices in Rutland Square were literally next door to the Gogarty home.

My aunt waited until Eliza sighed and then said:

—Ah, well, he's gone to a better world—

Eliza sighed again and bowed her head in assent. My aunt fingered the stem of her wine glass before sipping a little.

a —Did he . . . peacefully? she asked—

b —O, quite peacefully, ma'am, said Eliza. You couldn't tell
c when the breath went out of him. He had a beautiful death, God be praised—

d —And everything . . . ?—

e —Father O'Rourke was in with him a Tuesday and anointed him and prepared him and all—

—He knew then?—

—He was quite resigned—

f —He looks quite resigned, said my aunt—

—That's what the woman we had in to wash him said. She said he just looked as if he was asleep, he looked that peaceful and resigned. No one would think he'd make such a beautiful corpse.

—Yes, indeed, said my aunt—

She sipped a little more from her glass and said:

—Well, Miss Flynn, at any rate it must be a great comfort for you to know that you did all you could for him. You were both very kind to him, I must say—

Eliza smoothed her dress over her knees.

—Ah, poor James! she said. God knows we done all we could, as poor as we are – we wouldn't see him want anything
g while he was in it—

Nannie had leaned her head against the sofa-pillow and
h seemed about to fall asleep.

—There's poor Nannie, said Eliza, looking at her, she's wore out. All the work we had, she and me, getting in the woman
i to wash him and then laying him out and then the coffin and
j then arranging about the mass in the chapel. Only for Father O'Rourke I don't know what we'd have done at all. It was him brought us all them flowers and them two candlesticks out of the chapel and wrote out the notice for the *Freeman's*
kl *General* and took charge of all the papers for the cemetery and poor James's insurance—

—Wasn't that good of him? said my aunt—

Eliza closed her eyes and shook her head slowly.

—Ah, there's no friends like the old friends, she said, when

Dublin parish confession-box (9)

(*h*)

a) *that a body can trust*: She means 'that anyone can trust', but the awkwardness of the conversation makes her produce a macabre pun.

b) *beef-tea*: A concoction made from an infusion of shin beef. It is similar to Bovril – which takes its name from Latin *bos* ('bullock' or 'cow') + vril, Bulwer-Lytton's invented word for the embodiment of that 'unity of natural energic agencies, which has been conjectured by many philosophers'. It is a great deal to ask of beef tea.

c) *breviary*: The book containing the canonical prayers for each day, which those who are in holy orders are bound to recite.

d) *and his mouth open*: Fr Flynn was not the only disturbed Dublin cleric. Jonathan Swift comes to mind. Indeed, in a workbook for *FW* (published as *Scribbledehobble*), Joyce has a direct reference to Dublin's Dean under the heading of 'The Sisters': '... fish stinks first at head, oak withers at top'.

e) *She laid a finger against her nose*: Body language: say no more in front of the boy.

f) *Irishtown*: An area of Dublin just south of the Liffey. It has never been prosperous, and in the 1830s (while the Flynns would have been growing up) there was an outbreak of cholera there. The parish of Irishtown, which included Ringsend, had a population of c. 5,000 in 1895, of which a surprising 1,100 were members of the Church of Ireland, descendants of English fishermen who settled in the eighteenth century. Although Fr Flynn never makes this final pilgrimage, the boys in 'An Encounter' go there.

g) *new-fangled carriages*: These are not motor-cars but horse-drawn carriages with airfilled rubber tyres.

h) *rheumatic wheels*: Another malapropism. Pneumatic tyres were invented by the Irishman, J. B. Dunlop, who is described in *FW* (497/8) as 'the best tyrent of ourish times'. The word 'rheumatic' is not in the first version of the story in the *Irish Homestead*, but it can be seen in an advertisement for a patent medicine printed underneath it on the page (10).

i) *Johnny Rush's*: Francis Rush, cab and car proprietor, had a business at 10 Findlater's Place, between Upper Sackville Street and Marlborough Street. This was a short walk from the drapery.

j) *He was too scrupulous always*: Eliza uses the expression in a probable echo of Fr O'Rourke: Joyce was aware of its theological signification: 'prone to unreasonable doubts about sin'.

k) *crossed*: An angular pun. Eliza means her brother was thwarted or afflicted. But there are other meanings of this word, which was again strangely used in the opening sentence of *U*.

a all is said and done, no friends that a body can trust—

—Indeed, that's true, said my aunt. And I'm sure now that he's gone to his eternal reward he won't forget you and all your kindness to him—

—Ah, poor James! said Eliza. He was no great trouble to us. You wouldn't hear him in the house any more than now. Still, I know he's gone and all to that . . .—

—It's when it's all over that you'll miss him, said my aunt—

—I know that, said Eliza. I won't be bringing him in his cup
b of beef-tea any more, nor you, ma'am, sending him his snuff. Ah, poor James!—

She stopped, as if she were communing with the past, and then said shrewdly:

—Mind you, I noticed there was something queer coming over him latterly. Whenever I'd bring in his soup to him there
c I'd find him with his breviary fallen to the floor, lying back in
d the chair and his mouth open—

e She laid a finger against her nose and frowned: then she continued:

(h)

—But still and all he kept on saying that before the summer was over he'd go out for a drive one fine day just to see the
f old house again where we were all born down in Irishtown and take me and Nannie with him. If we could only get one
g of them new-fangled carriages that makes no noise that Father
h O'Rourke told him about, them with the rheumatic wheels
i – for the day cheap, he said, – at Johnny Rush's over the way there and drive out the three of us together of a Sunday evening. He had his mind set on that . . . Poor James!—

—The Lord have mercy on his soul! said my aunt—

Eliza took out her handkerchief and wiped her eyes with it. Then she put it back again in her pocket and gazed into the empty grate for some time without speaking.

j —He was too scrupulous always, she said. The duties of the priesthood was too much for him. And then his life was, you
k might say, crossed—

—Yes, said my aunt. He was a disappointed man. You could see that—

A silence took possession of the little room and, under cover of it, I approached the table and tasted my sherry and then returned quietly to my chair in the corner. Eliza seemed to have fallen into a deep revery. We waited respectfully for her

8

JULY, 1895.—31 DAYS.

Week-days and Remarkable days.	Sun rises H.M.	Sun sets H.M.	Dublin Bar. Morn. H.M.	Dublin Bar. Aft. H.M.	Moon rises H.M.	M. Age
1 M Irish Parliamentary Party suspended.	3 39	8 28	5 48	6 17	3 a 10	9
2 Tu Death of Father Burke, 1883. [1882	3 39	8 28	6 45	7 16	4 36	10
3 W John Kenny shot, Dublin, '82. [Dog	3 40	8 28	7 48	8 19	6	2 11
4 Tu American Independence, 1782. [days b.	3 41	8 27	8 52	9 24	7	20 12
5 F Smith O'Brien transported, 1849.	3 42	8 27	9 51	10 16	8	19 13
6 S Full Moon, 11.4 p.m.	3 43	8 26	10 37	10 57	9	1 14
7 ☼ 4th Sunday past Trinity.	3 44	8 26	11 17	11 35	9	29 15
8 M O'Connell elected for Clare, 1828.	3 45	8 25	11 55	—	9	47 16
9 Tu (6) Samuel Lover died, 1868.	3 46	8 24	0 14	0 33	10	1 17
10 W Election for South Louth, 1886.	3 47	8 23	0 52	1 11	10	18 18
11 Tu Bombardment of Alexandria, 1882.	3 48	8 22	1 29	1 46	10	20 19
12 F Battle of Aughrim, 1691.	3 49	8 21	2 4	2 22	10	27 20
13 S Berlin Treaty signed, 1878.	3 50	8 20	2 40	2 59	10	35 21
14 ☼ 5th Sunday past Trinity.	3 51	8 19	3 20	3 41	10	43 22
15 M Last Quarter, 3.6 a.m. [St. Swithin.	3 52	8 18	4 2	4 28	10	55 23
16 Tu Sir Joshua Reynolds born, 1723.	3 54	8 17	4 56	5 25	11	9 24
17 W (14) The Bastille destroyed, 1789.	3 55	8 16	5 55	6 27	11	29 25
18 Tu Papal Infallibility, 1870.	3 56	8 15	6 58	7 32	—	26
19 F Battle of Bull's Run, 1861.	3 58	8 14	8 5	8 39	0 m 2	27
20 S Miss Fanny Parnell died, 1882.	3 59	8 13	9 13	9 44	0	54 28
21 ☼ 6th Sunday past Trinity.	4 1	8 12	10 10	10 34	2	8 29
22 M New Moon, 5.7 a.m. [Mary Magdalen.	4 2	8 11	10 57	11 21	3	41 N
23 Tu Death of General Grant, 1885.	4 4	8 9	11 45	—	5	19 1
24 W Window Tax repealed, 1851. [Fast.	4 5	8 8	0 9	0 35	6	56 2
25 Tu Smith O'Brien's rising, '48. [St. James.	4 7	8 6	0 58	1 21	8	30 3
26 F Rothschild elected M.P. '58. [St. Anne	4 8	8 4	1 46	2 8	10	0 4
27 S Atlantic Cable laid, 1866.	4 10	8 3	2 33	2 55	11	29 5
28 ☼ 7th Sunday past Trinity. [First Quarter.	4 11	8 1	3 18	3 40	0 a 9	6
29 M Carey, informer, shot, '83. [8.10 p.m.	4 13	7 59	4 8	4 36	2 25	7
30 Tu French Revolution, 1830.	4 14	7 58	5 7	5 40	3 51	8
31 W Trinity Law Sitting ends.	4 16	7 56	6 14	6 51	5 11	9

WEATHER GUIDE.—Fair to the 15th; showery to end of month.

Predictions for July.

Sol and Mercury in conjunction on the 1st, preparatory to the former's backward
progress from Apogee on the 2nd. Saturn stationary, and hovering on the con-
fines of Scorpio and Libra. Conflicting election rumours; both political parties
thoroughly in accord in indefinitely postponing the just demands of Ireland. Our
national members should now unite in combatting the common foe. Meetings held
throughout Ireland, as landlordism is once more trying to raise its hydra head.
Jupiter's conjunction with Sol in Cancer on the 10th, brings the two conflicting
powers in the British Senate once more face to face in deadly hostility. Venus at her
greatest elongation and in her descending node in the Dragon's Tail in Leo. Saturn's
great square with the Sun in the ominous Scorpio near midnight on the 23rd, may
bring about reverses to some of John Bull's troops abroad. Earthquakes, cyclones,
railway accidents and floods.

Predictions published in 1894

a) *it contained nothing*: The suggestion is not that Fr Flynn had a drink problem. The 'crime' of breaking a chalice was not too serious unless it contained consecrated wine, and theologians decree that even then what would be spilt is not the Blood of Christ, but merely wine, or rather the *appearance* of it.

b) *They say it was the boy's fault*: i.e. the server at Mass, not the young narrator, but implicating him by association. At Clongowes, Joyce, aged seven, had been an altarboy.

c) *so nervous*: The narrator wonders how anyone could have the courage to undertake the rituals of the Mass: Fr Flynn had lost that courage – perhaps knowing that he was guilty of some sin that he felt he could not confess to another priest. In the boy's dream, the priest seems to want to confess, and again, at the end of this story, he may in his madness have gone to his own confessional for the same purpose.

d) *wanted for to go*: Irish idiom, as later in 'a light for to look'.

e) *a call*: A visit to the sick or dying.

f) *as if to listen*: This is almost an invitation for the dead to return, arguably something that happens in the final story. Joyce makes good use of the ambiguities of the 'as if' construction in *D*.

g) *chalice*: Another empty chalice: Fr Flynn cannot escape from the ostensible cause of his breakdown, even in death.

h) *gone wrong with him . . .*: The use of ellipses (or dots) often signposts the Joycean epiphany, which he defined as the 'revelation of the whatness of a thing', when 'the soul of the commonest object . . . seems to us radiant'. It can be argued that the ending of each of the stories constitutes an epiphany.

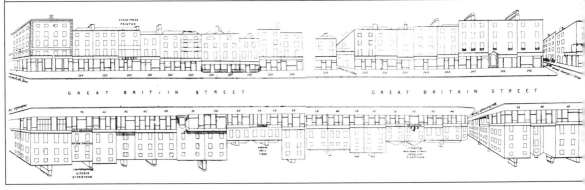

The street in 1850

9

to break the silence: and after a long pause she said slowly:

—It was that chalice he broke ... That was the beginning of it. Of course, they say it was all right, that it contained nothing, I mean. But still ... They say it was the boy's fault. But poor James was so nervous, God be merciful to him!—

—And was that it? said my aunt. I heard something ...—

Eliza nodded.

—That affected his mind, she said. After that he began to mope by himself, talking to no one and wandering about by himself. So one night he was wanted for to go on a call and they couldn't find him anywhere. They looked high up and low down; and still they couldn't see a sight of him anywhere. So then the clerk suggested to try the chapel. So then they got the keys and opened the chapel and the clerk and Father O'Rourke and another priest that was there brought in a light for to look for him ... And what do you think but there he was, sitting up by himself in the dark in his confession-box, wide-awake and laughing-like softly to himself?—

She stopped suddenly as if to listen. I too listened; but there was no sound in the house: and I knew that the old priest was lying still in his coffin as we had seen him, solemn and truculent in death, an idle chalice on his breast.

Eliza resumed:

—Wide-awake and laughing-like to himself ... So then, of course, when they saw that, that made them think that there was something gone wrong with him ...—

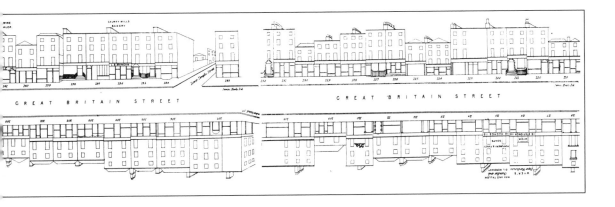

O, King of Glory, is it not a great change
  Since I was a young man, long, long ago?
When the heat of the sun made my face glow
  As I cut the grass, on a fine cloudless day;
Fair girls laughing
  All through the field raking hay,
Merry in the fragrant morning,
  And the sound of their voices like music in the air.

The bees were after the honey,
  Taking it to their nests among the hay,
Flying against us nimbly and merrily,
  And disappearing from sight with small keen buzz.
And the butterflies on the thistles,
  And on the meadow daisies, and from flower to flower,
On light wing lying and rising up,
  Moving through the air—they were fine.

The blackbird and the thrush were in the small nut wood,
  Making sweet music like the songs of the bards,
And the sprightly lark with a song in her little mouth
  Poising herself in the air aloft.
The beautiful thrush was on top of the branch,
  His throat stretched out in melodious song.
And, O, God of Grace, it was fine to be
  In beauteous Ireland at that time!

OUR WEEKLY STORY.

THE SISTERS.

By STEPHEN DÆDALUS.

Three nights in succession I had found myself in Great Britain-street at that hour, as if by Providence. Three nights also I had raised my eyes to that lighted square of window and speculated. I seemed to understand that it would occur at night. But in spite of the Providence that had led my feet, and in spite of the reverent curiosity of my eyes, I had discovered nothing. Each night the square was lighted in the same way, faintly and evenly. It was not the light of candles, so far as I could see. Therefore, it had not yet occurred.

On the fourth night at that hour I was in another part of the city. It may have been the same Providence that led me there—a whimsical kind of Providence to take me at a disadvantage. As I went home I wondered was that square of window lighted as before, or did it reveal the ceremonious candles in whose light the Christian must take his last sleep. I was not surprised, then, when at supper I found myself a prophet. Old Cotter and my uncle were talking at the fire, smoking. Old Cotter is the old distiller who owns that batch of prize setters. He used to be very interesting when I knew him first, talking about "faints" and "worms." Now I find him tedious.

While I was eating my stirabout I heard him saying to my uncle:

"Without a doubt. Upper storey—(he tapped an unnecessary hand at his forehead)—gone."

"So they said. I never could see much of it. I thought he was sane enough."

"So he was, at times," said old Cotter.

I sniffed the "was" apprehensively, and gulped down some stirabout.

"Is he better, Uncle John?"

"He's dead."

"O . . . he's dead?"

"Died a few hours ago."

"Who told you?"

"Mr. Cotter here brought us the news. He was passing there."

"Yes, I just happened to be passing, and I noticed the window . . . you know."

"Do you think they will bring him to the chapel?" asked my aunt.

"Oh, no, ma'am. I wouldn't say so."

"Very unlikely," my uncle agreed.

So old Cotter had got the better of me for all my vigilance of three nights. It is often annoying the way people will blunder on what you have elaborately planned for. I was sure he would die at night.

The following morning after breakfast I went down to look at the little house in Great Britain-street. It was an unassuming shop registered under the vague name of "Drapery." The drapery was principally children's boots and umbrellas, and on ordinary days there used to be a notice hanging in the window, which said "Umbrellas recovered." There was no notice visible now, for the shop blinds were drawn down and a crape bouquet was tied to the knocker with white ribbons. Three women of the people and a telegram boy were reading the card pinned on the crape. I also went over and read :—"July 2nd, 189— The Rev. James Flynn (formerly of St. Ita's Church), aged 65 years. R.I.P."

Only sixty-five ! He looked much older than that. I often saw him sitting at the fire in the close dark room behind the shop, nearly smothered in his great coat. He seemed to have almost stupefied himself with heat, and the gesture of his large trembling hand to his nostrils had grown automatic. My aunt, who is what they call good-hearted, never went into the shop without bringing him some High Toast, and he used to take the packet of snuff from her hands, gravely inclining his head for sign of thanks. He used to sit in that stuffy room for the greater part of the day from early morning, while Nannie (who is almost stone deaf) read out the newspaper to him. His other sister, Eliza, used to mind the shop. These two old women used to look after him, feed him, and clothe him. The clothing was not difficult, for his ancient, priestly clothes were quite green with age, and his dogskin slippers were everlasting. When he was tired of hearing the news he used to rattle his snuff-box on the arm of his chair to avoid shouting at her, and then he used to make believe to read his Prayer Book. Make believe, because, when Eliza brought him a cup of soup from the kitchen, she had always to waken him.

As I stood looking up at the crape and the card that bore his name I could not realise that he was dead. He seemed like one who could go on living for ever if he only wanted to ; his life was so methodical and uneventful. I think he said more to me than to anyone else. He had an egoistic contempt for all women-folk, and suffered all their services to him in polite silence. Of course, neither of his sisters were very intelligent. Nannie, for instance, had been reading out the newspaper to him every day for years, and could read tolerably well, and yet she always spoke of it as the Freeman's General. Perhaps he found me more intelligent, and honoured me with words for that reason. Nothing, practically nothing, ever occurred to remind him of his former life (I mean friends or visitors), and still he could remember every detail of it in his own fashion. He had studied at the college in Rome, and he taught me to speak Latin in the Italian way. He often put me through the responses of the Mass, he smiling often and pushing huge pinches of snuff up each nostril alternately. When he smiled he used to uncover his big, discoloured teeth, and let his tongue lie on his lower lip. At first this habit of his used to make me feel uneasy. Then I grew used to it.

That evening my aunt visited the house of mourning and took me with her. It was an oppressive summer evening of faded gold. Nannie received us in the hall, and, as it was no use saying anything to her, my aunt shook hands with her for all. We followed the old woman upstairs and into the dead-room. The room, through the lace end of the blind, was suffused with dusky golden light, amid which the candles looked like pale, thin flames. He had been coffined. Nannie gave the lead, and we three knelt down at the foot of the bed. There was no sound in the room for some minutes except the sound of Nannie's mutterings—for she prays noisily. The fancy came to me that the old priest was smiling as he lay there in his coffin.

But, no. When we rose and went up to the head of the bed I saw that he was not smiling. There he lay solemn and copious in his brown habit, his large hands loosely retaining his rosary. His face was very grey and massive, with distended nostrils and circled with scanty white fur. There was a heavy odour in the room—the flowers.

We sat downstairs in the little room behind the shop, my aunt and I and the two sisters. Nannie sat in a corner and said nothing, but her lips moved from speaker to speaker with a painfully intelligent motion. I said nothing either, being too young, but my aunt spoke a good deal, for she is a bit of a gossip—harmless.

"Ah, well! he's gone!"

"To enjoy his eternal reward, Miss Flynn, I'm sure. He was a good and holy man."

"He was a good man, but, you see . . . he was a disappointed man. . . . You see, his life was, you might say, crossed."

"Ah, yes! I know what you mean."

"Not that he was anyway mad, as you know yourself, but he was always a little queer. Even when we were all growing up together he was queer. One time he didn't speak hardly for a month. You know, he was that kind always."

"Perhaps he read too much, Miss Flynn?"

"O, he read a good deal, but not latterly. But it was his scrupulousness, I think, affected his mind. The duties of the priesthood were too much for him."

"Did he . . . peacefully?"

"O, quite peacefully, ma'am. You couldn't tell when the breath went out of him. He had a beautiful death, God be praised."

"And everything . . . ?"

"Father O'Rourke was in with him yesterday and gave him the Last Sacrament."

"He knew then?"

"Yes; he was quite resigned."

Nannie gave a sleepy nod and looked ashamed.

"Poor Nannie," said her sister, "she's worn out. All the work we had, getting in a woman, and laying him out; and then the coffin and arranging about the funeral. God knows we did all we could, as poor as we are. We wouldn't see him want anything at the last."

"Indeed you were both very kind to him while he lived."

"Ah, poor James; he was no great trouble to us. You wouldn't hear him in the house no more than now. Still I know he's gone and all that. . . . I won't be bringing him in his soup any more, nor Nannie reading him the paper, nor you, ma'am, bringing him his snuff. How he liked that snuff! Poor James!"

"O, yes, you'll miss him in a day or two more than you do now."

Silence invaded the room until memory reawakened it, Eliza speaking slowly—

"It was that chalice he broke. . . . Of course, it was all right. I mean it contained nothing. But still . . . They say it was the boy's fault. But poor James was so nervous, God be merciful to him."

"Yes, Miss Flynn, I heard that . . . about the chalice. . . He . . . his mind was a bit affected by that."

"He began to mope by himself, talking to no one, and wandering about. Often he couldn't be found. One night he was wanted, and they looked high up and low down and couldn't find him. Then the clerk suggested the chapel. So they opened the chapel (it was late at night), and brought in a light to look for him. . . And there, sure enough, he was, sitting in his confession-box in the dark, wide awake, and laughing like softly to himself. Then they knew something was wrong."

"God rest his soul!"

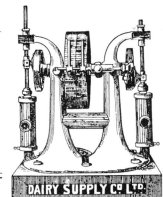

'The Sisters' is the first of the 'Childhood' group of stories in the collection, all narrated anonymously in the first person. These three are the only stories to give the illusion that it is Joyce speaking directly to the reader of his own experiences. And there is some truth in the illusion, for there is no doubt that Joyce drew on his own life in everything he wrote. However, 'The Sisters' is no mere 'slice of life'. It has a much more important function to perform.

One of Joyce's aims in *Dubliners* was to diagnose, and perhaps even to help cure, what he saw was wrong with Dublin life. In the later stories he would be specific, examining symptoms, charting ailments, making detailed reports. The role of 'The Sisters' is to state the problem to be addressed. The last line of the story says it: 'there was something gone wrong with him'. Nothing is explicit – we never discover precisely what it is that has 'gone wrong' with Father Flynn, nor does the boy know. There are hints from Old Cotter and an unclear story from Eliza, but they may not know either. But it is a fair bet that whatever it is, the same thing is wrong with Dublin life.

So what is it? Father Flynn is the key. It is he who has been ill, who has died after his third stroke. A stroke will usually cause some degree of paralysis, and that this has happened to the priest is suggested by the word that the boy says softly to himself as he gazes up at the old man's window: *paralysis*. The word reminds the boy of two other strange-sounding words, *gnomon* and *simony*. Together, these three words, the meanings of which the boy may not quite grasp, announce the concerns of the book. None of

them reappears in later stories, but they state what is wrong with people in Dublin, and perhaps even, for we are all human beings, with the whole of mankind.

The most important of the three key words is 'simony'. Its religious meaning is 'the sin of dealing for personal gain in things spiritual', but Joyce uses it as a sign for many 'sins against the light', and tacitly accuses many of his characters of it. In *Stephen Hero*, for instance, Joyce comments that prostitution is simony, since the body is 'what they call the temple of the Holy Ghost'. Exchanging love for money or status, betraying or buying friendship, exploitation of the poor, lonely or miserable, reneging on political principles, abuse of high office, nepotism, and many forms of pandering and hypocrisy are all covered by the term. For Joyce, it is no longer merely a personal sin; it is also a crime against society and against life. This expanded simony is the root cause of much that will follow in the book, and the reader, like the boy, will 'look upon its deadly work'.

Not all the 'Dubliners' are simoniacs. Many are victims of simony. Joyce, while he was writing *Dubliners*, professed himself a socialist. He believed that corruption and class greed were hand in hand with the triumphalism and superstition of the Roman Catholic Church. The sisters, for example, whom Gabriel (of 'The Dead') might with justice have called 'only two ignorant old women', are poor and ill-educated, and yet remain unresentful of – even grateful to – the church that banished their 'poor James'. By being kept in a constant state of poverty and fear by these combined forces, the ordinary

Dubliner was in effect imprisoned, or paralysed, both in mind and body. Images of paralysis, imprisonment and attempted escape are everywhere in the book. The best that can be achieved by Joyce's paralytics until the final story is the illusion of motion, an endless circling round and round an empty centre.

The correct place of the third strange-sounding word, 'gnomon', is in between 'paralysis' and 'simony'. It is applicable to both the paralytic and the simoniac. Although it has a variety of meanings, several of which Joyce will allude to in later stories, 'it is the word *gnomon* in the Euclid' (as we are told) that is primary here. At its simplest, it is a regular four-sided figure with a smaller piece of the same shape missing from one corner. Cirlot's *Dictionary of Symbols* describes it as a damaged rectangle, signifying suffering and inner irregularity, but it should also be said that the gnomon is by definition incomplete. In 'The Sisters', the damaged Father Flynn tries to 'complete' himself by teaching the boy, making a smaller replica of himself, but he also can be seen as the missing piece in the gnomon of the damaged church which has rejected him. The image of incompleteness runs through the stories, from the deafness of Nannie to the metaphorical blindness of Gabriel Conroy. As the simoniacs have lost their 'wholeness' through their simony, so too the paralytics are incomplete by virtue of their paralysis.

Two versions of 'The Sisters' are printed here, one from the *Irish Homestead* (August 1904), and the other as published in *Dubliners* ten years later. They are strikingly different, and a comparison can give rewarding insights into Joyce's creative methods. Missing from the earlier text are the orientalism, dreams, confession and the all-important triple idea of paralysis, the gnomon and simony, and Joyce made many other changes, additions and subtractions, whose effect is often both to distance the narrator from the events of the story, and to stress his central position within it. 'The Sisters', once simple enough in itself, became an essential introduction to the collection. The interrelationship between the living and the dead, for example, is one of the central themes of *Dubliners*, and is the subject of the first story as well as the last.

Occasionally, as here, Joyce's choice of title is puzzling. ('The Dead' and 'The Sisters' could easily exchange theirs.) The word 'sisters' is used both for nuns and for nurses, and the ladies share characteristics with both vocations, but the story's main concern is actually with the narrator and the old priest. Hence, various commentators have speculated that the title might hint at homosexuality ('sisters' in late Victorian slang could mean a gay male couple), or that the female pair is to be seen as a Dublin counterpart to the biblical Mary and Martha, sisters of Lazarus of Bethany (which could even be seen encoded in their names, Eliz*abeth* + N*annie*). However, Joyce's maiden aunts, Elizabeth and Annie Flynn, lived for a time at least with their married sisters at 15 Usher's Island (158f). Furthermore, in Irish locution the title would mean simply 'The Sisters' House', as in the idiom 'I'm just going down to the sisters' '. And that is where everything begins.

a) AN ENCOUNTER: The main meanings of the title-word are: 1) a battle, 2) a meeting, 3) a sexual episode. All three are relevant. The word occurs nowhere else in the book.

b) *Joe Dillon*: He was actually Joe Wilkins, and it is true that he became a priest. His brother Leo Wilkins was a classmate of the young James Joyce. The fictional surname recalls the leader of one of the post-Parnellite factions.

c) *a little library*: These periodicals were all published by the future Lord Harmsworth, who was born in Chapelizod, Dublin (95c) in 1865, and went on to own *The Times*. *The Union Jack* was established in April 1894 as a 'wholesome read' and lasted until February 1933. *The Halfpenny Marvel* was founded in November 1893 as a reaction to the Penny Dreadfuls: its title succinctly offers cheap thrills (though long before its demise it had become *The Marvel*). Both main characters of 'A Little Cloud' and of 'A Painful Case' also turn out to have little libraries.

d) Pluck: Its first number was in November 1894. Depending one one's view of Joycean mimesis, this could set the story in the summer of 1895 or even later. The *Pluck* Library was:

A High-Class Weekly Library of Adventure at Home and Abroad, on Land and Sea: Being the Daring Deeds of Plucky Sailors, Plucky Soldiers, Plucky Firemen, Plucky Explorers, Plucky Detectives, Plucky Railwaymen, Plucky Boys, Plucky Girls, and All Sorts and Conditions of British Heroes.

It finally folded in October 1924.

e) *battles*: On their journey towards the north bank of the Liffey, the boys will cross the site of the Battle of Clontarf in 1014, a rare Irish victory – over the Danes. On the south bank they will be near where many invaders landed, such as the Vikings and, in 1649, Oliver Cromwell.

f) *we*: Joyce's actual brother (Stanislaus) is fictionalised but still goes unnamed. As Maurice, he was also excised in the transition from *SH* to *P*.

g) *carry ... siege or battle*: The idiom here is in the style of a Latin 'trans' and the detail anticipates the imminent Latin lesson.

h) *Gardiner Street*: Saint Francis Xavier's church, Upper Gardiner Street, a Jesuit church founded in the year of Catholic Emancipation, 1829. *The Belvederian* of 1928 reports that 'Joe Dillon's' father – Mr Wilkins – did indeed go to eight-o'clock Mass every morning there. The church is also featured in 'Grace' and in *SH* (where Stephen attends a dismal Good Friday service given by a Father Dillon). The Spanish saint (1506–52), after whom the church was named, was one of the first and greatest of Jesuits: he was both an ascetic and a mystic, and was widely travelled in the Far East. He was recruited by Saint Ignatius Loyola (63p), the founder of the Jesuits and the patron of Belvedere College, after an intense religious experience.

i) *He looked like some kind of an Indian:* Stanislaus in 1903 described his elder brother similarly, that with

his long face red as an Indian's in the reflexion of the fire, there was a look of cruelty in his face.

j) *capered round the garden*: Some rare film footage of James Joyce shows him in 1937 smiling indulgently at his grandson Stephen, who is similarly prancing around in his Indian head-dress.

k) *Everyone was incredulous ... Nevertheless it was true*: Priests can be worldly as well as secular. One of the more obvious ironies in the surviving part of *SH* is that Wells (who in *P* (I.2) shoulders Stephen into the square ditch and otherwise intimidates him) reappears as a spotty and loud-voiced seminarian, the inmate of 'an ecclesiastical barracks'.

l) *vocation*: A calling for the priesthood, such as the one Stephen Dedalus contemplates in *P* (IV.2). Joyce's younger brother Charles went off to a seminary, but returned after a year and went to work at a wine merchant's before becoming a hard-drinking actor instead.

m) *the literature of the Wild West*: There is no inherent reason why the Wild West should not produce good literature, but the schoolboys feel the importance of the need to be sanctified by tradition.

n) *doors of escape*: In this and the next story, freedom from school is analogous to escape from the Ireland of *D*.

o) *circulated*: The secret circulation of these narratives

An Encounter

IT WAS JOE DILLON who introduced the Wild West to us. He had a little library made up of old numbers of *The Union Jack, Pluck* and *The Halfpenny Marvel*. Every evening after school we met in his back garden and arranged Indian battles. He and his fat young brother Leo, the idler, held the loft of the stable while we tried to carry it by storm; or we fought a pitched battle on the grass. But, however well we fought we never won siege or battle and all our bouts ended with Joe Dillon's war dance of victory. His parents went to eight-o'clock mass every morning in Gardiner Street and the peaceful odour of Mrs Dillon was prevalent in the hall of the house. But he played too fiercely for us who were younger and more timid. He looked like some kind of an Indian when he capered round the garden, an old tea-cosy on his head, beating a tin with his fist and yelling:

—Ya! yaka, yaka, yaka!—

Everyone was incredulous when it was reported that he had a vocation for the priesthood. Nevertheless it was true.

A spirit of unruliness diffused itself among us and, under its influence, differences of culture and constitution were waived. We banded ourselves together, some boldly, some in jest and some almost in fear: and of the number of these latter, the reluctant Indians who were afraid to seem studious or lacking in robustness, I was one. The adventures related in the literature of the Wild West were remote from my nature but, at least, they opened doors of escape. I liked better some American detective stories which were traversed from time to time by unkempt fierce and beautiful girls. Though there was nothing wrong in these stories and though their intention was sometimes literary they were circulated secretly at school. One day when Father Butler was hearing the four pages of Roman History, clumsy Leo Dillon was discovered with a copy of *The Halfpenny Marvel*.

—This page or this page? This page? Now, Dillon, up! *Hardly had the day...* Go on! What day? *Hardly had the day dawned ...* Have you studied it? What have you there in your pocket?—

configures the circular excitements spoken of near the end of the story (17h).

p) *Father Butler*: He was based on Fr William Henry, who was the Rector and Prefect of Studies at Belvedere from September 1894 to 1900. Joyce later told his biographer Herbert Gorman that he 'got on ... very well' with Fr Henry. As the rector/director, he is described in *P*. In his Trieste Notebook, Joyce wrote under the entry 'Henry':

> In translations of Ovid he spoke of porkers and potsherds and of chines of bacon. When I listen I can still hear him read sonorously: *In tanto discrimine ... Implere ollam denariorum ... India mittit ebur.*

q) *the four pages*: Which should have been prepared the night before as homework.

r) Hardly had the day dawned: Thus the reader can expect the unexpected. The passage appears to be from Julius Caesar's *De Bello Gallico*, a set text for the intermediate examination which Joyce took in June 1895, having been taught by Father Henry. Gaul was divided into three, and this is a mute allusion to the story's persistent theme of three.

a) *everyone assumed an innocent face*: More dissembling, and a hint of the corruption that awaits the boy.

b) *Apache*: The word is also French slang for an urban hooligan or street arab.

c) *this college*: In April 1893, James and Stanislaus Joyce entered Belvedere College, Denmark Street, in central Dublin. Because of the intercession of Father Conmee (of *P* and *U*, 'Wandering Rocks' 1), they were non-fee-paying pupils. James was eleven and Stanislaus seven. Belvedere was for the sons of the middle classes, a day-school near in status to Joyce's previous school, Clongowes Wood College in County Kildare. Among his schoolfriends were the Sheehy brothers, sons of a Member of Parliament – which is how Joyce came to know the celebrated Sheehy sisters (168b). Joyce at school was not the recipient of charity, however. Rather, he was the conferrer of it, as the scholarships he won paid his way and he brought prestige to the school throughout Ireland. Stanislaus later recalled how through some sharp practice the Dominicans also tried to recruit the exceptional talent they had heard about.

d) *some wretched scribbler . . .*: The original version was 'some wretched fellow'. There is a passing resemblance to Joyce himself. Harmsworth claimed that his magazines were 'Started to Suppress Bad Books for Boys' – by which he meant the Penny Dreadfuls. An article in *The Boy's Friend* in 1895 objected to the Penny Dreadfuls, saying that their writers were 'miserable beer-swilling wretches', who wrote their drivelling stories in seedy lodging houses, and whose readers were led into a life of degradation and crime. In fact the scribblers would tend to provide material for whatever the market wanted.

e) *National School boys*: Educated in state schools, which were in practice run by the Catholic clergy.

f) *paled . . . face*: In the manuscript, 'paled' read 'blenched'. Joe might be some kind of an Indian, but as yet Leo and the narrator are palefaces at heart.

g) *abroad*: A typical Joycean ambiguity, inasmuch as there is such a thing. Other instances include *FW passim,* or the droll 'forge' of the final passage of *P*.

h) *near at hand*: Possibly an allusion from Luke XXI. 30: '. . . summer is now nigh at hand'. In the September 1901 edition of the *International Theosophist*, published in Dublin, there is this:

> Mr Tingley . . . enthusiastically supported Mrs Tingley in her appreciation of California, and in her belief that it had a great future and would ultimately be the star state of America. In this connection she said the glory of San Diego was close at hand . . .

Given that the boys will be free from school soon, their illegal expedition is particularly defiant.

i) *Mahony*: In Dublin the ordinary pronunciation would be Mà-henny, but the Anglo–Irish version would be Mahnee. Americans say Ma-hòany. The name recalls the notorious Clongownian teacher of the 1860s, the Rev. Francis Sylvester Mahony, who was dismissed for impropriety. Joyce knew of this Corkman of letters and of his literary fame as 'Father Prout': he is described in Herbert Gorman's biography of Joyce as

> a bright-eyed scholarly little rascal, with a store of ribald stories and an unslakeable thirst.

j) *miching*: A Dublin (and Elizabethan) word for playing truant (14u). It is still used there (as is 'the jakes'). In *Hamlet* (III. ii), Hamlet says to Ophelia, 'this is miching malecho: it means mischief'. The echo ran on to Buck (Malachi) Mulligan in *U*. In *FW* (16), HCE is described as 'the michindaddy'.

k) *the Canal Bridge*: This is Newcomen Bridge, on the Royal Canal. It was named after Sir William Newcomen, an eminent banker, director of the Royal Canal Company, and an Irish MP in the 1790s.

l) *an excuse*: The boy's stratagem is not revealed.

m) *ferryboat*: One of several that crossed the Liffey. Benson's ferry, mentioned in *U,* 'Wandering Rocks' 16, was the easternmost one (landing near Grand Canal Dock), and would expedite the boys' mission to the Pigeon House, but their meandering means that they board another one (15d).

n) *the Pigeon House*: The road to it begins at Ringsend and runs east on the south side of Dublin Bay. It is an appropriate destination for the young travellers as it was once Dublin's main entry and exit point for passengers to and from England. Later it was a barracks (known as Pigeonhouse Fort), and eventually it became an electricity and drainage station. The name is derived from one John Pigeon, an eighteenth-century caretaker or official, who was murdered by thieves. The building became an inn and later a hotel, but it was dismantled in 1897. By the time of the writing of this story, it was a municipal waste tip (because the site minimised the stench for Dubliners). Symbolic interpretations regarding the Holy Ghost and the Pigeon House are sometimes overblown in Joycean studies, as both recur in his novels. In *SH* for example, Christ is described to Emma by Stephen as 'the middle-aged gentleman with the aviary – Jehovah the Second'.

o) *first stage of the plot*: The boys are enacting their romantic comics.

a Everyone's heart palpitated as Leo Dillon handed up the paper and everyone assumed an innocent face. Father Butler turned over the pages, frowning.

b —What is this rubbish? he said. *The Apache Chief!* Is this what you read instead of studying your Roman History? Let

c me not find any more of this wretched stuff in this college.

d The man who wrote it, I suppose, was some wretched scribbler who writes these things for a drink. I'm surprised at boys like you, educated, reading such stuff. I could understand it if you

e were ... National School boys. Now, Dillon, I advise you strongly, get at your work or ...—

f This rebuke during the sober hours of school paled much of the glory of the Wild West for me, and the confused puffy face of Leo Dillon awakened one of my consciences. But when the restraining influence of the school was at a distance I began to hunger again for wild sensations, for the escape which those chronicles of disorder alone seemed to offer me. The mimic warfare of the evening became at last as wearisome to me as the routine of school in the morning because I wanted real adventures to happen to myself. But real adventures, I reflected, do not happen to people who remain at home: they must be

g sought abroad.

h The summer holidays were near at hand when I made up my mind to break out of the weariness of school-life for one

i day at least. With Leo Dillon and a boy named Mahony I

j planned a day's miching. Each of us saved up sixpence. We

k were to meet at ten in the morning on the Canal Bridge.

l Mahony's big sister was to write an excuse for him and Leo Dillon was to tell his brother to say he was sick. We arranged to go along the Wharf Road until we came to the ships, then

mn to cross in the ferryboat and walk out to see the Pigeon House. Leo Dillon was afraid we might meet Father Butler or some one out of the college; but Mahony asked, very sensibly, what would Father Butler be doing out at the Pigeon House. We

o were reassured: and I brought the first stage of the plot to an

p end by collecting sixpence from the other two, at the same time showing them my own sixpence. When we were making

q the last arrangements on the eve we were all vaguely excited. We shook hands, laughing, and Mahony said:

r —Till to-morrow, mates!—

s That night I slept badly. In the morning I was first-comer

p) *collecting sixpence:* A device of complicity and a suggestion of simony — perhaps for the privilege in prospect.

q) *on the eve:* The title of a novel by Ivan Turgenev (1860). The Russian was notorious as a corrupter of young minds, because of his nihilist novel *Fathers and Sons* (1862). In *SH,* Stephen has clearly read more 'Turgénieff' than Father Butt.

r) *mates!:* Note the language of adventure, the nautical theme. J. F. Byrne (16n) told the story of Parnell travelling westward on the quays, going to Kings-bridge Station (103f), and a coal porter calling out:

> Do ye know what it is mates! Be the livin' jingo I think every man in Ireland ought to stand that man a pint!

s) *first-comer to the bridge:* A Joycean joke, as it was New-comen Bridge. Stephen Dedalus crosses Newcomen Bridge during his morning walk in *P* (V. 1), and associates going along the North Strand Road with thinking of Guido Cavalcanti, poet and friend of Dante. On the same walk, near the canal, Stephen meets 'the consumptive man with the doll's face and the brimless hat' walking with small steps and an outheld umbrella — very much like the old man of this story.

a) *ashpit*: A hole in waste ground for dumping the residue of the domestic hearth. With good reason, Joyce wrote to Grant Richards in June 1906 that the odour of ashpits and weeds and offal hung around his stories. Stanislaus reported finding songs and gospels at the end of the garden of his home in Royal Terrace – material known as 'the ashpit books'.

b) *coping*: Top course of masonry.

c) *pipeclayed*: Made from the fine white clay used for making pipes. When mixed into a paste with water, it could serve to whiten canvas shoes and sailors' trousers (such as those worn by Joyce during his 'Scandinavian sailor' phase in the summer of 1904 – while he was writing this story).

d) *horses pulling a tramload*: Horsedrawn trams (as in *P* II. 2) had given way to electric ones by the turn of the century (as in the opening of *U*, 'Aeolus').

e) *the mall*: Charleville Mall, on the Royal Canal.

f) *air*: A melody (with a suggestion of Hamlet's remark, 'I eat the air, promise-crammed' (III. ii)).

g) *grey suit*: Mahony has been obliged to set out wearing his school clothes.

h) *gas*: A Dublin word for fun. Again the theme of birds and a web of conceit. The gaseous swerve of thought anticipates Bloomean stream-of-consciousness. The expression, and compounds such as 'great gas' and 'a gas man', remain current in Dublin. In the National Library scene in *U*, Shakespeare is jokingly referred to as 'the gaseous vertebrate' by Buck Mulligan.

i) *Old Bunser*: The text was improved from 'Bunsen Burner', which is hardly a nickname. The device was named after R. W. E. Bunsen (1811–1899) of Heidelberg. Joyce began studying chemistry at Belvedere in 1894. Eighteen years later he wrote 'Gas from a Burner'.

j) *funk*: To fail from fear.

k) *a bob and a tanner*: A shilling and sixpence, i.e. 1/6d, today 7 ½p.

l) *Vitriol Works*: They were operated by the Dublin and Wicklow Manure Company Limited, on the north bank of the River Tolka, between Ballybough Bridge and Annesley Bridge. The company flourished in the late nineteenth century, manufacturing a range of agricultural products. Ballybough is derived from the Irish *Baile bocht*, Poortown.

m) *Wharf Road*: Named after the long bathing slip which had been built beside the road – on part of which was the Smoothing Iron (s). It is now the East Wall Road.

n) *out of public sight*: The ragged children do not matter, but it is important not to be seen skipping school. This may explain the boys' extremely roundabout route.

o) *the ragged troop*: Girls and boys of the poorest class went to what were officially called Ragged Schools, which were free. Such a troop would also be known as 'town sparrows'. The Smyly family were on the committees of most of them. The biggest, 'the Birds' Nest', was in York Road, Kingstown. On Dublin's north side, Lurgan Street Ragged Schools (which at about this time has seventy-six boys, forty-six girls and 118 'infants') offered a meal of bread and cocoa in the morning. Thirty shillings paid for breakfast for one child for one year.

p) *Swaddlers!*: Protestants, originally Methodists. In his *Journal* in September 1747, Charles Wesley wrote:

> We din'd with a gentleman who explained our name to us. It seems we are beholden to Mr Cennick for it, who abounds in suchlike expressions as 'I curse and blaspheme all the gods in heaven but the babe that lay in Mary's lap, the babe that lay in swaddling clouts &c'. Hence they nicknamed him Swaddler or Swaddling John and the word sticks to us all not excepting the clergy.

q) *dark-complexioned*: In *D* Joyce seems to link dark skin with Protestantism. Mr Browne in 'The Dead' is also swarthy. Possibly he is seen as a rebus of the common expression 'black Protestant' – used in *Exiles* of Miss Justice, who plays Beatrice to Richard Rowan's Dante.

r) *a cricket club*: Cricket was primarily – though by no means exclusively – a 'Protestant' game at this time in Ireland. It was often played at the better schools, as the end of *P* (I) shows. At Belvedere, Joyce was 'a useful bat', and studied the achievements of contemporary cricketers such as Trumper, Fry, Spofforth and Ranjitsinhji Vibhaji – the great 'Ranji'.

s) *the Smoothing Iron*: It was constructed c.1800 as a diving platform and a bathing-place on the East Wall. Now long gone, its site is under the office building of the Stewart and Lloyd Iron Works, near Merchant's Road.

t) *three o'clock*: The traditional time for punishment in Belvedere. Some commentators have also linked it with the hour of the Crucifixion.

u) *Mr Ryan*: He was a real person, one disliked by Joyce. Francis Ryan taught him French and Italian, and was at Belvedere from 1894 to 1897. Joycean accuracy being what it is, 'Mr' Ryan is correct as he was not ordained a priest until the end of 1894, six months later. Stanislaus recorded of October 1894:

to the bridge, as I lived nearest. I hid my books in the long grass near the ashpit at the end of the garden where nobody ever came and hurried along the canal bank. It was a mild sunny morning in the first week of June. I sat up on the coping of the bridge admiring my frail canvas shoes which I had diligently pipeclayed overnight and watching the docile horses pulling a tramload of business people up the hill. All the branches of the tall trees which lined the mall were gay with little light green leaves and the sunlight slanted through them on to the water. The granite stone of the bridge was beginning to be warm and I began to pat it with my hands in time to an air in my head. I was very happy.

When I had been sitting there for five or ten minutes I saw Mahony's grey suit approaching. He came up the hill, smiling, and clambered up beside me on the bridge. While we were waiting he brought out the catapult which bulged from his inner pocket and explained some improvements which he had made in it. I asked him why he had brought it and he told me he had brought it to have some gas with the birds. Mahony used slang freely, and spoke of Father Butler as Old Bunser. We waited on for a quarter of an hour more but still there was no sign of Leo Dillon. Mahony, at last, jumped down and said:

—Come along. I knew Fatty'd funk it—

—And his sixpence . . .? I said—

—That's forfeit, said Mahony. And so much the better for us – a bob and a tanner instead of a bob—

We walked along the North Strand Road till we came to the Vitriol Works and then turned to the right along the Wharf Road. Mahony began to play the Indian as soon as we were out of public sight. He chased a crowd of ragged girls, brandishing his unloaded catapult and, when two ragged boys began, out of chivalry, to fling stones at us, he proposed that we should charge them. I objected that the boys were too small, and so we walked on, the ragged troop screaming after us *Swaddlers! Swaddlers!* thinking that we were Protestants because Mahony, who was dark-complexioned, wore the silver badge of a cricket club in his cap. When we came to the Smoothing Iron we arranged a siege; but it was a failure because you must have at least three. We revenged ourselves on Leo Dillon by saying what a funk he was and guessing how many he would get at three o'clock from Mr Ryan.

... at Belvedere a boy mitched and was found out. A Jesuit named Fr. Ryan did the flogging ...

In a sneering revenge for his classroom experiences, James Joyce had Herbert Gorman record that Father Ryan should have been a Christian Brother.

The Pigeonhouse, 1895

14

a) *Ringsend*: Now part of the Dublin conurbation, Ringsend was a fishing village which had been colonised by bottle-factories (189m) and sawmills. At about this time it was the scene of an unusual encounter: a tram going over the swing-bridge collided with a two-masted sailing vessel going under it. The name of the village chimes commodiously with the idea of circularity and destination, both in the story and in the collection. Ringsend

> was from the seventeenth to the nineteenth century the chief place of embarkation and disembarkation for Dublin's passenger traffic.

(Ball's *History of the County Dublin* (1903)).

b) *right skit*: Great fun. The word still survives in 'skit', a humorous dramatic sketch or burlesque.

c) *influences . . . seemed to wane*: The gravitational and navigational motif is developed later with the boys' future interlocutor and his orientation.

d) *ferryboat*: The last ferry on this run, from Spencer Dock south to Cardiff's Lane, finally ceased in 1984 and was superseded by the new toll-bridge, the East Link. Another ferry ran between 'the steps' at East Wall and 'the point' at Ringsend. Upstream in 1386, after the Old Bridge (close to the modern Father Mathew Bridge, near Stonybatter (158k)) was swept away, the right to maintain a ferry was granted to the men of Dublin for four years. The modern ferry service was founded by a 1665 charter issued to Dublin Corporation by Charles II.

e) *transported*: An ironic hint of a long voyage and of continuing captivity. It was not long since Irish rebels (such as John Mitchel and William Smith O'Brien) had been transported to Australia.

f) *little Jew with a bag*: Ned Lambert in *U*, 'Hades' remarks that Bloom was once a 'traveller for blottingpaper'.

g) *the graceful three-master*: If, like 'Araby', this story is remembered from and set in 1894, the ship can be tentatively identified: in the first week of June that year, the only Norwegian ship in Dublin Port was the *Alma*, 433 tons, of Berg, Hernosund, bringing in 660 loads of split firwood for G. Perry & Co, portmanteau, trunk and packing-case makers, who had an outlet in Grafton Street. The *Rosevean* in *U* is also a 'threemaster'.

h) *green eyes*: The narrator seeks the green eyes of an adventurer and unexpectedly finds them. Joyce, in his earliest surviving piece of prose, 'Trust Not Appearances' (c. 1896), wrote:

> It is the eye that reveals to man the guilt or innocence, the vices or the virtues of the soul.

i) *All right!*: Having failed to decipher the legends on the sterns of the ships, the boy is either hearing a foreign sailor saying something sounding like this, or an Irish sailor looking like W. B. Murphy in *U*, 'Eumaeus' (16 h).

j) *bleaching*: Becoming white in the sun. The biscuits and the raspberry lemonade have led critics who take their cue from the cream crackers and sherry in 'The Sisters' to see another symbolic communion service here.

k) *sedulously*: An indication of a precocious – even

Liffey ferry

Belvedere College

We came then near the river. We spent a long time walking about the noisy streets flanked by high stone walls, watching the working of cranes and engines and often being shouted at for our immobility by the drivers of groaning carts. It was noon when we reached the quays and, as all the labourers seemed to be eating their lunches, we bought two big currant buns and sat down to eat them on some metal piping beside the river. We pleased ourselves with the spectacle of Dublin's commerce – the barges signalled from far away by their curls

a of woolly smoke, the brown fishing fleet beyond Ringsend, the big white sailing-vessel which was being discharged on the

b opposite quay. Mahony said it would be right skit to run away to sea on one of those big ships and even I, looking at the high masts, saw or imagined the geography which had been scantily dosed to me at school gradually taking substance under my eyes. School and home seemed to recede from us and their

c influences upon us seemed to wane.

d   We crossed the Liffey in the ferryboat, paying our toll to be

e transported in the company of two labourers and a little Jew

f with a bag. We were serious to the point of solemnity, but once during the short voyage our eyes met and we laughed. When we landed we watched the discharging of the graceful

g three-master which we had observed from the other quay. Some bystander said that she was a Norwegian vessel. I went to the stern and tried to decipher the legend upon it but, failing to do so, I came back and examined the foreign sailors to see

h had any of them green eyes for I had some confused notion ... The sailors' eyes were blue and grey and even black. The only sailor whose eyes could have been called green was a tall man who amused the crowd on the quay by calling out cheerfully every time the planks fell:

i   —All right! all right!—

When we were tired of this sight we wandered slowly into Ringsend. The day had grown sultry, and in the windows of

j the grocers' shops musty biscuits lay bleaching. We bought

k some biscuits and chocolate which we ate sedulously as we

l wandered through the squalid streets where the families of the

m fishermen live. We could find no dairy and so we went into a

n huckster's shop and bought a bottle of raspberry lemonade

o each. Refreshed by this, Mahony chased a cat down a lane but

p the cat escaped into a wide field. We both felt rather tired and

exhibitionist – understanding of 'good English' in the narrator (4 l).

l) *wandered through the squalid streets*: A paradigm of *D*, but actually the boys go south into Irishtown, the childhood home of Father Flynn of 'The Sisters'. There is also a suggestion of the poem by William Blake that Stephen thinks of in *U*, 'Nestor':

> I wander through each
>   charter'd street,
> Near where the charter'd
>   Thames does flow,
> And mark in every face I
>   meet
> Marks of weakness, marks
>   of woe ...

m) *We could find no dairy*: In fact at No 4 Thomas Street was Thomas Doyle, dairy, but the boys may have gone another way, down Fitzwilliam Street.

n) *huckster's*: This was the local name for a general store. Lowliness is implied but not dishonesty.

o) *cat*: Having bought a catapult to hunt birds (and pursue a journey to the Pigeon House) Mahoney ends up using it to chase their natural predators. The word subliminally suggests an instrument of nautical whipping – the cat-o'-nine-tails. A letter from Joyce to his young grandson was later published as *The Cat and the Devil*: in it, the lord mayor of the town of Beaugency (M. Alfred Byrne) outwits the devil with the help of a very wet cat. Here it will be rather different.

p) *a wide field*: The field is no longer there, as Aikenhead Terrace has been built over it. Directly across the Dodder is the Dublin Morgue (47b).

a) *the Dodder*: The river, mostly scenic, runs from the Wicklow Hills, and flows into the Liffey near Hanover Quay, just east of the Grand Canal Docks. One of the Dodder's mysteries has a bearing on 'Two Gallants'.

b) *home by train*: They have wandered so far into Irishtown that they are close to Lansdowne Road Station, whence regular trains went to Amiens Street Station. (Joyce and some cartographers happily wrote 'Landsdowne'.)

c) *jaded*: Exhausted, from 'jade', a worn-out or inferior horse. It is also of course a green mineral from the East.

d) *man approaching*: Possibly an allusion to the *Inferno* XV (from the Canto of the Sodomites). This describes the disquiet of one being recognised by another proceeding along a bank.

e) *girls tell fortunes*: The stem was probably from some form of wild rye-grass. The *Oxford Dictionary of Superstitions* explains that one popped off the seeds one by one to see whom one would marry: 'Tinker, Tailor, Soldier, Sailor, Rich man, Poor man, Beggarman, Thief'. The idea anticipates 'Clay'.

f) *greenish-black*: A clear echo of Father Flynn's attire in 'The Sisters'.

g) *jerry hat*: A hard round hat, popular in the mid-nineteenth century. The full name was Tom-and-Jerry hat, from the fashionable characters in Pierce Egan's *Life in London* (1821). When it was dramatised at the Theatre Royal Dublin in 1822, the play was described as a

New Classic – Comic – Didactic – Moralistic – Aristophanic – Localic – Analytic – Terpsichoric – Panoramic – Camarac – Obscuric Extravaganza, or Melange, in Twenty New Scenes.

Like Ignatius Gallaher of 'A Little Cloud', Egan was an Irish sports journalist, one who wrote on boxing as well as on London's low life. He is referred to in *FW* (447).

h) *fifty paces*: A common expression in Latin literature, often in a military context. In *U*, 'Eumaeus', the implausible sailor W. B. Murphy tells Bloom how one Simon Dedalus shot (over his shoulder) two eggs off two bottles from a similar distance, at a circus in Stockholm.

i) *looking for something in the grass*: A snake perhaps, if Ireland had any.

j) *bade us good-day*: See 19c.

k) *the seasons had changed*: As well as having a natural sympathy for his own halcyon youth, the man is perhaps thinking of details such as the cold snap of 1893 (mentioned by Mrs Bellingham in *U*, 'Circe'), and the excessively hot summer of 1846.

l) *Thomas Moore*: Irish poet (1779–1852) and friend of Byron, who was born in Aungier Street, Dublin, the son of a grocer. He and the publisher John Murray burnt Byron's memoirs – loosely for the foolish reason given in *P* (II. 3), that Byron was a bad man. Moore's commemorative statue (which was ridiculed when first erected and had to have its head removed and two inches of neck added) still stands in College Street, over a public convenience: 'meeting of the waters' thinks Bloom in *U* as he passes – though it was an old joke.

m) *Sir Walter Scott*: Poet and novelist (1771–1832), who wrote many romantic tales of chivalry and faraway places. Among them are *The Lady of the Lake, Ivanhoe, Redgauntlet*, 'Harold the Dauntless' and *The Abbot*. Scott is also the favourite writer of the perverse old dwarfish 'captain' of *P* (V. 3), with whom the so-called pervert of 'An Encounter' has some similarities. According to Stanislaus, his brother 'could not stand' Scott.

n) *Lord Lytton*: A prolific novelist (1803–73) with, for the times, a mildly scandalous private life. His wife, Rosina Doyle Wheeler, was an Irish novelist. He wrote as Edward Bulwer-Lytton and should not be confused with his son (1831–91), Viceroy of India and poetaster. Lytton's many books ran to about 110 volumes. Perhaps *The Last Days of Pompeii* (of which Joyce had a copy) or *Eugene Aram* (about a schoolmaster murderer) may be considered unsuitable for boys. J. F. Byrne (*P*'s 'Cranly') records how, at Belvedere in 1893, reading practice was done from *Eugene Aram, Ivanhoe* and the like – though this was just before James Joyce joined the class. Even John Joyce had a Bulwer-Lytton in his little library (*Pelham, or the Adventures of a Gentleman*), though he often thought the author was Lytton-Bulwer. In the mid-nineteenth century, Bulwer-Lytton and Scott had extremely high popular reputations, both of which rapidly declined.

when we reached the field we made at once for a sloping bank
over the ridge of which we could see the Dodder.

It was too late and we were too tired to carry out our project
of visiting the Pigeon House. We had to be home before
four o'clock lest our adventure should be discovered. Mahony
looked regretfully at his catapult and I had to suggest going
home by train before he regained any cheerfulness. The sun
went in behind some clouds and left us to our jaded thoughts
and the crumbs of our provisions.

There was nobody but ourselves in the field. When we had
lain on the bank for some time without speaking I saw a man
approaching from the far end of the field. I watched him lazily
as I chewed one of those green stems on which girls tell
fortunes. He came along by the bank slowly. He walked with
one hand upon his hip and in the other hand he held a stick
with which he tapped the turf lightly. He was shabbily dressed
in a suit of greenish-black and wore what we used to call a
jerry hat with a high crown. He seemed to be fairly old, for
his moustache was ashen-grey. When he passed at our feet he
glanced up at us quickly and then continued his way. We
followed him with our eyes and saw that when he had gone
on for perhaps fifty paces he turned about and began to retrace
his steps. He walked towards us very slowly, always trapping
the ground with his stick, so slowly that I thought he was
looking for something in the grass.

He stopped when he came level with us and bade us good-
day. We answered him and he sat down beside us on the slope
slowly and with great care. He began to talk of the weather,
saying that it would be a very hot summer and adding that the
seasons had changed greatly since he was a boy—a long time
ago. He said that the happiest time of one's life was undoubtedly
one's schoolboy days and that he would give anything to be
young again. While he expressed these sentiments, which bored
us a little, we kept silent. Then he began to talk of school and
of books. He asked us whether we had read the poetry of
Thomas Moore or the works of Sir Walter Scott and Lord
Lytton. I pretended that I had read every book he mentioned
so that in the end he said:

—Ah, I can see you are a bookworm like myself. Now, he
added, pointing to Mahony who was regarding us with open
eyes, he is different. He goes in for games—

16

NOW ON SALE!

A Rattling New Complete Sea Novel, entitled:

THE MUTINY OF THE 'POLE STAR'

He stood fierce and calm and resolute, waiting for his foes.

By E. Harcourt Burrage, the favourite Author, in the

MARVEL

ONE HALFPENNY.
Of all Newsagents.

(12c)

a) *great gaps ... yellow teeth*: They are clearly reminiscent of Father Flynn's 'big discoloured teeth', and are also like Stephen's 'mouth of decay' in *U*, 'Proteus'. In the tradition of sinister strangers, the man also recalls Dickens' description of Daniel Quilp in Chapter III of *The Old Curiosity Shop* (1841):

> His black eyes were restless, sly, and cunning; his mouth and chin bristly with the stubble of a coarse-haired beard; and his complexion was one of that kind which never looks clean or wholesome. But what added most to the grotesque expression of his face was a ghastly smile, which, appearing to be the mere result of habit and to have no connection with any mirthful or complacent feeling, constantly revealed the few discoloured fangs that were yet scattered in his mouth, and gave him the aspect of a panting dog. His dress consisted of a large high-crowned hat, a worn dark suit ...

PENNY NOVELS.

No. 1.—" She." By Rider Haggard.
.. 2.—" Monte Christo." By Dumas. Part I.
.. 3.—" The True History of Joshua Davidson." By Mrs. Lynn Linton
.. 4.—" The Vengence of Monte Christo."
.. 5.—" The Scarlet Letter." Hawthorne.
.. 6.—" Little Emily," (From " David Copperfield,") by Dickens.
.. 7.—" Ben Hur." By Gen. Lew Wallace.
.. 8.—" It is never too Late to Mend." Charles Reade.
.. 9.—" Mary Barton." Mrs. Gaskell.
.. 10.—" Lay Down Your Arms " Baroness Von Suttner.
.. 11.—" Coningsby." Benjamin Disraeli.
.. 12.—" The Tower of London." Harrison Ainsworth.
.. 13.—" The Last Days of Pompeii. Bulwer Lytton.
.. 14.—" Jane Eyre." Charlotte Bronte
.. 15.—" The Chronicles of the Schonberg-Cotta Family," by Elizabeth R. Charles.
.. 16.—" Pride and Prejudice." Jane Austen.
.. 17.—" Hypatia." Charles Kingsley.
.. 18.—" Charles O'Malley, the Irish Dragoon." By Charles Lever.
.. 21.—" The Queen Diamonds." (From " The Three Musketeers.") By Alexander Dumas.
.. 26.—" Robert Falconer." By George Macdonald.
.. 27.—" Fantine." (From " Les Miserables.") By Victor Hugo.
.. 29.—" Ivanhoe." Sir W. Scott.
.. 33.—" Valentine Vox." By Robert Cockton.
.. 34.—" The Scalp Hunters."
.. 35.—" The Hour and the Man." By Harriet Martineau.
.. 36.—" Cosette." (From " Les Miserables.") By Victor Hugo.
.. 37.—" Tales of Horror and Mystery. By. E. A. Poe.
.. 38.—" Adventures of Jimmy Brown.
.. 39.—" The Last of the Mohicans." By J. Fennimore Cooper.
.. 40.—" The History of a Conscript." (Erckmann Chatrian).
.. 41.—" The Scottish Chiefs." By Jane Porter.
.. 42.—" Tartarian of Tarascon." By Alphonse Daudet.
.. 43.—Three popular Novels, " The Art of Marriage," by Mrs. Ward; " The Sorrows of Satan," by Marie Corelli, and " Trilby," by Du Marier.
.. 45.—" Guy Fawkes " By Harrison Ainsworth.
.. 46.—" Marius." (From " Les Miserables.") By Victor Hugo.

Any of the foregoing can be had post free for 2d each.

Novels for Twopence

He said he had all Sir Walter Scott's works and all Lord Lytton's works at home and never tired of reading them. Of course, he said, there were some of Lord Lytton's works which boys couldn't read. Mahony asked why couldn't boys read them – a question which agitated and pained me because I was afraid the man would think I was as stupid as Mahony. The man, however, only smiled. I saw that he had great gaps in his
a mouth between his yellow teeth. Then he asked us which of us had the most sweethearts. Mahony mentioned lightly that
bc he had three totties. The man asked me how many had I.
d I answered that I had none. He did not believe me and said he was sure I must have one. I was silent.

—Tell us, said Mahony pertly to the man, how many have you yourself?—

The man smiled as before and said that when he was our age he had lots of sweethearts.

—Every boy, he said, has a little sweetheart—

His attitude on this point struck me as strangely liberal in a
e man of his age. In my heart I thought that what he said about boys and sweethearts was reasonable. But I disliked the words in his mouth and I wondered why he shivered once or twice as if he feared something or felt a sudden chill. As he proceeded
f I noticed that his accent was good. He began to speak to us
g about girls, saying what nice soft hair they had and how soft their hands were and how all girls were not so good as they seemed to be if one only knew. There was nothing he liked, he said, so much as looking at a nice young girl, at her nice white hands and her beautiful soft hair. He gave me the impression that he was repeating something which he had learned by heart or that, magnetized by some words of his
h own speech, his mind was slowly circling round and round in the same orbit. At times he spoke as if he were simply alluding to some fact that everybody knew, and at times he lowered his voice and spoke mysteriously, as if he were telling us something secret which he did not wish others to overhear. He repeated his phrases over and over again, varying them and surrounding them with his monotonous voice. I continued to gaze towards the foot of the slope, listening to him.

After a long while his monologue paused. He stood up slowly, saying that he had to leave us for a minute or so, a few minutes, and, without changing the direction of my gaze, I

b) *totties*: Partridge's *Slang* defines a tottie as a high-class whore, from c.1880. It can also mean a little girl. Graham Greene lost a famous libel case in 1937 after referring to Shirley Temple as 'a little totsie'.
c) *had I*: An Irish idiom. Joyce improved the line from 'I had'.
d) *that I had none*: In Joyce's fair copy of the manuscript, he wrote 'I had one' and then inserted an 'n'.
e) *In my heart*: See 19h.
f) *his accent was good*: Then as now, accents mattered greatly in Dublin. The thought reflects the Joycean pre-occupation with the relationship between sound and meaning, firmly announced at the beginning of *D*. Accents are mentioned in many of the stories. (Note too the narrator's immediately previous comment about the words in the other's mouth.)
g) *nice soft hair*: The expression and variants of it recur here. (In 'Araby' there will be 'the soft rope of her hair' (22a).) Compare Mahony as a 'rough boy'. But the narrator is not rough.
h) *mind . . . orbit*: The old man's mind has a planetary or sat-ellite logic of its own. The image is repeated later in the story. Like the green-eyed sailors of the boy's imagin-ation, the pervert seems to steer by the stars.

a) *Look what he's doing!*: In a letter to Grant Richards in June 1906, Joyce acknowledged the 'enormity' (nothing to do with size) of 'An Encounter'. The boy never looks, so his and the reader's imagination can have full scope. Public masturbation is the commonest suggestion, a deed repeated by that quintessential advertising man, Leopold Bloom.

b) *queer*: No homosexual connotation had as yet attached itself to this word. In Ireland it remains a common expression – as in Brendan Behan's *The Quare Fellow*. In *P* (I.2), Stephen thinks of Brother Michael while in the infirmary:

> he had reddish hair mixed with grey and a queer look. It was queer that he would always be a brother. It was queer too that you could not call him sir . . .

c) *old josser*: A simpleton or an old roué – from c. 1890. Now in Dublin it merely means 'fellow' or 'layabout'. But consider also 'Joss', a Chinese figure of a deity, from the Portuguese '*deos*'. 'Joss-pidgin' means a religious ceremony, and 'joss-pidgin-man' is a minister of religion. In *FW* (611) there is 'Lord Joss'.

d) *let you be*: Again the boy reflects his education. The phrase recalls Euclid's *Elements*, Proposition 8: Let ABC and DEF be two triangles . . .

e) *Murphy . . . Smith*: He has chosen the commonest Irish and English surnames. Changing names was also a course of action adopted by Odysseus, by Leopold Bloom, by Madame Marion Tweedy, by Rudolph Virag, by Charles Stewart Parnell, by James Joyce and by many of the Guinnesses. One of Samuel Beckett's most famous alter egos was Murphy. Bloom is told in *U* in the cabman's shelter:

> Sounds are impostures, Stephen said after a pause of some little time. Like names, Cicero, Podmore, Napoleon, Mr Goodbody, Jesus, Mr Doyle. Shakespeares were as common as Murphies.

f) *Hardly had he sat down*: A parody of 'Hardly had the day dawned' (12r).

g) *escaladed*: What seems and is Latinist preciousness is also accurate military jargon, in keeping with the battle/siege motif. (The journey is to the Pigeon House Fort.)

h) whipped: At Belvedere boys had the dignity of being punished with a leather strap strengthened with whalebone – the notorious 'pandybat', which Joyce and Stephen never forgot. In this passage there are ten references to whipping (not including 'chastising' and 'twitching'). In 1909 Joyce wrote to Nora that he felt he would like to be flogged by her. Bloom is similarly chastisable – notably by the honourable Mrs Mervyn Talboys in *U*, 'Circe'. Contemporary whipping enthusiasts included A. C. Swinburne (Buck Mulligan's 'Algy'), Mr Gladstone, and J. Gordon Bennett's famous employee, H. M. Stanley. In his Intermediate Exam in June 1894, Joyce sat a paper on Charles Lamb's *Adventures of Ulysses* (1808). Question 4 was:

> Mention a peculiar prejudice of the Phaecians about whips, and the incident from which it arose.

Some of the Dublin Poor

saw him walking slowly away from us towards the near end of the field. We remained silent when he had gone. After a silence of a few minutes I heard Mahony exclaim:

a   —I say! Look what he's doing!—

As I neither answered nor raised my eyes Mahony exclaimed again:

bc   —I say ... he's a queer old josser!—

d   —In case he asks us for our names, I said, let you be Murphy
e and I'll be Smith—

We said nothing further to each other. I was still considering whether I would go away or not when the man came back
f and sat down beside us again. Hardly had he sat down when Mahony, catching sight of the cat which had escaped him, sprang up and pursued her across the field. The man and I watched the chase. The cat escaped once more and Mahony
g began to throw stones at the wall she had escaladed. Desisting from this, he began to wander about the far end of the field, aimlessly.

After an interval the man spoke to me. He said that my friend was a very rough boy and asked did he get whipped often at school. I was going to reply indignantly that we were
h not National School boys to be *whipped* as he called it; but I
i remained silent. He began to speak on the subject of chastising boys. His mind, as if magnetized again by his speech, seemed to circle slowly round and round its new centre. He said that when boys were that kind they ought to be whipped and well whipped. When a boy was rough and unruly there was nothing would do him any good but a good sound whipping. A slap on the hand or a box on the ear was no good: what he wanted was to get a nice warm whipping. I was surprised at this sentiment and involuntarily glanced up at his face. As I did so
j I met the gaze of a pair of bottle-green eyes peering at me from under a twitching forehead. I turned my eyes away again.

k   The man continued his monologue. He seemed to have
l forgotten his recent liberalism. He said that if ever he found a boy talking to girls or having a girl for a sweetheart he would whip him and whip him: and that would teach him not to be
m talking to girls. And if a boy had a girl for a sweetheart and told lies about it then he would give him such a whipping as no boy ever got in this world. He said that there was nothing in this world he would like so well as that. He described to me

i) *chastising*: The word can also have the sense of 'to repress'. Robert Boyle, 'The Father of Chemistry and Brother of the Earl of Cork', appropriately remarked:

> I am glad to see the vanity or envy of the canting chymists thus discovered and chastised.

j) *bottle-green eyes*: Joyce at first wrote 'sage green', but this is more appropriate with its hint of drink. The narrator has found the green eyes he sought earlier. There was a tradition that Odysseus, another great sailor, had green eyes.

k) *monologue*: The mystery and ritual of sex are added to those of religion from 'The Sisters', a process comparable with the explanation of the mysteries of the Mass. All sorts of unexpected things are 'complex and mysterious' (5h).

l) *forgotten his recent liberalism*: Perhaps a post-orgasmic mood-change, reminiscent of the one Bloom has close to the same place, in *U*, 'Nausicaa'.

m) *not to be talking*: A common Irish construction, which stems from the Gaelic present continuous tense – demonstrated e.g. in Anna Livia Plurabelle's 'don't be dabbling', in the eponymous chapter of *FW* (196), or, in *U*, 'Lestrygonians', where Josie Breen's replies to Bloom's enquiry about her eccentric husband:

> – O, don't be talking, she said. He's a caution to rattlesnakes.

18

The Dodder at Ringsend

WHIPPING IMPLEMENTS.

The figures in the upper half of this plate represent the Prison-Rod and Whipping-Post. The Rattan, Birch, and Loose Garment belong to ladies' boarding Schools in the last century. The Rule and Spatula (or "Jonathan") were used in boys' Schools. The holes in the spatula raised blisters. Beneath are the modern Jesuit discipline with the Whipping-Post or Hurdle in Wandsworth House of Correction. On either side are Knouts of leather and of twisted cord.

a) *as if he were unfolding*: The conditionality matters. The verb is similarly used by Milton in his *Eikonoklastes* (XXVI) (1649):

> But to counterfet the hand of God is the boldest of all forgery: And he, who without warrant but his own fantastic surmise, takes upon him perpetually to unfold the secret and unsearchable Mysteries of high Providence, is likely for the most part to mistake and slander them; and approaches to the madness of those reprobate thoughts . . .

b) *pretending to fix my shoe properly*: The tying of a lace is meant, but more is implied. The expression 'fixing my shoe' was more noticeably colloquial a century ago, and (properly) carries with it the Latin connotation of staying (fast) in the same place – in this case together with the old man. And how does one pretend properly? There is much confusion and contradiction in this final passage – e.g. in the calling of untruths and in despising 'a little'.

c) *I bade him good-day*: The expression recalls the leavetaking at *Inferno* XV. 115–6:

> I would say more but I cannot go farther talking with thee, for I see there a new cloud rising . . .

The pervert and the boy have both failed in their quest. Note also, however, that the boy's formula for saying goodbye is identical to the man's formula for saying hello.

d) *forced bravery*: The boy is again a 'reluctant Indian'.

e) *hallooed*: The homophone with 'hallowed' would not have escaped Joyce.

f) *as if*: Note the insinuation in this construction, which has already been used of the josser (a), and which recurs in *D*.

g) *bring me aid*: Possibly based on *Inferno* XV. 121–4, on running after the green cloth (in the field at Verona). Aspects of the (Irish) green cloth are treated elsewhere in *D*, as in 'Ivy Day' and 'The Dead'. The boy has been made aware of a defect of love possibly like that of the old man.

h) *And I was penitent, for in my heart I had always despised him*: 'Penitent' because of the 'as if'? The arrogant statement of remorse is quite ambiguous. There is a suggestion of Antony's remark to Caesar, in *Antony and Cleopatra* (II.ii):

> As nearly as I may,
> I'll play the penitent to you. But mine honesty
> Shall not make poor my greatness, nor my power
> Work without it.

a how he would whip such a boy as if he were unfolding some
elaborate mystery. He would love that, he said, better than
anything in this world; and his voice, as he led me mono-
tonously through the mystery, grew almost affectionate and
seemed to plead with me that I should understand him.

I waited till his monologue paused again. Then I stood up
abruptly. Lest I should betray my agitation I delayed a few
b moments pretending to fix my shoe properly and then, saying
c that I was obliged to go, I bade him good-day. I went up the
slope calmly but my heart was beating quickly with fear that
he would seize me by the ankles. When I reached the top of
the slope I turned round and, without looking at him, called
loudly across the field:

—Murphy!—

d My voice had an accent of forced bravery in it, and I was
ashamed of my paltry stratagem. I had to call the name again
e before Mahony saw me and hallooed in answer. How my heart
f beat as he came running across the field to me! He ran as if to
g bring me aid. And I was penitent, for in my heart I had always
h despised him a little.

The second half of the sentence is possibly a recollection of 2 Samuel VI.16, where Michal sees David, and she despises him in her heart, for leaping and dancing before the Lord.

Afterword: 'An Encounter'

Buried under its freight of symbolism, this story is nevertheless a 'true one'. As Stanislaus Joyce confirmed in *My Brother's Keeper*, the incident (or something very like it) 'really happened' one strange day in the mid-1890s. But the literature lies in the treatment, not in the veracity or slightness of the subject-matter.

It was Stanislaus himself who in a letter of October 1905 pointed out that this is not one story, but two half-stories. A narrative that starts out 'about' the Dillon brothers loses one of them, then the other: the business of miching from school is then bolted on to the account of the strange meeting. Most exasperating of all for contemporary readers of 'the short story' (where style and plot were of great importance), this one had no obvious ending. The inconclusive petering out shows how much Joyce needed catching up with by the contemporary reader. He still does.

The narrator of 'An Encounter' is anonymous. Whether he is the narrator of the first story is unknowable, and if he is not young James Joyce, in many respects he might as well be. In the first story, a journey across the Liffey to the south side was mooted but not begun. Here, such a journey is actually begun, though the goal is not arrived at. (In 'Araby', another young anonymous narrator will travel in the same direction, and though he reaches his destination, he will be the most disillusioned of the three.)

The language of the young adventurer in 'An Encounter' tells us of his pretentiousness and notional superiority (as the detail of the failed sieges tell us about the bullying vigour of the future priest, Joe Dillon). His necessary Dublin cunning is a mundane version of the wiles of Odysseus: he pretends not to know about *The Halfpenny Marvel* when Leo Dillon, the fat idler, is caught out; he extracts hostage sixpences from his co-michers; he chooses not to reveal his excuse for being off school; his statement about his lack of totties may be ambiguous; he has a subterfuge to lie about names. Most importantly perhaps (and most cunningly), he chooses not to know what it is that the josser actually does. Joyce in his wrangles with his potential publisher virtually told us. (It has also been suggested, however, that the josser's marked change of tone is due to a change of tactics while talking to the narrator alone, seeking to enlist his support in physical punishment for the boorish Mahony.) In 'An Encounter', the snares and disappointments of the adult world become more substantial than in the first story. What is yet more fearful is the growing realisation by the boy of the enemy inside himself – what Stephen (quoting William Blake in *Ulysses* ('Circe')) was to call 'the priest and the king' in one's own mind.

It is a part, then, of the boy's development that the josser can be what he most dislikes or fears in himself. Both Father Flynn and the josser were clever young boys once. The boy can sense a possible future even without understanding it; in claiming to have read every book mentioned by the josser he is at risk of being identified with him, his 'good-day' of farewell to the josser echoes the josser's earlier 'good-day' to him, and he certainly has enough Latin to know the terror of being 'fixed' to the ground (if only by a shoe). Being trapped in Ringsend with such a person is a terrible fate. That does not happen, but the narrator has learnt something about his attitude to Mahony and others that he had not expected. The extent of his penitence remains an open question.

Despite Joyce's own peculiar psychopathology (the *locus classicus* of which is the 1909 letters to Nora), Joyce was not just writing about himself in 'An Encounter': he was also addressing the society of which he was a part. The small city of Dublin had twelve lunatic asylums at this time. Some of them were private (such as Bloomfield, in Morehampton Road) and at least one was the preserve of the female insane, St Vincent's in Fairview, described (autobiographically) in *A Portrait* (V.1) as Stephen sets out on his walk to the university:

... he heard a mad nun screeching in the nuns' madhouse beyond the wall,
   – Jesus! O Jesus! Jesus!
He shook the sound out of his ears by an angry toss of his head and hurried on, stumbling through the mouldering offal, his heart already bitten by an ache of loathing and bitterness.

Yet people such as Endymion (in *Ulysses* under his multiple names) and the captain of *A Portrait* (V.1 and 3) were still roaming the streets of Dublin. Green-eyed perverts were not a rarity in such a place, but the boy has yet to learn this. The josser's masturbation is the epitome of sexual paralysis, and he can also be seen as a perverted God or a perverted father.

As for the priggish narrator (ever more clearly a Dedalus *in vitro*), Joyce does not tell us what to think of him, but the potential whipster comes out of it less well than the uncomplicated, catapult-wielding (seriously normal) Mahony. The boy's quest has been a failure (though worse is to follow in the next story), and in recoiling from the mystery which the josser wishes to explain to him, he is forced to rely on the worldly existence of his inferior associate.

Just as in Chaucer's 'Pardoner's Tale', in which some young men meet Death in a field, the boy has had an intimation of his own mortality (in a stunted and corrupt society). In this spiritual death, where his search for wisdom and adventure ('some confused notion . . .') has led to a lesson in cruelty, his Dublin future seems now to be one of future complicity, and of more defeats by authority (including Father Joseph Dillon).

Whether the ending of 'An Encounter' suggests the boy's rejection of paternal or religious authority, or collaboration with it at the cost of spiritual death, the genuineness of his shame (for having scorned Mahony) is even more perplexing: the penitence is possibly opportunistic, and the shame of having to rely on Mahony is probably greater. Some Dubliners might feel that such self-knowledge was not worth having.

a) ARABY: A charity bazaar held in Dublin in 1894. The title of the story is discussed in the Afterword.

b) *North Richmond Street*: Built in 1829, and named after Charles Lennox, Fourth Duke of Richmond, who was Lord Lieutenant of Ireland 1807–13. The Joyces lived here at No 13. (See Afterword.)

c) *blind*: A cul-de-sac: the Royal Canal runs behind the end house in the street. The theme of blindness and sight runs through all Joyce's work, including *D*. See the final sentence of this story.

d) *Christian Brothers' School*: The Christian Brothers were (and are) Catholic laymen, teaching under temporary vows. Daniel O'Connell contributed to the school's building fund and laid the foundation stone in 1828, the year before Catholic Emancipation. By 1910 there were 2,000 pupils. James and Stanislaus went to this school in early 1893, but only for a few months as their father had no time for the Christian Brothers, calling it – according to Joyce's representation of a view that was very much his own – a school for 'Paddy Stink and Micky Mud' (*P* II.2). Both father and son preferred the Jesuits (who ran Belvedere and Clongowes).

e) *a priest, had died*: A look back to the theme of 'The Sisters'. There may have been several models for this priest. The most likely seems to be a Fr Quaid, who died in March 1895 of erysipelas and pneumonia. He had lived at No 13 North Richmond Street.

f) The Abbot [etc]: The second mention of Scott in *D*. *The Abbot* (1820) was a sequel to *The Monastery* (1820), and features a young boy and his involvement with Mary Queen of Scots (16m). *The Devout Communicant* by Pacificus Baker was published in 1813. Baker was an English Franciscan friar, of whose books the *Dictionary of National Biography* states:

> Without much originality, all these works are remarkable for unction, solidity, and moderation; but we wish the style was less diffuse and redundant of words.

The Memoirs of Vidocq: This unreliable book was first published in four volumes in 1828. The ostensible author was François-Eugène Vidocq (1775–1857), a criminal who, because of his knowledge of crime, was appointed to run a branch of the French police – a thief to catch a thief.

g) *a central apple-tree*: The imagery cannot but recall the Garden of Eden, and is perhaps also an echo of the mood of Malory's *Le Morte D'Arthur* (VI.1):

So they mounted on their horses, armed at all rights, and rode into a deep forest, and so into a deep plain. And then the weather was hot about noon, and Sir Launcelot had great lust to sleep. Then Sir Lionel espied a great apple tree that stood by an hedge, and said, Brother, yonder is a fair shadow, there we may rest us and our horses.

h) *the late tenant's rusty bicycle pump*: Details such as this in *D* are rarely without significance. This is perhaps a private joke: the first local bicycle with 'rheumatic wheels' belonged to Eddie Boardman (brother of the original of Edy Boardman of *U*, 'Nausicaa') who lived at No 1 North Richmond Street. It is unlikely that an old priest would have ridden such an up-to-date model. However, note the musty air enclosed in the house. Some commentators have seen a (rusty) sexual symbol in the pump or have spoken of 'divine afflatus'; one has mentioned that an ancient wind instrument under an Edenic apple tree might be called a serpent.

i) *a very charitable priest*: i.e. charitable to institutions of the Church. This form of charity, as Joyce was well aware, was rewarded generously by Masses for the Repose of the Soul, which, in turn, would allow the soul to ascend from Purgatory to Paradise with greater alacrity than might otherwise be the case.

j) *When the short days of winter . . .*: The boy will have loved Mangan's sister from afar for some six months before they speak.

k) *lamps . . . lanterns*: The Araby Bazaar Catalogue featured:

> The Eiffel Search-Light Tower,
> EIGHTY FEET HIGH.
> This powerful light will turn
> night into day, and when flashed
> on the Moon at 9 pm at night,
> the Man will be distinctly visible
> to the naked eye.

The effect might be spectacular when the narrator plans to visit Araby, for almanacs confirm that there was a full moon that night.

l) *gantlet*: Obsolete form of 'gauntlet'. Joyce specified this spelling, perhaps to bring a mediaeval tone to the story. The word is unrelated to 'glove', but came into English from Old Swedish as 'gantlope', a double row of stick-toting men, whacking at a victim forced to run between them.

m) *the cottages*: A lane called Richmond Cottages opened into a maze of small dwellings to the east side of North Richmond Street.

ARABY

NORTH RICHMOND STREET, being blind, was a quiet street except at the hour when the Christian Brothers' School set the boys free. An uninhabited house of two storeys stood at the blind end, detached from its neighbours in a square ground. The other houses of the street, conscious of decent lives within them, gazed at one another with brown imperturbable faces.

The former tenant of our house, a priest, had died in the back drawing-room. Air, musty from having been long enclosed, hung in all the rooms, and the waste room behind the kitchen was littered with old useless papers. Among these I found a few paper-covered books, the pages of which were curled and damp: *The Abbot* by Walter Scott, *The Devout Communicant* and *The Memoirs of Vidocq*. I liked the last best because its leaves were yellow. The wild garden behind the house contained a central apple-tree and a few straggling bushes, under one of which I found the late tenant's rusty bicycle pump. He had been a very charitable priest; in his will he had left all his money to institutions and the furniture of his house to his sister.

When the short days of winter came, dusk fell before we had well eaten our dinners. When we met in the street the houses had grown sombre. The space of sky above us was the colour of ever-changing violet and towards it the lamps of the street lifted their feeble lanterns. The cold air stung us and we played till our bodies glowed. Our shouts echoed in the silent street. The career of our play brought us through the dark muddy lanes behind the houses, where we ran the gantlet of the rough tribes from the cottages, to the back doors of the dark dripping gardens where odours arose from the ashpits, to the dark odorous stables where a coachman smoothed and combed the horse or shook music from the buckled harness. When we returned to the street, light from the kitchen windows had filled the areas. If my uncle was seen turning the corner we hid in the shadow until we had seen him safely housed. Or if Mangan's sister came out on the doorstep to call

n) *the dark odorous stables*: It is appropriate, before the boy goes on his romantic quest, that the story mentions the traditional mode of transport for all knights errant. At the end of *P* (II.3), Stephen inhales the 'rank heavy air' of a laneway to calm himself:

> – That is horse piss and rotted straw, he thought. It is a good odour to breathe. It will calm my heart.

o) *the areas*: An area was, and is, a space below street level between the railings and the front of many Dublin houses.

p) *we hid in the shadow*: Notable in this paragraph is Joyce's use of what might be called chiaroscuro. Images of light and shade predominate – thus: dusk, sombre, lamps, feeble lanterns, glowed, dark, dark, dark, light, shadow, shadow, shadow, light. The fact that this device remains unobtrusive is a measure of Joyce's skill in weighting, though not burdening, his stories with symbolic pointers.

q) *Mangan's sister*: Although Mangan's sister is in the light, there may also be an echo here of that personification of Ireland, 'Dark Rosaleen', from the poem by James Clarence Mangan (1803–49). Joyce had a longstanding interest in Mangan and in 1902 published a paper on him in the University College magazine, *St Stephen's*. It mentions Mangan's orientalism:

> The love of many lands goes with him always, eastern tales and the memory of curiously printed books which have rapt him out of time . . .

a) *the soft rope of her hair*: The name Mangan is a version of the Gaelic Ó Mongáin. *Mongán* means someone with a luxurious head of hair.

b) *her name*: She remains unnamed, mysterious, perhaps as much an idea as a person. James Clarence Mangan, in his unfinished *Autobiography*, does not name his sister either, but says that their father 'led my sister such a life that she was obliged to leave the house'. There are several interesting parallels with Joyce in these chapters. The poet could be Stephen Dedalus describing his father when he writes:

> My father's grand worldly fault was *improvidence* ... I ... came into the world surrounded ... by an atmosphere of curses and intemperance ... Year by year his property melted away ... Step by step he sank, until, as he himself expressed it only 'the desert of perdition' lay before him ... For me, I sought refuge in books and solitude, and days would pass during which my father seemed neither to know nor care whether I were living or dead.

c) *romance*: In some ways 'Araby' is a parody of the *amour courtois* quest literature of the Middle Ages (which itself has affinities to ancient Arabic writing), where the lover is gripped by a religious passion chastely to worship his beloved. When they were both extremely young, Dante met and fell in love with Beatrice, a relationship that remained high-minded and pure, and hints can be seen here of his *Vita nuova*, which is part of this courtly-love tradition. Some of Walter Scott's novels (21f) drew on similar material.

d) *a come-all-you about O'Donovan Rossa*: a 'come-all-you' is a ballad, many of which begin with a variant of the phrase. In 1937 Joyce wrote one which began:

> Come all you lairds and ladies and listen to my lay!
>
> I'll tell of my adventures upon last Thanksgiving Day ...

'Rossa's Farewell to Erin' is the most anthologised ballad about Rossa, but there are others. 'O Donnabhain Rosa' by Brian na Banban (Brian O'Higgins) begins:

> Diarmuid O Donnabhain Rosa!
>   Honour and love to thy name!
> There is nought in it mean or ignoble,
>   It speaks not of serfdom or shame;

It tells of a life lived for Ireland,
   Of a heart fond and fearless and true,
Of a spirit untamed and defiant,
   That the foeman could never subdue.

His crime was that Ireland, his Mother,
   Had called him to dare and to dree,
That one day her bonds might be riven,
   That one day her limbs might be free
From the chains of the English enslaver –
   And proudly he answered her call,
Nor cared what the future might bring him,
   So Ireland were freed from her thrall.

One can almost see the British Bulldog enslavering. Mr Hynes' tribute to Parnell in 'Ivy Day in the Committee Room' is, of course, far superior.

Jeremiah O'Donovan Rossa (1831–1915), Fenian, whose followers were jocularly known as 'Rossacrucians', was sentenced to penal servitude for life (with John O'Leary, Charles Kickham and others). Amnestied, he went to America, where he edited the *United Irishman*. His body was returned to Glasnevin Cemetery, and Patrick Pearse gave an influential panegyric over his grave:

> The fools, the fools, the fools! – they have left us our Fenian dead, and while Ireland holds these graves, Ireland, unfree, shall never be at peace.

Pearse taught Joyce Irish for a time, but Joyce abandoned the class because he felt that to be anti-English was not the best way of being Irish. Fittingly, in view of the equine emphasis of 'Araby', *ros* is an early Irish word for 'horse'.

e) *I bore my chalice ... strange prayers and praises ...*: The imagery of religion, so familiar to the boy, has been adapted to become the language of love. The image of the chalice is a link with 'The Sisters'.

f) *full of tears*: There are more unexpected tears at the end of several stories in *D*. The phrase also appears in the Yeats poem that Joyce used to sing ('Down by the Salley Gardens'):

> She bid me take life easy, as the grass grows on the weirs;
> But I was young and foolish, and now am full of tears.

g) *my body was like a harp*: The harp is an ancient symbol of Ireland and a less ancient one of Guinness. (In 'Two Gallants' there will be a harp like a body.)

her brother in to his tea we watched her from our shadow peer up and down the street. We waited to see whether she would remain or go in and, if she remained, we left our shadow and walked up to Mangan's steps resignedly. She was waiting for us, her figure defined by the light from the half-opened door. Her brother always teased her before he obeyed, and I stood by the railings looking at her. Her dress swung as she moved her body and the soft rope of her hair tossed from side to side.

Every morning I lay on the floor in the front parlour watching her door. The blind was pulled down to within an inch of the sash so that I could not be seen. When she came out on the doorstep my heart leaped. I ran to the hall, seized my books and followed her. I kept her brown figure always in my eye and, when we came near the point at which our ways diverged, I quickened my pace and passed her. This happened morning after morning. I had never spoken to her, except for a few casual words, and yet her name was like a summons to all my foolish blood.

Her image accompanied me even in places the most hostile to romance. On Saturday evenings when my aunt went marketing I had to go to carry some of the parcels. We walked through the flaring streets, jostled by drunken men and bargaining women, amid the curses of labourers, the shrill litanies of shop-boys who stood on guard by the barrels of pigs' cheeks, the nasal chanting of street-singers, who sang a *come-all-you* about O'Donovan Rossa or a ballad about the troubles in our native land. These noises converged in a single sensation of life for me: I imagined that I bore my chalice safely through a throng of foes. Her name sprang to my lips at moments in strange prayers and praises which I myself did not understand. My eyes were often full of tears (I could not tell why) and at times a flood from my heart seemed to pour itself out into my bosom. I thought little of the future. I did not know whether I would ever speak to her or not, or if I spoke to her, how I could tell her of my confused adoration. But my body was like a harp and her words and gestures were like fingers running upon the wires.

One evening I went into the back drawing-room in which the priest had died. It was a dark rainy evening and there was no sound in the house. Through one of the broken panes I heard the rain impinge upon the earth, the fine incessant needles

Mangan

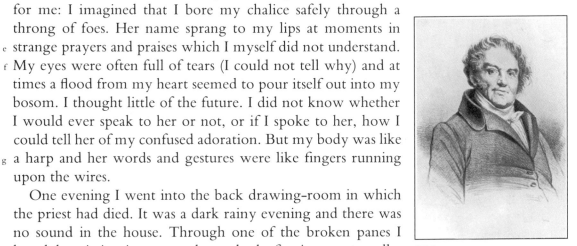

Vidocq

No 12 North Richmond St, where Joyce placed Stephen's old home

The upstairs windows of No 13, from where the boy gazes down on the street

a) *O love! O love!*: Joyce's poem 'I hear an army charging on the land' (*Chamber Music* XXXVI) ends: 'My love, my love, my love, why have you left me alone?' (itself reminiscent of Christ's words on the Cross: 'My God, my God, why hast Thou forsaken Me?')

b) *She asked me was I going to* Araby: There were frequent bazaars in Dublin around this time, the 1904 Mirus Bazaar being mentioned in *U*. 'Araby' was held in the Royal Dublin Society's premises in Ballsbridge, where the Dublin Horse Show is held each August. It was officially opened on Tuesday 15 May by the Lord Lieutenant of Ireland. The theme-song of the bazaar, by W. G. Wills and F. Clay, began:

> I'll sing thee songs of Araby,
> And tales of fair Cashmere,
> Wild tales to cheat thee of a sigh,
> Or charm thee to a tear.
> And dreams of delight shall on thee break,
> And rainbow visions rise,
> And all my soul shall strive to wake
> Sweet wonder in thine eyes.

Although Stanislaus in *MBK* says that 'Araby' has no basis in fact, William Fallon, a contemporary, claimed to have spotted the young Joyce on his real-life visit to the bazaar. However, in *P* (II.2) Stephen is sneered at by his enemy Heron: 'He doesn't smoke and he doesn't go to bazaars and he doesn't flirt . . .'

c) *a retreat that week in her convent*: Retreats, or quiet periods for devotional exercises, were frequently held in Dublin, and were described several times by Joyce, e.g. in 'Grace'.

d) *one of the spikes*: This, coupled with the silver bracelet above, has given rise to furious speculation along sexual and heraldic lines among certain classes of reader.

e) *the white curve of her neck*: See line 2 of 'The Arab's Farewell to his Steed' (25c).

f) *the white border of a petticoat*: The detail confirms Robert Herrick's famous observations:

> A sweet disorder in the dress
> Kindles in clothes a wantonness . . .
> A winning wave (deserving note)
> In the tempestuous petticoat . . .

g) *It's well for you*: Irish idiom: You're all right, Jack.

h) *some Freemason affair*: The aunt's concern is reasonable as the previous year the Catholic Archbishop of Dublin had announced that any of his flock caught attending a Masonic bazaar would be liable to

of water playing in the sodden beds. Some distant lamp or lighted window gleamed below me. I was thankful that I could see so little. All my senses seemed to desire to veil themselves and, feeling that I was about to slip from them, I pressed the palms of my hands together until they trembled, murmuring:

a   *O love! O love!* many times.

At last she spoke to me. When she addressed the first words to me I was so confused that I did not know what to answer.

b   She asked me was I going to *Araby*. I forgot whether I answered yes or no. It would be a splendid bazaar, she said; she would love to go.

—And why can't you? I asked—

While she spoke she turned a silver bracelet round and round her wrist. She could not go, she said, because there would be

c   a retreat that week in her convent. Her brother and two other boys were fighting for their caps and I was alone at the railings.

d   She held one of the spikes, bowing her head towards me. The light from the lamp opposite our door caught the white curve

e   of her neck, lit up her hair that rested there and, falling, lit up the hand upon the railing. It fell over one side of her dress and

f   caught the white border of a petticoat, just visible as she stood at ease.

g   —It's well for you, she said—

—If I go, I said, I will bring you something—

What innumerable follies laid waste my waking and sleeping thoughts after that evening! I wished to annihilate the tedious intervening days. I chafed against the work of school. At night in my bedroom and by day in the classroom her image came between me and the page I strove to read. The syllables of the word *Araby* were called to me through the silence in which my soul luxuriated and cast an Eastern enchantment over me. I asked for leave to go to the bazaar on Saturday night. My

h   aunt was surprised and hoped it was not some Freemason affair. I answered few questions in class. I watched my master's face pass from amiability to sternness; he hoped I was not beginning to idle. I could not call my wandering thoughts together. I had hardly any patience with the serious work of life which, now that it stood between me and my desire, seemed to me child's play, ugly monotonous child's play.

On Saturday morning I reminded my uncle that I wished to go to the bazaar in the evening. He was fussing at the

excommunication. In *U*, 'Hades', the suspected Mason Bloom himself suspects Mr Kernan (also in 'Grace') of being a Mason. The Freemason's Hall in Molesworth Street, close to the National Library, boasts a sculpted gnomon (or T-square) on its fascia. In the 'square ground' of the fourth line of this story could perhaps be seen an allusion to Masonic ritual, though whether this would enhance appreciation of 'Araby' is extremely moot.

By the Gulf of Persia sail,
Where the true-love nightingale
Woos the rose in every vale.

Though Arabia charge the breeze
With the incense of her trees,
On I press through southern seas.

The lure of the Orient

(*a*)

a) *looking for the hatbrush*: The uncle believes in 'passing muster' (138e), even if he will become pixillated later in the day.

b) *I could not go into the front parlour*: The 'front parlour', by strong social convention, was used in Ireland as a 'room for visitors'.

c) *my heart misgave me*: I was apprehensive; a now obsolescent usage. (It appears, however, on page one of Ruth Rendell's *Going Wrong* (1990).)

d) *by my imagination*: The watching boy has produced a phantasm – not the last ghost in *D*.

e) *this night of Our Lord*: Emptily pious phrase on the lines of 'in the year of Our Lord ...'; it is actually Saturday 19 May 1894, the last scheduled night of the bazaar.

f) *I could interpret these signs*: Interpretative skills have been learnt over these three stories.

g) *after their first sleep*: Ambiguous – the uncle means either that they have been asleep for a while or that they are intending to go to sleep. Either way, the observation is unlikely to make the boy smile.

a hallstand, looking for the hatbrush, and answered me curtly:

—Yes, boy, I know—

b   As he was in the hall I could not go into the front parlour and lie at the window. I left the house in bad humour and walked slowly towards the school. The air was pitilessly raw

c and already my heart misgave me.

When I came home to dinner my uncle had not yet been home. Still it was early. I sat staring at the clock for some time and, when its ticking began to irritate me, I left the room. I mounted the staircase and gained the upper part of the house. The high cold empty gloomy rooms liberated me and I went from room to room singing. From the front window I saw my companions playing below in the street. Their cries reached me weakened and indistinct and, leaning my forehead against the cool glass, I looked over at the dark house where she lived. I may have stood there for an hour,

d seeing nothing but the brown-clad figure cast by my imagination, touched discreetly by the lamplight at the curved neck, at the hand upon the railings and at the border below the dress.

When I came downstairs again I found Mrs Mercer sitting at the fire. She was an old garrulous woman, a pawnbroker's widow, who collected used stamps for some pious purpose. I had to endure the gossip of the tea-table. The meal was prolonged beyond an hour and still my uncle did not come. Mrs Mercer stood up to go: she was sorry she couldn't wait any longer, but it was after eight o'clock and she did not like to be out late, as the night air was bad for her. When she had gone I began to walk up and down the room, clenching my fists. My aunt said:

e   —I'm afraid you may put off your bazaar for this night of Our Lord—

At nine o'clock I heard my uncle's latchkey in the halldoor. I heard him talking to himself and heard the hallstand rocking

f when it had received the weight of his overcoat. I could interpret these signs. When he was midway through his dinner I asked him to give me the money to go to the bazaar. He had forgotten.

g   —The people are in bed and after their first sleep now, he said—

I did not smile. My aunt said to him energetically:

a) All work and no play makes Jack a dull boy: This English proverb was first recorded in James Howell's *Proverbs ... in English ...* (1659). Samuel Smiles quotes it:

All work and no play makes Jack a dull boy;
But all play and no work makes him something greatly worse.

b) *when I had told him a second time*: The uncle is clearly squiffy: he has certainly not been observing the fast exhorted by the priesthood for holy days, and has perhaps forgotten that today, 19 May 1894, is an Ember Day.

c) The Arab's Farewell to his Steed: This popular romantic poem and recitation is by the Hon. Mrs Caroline Norton (1808–1877), grand-daughter of the playwright and Dubliner Richard Brinsley Sheridan, and the original of the feminist heroine of George Meredith's *Diana of the Crossways*. She married a 'blackguard'. Her verse resembles that of Mrs Felicia ('The boy stood on the burning deck') Hemans (who was buried in Dublin), but none of it can match that of Caroline's sister, Lady Dufferin (1807–1867), whose *Lispings from Low Latitudes, or Extracts from the Journal of the Hon. Impulsia Gushington*, has been entirely forgotten. The opening lines of 'The Arab's Farewell' are:

My beautiful! my beautiful! that standest meekly by,
With thy proudly arch'd and glossy neck, and dark and fiery eye,
Fret not to roam the desert now with all thy wingèd speed!
I may not mount on thee again – thou art sold, my Arab steed;
Fret not with that impatient hoof, snuff not the breezy wind—
The further that thou fliest now, so far am I behind.

Joyce's mention of the poem is a direct hint that its imagery informs the story (23e and 26e).

d) *a florin*: Two shillings, twenty-four old pence – now 10p. The name was derived from a coin of Florence, the city that gave birth to and later banished Dante. Joyce's broadside, 'The Holy Office' (1904), makes plain his view that the relationship between himself and Dublin was comparable.

e) *Buckingham Street*: Like several Dublin streets it was named after an eighteenth-century Lord Lieutenant of Ireland: here, George Grenville Temple, Marquess of Buckingham.

f) *the station*: Amiens Street Station, now Connolly Station.

g) *glaring with gas*: A pathetic fallacy for the narrator's ardent ways.

h) *onward among ruinous houses*: A journey on horseback through desolate lands is a standard scene in mediaeval descriptions of gallant questing knights.

i) *Westland Row Station*: Now Pearse Station, but usually known by Dubliners as Pearse Street Station.

j) *special train*: The Royal Dublin Society had recently spent £7,000 on a private siding from Lansdowne Road Station to their main entrance, and arrangements had been made to run special through-trains via the 'Loop Line', which linked Amiens Street with Westland Row Station over the Liffey. Carrying both passengers and livestock, the new siding served the many shows and exhibitions, as well as the 'Monster Charity Bazaars' that were held during the 'Season'. A proper platform was not built until 1902, and the line has now gone. The journey from Amiens Street Station took ten minutes.

k) *the lighted dial of a clock*: On the original entrance to the RDS in Ballsbridge. Early in this century, the premises were rebuilt.

l) *sixpenny entrance*: For all his disdain of 'child's play', the boy hopes to save money by being eligible for a half-price ticket. But there are no concessions.

m) Café Chantant: Singing Café. From the Araby Bazaar Catalogue:

CAFÉ CHANTANT
Under management of
Mr Houston

French songs	
German songs	Piano and Violin Solos
Italian songs	
Spanish songs	Orpheus Glees
English songs	
Irish songs	

n) *two men were counting money on a salver*: A salver is literally a 'saviour', a plate or tray to catch wine etc spilt from a cup or chalice standing on it. Other religious parallels suggest themselves, including the moneychangers in the temple, and the counting of money after Mass by the clergy (see Afterword).

o) *porcelain vases and flowered tea-sets*: The alluring bazaar turns out to be selling just the usual late-Victorian domestic kitsch.

p) *I remarked their English accents*: Probably they are not English but Irish Protestant middle-class accents, which very well might be unfamiliar to the young boy.

q) —*O*: Joyce preferred the elegant and economical 'O' to the more usual 'Oh'.

—Can't you give him the money and let him go? You've kept him late enough as it is—

My uncle said he was very sorry he had forgotten. He said he believed in the old saying: *All work and no play makes Jack a dull boy.* He asked me where I was going and, when I had told him a second time he asked me did I know *The Arab's Farewell to his Steed.* When I left the kitchen he was about to recite the opening lines of the piece to my aunt.

I held a florin tightly in my hand as I strode down Buckingham Street towards the station. The sight of the streets thronged with buyers and glaring with gas recalled to me the purpose of my journey. I took my seat in a third-class carriage of a deserted train. After an intolerable delay the train moved out of the station slowly. It crept onward among ruinous houses and over the twinkling river. At Westland Row Station a crowd of people pressed to the carriage doors; but the porters moved them back, saying that it was a special train for the bazaar. I remained alone in the bare carriage. In a few minutes the train drew up beside an improvised wooden platform. I passed out on to the road and saw by the lighted dial of a clock that it was ten minutes to ten. In front of me was a large building which displayed the magical name.

I could not find any sixpenny entrance and, fearing that the bazaar would be closed, I passed in quickly through a turnstile, handing a shilling to a weary-looking man. I found myself in a big hall girdled at half its height by a gallery. Nearly all the stalls were closed and the greater part of the hall was in darkness. I recognized a silence like that which pervades a church after a service. I walked into the centre of the bazaar timidly. A few people were gathered about the stalls which were still open. Before a curtain, over which the words *Café Chantant* were written in coloured lamps, two men were counting money on a salver. I listened to the fall of the coins.

Remembering with difficulty why I had come, I went over to one of the stalls and examined porcelain vases and flowered tea-sets. At the door of the stall a young lady was talking and laughing with two young gentlemen. I remarked their English accents and listened vaguely to their conversation.

—O, I never said such a thing!—

—O, but you did!—

—O, but I didn't!—

(c)

25

The exotic transports of the east

A representation of the back of the 'Araby' catalogue

—Didn't she say that?—

—Yes. I heard her—

a   —O, there's a . . . fib!—

Observing me the young lady came over and asked me did I wish to buy anything. The tone of her voice was not encouraging: she seemed to have spoken to me out of a sense of duty. I looked humbly at the great jars that stood like eastern guards at either side of the dark entrance to the stall and murmured:

—No, thank you—

The young lady changed the positon of one of the vases and went back to the two young men. They began to talk of the same subject. Once or twice the young lady glanced at me over her shoulder.

I lingered before her stall, though I knew my stay was useless, to make my interest in her wares seem the more real. Then I turned away slowly and walked down the middle of the bazaar. b I allowed the two pennies to fall against the sixpence in my pocket. I heard a voice call from one end of the gallery that c the light was out. The upper part of the hall was now completely dark.

d   Gazing up into the darkness I saw myself as a creature driven e and derided by vanity; and my eyes burned with anguish and anger.

a) *O, there's a . . . fib!*: A possible reworking of the Eccles Street epiphany in *SH*: 'O . . . but you're . . . ve . . . ry . . . wick . . . ed . . .'

b) *the two pennies . . .*: A return ticket over that distance cost fourpence in 1894. As can be seen from the catalogue, entrance was one shilling, or 12d. From his initial two shillings he had only 8d to spend.

c) *the light was out*: Closing time was 10.30 pm – he has no time to spend his money in any case.

d) *a creature driven . . .*: Hints and mentions of horses are common in 'Araby': it is tempting to read the first five words of the previous paragraph in this context.

e) *my eyes burned . . .*: The light and dark are again contrasted at the end of the story – consider the 'fiery eyes' of the Arab steed in the Hon. Caroline Norton's poem (25c). The heightened, almost melodramatic language here contrasts sharply with the tone at the beginning of the story – a device later to be seen in 'Eveline', 'Counterparts', 'A Painful Case' and even 'The Dead'.

Afterword: 'ARABY'

'Araby' is the third and last of the anonymously 'autobiographical' childhood sections of *Dubliners*. It was finished by the autumn of 1905. In the story we are told for the first time that the narrator's home is in North Richmond Street, where the Joyces went to live during the mid-1890s. No 17 is usually given as the Joyce residence, but by a confusing coincidence this house was in fact occupied by an altogether different John Joyce. This John Joyce died, as the Dublin Joycean Peter Costello has discovered, in 1898, while John Stanislaus Joyce lived until 1931. His son twice explicitly (but misleadingly) mentions the house in his writings. Stephen in *Ulysses* ('Ithaca') remembers 'his mother Mary . . . in the kitchen of number twelve North Richmond street on the morning of the feast of Saint Francis-Xavier 1898', and in *Finnegans Wake* (420) Joyce again identifies the house (as '12 Norse Richmound'). No 12 was in fact occupied by the very elderly Hon. Mrs Michell, relict of a Dublin doctor, one Humfrey Michell, and by their son. It was perhaps superstition that led Joyce fictionally to alter the number from No 13 where the Joyces lived after the death of the priest, Father Quaid.

However long the Joyce family occupied the house, it and the area round it left a strong impression on the young James. Great Britain Street, where the fictional Flynns' drapery is, was a short walk from North Richmond Street, and would have been the nearest good shopping street. But the young Joyce made at least two rather more daring excursions from his home.

In 'An Encounter', the expedition towards the Pigeon House is a boyish search for adventure, inspired by exciting stories read under the desk at school. However, the trip to the Araby Bazaar has quite another purpose. The boy seems slightly older, and has perhaps grown up a little. The priest who died is mentioned almost in passing, as if a lesson learnt in 'The Sisters' has been assimilated. But a question has been asked in 'An Encounter' which the boy wishes to address: 'The man asked me how many (totties) had I. I answered that I had none.' After some six months of distant worship, the boy is now firmly in love with Mangan's sister, and after she speaks casually to him, he decides to act. Soon he is on a romantic quest.

The story is based on the young Joyce's visit to the Araby Bazaar in 1894. The name 'Araby', a romantic and poetic version of 'Arabia', breathes all the perfumes and mystery of the Orient. At the bazaar, Joyce may have noticed the stall from Galway, decorated with Eastern hangings, and offering for sale china and other rather unexotic household trinkets. The stall was called 'Algeciras' in honour of the long historical connection between the city and Moorish Spain. Galway was of course Nora Barnacle's native city, while in Molly Bloom's soliloquy in *Ulysses*, memories of her Gibraltar days include 'looking across the bay from Algeciras'. 'Araby', which was primarily a Protestant affair, received a great deal of publicity in contemporary magazines and papers. It imported an unwonted sense of the exotic into the circumscribed life of 'old jog-along Dublin' and nobody seems to have noticed that it was really rather a sham. To the boy it assumes a talismanic importance.

27

The nineteenth century had imported a rapid growth of interest in things oriental. The British Empire was at its peak, and foreign influences floated into the British Isles along the eastern trade routes. Little boys leaning over Liffey bridges would shout to the Guinness barges that plied to and fro (see 176) from the brewery to the Port of Dublin: 'Hey mister, bring us back a monkey'. Edward Fitzgerald's 'translation' of the *Rubáiyát of Omar Khayyám* (1859) had combined the exotic with the erotic to an extent only surpassed by Sir Richard Burton's version of the *Arabian Nights* (1885–8); Thomas Moore had celebrated the allure of the East with his long and then still popular Byronic poem, *Lalla Rookh* (1817); Mangan himself had published large numbers of poems that purported to be 'From the Ottoman' or 'From the Arabic'. However, the earliest (twelfth-century) meaning of 'Araby' was 'Arab horse', and it is therefore appropriate that the poem mentioned in Joyce's story is 'The Arab's Farewell to his Steed'. This was Caroline Norton's most celebrated work, and images from the poem are used at key points in Joyce's narrative. It forms a focus for the repeated equine references in the story, and the theme of the East is linked through the horse with another important element of 'Araby', that of knightly chivalry.

Several passages in the story are written in a style that is reminiscent of the mediaeval tales of courtly love and adventure that Chaucer may have been parodying in 'The Knight's Tale'. The boy promises to seek a prize for his fair lady, and the quest will test his abilities to overcome the obstacles in front of him – notably the lateness, drunkenness and possible stinginess of his uncle. Like many a knight of yore, riding through solitary lands and crossing distant and nameless rivers, the boy journeys alone amid ruinous houses until he reaches the place with 'the magical name', 'Araby'. Perhaps he will return with his trophy to the arms of his beloved.

Woven into these three linked motifs, the East, the horse and the mediaeval quest, is another. The boy's somewhat voyeuristic passion for Mangan's sister is expressed in the powerful language of the Church. His love is a chalice, borne through a throng of foes, and her name is invoked 'in strange prayers and praises'. The boy is not simply a questing knight: he is on a holy quest. His search is as serious as that of the Knights of Arthur's Round Table for the Holy Grail – not just a cup but also the plate that was used by Jesus at the Last Supper, which later received His Blood at the Cross. When he reaches the bazaar, it reminds him of an empty church. There, surrounded by darkness, but significantly lit by a pool of coloured light, the first people he sees are two men counting money on a salver. The boy is too late. If this is the Holy Grail, it has been debased by the commerce of Dublin. He will return to his beloved empty-handed.

Debased also is the ideal of adoring love that sent him on his mission. Romance is an illusion, and the reality of love is overheard in the flirtatious conversation between the young lady and the two young men. The boy gazes into the darkness and sees only himself, 'a creature driven and derided by vanity'. Another painful lesson in Dublin life has been learned.

Young Adulthood

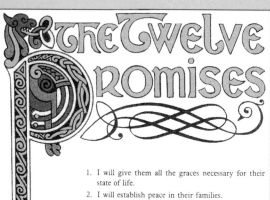

The Twelve Promises

1. I will give them all the graces necessary for their state of life.
2. I will establish peace in their families.
3. I will console them in all their difficulties.
4. I will be their assured refuge in life and more especially at death.
5. I will pour out abundant benedictions on all their undertakings.
6. Sinners shall find in My Heart a boundless ocean of mercy.
7. Tepid souls shall become fervent.
8. Fervent souls shall advance rapidly to great perfection.
9. I will bless the houses in which the image of My Heart shall be exposed and honoured.
10. I will give to priests the power of touching the most hardened hearts.
11. Those who propagate this devotion shall have their names written in My Heart and they shall never be effaced.
12. I promise thee, in the excess of the mercy of My Heart, that Its all-powerful love will grant to all those who receive Communion on the First Friday of every month, for nine successive months, the grace of final repentance, and that they shall not die under My displeasure, nor without receiving the Sacraments, and My Heart shall be their secure refuge at that last hour.

THE GREAT MOTOR RACE.

CONTEST FOR GORDON-BENNETT CUP.

VICTORY FOR GERMANY.

INTERVIEW WITH THE WINNER.

SCENES AND INCIDENTS ON THE COURSE

ACCIDENT TO JARROTT.

ENTHUSIASM IN DUBLIN.

Clockwise from top left:

★ *A 'Celtic Deco' setting for the promises of the Blessed Margaret Mary Alacoque*
★ *Young James Joyce*
★ *A 'motor establishment in Paris' (35r)*
★ *The other side of Stephen's Green*
★ *Irish newspaper headlines, July 1903 (35a)*

28

a) EVELINE: The title is discussed in the Afterword.

b) *She sat at the window*: The Lady of Shalott in Tennyson's poem, who was to take an all too final voyage herself, seals her fate by looking out of the window. The image of the lovelorn woman at the window was a common one in Victorian art. (Not until the last few lines of the story is Eveline's name actually used.)

c) *invade*: The image of invasion and migration is a theme in this story.

d) *the avenue*: This was in the suburb of Fairview, to the north-east of North Richmond Street. Here, the Joyces had three addresses in the years up to 1900. The most likely setting for the story is Richmond Avenue (where red-brick houses had recently been built).

e) *cretonne*: Printed material of stout unglazed cotton, named after the Normandy village of Creton.

f) *the new red houses*: The *Evening Mail* in December 1903 reported that in this area a new house with hot and cold water, scullery, and kitchen with copper fittings cost £280. *SH* refers to 'those brown brick houses which seem the very incarnation of Irish paralysis', but in fact the Joyces lived in one of the new red houses, No 13.

g) *the Devines* [etc]: The names of these lost playmates from Eveline's past are not irrelevant. The Waters come from 'across the water', in contrast to the Dunns (from the Irish *donn*, brown). The Devines and crippled little Keogh could be seen to represent religious elements in the story: 'Brother Keogh' in *P* (IV.3) is one of Stephen's names for a typical Christian Brother. In Upper Sherrard Street, however, quite close to Glengariff Parade where the Joyces moved in 1901, lived Devines, Waters and Keoghs, as well as the journalist William O'Leary Curtis (mentioned in 'Gas From a Burner'), who is the model for Mr O'Madden Burke of 'A Mother' (129b).

h) *her brothers and sisters*: According to this part of the story, Eveline has at least two sisters and one brother (apart from Harry and Ernest – who was 'too grown up' to play, and who is now dead). Of this family of six or more children, only two now appear to have any dealings whatever with Eveline's father. But see 30(o).

i) *Her father ...*: Mr Hill is based upon John Joyce. Like the God of Genesis, he banishes his children from their Garden of Eden – a fallen world already glimpsed in 'Araby' (21g). The scene is also reminiscent of Nora's experiences of being hunted by her uncle Tom Healy in Galway. The blackthorn was a tree of magical druidic potency in Celtic mythology, and the blackthorn stick (or shillelagh) is the clichéd weapon of the stage-Irishman.

j) *to keep* nix: To keep watch. Probably not from German *nichts* ('nothing'), but from Romany *nisser*, 'to avoid'. Little Keogh would have hissed the word 'nix' to warn them. What it was that would have been disapproved of is unstated, but Keogh's disability made him suitable for the role of lookout.

k) *Tizzie Dunn*: In the *Irish Homestead* version, Mrs Dunn. Tizzie is a likely diminutive of 'Teresa'.

l) *Everything changes*: In Cork (*P* 11.4) Stephen is asked whether *Tempora mutantur nos et mutamur in illis* or *Tempora mutantur et nos mutamur in illis* is correct.

m) *Home!*: One of the key words of *P*, unchangeable and ever-changing. Stephen reflects on the dean of studies' pronunciation, but goes on to speak of his own determination to surpass nationality, language and religion.

n) *reviewing*: Literally, seeing again. Joyce changed this from the *Irish Homestead* version, which reads 'passing in review'.

o) *during all those years*: According to the *Homestead* text, she had 'known the room for ten years – more – twelve years ...'

p) *the broken harmonium*: A symbol of family discord. The theme of music and song runs through 'Eveline'.

q) *Blessed Margaret Mary Alacoque*: She is a late interpolation into the text, and of some importance in the story. 'Margaret Mary Anycock', as Buck Mulligan (and very likely Gogarty before him) unfairly called her, was a French seventeenth-century Visitandine nun in the convent at Paray-le-Monial. Her devotion and self-mortification were surprisingly ardent: she preferred to drink only water in which laundry had been boiled, and consumed pus in preference to tea. She has since been canonised. Her fame sprang from the 'Great Revelations of the Sacred Heart' in which Christ made the twelve promises to her (28).

EVELINE

SHE SAT AT the window watching the evening invade the avenue. Her head was leaned against the window curtains and in her nostrils was the odour of dusty cretonne. She was tired.

Few people passed. The man out of the last house passed on his way home; she heard his footsteps clacking along the concrete pavement and afterwards crunching on the cinder path before the new red houses. One time there used to be a field there in which they used to play every evening with other people's children. Then a man from Belfast bought the field and built houses in it – not like their little brown houses but bright brick houses with shining roofs. The children of the avenue used to play together in that field – the Devines, the Waters, the Dunns, little Keogh the cripple, she and her brothers and sisters. Ernest, however, never played: he was too grown up. Her father used often to hunt them in out of the field with his blackthorn stick; but usually little Keogh used to keep *nix* and call out when he saw her father coming. Still they seemed to have been rather happy then. Her father was not so bad then; and besides, her mother was alive. That was a long time ago; she and her brothers and sisters were all grown up; her mother was dead. Tizzie Dunn was dead, too, and the Waters had gone back to England. Everything changes. Now she was going to go away like the others, to leave her home.

Home! She looked round the room, reviewing all its familiar objects which she had dusted once a week for so many years, wondering where on earth all the dust came from. Perhaps she would never see again those familiar objects from which she had never dreamed of being divided. And yet during all those years she had never found out the name of the priest whose yellowing photograph hung on the wall above the broken harmonium beside the coloured print of the promises made to Blessed Margaret Mary Alacoque. He had been a school friend of her father. Whenever he showed the photograph to a visitor her father used to pass it with a casual word:

—He is in Melbourne now—

(*b*).

r) *He is in Melbourne now*: This, 'a better place', is capital of Victoria, Australia. The question of whether or not to emigrate is underlined by repeated mentions of distant places in the story: at first only Belfast and England, but to come are Buenos Ayres, Bohemia, Canada, the Straits of Magellan, Patagonia and Italy. Priests often emigrated to Melbourne: Fr Thomas P. Brown, who in 1888 wrote to Mrs Joyce about her son's progress at Clongowes, shortly afterwards became Rector of the Xavier College, Kew, Melbourne, and later Superior of the Irish Jesuit Mission in Australia. In 1912 the Irishman Daniel Mannix became Coadjutor Bishop of Melbourne and in 1917 Archbishop.

29

CLERY & COMPANY, LIMITED, DUBLIN.

(b)

A postcard in Irish of His Grace the Archbishop of Melbourne (29r)

a) *Was that wise?*: Significantly, this has been changed from the first version, which read: 'Was it wise – was it honourable?'

b) *the Stores*: Perhaps Pim's (43r), or more likely, Clery & Co., which had previously been M'Swiney's, who were cousins of John Joyce (or so he said). *Thom's Directory* (1902) describes the shop as

> drapers, silk mercers, hosiers, glovers, haberdashers, jewellers, boot and shoe makers, tailors, woollen drapers, and general warehousemen, 21 to 27 Sackville Street Lower.

c) *an edge on her*: A sharp, sarcastic manner.

d) *Miss Hill*: We learn Eveline's surname. It is surely fanciful to find the Garden of Eden combined with the Hill of Calvary in her name, but Joyce's names are always worth examining. This one also recalls John Cleland's enterprising heroine, Fanny Hill.

e) *Look lively, Miss Hill, please*: Originally, 'A little bit smarter, Miss Hill, if you please'. The change shows Eveline being forced to appear to be alive (as opposed to dead).

f) *over nineteen*: An over-defensive assertion, meaning 'nineteen'.

g) *the palpitations*: This is either a colloquial usage, deriving from the lack of an indefinite article in Irish, as in 'She has the varicose veins,' or else Eveline is thinking of a particular attack. It is sufficient to note that palpitations are a condition of the heart (33a) and that the danger of classroom violence from Father Butler has the same effect on the schoolboys in 'An Encounter'.

h) *Harry and Ernest*: Suggestions have been made that there is a link in this story with Wilde's *The Importance of Being Ernest*, but, apart from the absent Ernest's influence upon Eveline and her search for a stable and happy relationship, it is hard to discern any tenable allusion. A black leather purse is not quite a handbag, nor is a porthole exactly a prism. However, Joyce had by accident been baptised with the same name (Augusta) as Lady Bracknell (and, indeed, as Lady Gregory).

i) *the church decorating business*: At this time a great deal of money was being spent on building and decorating Catholic churches. Harry's employer's business was likely to be prosperous.

j) *She always gave her entire wages – seven shillings*: The implication is not that she gave them to her father, but that they went on the upkeep of the house and on the children left to her charge. Were it not for her family expenses, Eveline would be

She had consented to go away, to leave her home. Was that
a wise? She tried to weigh each side of the question. In her home
anyway she had shelter and food; she had those whom she had
known all her life about her. Of course she had to work hard,
both in the house and at business. What would they say of her
b in the Stores when they found out that she had run away with
a fellow? Say she was a fool, perhaps; and her place would be
filled up by advertisement. Miss Gavan would be glad. She
c had always had an edge on her, especially whenever there were
people listening.

d   —Miss Hill, don't you see these ladies are waiting?—

e   —Look lively, Miss Hill, please—

She would not cry many tears at leaving the Stores.

But in her new home, in a distant unknown country, it
would not be like that. Then she would be married – she,
Eveline. People would treat her with respect then. She would
not be treated as her mother had been. Even now, though she
f was over nineteen, she sometimes felt herself in danger of her
father's violence. She knew it was that that had given her the
g palpitations. When they were growing up he had never gone
h for her, like he used to go for Harry and Ernest, because she
was a girl; but latterly he had begun to threaten her and say
what he would do to her only for her dead mother's sake. And
now she had nobody to protect her. Ernest was dead and Harry,
i who was in the church decorating business, was nearly always
down somewhere in the country. Besides, the invariable squab-
ble for money on Saturday nights had begun to weary her
unspeakably. She always gave her entire wages – seven shil-
j lings – and Harry always sent up what he could, but the trouble
was to get any money from her father. He said she used to
k squander the money, that she had no head, that he wasn't going
to give her his hard-earned money to throw about the streets,
l and much more, for he was usually fairly bad of a Saturday
night. In the end he would give her the money and ask her
had she any intention of buying Sunday's dinner. Then she had
m to rush out as quickly as she could and do her marketing,
n holding her black leather purse tightly in her hand as she
elbowed her way through the crowds, and returning home
late under her load of provisions. She had hard work to keep
o the house together and to see that the two young children who
had been left to her charge went to school regularly and got

earning quite a satisfactory
wage in the Stores for
someone who pays no rent.
k) *she had no head*: No brains,
no common sense.
l) *he was usually fairly bad of a
Saturday night*: What he
accuses her of is precisely what
he himself is guilty of – and if
she had no head for money,
he had none for drink.
m) *marketing*: Groceries were
cheaper in markets (e.g.
Moore Street) than in shops.
n) *black leather purse*: The
colours which dominate his
story are two of Joyce's archetypal Dublin colours: black
and brown (the third being
yellow).
o) *the two young children*: We
have been told that Eveline's
brothers and sisters have all
grown up. Who these are is a
mystery. Eveline and, reluctantly, her father are supporting them. Perhaps we are
to suppose that they are
orphaned cousins or the like
who have been taken in
through family loyalty, as
may be the case in the first
three stories of the collection.
It seems to be one of Joyce's
rare and uncharacteristic loose
ends.

30

a) *a hard life*: Flann O'Brien's novel *The Hard Life: An Exegesis of Squalor* (1961) can be seen as an extended parody of *D*.

b) *open-hearted*: An adjective that could equally be applied to representations of Christ and the Sacred Heart. Eveline will have to choose which suitor to espouse.

c) *the night-boat*: This really is a journey into the dark, into the future. Perhaps it is also a journey towards death, a last passage on the ferry-boat across the Styx.

d) *Buenos Ayres*: The capital of the Argentine. The spelling is now standardised as 'Aires', and the name means 'Good Air(s)', in contrast to the stifling atmosphere of Dublin (which means 'Black Pool'). Stanislaus in *MBK* identifies the city as where the husband of Joyce's aunt, 'Dante' Conway (an early influence in *P* and also in *U* as Mrs Riordan), went with all her savings. 'To go to Buenos Aires' used to mean to become a prostitute, particularly through a pimp.

e) *a house on the main road*: Probably on Richmond Road, which leads from Ballybough Bridge to Drumcondra Road. It is not, in any case, the eponymous boarding house in Hardwicke Street.

f) *It seemed a few weeks ago*: How long Frank has been in 'the old country just for a holiday' is hard to tell. If, as he said, he 'had a home waiting for her' in Buenos Aires, it seems that he was determined to wait as long as it took to find a wife. If not, which appears to be just as likely, the duration of his stay could only be guessed at by the fading tan of his bronzed face.

g) *his peaked cap pushed back on his head*: The mannerism is found again in 'Two Gallants' and 'Ivy Day'. It is also a trait of Lynch in *SH*, who 'destroyed the illusion of imperialism by wearing his cap very far back from a shock forehead'. Joyce, like Frank, 'sang a little'. With his cap, he was at first taken by Nora to be a sailor.

h) The Bohemian Girl: An opera (1843) by one of Joyce's favourite composers, the Dubliner Michael Balfe (1808–70), who is mentioned in 'Clay'. It contains a heroine ready to run away with the hero.

i) *the lass that loves a sailor*: The early nineteenth-century song is by Charles Dibdin. It begins:

The moon on the ocean was dimmed by a ripple,
Affording a chequered delight,
The gay jolly tars passed the word for a tipple,
And the toast, for 'twas Saturday night.
Some sweetheart or wife he loved as his life,
Each drank and wished he could hail her;
But the standing toast that pleased the most
Was 'The wind that blows,

The ship that goes,
And the lass that loves a sailor'.

Frank and Mr Hill have similar Saturday nights, perhaps. The song is mentioned in *FW*.
The Lass that Loved a Sailor was also the subtitle of Gilbert and Sullivan's *HMS Pinafore*.

j) *Poppens*: See Afterword.

k) *He had tales of distant countries*: Othello (I. iii) woos Desdemona in a similar fashion, telling her father of incidents

... in my travel's history ...
And of the Cannibals that each other eat,
The Anthropophagi, and men whose heads
Do grow beneath their shoulders. This to hear
Would Desdemona seriously incline;
But still the house-affairs would draw her thence;
Which ever as she could with haste dispatch,
She'd come again, and with a greedy ear
Devour up my discourse.

l) *the Allan Line*: This British steamship company was founded in 1852 by Sir Hugh Allan. It made weekly sailings from Liverpool to the west coast of Canada, calling at Buenos Aires, Cape Horn and elsewhere.

m) *the terrible Patagonians*: The only direct indication in the story that Frank might be lying: the myth of the giants who dwelt on Tierra del Fuego, and who had been 'sighted' on Magellan's first circumnavigation of the world, was quite exploded by 1900. Shakespeare's Caliban (in *The Tempest*) was based on early reports of Patagonians.

n) *fallen on his feet in Buenos Ayres, he said,*: Hugh Kenner has made a great deal of the significance of these two commas enclosing 'he said', and suggests that they imply that Frank is lying, especially as the language resembles that of romantic novels. The sentence can also be read much more innocently, however.

o) *just for a holiday*: This throwaway remark begs several questions. Has Frank no real past? Who were/are his family? Why is he lodging in a boarding-house on Richmond Road, scarcely the most luxurious of places for one who has 'fallen on his feet'?

p) *a ghost story and made toast*: Memories of a Dublin childhood. A common skipping-rhyme goes:

Mrs White
Had a fright
In the middle of the night:
Saw a ghost
Eating toast
Sliding down the lamp-post.

their meals regularly. It was hard work – a hard life – but now that she was about to leave it she did not find it a wholly undesirable life.

She was about to explore another life with Frank. Frank was very kind, manly, open-hearted. She was to go away with him by the night-boat to be his wife and to live with him in Buenos Ayres where he had a home waiting for her. How well she remembered the first time she had seen him; he was lodging in a house on the main road where she used to visit. It seemed a few weeks ago. He was standing at the gate, his peaked cap pushed back on his head and his hair tumbled forward over a face of bronze. Then they had come to know each other. He used to meet her outside the Stores every evening and see her home. He took her to see *The Bohemian Girl* and she felt elated as she sat in an unaccustomed part of the theatre with him. He was awfully fond of music and sang a little. People knew that they were courting and, when he sang about the lass that loves a sailor, she always felt pleasantly confused. He used to call her Poppens out of fun. First of all it had been an excitement for her to have a fellow and then she had begun to like him. He had tales of distant countries. He had started as a deck boy at a pound a month on a ship of the Allan Line going out to Canada. He told her the names of the ships he had been on and the names of the different services. He had sailed through the Straits of Magellan and he told her stories of the terrible Patagonians. He had fallen on his feet in Buenos Ayres, he said, and had come over to the old country just for a holiday. Of course, her father had found out the affair and had forbidden her to have anything to say to him.

—I know these sailor chaps, he said—

One day he had quarrelled with Frank and after that she had to meet her lover secretly.

The evening deepened in the avenue. The white of two letters in her lap grew indistinct. One was to Harry; the other was to her father. Ernest had been her favourite but she liked Harry too. Her father was becoming old lately, she noticed; he would miss her. Sometimes he could be very nice. Not long before, when she had been laid up for a day, he had read her out a ghost story and made toast for her at the fire. Another day, when their mother was alive, they had all gone for a picnic to the Hill of Howth. She remembered her father putting on

q) *a picnic to the Hill of Howth*: Leopold Bloom and Molly Tweedy also picnicked memorably on the Howth peninsula, near Dublin (*U*, 'Lestrygonians', 'Penelope'). Howth's geographical features include Bloody River and Doldrum Bay.

Old Buenos Aires (31d)

a) *Her time was running out*: This sentence is a reprise of the beginning of the story, subtly changed. The verbs are now active: Eveline seems ready to move.

b) *a street organ playing*: This instrument works, unlike the broken harmonium at home. Shortly before the story was written, Italian organ-grinders had been involved in a plot to irritate George Moore, which it is tempting to imagine was masterminded by Joyce and Gogarty (51a).

c) *the promise to her mother*: See Afterword.

d) *a melancholy air of Italy*: Comparable with the 'good air' of Buenos Aires, the phrase returns to the motifs of music and foreignness.

e) *Damned Italians!*: The influence in Ireland of Rome, through the Catholic Church, is certainly commented on here, but this may also be a dig at Luigi Denza, composer of 'Funiculi-Funicula', who intended (but failed) to give Joyce a gold medal at the 1904 Feis (music festival). Another Italian known by the Joyces was Professor Michele Esposito of the Royal Irish Academy of Music, who was a leading light in musical circles. There are to be many musical Italians spoken of in 'The Dead'. Had Eveline ever got to Argentina, she would have found many immigrants from Italy there, who would no doubt have said similar things about her.

f) *final craziness*: Like that reported at the end of 'The Sisters'.

g) *Derevaun Seraun!*: What this might mean is obscure, and is almost a party game among Joyceans. It probably either means nothing, or parrots what Joyce's own mother repeated on her death-bed. There have been several other suggestions. It might be garbled Irish: Patrick Henchy of the National Library, Dublin, heard it as meaning 'The end of pleasure is pain'; other ideas have been 'Farewell to the white oak-woods' and 'My own little one, grasp my hand'. It might also possibly be:

Deireadh amháin seráin: There is one end: maggots; *Deireadh fan saorán*: The end of the free person; *Deirbhfhine 's arán*: Bloodline and bread-(line); *Do raibh únsa aráin*: There was an ounce of bread; *Deirbh an soirean*: The real laughing-stock; *Dearbhán sarán*: The right louse; *Deireadh amhráin siabhrán*: The end of song is derangement; *Deirbh an sorn*: Certain is the furnace; *Deireadh amháin siarain*: The only end is westwards.

It could be bad French: *Devrons serons*, We ought to be what we will be. It could even be English: There, a fancy run!; Dare advance, or run; The reforms are on; The reverends are wrong. One hesitates to

her mother's bonnet to make the children laugh.

a   Her time was running out, but she continued to sit by the window, leaning her head against the window curtain, inhaling the odour of dusty cretonne. Down far in the avenue she could

b hear a street organ playing. She knew the air. Strange that it should come that very night to remind her of the promise to

c her mother, her promise to keep the home together as long as she could. She remembered the last night of her mother's illness; she was again in the close dark room at the other side

d of the hall and outside she heard a melancholy air of Italy. The organ-player had been ordered to go away and given sixpence. She remembered her father strutting back into the sickroom saying:

e   —Damned Italians! coming over here!—

As she mused the pitiful vision of her mother's life laid its spell on the very quick of her being – that life of commonplace

f sacrifices closing in final craziness. She trembled as she heard again her mother's voice saying constantly with foolish insistence:

g   —Derevaun Seraun! Derevaun Seraun!—

She stood up in a sudden impulse of terror. Escape! She must escape! Frank would save her. He would give her life, perhaps love, too. But she wanted to live. Why should she be unhappy? She had a right to happiness. Frank would take her in his arms, fold her in his arms. He would save her.

.   .   .   .

She stood among the swaying crowd in the station at the

h North Wall. He held her hand and she knew that he was speaking to her, saying something about the passage over

i and over again. The station was full of soldiers with brown

j baggages. Through the wide doors of the sheds she caught a

k glimpse of the black mass of the boat, lying in beside the quay wall, with illumined portholes. She answered nothing. She felt her cheek pale and cold and, out of a maze of distress, she prayed to God to direct her, to show her what was her duty. The boat blew a long mournful whistle into the mist. If she

l went, to-morrow she would be on the sea with Frank, steaming towards Buenos Ayres. Their passage had been booked. Could she still draw back after all he had done for her? Her distress awoke a nausea in her body and she kept moving her lips in silent fervent prayer.

suggest that if she really was saying the words constantly, she might have been saying 'Seraun Derevaun!' Like Eveline, you make your choice.

h) *the North Wall*: The embarkation point from Dublin, as it was for Joyce and Nora.

i) *something about the passage over and over again*: Eveline's mother also repeated something unidentifiable about her own impending passage to the next world.

j) *soldiers with brown baggages*: British soldiers from Irish garrisons were a common sight on ships bound for England.

k) *black mass*: The phrase underlines Eveline's fear of the unknown, and of sinning against the responsibilities of Church and family. Note also the juxtaposition of brown (j) and black again.

l) *to-morrow*: Eveline is right: Most sailings went via Liverpool, and it would probably not be until the next day that they would be truly on their way to Buenos Ayres.

From an old Irish song-sheet

Christ appearing to the Blessed Margaret Mary Alacoque

The Sacred Heart of Jesus

a) *A bell clanged upon her heart*: As with the long mournful whistle above, a form of music has accompanied her through the story. Eveline's heart is at the mercy of many influences – the bell, the sea, open-hearted Frank and the Sacred Heart of Jesus.

b) *Come!*: The climax of the story brings in a note of melodrama, in stark contrast to the stasis of the opening. There is a similarity with *U*, 'Sirens':

> *Co-ome thou lost one!*
> *Co-ome thou dear one! . . .*
> *Come!*

c) *All the seas of the world*: Joyce had read the farewell letter of Evelyn Innes's lover Ulick in his copy of George Moore's 1898 novel:

> I see you like a ship that has cleared the harbour bar, and is already amid the tumult of the ocean . . . We are ships . . . we part, drawn apart by the eternal magnetism of the sea . . .

From *Evelyn Innes* (Ch XXXII). Its sequel, *Sister Teresa* (1901), describes Evelyn Innes' life as a nun.

d) *She set her white face . . .*: She is like the snowy statue in 'The Dead' (199(0)), and at the same time like the boy at the end of 'Araby'. Amidst the turmoil, she is as motionless at the end of the story as she has been at the beginning, incapable of leaving behind this city and its all-pervading paralysis.

e) *passive*: For the Blessed Margaret Mary Alacoque (29q), passivity was a positive virtue. On one occasion 'our Lord showed her his sacred Body, covered with wounds which He had suffered for her . . . [and He] told her that if she placed [her will] in the Wound of His Sacred Side she would no longer find any difficulty in overcoming herself'. When she was twenty she had refused an offer of marriage, but later, when she had made her profession in November 1672 she wrote that 'my Divine Lord was pleased to receive me as His spouse in a manner I am unable to express'. Her autobiography continues:

> Penetrated with respect for His infinite majesty, my own inclination would have led me to remain constantly prostrate on my face before Him . . . I never dared to remain seated when alone . . . On a Friday, He placed my mouth to the Wound in His Side, and held me close to Him, with delights which I cannot express.

f) *no sign*: Paralysis. The Blessed Margaret Mary similarly despised and suppressed her own honest reactions to people around her.

a   A bell clanged upon her heart. She felt him seize her hand:

b   —Come!—

c   All the seas of the world tumbled about her heart. He was drawing her into them: he would drown her. She gripped with both hands at the iron railing.

—Come!—

No! No! No! It was impossible. Her hands clutched the iron in frenzy. Amid the seas she sent a cry of anguish.

—Eveline! Evvy!—

He rushed beyond the barrier and called to her to follow. He was shouted at to go on but he still called to her. She set
de   her white face to him, passive, like a helpless animal. Her eyes
f   gave him no sign of love or farewell or recognition.

Come!

Afterword: 'Eveline'

Written in the summer of 1904, 'Eveline' was the second of the three stories to be published in the *Irish Homestead*, where it appeared on 10 September 1904, a month before Mr Joyce eloped with Miss Barnacle. It was later revised – probably in 1905 – when Joyce inserted the guiding presence of the Blessed Margaret Mary Alacoque. The story is the first narrative in *Dubliners* to be written in the third person, and it contains Joyce's earliest surviving use of a device which he was to perfect in *Ulysses*, the interior monologue. It was also his first attempt to write from the point of view of a woman.

Eveline is a victim, a sufferer from the paralysis of Dublin. She bears an unusual form of the Christian name, meaning 'little Eve'. A nineteenth-century pornographic novel shared the name and Fanny Burney wrote a novel called *Evelina, or a Young Lady's Entrance into the World* (1778), but 'Eveleen's Bower', one of the ubiquitous *Melodies* of Tom Moore, is more likely to have influenced Joyce's choice of name:

Oh! weep for the hour,
When to Eveleen's bower
The Lord of the Valley with false vows came;
The moon hid her light
From the Heavens that night,
And wept behind her clouds o'er the maiden's
shame.

The clouds past soon
From the chaste cold moon,
And Heav'n smiled again with her vestal flame:
But none will see the day

When the clouds shall pass away,
Which that dark hour left upon Eveleen's fame.

The white snow lay
On the narrow pathway
When the Lord of the Valley cross'd over the
moor,
And many a deep print
On the white snow's tint
Show'd the track of his footsteps to Eveleen's door.
The next sun's ray
Soon melted away
Every trace on the path where the false Lord came,
But there's a light above
Which alone can remove
That stain upon the snow of fair Eveleen's fame.

Joyce and Nora had known each other for less than three months when he wrote 'Eveline'. Would he prove to be a 'false Lord'? Stanislaus reported that AE (George Russell) at least thought that Joyce would abandon Nora when they reached the Continent. Would she too change her mind at the last minute? 'Eveline' describes a possible outcome of the suggestion that they leave Ireland together.

How did Joyce ensure that Nora would trust him? The knowledgeable Dublin critic and diarist Arland Ussher may have provided an answer. In *Three Great Irishmen* (1952) he states that on the night before they sailed the couple stayed together in the Grosvenor Hotel, Westland Row. If they did, it was a chaste night, for it wasn't until they had reached Zürich later in October 1904 that Joyce announced in a letter to his brother that Nora *'n'est pas encore vierge'*. Joyce was very broke, but the Grosvenor was around the corner from Finn's Hotel where Nora had been working, and she would almost certainly have known members of the hotel staff who would have lent a spare room to the couple for that last night in Ireland. There Joyce could prove to Nora his good faith by exercising a very considerable degree of chastity.

The detail is not in Richard Ellmann's biography, but Ussher was no pub gossip. It would certainly explain the otherwise mysterious sighting by Bloom (in *Ulysses*, 'Lotus Eaters') of a young couple emerging from the hotel on the morning of Bloomsday: notably, both have very little change as they set out on their journey. She is attractive, standing carelessly, 'Reserved about to yield', while he is ambiguously described (in a late addition to the manuscript of *Ulysses*) as 'the man, husband, brother'. The facts of the matter are probably now unprovable, though certainly if Frank had organised such a night for Eveline, she would have gone with him.

Clearly, the plot of the story is partly borrowed from the emigration plans of Joyce and Nora. But Eveline was not based on Nora. According to Ellmann, her life-model was the daughter of Ned Thornton (who contributes to Mr Kernan's character in 'Grace'). She had a brother who worked not in church furnishings but at Telfords (makers of the organ played by Mary Jane Morkan (of 'The Dead'), and she fell in love with a sailor. However, they settled in Dublin and produced a large number of children, and she predeceased her mother.

Although Joyce took certain details from Thornton's daughter, the main source for Eveline was actually Joyce's own sister, Margaret (1884–1964), known to all as 'Poppie'. Frank calls Eveline 'Poppens'. This babytalk suffix of the Joyces, '-ens', appears also in *A Portrait* ('nicens') and in *Ulysses* ('Calypso'), where Bloom addresses his cat as 'Pussens'. Poppie displayed striking similarities with Eveline: at twenty, keeping a promise made to her dying mother, she took over the running of the house and, with the help of the little money she could worm out of her father, she brought up the younger children. One night, sitting up with Joyce, she claimed to see a vision of her dead mother in a brown habit. She argued against Joyce's elopement with Nora, and (though he could not have known it when the story was being written), she was never to marry. Poppie became a nun, joining the Sisters of Mercy in 1909, and emigrated to New Zealand, where she taught the piano and the violin. She died in Auckland fifty-four years later at the age of eighty.

Poppie may have shown signs of religious fervour by the time the story was written or revised. Her final choice was made in 1909. At the North Wall, Eveline too makes her final choice, between – on the one hand – the opportunity of a life with Frank, marriage, and a home far from the brown houses of Dublin, and – on the other – the responsibilities laid upon her by her mother and her father, by the children in her care, and above all by the prospect of the pseudo-marriage to Christ offered by the Blessed Margaret Mary Alacoque.

a) AFTER THE RACE: The race happened on 2 July 1903. Joyce took the phrase directly from his own Paris interview, which is discussed in the Afterword. It remains a matter of debate how far in his Irishness Jimmy takes after the race.

b) *scudding*: The word is cognate with skidding. A report of the race in *The Constabulary Gazette* (by 'ONE WHO WAS THERE') says:

> Before the stoppage of the highway, motors of all kinds were to be seen scudding along to various chosen points to view the great race.

c) *running evenly like pellets in the groove*: There is no hurry, as the race is already over. The route was in the Irish Midlands and went through Castledermot, Carlow, Athy, Kildare, Monasterevan, and Stradbally. (Additionally, there were to be time trials in the Phoenix Park two days later.) Ségouin's car, with its cosmopolitan cargo, was not competing, only observing.

d) *Naas Road*: Naas rhymes with 'grace', and is a town to the south-east, in County Kildare. The road runs into Dublin between Kilmainham Gaol and Richmond Barracks – both symbols of Irish subjugation. Being hanged was once known as doing the Kilmainham minuet.

e) *Inchicore*: Then a village on the south bank of the Liffey, near Chapelizod.

f) *poverty and inaction ... wealth and industry*: The groupings are wholly deliberate, and the Irish lack of capital foretells the discussion in 'Ivy Day in the Committee Room'.

g) *the cheer of the gratefully oppressed*: This sardonic detail recalls that when Queen Alexandra visited Dublin with Edward VII in 1904, she observed of the crowds that 'the poorer they are the more they cheer'.

h) *blue cars*: The French colour, distinguished from (say) British Racing Green.

i) *their friends, the French*: Irish-French relations are deep. The invasion of 1798 is only one instance, remembered in the songline 'The French are on the Say, says the Shan Van Vocht'. In *P* (V.1), Stephen remembers the politically naïve Frenchmen who appeared at the abortive Wolfe Tone memorial sculpture ceremony.

j) *second and third*: Both these cars were Panhards. A Mors was fourth, and though Joyce had mentioned the *marque* in his original article, he chose to make nothing of its Latin meaning.

k) *the winning German car*: A Mercédès, at a time of six hours thirty-nine minutes and nine seconds, over a course of 370 miles. Only five of the twelve starters finished.

l) *a Belgian*: M. Jenatzy, who won the race, was indeed a Belgian and he spoke no German – grounds for Francophile pleasure, therefore. He was described in the Dublin *Daily Express* (37f) as 'that plucky and daring automobilist' (12d), and is also mentioned towards the end of *U*, 'Oxen of the Sun':

> Lay you two to one Jenatzy licks him ruddy well hollow.

m) *a double measure of welcome*: 'measure' was amended by Joyce from the similarly bibulous 'round'.

n) *successful Gallicism*: A Gallicism is usually a word or phrase, though occasionally it is a characteristic. Because of their *bons mots* and the day's adventure, the young observers are sharing in the success of the virtual victors. In this rerun of the Gallic Wars (12r), it is the Gauls who do well.

o) *Ségouin*: The name was possibly adapted by Joyce from *sagouin*, which is French for a dirty fellow, either physically or morally. Here, after a drive on the dusty roads, both meanings apply. Paul de Kock, much read by the Blooms, wrote in *Ni jamais, ni toujours* (1835) '*c'est un affreux, un vrai sagouin*'.

p) *Rivière*: Joyce had an hospitable medical acquaintance in Paris of this name from 1902, whom he had met through Lady Gregory.

q) *Villona*: Also named after a Paris-based acquaintance from Joyce's first flight in 1902–3, though one who was French rather than Hungarian.

r) *a motor establishment*: Henri Fournier, whom Joyce had interviewed (a), was the manager of Paris-Automobile, in the rue d'Anjou. There were many others, as the industry was immature.

s) *His father*: Mr Doyle is based on William Field (1848–1935), who owned a chain of butcher's shops

AFTER THE RACE

THE CARS CAME scudding in towards Dublin, running evenly like pellets in the groove of the Naas Road. At the crest of the hill at Inchicore sightseers had gathered in clumps to watch the cars careering homeward and through this channel of poverty and inaction the Continent sped its wealth and industry. Now and again the clumps of people raised the cheer of the gratefully oppressed. Their sympathy, however, was for the blue cars – the cars of their friends, the French.

The French, moreover, were virtual victors. Their team had finished solidly; they had been placed second and third and the driver of the winning German car was reported a Belgian. Each blue car, therefore, received a double measure of welcome as it topped the crest of the hill and each cheer of welcome was acknowledged with smiles and nods by those in the car. In one of these trimly built cars was a party of four young men whose spirits seemed to be at present well above the level of successful Gallicism: in fact, these four young men were almost hilarious. They were Charles Ségouin, the owner of the car; André Rivière, a young electrician of Canadian birth; a huge Hungarian named Villona and a neatly groomed young man named Doyle. Ségouin was in good humour because he had unexpectedly received some orders in advance (he was about to start a motor establishment in Paris) and Rivière was in good humour because he was to be appointed manager of the establishment; these two young men (who were cousins) were also in good humour because of the success of the French cars. Villona was in good humour because he had had a very satisfactory luncheon; and besides he was an optimist by nature. The fourth member of the party, however, was too excited to be genuinely happy.

He was about twenty-six years of age, with a soft, light brown moustache and rather innocent-looking grey eyes. His father, who had begun life as an advanced Nationalist, had modified his views early. He had made his money as a butcher in Kingstown and by opening shops in Dublin and in the

which grew from his original establishment near Kingstown. After attending school in Blackrock, he graduated from the Catholic University (169c). He was one of the official party at the catafalque when Parnell's body was brought back to Kingstown in 1891, an occasion imagined by Stephen in *P* (I.2).

t) *advanced Nationalist*: A strong supporter of Home Rule and of Parnell.

u) *modified his views*: The father has become a 'Castle Catholic', and has clearly gone to some trouble to make Jimmy as pro-British as possible. Arthur Griffith's paper, the *United Irishman*, labelled Field as a 'flunkey' of the crown.

v) *money as a butcher*: Like Polly Mooney's father and grandfather in 'The Boarding House', though considerably more successful. Cardinal Wolsey, Henry VIII's mighty henchman who is thought of by young Stephen Dedalus, was the son of a butcher.

w) *Kingstown*: Formerly Dunleary, it was renamed in 1821 after George IV's visit, and is now Dún Laoghaire. The vicissitudes are mentioned in *FW* (428). Long a solidly prosperous area, it is twelve miles south-east of Dublin.

a) *police contracts*: Large butchers often styled themselves 'victuallers and contractors'. Providing chops for the constabulary (especially the Royal Irish Constabulary depot near Phoenix Park) would have been a useful source of bulk business. Mr Doyle has changed politically so much that he now feeds (and feeds off) his former enemies. When revising the story, Joyce wrote to his faithful gofer Stannie in September 1905 asking whether the police were supplied with provisions by government or by private contracts. The latter assumption was allowed to prevail.

b) *a merchant prince*: Appropriately, given the riskiness of Mr Doyle's latest venture, the expression comes from Isaiah (XXIII. 6–8), on the overthrow of the biblical city of Tyre:

> howl, ye inhabitants of the isle. Is this your joyous city, whose antiquity is of ancient days? Her own feet shall carry her afar off to sojourn. Who hath taken this counsel against Tyre, the crowning city, whose merchants are princes, whose traffickers are the honourable of the earth?

c) *England . . . college*: Not an unusual background. Oliver St John Gogarty went to the Jesuit-run Stonyhurst College in Lancashire (once the school of the lamentable Poet Laureate, Alfred Austin), and then to university in Dublin. Father Henry (12p) also went to an English school followed by an Irish college. Even Charles Stewart Parnell, born in Wicklow, went to school in England.

d) *Dublin University*: The less common name for Trinity College, Dublin, founded by Elizabeth I in 1591. By tradition it was strongly Protestant and Unionist, but its foundation statutes made no mention of religious discrimination, and indeed, many local Catholics had contributed to its establishment. Trinity's central location in Dublin helps Stephen to think of it as 'set heavily in the city's ignorance like a great dull stone set in a cumbrous ring' (*P* V.1). When in 1873, the College ended the last of the religious tests that excluded Catholics – and Presbyterians and Jews and others – from academic achievement, the Catholic bishops brought in 'the ban', which forbade Catholics to enrol there without special episcopal dispensation. Assertive middle-class families (such as the Gogartys) ensured that there were always some Catholic students at Trinity.

e) *bad courses*: 'course' is French for race. The term recalls Shakespeare's *Henry V* (I.i):

> His addiction was to courses vain;
> His companies, unletter'd, rude and shallow;
> His hours fill'd up with riots, banquets, sports.

f) *musical . . . circles*: Although *D* has been seen as a cross-section of Dublin life, it draws heavily on Joyce's own milieux. Many of his acquaintances were involved in music in some way, and can be seen in 'A Mother', 'The Dead' and elsewhere.

g) *Cambridge*: Spending only a term at Cambridge University was quite easily done at this time. Clearly Doyle senior has strong aspirations that his son meet the right people – Englishmen. There is an ironic contrast with Parnell (c), who had attended Magdalene College, Cambridge in the 1860s, and not graduated.

h) *see a little life*: The unfulfilled aspiration of many of these Dubliners, e.g. Eveline, or Little Chandler.

Irish Travellers (38)

suburbs he had made his money many times over. He had also
a been fortunate enough to secure some of the police contracts
and in the end he had become rich enough to be alluded to in
b the Dublin newspapers as a merchant prince. He had sent his
c son to England to be educated in a big Catholic college and
d had afterwards sent him to Dublin University to study law.
e Jimmy did not study very earnestly and took to bad courses
for a while. He had money and he was popular; and he divided
f his time curiously between musical and motoring circles. Then
gh he had been sent for a term to Cambridge to see a little life.
i His father, remonstrative, but covertly proud of the excess,
had paid his bills and brought him home. It was at Cambridge
that he had met Ségouin. They were not much more than
acquaintances as yet but Jimmy found great pleasure in the
society of one who had seen so much of the world and was
reputed to own some of the biggest hotels in France. Such a
person (as his father agreed) was well worth knowing, even if
he had not been the charming companion he was. Villona was
entertaining also – a brilliant pianist – but, unfortunately, very
poor.

The car ran on merrily with its cargo of hilarious youth.
The two cousins sat on the front seat; Jimmy and his Hungarian
friend sat behind. Decidedly Villona was in excellent spirits; he
kept up a deep bass hum of melody for miles of the road. The
Frenchmen flung their laughter and light words over their
shoulders and often Jimmy had to strain forward to catch the
quick phrase. This was not altogether pleasant for him, as he
had nearly always to make a deft guess at the meaning and
j shout back a suitable answer in the teeth of a high wind. Besides
Villona's humming would confuse anybody: the noise of the
car, too.

k Rapid motion through space elates one; so does notoriety;
so does the possession of money. These were three good reasons
for Jimmy's excitement. He had been seen by many of his
friends that day in the company of these continentals. At
l the control Ségouin had presented him to one of the French
competitors and, in answer to his confused murmur of compliment, the swarthy face of the driver had disclosed a line of
shining white teeth. It was pleasant after that honour to return
m to the profane world of spectators amid nudges and significant
n looks. Then as to money – he really had a great sum under his

i) *remonstrative*: The unusual word is possibly a theological joke by Joyce. Mr Doyle as a Remonstrant suggests that he has come a long way from his background. The term was used of a Protestant group of the early seventeenth century, who gave a new direction to Calvinism (181i).

j) *teeth of a high wind*: Originally 'face'.

k) *Rapid motion through space*: As in 'An Encounter', an expression derived from physics or astronomy. Jimmy is being subjected to layers of disorientation. At least six factors of confusion are mentioned: speed, wind, humming, car noise, notoriety, money.

l) *the control*: One of the timing stages in the race.

m) *the profane world*: Not necessarily unholy, but the implication is that the experiences of the day have assumed an almost religious importance in Jimmy's mind. This is his chance to 'improve' himself.

n) *he really had a great sum under his control*: Actually the money was still under his father's control. Jimmy, careering along, does not yet seem to have earned anything.

a) *the inheritor of solid instincts*: Joyce is being sardonic: *solidus* is the Latin for shilling, and still found in the expression '£.s.d.' – pounds, shillings and pence.

b) *labour latent in money*: A hint of Joyce's socialist sympathies at this time. Had it not been for its involvement in the Irish language revival, Joyce might at this time actually have supported the Irish Socialist Republican Party, then part-led by James Connolly (who also argued 'You cannot teach starving men Gaelic' (97k)).

c) *money … pots of money*: Pots of money can easily be confused with crocks of gold, which can never be found, situated as they are at the ends of rainbows (134). This is the authentic voice of Jimmy's father.

d) *machinery of human nerves … swift blue animal*: Joyce had possibly detected in the Italian *Zeitgeist* the Futurist and pre-Fascist obsession with speed.

e) *Dame Street*: It runs east from Dublin Castle, to College Green, and got its name from the dam there on what was then called the River Anliffe. Peg Woffington, later the *inamorata* of David Garrick, was born in Dame Street in 1719.

f) *unusual traffic*: The *Daily Express* (168h) described it thus:

> At numerous corners little knots of people were to be seen gathered showing in their demeanour an anxiety to glean the latest details of the contest, and at Cork Hill, perhaps, the largest number had assembled to discuss the race, and eagerly scrutinise the occupants of some automobiles, the first of a procession which entered the city a little before five o'clock. From this time the assemblages at various points of vantage in the city commenced to increase…
>
> Towards six o'clock enthusiasm ran high, and at this time there was a fairly consistent string of automobiles making their entry into the city by way of Lord Edward and Dame street. When the result was published the spectators instead of diminishing, kept on increasing, and in many places, notably College Green and the vicinity of the Shelbourne Hotel, where many of the visitors stayed, the policemen on duty had occasionally a busy time, preserving clear space for the progress of the ordinary and motor traffic … the crowds at every point were of a most enthusiastic character, and on many occasions during the early portion of the evening the motors containing officials and well-known automobilists were lustily cheered as they passed to their quarters in the city. By seven o'clock the thoroughfares were lined in every direction by eager crowds…

g) *the Bank*: The Bank of Ireland, facing the main gates of Trinity, was the Irish Parliament until 1800. It is where Stephen Dedalus collects his prize monies in *P* (II.5). The 'homerule sun' that was the *Freeman's* 'device' (120d) was another statement of the Bank's importance.

h) *to pay homage to the snorting motor*: In the city, as in the countryside, there is subservience in the face of arrogance. The worship of anything but God is, like simony, an offence against the First Commandment. Robert in *Exiles* says to Richard that a kiss is an act of homage.

control. Ségouin, perhaps, would not think it a great sum but Jimmy who, in spite of temporary errors, was at heart the
a inheritor of solid instincts, knew well with what difficulty it had been got together. This knowledge had previously kept his bills within the limits of reasonable recklessness and, if he
b had been so conscious of the labour latent in money when there had been question merely of some freak of the higher intelligence, how much more so now when he was about to stake the greater part of his substance! It was a serious thing for him.

Of course, the investment was a good one and Ségouin had managed to give the impression that it was by a favour of friendship the mite of Irish money was to be included in the capital of the concern. Jimmy had a respect for his father's shrewdness in business matters and in this case it had been his
c father who had first suggested the investment; money to be made in the motor business, pots of money. Moreover, Ségouin had the unmistakable air of wealth. Jimmy set out to translate into days' work that lordly car in which he sat. How smoothly it ran! In what style they had come careering along the country roads! The journey laid a magical finger on the genuine pulse
d of life and gallantly the machinery of human nerves strove to answer the bounding courses of the swift blue animal.

e They drove down Dame Street. The street was busy with
f unusual traffic, loud with the horns of motorists and the gongs
g of impatient tram-drivers. Near the Bank Ségouin drew up and Jimmy and his friend alighted. A little knot of people
h collected on the footpath to pay homage to the snorting motor. The party was to dine together that evening in Ségouin's hotel and, meanwhile, Jimmy and his friend, who was staying with him, were to go home to dress. The car steered out slowly for
i Grafton Street while the two young men pushed their way
j through the knot of gazers. They walked northward with a curious feeling of disappointment in the exercise, while the city hung its pale globes of light above them in a haze of summer evening.

In Jimmy's house this dinner had been pronounced an occasion. A certain pride mingled with his parents' trepidation,
k a certain eagerness, also, to play fast and loose, for the names
l of great foreign cities have at least this virtue. Jimmy, too,
m looked very well when he was dressed and, as he stood in the

i) *Grafton Street*: The most fashionable street in Dublin. *Dignam's Dublin Guide* (1891) describes it thus:

> Poverty cares not to come from the back lanes ... and only the puff, powder, and shave of high society crawl along, begloved and bejewelled, with the real quality voice on.

The cousins are staying at the Shelbourne Hotel on Stephen's Green, around which they are to stroll after their meal. (The other hotel on the Green at this time was the Russell Temperance Hotel – clearly unsuitable.)

j) *walked northward ... pale globes of light*: These young men in O'Connell Street on a summer evening provide a variant to the opening of 'Two Gallants'.

k) *fast and loose*: Significantly, this is the name of an old swindling game.

l) *the names of great foreign cities*: So too in 'A Little Cloud' and 'The Dead'.

m) *Jimmy, too, looked very well when he was dressed*: In *U*, 'Telemachus', Buck Mulligan tells Stephen:

> You look damn well when you're dressed.

The 'too' is not in addition to other characters, but an enthusiastic and subjective statement of Jimmy's suitability for this company.

a) *a last equation*: A metaphor for the ends of his bow tie, (which unlike Jimmy are egalitarian). The algebraic '*x*' even looks like a bow tie.

b) *qualities often unpurchasable*: In the *Irish Homestead*, this read 'unpurchasable qualities'. The change suggests that these qualities *were* purchased in this case.

c) *The dinner*: Jimmy and Villona have rejoined the others at their hotel. Present are Rivière, Routh, Villona, Jimmy, and Ségouin (who is the alert host).

d) *Ségouin, Jimmy decided, had a very refined taste*: The punctuation recalls the trickiness of 'Eveline'(31n).

e) *Routh*: The name was that of yet another Paris associate of Joyce, a smug Cambridge version of 'Haines' of *U*, who was an Oxford man. Gorman suggested that Joyce and Villona spoke to one another in Latin – something that students and ex-students and medical students' pals could do in 1902.

f) *electric candle lamps*: Public electricity began in Dublin in the Mansion House and Dawson Street in 1881 (191i). This was some decades after Cardinal Newman wrote:

> Lead kindly light
> Amid the encircling gloom . . .

g) *volubly*: In the first version, 'a great deal'.

h) *twined elegantly*: In the story there are no hints that any of the men are interested in women, and several

that they are not. The homosexual traditions of a part of Cambridge, or of European decadence, might have a bearing on this.

i) *host*: 'entertainer' in the *Irish Homestead*.

j) *began to discover*: A deliberately old-fashioned usage, or perhaps Hungarian inexact English. Flann O'Brien mentioned how he had discovered and then recovered James Joyce.

k) *English madrigal ... old instruments*: Always an enthusiasm of Joyce, as shown in a letter to Gogarty of June 1904. Joyce hoped to obtain a lute from the London instrument-maker Arnold Dolmetsch, who had made a psaltery for Yeats, but on this occasion English charity began at home. The interest was instead later bestowed on Bloom.

l) *not wholly ingenuously*: Rivière is expatiating on French expertise, and being economical with the truth (a phrase coined by Edmund Burke) about the likely success of the motor business, in order to stiffen Jimmy's resolve to invest in it.

m) *the spurious lutes of the romantic painters*: The point is that the lutes as pictured were anachronistic in style. Anachronism is an occupational hazard of the artist.

n) *generous influences*: They would include alcohol, and the likely political ideas of Villona, who would

More Irish Travellers (*36*)

a hall giving a last equation to the bows of his dress tie, his father
may have felt even commercially satisfied at having secured
b for his son qualities often unpurchasable. His father, therefore,
was unusually friendly with Villona and his manner expressed
a real respect for foreign accomplishments; but this subtlety of
his host was probably lost upon the Hungarian, who was
beginning to have a sharp desire for his dinner.
c The dinner was excellent, exquisite. Ségouin, Jimmy
d decided, had a very refined taste. The party was increased by
e a young Englishman named Routh whom Jimmy had seen
with Ségouin at Cambridge. The young men supped in a snug
fg room lit by electric candle lamps. They talked volubly and
with little reserve. Jimmy, whose imagination was kindling,
h conceived the lively youth of the Frenchmen twined elegantly
upon the firm framework of the Englishman's manner. A
graceful image of his, he thought, and a just one. He admired
i the dexterity with which their host directed the conversation.
The five young men had various tastes and their tongues
had been loosened. Villona, with immense respect, began to
j discover to the mildly surprised Englishman the beauties of
k the English madrigal, deploring the loss of old instruments.
l Rivière, not wholly ingenuously, undertook to explain to
Jimmy the triumph of the French mechanicians. The resonant
voice of the Hungarian was about to prevail in ridicule of the
m spurious lutes of the romantic painters when Ségouin
shepherded his party into politics. Here was congenial ground
n for all. Jimmy, under generous influences, felt the buried zeal
of his father wake to life within him: he aroused the torpid
Routh at last. The room grew doubly hot and Ségouin's task
grew harder each moment: there was even danger of personal
o spite. The alert host at an opportunity lifted his glass to
p Humanity and, when the toast had been drunk, he threw open
a window significantly.
q That night the city wore the mask of a capital. The five
r young men strolled along Stephen's Green in a faint cloud of
aromatic smoke. They talked loudly and gaily and their cloaks
dangled from their shoulders. The people made way for them.
At the corner of Grafton Street a short fat man was putting
s two handsome ladies on a car in charge of another fat man.
The car drove off and the short fat man caught sight of the
party.

probably have sympathies
with Arthur Griffith's 'Two
Crowns' approach (40h), itself
based on Hungary's relationship with the Habsburg
Empire.
o) *personal spite*: Piquantly, the
Irish Homestead gives 'personal
spice'.
p) *Humanity*: The unob-
jectionable toast is a frequent
ploy used to cool a political
disagreement. John Locke,
friend of John Anthony
Collins (57c), wrote:

> All men ought to maintain
> peace, and the common
> offices of humanity and
> friendship, in the diversity
> of opinions.

q) *mask of a capital*: Joycean
waspishness, and a great
improvement from his pre-
vious 'air of a capital'. There
is self-deception too, as with
Jimmy. Dublin, though the
capital of a country, had not
for over a century been the
capital of a state. The drive to
the bank (37g) is mute tes-
timony of this.
r) *Stephen's Green*: Much featured in *SH* and *P* as 'my
Green'. In 1700 Captain
William Phillips published in
Dublin his only comedy, *St
Stephen's Green, Or The Generous Lovers*. The characters
included   Wormwood,
Vanity, Trickwell, and Feign-
youth.   The   later   writer
Stephen Phillips (whose work
Joyce knew) was perhaps a
kinsman: in 1902 he published
a play – *Ulysses*.
s) *two handsome ladies*: There
is an innuendo of prostitution
here (especially given the rich-
ness or fatness of the two
men), though it may be significant that Farley does not
accompany the ladies.

38

a) *It's Farley!*: Joyce knew of the Rev. Charles Farley, who was attached to St Francis Xavier's (12h). The name is not uncommon in Ireland, and the suggestion is that Farley was an Irish-American. In Middle-English however, the word meant 'surprising' or 'strange', so the exclamation mark is doubly appropriate.

b) *squeezing themselves together*: It would be difficult to fit six, as well as the driver, on an outsider, particularly when one is 'fat' and another 'huge'.

c) *Westland Row*: In *U*, between 'Oxen of the Sun' and 'Circe', the station is again the setting for a high-spirited departure, when Stephen has a drunken quarrel with Mulligan and Haines. Three gaseous products of this short street are Oscar Wilde (born at No 21), soda water (65n) and pneumatic tyres (8h).

d) *in a few seconds*: The railway to Kingstown was begun in 1832, and was the oldest and most frequent in Ireland (158s). The train took fifteen minutes to reach Kingstown.

e) *saluted*: The meaning is merely 'greeted' or 'acknowledged non-verbally'. The word is used throughout Joyce's work.

f) *he was an old man*: Presumably he remembers Jimmy (who alone is treated thus) from the days before his father had expanded his business from Kingstown and moved into Dublin.

g) *the harbour*: Four days after the race there was a story in the *Evening Mail*:

ACCIDENT TO A DUBLIN LADY AND GENTLEMAN

An alarming boating accident occurred last evening at Kingstown Harbour. Mr. Sebastian Nolan of St Stephen's Green Club, and the Edward Yachting Club, Kingstown, was out for a sail in the bay in his yacht Concha, accompanied by a Dublin gentleman and lady – Mr. and Mrs. Bloom. When the party returned to the harbour, the Concha was made fast to her moorings, and Mr. and Mrs. Bloom proceeded to go ashore, a yacht's punt being requisitioned for the purpose. When they got into the punt, however, it capsized, Mr. and Mrs. Bloom being thrown into the water ... Mr. and Mrs. Bloom managed to cling to the capsized boat – which was drifting – until assistance arrived, and eventually they were rescued, and taken to the Edward Yacht Club. Later in the evening, Mr. and Mrs. Bloom returned to town, apparently not any the worse for their adventure.

h) *like a darkened mirror*: As they go down the hill from the station they can see the symmetrical arms of the harbour walls making a mirror-like polygonal shape. But Jimmy has little capacity for introspection. Mirrors are one theme of the book, and this image cannot but recall I Corinthians (XIII. 12):

> For now we see through a glass, darkly; but then face to face: now I know in part; but then shall I know even as also I am known.

In *Krapp's Last Tape*, Samuel Beckett recalled the intense spiritual experience he had here one memorable night not long after the Second World War (169l)

> at the end of the jetty, in the howling wind, never to be forgotten, when suddenly I saw the whole thing. The vision at last.

i) Cadet Rousselle: A French cabaret song, one of the Paris fads which Joyce brought back to Dublin in 1903. Padraic Colum reported that Gogarty for a while called Joyce by the name. The chorus translates as, 'Ah, ah, but it's true, Rousselle junior is good-natured': Doyle junior is going to need to be, too.

j) *cavalier*: A gallant.

k) *lady*: As a waltz involves a stylised embrace, one partner has to 'lead' and the 'lady' to 'follow'.

l) *square dance*: A type of dance done in square formation. There are several in the stories. As Villona is playing the piano, there are five men for the square dance, so it is hardly surprising that they devise 'original figures' – and perhaps some gnomons. This is a musical precursor of the quincunx (153g).

m) *this was seeing life*: Improved from 'this was life'. The idea is repeated in 'A Little Cloud'.

n) *Farley ... cried Stop!*: In the *Irish Homestead*, 'and they cried 'Stop!''. The changed detail reflects Farley's fatness.

o) *for form' sake*: This was Joyce's preferred usage. A sacrament required matter (such as bread and wine), and also form – in this case the social context rather than the nutritious aspect of the supper. The Oxonian Anthony Wood in 1672 referred to:

> A fellow of little or no religion only for forme-sake.

p) *Bohemian*: Jimmy thinks of himself as the Bohemian boy, a parallel with Eveline (31h) and Ignatius Gallaher (67b).

q) *Ireland ... the United States*: It is an imperial detail that André does not toast his own Canada.

—André—

a　—It's Farley!—

A torrent of talk followed. Farley was an American. No one knew very well what the talk was about. Villona and Rivière were the noisiest, but all the men were excited. They got up

b　on a car, squeezing themselves together amid much laughter. They drove by the crowd, blended now into soft colours, to

c　a music of merry bells. They took the train at Westland Row

d　and in a few seconds, as it seemed to Jimmy, they were walking

e　out of Kingstown Station. The ticket-collector saluted Jimmy;

f　he was an old man:

—Fine night, sir!—

g　It was a serene summer night; the harbour lay like a darkened

h　mirror at their feet. They proceeded towards it with linked

i　arms, singing *Cadet Rousselle* in chorus, stamping their feet at every:

—*Ho! Ho! Hohé, vraiment!*—

They got into a rowboat at the slip and made out for the American's yacht. There was to be supper, music, cards. Villona said with conviction:

—It is delightful!—

There was a yacht piano in the cabin. Villona played a waltz

j　for Farley and Rivière, Farley acting as cavalier and Rivière as

kl　lady. Then an impromptu square dance, the men devising original figures. What merriment! Jimmy took his part with a

m　will; this was seeing life, at least. Then Farley got out of breath

n　and cried *Stop!* A man brought in a light supper, and the young

o　men sat down to it for form' sake. They drank, however: it was

p　Bohemian. They drank Ireland, England, France, Hungary, the

q　United States of America. Jimmy made a speech, a long speech,

r　Villona saying *Hear! hear!* whenever there was a pause. There was a great clapping of hands when he sat down. It must have been a good speech. Farley clapped him on the back and laughed loudly. What jovial fellows! What good company they were!

s　Cards! cards! The table was cleared. Villona returned quietly to his piano and played voluntaries for them. The other men played game after game, flinging themselves boldly into the

t　adventure. They drank the health of the queen of hearts and of the queen of diamonds. Jimmy felt obscurely the lack of an audience: the wit was flashing. Play ran very high and paper

r) Hear! hear!: This recurs in 'The Dead' from Mr Browne, and is still the conventional cry of endorsement.

s) *Cards! cards!*: Which these cavaliers and gallants are. Bishop Berkeley (40c) in his excellent series of musings, *The Querist* (1737), wondered in No 552:

> Whether there be not every year more cash circulated at the card tables of Dublin than at all the fairs of Ireland.

The popular games of Edwardian Dublin included bezique (which Bloom played with Dante Riordan in 1893 and 1894), baccarat, faro and Nap (short for Napoleon).

t) *queen of hearts. . . queen of diamonds*: Both red, and stimulating. That seventeenth-century Bohemian girl, Elizabeth Stuart (Queen thereof, and daughter of James VI and I), was known as the Queen of Hearts. Hearts and diamonds are of course symbolic of love and money respectively.

39

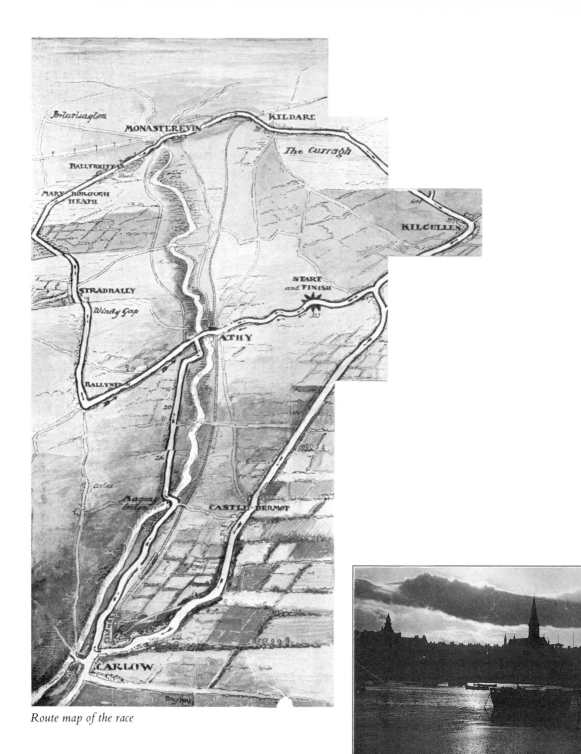

Route map of the race

Kingstown Harbour by night

a began to pass. Jimmy did not know exactly who was winning but he knew that he was losing. But it was his own fault for

b he frequently mistook his cards and the other men had to calculate his I.O.U.'s for him. They were devils of fellows but he wished they would stop: it was getting late. Some one gave

c the toast of the yacht *The Belle of Newport*, and then some one

d proposed one great game for a finish.

The piano had stopped; Villona must have gone up on deck. It was a terrible game. They stopped just before the end of it to drink for luck. Jimmy understood that the game lay between Routh and Ségouin. What excitement! Jimmy was excited too; he would lose, of course. How much had he written away? The men rose to their feet to play the last tricks, talking and

e gesticulating. Routh won. The cabin shook with the young men's cheering and the cards were bundled together. They began then to gather in what they had won. Farley and Jimmy

f were the heaviest losers.

g He knew that he would regret in the morning, but at present he was glad of the rest, glad of the dark stupor that would cover up his folly. He leaned his elbows on the table and rested his head between his hands, counting the beats of his temples. The cabin door opened and he saw the Hungarian standing in a shaft of grey light:

h —Daybreak, gentlemen!—

a) *paper began to pass*: The players are gambling with banknotes or cheques or (in Jimmy's case) IOUs.

b) *mistook*: Misunderstood, and thus made a mistake.

c) The Belle of Newport: The famous town in Rhode Island was praised, in different degrees, by Berkeley, Wilde, Trollope and Henry James. There are connotations here of hedonism, plutocracy and arch-capitalism.

d) *one great game*: Undercover diplomacy in the nineteenth century was known as the 'Great Game', involving spies, disguises and treachery.

e) *Routh won*: Just as in the early twentieth century, Great Britain was the clear winner in the Great Game.

f) *Farley and Jimmy were the heaviest losers*: They are also the only ones with Irish blood.

g) *he would regret*: The construction is strangely intransitive.

h) *Daybreak, gentlemen!*: A Hungarian telling an audience in Ireland of a new day dawning has been seen by some as a symbol of Arthur Griffith's Irish programme. He had published *The Resurrection of Hungary* in 1904, in which the Habsburg 'Two Crowns' formula was adopted as a model for the local problem, so that Dublin could be Budapest to imperial London's Vienna. In *U*, the source of Griffith's Hungarianism is said to be Leopold Bloom, son of Rudolph Virag, formerly of Szombathely.

DEPARTURE OF THE KING. *Inconsolable Grief of the Hibernians*

George IV leaves Kingstown in 1821: Inconsolable Grief of the Hibernians
(*35 g and w*)

The story appeared in the *Irish Homestead* of 17 December 1904, by which time Joyce and Nora were far away in polyglot Pola. 'After the Race' was the third and last of the stories to appear independently in this way.

Unusually, given Joyce's reputation as a writer about the prosaic (and the universal), this story is concerned with an internationally renowned event. The Gordon Bennett Cup was the forerunner of the modern Grand Prix series of races. It was established in 1900 as the Coupe Internationale de l'Automobile and named (informally) after the eccentric, Paris-based proprietor of the *New York Herald* (whose flair for publicity – and circulation-building – caused him to send H. M. Stanley to find David Livingstone).

A British subject named Edge had won the 1902 race, and so the United Kingdom had the right to stage the 1903 race. Because of Ireland's lesser density of population than England, it was chosen as the site of the road race. The Westminster Parliament passed the Light Locomotives (Ireland) Act 1903, a small and temporary measure to enable the authorities to stage the race with due concern for public safety (e.g. by having the right to close roads). Anticipation was keen. In Paris that April, Joyce had made some money (actually 13/9d – less than 70p) by selling to the *Irish Times* an interview with a much-fancied competitor, M. Henri Fournier (who did not in fact complete). His piece included this story's title, and some incisive questioning:

"Will you remain any time in Ireland?"

"After the race?"

"Yes."

"I am afraid not. I should like to, but I don't think I can."

"I suppose you would not like to be asked your opinion of the result?"

"Hardly."

"Yet, which nation do you fear most?"

"I fear them all – Germans, Americans, and English. They are all to be feared."

"And how about Mr. Edge?"

No answer.

By the end of June the police and the railways were ready. So too were the motoring clubs and the hotels and the hospitals and the steam-packet companies. There were to be seven circuits of the route, in the Irish midlands. The race began at about 6.30 am, when the twelve competitors were sent off at seven-minute intervals. The roads were reopened at 7.25 pm, and the day was a resounding success (except perhaps for the hapless Edge, who was disqualified). When the crowds surged into Dublin that evening, it is hardly surprising that the mood was one of exhilaration: high-spirited, festive, Continental.

But Jimmy Doyle's poise and sophistication are not deep. He does not speak French very well. He is taken for a ride by his European 'friends'. Not only is he too excited to be genuinely happy, he is also too excited to understand them or Dublin or himself. Even though he makes a speech, we hear nothing of Jimmy's utterances. Like Little Chandler later (but unlike Miss Ivors), he allows himself to be patronised by exponents of continental ways. Rivière is similarly deracinated but has come to terms with the dominant culture (in his case, metropolitan France), whereas Jimmy – in his cups – feels more compromised about his status as a British subject than his father does (or is).

It is a casually eloquent historical detail that the model for Mr Doyle was William Field, Member of Parliament for the Saint Patrick's Division of Dublin since 1892: he was superseded in 1918 by Countess Markiewicz, the United Kingdom's first elected woman MP. Field in his day had been President of the Irish Cattle Traders and Stock Owners Association, Honorary Secretary of the Dublin Victuallers Association, Vice-President of the National Federation of Meat Traders of the United Kingdom, Governor of the Royal Irish Veterinary College, Chairman of the Blackrock Technical Instruction Committee, and had held other positions of considerable power and influence.

Joyce in the summer of 1912 wrote about foot and mouth disease to Field, who did not reply. It was part of a rigmarole again treated in *Ulysses.*

While the story's exotic group of automobilists can accommodate Villona (because of his talent), Jimmy is not obviously welcome among them except for his money. The whole story is sprinkled with the vocabulary of commercial worth, (a theme re-encountered in 'Grace'). Whatever the shortcomings and depredations of Dublin reflected in 'After the Race', its satire extends to European targets.

Joyce himself was not happy with this story, and regarded it as the joint worst in the collection. In 1906 he intended to rewrite it, but the stressful correspondence with Grant Richards, and the demands of stories such as 'The Dead' and 'Ulysses' soon prevented this. Though Jimmy Doyle is the nearest contemporary in *Dubliners* to Joyce himself, the delineation of Jimmy lacks depth. Unlike in other stories (notably 'Clay') the subjectivity of the character – what has been called the 'Uncle Charles Principle' – is not successfully rendered.

While some of the boys of 'An Encounter' got most of the way to Dublin Bay, and Eveline very nearly reached the gangplank, in 'After the Race' – for the only time in the book – we go offshore, in Kingstown Harbour. Stephen in his diary for 3 April (*P* V.4) has told Davin that the shortest way to Tara is '*via* Holyhead'. This is no fruitful exile for Jimmy, however. Despite the speed and travel in the story – automobile, train, yacht – the theme of paralysis is still marked. Jimmy's notion of 'life' is no more developed than Eveline's. His adolescence, like hers or Lenehan's, is a state of mind (a paralysed one) rather than a statement of his youth.

Homer often gave his seafarers a rosy-fingered dawn, but here Joyce has young Doyle make do with a grey one. Jimmy in his crapulous misery is best described in the second-last stanza of Joe Hynes' poem in 'Ivy Day in the Committee Room', though Irish history offers little encouragement.

a) Two Gallants: For some implications of the title, see the Afterword.

b) *The grey warm evening . . .* : The opening paragraph of this story is a good example of Joyce's use of repetition and echo to set an almost hypnotic tone. In these few lines the sounds repeat: grey, warm, evening, air, memory, murmur, summer, summit, swarmed, streets, unceasing, unchanging. The last eight words of the paragraph all have earlier counterparts. The influence of Flaubert is noticeable in passages such as this.

c) *the streets, shuttered for the repose of Sunday*: *The Real Charlotte* (1894) is perhaps the best novel by Edith Somerville and Martin Ross. It opens with a description:

> An August Sunday afternoon in the north side of Dublin. Epitome of all that is hot, arid, and empty. Tall brick houses, browbeating each other in gloomy respectability across the white streets; broad pavements, promenaded mainly by the nomadic cat; stifling squares . . . Few towns are duller out of the season than Dublin, but the dullness of its north side neither waxes nor wanes; it is immutable, unchangeable, fixed as the stars. So at least it appears to the observer whose impressions are only eye-deep . . .

d) *Rutland Square*: After independence this was renamed Parnell Square. Its east side (where Oliver Gogarty was born at No 5) is a northward continuation of O'Connell Street. Built between 1753 and 1769, it is named after the Fourth Duke of Rutland, Lord Lieutenant of Ireland 1784–7. Lenehan and Corley are passing the point where the photograph on the jacket of this book was taken.

e) *A yachting cap*: Similar attire is worn by Frank in 'Eveline'. Since Joyce also wore one, there is a hint that Lenehan contains elements of what Joyce felt he might have become if he had not left Dublin. Lenehan may be dressed as a yachtsman but he's not going anywhere.

f) *waterproof*: The largest and most successful waterproof manufacturers in rainy Ireland was the Dublin Rubber Company, 37 Lower Kevin Street. Some critics have seen the frequent water-repellent gar-

ments in *D* as symbols of unwillingness to accept the benefit of natural (or baptismal) and life-giving water, or of prophylactics.

g) *his figure fell into rotundity*: Suitably – because he is passing the Rotunda (96s).

h) *That takes the biscuit!*: A catchphrase meaning 'That takes first prize'. It has some delightful variants – in place of 'biscuit' can be 'Huntley and Palmer', 'cake', 'bun' or even 'kettle'. Australians have even been known to cry: 'That captures the pickled biscuit'. Various enthusiastic readers have seen the Communion wafer alluded to here, as in the cream crackers of 'The Sisters'. In *SH* Moynihan tells Stephen that 'the *Decameron* took the biscuit for "smut"'.

i) *recherché*: Much sought after, and hence scarce. This baroque verbal flourish foreshadows the conversational eccentricities of characters in the novels of James Stephens, Eimar O'Duffy, Flann O'Brien and many others.

j) *Dorset Street*: Another street named after a Lord Lieutenant. Seán O'Casey, two years before Joyce, was born here, and this area provided the setting for his best plays. From this area too came Boucicault and Behan. The street had several pubs: given the trajectory of the walkers, they could have been in Ryan's at No 4, Masterson's at No 20, O'Loughlin's at No 28, or Thomas M'Auley's at No 39 (145b), all on Lower Dorset Street, or if they had been drinking in Upper Dorset Street, they could have patronised the Dorset House at No 71 or Larry O'Rourke's

YACHTING HATS AND CAPS,
For Ladies and Gentlemen.

Royal Yacht Squadron. cloth peak, 8s. 6d., 10s.;6d.
The Jersey Cap, in all Colours, Spun Silk, 4s. 6d. ; Merino Wool,
2s. 6d., 1s. 6d. Straw Hats, club make, 4s. 6d., 5s. 6d., &c.
FORWARDED POST FREE.

TWO GALLANTS

THE GREY WARM evening of August had descended upon the city and a mild warm air, a memory of summer, circulated in the streets. The streets, shuttered for the repose of Sunday, swarmed with a gaily coloured crowd. Like illumined pearls the lamps shone from the summits of their tall poles upon the living texture which below, changing shape and hue unceasingly, sent up into the warm grey evening air an unchanging, unceasing murmur.

Two young men came down the hill of Rutland Square. One of them was just bringing a long monologue to a close. The other, who walked on the verge of the path and was at times obliged to step on to the road, owing to his companion's rudeness, wore an amused listening face. He was squat and ruddy. A yachting cap was shoved far back from his forehead and the narrative to which he listened made constant waves of expression break forth over his face from the corners of his nose and eyes and mouth. Little jets of wheezing laughter followed one another out of his convulsed body. His eyes, twinkling with cunning enjoyment, glanced at every moment towards his companion's face. Once or twice he rearranged the light waterproof which he had slung over one shoulder in toreador fashion. His breeches, his white rubber shoes and his jauntily slung waterproof expressed youth. But his figure fell into rotundity at the waist, his hair was scant and grey and his face, when the waves of expression had passed over it, had a ravaged look.

When he was quite sure that the narrative had ended he laughed noiselessly for fully half a minute. Then he said:

—Well! . . . That takes the biscuit!—

His voice seemed winnowed of vigour; and to enforce his words he added with humour:

—That takes the solitary, unique, and, if I may so call it, *recherché* biscuit!—

He became serious and silent when he had said this. His tongue was tired for he had been taking all the afternoon in a public-house in Dorset Street. Most people considered Lenehan

(who and which features briefly in *U*, 'Calypso') opposite it. Wright's at No 93a is perhaps too close for Corley to have achieved a very long monologue since leaving the pub.

k) *Lenehan*: Matt Lenehan is thought to be based on a friend of John Joyce, one Michael Hart, who died of phthisis (pulmonary consumption) in the Mater Hospital at the turn of the century. His wheezing laughter would indicate that he is not in the best of health, but he is lively enough in *U*, where his bad jokes ('I caught a cold in the park. The gate was open'), his 'work' as an inept racing tipster, and his groping of the Molly Bloom bosom are all described. In 'Aeolus', where Bloom literally bumps into him, he cadges cigarettes by the clever expedient of offering lights from the box of matches he always carries. Writing from Italy in October 1906, Joyce referred to a local ne'er-do-well as 'a Roman Lenehan'.

a) *a leech*: Joyce had leeches used on his eyes for bloodletting as late as the 1920s. The word has also meant 'doctor', which led to its being used as an epithet for the deity: Chaucer's *Summoner's Tale* uses it thus: 'God, that is our lyves leche'.

b) *a round*: A round of drinks, which is usually offered on the understanding that the recipients will each reciprocate. Lenehan, though, would not have stood a round, but merely stood around.

c) *racing tissues*: Lists of horses running, printed on flimsy paper. These were also known as 'tipsheets', as they gave betting prices and recommended likely winners. Off-course betting was frequent, though then still illegal, in Ireland.

d) *Corley*: The name is an anglicised version of the Irish *Toirdhealbhach*, meaning 'in the shape of Thor'. Joyce knew a (Michael) Corley who lived on the North Circular Road, and after meeting him while on one of his trips to Dublin reported that Corley was delighted to hear that he was in one of his stories. In *U*, 'Eumaeus', however, he is less lucky. 'Lord John Corley', as he is jokingly known, drunkenly meets Stephen near the cabman's shelter and cadges money from him. Bloom sums him up as one of Stephen's 'hangerson', noticing his hat to be very dilapidated, and his clothes no better. He has had a row with Lenehan, 'a mean bloody swab'. To cap it all, Corley's counterpart in Homer's epic, Odysseus's goatherd, Melanthius, not only has his genitals devoured by dogs but also loses his nose, ears, hands and feet for betraying his master.

e) *Dame Street*: See 37e.

f) *tart*: Generally a prostitute, but in low milieux sometimes an attractive girlfriend. In Dublin it is still a pejorative epithet for a woman likely to be free with her favours. George Orwell in 1931 said that the word had become interchangeable with 'girl'.

g) *Waterhouse's clock*: One of Dublin's landmarks and rendezvous points, it was at 25–6 Dame Street, between the bottom of George's Street and Hely's stationers. From *Thom's Directory* (1902):

> Waterhouse and Co. gold and silver smiths, electro platers, jewellers and watchmakers to His Majesty, and the Irish court.

The shop closed down in the month of Joyce's exile with Nora.

h) *round by the canal*: The Grand Canal.

i) *slavey*: This dismissive term for a lowly female was current throughout the nineteenth century. (Pierce Egan's *Life in London* (1821) uses it: 'He is only fond of the Slaveys!') In 1904 Gogarty wrote to Dermot Freyer: 'The Bard Joyce has fled to Pola, on the Adriatic. A slavey shared his flight.' Employment agencies for domestic staff were jokingly called 'slavey markets', while a popular melodrama of the time was entitled *The Lady Slavey*.

j) *Baggot Street*: Formerly named Gallows Road, Lower Baggot Street leads southeast from near St Stephen's Green to the Grand Canal. The Parliamentarians defeated the Royalists here in 1649, allowing Cromwell and his troops to land unscathed in Ireland. Much later, the poet Patrick Kavanagh lived near here and would write about the area.

k) *Donnybrook*: A suburb on the River Dodder near Ballsbridge, a couple of miles south-east of the centre. Anthony Trollope lived here in the 1850s.

l) *a field there*: The fields along the banks of the Dodder were the site of the famous 'Donnybrook Fair', a great carnival which was finally suppressed in 1855 for being a 'public nuisance', having been held every August since the time of King John. More marriages were said to take place in the week after the fair than in any other two months. Sir Jonah Barrington (81n) described it and the customary shillelagh battles which took place each evening:

> No one was disfigured thereby or rendered fit for a doctor . . . small hurts were frequent, but did not interfere with the song, the dance, the frolicking or general good humour.

m) *a dairyman*: It is hard to realise it now, but in the first decade of this century Dublin had a large population of cattle. Most shopping streets had more than one dairy which sold unpasteurised milk from cows kept behind the shop. Flies spread disease, and many Dublin families, the Joyces included, lost children to infections probably picked up from contaminated milk. In his 1939 memoir *Tumbling in the Hay* (58b), describing this period, Oliver Gogarty mentions a large 'moving' mass of unspecified ordure at the bottom of Grafton Street. *U* resounds to the thud of bovine hooves (53h).

n) *tram out and back*: There were Donnybrook trams every ten minutes in each direction.

o) *the real cheese*: The best, the height of fashion. 'I have heard Nudity is not the cheese on public occasions' (Charles Reade, *Hard Cash* (1863)).

p) *the old fellow*: Corley's father (t).

q) *up to the dodge*: Corley is unlikely to practise *coitus interruptus*, but perhaps he could be persuaded to use a 'french letter'. As a last resort, there were various unreliable and dangerous methods of inducing abortions.

a a leech but, in spite of this reputation, his adroitness and eloquence had always prevented his friends from forming any general policy against him. He had a brave manner of coming up to a party of them in a bar and of holding himself nimbly

b at the borders of the company until he was included in a round. He was a sporting vagrant armed with a vast stock of stories, limericks and riddles. He was insensitive to all kinds of discourtesy. No one knew how he achieved the stern task of

c living, but his name was vaguely associated with racing tissues.

d —And where did you pick her up, Corley? he asked—
Corley ran his tongue swiftly along his upper lip.

e —One night, man, he said, I was going along Dame Street
fg and I spotted a fine tart under Waterhouse's clock and said
h good-night, you know. So we went for a walk round by the
i canal and she told me she was a slavey in a house in Baggot
j Street. I put my arm around her and squeezed her a bit that night. Then next Sunday, man, I met her by appointment. We
kl went out to Donnybrook and I brought her into a field there.
m She told me she used to go with a dairyman ... It was fine, man. Cigarettes every night she'd bring me and paying the
n tram out and back. And one night she bought me two bloody
op fine cigars – O, the real cheese, you know, that the old fellow used to smoke ... I was afraid, man, she'd get in the family
q way. But she's up to the dodge—
—Maybe she thinks you'll marry her, said Lenehan—

r —I told her I was out of a job, said Corley. I told her I was
s in Pim's. She doesn't know my name. I was too hairy to tell her that. But she thinks I'm a bit of class, you know—
Lenehan laughed again, noiselessly.
—Of all the good ones ever I heard, he said, that emphatically takes the biscuit—
Corley's stride acknowledged the compliment. The swing of his burly body made his friend execute a few light skips from the path to the roadway and back again. Corley was the

t son of an inspector of police and he had inherited his father's frame and gait. He walked with his hands by his sides, holding

u himself erect and swaying his head from side to side. His head was large, globular and oily; it sweated in all weathers; and his large round hat, set upon it sideways, looked like a bulb which had grown out of another. He always stared straight before him as if he were on parade and, when he wished to gaze after

r) *I was in Pim's*: A large department store, Pim Bros Ltd, was at 75–88 South Great George's Street. As a young man, George Russell (AE), who was to commission stories from Joyce for his *Irish Homestead*, worked there, and several girls from Pim's later joined his Theosophist group in the 'Yogibogeybox in Dawson Chambers'.

s) *hairy*: Dublin slang: careful, cute. The *Oxford English Dictionary* (Second Edition), which quotes this very instance of the word, defines it wrongly as 'angry, excited'. In Joyce's early letters his co-pamphleteer Francis Sheehy-Skeffington (169c) is usually called 'Hairy Jaysus', but this was more for the shagginess of his appearance than for any calculating shrewdness.

t) *son of an inspector of police*: According to Ellmann, Michael Corley was in real life the son of a policeman.

u) *erect*: The description that follows is indisputably phallic.

Dublin Castle

War and peace at Donnybrook Fair

a) *about town*: Euphemistically, out of a job, as he is when he meets Stephen on the night of Bloomsday in *U* 'Eumaeus', but see c.

b) *the hard word*: A hot tip (for the horses, etc); reliable insider knowledge.

c) *policemen in plain clothes*: The implication is that he was not averse to earning a little money by informing Dublin Castle of anything incriminating or politically useful that he heard.

d) *after the manner of Florentines*: The manner is a long way from that of Dante and Beatrice. Corley pronounces the initial 'C' as an 'H', as is done in Florence. No Irish pronunciation corresponds with this: ergo, Corley is making a Lenehanian pun on his own name, and 'Corley' becomes 'Whore-ly'. The Florentine monk and artist, Fra Filippo Lippi, was noted for his sexual rapaciousness. Vasari in his *Lives* reports that the monk even abducted a beautiful young nun and married her. Both Robert Boyle and Montaigne were among those who visited brothels in the city.

e) *smile at some of the passing girls*: Swift in 1732 wrote *The humble PETITION of the Footmen in and about the City of Dublin*, mentioning

> ... that certain *lewd, idle* and *disorderly* persons, for several months past, as it is notoriously known, have been daily seen in the publick Walks of this City ... in hopes to procure favour ... with a great number of ladies who frequent those Walks; pretending and giving themselves out to be genuine *Irish footmen.*

f) *the large faint moon*: Joyce paid close attention in this story, probably with symbolic intent, to sources of light.

g) *pull it off*: While no dirty jokes are actually made, the conversations between the two cronies contain frequent *doubles-entendres*, which would be appreciated by Lenehan at least.

h) *a gay Lothario*: A mock-heroic name for a seductive young blade. Tom Moore in *Intercepted Letters* VIII (1812) mentions 'Both gay Lotharios', and the word is used in *FW*. It is also the name of the seducer in the opera *Mignon* (177k). The word originated in 1630 with Davenant – already connected with Dublin and Shakespeare (177e).

i) *unbosoming*: Deliberately physiological.

j) *South Circular*: The South Circular Road, part of the fine legacy of the eighteenth-century Wide Streets Commission, runs more or less parallel to the Grand Canal, as the North Circular Road does with the Royal Canal. These thoroughfares give central Dublin its elegant oval shape.

some one in the street, it was necessary for him to move his
body from the hips. At present he was about town. Whenever
any job was vacant a friend was always ready to give him the
hard word. He was often to be seen walking with policemen
in plain clothes, talking earnestly. He knew the inner side of
all affairs and was fond of delivering final judgments. He
spoke without listening to the speech of his companions. His
conversation was mainly about himself: what he had said to
such a person and what such a person had said to him and what
he had said to settle the matter. When he reported these
dialogues he aspirated the first letter of his name after the
manner of Florentines.

Lenehan offered his friend a cigarette. As the two young
men walked on through the crowd Corley occasionally turned
to smile at some of the passing girls but Lenehan's gaze was
fixed on the large faint moon circled with a double halo. He
watched earnestly the passing of the grey web of twilight across
its face. At length he said:

—Well . . . tell me, Corley, I suppose you'll be able to pull
it off all right, eh?—

Corley closed one eye expressively as an answer.

—Is she game for that? asked Lenehan dubiously. You can
never know women—

—She's all right, said Corley. I know the way to get around
her, man. She's a bit gone on me—

—You're what I call a gay Lothario, said Lenehan. And the
proper kind of a Lothario, too!—

A shade of mockery relieved the servility of his manner. To
save himself he had the habit of leaving his flattery open to the
interpretation of raillery. But Corley had not a subtle mind.

—There's nothing to touch a good slavey, he affirmed. Take
my tip for it—

—By one who has tried them all, said Lenehan—

—First I used to go with girls, you know, said Corley,
unbosoming; girls off the South Circular. I used to take them
out, man, on the tram somewhere and pay the tram or take
them to a band or a play at the theatre or buy them chocolate
and sweets or something that way. I used to spend money on
them right enough, he added, in a convincing tone, as if he
was conscious of being disbelieved—

But Lenehan could well believe it; he nodded gravely.

A flavour of Donnybrook
Fair (43k) can be got from
Exshaw's *Gentlemen's and
London Magazine* for 1790,
which prints this
celebration, 'Why go to
Donnybrook?':

Boys in rags
Swarthy hags
Buckish wags
Who ride their nags
Girls in tatters
Wives in shatters
Hosiers, hatters,
Mending matters
Cheating bakers
Pulpit shakers
Money stakers
Mantua makers
Drunken sailors
Valiant tailors
Undertakers
Sabbath breakers
(God's forsakers)
Midnight wakers
Thieves, thief-takers...

Lenehan and Corley pass the Pillar and cross the bridge

Looking towards Trinity from the end of Nassau Street

—I know that game, he said, and it's a mug's game—

—And damn the thing I ever got out of it, said Corley—

—Ditto here, said Lenehan—

—Only off of one of them, said Corley—

He moistened his upper lip by running his tongue along it. The recollection brightened his eyes. He too gazed at the pale disc of the moon, now nearly veiled, and seemed to meditate.

—She was . . . a bit of all right, he said regretfully—

He was silent again. Then he added:

ab —She's on the turf now. I saw her driving down Earl Street one night with two fellows with her on a car—

—I suppose that's your doing, said Lenehan—

—There was others at her before me, said Corley philosophically—

This time Lenehan was inclined to disbelieve. He shook his head to and fro and smiled.

—You know you can't kid me, Corley, he said—

—Honest to God! said Corley. Didn't she tell me herself?—

Lenehan made a tragic gesture.

c —Base betrayer! he said—

d As they passed along the railings of Trinity College, Lenehan skipped out into the road and peered up at the clock.

—Twenty after, he said—

—Time enough, said Corley. She'll be there all right. I always let her wait a bit—

Lenehan laughed quietly.

e —Ecod! Corley, you know how to take them, he said—

—I'm up to all their little tricks, Corley confessed—

—But tell me, said Lenehan again, are you sure you can bring it off all right? You know it's a ticklish job. They're

f damn close on that point. Eh? . . . What?—

His bright, small eyes searched his companion's face for reassurance. Corley swung his head to and fro as if to toss aside an insistent insect, and his brows gathered.

—I'll pull it off, he said. Leave it to me, can't you?—

Lenehan said no more. He did not wish to ruffle his friend's temper, to be sent to the devil and told that his advice was not wanted. A little tact was necessary. But Corley's brow was soon smooth again. His thoughts were running another way.

—She's a fine decent tart, he said, with appreciation; that's what she is—

a) *She's on the turf*: She is a prostitute – after the analogy of a racehorse. There were other euphemisms. In September 1900 the *Daily Express* reported the last Gannon inquest (47b) in which the Coroner asked one Lizzie Kavanagh:

> . . . are you a respectable girl?
> *Yes, I assume so.*
> Are you of the unfortunate class?
> *No, sir. I don't think so anyway.*

b) *down Earl Street*: North Earl Street, off Sackville Street, is implied. Heading east along Earl Street will bring the (horsedrawn) car into the brothel area known as 'Monto' (Joyce's 'Nighttown'), including Montgomery, Purdon, Mabbot and Beaver Streets, and Faithful Place.

c) *Base betrayer!*: Although Lenehan is not being serious, the accusation is just, and germane to the story.

d) *Trinity College*: See 36d. In fact the blue and gold face of the clock can be read perfectly well from the pavement.

e) *Ecod!*: A mild eighteenth-century oath. For example: 'It's well I have a husband acoming, or ecod I'd marry the baker.' (R. B. Sheridan, *A Trip to Scarborough* (1777).)

f) *close*: Uncommunicative.

a) *Nassau Street*: Flanking the south side of Trinity, this is a prosperous shopping street. It was constructed on the site of the seventeenth-century St Patrick's Well Lane from the soil obtained from the razing of the nearby meeting-place of Norse Dublin, the Thingmote, or Thing Mount.

b) *Kildare Street . . . club*: At the north-east corner of the street was this most patrician of Dublin gentlemen's clubs, a bastion of the Anglo-Irish ascendancy. Edward Martyn, one of the few Catholic members, called it 'The Cod Bank' in honour of its pop-eyed denizens whose 'silver heads shoaled high in its great windows', as Gogarty said. The club's façade displays interesting carvings of billiard-playing animals.

c) *a harpist*: At the beginning of the century there were still several professional harpists in the Dublin streets. This man is a memory of the old court harpists, who, like the bards, were an important element in the great houses of old Ireland. Blind Carolan (some of whose tunes were lifted for Tom Moore's *Melodies*) was the most celebrated of these. In mid-1935 Joyce wrote to his daughter Lucia, saying that for many years he had wanted her to learn the harp.

d) *His harp*: Here the personification of the harp, symbol of Ireland, links it, and accordingly the nation, with the woman whom Corley is going to meet and betray, and over whom his hands will wander (47g).

e) *Silent, O Moyle*: This, a frequent nickname for a reticent Dubliner, is one of Moore's most familiar *Melodies*, and was to be played, 'mournfully', to the tune 'Arrah, My Dear Eveleen' – a musical hint of 'Eveline'. The song is based on the legend of Fionnghuala, one of the children of the chieftain, Lir, who all were turned to swans by a jealous stepmother, not to be released until either the first Mass-bell should sound or until a noblewoman from the south should marry a nobleman from the north. Whichever it was, it took a while to arrange, but after 900 years the children were restored, and, now old and withered, were rapidly baptised and soon

afterwards buried. The 'Moyle' is the stretch of water between Antrim and Scotland where the 'children' had floated for centuries. The song begins:

> Silent, O Moyle! be the roar of thy water,
> Break not, ye breezes! your chain of repose,
> While, murmuring mournfully, Lir's lonely
>   daughter
> Tells to the night-star her tale of woes.
> When shall the Swan, her death-note singing,
> Sleep with wings in darkness furl'd?
> When will Heav'n, its sweet bell ringing,
> Call my spirit from this stormy world?

f) *Stephen's Green*: See 38r.

g) *Hume Street*: A prosperous and elegant eighteenth-century red-brick street leading east from the Green, untouched until 1969 when several houses were pulled down and replaced with modern offices hiding behind a mock-Georgian mask. The street is named not after the Scottish sceptic but after the daughter of the Georgian developer.

h) *a blue dress and a white sailor hat*: Wearing colours like the sea, the slavey is linked to the harpist's tune, and so to the harp and to Ireland itself. Her 'umbrella' was previously a 'sunshade'.

i) *to get inside me*: This is a sporting idiom from the game of bowls. Bloom at Glasnevin Cemetery remembers how he once annoyed Paddy Dignam's boss, John Henry Menton: 'Got his rag out that evening on the bowling green because I sailed inside him.'

j) *leg over the chains*: The area was clearly one which Joyce associated with affairs of the flesh: Stephen Daedalus propositions Emma Clery here in *SH*. Joyce himself was assaulted in the Green in June 1904 for being too forward with a young lady. The chains, which no longer exist, were hung from bollards, which still do, known as the 'höhenzollerns'.

k) *Corner of Merrion Street*: At the junction of Merrion Row and Lower Baggot Street. The Duke of Wellington is said to have been born at No 24 (55b).

l) *the conqueror*: See 49f.

They walked along Nassau Street and then turned into Kildare Street. Not far from the porch of the club a harpist stood in the roadway, playing to a little ring of listeners. He plucked at the wires heedlessly, glancing quickly from time to time at the face of each new-comer and from time to time, wearily also, at the sky. His harp too, heedless that her coverings had fallen about her knees, seemed weary alike of the eyes of strangers and of her master's hands. One hand played in the bass the melody of *Silent, O Moyle*, while the other hand careered in the treble after each group of notes. The notes of the air throbbed deep and full.

The two young men walked up the street without speaking, the mournful music following them. When they reached Stephen's Green they crossed the road. Here the noise of trams, the lights and the crowd released them from their silence.

—There she is! said Corley—

At the corner of Hume Street a young woman was standing. She wore a blue dress and a white sailor hat. She stood on the kerbstone, swinging an umbrella in one hand. Lenehan grew lively.

—Let's have a squint at her, Corley, he said—

Corley glanced sideways at his friend and an unpleasant grin appeared on his face.

—Are you trying to get inside me? he asked—

—Damn it! said Lenehan boldly, I don't want an introduction. All I want is to have a look at her. I'm not going to eat her—

—O . . . A look at her? said Corley, more amiably. Well . . . I'll tell you what. I'll go over and talk to her and you can pass by—

—Right! said Lenehan—

Corley had already thrown one leg over the chains when Lenehan called out:

—And after? Where will we meet?—

—Half ten, answered Corley, bringing over his other leg—

—Where?—

—Corner of Merrion Street. We'll be coming back—

—Work it all right now, said Lenehan in farewell—

Corley did not answer. He sauntered across the road swaying his head from side to side. His bulk, his easy pace and the solid sound of his boots had something of the conqueror in them.

pé áit 'ran doṁan 'na bḟuil na Ṡaeḋil
ní éagṗaiḋ cuiṁne Éireann coiḋċe.

WHERE IRISH HEARTS AND HANDS ARE FOUND THE GREEN SHALL NEVER PERISH.

A common symbol of Ireland. The Irish message reads surprisingly like a bad translation of the English one

A 'höhenzollern' (j)

46

a) *tulle*: A delicate silk fabric, originally French.

b) *a big bunch of red flowers*: The colour is that of blood. Hidden behind this story is a true one, which Joyce knew well.

In August 1900 the half-clothed body of an unidentified young woman was taken from the shallow water of the River Dodder near Irishtown by three members of the Dublin Metropolitan Police. On the bank were strewn the shredded remnants of a flower, later found to have been worn by the deceased. One of the policemen, Constable Henry Flower, 'made a swift anxious scrutiny of the young woman's appearance', and muttered something under his breath. After a perfunctory inquest, a maid-servant, Margaret Clowry, testified that the dead woman was Bridget Gannon, a serving-girl, or slavey, of No 124 Baggot Street. Further, on the day of her death, Clowry had accompanied her and Constable Flower to her previous place of work, from where, following a request by Flower, Gannon had collected an item of property. And so there was another inquest. The case became a *cause célèbre* and the coroner's court was crowded. Even the highly respectable *Daily Express* (168h) gave it many closely-printed columns of coverage. The exhumation at Clonsilla burial ground certainly caused a frisson of necrophiliac fear in Dublin.

At the later inquest, Flower was represented by no less a figure than Mr Timothy Harrington MP, later thrice Lord Mayor of Dublin, who had known John Joyce for at least twenty years. The medical evidence was that Miss Gannon had drowned, and that there had been no violence before death, but perhaps afterwards.

The greatest sensation occurred when the Coroner attempted to cross-examine Constable Flower:

Mr. Harrington (to witness) – And I take the responsibility of advising him not to answer.

The Coroner (to witness) – Tell me, did you know Bridget Gannon, the deceased?

Constable Flower – I did not, sir.

Mr. Harrington (to witness) – I advise you to make no further statement.

The Coroner – You say you did not know Bridget Gannon?

Constable Flower – I decline to answer.

The policeman's later (and persistent) statement that he did not know Miss Gannon was flatly contradicted by Margaret Clowry's evidence. Eventually the jury reached a verdict:

That death was due to drowning, and that the deceased was unconscious previous to, or immediately on her immersion in water. They added that the deceased was last seen in company of Constable Henry Flower, 94E, but they had no positive evidence as to how the body came into the water.

Flower was arrested. Shortly afterwards, a sergeant at Irishtown police station cut his throat out of mental distress. A month later the legal system produced a decision that Flower would not stand trial.

Henry Flower, some of whose family, like Corley's, were also policemen, quickly left Dublin, but he left traces in this story and in *U*, providing Bloom's pseudonym in his flirtatious correspondence with Martha Clifford (who shares initials with Margaret Clowry). The field in 'An Encounter' was just downriver from where the body was found, and was opposite the morgue to which it was brought. Other unverifiable facts about the case were to emerge (notably via the late John Garvin), but it seems likely that Joyce learned Flower's version of the story through his father's connection with Tim Harrington, and there may be further hints of the truth, which never became public, embedded in 'Two Gallants'.

c) *stems upwards*: Perhaps these, and 46i and j, and even the pronunciation of 47a, are yet more sexual innuendos. Certainly, it is an odd way to wear flowers, and can be a sign of distress.

d) *Shelbourne Hotel*: Dublin's most prestigious hotel, where Bloom had bought Mrs Dandrade's black underthings (*U*, 'Lestrygonians'). Among its galaxy of literary and historical associations is the story that Hitler's half-brother worked there for a short time. It also has the honour of appearing in the works of probably the worst novelist ever published, Joyce's contemporary, Amanda M'Kittrick Ros.

e) *Merrion Square*: The epicentre of what remains of Georgian Dublin, where (*inter alios*) Daniel O'Connell, W. B. Yeats, AE, Mrs Hemans (25c) and Oscar Wilde at one time or another all lived. In *U*, 'Sirens', Simon Dedalus in the Ormond muses on 'Merrion Square style. Balldresses, by God, and court dresses.'

f) *the Duke's Lawn*: In front of Leinster House, outside the National Gallery.

g) *harpist*: Lenehan, in emulating the harpist, is vicariously emulating Corley's amorous fingerwork. There is also an echo of the narrator of 'An Encounter' 'playing' the bridge (14f), and the singing of the lovelorn boy in 'Araby'.

He approached the young woman and, without saluting, began at once to converse with her. She swung her umbrella more quickly and executed half turns on her heels. Once or twice when he spoke to her at close quarters she laughed and bent her head.

The morgue on the Dodder bank (b)

Lenehan observed them for a few minutes. Then he walked rapidly along beside the chains to some distance and crossed the road obliquely. As he approached Hume Street corner he found the air heavily scented and his eyes made a swift anxious scrutiny of the young woman's appearance. She had her Sunday finery on. Her blue serge skirt was held at the waist by a belt of black leather. The great silver buckle of her belt seemed to depress the centre of her body, catching the light stuff of her white blouse like a clip. She wore a short black jacket with mother-of-pearl buttons and a ragged black boa. The ends of her tulle collarette had been carefully disordered and a big bunch of red flowers was pinned in her bosom stems upwards. Lenehan's eyes noted approvingly her stout short muscular body. Frank rude health glowed in her face, on her fat red cheeks and in her unabashed blue eyes. Her features were blunt. She had broad nostrils, a straggling mouth which lay open in a contented leer, and two projecting front teeth. As he passed Lenehan took off his cap and, after about ten seconds, Corley returned a salute to the air. This he did by raising his hand vaguely and pensively changing the angle of position of his hat.

Lenehan walked as far as the Shelbourne Hotel where he halted and waited. After waiting for a little time he saw them coming towards him and, when they turned to the right, he followed them, stepping lightly in his white shoes, down one side of Merrion Square. As he walked on slowly, timing his pace to theirs, he watched Corley's head which turned at every moment towards the young woman's face like a big ball revolving on a pivot. He kept the pair in view until he had seen them climbing the stairs of the Donnybrook tram; then he turned about and went back the way he had come.

Now that he was alone his face looked older. His gaiety seemed to forsake him and, as he came by the railings of the Duke's Lawn, he allowed his hand to run along them. The air which the harpist had played began to control his movements. His softly padded feet played the melody while his fingers

From an old ballad broadsheet (46d)

47

(47f)

(h)

(47d)

a) *round Stephen's Green*: Lenehan has a great deal of time to kill. He is to walk quite a distance in the story. The shortest route towards Grafton Street is along the north side, but he travels the other three sides of the square. St Stephen's Green is said by Dubliners to be the largest square in Europe, and O'Connell Street the widest main street.

b) *Grafton Street*: See 37i.

c) *trivial*: Much later, when Joyce was charged that the wordplay in *FW* was trivial, he agreed, but went on to say that some of it was quadrivial.

d) *the corner of Rutland Square*: Lenehan is now back near where the story opened, and is heading west along Great Britain Street.

e) *sombre look*: This 'dark quiet street' is where 'The Sisters', and the book, begin.

f) *Refreshment Bar*: At No 183 there was a bakery, and there were several dairies on Great Britain Street at the time, any of which might have served a simple sit-down meal. The only suitably cheap restaurant on Great Britain Street was the Parnell Restaurant at No 158, to the east not west of Upper Sackville Street.

g) *flying inscriptions*: Slogans in ceramic lettering affixed to shop-windows.

h) Ginger Beer *and* Ginger Ale: Although Elizabethan travellers reported that American Indians drank beverages 'sodden with ginger', ginger beer proper, a cloudy liquid sometimes with an admixture of brandy, first became popular in the early nineteenth century. Ginger ale was invented in the 1870s in Ireland, with the 'world-famous Belfast Ginger Ales'; it was a clearer and more sophisticated drink, which never contained alcohol (unless added by consumer or curate). It is impossible to determine whether Lenehan has alcohol in his brew, but perhaps worth noting is a report in *Punch* (March 1904): 'A contemporary is offering £100 for the "best Temperance story". We always think the assertion that there is no alcohol in ginger-beer is hard to beat'.

i) *cut ham ... blue dish ... light plum-pudding*: It may be noted that the colours in the window could be emblematic of Great Britain, while Lenehan's choices (peas and ginger beer) are Ireland's green and orange.

j) *curates*: The word is not slang, but jargon. In June 1914 the *Times Literary Supplement* review of *D* (mocked in *FW* (116)), commented:

> The reader's difficulty will be enhanced if he is ignorant of Dublin customs; if he does not know, for instance, that 'a curate' is a bringer of strong waters.

swept a scale of variations idly along the railings after each group of notes.

a He walked listlessly round Stephen's Green and then down
b Grafton Street. Though his eyes took note of many elements of the crowd through which he passed they did so morosely.
c He found trivial all that was meant to charm him and did not answer the glances which invited him to be bold. He knew that he would have to speak a great deal, to invent and to amuse, and his brain and throat were too dry for such a task. The problem of how he could pass the hours till he met Corley again troubled him a little. He could think of no way of passing them but to keep on walking. He turned to the left when he
d came to the corner of Rutland Square and felt more at ease in
e the dark quiet street, the sombre look of which suited his mood. He paused at last before the window of a poor-looking
f shop over which the words *Refreshment Bar* were printed in
g white letters. On the glass of the window were two flying
h inscriptions: *Ginger Beer* and *Ginger Ale*. A cut ham was exposed on a great blue dish while near it on a plate lay a segment of
i very light plum-pudding. He eyed this food earnestly for some time and then, after glancing warily up and down the street, went into the shop quickly.

He was hungry for, except some biscuits which he had asked
j two grudging curates to bring him, he had eaten nothing since breakfast-time. He sat down at an uncovered wooden table opposite two work-girls and a mechanic. A slatternly girl waited on him.

—How much is a plate of peas? he asked—
k —Three halfpence, sir, said the girl—
—Bring me a plate of peas, he said, and a bottle of ginger beer—

He spoke roughly in order to belie his air of gentility for his entry had been followed by a pause of talk. His face was heated. To appear natural he pushed his cap back on his head and planted his elbows on the table. The mechanic and the two work-girls examined him point by point before resuming their conversation in a subdued voice. The girl brought him a plate
l of hot grocer's peas, seasoned with pepper and vinegar, a fork and his ginger beer. He ate his food greedily and found it so good that he made a note of the shop mentally. When he had eaten all the peas he sipped his ginger beer and sat for some

k) *Three halfpence*: Pronounced as an amphibrach, the central syllable 'hape'. It is interesting to note that Lenehan has enough money for a pint of Guinness, which is considered in Ireland to be food, for the 'eating and drinking in it'. Overheard recently in Dublin, a stout and bibulous worthy, on being pressed to have some soup at least, said: 'Ah, for God's sake,' (brandishing pint), 'isn't this all the soup I need?'

l) *hot grocer's peas*: Joyce was vainly insistent that a misprint in the 1914 proofs ('grocer's hot peas') be corrected. Grocer's peas are large, pale processed peas, closer to pease pudding than to the fresh variety.

The City Markets (p)

a) *gallantries*: A leering invocation of the title.

b) *pulling the devil by the tail*: Battling continually for survival. Joyce would have been aware that a Scandinavian form of 'Dublin' was 'Divelina'. So was Robert Burns: 'it's just as true's the devil's in hell/Or Dublin City' ('Death and Doctor Hornbrook'). (There was a notorious catacomb called 'Hell' in Dublin, the haunt of lawyers.)

c) *shifts*: Ingenious dodges. There are several echoes of sex and sin in this short sentence, with 'knocking', 'pulling', 'devil', 'tail', 'intrigues' and indeed 'shifts' itself, maybe, which was also the word that was to begin the *Playboy* riots in the Abbey Theatre in 1907 when the audience violently objected to J. M. Synge's vision of

> a drift of chosen females, standing in their shifts itself, maybe, from this place to the eastern world.

d) *thirty-one*: This falls cheeringly into the *adulescentia* bracket of Joyce's system of age-division.

e) *with friends and with girls*: They do not overlap in Lenehan's life. For more 'friends', see the opening section of 'Grace'.

f) *vanquished*: There is a good case to be made that Joyce intended Corley to represent England and the almost vanquished Lenehan with his green peas to symbolise Ireland. Corley is described (46l) as having 'something of the conqueror' and we know that he

is on good terms with the agents of the Crown (44c). The course of his relationship with the slavey too can be seen as analogous to John Bull's treatment of Kathleen ní Houlihan: he violates her and then he takes her money. And accordingly Lenehan is then the 'base betrayer', the Irishman enjoying the spoils of Ireland's debasement, as traitors and informers have done throughout the centuries.

g) *simple-minded*: Necessarily so.

h) *the ready*: Ready money, cash.

i) *Capel Street*: Austin Clarke reliably reported in *Twice Around the Black Church* (1960) that this was Joyce's favourite street in Dublin. Lenehan follows most of the route that will be taken by Chandler in 'A Little Cloud'. Just as at the beginning the air circulates in the streets, so Lenehan is on a circular path around the city, whose only aim is to pass the time.

j) *the City Hall*: The centre of Dublin's municipal government, on Cork Hill at the end of Dame Street.

k) *George's Street*: South Great George's Street was then dominated by the department store Pim Brothers (43r) which was demolished in the 1970s. The Pim family, who were Quakers, built extensively in the street in the 1850s.

l) *Mac*: Unsurprisingly, a common nickname in Ireland. *SH* refers to 'Mac – you know – the Gaelic League chap. He brought us down to the kips last

49

time thinking of Corley's adventure. In his imagination he beheld the pair of lovers walking along some dark road; he heard Corley's voice in deep energetic gallantries and saw again the leer of the young woman's mouth. This vision made him feel keenly his own poverty of purse and spirit. He was tired of knocking about, of pulling the devil by the tail, of shifts and intrigues. He would be 'thirty-one in November. Would he never get a good job? Would he never have a home of his own? He thought how pleasant it would be to have a warm fire to sit by and a good dinner to sit down to. He had walked the streets long enough with friends and with girls. He knew what those friends were worth: he knew the girls too. Experience had embittered his heart against the world. But all hope had not left him. He felt better after having eaten than he had felt before, less weary of his life, less vanquished in spirit. He might yet be able to settle down in some snug corner and live happily if he could only come across some good simple-minded girl with a little of the ready.

He paid twopence halfpenny to the slatternly girl and went out of the shop to begin his wandering again. He went into Capel Street and walked along towards the City Hall. Then he turned into Dame Street. At the corner of George's Street he met two friends of his and stopped to converse with them. He was glad that he could rest from all his walking. His friends asked him had he seen Corley and what was the latest. He replied that he had spent the day with Corley. His friends talked very little. They looked vacantly after some figures in the crowd and sometimes made a critical remark. One said that he had seen Mac an hour before in Westmoreland Street. At this Lenehan said that he had been with Mac the night before in Egan's. The young man who had seen Mac in Westmoreland Street asked was it true that Mac had won a bit over a billiard match. Lenehan did not know: he said that Holohan had stood them drinks in Egan's.

He left his friends at a quarter to ten and went up George's Street. He turned to the left at the City Markets and walked on into Grafton Street. The crowd of girls and young men had thinned and on his way up the street he heard many groups and couples bidding one another good-night. He went as far as the clock of the College of Surgeons: it was on the stroke of ten. He set off briskly along the northern side of the Green,

night.' There, conveniently, lived Mrs Mack of 'Night-town', Dublin's best-known madam, who is asked about by Bloom in U, 'Circe', and who appears in Gogarty's *Tumbling in the Hay*. In a page of notes 'For "Dubliners"', Joyce jotted down an unused fragment of Dublinese relating to Mac: 'Be Jaze, that put the kybosh on me'.

m) *Westmoreland Street*: A wide street that links O'Connell Bridge with College Green. It is not common knowledge that Westmoreland Street is the length, breadth and height of Noah's Ark (Genesis VI. 15).

n) *Egan's*: Probably The Oval public house, 78 Middle Abbey Street, a haunt of pressmen. In the oral culture of Dublin, pub names are often different from their signs. There were, however, several other pubs called Egan's.

o) *Holohan*: If this is Hoppy Holohan, he reappears in 'A Mother'.

p) *the City Markets*: The South City Market Arcade, between 19 and 22 South Great George's Street, leads into Drury Street. It now contains bookshops and small boutiques, though then there were cafés, fruit and fish shops etc.

q) *College of Surgeons*: Once more he has set off on the longer way from a to b. At No 123, seeing the clock above the door of the Royal College of Surgeons, on the west side of Stephen's Green, he turns back and traverses the north side (inside the Green traditionally known as 'Beaux' Walk'). This is the only side of the Green which he has not yet wholly tramped.

49

124 Baggot St (b)

The College of Surgeons and its clock (49q)

Lenehan was never without matches (42k)

hurrying for fear Corley should return too soon. When he reached the corner of Merrion Street he took his stand in the shadow of a lamp and brought out one of the cigarettes which he had reserved and lit it. He leaned against the lamp-post and kept his gaze fixed on the part from which he expected to see Corley and the young woman return.

His mind became active again. He wondered had Corley managed it successfully. He wondered if he had asked her yet or if he would leave it to the last. He suffered all the pangs and thrills of his friend's situation as well as those of his own. But the memory of Corley's slowly revolving head calmed him somewhat: he was sure Corley would pull it off all right. All at once the idea struck him that perhaps Corley has seen her home by another way and given him the slip. His eyes searched the street: there was no sign of them. Yet it was surely half-an-hour since he had seen the clock of the College of Surgeons. Would Corley do a thing like that? He lit his last cigarette and began to smoke it nervously. He strained his eyes as each tram stopped at the far corner of the square. They must have gone home by another way. The paper of his cigarette broke and he flung it into the road with a curse.

Suddenly he saw them coming towards him. He started with delight and keeping close to his lamp-post tried to read the result in their walk. They were walking quickly, the young woman taking quick short steps, while Corley kept beside her with his long stride. They did not seem to be speaking. An intimation of the result pricked him like the point of a sharp instrument. He knew Corley would fail; he knew it was no go.

They turned down Baggot Street and he followed them at once, taking the other footpath. When they stopped he stopped too. They talked for a few moments and then the young woman went down the steps into the area of a house. Corley remained standing at the edge of the path, a little distance from the front steps. Some minutes passed. Then the halldoor was opened slowly and cautiously. A woman came running down the front steps and coughed. Corley turned and went towards her. His broad figure hid hers from view for a few seconds and then she reappeared running up the steps. The door closed on her and Corley began to walk swiftly towards Stephen's Green.

Lenehan hurried on in the same direction. Some drops of

a) *asked her yet*: This is the first definite hint that Corley's expedition has an aim other than carnal.

b) *the halldoor*: On the south side of Lower Baggot Street, opposite to where Lenehan has walked, was No 124, with steps down to the servants' entrance (47b). At this time it was occupied by an eminent solicitor, Ernest W. Harris, who had a practice in St Andrew Street.

c) *A woman*: Joyce several times uses the indefinite article in *D* when a definite article would seem more appropriate. It is clearly the same woman, so (as we are looking through Lenehan's eyes) the usage may indicate that he cares about the impersonal cash, not the human courier.

d) *His broad figure hid hers*: It is to be presumed that Corley is dispensing a kiss in exchange for her offering. Judas comes to mind.

The area railings and gate to the servants' entrance of 124 Baggot St (b)

50

a) *Ely Place*: Joyce's erstwhile friend, Oliver Gogarty, later moved to No 15. As he grew up in Rutland Square, the story, oddly, has been framed by his addresses. Poignantly, the two gallants are now standing almost opposite the home of the Young Women's Christian Association. At the other end of the street, No 4 Upper Ely Place is where George Moore was living at this time (32b). See below.

b) *his disciple*: The use of this word makes explicit the biblical parallel. In the first act of *Exiles*, Richard (very much Joyce) tells Robert (partly Gogarty):

> There is a faith still stranger than the faith of a disciple in his master.
> *Robert:* And that is?
> *Richard:* The faith of a master in the disciple who will betray him.

There are several layers of betrayal in this story. Just as, with a kiss, the disciple Judas betrayed Christ for thirty pieces of silver, Corley likewise betrays the slavey, who is herself identified, through the harp, with Ireland. He is also implicated in the betrayal of

Ireland through his police contacts. To see the now menacing Lenehan as a corrupt disciple puts Corley in the position of a corrupt Christ. A complex nexus of symbols is completed in these last lines.

c) *A small gold coin*: A sovereign (as depicted below) or a half-sovereign. Some have felt that the slavey's covertness suggests that she has stolen the coin, which even if only a half-sovereign is half as much again as Eveline earns in a week, and a great deal of money for a maid-servant to have to hand. However, one cannot say more than that her principles are uncertain. The money is revealed to be the main object of Corley's evening, and the sole object of Lenehan's: they now have money for several days' drinking. The coin is the last of many circles in the story, a sun-like counterpart to the moon earlier, and it is held up to Lenehan as the communion wafer is held up in the Eucharist. Notwithstanding all these interweaving significances, 'Two Gallants' ends uniquely for *D*: it has a revelatory twist of the sort that is almost mandatory in the stories of many other writers.

PERSECUTING A NOVELIST
MR MOORE AND THE ORGAN GRINDER

In the Southern Division Police Court today before Mr. Drury, Carmaud Nordani and Giovanni Cafeldi, organ-grinders from Italy, were charged with having caused a nuisance by playing an organ in front of the residence of Mr. George Moore, the novelist, at Ely place, and refusing to go away when requested to do so.

Mr. Moore told the court that the defendants insisted on grinding their instruments opposite his residence, this giving him annoyance while he was engaged in his writing. He had already warned one of the men.

Mr. Drury (to the defendants) - Why do you annoy this gentleman?

Cafeldi - I cannot speak English.

Mr. Drury - You seem to speak it very well.

Mr. Moore - The whistling of the defendants at the organ was intolerable.

An interpreter, a compatriot of the defendants, asked the defendants why they did not move away when requested to do so.

Cafeldi in reply said that he only wanted to finish the tune. (A laugh.)

Mr. Moore - He played for ten minutes after I asked him to go away.

The defendant promised the Court not to repeat the offence.

Mr. Drury ordered that the defendants should give security in £5 to be of good behaviour, and undertake to refrain from a course of conduct, which seemed to have been deliberately adopted for the purpose of persecution.

CASUAL NOTES

Mr. George Moore in the role of a persecutor of the Arts is a sight for the gods, yet it was in this guise that he appeared to-day in the Police Court to lay heavy indictment against a couple of itinerant musicians for having invaded the sacred precincts of Ely Place and smashed its solemn silence into smithereens. These two musicians bore the picturesque names of Nordani and Cafeldi – what glorious visions of the Italy of Medici and the Renaissance do they not conjure up! – and they wandered into Ely Place with a barrel organ trailing casually behind. From this instrument of torture they proceeded to extract what Kipling calls "common tunes which make you choke and blow your nose." The effect upon Mr. Moore, however, was very different – he seems to have been more inclined to choke the olive-tinted sons of the South. He suggested in his best Italian that they should "clear out," but they seem to have mistaken his denunciatory remarks for compliments, and they only ground their organ the harder and whistled joyously. Then Mr. Moore registered a mighty vow by Esther Waters and Evelyn Innes and Sister Teresa, and haled them before Mr. Drury, to whom they have given security for £5 that for the future they will regard Ely Place as out of bounds. No doubt they think that they have been treated harshly, but, after all, there is a difference between music and "music."

A painful case in Ely Place (32b), reported in the Press

light rain fell. He took them as a warning and, glancing back towards the house which the young woman had entered to see that he was not observed, he ran eagerly across the road. Anxiety and his swift run made him pant. He called out:

—Hallo, Corley!—

Corley turned his head to see who had called him, and then continued walking as before. Lenehan ran after him, settling the waterproof on his shoulders with one hand.

—Hallo, Corley! he cried again—

He came level with his friend and looked keenly in his face. He could see nothing there.

—Well? he said. Did it come off?—

a   They had reached the corner of Ely Place. Still without answering Corley swerved to the left and went up the side street. His features were composed in stern calm. Lenehan kept up with his friend, breathing uneasily. He was baffled, and a note of menace pierced through his voice.

—Can't you tell us? he said. Did you try her?—

Corley halted at the first lamp and stared grimly before him. Then with a grave gesture he extended a hand towards the

b light and, smiling, opened it slowly to the gaze of his disciple.

c A small gold coin shone in the palm.

Afterword: 'Two Gallants'

'Two Gallants' was completed in February 1906, and was one of Joyce's favourites. One of the last stories to be written, it is a rich and symbolic brew, and its polyguity has led to several intelligent interpretations (the best of which is by the dependable Florence L. Walzl). Most of these exegeses seem reasonable when read separately, but few can satisfactorily coexist.

Even the title itself is not easily elucidated. The word 'gallant' has a wide variety of meanings and references. It can also be used ironically, as here. Charles II has been quoted as using it: 'A handsome face without mony has but few galants'. Loosely, when pronounced 'gàllant' it indicates bravery or chivalry, and when pronounced 'gallànt' there is some additional amatory intent. The word comes from the Old French verb *galer*, to make merry, which itself has been thought to derive from Old High German, either from a noun meaning 'wanton' or from a verb meaning 'to wander about, to go on pilgrimage'. The Irish word *gall* means 'foreigner' and by extension 'Englishman'. 'Gallant' in English has two further relevant subsidiary meanings: a naval flag, and a military follower. It could be said that Corley is an amorous blade (or gallant) and that Lenehan is his follower (or gallant). A final point about the title: Coleridge's 'The Ancient Mariner' has this rubric beside the first verse:

An ancient Mariner meeteth three Gallants bidden to a wedding-feast, and detaineth one.

As with interpretations, the story has a variety of sources. In May 1906, Joyce wrote to his would-be publisher Grant Richards, whose printer had refused to print 'Two Gallants':

... Is it the small gold coin ... or the code of honour which the two gallants live by which shocks him? ... I would strongly recommend to him the chapters [in *Europa Giovane*] wherein [Guglielmo] Ferrero examines the moral code of the soldier and (incidentally) of the gallant.

Joyce later confirmed to Stanislaus that Ferrero, the Italian historian and polemicist, 'gave' him 'Two Gallants'. A second element in the genesis of the story, as we have seen, is the 'Dodder Mystery' (47b). A third came, as ever, from Joyce's own life.

During the course of the story Lenehan covers some four and a half miles (passing, as Donald Torchiana has pointed out, many of the legacies of British rule in Ireland – though admittedly it would be difficult not to). Joyce, too, was a walker of Dublin, going on long conversational perambulations around the city with his brother Stanislaus, or with the friends who are lightly disguised as Cranly and Lynch in *A Portrait*. When there was money, these walks would be punctuated by drinks, and sometimes girls were followed quite long distances. 'Two Gallants' is a memory of those days.

However, such peripatesis was not confined to Joyce and his friends, particularly when the route involved meandering into 'Nighttown' beyond the end of North Earl Street. There was an obscure Dublin publication entitled *Startlers*, a tiny privately printed magazine run from Merrion Road by a Henry Johnston. The November 1892 issue contains part of a novel by one Jean Dubois, which startles only by its similarity to this story in tone and setting. From Chapter II:

Along Sackville Street – as O'Connell Street was then called – two young men were progressing in the direction of Carlisle Bridge.

As they passed beneath the street lamps the faint glimmer of light thrown out by them showed their faces indistinctly, yet sufficiently well for anyone passing to know them again if necessary.

The older of the two was probably twenty-two, and walked with unsteady gait which betokens too much indulgence in the cup which inebriates. Though his features bore traces of dissipation and debauchery, he was by no means ill-looking. There was, however, sometimes to be seen an ugly glitter in his eyes which denoted a determination to succeed in any object, good or bad, on which he set his mind . . .

'Come along home, Joe!' Bramley was saying to his inebriated companion, who seemed disposed to turn down North Earl Street, instead of keeping straight on.

'Yesh, old feller! When we go to Mac's.'

While not a work of much merit, Dubois' novel (which was probably never published in its entirety) is part of a minor branch of Irish writing that was to have other exponents including James Stephens, Samuel Beckett, Gogarty, Ralph Cusack, J. P. Donleavy, Anthony Cronin, James Plunkett, Roddy Doyle *et al*. The tradition might be called 'Dublin Street Literature' and 'Two Gallants' is part of it. The story can be seen as a trial piece for the masterpiece of the genre, *Ulysses*.

What the story does not share with *Ulysses*, however, is its humanity. Although 'Two Gallants' is a love story of a kind, no real love is evident, and though Lenehan is said to be witty, there is no real humour. All the characters are very unattractive, even the slavey in her subservience. It is significant that her point of view is not rendered, unlike that of her male counterpart, Bob Doran in 'The Boarding House'. *Dubliners* was conceived as a polemical work, which would hold up a 'mirror' wherein the city's inhabitants could see themselves. Before Joyce began 'The Dead', he wrote (in September 1906) to his brother:

Sometimes thinking of Ireland it seems to me that I have been unnecessarily harsh. I have reproduced (in 'Dubliners', at least) none of the attraction of the city . . . its ingenuous insularity and its hospitality; the latter 'virtue', so far as I can see, does not exist elsewhere in Europe. I have not been just to its beauty: for it is more beautiful naturally, in my opinion, than what I have seen of England, Switzerland, France, Austria and Italy. And yet I know how useless these reflections are. For was I to rewrite the book as G[rant] R[ichards] suggests . . . I am sure I should find again what you call the Holy Ghost sitting in the ink-bottle and the perverse devil of my literary conscience sitting on the hump of my pen. And, after all, 'Two Gallants' – with the Sunday crowds and the harp in Kildare Street and Lenehan – *is* an Irish landscape.

With 'The Dead', and above all with *Ulysses*, Joyce was to atone for his harshness. In the meantime, 'Two Gallants' is one of the most scrupulously reflective of all Joyce's mirrors.

a) THE BOARDING HOUSE: As a family-sized enterprise (together with a slavey or two), a boarding house was a common use for the formerly grand Georgian mansions of Dublin. The pressures of population also meant housing needs could be met by 'rooming' or taking permanent lodgings in such establishments. They varied hugely. The expression was also nineteenth-century slang for a prison or house of correction. 'Boarding' also has Shakespearean (sub-nautical) connotations of making sexual advances:

> Boarding, call you it? I'll be sure to keep him above deck.

(Mistress Ford to Mistress Page, in *The Merry Wives of Windsor* (II.i).) Joyce's story is rife with innuendo.
b) *Mrs Mooney*: One ironic derivative of the name is derived from the Irish *maoineach*, 'rich', 'prosperous' (but compare 88h).
c) *butcher's daughter*: An echo of Jimmy Doyle in 'After the Race'. In a deliberately misleading reference to a biographical error of John Aubrey's, Stephen, in *U*, 'Scylla and Charybdis', sneers about Shakespeare (35v):

> Not for nothing was he a butcher's son, wielding the sledded poleaxe and spitting in his palm.

(This itself is a misquotation from *Hamlet* (I.i).)
d) *near Spring Gardens*: An area on the north side around Spring Garden Street, off North Strand Road, between the Tolka and the Royal Canal. Spring Garden Parade formed part of Ballybough Road. Joyce originally wrote 'in Fairview'.
e) *plundered the till*: In a letter to his brother in December 1904, Joyce wrote of Nora's baker father:

> Papa had a shop but drank all the buns and loaves like a man. The mother's family are 'toney'.

f) *the pledge*: An oath to become teetotal.
g) *to break out*: To renege on the pledge – as will Freddy in 'The Dead'.
h) *by buying bad meat*: In 1881 the Corporation abattoir was opened, which was intended to replace the many private slaughterhouses that befouled residential areas of the city. In the new, County Mayo jargon of the time, the new abattoir was 'boycotted'. The regulation of the sale of meat was a continuing municipal problem: meat condemned by Corporation inspectors often found its way back on to the market, so Dublin putrefaction was not only moral. Contemporary newspapers often reported cases of 'passing off' – e.g. margarine as butter, or adulterated buttermilk as the real thing.
i) *he went for his wife with the cleaver*: It is not suggested that his standards had slipped so low that he intended to offer choice cuts of her haunches – or not quite. Joyce is perhaps drolly invoking the formula of Christian marriage (in Matthew XIX.5):

> For this cause shall a man leave father and mother, and shall cleave to his wife: and they twain shall be one flesh?

j) *She went to the priest*: Social regulation (as in 'Grace') was shared between the police and the clergy. Joyce originally wrote 'priests'.
k) *separation*: As divorce was not allowed to Catholics, the only possibilities were an annulment (which required a demonstration that there had never been a proper marriage to begin with, and was in practice only open to the rich and powerful), or a separation. Having children made even the latter less likely. Ireland, free since 1922, still forbids divorce.
l) *a sheriff's man*: A bumbailiff, i.e. a menial functionary of law-enforcement in Dublin, in such matters as debt-collection (often through the forceable seizure of assets). It was an ill-regarded occupation, being dependent on the misery of others.
m) *a boarding house*: Although it has been suggested that this establishment was based on Waverley House, 4 Hardwicke St, this was at the far end of the street. Overlooking 'the little circus' that fronted St George's Church were Maurice Whelan, hotel proprietor, at No 28 and Mrs Doyle at No 27.
n) *Hardwicke Street*: According to Stanislaus, the Joyce family lived at No 29 Hardwicke St in 1894. Appropriately, the name also suggests the Hardwicke Act of 1754, which regulated marriage. J. P. Nannetti of *U* (MP, and – as predicted by Bloom – future Lord Mayor of Dublin), lived at No 19 for many years.

THE BOARDING HOUSE

MRS MOONEY WAS a butcher's daughter. She was a woman who was quite able to keep things to herself: a determined woman. She had married her father's foreman and opened a butcher's shop near Spring Gardens. But as soon as his father-in-law was dead Mr Mooney began to go to the devil. He drank, plundered the till, ran headlong into debt. It was no use making him take the pledge: he was sure to break out again a few days after. By fighting his wife in the presence of customers and by buying bad meat he ruined his business. One night he went for his wife with the cleaver and she had to sleep in a neighbour's house.

After that they lived apart. She went to the priest and got a separation from him with care of the children. She would give him neither money nor food nor house-room; and so he was obliged to enlist himself as a sheriff's man. He was a shabby stooped little drunkard with a white face and a white moustache and white eyebrows, pencilled above his little eyes, which were pink-veined and raw; and all day long he sat in the bailiff's room, waiting to be put on a job. Mrs Mooney, who had taken what remained of her money out of the butcher business and set up a boarding house in Hardwicke Street, was a big imposing woman. Her house had a floating population made up of tourists from Liverpool and the Isle of Man and, occasionally, *artistes* from the music halls. Its resident population was made up of clerks from the city. She governed her house cunningly and firmly, knew when to give credit, when to be stern and when to let things pass. All the resident young men spoke of her as *The Madam*.

Mrs Mooney's young men paid fifteen shillings a week for board and lodgings (beer or stout at dinner excluded). They shared in common tastes and occupations and for this reason they were very chummy with one another. They discussed with one another the chances of favourites and outsiders. Jack Mooney, the Madam's son, who was clerk to a commission agent in Fleet Street, had the reputation of being a hard case. He was fond of using soldiers' obscenities: usually he came

o) *Liverpool*: Then the main English seaport, opposite Dublin on the Irish Sea. Its emigrant population (97k) was so sizeable that the city was sometimes known as the second capital of Ireland. The famous trade union leader Jim Larkin, active both in Great Britain and Ireland, was born there in 1876.

p) *Isle of Man*: See 66 m.

q) The Madam: The young men are making a joke, and the innuendo is unavoidable, especially given the street name and its location – near Mountjoy Square.

r) *fifteen shillings*: i.e. $\frac{3}{4}$ of a £ (now 75p). This was at the upper end of the middle range.

s) *beer or stout*: As to the latter, Guinness's brewery at St James's Gate was the biggest in the world at this time.

t) *favourites and outsiders*: Jargon from the ordinary Dublin pastimes of horse-racing and betting.

u) *a commission agent*: They had a variety of commercial tasks, and took an agreed percentage of the revenues from a client. Dublin had many 'commission agents', it should be noted, but very few 'accountants'.

v) *Fleet Street*: See 81g.

w) *a hard case*: A euphemism for a heavy drinker, or a violent man, too fond of the hard stuff. Stanislaus claimed a reputation as a 'hard case' for his effrontery at school.

x) *soldiers' obscenities*: e.g. the earholing Privates Carr and Compton give Stephen at the end of *U*, 'Circe'.

A fast couple from the Isle of Man

a) *a good one*: A joke, presumably coarse.

b) *a good thing*: Boorish reification, as with Corley's 'a fine thing' in 'Two Gallants'.

c) *handy with the mits*: Given to, and adept at, fisticuffs (Joyce originally wrote 'an amateur boxer'). In *SH*, there is a report of a set-to where a medical student made derisive laughs, and remarks such as . . . 'Is he handy with the mits?' 'Can he put up his props?' 'Is he a good man with the mits?'

d) *a reunion*: A gathering of residents and friends (sometimes musical, sometimes not), like those often attended by Joyce and his sister Poppie (34) at the Sheehys' house in Belvedere Place.

e) *Sheridan*: One of the most celebrated Dublin names, ironically here evocative of the past glories of theatrical and cultural and artistic Dublin. The Rev. Thomas Sheridan was a friend of Swift. His son was Thomas Sheridan, famous actor and teacher of elocution, who married Frances Chamberlaine, later a novelist and playwright. Their son, Richard Brinsley Sheridan, was born in Dublin in 1751, and wrote *The Rivals*, *The School for Scandal* and *The Critic*. He is buried in Westminster Abbey, near the Dublin University graduates Oliver Goldsmith, William Congreve and Samuel Johnson, whose doctorate was an honorary one.

f) *vamped*: Improvised on the piano. There is also perhaps a suggestion of 'vamp', a seductive, parasitic woman.

g) *Polly*: The names evokes Polly Peachum, the saucy heroine of *The Beggar's Opera* (1728), whose surname means 'betrayer'. (Polly Peachum was often played to acclaim in Dublin by Peg Woffington (37e).) Much of the Mooney set-up also recalls the *Opera* (e.g. Mrs Peachum saying 'What of Bob Booty? . . . he's a favourite Customer of mine'). There was a sequel set in Dublin, Charles Coffey's *The Beggar's Wedding*, in which Bob Doran would no doubt find familiar scenes.

h) *the Madam's daughter*: Something of the status of single women can be inferred from this and from expressions such as 'a butcher's daughter' and 'the caretaker's daughter', elsewhere in *D*. There is also an echo of Ophelia's derangement (*Hamlet* IV.v):

> They say the owl was a baker's daughter. Lord, we know what we are, but know not what we may be.

i) *I'm a . . . naughty girl*: According to Zack Bowen, the song runs on:

> Rome is in a whirl
> Because they're all afraid
> Of this naughty little maid.

This seems appropriate for a perverse madonna.

j) *like a little perverse madonna*: Quite. The green in her eyes recalls the old man of 'An Encounter'. Though the manuscript reads 'like a little hypocritical

(*j*)

home in the small hours. When he met his friends he had always a good one to tell them and he was always sure to be on to a good thing – that is to say, a likely horse or a likely *artiste*. He was also handy with the mits and sang comic songs. On Sunday nights there would often be a reunion in Mrs Mooney's front drawing-room. The music-hall *artistes* would oblige; and Sheridan played waltzes and polkas and vamped accompaniments. Polly Mooney, the Madam's daughter, would also sing. She sang:

> *I'm a . . . naughty girl.*
> *You needn't sham:*
> *You know I am.*

Polly was a slim girl of nineteen; she had light soft hair and a small full mouth. Her eyes, which were grey with a shade of green through them, had a habit of glancing upwards when she spoke with anyone, which made her look like a little perverse madonna. Mrs Mooney had first sent her daughter to be a typist in a corn-factor's office but, as a disreputable sheriff's man used to come every other day to the office, asking to be allowed to say a word to his daughter, she had taken her daughter home again and set her to do housework. As Polly was very lively the intention was to give her the run of the young men. Besides, young men like to feel that there is a young woman not very far away. Polly, of course, flirted with the young men but Mrs Mooney, who was a shrewd judge, knew that the young men were only passing the time away: none of them meant business. Things went on so for a long time and Mrs Mooney began to think of sending Polly back to typewriting when she noticed that something was going on between Polly and one of the young men. She watched the pair and kept her own counsel.

Polly knew that she was being watched, but still her mother's persistent silence could not be misunderstood. There had been no open complicity between mother and daughter, no open understanding but, though people in the house began to talk of the affair, still Mrs Mooney did not intervene. Polly began to grow a little strange in her manner and the young man was evidently perturbed. At last, when she judged it to be the right moment, Mrs Mooney intervened. She dealt with moral

Madonna', this may be the story's neat phrase of five words which Joyce in July 1905 challenged Stanislaus to find, as he was 'uncommonly pleased' with it.

k) *to be a typist*: In the manuscript, 'to be a typewriter' (76g).

l) *a corn-factor's office*: A corn-factor was an agent, buying and selling according to the market. Lily in 'The Dead' works in a house also containing a corn-factor's office, and is seriously disillusioned (163).

m) *Polly was very lively*: There is a contrast with Eveline, who is exhorted to 'Look lively' (30e).

n) *the run of the young men*: To allow her to find a suitable suitor (among other meanings).

o) *kept her own counsel*: Legal metaphor. We already know that 'she was able to keep things to herself'.

p) *no open understanding*: In Ireland, an 'understanding' is also the step before an engagement. Each stage could last a decade or more before marriage, unless, as here, something untoward took place.

q) *moral problems ... cleaver*: Perhaps a comparison with her husband's behaviour is intended (53h).

a) *raised sashes*: Open windows. Swift wrote (in 'Progress of Beauty'):

> She ventures now to lift the sash;
> The window is her proper sphere.

b) *The belfry of George's Church*: It was famous for its bells, the loud dark iron of which is a motif of *U*. The church (now defunct) was a Church of Ireland one, where the Duke of Wellington (158m) was married in April 1806. Before the wedding his fiancée wrote to him offering release from their engagement because of her smallpox. He refused, however, and they had a disappointing married life. Wellington was formerly an MP in the Irish Parliament, and after the Union became Chief Secretary for Ireland. When he resumed his political career after defeating Napoleon, he eventually became Prime Minister of the United Kingdom. According to Joyce's friend Stuart Gilbert, the church was the only one in Dublin with a Greek inscription, hence its appearance in *FW* (569) as 'S. George-le-Greek'.

c) *revealing their purpose*: For some it was to worship God, for others it was to be seen to be doing so (6g).

d) *Tuesday's bread pudding*: Sunday's leftovers cooked on Monday. The recipe involved stale buttered bread, milk, raisins, eggs and sugar.

e) *as she had suspected*: As with Old Cotter in 'The Sisters', it is never made clear what she suspects. Polly might be *virgo intacta* still, or she might be pregnant.

f) *the news*: There is certainly *some* news: it cannot be that they simply have a crush on one another.

g) *seem to have connived*: She has and she has not. Though the root meaning of the word is to shut one's eyes, Mrs Mooney's have been culpably open.

h) *allusions of that kind always made her awkward*: Polly's knowingness might extend to promiscuity.

i) *her wise innocence*: Joyce of course means the very opposite. But it is appropriate for a 'perverse madonna', living as she does in an environment of insinuation and sarcasm.

j) *revery*: Joyce's variant of reverie. In *Chamber Music* IV is 'O bend no more in revery'. John Locke (38p) defined it expertly:

> Revery is when ideas float in our mind, without any reflection or regard of the understanding.

k) *lots of time*: It leaves a little over half an hour to resolve her daughter's destiny, before she goes to Mass.

l) *Mr Doran*: At last the suitor's name is mentioned. The Irish *deoradh* means 'exile' or 'stranger', but the Greek *doron* means 'gift', and Polly (like her mother) sounds carnivorous enough to be a snapper-up of unconsidering trifles.

m) *short twelve*: The last Mass of a busy Sunday was an expedited one, so this is very much Mrs Mooney's kind of service. A contemporary account was given by a Catholic witness in 1901:

> The most absurd and irreverent sight possible is to be witnessed, for instance, every Sunday at the Pro-Cathedral in Marlborough-street. A High Mass and a Low Mass both begin at different altars at twelve o'clock, and the church is generally filled. When the Low Mass is finished at about half-past twelve, the preacher at High Mass is always mounting, or has just mounted, the pulpit. At that instant, the entire congregation, *sixpenny*, *threepenny*, and *penny*, all get up and crowd out of the church, leaving the preacher to make his discoures to empty benches, and leaving High Mass to be finished in an almost desolate church ...

(Michael McCarthy, *Five Years in Ireland, 1895–1900*, Ch XXIII.)

In *SH* Stephen admits to his brother that when his mother gives him money to attend short twelve at 'Marlboro' Street' he does not go. He does, however, attend Tenebrae here with Cranly on the Wednesday of Holy Week, but he likes neither the ceremony nor the surroundings, which he compares to an insurance office.

The Pro-Cathedral

problems as a cleaver deals with meat: and in this case she had made up her mind.

It was a bright Sunday morning of early summer, promising heat, but with a fresh breeze blowing. All the windows of the boarding house were open and the lace curtains ballooned gently towards the street beneath the raised sashes. The belfry of George's Church sent out constant peals, and worshippers, singly or in groups, transversed the little circus before the church, revealing their purpose by their self-contained demeanour no less than by the little volumes in their gloved hands. Breakfast was over in the boarding house and the table of the breakfast-room was covered with plates on which lay yellow streaks of eggs with morsels of bacon-fat and bacon-rind. Mrs Mooney sat in the straw arm-chair and watched the servant Mary remove the breakfast things. She made Mary collect the crusts and pieces of broken bread to help to make Tuesday's bread-pudding. When the table was cleared, the broken bread collected, the sugar and butter safe under lock and key, she began to reconstruct the interview which she had had the night before with Polly. Things were as she had suspected: she had been frank in her questions and Polly had been frank in her answers. Both had been somewhat awkward, of course. She had been made awkward by her not wishing to receive the news in too cavalier a fashion or to seem to have connived, and Polly had been made awkward not merely because allusions of that kind always made her awkward but also because she did not wish it to be thought that in her wise innocence she had divined the intention behind her mother's tolerance.

Mrs Mooney glanced instinctively at the little gilt clock on the mantelpiece as soon as she had become aware through her revery that the bells of George's Church had stopped ringing. It was seventeen minutes past eleven: she would have lots of time to have the matter out with Mr Doran and then catch short twelve at Marlborough Street. She was sure she would win. To begin with she had all the weight of social opinion on her side: she was an outraged mother. She had allowed him to live beneath her roof, assuming that he was a man of honour, and he had simply abused her hospitality. He was thirty-four or thirty-five years of age, so that youth could not be pleaded as his excuse; nor could ignorance be his excuse since he was a man who had seen something of the world. He had simply

n) *Marlborough Street*: It was typical Dublinese to refer to churches by their addresses (158p). St Mary's Pro-Cathedral of the Immaculate Conception was not far from Hardwicke Street. (Also nearby was Monto, the red-light district, which gave the church the nickname of 'the pros' cathedral'.) Contrary to some suggestions, this is Mrs Mooney's parish church. The street is named after the Great Duke of Marlborough, who was attacked by Swift in his excoriating pamphlet *The Conduct of the Allies* (1711). The duke's daughter and heir, Henrietta, Duchess of Marlborough, had a child in 1723 by that other famous Trinity man, William Congreve. Marlborough, like his descendant, Sir Winston Churchill (174b), spent several years of his childhood in Dublin.

o) *She was sure she would win*: It being a Sunday morning, her hefty son will be on hand if needed.

p) *an outraged mother*: 'Outrage' could also mean extra-marital sexual activity. In c. 1590, Edmund Spenser, sometime Irish resident, wrote in *The Faerie Queene* (I. VI):

Ah heavens! that do this
  hideous act behold,
And heavenly virgin thus
  out·agèd see;
How can the vengeance just
  so long withhold!

q) *youth could not be pleaded as his excuse*: Notwithstanding this fact, and Bob's age of thirty-four or thirty-five, Joyce included the story in his *adulescentia* or 'young adulthood' group.

Outside the Pro-Cathedral (above and below)

a) *reparation*: The word is used five times in the story (and nowhere else), with different emphases. Its basic meaning is 'repair' rather than 'recompense'. To repair a lost reputation is difficult; to repair a lost virginity is impossible. Marriage here would seem to be the only solution, and it too satisfies the theological meaning of the word, the reparation for sin effected through confession. Joyce, however, had a deep contempt for both marriage and confession.

b) *Mr Meade*: It is presumably he who reappears in 'A Mother' (123q). The name was also that of an important Dublin alderman of the day.

c) *Bantam Lyons*: Another inmate of Mrs Mooney's, who reappears in 'Ivy Day' (and in *U* as a friend of Lenehan). His misunderstanding with Bloom over a racehorse leads to hilarious complications.

d) *a great Catholic wine-merchant's office*: Unsurprisingly, there were several. J. M'Carthy and Sons Limited, Wholesale Wine and Tea Merchants, were at 12 Swift's Row (near Ormond Quay): their telegraphic address was 'POTHEEN, Dublin'. W. & A. Gilbey were wine growers and shippers, with branches all around Dublin. Kelly's were noted for selling a great deal of altar wines. J. F. Byrne (16n) had indirect associations with 'the Allingham family, the immensely rich wine and spirit merchants of 99 and 100 Capel Street'. Bloom's advertising clients include Alexander Keyes, tea, wine and spirit merchant, 5 and 6 Ball's Bridge. Joyce was familiar with the trade as his maternal grandfather, John Murray, was in it.

e) *the loss of his job*: Joyce at one stage amended this to 'his sit', but it seems he thought better of it. See 66h.

f) *a good screw*: Mainly a reference to Bob Doran's adequate income, though Joyce was well aware of other connotations, including perhaps the Anglo-Irish slang for 'a bottle of wine'.

g) *a bit of stuff put by*: Mrs Mooney's typically grasping idiom for Doran's savings.

h) *the pier-glass*: A long mirror on the 'pier' between two windows. The imagery recalls 'After the Race' (39h).

i) *who could not get their daughters off their hands*: The theme is revisited in 'A Mother'.

j) *Three days' reddish beard*: The evidence is ambiguous as to whether Bob Doran shaved on Friday or not: if he did not, then he would not have been at work either.

k) *a mist gathered on his glasses*: With his spectacles and his implied hangover, he is one of several projections of the author in *D* (who was well aware what *Mist* is

taken advantage of Polly's youth and inexperience: that was evident. The question was: What reparation would he make?

There must be reparation made in such cases. It is all very well for the man: he can go his ways as if nothing had happened, having had his moment of pleasure, but the girl has to bear the brunt. Some mothers would be content to patch up such an affair for a sum of money; she had known cases of it. But she would not do so. For her only one reparation could make up for the loss of her daughter's honour: marriage.

She counted all her cards again before sending Mary up to Mr Doran's room to say that she wished to speak with him. She felt sure she would win. He was a serious young man, not rakish or loud-voiced like the others. If it had been Mr Sheridan or Mr Meade or Bantam Lyons her task would have been much harder. She did not think he would face publicity. All the lodgers in the house knew something of the affair; details had been invented by some. Besides, he had been employed for thirteen years in a great Catholic wine-merchant's office and publicity would mean for him, perhaps, the loss of his job. Whereas if he agreed all might be well. She knew he had a good screw for one thing and she suspected he had a bit of stuff put by.

Nearly the half-hour! She stood up and surveyed herself in the pier-glass. The decisive expression of her great florid face satisfied her and she thought of some mothers she knew who could not get their daughters off their hands.

Mr Doran was very anxious indeed this Sunday morning. He had made two attempts to shave but his hand had been so unsteady that he had been obliged to desist. Three days' reddish beard fringed his jaws and every two or three minutes a mist gathered on his glasses so that he had to take them off and polish them with his pocket-handkerchief. The recollection of his confession of the night before was a cause of acute pain to him: the priest had drawn out every ridiculous detail of the affair and in the end had so magnified his sin that he was almost thankful at being afforded a loophole of reparation. The harm was done. What could he do now but marry her or run away? He could not brazen it out. The affair would be sure to be talked of and his employer would be certain to hear of it. Dublin is such a small city: everyone knows everyone else's business. He felt his heart leap warmly in his throat as he heard

German for, 'dung'). Bob's failure of vision reiterates the book's theme of faulty sight and false perspective.

l) *his confession of the night before*: Going to confess to the priest on a Saturday evening was common practice, but with a two-day beard, perhaps Bob was drunk. Bloom in church (*U*, 'Lotus Eaters') captures the essence of confession:

And I schschschschschsch. And did you chacha-chachacha? And why did you?

m) *magnified his sin*: There is a suggestion of a vicarious thrill for the priest, as he questions the sinner. It is an ironic counterpart of the Magnificat (Luke I. 46–55), the Madonna's hymn of praise: 'My soul doth magnify the Lord, and my spirit doth rejoice in God my Saviour . . .'

56

a) *old Mr Leonard*: Not he of 'Counterparts', but perhaps a relative. He epitomises the Catholic middle-class morality of early twentieth-century Dublin. Nobody who had caused a scandal could work in a wine merchant's – in part because of the sizeable business to be gained by supplying altar wine to Dublin's army of priests and 'religious'.

b) *sown his wild oats*: Wild oats are bad grain, as opposed to cultivated grain. The Dublin playwright John O'Keeffe wrote the highly successful play *Wild Oats* (1791), still occasionally revived. In *U*, 'Nestor', Stephen thinks:

> Riddle me, riddle me, randy ro,
> My father gave me seeds to sow.

c) *free-thinking*: A sub-Nietzschean vogue of the period, meaning the rejection of any intellectual values imposed by an institution (such as the university or the Vatican). Any belief-system develops its own orthodoxy, however, which is why Stephen can tell the dean of studies in *P* (V.i):

> I also am sure that there is no such thing as free thinking inasmuch as all thinking must be bound by its own laws.

By the morning of Bloomsday (in *U*, 'Telemachus'), Haines hears about it differently:

> You behold in me, Stephen said with grim displeasure, a horrible example of free thought.

Cognate is the Swiftian warning that when people cease to believe in something, they do not believe in nothing, they believe in anything. Swift himself wrote a parody of the deism of the day in his *Mr. Collins's Discourse of Free-Thinking* (1713). Anthony Collins (38p) is championed by Temple, the poltroon, in *P* (V.1).

d) *existence of God*: Nietzsche's ideas on the Death of God (or debased versions of them) were in circulation during this period (99b). That Bob is doing his denying 'in public houses' mordantly suggests that his freethinking seems to lack rigour.

e) *Reynolds's Newspaper*: A radical newspaper published in London in various forms for a century after 1850. The name also recalls Thomas Reynolds (1771–1832), who betrayed the national cause, and whose similarity in this respect to Gogarty is mentioned by Joyce in a letter to Stanislaus in November 1906. Here, however, Bob Doran betrays himself.

f) *his religious duties*: According to the *Maynooth Catechism*, there were then six 'Precepts of the Church', as well as the Ten Commandments of God. These were:

1 To hear Mass on Sundays and all Holydays of Obligations.
2 To fast and abstain on the days commanded.
3 To confess our sins at least once a year.
4 To receive *worthily* the Blessed Eucharist at Easter within the time appointed.
5 To contribute to the support of our pastors.
6 Not to solemnize marriage at the forbidden times – nor to marry persons within the forbidden degrees of kindred – nor otherwise prohibited by the Church – nor clandestinely.

Stephen argues with his mother about his Easter Duty in *SH* and *P*.

g) *nine-tenths of the year*: It is as if Bob Doran pays temporal tithes to or for his freethinking. In *U*, 'Cyclops', the narrator visits Barry Kiernan's pub in Little Britain Street:

> And who was sitting up there in the corner that I hadn't seen snoring drunk blind to the world only Bob Doran.

h) *If I had've known*: The idiom is still current in Ireland.

i) *if he really loved her*: In Congreve's *The Way of the World*, Mirabell has decided that he loves Millimant:

> with all her faults; nay liked her for her faults ...which were so natural that they became her.

j) *Once you are married you are done for*: Joyce himself forestalled matrimony until 1931, when he was forty-nine – and only then did it 'for testamentary reasons'. He chose to marry Nora on 4 July, his father's birthday: Stanislaus a few years earlier had married Nellie Lichtensteiger on 13 August – the anniversary of his mother's death. In *All's Well That Ends Well* (II.iii), Parolles advises:

> A young man married is a man that's marr'd ...

k) *helplessly*: Bob's helpless immobility is similar to Eveline's helplessness when faced with impending marriage, though it has the opposite result.

l) *Bob! Bob!*: Among the word's slang meanings were: to cheat or obtain by cheating, to taunt, to thump. In *Othello* (V.i), there is Desdemona's Polly-like sentiment:

> He calls me to a restitution large
> Of gold and jewels that I bobb'd from him.

m) *She would put an end to herself, she said*: A slight hint of Mrs Sinico of 'A Painful Case', in the style of

a in his excited imagination old Mr Leonard calling out in his
rasping voice: *Send Mr Doran here, please.*

b All his long years of service gone for nothing! All his industry
and diligence thrown away! As a young man he had sown his
c wild oats, of course; he had boasted of his free-thinking and
d denied the existence of God to his companions in public-houses.
But that was all passed and done with . . . nearly. He still bought
e a copy of *Reynolds's Newspaper* every week but he attended to
fg his religious duties and for nine-tenths of the year lived a
regular life. He had money enough to settle down on; it was
not that. But the family would look down on her. First of all
there was her disreputable father and then her mother's boarding house was beginning to get a certain fame. He had a notion
that he was being had. He could imagine his friends talking of
the affair and laughing. She *was* a little vulgar; sometimes she
h said *I seen* and *If I had've known*. But what would grammar
i matter if he really loved her? He could not make up his mind
whether to like her or despise her for what she had done. Of
course, he had done it too. His instinct urged him to remain
j free, not to marry. Once you are married you are done for, it
said.

k While he was sitting helplessly on the side of the bed in shirt
and trousers she tapped lightly at his door and entered. She
told him all, that she had made a clean breast of it to her mother
and that her mother would speak with him that morning. She
cried and threw her arms round his neck, saying:

l —O, Bob! Bob! What am I do to? What am I to do at all?—

m She would put an end to herself, she said.

He comforted her feebly, telling her not to cry, that it would
be all right, never fear. He felt against his shirt the agitation of
her bosom.

It was not altogether his fault that it had happened. He
remembered well, with the curious patient memory of the
no celibate, the first casual caresses her dress, her breath, her fingers
had given him. Then late one night as he was undressing for
bed she had tapped at his door, timidly. She wanted to relight
her candle at his, for hers had been blown out by a gust. It was
p her bath night. She wore a loose open combing-jacket of
printed flannel. Her white instep shone in the opening of
q her furry slippers and the blood glowed warmly behind her
perfumed skin. From her hands and wrists too as she lit and

Eveline's Frank (31n). The
sentence originally had the two
clauses transposed.

n) *celibate*: The word means
unmarried rather than chaste.
George Moore (who memo-
rably 'told but did not kiss')
wrote *Celibates* in 1895. Joyce
translated some of it in Trieste
to improve his Italian.

o) *her fingers*: Much more
seductive than the original
'her arms'.

p) *open combing-jacket*: A lady's
garment for wearing at the
dressing-table.

q) *the opening of her furry slippers*: Like the open jacket, an
incidental detail of Polly's
sexuality. The whole passage
drips with suggestion, each
word reinforcing the effect of
the last.

A Bawdy-house of Old Dublin

a) *anyway cold*: i.e. to any extent cold.

b) *tumbler of punch*: Both these words are sexually charged. In *U*, 'Scylla and Charybdis', Joyce was to refer to Ann Hathaway as

> a bold faced Stratford wench who tumbles in a cornfield a lover younger than herself.

Similarly, Gogarty was to write *Tumbling in the Hay* (itself a quotation from *The Winter's Tale*). As for 'punch', it was eighteenth-century slang for to deflower. For the drink, see 79f.

c) *Perhaps they could be happy together*: The dead weight of Dublin matrimonial tradition includes a production c. 1694 of Thomas Southerne's *The Fatal Marriage, or the Innocent Adultery*. His earlier work, *The Disappointment, or the Mother in Fashion* was also performed there.

d) *his delirium* . . .: As in 'An Encounter', the offence is veiled from the reader.

e) *Going down the stairs his glasses* . . .: Very unusually for Joyce, this sentence is grammatically inelegant: the glasses are not descending under their own steam.

f) *dimmed*: Originally 'snuffed'.

g) *to ascend through the roof*: Bob's Ascension is doomed, in contrast to 'Ben Bloom Elijah's' at the end of *U*, 'Cyclops', 'like a shot off a shovel'.

h) *fly away to another country*: A hint of Stephen Dedalus in *P* (V.1) resolving to fly beyond those nets in Ireland constraining his soul. If Bob had been able to run away on his own, he might have emulated Barabas in his famous rejoinders in Marlowe's *The Jew of Malta* (IV.i):

> Thou has commited –
>
> Fornication: But that was in another country,
> And besides, the wench is dead . . .
> She has confest, and we are both undone,
> My bosom inmate, but I must dissemble . . .

i) *downstairs step by step*: The descent at the beginning of 'Grace' is steeper and swifter, but probably less disastrous.

j) *discomfiture*: The meaning is not 'discomfort' but 'defeat'.

steadied her candle a faint perfume arose.

On nights when he came in very late it was she who warmed up his dinner. He scarcely knew what he was eating, feeling her beside him alone, at night, in the sleeping house. And her
a thoughtfulness! If the night was anyway cold or wet or windy
b there was sure to be a little tumbler of punch ready for him.
c Perhaps they could be happy together ...

They used to go upstairs together on tiptoe, each with a candle, and on the third landing exchange reluctant goodnights. They used to kiss. He remembered well her eyes, the touch of
d her hand and his delirium ...

But delirium passes. He echoed her phrase, applying it to himself: *What am I to do?* The instinct of the celibate warned him to hold back. But the sin was there; even his sense of honour told him that reparation must be made for such a sin.

While he was sitting with her on the side of the bed Mary came to the door and said that the missus wanted to see him in the parlour. He stood up to put on his coat and waistcoat, more helpless than ever. When he was dressed he went over to her to comfort her. It would be all right, never fear. He left her crying on the bed and moaning softly: *O my God!*

ef Going down the stairs his glasses became so dimmed with moisture that he had to take them off and polish them. He
g longed to ascend through the roof and fly away to another
h country where he would never hear again of his trouble, and
i yet a force pushed him downstairs step by step. The implacable faces of his employer and of the Madam stared upon his
j discomfiture. On the last flight of stairs he passed Jack Mooney who was coming up from the pantry nursing two bottles of
k *Bass*. They saluted coldly; and the lover's eyes rested for a second or two on a thick bulldog face and a pair of thick short arms. When he reached the foot of the staircase he glanced
l up and saw Jack regarding him from the door of the return-room.
m Suddenly he remembered the night when one of the music-hall *artistes*, a little blond Londoner, had made a rather free allusion to Polly. The reunion had been almost broken up on account of Jack's violence. Everyone tried to quiet him. The music-hall *artiste*, a little paler than usual, kept smiling and saying that there was no harm meant: but Jack kept shouting at him that if any fellow tried that sort of a game on with *his*

k) Bass: A well-known British ale, pronounced like the fish rather than the musical term. In *U*, 'Oxen of the Sun', the red triangle of Bass (the UK's oldest trade mark) serves as a symbol of Sicily, where the Homeric scene is set.

l) *return-room*: The room of the house on the half-landing, at the rere (which is the usual Dublin spelling of 'rear').

m) *one of the music-hall* artistes: This sounds very like Weathers from 'Counterparts' (82k).

Hardwicke Street and St George's

a) *he'd bloody well put his teeth down his throat*: Joyce was understandably adamant that this 'bloody' could not be deleted. In a letter to his would-be publisher in May 1905, he said it was

> the one expression in the English language which can create on the reader the effect which I wish to create.

This was nearly a decade before Bernard Shaw's sensational 'Not bloody likely' in *Pygmalion* – played by 'Mrs Pat' (130d).

b) *so he would*: Irish idiom of emphasis.

c) *looking-glass*: In a letter of June 1906 to Grant Richards, Joyce wrote that he believed that his publisher would retard the course of civilisation in Ireland if he prevented the Irish people from having one good look at themselves 'in my nicely-polished looking-glass'.

d) *She looked at herself*: So too Maria in 'Clay'. Polly's profile and manner hardly suggest 'outrage' (55p) and she seems quite familiar with the bed.

e) *a revery*: See 55j. Originally Joyce had 'a mood of reminiscence'.

f) *started to her feet*: Originally 'jumped up'.

59

a sister he'd bloody well put his teeth down his throat, so he
b would.

. . . .

Polly sat for a little time on the side of the bed, crying. Then
c she dried her eyes and went over to the looking-glass. She
dipped the end of the towel in the water-jug and refreshed her
d eyes with the cool water. She looked at herself in profile and
readjusted a hairpin above her ear. Then she went back to the
bed again and sat at the foot. She regarded the pillows for a
long time and the sight of them awakened in her mind secret
amiable memories. She rested the nape of her neck against the
e cool iron bedrail and fell into a revery. There was no longer
any perturbation visible on her face.

She waited on patiently, almost cheerfully, without alarm,
her memories gradually giving place to hopes and visions of
the future. Her hopes and visions were so intricate that she no
longer saw the white pillows on which her gaze was fixed or
remembered that she was waiting for anything.

f At last she heard her mother calling. She started to her feet
g and ran to the banisters.

—Polly! Polly!—

—Yes, Mamma?—

—Come down, dear. Mr Doran wants to speak to you—

h Then she remembered what she had been waiting for.

g) *ran to the banisters*: Echoed in *FW* (159):

> Then Nuvoletta reflected for the last time in her little long life and she made up all her myriads of drifting minds in one. She cancelled all her engauzements. She climbed over the bannistars; she gave a childy cloudy cry: *Nuée! Nuée!* A lightdress fluttered. She was gone.

The Italian version of *D* renders 'A Little Cloud' as 'Nuoveletta'.

h) *what she had been waiting for*: The manuscript continued with the unnecessary phrase: 'this was it'.

The story is an asymmetrical companion-piece for 'Two Gallants'. The earlier story shows male morality in a bad light. This one reflects badly on the venality of women. Instead of two men exploiting a woman (and we have been spared in 'Two Gallants' an exploration of the slavey's psyche), two women conspire to take advantage of a convention-bound man. As in 'A Mother' there can be extenuating circumstances for any individual in such a society, but only to a limited extent. The situation is not an attractive one.

Bob, at thirty-four or thirty-five, is rapidly disintegrating. He is reasonably well-off, but because of 'an indiscretion' he is being blackmailed into matrimony, even though he has 'a notion that he was being had'.

As *Ulysses* confirms, Bob goes on to marry Polly. Only a year or two after 'The Boarding House', the evidence of another June day is both chilling and hilarious. In 'Cyclops', the narrator is brightly scathing in his best broad Dublinese, as Bob in Barney Kiernan's gets ludicrously maudlin about 'poor little Willy Dignam':

Talking through his bloody hat. Fitter for him to go home to the little sleepwalking bitch he married, Mooney, the bumbailiff's daughter. Mother kept a kip in Hardwicke street that used to be stravaging about the landings Bantam Lyons told me that was stopping there at two in the morning without a stitch on her, exposing her person, open to all comers, fair field and no favour.

Later, the detail accumulates, and we have already been told that Bob Doran is the 'lowest blackguard in Dublin when he's under the influence'. After trying to shake paws with the citizen's mangy dog and nearly falling off his stool onto the animal, he shakes hands with Bloom and starts 'doing the tragic' to ask him to tell Mrs Dignam all the things he was sorry for (though not including getting Paddy Dignam's name wrong). The narrator continues:

And off with him and out trying to walk straight. Boosed at five o'clock. Night he was near being lagged only Paddy Leonard knew the bobby, 14 A. Blind to the world up in a shebeen in Bride street after closing time, fornicating with two shawls and a bully on guard, drinking porter out of teacups. And calling himself a Frenchy for the shawls, Joseph Manuo, and talking against the catholic religion and he serving mass in Adam and Eve's when he was young with his eyes shut who wrote the new testament and the old testament and hugging and smugging. And the two shawls killed with the laughing, picking his pockets the bloody fool and he spilling the porter all over the bed and the two shawls screeching laughing at one another. *How is your testament? Have you got an old testament?* Only Paddy was passing there, I tell you what. Then see him of a Sunday with his little concubine of a wife, and she wagging her tail up the aisle of the chapel, with her patent boots on her, no less, and her violets, nice as pie, doing the little lady. Jack Mooney's sister. And the old prostitute of a mother procuring rooms to street couples. Gob, Jack made him toe the line. Told him if he didn't patch up the pot, Jesus, he'd kick the shite out of him.

These statements (like the *Wake*'s telling reference (186) to the 'boardelhouse') need not be taken at face value, but Bob's failure is manifest. Joyce's own antics in Istria and Italy between 1904 and 1912 were not so very different. He and Nora were sometimes virtually a street couple, behind on current and previous rents, with Stanislaus exasperatedly trying to help feed two children not his own and feeling bled white for his pains. The situation was dramatised in Act I of Tom Gallacher's play, *Mr Joyce is Leaving Paris* (1970). What the drunken Bob does not have that his creator did (drunken leech though he may have been), is integrity, or a sense of purpose. Bob has imploded morally, culpably so, and he has to pay the price. Polly Mooney's intentions are no better than Bob's. In offering sexual pleasure for her own material comfort, she is guilty of a form of simony.

Nevertheless, at a stroke she has found a moderately prosperous husband, and has satisfied the rules of Dublin propriety. The tarty detail from 'Cyclops' about her patent boots, and the remark about her mother's 'kip', confirm that she is her mother's daughter – a perverse madonna. In these brown houses that Joyce writes of, the generations repeat themselves, making old mistakes in new ways. So Bob the wineman has much in common with his father-in-law, a failed meatman. Polly's brother Jack works for a commission agent, while his father is a bumbailiff paid on a job-by-job basis: both are given to alcohol and violence. Polly will repeat her mother's mistake of marriage to a weak man. A Sheridan (as so often) provides the Dublin entertainment here. 'Old' Mr Leonard implies the existence of a young one.

That Jack can boast about being 'on to' a likely *artiste*, yet object to anyone being too free about Polly reveals his hypocrisy more than it does any concern for domestic protocol. The activities of the boarding house are a microcosm of Dublin society: the florid-faced missus looks in the mirror (as her daughter is later to do), the servant Mary hoards the crusts, the inmates come and go – tourists, *artistes*, clerks, commercial travellers, improvisers. (The luckless Bantam Lyons is also recognisable in Dublin folklore: in *Ulysses* he is about to back the winner of the Ascot Gold Cup until talked out of it by the professional tipster, Lenehan.) In a world where one's duty is to be seen at a token Mass and to mumble louder in the confessional, where happiness consists of a few drinks or comic songs, desperate measures are unlikely to be far away, as Bob knows. Although his Bloomsday bender is the one-a-year fling mentioned in the story (and even if the evidence of *Ulysses* did not exist), the sense, in 'The Boarding House', of despair as well as desperation is strong.

The story exudes moral squalor. Bob's three-day beard has been interpreted as a hint that he is dead, like an unrisen Christ, but his reluctant, slow descent to his destiny prefigures no resurrection. The cross he will bear on his 'bottle shoulders' (*U*, 'Lestrygonians') is one of his own making. Dublin (as seen by Joyce c. 1905) did not allow for redemption. Bob Doran, 'the lover', who longs to escape to another country, has indeed been had. These are country matters, and Bob has embraced his own doom, precisely Mrs Mooney's intention ever since the opportunity arose. Now her naughty daughter has at last made him *her* intended.

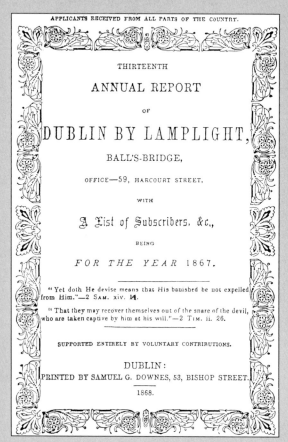

APPLICANTS RECEIVED FROM ALL PARTS OF THE COUNTRY.

THIRTEENTH

ANNUAL REPORT

OF

DUBLIN BY LAMPLIGHT,

BALL'S-BRIDGE,

OFFICE—59, HARCOURT STREET,

WITH

A List of Subscribers, &c.,

BEING

FOR THE YEAR 1867.

"Yet doth He devise means that His banished be not expelled from Him."—2 SAM. xiv. 14.

"That they may recover themselves out of the snare of the devil, who are taken captive by him at his will."—2 TIM. ii. 26.

SUPPORTED ENTIRELY BY VOLUNTARY CONTRIBUTIONS.

DUBLIN:
PRINTED BY SAMUEL G. DOWNES, 53, BISHOP STREET.
1868.

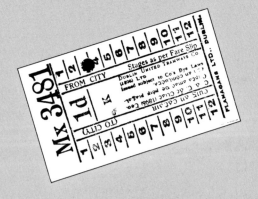

Clockwise from top left:

★ Maria's Institution (89c)
★ Mulligan's of Poolbeg Street (83b)
★ Ballsbridge welcomes Edward VII
★ Dublin diet (95(o))
★ A view of the 'old sombre house' (by the churchyard),
where Mr Duffy lives (95d)
★ King's Inns (62j)
★ Travel from the city

a) A LITTLE CLOUD: For significances of the title, see Afterword.

b) *Eight years before*: In about 1895: this story is set in about 1903.

c) *the North Wall*: Where Frank tried to embark with Eveline (32h). There is a similarity between Frank and Ignatius Gallaher, both active and much-travelled, as there is between the passive, immobile Eveline and Little Chandler.

d) *Gallaher*: Ignatius Gallaher combines unsympathetic elements of Oliver Gogarty (who is also the bedactylled Malachi Mulligan of *U*) with memories of a Dublin journalist whom the Joyces knew, Fred Gallaher. Ignatius Gallaher, now an employee of Lord Northcliffe, appears by name in *U*, 'Aeolus', where he is celebrated for his ingenious scoop in the *New York World* reporting the Phoenix Park Murders of 1882. The name derives from the Irish *Gallchobar*, from *gall*, 'foreign' + *cabhair*, 'help'.

e) *fearless accent*: In *D*, accents are indicative of character and status. The expression here is mostly a euphemism for Gallaher's scope for impudence.

f) *Little Chandler*: Obviously the name Chandler signifies 'candlemaker', and thus fortifies the recurrent image of candles in *D*, but the nickname 'Little' is important: he is not a provider of light but a provider of little light. (The word 'little' has the same effect on 'light' as the word 'minor' has on 'poet'.) One commentator derives the name from an Anglo-Irish word for 'maggot'. Aptly, 'Chandler's Wobble', which affects slightly the rotation of the earth, was discovered in the 1890s. The name is not common in Dublin, but a Mr H. Chandler lived at Windsor Avenue, Fairview, five houses along from No 29, where the Joyces were in 1899.

g) *fair silken hair*: Silken Thomas, Tenth Earl of Kildare, in 1534 rose against Henry VIII (as mentioned in *U*, 'Wandering Rocks' 8). He and his garrison were defeated at his stronghold at Maynooth the next year, and his men were given what was called a 'Maynooth Pardon': they (as he was later to be) were executed after a promise of safety. Little Thomas Chandler, however, will lead no rebellions.

h) *half-moons of his nails*: Some have suggested that this may be a half-identification of Chandler with the feminine moon, while Gallaher could be linked with the masculine sun. In *P* (V.1) the artist (by Stephen's criteria) must remain 'indifferent, paring his fingernails'.

i) *childish white teeth*: This is almost the only decent set of teeth mentioned in *D*. Throughout the story, Chandler's immaturity is emphasised. As a Flaubertian detail, however, the teeth also recall Emma Bovary, a character similarly limited.

j) *King's Inns*: These legal and archival offices, designed by James Gandon just before the Union, and named after Henry VIII, are situated north of the river. Representations of 'Plenty' and a Bacchante adorn doorways in the north wing. The poet James Clarence Mangan worked here, as did Joyce's college friend, C. P. Curran (167m). For a brief period it was a copyright library under the Crown.

k) *his tiresome writing*: The would-be writer Chandler is little better than a scrivener, like Farrington of 'Counterparts' or Mr Callanan of 'Christmas Eve' (94) and his friend Hooper: 'Hooper was a clerk in a solicitor's office in Eustace St and Mr Callanan was a clerk in a solicitor's office close by on Wellington Quay'.

l) *a shower of kindly golden dust*: The decrepit old man Father Flynn ('The Sisters') similarly showers himself with snuff. This weather report reads like a parody of the end of 'The Dead'.

m) *life ... sad*: A clear contrast with the *saeva indignatio* (savage indignation) of Swift which is mentioned in his epitaph. Loving or loathing life (even alternately) is one thing, but 'gentle melancholy' is a shallow pose.

n) *the burden of wisdom ...*: The narrative is filtered through the mind of Little Chandler, and so passages of 'fine writing' in this vein appear regularly. Often, however, when Chandler is thinking of Gallaher, the style takes on some of the journalist's brashness. This device, a form of 'literary chameleonism', allows Joyce to produce a wide range of ironic effects, promise-crammed airs and gracenotes.

A LITTLE CLOUD

EIGHT YEARS BEFORE he had seen his friend off at the North Wall and wished him godspeed. Gallaher had got on. You could tell that at once by his travelled air, his well-cut tweed suit and fearless accent. Few fellows had talents like his and fewer still could remain unspoiled by such success. Gallaher's heart was in the right place and he had deserved to win. It was something to have a friend like that.

Little Chandler's thoughts ever since lunch-time had been of his meeting with Gallaher, of Gallaher's invitation and of the great city London where Gallaher lived. He was called Little Chandler because, though he was but slightly under the average stature, he gave one the idea of being a little man. His hands were white and small, his frame was fragile, his voice was quiet and his manners were refined. He took the greatest care of his fair silken hair and moustache, and used perfume discreetly on his handkerchief. The half-moons of his nails were perfect and when he smiled you caught a glimpse of a row of childish white teeth.

As he sat at his desk in the King's Inns he thought what changes those eight years had brought. The friend whom he had known under a shabby and necessitous guise had become a brilliant figure on the London Press. He turned often from his tiresome writing to gaze out of the office window. The glow of a late autumn sunset covered the grass plots and walks. It cast a shower of kindly golden dust on the untidy nurses and decrepit old men who drowsed on the benches; it flickered upon all the moving figures – on the children who ran scream-ing along the gravel paths and on everyone who passed through the gardens. He watched the scene and thought of life; and (as always happened when he thought of life) he became sad. A gentle melancholy took possession of him. He felt how useless it was to struggle against fortune, this being the burden of wisdom which the ages had bequeathed to him.

He remembered the books of poetry upon his shelves at home. He had bought them in his bachelor days and many an evening, as he sat in the little room off the hall, he had been

(63c).

62

a) *But shyness . . .*: Shyness is a condition of childhood or immaturity, beyond which it becomes the higher selfishness.

b) *he repeated lines to himself*: Which James Joyce also did on his walks in Dublin, Trieste, Zürich and Paris.

c) *under the feudal arch*: One of the difficulties for any reader (or annotator) of *D* can be seen here: (i) Is the arch truly a feudal arch, whatever that may be? (ii) Is Joyce using the arch as a comment on the serf-like Chandler? (iii) Does Chandler himself do this? (iv) Or is it an example of 'Chandleresque' 'fine writing', and hence an empty cliché?

d) *Henrietta Street*: Named after the wife of the Second Duke of Grafton, Lord Lieutenant in the early eighteenth century, it was for many years the most fashionable street in Dublin. By 1900 the grand houses had deteriorated to tenements, whose squalor was relieved only by the King's Inns entrance and by the 'Discharged Female Aid Society' at No 10, a house once owned by the Countess of Blessington and still with interiors containing very early and beautiful stucco and carved work.

e) *roistered*: Noisy revelling is something that Chandler is incapable of. As a clerk, he is perhaps better suited to rostering.

f) *memory of the past*: The phrase comes from a song in the opera *Maritana*, composed by the Waterford-born William Vincent Wallace (1812–1865). With *The Bohemian Girl* and *The Lily of Killarney* it was part of the so-called 'Irish' (or 'English') 'Ring' (127d). The words are by Edward Fitzball (who also worked with Balfe):

> There is a flower that bloometh
> When autumn leaves are shed.
> With the silent moment it weepeth,
> The spring and summer fled.
> The early frost of winter
> Scarce one tint hath overcast.
> Oh, pluck it ere it wither,
> 'Tis the memory of the past!
>
> It wafted perfume o'er us
> Of sweet, though sad regret
> For the true friends gone before us,
> Whom none would e'er forget.
> Let no heart brave its power,
> By guilty thoughts o'ercast,
> For then, a poison flow'r
> Is – the memory of the past!

g) *Corless's*: The Burlington Hotel and Restaurant, 26 & 27 St Andrew Street, which had been taken over in 1900 by the Jammet Brothers. With an entrance just off Dame Street, it was a popular but expensive venue for fashionable Dublin until its closure in 1967.

h) *oysters*: Bloom has a jaundiced meditation on this subject in *U*, 'Lestrygonians'. 'Effect on the sexual', he thinks. In 'Circe' and 'Penelope' there are reports of the Blooms' serving girl Mary Driscoll who was suspected of stealing oysters, an issue which caused the connubial alliance to split.

i) *cavaliers*: Another reference to the splendours of Georgian Dublin, and to its 'gallants'.

j) *alarmed Atalantas*: According to Ovid (*Metamorphoses* VIII, close to the epigraph of *P*), Atalanta, a princess from Greek mythology, was dedicated to virginity. She refused to marry until she had been beaten in a running race. Finally Hippomenes distracted her by dropping golden apples in her path, winning the race and her hand. In Victorian prints she is shown holding up her long dress as she runs.

k) *without turning his head*: A hint here of another Greek myth, that of Orpheus and Eurydice. Orpheus in the end turns his head, with terrible results, including the loss of Eurydice.

l) *He chose the darkest and narrowest streets*: Chandler presumably walks in or near 'Nighttown' and flirts with the thought of going to a prostitute, just as in *P* (II.5) the young Stephen wanders about with slightly bolder purpose.

m) *boldly*: The word 'bold' is applied to Little Chandler several times: in Ireland it has an extra meaning, being very commonly used to connote naughtiness in a child. 'You're a bold boy!' and 'Don't be bold, now' reverberate through most Irish childhoods.

n) *low fugitive laughter*: Whether the laughter is directed at this jejune and dapper little figure, or whether it is the offspring of street-corner romance, it has a powerful (and ambiguous) effect on Chandler. (In his last poem, Yeats was to celebrate 'Porter-drinkers' randy laughter'.)

o) *Capel Street*: Now (and then) a busy shopping street, Capel Street (the name rhymes with 'papal') was once part of the main artery through the city. It is named after Arthur Capel, Earl of Essex, whose throat was cut in 1683 after his incarceration in the Tower of London for conspiracy. In 1849, No 33 was the premises of 'John Clifford, wax and spermaceti chandler, oil merchant and perfumer', but there were none of his profession left in Capel Street by 1900 (49i).

p) *Ignatius*: The name is surely an ironic allusion to Ignatius Loyola (1491–1556), founder of the Jesuits

tempted to take one down from the bookshelf and read out
a something to his wife. But shyness had always held him back;
and so the books had remained on their shelves. At times he
b repeated lines to himself and this consoled him.

When his hour had struck he stood up and took leave of his
desk and of his fellow-clerks punctiliously. He emerged from
c under the feudal arch of the King's Inns, a neat modest figure,
d and walked swiftly down Henrietta Street. The golden sunset
was waning and the air had grown sharp. A horde of grimy
children populated the street. They stood or ran in the roadway
or crawled up the steps before the gaping doors or squatted
like mice upon the thresholds. Little Chandler gave them no
thought. He picked his way deftly through all that minute
vermin-like life and under the shadow of the gaunt spectral
e mansions in which the old nobility of Dublin had roistered.
f No memory of the past touched him, for his mind was full of
a present joy.

g He had never been in Corless's but he knew the value of the
name. He knew that people went there after the theatre to eat
h oysters and drink liqueurs; and he had heard that the waiters
there spoke French and German. Walking swiftly by at night
he had seen cabs drawn up before the door and richly dressed
i ladies, escorted by cavaliers, alight and enter quickly. They
wore noisy dresses and many wraps. Their faces were powdered
and they caught up their dresses, when they touched earth, like
j alarmed Atalantas. He had always passed without turning his
k head to look. It was his habit to walk swiftly in the street even
by day, and whenever he found himself in the city late at
night he hurried on his way apprehensively and excitedly.
Sometimes, however, he courted the causes of his fear. He
lm chose the darkest and narrowest streets and, as he walked boldly
forward, the silence that was spread about his footsteps troubled
him, the wandering silent figures troubled him; and at times a
n sound of low fugitive laughter made him tremble like a leaf.

op He turned to the right towards Capel Street. Ignatius Gallaher on the London Press! Who would have thought it possible
eight years before? Still, now that he reviewed the past, Little
Chandler could remember many signs of future greatness in
q his friend. People used to say that Ignatius Gallaher was wild.
Of course, he did mix with a rakish set of fellows at that time,
drank freely and borrowed money on all sides. In the end he had

(in 1540) and patron saint of Belvedere College. Loyola formulated what are called the Ignatian Spiritual Exercises, much used in retreats. Like many of these stories, and like Gaul, the works of Dante, Hegel, St Jerome and whatever you're having yourself, these Exercises were generally in three parts: preparation, then meditation, and finally petition to (or conversation with) God. Though they do not agree, both Gallaher and Loyola issue instructions upon how to live.

q) *Ignatius Gallaher was wild*: Joyce, referring to Oliver Gogarty's marriage, wrote in August 1906 to his brother: 'We had better wish Mr and Mrs Ignatius Gallaher health and long life'. Gogarty, with his stylish bearing and epigrammatic wit, often imitated Oscar Wilde, and in 1904 accordingly entered a poem for the Newdigate Prize at Oxford. Unlike Wilde, however, as he once wrote to Joyce, he 'obtained but a 2nd place in the Newdigate, further cause for impecuniosity'. The other model for Ignatius, Fred Gallaher (62d) moved, as did both Oscar and Ignatius, from Dublin to London to Paris, and he was also touched by scandal. So in more ways than one, Ignatius Gallaher *was* Wilde.

Doorways in Henrietta Street (63d)

a) *a certain . . . something*: The remark and the halting style recall Old Cotter's comments on Father Flynn in 'The Sisters' (2l).

b) *out at elbows*: Ragged and impoverished. From *The Times*, in May 1885: 'There is an out-at-elbows look about some quarters of Dublin.' Also used by Smollett in *Humphry Clinker* (1771): 'Sir Ulic Mackilligut . . . is said to be much out at elbows.'

c) *a tight corner*: Suitably for a book one of whose presiding images is the gnomon, or imperfect parallelogram. Corners are frequently invoked by *D*. Joyce's own birthplace, Brighton Square, is paradoxically triangular.

d) *Half time, now*: Wait a minute. An expression from various sports – rugby, football – with two halves.

e) *considering cap*: A term used by Dickens in both *Great Expectations* and *Our Mutual Friend*. 'Thinking cap' is still heard in Ireland.

f) *all out*: all through. An idiom from the Irish – the mortal, cricketing, park-keeping and other connotations of the phrase would be invoked at the very end of Samuel Beckett's *Murphy* (1938).

g) *You could do nothing in Dublin*: In essence, the 'paralysis' theme of the book.

h) *Grattan Bridge*: Originally Essex Bridge; versions were built in 1676, 1755 and 1874. It was renamed after Henry Grattan (1746–1820), leader of the Patriot Party, who was instrumental in achieving an autonomous parliament for Dublin.

i) *a band of tramps*: Several times in *D* Joyce personifies houses. This phrase also recalls the 'decrepit old men' whom Chandler notices earlier.

j) *write a poem*: Chandler in the next dozen lines is confused: he thinks successively about how 'to express his idea', about 'what idea . . . to express', about how he has 'so many different moods and impressions . . . to express' and about 'the melancholy tone of his poems'.

k) *a poetic moment*: This moment is the description of the houses on the lower quays. Chandler's interior monologue recognises the 'qualities' of its own prose.

l) *nearer to London*: Nearer to Gallaher, representative of the London literary world, and also physically nearer, as Chandler is headed south-east. The combination of the literal with the symbolic, where neither interpretation invalidates the other one, is typical of *D*.

m) *thirty-two*: As the story is set in 1903 or 1904, between Joyce's return from his first visit to Paris and his elopement with Nora, Chandler was born about 1872, and is of Yeats' and Synge's generation.

Atalanta (63j)

got mixed up in some shady affair, some money transaction: at least, that was one version of his flight. But nobody denied

a him talent. There was always a certain . . . something in Ignatius Gallaher that impressed you in spite of yourself. Even when he

b was out at elbows and at his wits' end for money he kept up a bold face. Little Chandler remembered (and the remembrance brought a slight flush of pride to his cheek) one of Ignatius

c Gallaher's sayings when he was in a tight corner:

d —Half time, now, boys, he used to say light-heartedly.

e Where's my considering cap?—

f That was Ignatius Gallaher all out; and, damn it, you couldn't but admire him for it.

Little Chandler quickened his pace. For the first time in his life he felt himself superior to the people he passed. For the first time his soul revolted against the dull inelegance of Capel Street. There was no doubt about it: if you wanted to succeed you had to go away. You could do nothing in Dublin. As he

g

h crossed Grattan Bridge he looked down the river towards the lower quays and pitied the poor stunted houses. They seemed

i to him a band of tramps, huddled together along the river-banks, their old coats covered with dust and soot, stupefied by the panorama of sunset and waiting for the first chill of night to bid them arise, shake themselves and begone. He wondered

j whether he could write a poem to express his idea. Perhaps Gallaher might be able to get it into some London paper for him. Could he write something original? He was not sure what

k idea he wished to express, but the thought that a poetic moment had touched him took life within him like an infant hope. He stepped onward bravely.

l Every step brought him nearer to London, farther from his own sober inartistic life. A light began to tremble on the

m horizon of his mind. He was not so old – thirty-two. His temperament might be said to be just at the point of maturity. There were so many different moods and impressions that he wished to express in verse. He felt them within him. He tried to weigh his soul to see if it was a poet's soul. Melancholy was the dominant note of his temperament, he thought, but it was

n a melancholy tempered by recurrences of faith and resignation

o and simple joy. If he could give expression to it in a book of poems perhaps men would listen. He would never be popular: he saw that. He could not sway the crowd but he might appeal

n) *tempered*: Moderated. However, in connection with steel, the word means 'hardened'. It is one of those unusual words with two almost opposite meanings: 'cleaver' (in 'The Boarding House') and 'timorous' (in 'A Painful Case') are others.

o) *If he could*: Chandler's excuses and evasions prefigure Garret Deasy in *U*, 'Nestor': 'I am surrounded by difficulties, by . . . intrigues by . . . backstairs influence by . . .'.

a) *a little circle of kindred minds*: Chandler should reflect on AE's definition of a literary movement: 'five or six people who live in the same town and hate each other cordially'.

b) *The English critics*: Literary influence within the empire was dominated by the London prints and the ancient universities. Edmund Gosse, George Saintsbury, Maurice Hewlett, W. P. Ker and Arthur Quiller-Couch were among the reviewers of the time.

c) *the Celtic school*: Matthew Arnold in his book *On the Study of Celtic Literature* (1867) gave the 'Celtic' school an early definition outside Ireland. Its members at the turn of the century included W. B. Yeats, AE, A. P. Graves (father of Robert) and Lizzie Twigg (briefly in *U*). Earlier, Speranza (Oscar Wilde's mother) and a group of poets led by Thomas Davis had written patriotic poetry for the *Nation* newspaper and elsewhere.

d) *he would put in allusions*: Allusions are not to be added to a text, any more than, say, symbols are. They should be inherent. Oliver Gogarty was not a member of the 'Celtic' School, but he larded his verse with classical allusions. Joyce, no stranger to allusions, removed the chapter headings of *U*, only to divulge them later.

e) Mr Chandler ...: Now Chandler is writing reviews, not writing writing. The August 1901 issue of the *New Ireland Review* contains a sample of the genre. *A Light on the Broom* by William Dara (pseudonym of William Byrne, whom Joyce once thought of putting into a story) is reviewed:

> There is genuine poetry in this little volume, which makes only the modest demand of sixpence on the public purse. There are imperfections which indicate the work of a young man. Chief among these I would place a certain obscurity, a lack of clear-cut expression, which makes 'Laurel and Laburnum', and two or three other pieces somewhat unsatisfactory reading. One could wish, too, that youth had imparted a more hopeful tinge, a more auroral cheerfulness to *A Light on the Broom*. But there is here a real charm and undoubted promise ...The long poem, 'By the Turf Clamps of Almhuin', seems to contain a searching self-revelation; some of its couplets are good poetry, others are weak; not all of it is easily understood, *e.g.* the twelve lines beginning –
>
> > 'As pines upon a windy night
> > Pinion the darkness with delight,
> > And gnaw it with a tiger's moan,
> > I clutched at pain, alone, alone,' &c.

f) *Thomas Malone Chandler*: This device would have made the author of *D* James Murray Joyce. Several 'patriotic' Irish poets adopted similar high-sounding names: Stanislaus in *MBK* describes his brother reading 'with cold patient scorn' the poetical works of Thomas D'Arcy McGee and Denis Florence Mac-Carthy.

g) *overmaster*: A Nietzschean idea in reverse, if it has that effect on him. The word recurs in a more serious sense towards the end of 'The Dead' (193b).

h) *the shining of many red and green wine glasses*: Bright lights do not suit Chandler. The Dublin-born Iris Murdoch in *The Red and the Green* (1965) also uses these colours to convey England and Ireland.

i) *when his sight cleared*: Bob Doran has a similar problem with vision in 'The Boarding House' (58f).

j) *his feet planted far apart*: Following the 'fearless accent' and the 'bold face', Chandler's first glimpse of his friend establishes Gallaher's dominance. Early in his university career, in an essay on art, 'Ecce Homo', Joyce wrote that in early statuary the 'separation of the feet' was the 'first step towards drama'.

k) *Tommy, old hero*: By 1895 'Tommy' (from 'Thomas Atkins', an army specimen name like A. N. Other) was used for a private in the British Army. Taken with 'old hero', the phrase is an inaccurate way of addressing Little Chandler.

l) *whisky*: They are drinking Irish malt, which is usually spelt 'whiskey'. It is reported that Fred Gallaher (62d), like his namesake Ignatius, didn't take water in his whiskey.

m) *better stuff than we get across the water*: When Gogarty went up to Worcester College, Oxford, for a couple of terms in 1904, he brought with him a barrel of Guinness, as the Dublin brew was (and still is) by strong repute better than its London counterpart.

n) *Soda? Lithia? No mineral?*: Soda water as a manufactured product was invented in 1776 by a Dublin medical student, Augustine Thwaites. It is still sold by the bottle in Irish pubs, whereas in England a splash from a syphon is free. Lithia was a well-known mineral water, containing oxide of lithium, and was sometimes prescribed for gout. 'Mineral' is still a term used in Ireland for many non-alcoholic fizzy drinks.

o) garçon: 'Waiter', and more generally, 'boy'. Gallaher is of course showing off his cosmopolitanism, but it is true that until the outbreak of the First World War, many Continental staff were employed in Jammet's (and likewise in the Shelbourne Hotel).

p) *two halves*: Two small whiskies, each half the size

65

to a little circle of kindred minds. The English critics, perhaps, would recognize him as one of the Celtic school by reason of the melancholy tone of his poems; besides that, he would put in allusions. He began to invent sentences and phrases from the notices which his book would get. *Mr Chandler has the gift of easy and graceful verse . . . A wistful sadness pervades these poems . . . The Celtic note.* It was a pity his name was not more Irish-looking. Perhaps it would be better to insert his mother's name before the surname: Thomas Malone Chandler, or better still: T. Malone Chandler. He would speak to Gallaher about it.

He pursued his revery so ardently that he passed his street and had to turn back. As he came near Corless's his former agitation began to overmaster him and he halted before the door in indecision. Finally he opened the door and entered.

The light and noise of the bar held him at the doorway for a few moments. He looked about him, but his sight was confused by the shining of many red and green wine glasses. The bar seemed to him to be full of people and he felt that the people were observing him curiously. He glanced quickly to right and left (frowning slightly to make his errand appear serious), but when his sight cleared a little he saw that nobody had turned to look at him: and there, sure enough, was Ignatius Gallaher leaning with his back against the counter and his feet planted far apart.

—Hallo, Tommy, old hero, here you are! What is it to be? What will you have? I'm taking whisky: better stuff than we get across the water. Soda? Lithia? No mineral? I'm the same. Spoils the flavour . . . Here, *garçon*, bring us two halves of malt whisky, like a good fellow . . . Well, and how have you been pulling along since I saw you last? Dear God, how old we're getting! Do you see any signs of aging in me – eh, what? A little grey and thin on the top – what?—

Ignatius Gallaher took off his hat and displayed a large closely cropped head. His face was heavy, pale and clean-shaven. His eyes, which were of bluish slate-colour, relieved his unhealthy pallor and shone out plainly above the vivid orange tie he wore. Between the rival features the lips appeared very long and shapeless and colourless. He bent his head and felt with two sympathetic fingers the thin hair at the crown. Little Chandler shook his head as a denial. Ignatius Gallaher put on his hat again.

of a 'ball o' malt', which was one tenth of a bottle and very slightly more than a 'tailor'.

q) *vivid orange tie*: A strong symbol in this story: Gallaher is not an Orangeman, but the Orange Order, like Gallaher, valued the British connection.

r) *thin hair at the crown*: In *U*, 'Hades', Simon Dedalus is told of an old (balding) friend that there's now nothing between himself and heaven.

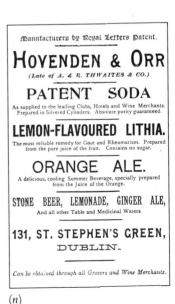

(*n*)

An early advertisement for Corless's (63g)

The pier at Douglas, in the Isle of Man (m)

a) *looking for copy*: The journalist's search for a story, or at least for something to fill space, is akin to Chandler's search for a subject for a poem.

b) *deuced*: Damned. The 'deuce' is an old word for the devil.

c) *the old country*: An epithet frequently used by exiles, it was also the title of the Christmas issues of the *Homestead*. In the 1980s Alan Bennett wrote a play with this title – set in Russia.

d) *dear dirty Dublin*: A phrase first popularised by Lady Morgan. It is still in common use, and although Dublin is no longer as dirty as it was, it is dearer than ever.

e) *old acquaintance*: The use of the singular confirms that Gallaher is quoting from Robert Burns' 'Auld Lang Syne':

> Should auld acquaintance be forgot
> And never brought to mind?
> Should auld acquaintance be forgot
> And auld lang syne?

f) *O'Hara*: The name could possibly be a rueful reference to Matthew O'Hara, who was helpful in persuading the *Irish Times* to publish Joyce's interview with Henri Fournier (41). Joyce failed, however, to obtain what he really hoped to see regularly in the paper: '*Irish Times* Paris Correspondent, Jas A. Joyce'.

g) *Hogan*: During this period more than one Hogan joined the Land Commission: two of them became Purchase Inspectors.

h) *a good sit*: A good job, or 'situation'. The word is still found in the newspapers: 'Sits Vac'.

i) *the Land Commission*: The Irish Land Commission was in Upper Merrion Street. Following the 1903 'Wyndham Act', its task was to oversee the breaking up of the great estates and the transfer of farmland to the tenants. A system of grants and bonuses meant that there was a great deal of money sloshing round the Commission, some of which, Joyce is implying, may have stuck to Hogan's fingers.

j) *Boose*: Drink – now spelt with a 'z'. The word has been current since Elizabethan times.

k) *Other things, too*: Chandler is too repressed to specify what these are. Women – or worse?

l) *you haven't changed an atom*: At the turn of the century atomic theory changed a great deal. This was partly due to the Dublin physicist, George Johnstone Stoney, who predicted the electron in a paper given to the RDS in 1891.

—It pulls you down, he said, Press life. Always hurry and scurry, looking for copy and sometimes not finding it: and then, always to have something new in your stuff. Damn proofs and printers, I say, for a few days. I'm deuced glad, I can tell you, to get back to the old country. Does a fellow good, a bit of a holiday. I feel a ton better since I landed again in dear dirty Dublin ... Here you are, Tommy. Water? Say when—

Little Chandler allowed his whisky to be very much diluted.

—You don't know what's good for you, my boy, said Ignatius Gallaher. I drink mine neat—

—I drink very little as a rule, said Little Chandler modestly. An odd half-one or so when I meet any of the old crowd: that's all—

—Ah, well, said Ignatius Gallaher cheerfully, here's to us and to old times and old acquaintance—

They clinked glasses and drank the toast.

—I met some of the old gang to-day, said Ignatius Gallaher. O'Hara seems to be in a bad way. What's he doing?—

—Nothing, said Little Chandler. He's gone to the dogs—

—But Hogan has a good sit, hasn't he?—

—Yes; he's in the Land Commission—

—I met him one night in London and he seemed to be very flush ... Poor O'Hara! Boose, I suppose?—

—Other things, too, said Little Chandler shortly—

Ignatius Gallaher laughed.

—Tommy, he said, I see you haven't changed an atom. You're the very same serious person that used to lecture me on Sunday mornings when I had a sore head and a fur on my tongue. You'd want to knock about a bit in the world. Have you never been anywhere, even for a trip?—

—I've been to the Isle of Man, said Little Chandler—

Ignatius Gallaher laughed.

—The Isle of Man! he said. Go to London or Paris: Paris, for choice. That'd do you good—

—Have you seen Paris?—

—I should think I have! I've knocked about there a little—

—And is it really so beautiful as they say? asked Little Chandler—

He sipped a little of his drink while Ignatius Gallaher finished his boldly.

—Beautiful? said Ignatius Gallaher, pausing on the word

m) *I've been to the Isle of Man*: Gallaher is recommending that the immature Chandler should grow up, but this is all Chandler can offer. There is a legend that the Isle of Man is part of Ireland anyway, because it was originally the land whose displacement caused Lough Neagh to come into being. Douglas was a popular holiday resort at the time: it was cheap to get there from Dublin, and it felt like 'abroad'.

n) *Paris*: When Joyce wrote this story he had his own experiences of Paris, although from the evidence of his letters, his lack of money meant that he had to choose the Bibliothèque Sainte-Géneviève rather than the more lurid centres of Parisian night-life. But he would recognise the boastful stance of a 'man-of-the-world'. In a notebook begun in Paris he jotted down the following, which appears to be an over-heard remark: 'Ah, Paris? What's Paris? The theatres, the cafés, *les petites femmes des boulevards*', and in the same notebook appears (under 'For "Dubliners"'): 'Paris – a lamp for lovers hung in the wood of the world'.

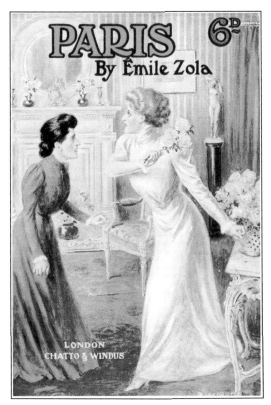

An early 20th century translation of a novel of Paris lowlife – whose hero is an unfrocked priest (66n)

Frolics at the Moulin Rouge (a)

a) *the Moulin Rouge*: From its foundation in 1889 until 1902, this most celebrated of Montmartre night-clubs combined cancan dancing indoors with music-hall features in the garden. From 1903 it concentrated on operetta and revue. The familiar drawings by Toulouse-Lautrec give a good impression of its glamour and loucheness. Of course, there were in Dublin nightly debaucheries no less sleazy in a score of tenement 'boarding houses'.

b) *Bohemian cafés*: These were meeting places for people of an often artistic or literary bent, who ignored, in the main, the usual rules of polite society. The apotheosis of Bohemian life was Puccini's opera *La Bohème*, but Dublin was far more familiar with *The Bohemian Girl*, Balfe's greatest success (31h).

c) *pious*: The tone of sanctimoniousness was generally absent from the word at this time. It meant simply 'holy'.

d) *gay*: Concurrently with its meaning of 'cheerful', this word has had a long history of sexual innuendo, from 'gay Lothario' (44h) to its current homosexual application. At the turn of the century, it was a slang term applied to prostitutes.

e) *they've a great feeling for the Irish there*: This trad-itional amity comes from both the common religion (Roman Catholicism) and the common enemy (England) (169k).

f) *man*: Gallaher addresses Chandler variously as 'man', 'Tommy', 'old chap', 'old man' and 'old hero', all of which may be seen as somewhat patronising, but his most frequent term of address is 'my boy'. The idiom here recalls Corley in 'Two Gallants'.

g) *immoral*: In this simoniac world, the word refers exclusively to matters sexual, a usage that continues in Ireland.

h) *a catholic gesture*: Gallaher embraces all the sins of the world with a broad sweep of the arm. The term ironically brings to mind the sign of the Cross, a Catholic gesture which does not indicate immorality.

i) *the students' balls*: The most celebrated of these was the bacchanalian 'Bal des Quat'z' Arts'. At this 'Four Arts' ball in the early hours of 10 February 1893, some students persuaded two girls to stand on tables in the Moulin Rouge to have their ankles judged. Then they had their knees judged. Soon, striptease was born.

j) *cocottes*: Prostitutes or loose women, part of the *demi-monde* of Paris.

k) *an immoral city*: Discussing Shakespeare in *U*, 'Scylla and Charybdis', Stephen remarks that 'Eliz-abethan London lay as far from Stratford as corrupt Paris lies from virgin Dublin'.

and on the flavour of his drink. It's not so beautiful, you know. Of course, it is beautiful ... But it's the life of Paris; that's the thing. Ah, there's no city like Paris for gaiety, movement, excitement ...—

Little Chandler finished his whisky and, after some trouble, succeeded in catching the barman's eye. He ordered the same again.

a —I've been to the Moulin Rouge, Ignatius Gallaher continued when the barman had removed their glasses, and I've
bc been to all the Bohemian cafés. Hot stuff! Not for a pious chap like you, Tommy—

Little Chandler said nothing until the barman returned with two glasses: then he touched his friend's glass lightly and reciprocated the former toast. He was beginning to feel somewhat disillusioned. Gallaher's accent and way of expressing himself did not please him. There was something vulgar in his friend which he had not observed before. But perhaps it was only the result of living in London amid the bustle and competition of the Press. The old personal charm was still there under this new gaudy manner. And, after all, Gallaher had lived, he had seen the world. Little Chandler looked at his friend enviously.

d —Everything in Paris is gay, said Ignatius Gallaher. They believe in enjoying life – and don't you think they're right? If you want to enjoy yourself properly you must go to Paris.
e And, mind you, they've a great feeling for the Irish there. When they heard I was from Ireland they were ready to eat
f me, man—

Little Chandler took four or five sips from his glass.

g —Tell me, he said, is it true that Paris is so ... immoral as they say?—

h Ignatius Gallaher made a catholic gesture with his right arm.

—Every place is immoral, he said. Of course you do find
i spicy bits in Paris. Go to one of the students' balls, for instance.
j That's lively, if you like, when the *cocottes* begin to let themselves loose. You know what they are, I suppose?—

—I've heard of them, said Little Chandler—

Ignatius Gallaher drank off his whisky and shook his head.

—Ah, he said, you may say what you like. There's no woman like the Parisienne – for style, for go—

k —Then it is an immoral city, said Little Chandler, with

A page from Maria Monk (*f*)

Little Chandler's inadequacies were not unique to him

68

a) *six of one and half a dozen of the other*: Both the same – what Byron (73a) in *Don Juan* (IV.93) called 'Arcades ambo – *id est*, blackguards both'.

b) *I say*: Gallaher, with this, and his 'old boy' and his 'what', uses the idioms of his adopted country.

c) *don't make punch ... liquor up*: Don't dilute it, and drink up.

d) François: Gallaher's jaunty use of this Gallicism is also a reference to one of the two Jammet brothers: François and Michel had recently founded Jammet's Restaurant, taking over the premises and business of Thomas Corless (63g).

e) *Berlin*: The reputation of Berlin later in the century became even more notorious for its decadent night-life and its tolerance of homosexuality. Joyce never visited the city.

f) *the secrets of religious houses*: *The History of the Rod*, the works of the Marquis de Sade and *The Awful Disclosures of Maria Monk: The Hidden Secrets of a Nun's Life in a Convent, Exposed*; ILLUSTRATED were among the many books that were then being clandestinely circulated which purported to reveal the reality behind life in convent and monastery. Maria Monk, as well as becoming rhyming slang for 'spunk', was mentioned in *U*.

g) *where nothing is known of such things*: The previous two stories give the lie to Chandler's statement. Dublin's more celebrated sexual scandals included one in which Sir William Wilde (Oscar's surgeon father) was accused of raping a patient. Joyce (as an Old Belvederian) once considered writing about another (eighteenth-century) episode in which the first Lady Belvedere was imprisoned by her husband for half a lifetime after being falsely accused of adultery with his brother.

h) *the old country, as they say, isn't it*: Gallaher has already used the expression. For a journalist, he is as accomplished at cliché as Chandler is.

i) *That's human nature*: Gallaher seems to be almost apologising for any residual affection for Ireland.

timid insistence, I mean, compared with London or Dublin?—

—London! said Ignatius Gallaher. It's six of one and half a
dozen of the other. You ask Hogan, my boy. I showed him a bit
about London when he was over there. He'd open your eye . . .

I say, Tommy, don't make punch of that whisky: liquor up—

—No, really . . .—

—O, come on, another one won't do you any harm. What
is it? The same again, I suppose?—

—Well . . . all right—

—*François*, the same again . . . Will you smoke, Tommy?—

Ignatius Gallaher produced his cigar-case. The two friends
lit their cigars and puffed at them in silence until their drinks
were served.

—I'll tell you my opinion, said Ignatius Gallaher, emerging
after some time from the clouds of smoke in which he had
taken refuge, it's a rum world. Talk of immorality! I've heard
of cases – what am I saying? – I've known them: cases of . . .
immorality . . .—

Ignatius Gallaher puffed thoughtfully at his cigar and then,
in a calm historian's tone, he proceeded to sketch for his friend
some pictures of the corruption which was rife abroad. He
summarized the vices of many capitals and seemed inclined to
award the palm to Berlin. Some things he could not vouch for
(his friends had told him), but of others he had had personal
experience. He spared neither rank nor caste. He revealed many
of the secrets of religious houses on the continent and described
some of the practices which were fashionable in high society:
and ended by telling, with details, a story about an English
duchess – a story which he knew to be true. Little Chandler
was astonished.

—Ah, well, said Ignatius Gallaher, here we are in old jog-
along Dublin where nothing is known of such things—

—How dull you must find it, said Little Chandler, after all
the other places you've seen!—

—Well, said Ignatius Gallaher, it's a relaxation to come over
here, you know. And, after all, it's the old country, as they
say, isn't it? You can't help having a certain feeling for it.
That's human nature . . . But tell me something about yourself.
Hogan told me you had . . . tasted the joys of connubial bliss.
Two years ago, wasn't it?—

Little Chandler blushed and smiled.

A jesuit at work. (*From* The
History of the Rod (*f*))

From here, Corless's is a short walk to the left

'a large gold watch'

a —Yes, he said. I was married last May twelve months—

—I hope it's not too late in the day to offer my best wishes,
b said Ignatius Gallaher. I didn't know your address or I'd have
done so at the time—

He extended his hand which Little Chandler took.

—Well, Tommy, he said, I wish you and yours every joy
in life, old chap, and tons of money, and may you never die
till I shoot you. And that's the wish of a sincere friend, an old
friend. You know that?—

—I know that, said Little Chandler—

—Any youngsters? said Ignatius Gallaher—

Little Chandler blushed again.

—We have one child, he said—

—Son or daughter?—

—A little boy—

Ignatius Gallaher slapped his friend sonorously on the back.

c —Bravo, he said, I wouldn't doubt you, Tommy—

Little Chandler smiled, looked confusedly at his glass and
bit his lower lip with three childishly white front teeth.

—I hope you'll spend an evening with us, he said, before
you go back. My wife will be delighted to meet you. We can
have a little music and—

—Thanks awfully, old chap, said Ignatius Gallaher, I'm sorry
we didn't meet earlier. But I must leave tomorrow night—

—To-night, perhaps . . . ?—

—I'm awfully sorry, old man. You see I'm over here with
d another fellow, clever young chap he is too, and we arranged
to go to a little card-party. Only for that . . .—

—O, in that case . . .—

—But who knows? said Ignatius Gallaher considerately.
Next year I may take a little skip over here now that I've
broken the ice. It's only a pleasure deferred—

—Very well, said Little Chandler, the next time you come
we must have an evening together. That's agreed now, isn't
it?—

—Yes, that's agreed, said Ignatius Gallaher. Next year if I
e come, *parole d'honneur*—

—And to clinch the bargain, said Little Chandler, we'll just
f have one more now—

Ignatius Gallaher took out a large gold watch and looked at
it.

a) *last May twelve months*: i.e.
nearly eighteen months
before. The phrase is pronounced with the emphasis on
'twelve'.

b) *I didn't know your address*:
But everyone in Dublin
knows King's Inns. Fur-
thermore, Gallaher could
easily have written via Hogan,
or otherwise inquired of 'the
old crowd'.

c) *I wouldn't doubt you*: The
phrase means 'I knew you had
it in you (to father a child)'.
When Bloom's family is being
discussed in *U*, 'Cyclops', the
Citizen's insults include
'Whom does he suspect?' and
'Did he ever put it out of
sight?' The immaturity of
Chandler (as seen in the next
sentence) almost leads the
reader to suspect.

d) *another fellow*: A reminder
of Routh in 'After The Race',
about to relieve the Irish of
their money. Chandler is not
invited to attend.

e) parole d'honneur: Word of
honour: a promise by a prisoner not to escape, and to
return to custody on time. If
Gallaher is a ticket-of-leave
man, then Dublin is a prison.
Chandler is later to realise this
(73f).

f) *one more now*: This is a
matter of honour for Little
Chandler, as it is his round.

From a 1903 magazine: Irish whisk(e)y was widely advertised

—Is it to be the last? he said. Because you know, I have an
a   a.p.—

—O, yes, positively, said Little Chandler—

—Very well, then, said Ignatius Gallaher, let us have another
b   one as a *deoc an doruis* – that's good vernacular for a small
whisky, I believe—

Little Chandler ordered the drinks. The blush which had
risen to his face a few moments before was establishing itself.
A trifle made him blush at any time: and now he felt warm
and excited. Three small whiskies had gone to his head and
Gallaher's strong cigar had confused his mind, for he was a
delicate and abstinent person. The adventure of meeting Gallaher after eight years, of finding himself with Gallaher in
Corless's surrounded by lights and noise, of listening to Gallaher's stories and of sharing for a brief space Gallaher's vagrant
and triumphant life, upset the equipoise of his sensitive nature.
He felt acutely the contrast between his own life and his friend's,
and it seemed to him unjust. Gallaher was his inferior in birth
and education. He was sure that he could do something better
than his friend had ever done, or could ever do, something
higher than mere tawdry journalism if he only got the chance.
What was it that stood in his way? His unfortunate timidity!
He wished to vindicate himself in some way, to assert his
manhood. He saw behind Gallaher's refusal of his invitation.
c   Gallaher was only patronizing him by his friendliness just as
he was patronizing Ireland by his visit.

The barman brought their drinks. Little Chandler pushed
one glass towards his friend and took up the other boldly.

—Who knows? he said, as they lifted their glasses. When
you come next year I may have the pleasure of wishing long
life and happiness to Mr and Mrs Ignatius Gallaher—

Ignatius Gallaher in the act of drinking closed one eye
expressively over the rim of his glass. When he had drunk he
smacked his lips decisively, set down his glass and said:

—No blooming fear of that, my boy. I'm going to have my
fling first and see a bit of life and the world before I put my
d   head in the sack – if I ever do—

—Some day you will, said Little Chandler calmly—

Ignatius Gallaher turned his orange tie and slate-blue eyes
full upon his friend

—You think so? he said—

a) *an a.p.*: This surely means an
appointment (with the card-
party) and not, as has been
suggested, an 'author's proof'
or an *ante prandium*. The nonce
abbreviation does not seem to
have survived.
b) deoc an doruis: Gallaher, or
Joyce, gets his aspiration
wrong. In Irish the first word
is correctly *deoch*. The phrase
is frequently used, meaning a
final drink, 'one for the road'
(literally, a 'drink of the
door'). This can involve,
though does not necessarily
mean, 'a small whisky'. (R. Y.
Tyrrell of Trinity, then Professor of Ancient History, was
famous for – *inter alia* –
observing that there was no
such thing as a large whiskey.)
c) *patronizing him*: Literally,
acting as his father. It can be
argued that, for all his faults,
Gallaher does not patronize
Chandler, but that Chandler
causes the imbalance in the
relationship by himself adopt-
ing the role of child.
d) *before I put my head in the
sack*: Bob Doran's sentiments
in 'The Boarding House' (57j)
are repeated. 'Sack' is traditionally said to be the last
word uttered before 'the Lord
did . . . confound the language
of all the earth' at the tower
of Babel – during the time of
Shem (Genesis XI).

(j)

a) *mooning and spooning*: Words used in early twentieth-century popular songs as indicators of callow romantic love. 'Mooning' means idling about in a lovelorn fashion, while 'spooning' indicates greater romantic success, though involving congruent embracing rather than congress.

b) *she'll have a good fat account . . .*: A suggestion of Miss Delacour of 'Counterparts' (78h).

c) *do you know what it is?*: Phrase meaning 'I'll tell you what'. Myles na Gopaleen used it often in his 'The Brother' pieces.

d) *rich Germans and Jews, rotten with money*: Stephen is patronized in *U*, 'Telemachus':

> – Of course I'm a Britisher, Haines's voice said, and I feel as one. I don't want to see my country fall into the hands of German jews either. That's our national problem, I'm afraid, just now.

e) *a bit stale*: Gallaher characteristically uses the image of eating to describe relations between men and women. Little Chandler's humiliation remains unstated.

f) *the room off the hall*: Where Chandler keeps his little library.

g) *a child*: Earlier in the story, he has seen children as 'minute vermin-like life' (63). This child is his son and heir, but there is no sign that he is any more interested in him than he is in the 'grimy . . . mice' of the streets.

h) *To save money*: Yet again, 'Trust Not Appearances'. Chandler prides himself on his superior birth and education but cannot afford proper servants. The device of using siblings as domestics is one that Joyce took to his various homes on the Continent. Stanislaus was pressed into service on many occasions, and in 1909 Joyce took his sister Eva back to Trieste with him, followed in 1910 by Eileen.

i) *Monica*: St Monica was the mother of St Augustine of Hippo, and by 'her prayers and tears' converted him from his dissolute ways. She features in his *Confessions*.

j) *Bewley's*: No book set in Dublin can be considered complete without a mention of Bewley's Oriental Cafés. At this time the family ran several competing businesses. Chandler has passed Samuel Bewley & Co., at No 6 Dame Street, who boasted of supplying the King, but who had missed Chandler's valued custom.

k) *short answers*: These are to be a recurring feature in *D* (81(o), 91(o), 159c).

71

—You'll put your head in the sack, repeated Little Chandler stoutly, like everyone else if you can find the girl—

He had slightly emphasised his tone and he was aware that he had betrayed himself; but, though the colour had heightened in his cheek, he did not flinch from his friend's gaze. Ignatius Gallaher watched him for a few moments and then said:

—If ever it occurs, you may bet your bottom dollar there'll be no mooning and spooning about it. I mean to marry money. She'll have a good fat account at the bank or she won't do for me—

Little Chandler shook his head.

—Why, man alive, said Ignatius Gallaher, vehemently, do you know what it is? I've only to say the word and to-morrow I can have the woman and the cash. You don't believe it? Well, I know it. There are hundreds – what am I saying? – thousands of rich Germans and Jews, rotten with money, that'd only be too glad . . . You wait a while, my boy. See if I don't play my cards properly. When I go about a thing I mean business, I tell you. You just wait—

He tossed his glass to his mouth, finished his drink and laughed loudly. Then he looked thoughtfully before him and said in a calmer tone:

—But I'm in no hurry. They can wait. I don't fancy tying myself up to one woman, you know—

He imitated with his mouth the act of tasting and made a wry face.

—Must get a bit stale, I should think, he said—

.   .   .   .

Little Chandler sat in the room off the hall, holding a child in his arms. To save money they kept no servant, but Annie's young sister Monica came for an hour or so in the morning and an hour or so in the evening to help. But Monica had gone home long ago. It was a quarter to nine. Little Chandler had come home late for tea and, moreover, he had forgotten to bring Annie home the parcel of coffee from Bewley's. Of course she was in a bad humour and gave him short answers. She said she would do without any tea but when it came near the time at which the shop at the corner closed she decided to go out herself for a quarter of a pound of tea and two pounds of sugar. She put the sleeping child deftly in his arms and said:

(*j*)

a) *A little lamp*: In Irish *lampa beag* means both 'a little lamp' and 'a little cloud'. That Joyce is indulging in a bilingual pun is unproven, but the significance of the word 'little' in the story can scarcely be overestimated: Little Chandler is belittled by Dublin's past, by Gallaher, by his wife and by himself. Furthermore, what little light there is falls onto others.

b) *crumpled horn*: Sexual inability (or even cuckoldry) is hinted at, as Chandler looks at the photograph of his wife. The phrase comes from a childish source, a nursery rhyme, 'The House that Jack Built':

> This is the farmer sowing his corn,
> That kept the cock that crowed in the morn,
> That waked the priest all shaven and shorn,
> That married the man all tattered and torn,
> That kissed the maiden all forlorn,
> That milked the cow with the crumpled horn,
> That tossed the dog, that worried the cat,
> That killed the rat, that ate the malt
> That lay in the house that Jack built.

c) *pale blue summer blouse*: Blue, like Gallaher's eyes. Blue is also the colour of the Virgin Mary. This final section of the story can be seen as parodying the Holy Family (74f). St Ignatius' nativity meditation advises contemplation of 'Our Lady, and Joseph, and the maidservant, and the infant Jesus' (63p).

d) *ten and elevenpence*: This was then a great deal of money. Eveline earns only seven shillings per week. In *U*, 'Circe', the maid Mary Driscoll testifies: 'I was in a situation, six pounds a year' (or ten shillings a month, but this sum included board).

e) *when she heard the price*: Annie is angry, unsurprisingly: her family is trying to save money – e.g. by having her sister in to help.

f) *Hm!*: Reveries of married life when it was better are indulged in by Gabriel Conroy in 'The Dead' and by both Blooms in *U*.

g) *Jewesses*: Not an offensive word at the beginning of the century, but times have changed. Joyce was always philosemitic, but his work often reported the endemic antisemitism of the times.

h) *Those dark Oriental eyes*: The Eastern strand of the book is returned to. *Giacomo Joyce* describes the latest object of Joyce's affections as having 'full dark suffering eyes, beautiful as the eyes of an antelope'.

i) *He found something mean*: A fellow citizen (Mr Duffy of 'A Painful Case') will find virtually all of Dublin mean.

j) *the hire system*: In Dublin, furniture was often bought by Hire Purchase, particularly by those whose income, though small, was regular. Firms such

—Here. Don't waken him—

a   A little lamp with a white china shade stood upon the table and its light fell over a photograph which was enclosed in a
b frame of crumpled horn. It was Annie's photograph. Little Chandler looked at it, pausing at the thin tight lips. She wore
c the pale blue summer blouse which he had brought her home
d as a present one Saturday. It had cost him ten and elevenpence; but what an agony of nervousness it had cost him! How he had suffered that day, waiting at the shop door until the shop was empty, standing at the counter and trying to appear at his ease while the girl piled ladies' blouses before him, paying at the desk and forgetting to take up the odd penny of his change, being called back by the cashier and, finally, striving to hide his blushes as he left the shop by examining the parcel to see if it was securely tied. When he brought the blouse home Annie kissed him and said it was very pretty and stylish; but when
e she heard the price she threw the blouse on the table and said it was a regular swindle to charge ten and elevenpence for that. At first she wanted to take it back but when she tried it on she was delighted with it, especially with the make of the sleeves, and kissed him and said he was very good to think of her.

f   Hm! ...

He looked coldly into the eyes of the photograph and they answered coldly. Certainly they were pretty and the face itself was pretty. But he found something mean in it. Why was it so unconscious and lady-like? The composure of the eyes irritated him. They repelled him and defied him: there was no passion in them, no rapture. He thought of what Gallaher had
gh said about rich Jewesses. Those dark Oriental eyes, he thought, how full they are of passion, of voluptuous longing! ... Why had he married the eyes in the photograph?

He caught himself up at the question and glanced nervously
i round the room. He found something mean in the pretty
j furniture which he had bought for his house on the hire system. Annie had chosen it herself and it reminded him of her. It too was prim and pretty. A dull resentment against his life awoke within him. Could he not escape from his little house? Was it too late for him to try to live bravely like Gallaher? Could he go to London? There was the furniture still to be paid for. If he could only write a book and get it published, that might open the way for him.

as H. Weiner & Co (of Talbot Street) and Pohlmann's (of Dawson Street) did not usually charge interest on such transactions, as inflation was low. However, discounts for cash were offered, which came to much the same thing.

From a contemporary fashion page

Byron and Tom Moore (a)

a) *Byron's poems*: Joyce always admired the poetic virility of Byron. In *P* (II.3) Stephen gets himself beaten up for championing Byron against Tennyson, and in *SH* he uses a quatrain of Byron's to illustrate his theories of stress in verse.

b) *He opened it*: The poem appeared on the first page of nearly all contemporary editions.

c) Hushed are the winds ...: The poem, 'On The Death Of A Young Lady', was written in memory of Margaret Parker, daughter of an admiral and cousin to Byron, to whom she was 'very dear'.

d) *keener*: More intense, but there is a strong alternative meaning: in Ireland, to cry for the death of a loved one is to 'keen'. Professional keeners were employed to mourn the dead by their wailing.

e) That clay where once ...: Having mutely announced a later story in *D*, the poem continues:

> ... such animation beamed;
> The King of Terrors seized her as his prey:
> Not worth, nor beauty, have her life redeemed.
>
> Oh! could that King of Terrors pity feel,
> Or Heaven reverse the dread decrees of fate!
> Not here the mourner would his grief reveal,
> Not here the muse her virtues would relate.

And so forth for another three verses, which speak of the 'endless pleasures' of Heaven and the inadvisability of challenging Providence. In most editions a note by Byron was appended to the poem:

> The author claims the indulgence of the reader more for this piece than perhaps any other in the collection; but as it was written at an earlier period than the rest (being composed at the age of fourteen), and his first essay, he preferred submitting it to the indulgence of his friends in its present state, to making either addition or alteration.

It is strongly ironic therefore that Little Chandler wishes that he could 'write like that', i.e. like a boy of fourteen.

f) *a prisoner for life*: Thinking of life always makes Little Chandler sad (62m). Gallaher has escaped, or at least has *parole d'honneur* (69e).

g) *Stop!*: This is Little Chandler's high point of rebellion. He is shouting not only at his son.

h) *The thin walls*: Another indicator of the Chandlers' insubstantial status.

i) *a young woman*: This distancing indefinite article is also used in 'Two Gallants' (50c) and elsewhere.

a A volume of Byron's poems lay before him on the table.
b He opened it cautiously with his left hand lest he should waken
the child and began to read the first poem in the book:

c
> *Hushed are the winds and still the evening gloom,*
> *Not e'en a Zephyr wanders through the grove,*
> *Whilst I return to view my Margaret's tomb*
> *And scatter flowers on the dust I love.*

He paused. He felt the rhythm of the verse about him in the
room. How melancholy it was! Could he, too, write like that,
express the melancholy of his soul in verse? There were so
many things he wanted to describe: his sensation of a few hours
before on Grattan Bridge, for example. If he could get back
again into that mood . . .

The child awoke and began to cry. He turned from the page
and tried to hush it: but it would not be hushed. He began to
d rock it to and fro in his arms but its wailing cry grew keener.
He rocked it faster while his eyes began to read the second
stanza:

e
> *Within this narrow cell reclines her clay,*
> *That clay where once . . .*

It was useless. He couldn't read. He couldn't do anything.
The wailing of the child pierced the drum of his ear. It was
f useless, useless! He was a prisoner for life. His arms trembled
with anger and suddenly bending to the child's face he shouted:
g —Stop!—

The child stopped for an instant, had a spasm of fright and
began to scream. He jumped up from his chair and walked
hastily up and down the room with the child in his arms. It
began to sob piteously, losing its breath for four or five seconds,
h and then bursting out anew. The thin walls of the room
echoed the sound. He tried to soothe it but it sobbed more
convulsively. He looked at the contracted and quivering face
of the child and began to be alarmed. He counted seven sobs
without a break between them and caught the child to his
breast in fright. If it died! . . .
i The door was burst open and a young woman ran in,
panting.
—What is it? What is it? she cried—
The child, hearing its mother's voice, broke out into a

How Chandler would have preferred a 'laughter-producing infant', and a 'really happy' home!

Jonathan Swift (d)

a) *his heart closed together*: This strange expression is scarcely English, but neatly describes both the distress and confusion felt by Chandler, and also his inability to be 'openhearted' and honest in the face of his wife's hatred.

b) *I didn't do anything*: Virtually Chandler's last words in the story, and they are a lie. Shouting into the face of an unhappy baby is not nothing. But with this short sentence, he might almost be writing his own epitaph.

c) *What?*: Chandler is so caught up in his own excuses that he thinks that his wife has said something to him. In fact she is by now murmuring to the child.

d) *My little man*: The baby is more a man to her than her husband is. In his *Journal to Stella*, Swift used a 'little language' reminiscent of Annie Chandler's in this speech.

e) *Lambabaun*: A nursery corruption of the Irish term of endearment *leanbhán*, which is often pronounced 'lannabawn', meaning something like 'babykins'.

f) *lamb of the world*: An epithet for Jesus Christ, as in 'Lamb of God (that taketh away the sins of the world)'.

g) *cheeks suffused with shame*: Chandler is shamed, not ashamed, and it is this, rather than shyness, drink or anger, as previously, that reddens his face.

Estella Solomons' drawing of King's Inns

paroxysm of sobbing.

—It's nothing, Annie . . . it's nothing . . . He began to cry . . .—

She flung her parcels on the floor and snatched the child from him.

—What have you done to him? she cried, glaring into his face—

Little Chandler sustained for one moment the gaze of her eyes and his heart closed together as he met the hatred in them. He began to stammer:

—It's nothing . . . He . . . he began to cry . . . I couldn't . . . I didn't do anything . . . What?—

Giving no heed to him she began to walk up and down the room, clasping the child tightly in her arms and murmuring:

—My little man! My little mannie! Was 'ou frightened, love? . . . There now, love! There now! . . . Lambabaun! Mamma's little lamb of the world! . . . There now!—

Little Chandler felt his cheeks suffused with shame and he stood back out of the lamplight. He listened while the paroxysm of the child's sobbing grew less and less: and tears of remorse started to his eyes.

h) *he stood back out of the lamp-light*: Little Chandler has reverted to photophobic type after the failure of the ambitions brought on by envy of Gallaher. The little cloud of hope on the horizon has failed to rain.

i) *tears of remorse*: Very like the end of 'Araby' and of 'The Dead'. Chandler has much to be remorseful about – and still there is no hint that he will make amends.

A 'little lamp' on Grattan Bridge, with the Four Courts behind

Afterword: 'A Little Cloud'

The centre story of *Dubliners*, 'A Little Cloud' was the fourteenth to be written, only 'The Dead' being added later. Joyce finished it in April 1906, when Grant Richards was already considering the publication of the book. It is the first of the four 'mature life' stories, and picks up from 'The Boarding House' the chronicle of Dublin marriage.

Joyce particularly liked the story: in October 1906 while he was arranging the publication of *Chamber Music*, he wrote to Stanislaus: 'A page of "A Little Cloud" gives me more pleasure than all my verses'. Joyce was aware of both his skills and his targets, and *Chamber Music*, though well written and wrought, was obviously slight. About a year after writing the story, he intended to deliver a lecture to the Università del Populo in Trieste on the subject of the Irish Literary Renaissance. Unfortunately the lecture was never written or given, but some of Joyce's views on the 'Celtic Twilight' – and particularly on its poetry – may be seen here. In 'The Holy Office' (1904), he took a swipe at Yeats and his pretentious (female) acolytes:

> . . . But I must not accounted be
> One of that mumming company –
> With him who hies him to appease
> His giddy dames' frivolities
> While they console him when he whinges
> With gold-embroidered Celtic fringes . . .

These sentiments do not differ greatly from the caustic commentary of his 1912 broadside, 'Gas from a Burner', where the words may be those of the printer who destroyed the 1910 edition of *Dubliners* while the sentiments are Joyce's:

> I printed mystical books in dozens:
> I printed the table book of Cousins
> Though (asking your pardon) as for the verse

> 'Twould give you a heartburn on your arse:
> I printed folklore from North and South
> By Gregory of the Golden Mouth:
> I printed poets, sad, silly and solemn:
> I printed Patrick What-do-you-Colm:
> I printed the great John Milicent Synge
> Who soars above on an angel's wing
> In the playboy shift that he pinched as swag
> From Maunsel's manager's travelling-bag.

As with many of the stories, 'A Little Cloud' is tripartite. The first part, where Chandler anticipates his meeting with Ignatius Gallaher and muses about his unlikely future as a successful poet with 'the Celtic touch', takes place almost entirely in Chandler's head. When he reaches Corless's, the narrative becomes more objective, while the third part returns to the viewpoint of Chandler, now home and half-drunk. The first and last sections are also linked through the poetry and the poetry books, while the child on the last page whose screams echo those of the children on the first brings the closed circle round on itself.

It has been suggested that the story is a study of envy, but while this emotion, or sin, is certainly present in the relationship between Little Chandler and Gallaher, the story also deals with Chandler's sloth, his cowardice, his self-delusion, and his final rage and humiliation. These aspects of Chandler's character and his plight are depicted by means of multiple contrasts.

Almost the first thing that we learn about Chandler is that he is 'Little'. He 'gave one the idea of being a little man'. If Chandler is 'little' and 'modest', Gallaher is 'wild'. His stamping ground is 'the great city London', while Chandler is stuck in 'old jog-along Dublin', and spends his evenings sitting 'in the little room off the hall'. When he first left Dublin, Gallaher already showed 'signs of future greatness', whereas Little Chandler tries to ignore his own timidity by such devices as stepping onward bravely along the street. Gallaher does not help matters by referring to his friend as 'my boy' and – ironically – as 'old hero'.

Another powerful device of comparison is one that is used elsewhere in *Dubliners*: light and dark. Gallaher is 'a brilliant figure', at home in the 'light and noise' of bars, where even the shining of wine-glasses confuses Chandler. He has a 'gaudy manner'. His blue eyes shine out above his vivid orange tie and he carries a gold watch.

By contrast, Chandler is a creature of the dark. His story takes place one autumn evening. By the time he leaves his office, the sunset he saw through the window is waning. His poetical ambitions, fanned by the thought of Gallaher, are 'a light' beginning 'to tremble on the horizon of his mind'. The 'little lamp' in the room off the hall illuminates not Chandler, but a photograph of his wife. He revels in melancholy (from the Greek for 'black bile'), and is inspired by the 'evening gloom' in Byron's dreadful poem. Finally, in misery, he stands back 'out of the lamplight'.

And the symbol of these contrasts is the 'little cloud'. The phrase 'a little cloud' appears in the Bible, at 1 Kings XVIII. 44: 'Behold, there ariseth a little cloud out of the sea, like a man's hand'. This cloud is the first sign to Elijah of welcome rain – there has been a drought for some years. The title does not at first sight seem to fit the story. However, in *A Portrait* (IV.3), Stephen thinks about the clouds:

They were voyaging across the deserts of the sky, a host of nomads on the march, voyaging high over Ireland, westward bound. The Europe they had come from lay out there beyond the Irish Sea, Europe of strange tongues and valleyed and woodbegirt and citadelled and of entrenched and marshalled races.

The only actual clouds in this story are those produced by the cigar of the Europeanised Gallaher, within which he uncharacteristically takes refuge. Gallaher can be seen as the little cloud because he finally casts a gloomy shadow on Chandler, making him realise that he is a prisoner. Conversely, the title may refer to hope: Gallaher's arrival from the east, telling of his plans eventually 'to marry money', kindles in Chandler hope of a career as a poet. It has been convincingly suggested (by Robert Spoo) that Joyce took the phrase from a passage in Guglielmo Ferrero's *L'Europa giovane* (*Young Europe*) (1897) which advises against making precise plans for the future: such conceptions are like a 'little cloud against the unbounded expanse of the sky; a breath disperses it and no human eye will see it more'. Chandler's (and Gallaher's) plans will most probably never succeed.

There may be something more to the title. One word (rarely used) in Irish for cloud, *lampa*, normally means 'lamp' (see 72a), but the usual Irish word is *néall*. Many other meanings of this common word (from Dinneen's *Irish-English Dictionary* – both Joyce and Fr Dinneen spent many hours in the National Library at the turn of the century) are in some way relevant to the story. They include: 'a swoon, trance, fit or mood; a "vapour," dizziness, rage, frenzy, exasperation; a notion, a wink of sleep, a glimpse of light'. *Néall dearmaid* means 'suspended animation', and *néall feirge* means 'a blinding fit of rage'. The 'little cloud' of the title embodies in its suitably complementary Anglo-Saxon and Celtic references and meanings the contrasts of the story: hope and gloom, light and shadow, paralysis and anger.

a) COUNTERPARTS: In legal language, a counterpart was the valid copy of a legal document, or a complementary part of one, such as a contract. Its metaphorical use here is clear: as Alleyne is to Farrington, so Farrington is to Little Tom.

b) *The bell rang furiously*: Mechanical anger is introduced even before the first character is. Throughout the story, the mechanical theme is repeated, as is that of anger.

c) *Miss Parker*: A link with the previous story, as it was a Miss Parker that was the dedicatee of Byron's 'On the Death of a Young Lady' (73e).

d) *the tube*: The voice-tube was an early type of office intercom.

e) *North of Ireland accent*: Noticeably different from the accents of other parts of Ireland. In *U*, 'Scylla and Charybdis', Stephen silently mocks Mr Best – 'He's from beyant Boyne water'. In *SH*, the Irish teacher (22d) has 'a cutting Northern accent'. So too had George Roberts, the potential publisher of *D*. In *P* (V.1), Stephen reflects on the 'sharp Ulster voice' of MacAlister:

> The voice, the accent, the mind of the questioner offended him and he allowed the offence to carry him towards wilful unkindness, bidding his mind think that the student's father would have done better had he sent his son to Belfast to study and have saved something on the train fare by so doing.

Though the sentiment is swiftly discarded it can be seen as an early instance of Conor Cruise O'Brien's 'Two Nations' theory of Irish history.

f) *Send Farrington here!*: A clear chime with old Mr Leonard's politer request (57). The character of Farrington is based on Joyce's uncle, William Murray. *Fear* in Irish means 'man' or 'husband'. Given this man's evident swinishness, the word also recalls the Middle English term *fearh* – a pig, seen again in Stephen's outburst in *P* (V.1):

> Ireland is the old sow that eats her farrow.

g) *her machine*: The tone of the narrative and of this workplace is to treat people as automatons. In the late 1890s, the writing machine would be operated by a 'typewriter' (54k).

h) *Mr Alleyne*: The name was taken from an associate of John Joyce (95e). There was also a C. W. Alleyne, a solicitor in Dame Street at this time, five doors away from where William Murray (88p) worked at Collis & Ward. Perhaps the suggestion of the German *allein*, meaning 'alone', appealed to Joyce. The character begins by being disembodied as well as alone. There is also an evocation of the power of Edward Alleyn, the Elizabethan actor, noted for forceful Marlovian roles such as Tamburlaine, Faustus and Barabas (of *The Jew of Malta* (58h)), and also famous as a bear-master and a bull-baiter. (He also gave his name to the Alleyn MS of Robert Greene's (84n) *Orlando Furioso*.)

i) *hanging face*: Given the summary execution at the end of the story, Farrington seems more like a hanging judge. The playwright George Farquhar was expelled from Trinity in 1695 for saying that Christ was 'a man born to be hanged'.

j) *dark wine-coloured*: A parody of Homeric idiom, repeated more than once in the story. The colour of the face is both 'like' and 'because of' wine.

k) *puffing with labour*: A symptom of Farrington's lack of fitness, as well as a joke about his laziness.

l) *Farrington?*: Friends could use surnames, but Dubliners also used them when addressing their domestic servants. Mr Alleyne is being pointedly unfriendly and superior.

m) *Kirwan*: The 'real' John Kirwan was a house-agent, of Shelbourne Road (No 54), where Farrington (84s) also lived. It seems likely that it was Kirwan who managed the sale of the Bodley house (77f) to John Joyce. Like the Joyces (and the Brownes), the Kirwans were one of the ancient tribes of Galway.

n) *what* Mr Shelley says, sir: Perhaps: 'I'll countermine him by a deeper plan' (Shelley's 'Homer's Hymn to Mercury', XXX). There were a few Dublin families of this name at the turn of the century, e.g. Samuel Shelley, a poor-rate collector, nearby in Dame Street. The poet Shelley came to Dublin early in 1812, to oppose the Union and to promote Catholic Emancipation. His principles included a renunciation of violence, and his tactics the throwing of copies of his *Address to the Irish People* to likely passers-

COUNTERPARTS

THE BELL RANG furiously and, when Miss Parker went to the tube, a furious voice called out in a piercing North of Ireland accent:

—Send Farrington here!—

Miss Parker returned to her machine, saying to a man who was writing at a desk:

—Mr Alleyne wants you upstairs—

The man muttered *Blast him!* under his breath and pushed back his chair to stand up. When he stood up he was tall and of great bulk. He had a hanging face, dark wine-coloured, with fair eyebrows and moustache: his eyes bulged forward slightly and the whites of them were dirty. He lifted up the counter and, passing by the clients, went out of the office with a heavy step.

He went heavily upstairs until he came to the second landing, where a door bore a brass plate with the inscription *Mr Alleyne*. Here he halted, puffing with labour and vexation, and knocked. The shrill voice cried:

—Come in!—

The man entered Mr Alleyne's room. Simultaneously Mr Alleyne, a little man wearing gold-rimmed glasses on a clean-shaven face, shot his head up over a pile of documents. The head itself was so pink and hairless that it seemed like a large egg reposing on the papers. Mr Alleyne did not lose a moment:

—Farrington? What is the meaning of this? Why have I always to complain of you? May I ask you why you haven't made a copy of that contract between Bodley and Kirwan? I told you it must be ready by four o'clock—

—But Mr Shelley said, sir . . .—

—*Mr Shelley said, sir* . . . Kindly attend to what I say and not to what *Mr Shelley says, sir.* You have always some excuse or another for shirking work. Let me tell you that if the contract is not copied before this evening I'll lay the matter before Mr Crosbie . . . Do you hear me now?—

—Yes, sir—

—Do you hear me now? . . . Aye and another little matter!

by from his balcony in Sackville Street. But his wild-eyed, free-thinking sincerity failed to transform the political situation as he had hoped. He soon wrote to a friend:

I am sick of this city, and long to be with you and peace. The rich *grind* the poor into abjectness, and then complain that they are abject. They goad them to famine, and hang them if they steal a loaf.

In Rome in 1906, Joyce was to give Shelley's grand-daughter £10 in his bank, noting that her name was Nora.

o) *Mr Crosbie*: The other partner, by implication more important and higher up. In 1785, the Irish Icarus, Richard Crosbie, made a sensational balloon journey across Dublin – before any Englishman had flown in this way.

76

a) *how many courses*: Farrington is a deadly glutton (80e).

b) *Do you mind me, now?*: An Ulster expression: the meaning is 'Do you heed me?', not 'Do you object?'

c) *a spasm of rage ...*: Farrington's deadly sin here recalls the Minotaur, the bull with a human head, in Dante's *Inferno* XII.14–15:

> he gnawed himself, like one that bursts with inward rage ...

d) *thirst*: Clearly not just a dryness of the throat, but a desire to get drunk.

e) *an order on the cashier*: An 'advance' on his meagre scrivener's salary.

f) the said Bernard Bodley: In October 1902, John Joyce (76m) brought 7 Peter's Terrace, Phibsborough, from a Mrs Bodley. At No 5 lived a Mr Bodley, perhaps her son, with whom she then moved in. These were probably the only family of Bodleys in Dublin at this time.

g) *they would be lighting the gas*: Each evening lamplighters came round to light the gaslamps, as electric light was still limited (though it expanded greatly in central Dublin in mid-1903).

h) *passing out*: A presage of death, which finds an echo in Anna Livia in *FW* (627):

> Loonely is me loneness. For all their faults, I am passing out. O bitter ending! I'll slip away ...

i) *As soon as he was on the landing*: As contemporary photographs show, headgear was worn by all adults out of doors (even workmen). Farrington's hat is hostage and 'proves' that he is somewhere in the building. The ploy is said to have been used later by certain literary civil servants. One other indication of the ubiquity and importance of headgear is that after Joyce had left the Martello Tower, Sandycove, he wrote to a friend in September 1904, asking him to retrieve

> ... a blue peaked cap, a black cloth cap, a black felt hat ... and the MS of my verses ...

j) *a shepherd's plaid cap*: See 82c.

See 76g

I might as well be talking to the wall as talking to you. Understand once for all that you get a half an hour for your lunch and not an hour and a half. How many courses do you want, I'd like to know . . . Do you mind me, now?—

—Yes, sir—

Mr Alleyne bent his head again upon his pile of papers. The man stared fixedly at the polished skull which directed the affairs of Crosbie & Alleyne, gauging its fragility. A spasm of rage gripped his throat for a few moments and then passed, leaving after it a sharp sensation of thirst. The man recognized the sensation and felt that he must have a good night's drinking. The middle of the month was passed and, if he could get the copy done in time, Mr Alleyne might give him an order on the cashier. He stood still, gazing fixedly at the head upon the pile of papers. Suddenly Mr Alleyne began to upset all the papers, searching for something. Then, as if he had been unaware of the man's presence till that moment, he shot up his head again, saying:

—Eh? Are you going to stand there all day? Upon my word, Farrington, you take things easy!—

—I was waiting to see . . .—

—Very good, you needn't wait to see. Go downstairs and do your work—

The man walked heavily towards the door and, as he went out of the room, he heard Mr Alleyne cry after him that if the contract was not copied by evening Mr Crosbie would hear of the matter.

He returned to his desk in the lower office and counted the sheets which remained to be copied. He took up his pen and dipped it in the ink but he continued to stare stupidly at the last words he had written: *In no case shall the said Bernard Bodley be . . .* The evening was falling and in a few minutes they would be lighting the gas: then he could write. He felt that he must slake the thirst in his throat. He stood up from his desk and, lifting the counter as before, passed out of the office. As he was passing out the chief clerk looked at him inquiringly.

—It's all right, Mr Shelley, said the man, pointing with his finger to indicate the objective of his journey—

The chief clerk glanced at the hat-rack but, seeing the row complete, offered no remark. As soon as he was on the landing the man pulled a shepherd's plaid cap out of his pocket, put it

77

a) *dark snug of O'Neill's shop*: J. J. O'Neill, tea and wine-merchant, had recently taken over the premises on the corner of Eustace St and East Essex St. The snug was a partitioned counter-area, as cosy as it sounds. The first draft referred to 'O'Reilly's shop'. Ironically, Farrington is exchanging the Ulster persecution of Mr Alleyne for the Red Hand of Ulster – part of the coat-of-arms of the O'Neills.

b) *a g.p.*: A glass of porter, as the context makes plain (d). But the expression also recalls 'g.p.i.' – general paralysis of the insane, the venereal complaint mentioned by Mulligan in *U*, 'Telemachus' (and which Lord Harmsworth (12c) died of).

c) *curate*: See 48j.

d) *glass of plain porter*: A glass is a half-pint measure. Dubliners still do not ask for half-pints. Porter is a weaker and cheaper form of Guinness than stout. It was originally called 'Porters' ale', being drunk chiefly by porters and the like. In 1734 Jonathan Swift (in *Mrs Delany's Life and Correspondence*) wrote of how he used to starve 'in London, with port-wine, or perhaps Porter's ale, to save charges'.

The best paean to porter comes from Flann O'Brien, in *At Swim-Two-Birds*. In *SH*, Mr Daedalus rails at Stephen:

Who taught you to drink pints of plain porter, might I ask? Is that considered the proper thing for an . . . artist to do?

When Joyce took up drinking, he soon abandoned the Elizabethan affectation of 'sack' for stout and porter.

e) *a caraway seed*: To hide the smell of drink on his breath.

f) *Eustace Street*: In a tavern here in the late eighteenth century, a bet was made that allegedly led to the introduction of a new word in the English language. The word was 'quiz'.

g) *moist pungent odour of perfumes*: An anticipation of Bloom's well-ordered sensuality in *U*, 'Lestrygonians':

Perfume of embraces all him assailed. With hungered flesh obscurely, he mutely craved to adore.

h) *Delacour*: There was an eighteenth-century Irish poet, James Delacour, who wrote the *Letter of Abelard to Eloisa*, modelled on Pope. He took Holy Orders, then to madness and the bottle. The name means literally, 'of the heart'.

i) *as if to intimate*: Farrington's stratagem supposes that these men have no familiarity with visiting a pub. As a ruse about a ruse it is hopeless.

j) *Five times in one day*: Mr Shelley may be exaggerating but there is no doubt that Farrington's standing with his superiors is low.

k) *he longed to spend it in the bars*: In a letter of August 1725, Swift wrote:

No men in Dublin go to Taverns who are worth sitting with.

W. B. Yeats was said never to have entered a Dublin pub.

O'Neill's in the middle of the Holy Hour

on his head and ran quickly down the rickety stairs. From the street door he walked on furtively on the inner side of the path towards the corner and all at once dived into a doorway. He was now safe in the dark snug of O'Neill's shop, and, filling up the little window that looked into the bar with his inflamed face, the colour of dark wine or dark meat, he called out:

—Here, Pat, give us a g.p., like a good fellow—

The curate brought him a glass of plain porter. The man drank it at a gulp and asked for a caraway seed. He put his penny on the counter and, leaving the curate to grope for it in the gloom, retreated out of the snug as furtively as he had entered it.

Darkness, accompanied by a thick fog, was gaining upon the dusk of February and the lamps in Eustace Street had been lit. The man went up by the houses until he reached the door of the office, wondering whether he could finish his copy in time. On the stairs a moist pungent odour of perfumes saluted his nose: evidently Miss Delacour had come while he was out in O'Neill's. He crammed his cap back again into his pocket and re-entered the office, assuming an air of absent-mindedness.

—Mr Alleyne has been calling for you, said the chief clerk severely. Where were you?—

The man glanced at the two clients who were standing at the counter as if to intimate that their presence prevented him from answering. As the clients were both male the chief clerk allowed himself a laugh.

—I know that game, he said. Five times a day is a little bit . . . Well, you better look sharp and get a copy of our correspondence in the Delacour case for Mr Alleyne—

This address in the presence of the public, his run upstairs and the porter he had gulped down so hastily confused the man and, as he sat down at his desk to get what was required, he realized how hopeless was the task of finishing his copy of the contract before half past five. The dark damp night was coming and he longed to spend it in the bars, drinking with his friends amid the glare of gas and the clatter of glasses. He got out the Delacour correspondence and passed out of the office. He hoped Mr Alleyne would not discover that the last two letters were missing.

The moist pungent perfume lay all the way up to Mr Alleyne's room. Miss Delacour was a middle-aged woman of

THE MAGIC PEN.

Every point hand-finished. Passes over the paper without the slightest scratch. Flexible as the quill. For rapid writers invaluable. Sample Box post-free for 12 stamps, to be had only of

PARKINS & GOTTO,

54, OXFORD-STREET, LONDON, W.

From the first edition of Pope's Dunciad (*above and below*) (*g*)

a) *Jewish appearance*: See 71d.

b) *or on her money*: Mr Alleyne might have a short-coming traditionally imputed to the Jews. The idea recapitulates the attitude of Gallaher in 'A Little Cloud'. Stanislaus in his diary observed in January 1905 (76e):

> These stupid Northerns. Nothing stirs their admir-ation but the 'finance' in a man spending a shilling and getting back one-and-six.

c) *The man*: From the point of view of the office staff, Farrington scarcely deserves a surname. Only when he gets to the pub does the narrator give him his name.

d) *to hurry Miss Parker*: Originally 'harry'.

e) *the public-house*: The convivial thought is reworked from the seventh of Vergil's *Eclogues* (82c):

> Here's a hearth, a roaring fire,
> A good smoky room, all winter long –
> A respite from sheep to shambles
> And threatening floods –
> Who cares about the cold north wind . . .

f) *hot punches*: One formula for the drink was a plain glass of whiskey with hot water, and sugar and cloves added. Its making is described in Joyce's unfinished story, 'Christmas Eve'.

g) Bernard Bernard: In Pope's *Dunciad*, the hulking bookseller Bernard Lintot races through London against his villainous rival, Edmund Curl:

> Here fortun'd Curl to slide; loud shout the band
> And 'Bernard! Bernard!' rings through all the
> Strand.
> Obscene with filth the miscreant lies bewray'd
> Fal'n in the plash his wickedness had lay'd.
> (Book II, 73–6)

A similar fate will later befall Tom Kernan, in 'Grace', though the allusion is derived from Vergil's *Eclogues* (VI. 44):

> . . .ut litus Hyla, Hyla, omne sonaret . . .

The Dunciad claimed (falsely) to have been first pub-lished in Dublin in 1728.

h) *clear out the whole office single-handed*: A fantasy of emulating Christ with the money changers (Mark XI. 15–17, Luke XIX. 41–46), or Hercules at the Augean Stables.

i) *Leonard*: Paddy Leonard, a lively friend of Bantam Lyons and Paddy Dignam, among many others. His mimicry of Tom Kernan is commended in *U*, 'Hades'. In Davy Byrne's pub, in *U*, 'Lestrygonians', he derides his teetotal alemates:

Jewish appearance. Mr Alleyne was said to be sweet on her or on her money. She came to the office often and stayed a long time when she came. She was sitting beside his desk now in an aroma of perfumes, smoothing the handle of her umbrella and nodding the great black feather in her hat. Mr Alleyne had swivelled his chair round to face her and thrown his right foot jauntily upon his left knee. The man put the correspondence on the desk and bowed respectfully but neither Mr Alleyne nor Miss Delacour took any notice of his bow. Mr Alleyne tapped a finger on the correspondence and then flicked it towards him as if to say: *That's all right: you can go.*

The man returned to the lower office and sat down again at his desk. He stared intently at the incomplete phrase: *In no case shall the said Bernard Bodley be ...* and thought how strange it was that the last three words began with the same letter. The chief clerk began to hurry Miss Parker, saying she would never have the letters typed in time for post. The man listened to the clicking of the machine for a few minutes and then set to work to finish his copy. But his head was not clear and his mind wandered away to the glare and rattle of the public-house. It was a night for hot punches. He struggled on with his copy, but when the clock struck five he had still fourteen pages to write. Blast it! He couldn't finish it in time. He longed to execrate aloud, to bring his fist down on something violently. He was so enraged that he wrote *Bernard Bernard* instead of *Bernard Bodley* and had to begin again on a clean sheet.

He felt strong enough to clear out the whole office single-handed. His body ached to do something, to rush out and revel in violence. All the indignities of his life enraged him ... Could he ask the cashier privately for an advance? No, the cashier was no good, no damn good: he wouldn't give an advance ... He knew where he would meet the boys: Leonard and O'Halloran and Nosey Flynn. The barometer of his emotional nature was set for a spell of riot.

His imagination had so abstracted him that his name was called twice before he answered. Mr Alleyne and Miss Delacour were standing outside the counter and all the clerks had turned round in anticipation of something. The man got up from his desk. Mr Alleyne began a tirade of abuse, saying that two letters were missing. The man answered that he knew nothing about them, that he had made a faithful copy. The tirade

Lord love a duck he said, look at what I'm standing drinks to! Cold water and gingerpop! Two fellows that would suck whisky off a sore leg.

j) *O'Halloran*: In *U*, 'Circe', the Papal Nuncio announces that 'Eunuch begat O'Halloran and O'Halloran began Guggenheim'.

k) *Nosey Flynn*: Another of the extras who go on to feature in *U*, where he is confirmed as a groinscratching regular at Davy Byrne's (81p), thought of by Bloom as 'Nosey numskull'.

l) *all the clerks had turned round*: The manuscript originally added the sub-Dickensian detail 'on their stools'.

79

'They do not kill time' (87)

Scotch and Irish (82i)

a) *manikin*: From the Dutch, *manniken*, 'little man'. The usage is of course contemptuous, with a slight suggestion of a model or tin man, repeating the mechanical theme. Swift's Gulliver, dwarfed in Brobdingnag, was at first suspected to be a clock-work 'mannikin'. There is a link with Mrs Chandler's words to her little son of a little father in 'A Little Cloud' (74d).

b) *glancing first for approval*: Mr Alleyne's foolishness will have a counterpart in Farrington's 'playing up' to his friends. The epitome of the *Dunciad* (79g) is given in Book III (135–38):

> . . . Mighty Dulness crown'd
> Shall take thro' Grub-street her triumphant round;
> And her Parnassus glancing o'er at once,
> Beheld a hundred sons, and each a Dunce.

c) *the hue of a wild rose*: Originally 'tea rose', but 'wild' better suggests an anger, manifestly crimson. There is an anticipation of young Stephen's song in *P* (I.1):

> O, the wild rose blossoms
> On the little green place.

d) *He shook his fist . . .*: Mr Alleyne and his emotion become indistinguishable, rather like Yeats' dancer and the dance, in 'Among School Children'.

e) *You impertinent ruffian!*: One of the many repetitions, though Farrington has no monopoly on impertinence. *Henry IV Part 2* (IV.v) has the question:

> Have you a ruffian that will swear? drink? dance?
> Revel the night? rob? murder? and commit
> The oldest sins the newest kinds of ways?

f) *instanter*: Lawyer's Latin – 'instantly', still a common usage in Ireland.

g) *You'll quit this . . . or*: A rhetorical inversion, a device known as 'chiasmus'.

h) *hornet's nest*: A cell of anger and aggression (131h).

i) *little Peake*: In *U*, 'Hades', the name is among the death notices on the way to Glasnevin Cemetery. Bloom wonders if it is the chap from Crosbie & Alleyne's: he decides against.

continued: it was so bitter and violent that the man could hardly restrain his fist from descending upon the head of the manikin before him.

—I know nothing about any other two letters, he said stupidly—

—*You – know – nothing*. Of course you know nothing, said Mr Alleyne. Tell me, he added, glancing first for approval to the lady beside him, do you take me for a fool? Do you think me an utter fool?—

The man glanced from the lady's face to the little egg-shaped head and back again; and, almost before he was aware of it, his tongue had found a felicitous moment:

—I don't think, sir, he said, that that's a fair question to put to me—

There was a pause in the very breathing of the clerks. Everyone was astounded (the author of the witticism no less than his neighbours) and Miss Delacour, who was a stout amiable person, began to smile broadly. Mr Alleyne flushed to the hue of a wild rose and his mouth twitched with a dwarf's passion. He shook his fist in the man's face till it seemed to vibrate like the knob of some electric machine:

—You impertinent ruffian! You impertinent ruffian! I'll make short work of you! Wait till you see! You'll apologize to me for your impertinence or you'll quit the office instanter! You'll quit this, I'm telling you, or you'll apologize to me!—

. . . .

He stood in a doorway opposite the office, watching to see if the cashier would come out alone. All the clerks passed out and finally the cashier came out with the chief clerk. It was no use trying to say a word to him when he was with the chief clerk. The man felt that his position was bad enough. He had been obliged to offer an abject apology to Mr Alleyne for his impertinence but he knew what a hornet's nest the office would be for him. He could remember the way in which Mr Alleyne had hounded little Peake out of the office in order to make room for his own nephew. He felt savage and thirsty and revengeful, annoyed with himself and with everyone else. Mr Alleyne would never give him an hour's rest; his life would be a hell to him. He had made a proper fool of himself this time. Could he not keep his tongue in his cheek? But they had never

a) *but sure*: See 107p.

b) *Higgins*: A very common Irish name. It is unclear whether this one is related to Miss Higgins of 'The Dead'. Bloom's maternal grandparents were named Higgins. When in *U*, 'Circe', the whore Zoe Higgins is asked if she is a Dublin girl, she says, 'No bloody fear. I'm English.'

c) *A man with two establishments to keep up*: Higgins' affairs are undoubtedly complicated, and the untold story adds verisimilitude to this one. This was one of the lines that was felt to be explicitly immoral and was proposed for deletion from *D*.

d) *touch Pat*: Borrow money from him.

e) *a bob*: A shilling (now 5p) – enough at this time to buy six pints of plain porter (eight at Hoey's near Merchant's Arch). Even the latter consumption would be insufficient to make a big man drunk enough to escape Dublin entrapment.

f) *Terry Kelly's pawn-office*: It was at No 48. Padraic Colum told how he and Joyce once tried to redeem an incomplete set of Walter Scott's works (16m) from Kelly, and sell it to George Webb (168n), but the wheeze was not successful.

g) *Fleet Street*: In the heart of Dublin's commercial district, just south of O'Connell Bridge. Despite the pawnbrokers and second-hand bookshops, the area was characterised more by the commission agents, solicitors, tailors and printers that abounded there.

h) *That was the dart!*: Dublin idiom, meaning 'the trick/solution/answer'. The word was to be recycled in the 1980s in the Dublin Area Rapid Transport railway – DART.

i) *Temple Bar*: Like Fleet Street, a London parallel (129d). This narrow street is said to be named after the Temples, the family of Lord Palmerston, the Victorian Prime Minister. Sir William Temple was Provost of Trinity in Jacobean times, and also MP for Dublin University in the Irish House of Commons. His namesake and grandson was the mentor and guardian of Swift.

j) *A crown!*: A unit, but not a current coin. There were four to a pound, each worth five shillings.

k) *consignor*: A technical commercial term for the pawner, and a word that does not rhyme with monsignor. Joyce originally wrote 'mortgagor'. Only later is it clear that Farrington's watch has been pawned. He is without his escapement, and a night on the tiles doesn't count.

l) *Westmoreland Street*: Running south-east off O'Connell Bridge. The Dublin street (49m, 137g) is

usually stressed on the second syllable – unlike the former English county. So too is Dorset Street (42j).

m) *ragged urchins ... evening editions*: Farrington's sighting of these urchins (literally 'hedgehogs') has its counterpart with Little Chandler's 'mice' (63d). There is a pre-echo of 'the whirl of wild newsboys' in *U*, 'Aeolus'. This whole passage (down to 'fumes of punch'), as well as rendering a Dublin street-scene, also evocatively conveys Farrington's high spirits. 'Evening editions' was previously 'evening papers'.

n) *he preconsidered the terms*: Sir Jonah Barrington, the eighteenth-century judge and sometime Irish MP, once said that in Dublin no one believes his own stories, only everyone else's.

o) *I don't think ...*: The statement seems *verbatim*, but the omission of the final 'sir' alters its tone hugely. So too will Farrington's timing and intonation, and he will not mention his apology.

The 'says I' is an Irish idiom. Percy French, the gifted entertainer, painter, and inspector of drains, imputed to Queen Victoria a monologue in broad Dublinese, in 'The Queen's After-Dinner Speech':

'An' I think there's a slate', sez she,
'Off Willie Yeats', sez she,
'He should be at home', sez she,
'French-polishin' a pome', sez she,
'An' not writin letters', sez she,
'About his betters', sez she,
'Paradin' me crimes', sez she,
'In the *Irish Times*', sez she.

p) *Davy Byrne's*: Still at 21 Duke Street (though *U*, 'Ithaca' unreliably says No 14). It was founded by the eponymous Wicklowman in 1889, who ran it for over fifty years. The 'moral pub' (as it is proud to call itself) can be revisited in *U*, 'Lestrygonians'.

q) *when he heard the story*: Farrington's vainglory is a form of rodomontade – a word derived from Ariosto's farrago of 1532, *Orlando Furioso* – a play reworked by Shelley, Robert Greene (84n), Wordsworth and others.

r) *Farrington*: At last the narrator gives him an identity. In the pub he achieves humanity of a kind.

s) *tailors of malt*: Large glasses of quality, unblended whiskey. In 1912, when Joyce first met James Stephens, they repaired to Pat Kinsella's (thought of by Bloom in 'Lestrygonians'), and Stephens ordered these, explaining gnomically that it took seven tailors to make a man, and two to make twins.

pulled together from the first, he and Mr Alleyne, ever since the day Mr Alleyne had overheard him mimicking his North of Ireland accent to amuse Higgins and Miss Parker: that had been the beginning of it. He might have tried Higgins for the money, but sure Higgins never had anything for himself. A man with two establishments to keep up, of course he couldn't . . .

He felt his great body again aching for the comfort of the public-house. The fog had begun to chill him and he wondered could he touch Pat in O'Neill's. He could not touch him for more than a bob – and a bob was no use. Yet he must get money somewhere or other: he had spent his last penny for the g.p. and soon it would be too late for getting money anywhere. Suddenly, as he was fingering his watch-chain, he thought of Terry Kelly's pawn-office in Fleet Street. That was the dart! Why didn't he think of it sooner?

He went through the narrow alley of Temple Bar quickly, muttering to himself that they could all go to hell because he was going to have a good night of it. The clerk in Terry Kelly's said *A crown!* but the consignor held out for six shillings; and in the end the six shillings was allowed him literally. He came out of the pawn-office joyfully, making a little cylinder of the coins between his thumb and fingers. In Westmoreland Street the footpaths were crowded with young men and women returning from business and ragged urchins ran here and there yelling out the names of the evening editions. The man passed through the crowd, looking on the spectacle generally with proud satisfaction and staring masterfully at the office-girls. His head was full of the noises of tram-gongs and swishing trolleys and his nose already sniffed the curling fumes of punch. As he walked on he preconsidered the terms in which he would narrate the incident to the boys:

—So, I just looked at him – coolly, you know, and looked at her. Then I looked back at him again – taking my time, you know. *I don't think that that's a fair question to put to me,* says I—

Nosey Flynn was sitting up in his usual corner of Davy Byrne's and, when he heard the story, he stood Farrington a half-one, saying it was as smart a thing as ever he heard. Farrington stood a drink in his turn. After a while O'Halloran and Paddy Leonard came in and the story was repeated to them. O'Halloran stood tailors of malt, hot, all round and told

A Money Office, or pawnbroker's

a) *Callan's*: There were several branches of this well-known commercial family.

b) *Fownes's Street*: Between Dame Street and the Liffey. The street was named after the philanthropist who persuaded Swift to leave his money to found a hospital 'for Fools and Mad'.

c) *liberal shepherds in the eclogues*: Vergil's *Eclogues* celebrate the simple, rustic life, so O'Halloran's back answer is more robust than witty. The classical parallel is one reason for Farrington's 'shepherd's plaid cap'. In *Eclogue* III, there is a rough 'flyte' between two of the shepherds:

Menalcas: Poor flock, whose ewes were drained
by you.
Damoetas: Shut up! I know what you've been up
to.
Menalcas: I suppose you saw *me* wreck them vines.
Damoetas: You broke the bow of Daphnis too.

In *Hamlet* (IV.vii), Gertrude mentions the flowers adorning the dead Ophelia:

... long purples
That liberal shepherds give a grosser name
But our cold maids do dead men's fingers call
them ...

d) *naming their poisons*: A drinking cliché, though many of the characters here and hereabouts are poisoned by their drink.

e) my nabs: Akin to the common expression, 'his nibs'.

f) *Duke Street*: Between Grafton and Dawson Streets, it was named after the Second Duke of Grafton, a seventeenth-century Viceroy. As well as Davy Byrne's, it has the Bailey, where the front door of 7 Eccles Street was taken in 1967. After it was mounted on the wall, the door was formally declared shut by Patrick Kavanagh.

g) *bevelled off to the left*: They go southwards, on Grafton Street, which Dublin style defines as travelling 'up' it. Farrington, Leonard and O'Halloran turn right and north. 'Bevel' comes from masonry and joinery, and is a reminder of the theme of geometry.

h) *Ballast Office*: On the corner of Aston Quay at O'Connell Bridge, it was the headquarters of the Dublin Port and Docks Board (1611). In *SH*, Cranly is told by Stephen that its clock – and by implication its famous timeball – is capable of an epiphany.

i) *the Scotch House*: A famous Dublin pub that was on Burgh Quay from 1840 until its demolition in the 1980s. At one stage in his struggle for the publication of *D*, Joyce agreed to disguise it as the Manx House. He knew the pub well, though not as well as his father did. In *U*, 'Wandering Rocks' 11, Stephen's needy sister questions the fictionalised John Joyce:

– Were you in the Scotch house now?
– I was not, then, Mr Dedalus said smiling.

Four or five decades later, the pub was widely regarded as the office of Myles na Gopaleen.

j) *whining match sellers*: Dublin in the early twentieth century was full of beggars and the unemployed. This is a rare Joycean reminder that the city's social hierarchy goes down as well as up. The extent of public squalor in Dublin was shown in an official inquiry of the time: see *Parliamentary Papers* 1900, Vol XXXIX. This poverty was part of Joyce's world too.

k) *Weathers*: A noticeably English name, from the Old English *weðer*, later *wether* or *weather*, 'castrated ram' – and hence somebody lacking in sexual prowess. It reflects badly on Farrington to be beaten by a eunuch. In *The Merchant of Venice* (IV.v), Antonio tells Bassanio:

I am a tainted weather of the flock.

l) *the Tivoli*: A music-hall theatre, close by on Burgh Quay, and formerly the Lyric. It had also been known as the Conciliation Hall, having been the scene of many of O'Connell's rallies. The site is now occupied by the offices of the *Irish Press*.

m) *knockabout*: See 117i.

n) *a small Irish and Apollinaris*: A whiskey and mineral water. The latter was imported from Germany (and therefore expensive). Edward VII was known to favour it, so Weathers appears to be aping his King. 'The Queen of Table Waters' is still available and its traditional pink equilateral triangle is noticeably similar to the trade mark of Bass (58k).

o) *He promised ...*: Weathers seems more inclined to act as a pimp.

p) *because he was a married man*: One of the gods of Thyrsis in *Eclogue* VII is Priapus. Menalcas (c) and others revel in their lust.

the story of the retort he had made to the chief clerk when he was in Callan's of Fownes's Street; but, as the retort was after the manner of the liberal shepherds in the eclogues, he had to admit that it was not so clever as Farrington's retort. At this Farrington told the boys to polish off that and have another.

Just as they were naming their poisons who should come in but Higgins! Of course he had to join in with the others. The men asked him to give his version of it, and he did so with great vivacity, for the sight of five small hot whiskies was very exhilarating. Everyone roared laughing when he showed the way in which Mr Alleyne shook his fist in Farrington's face. Then he imitated Farrington, saying, *And here was my nabs, as cool as you please*, while Farrington looked at the company out of his heavy dirty eyes, smiling and at times drawing forth stray drops of liquor from his moustache with the aid of his lower lip.

When that round was over there was a pause. O'Halloran had money but neither of the other two seemed to have any; so the whole party left the shop somewhat regretfully. At the corner of Duke Street Higgins and Nosey Flynn bevelled off to the left while the other three turned back towards the city. Rain was drizzling down on the cold streets and, when they reached the Ballast Office, Farrington suggested the Scotch House. The bar was full of men and loud with the noise of tongues and glasses. The three men pushed past the whining match-sellers at the door and formed a little party at the corner of the counter. They began to exchange stories. Leonard introduced them to a young fellow named Weathers who was performing at the Tivoli as an acrobat and knockabout *artiste*. Farrington stood a drink all round. Weathers said he would take a small Irish and Apollinaris. Farrington, who had definite notions of what was what, asked the boys would they have an Apollinaris too; but the boys told Tim to make theirs hot. The talk became theatrical. O'Halloran stood a round and then Farrington stood another round, Weathers protesting that the hospitality was too Irish. He promised to get them in behind the scenes and introduce them to some nice girls. O'Halloran said that he and Leonard would go, but that Farrington wouldn't go because he was a married man; and Farrington's heavy dirty eyes leered at the company in token that he under-

A Merchant's Arch legal doorway

a) *tincture*: Another drinking cliché. Joseph Addison (whose work Joyce disdained – in part because of the Augustan's hostility to the pun) pointed out:

> Malignant tempers, whatever kind of life they are engaged in, will discover their natural tincture of mind.

b) *Mulligan's in Poolbeg Street*: Still thriving near the south bank of the Liffey and (like many Dublin pubs) famous for 'the best pint of Guinness in Ireland'. The street is named after the part of Dublin Bay (which also gave its name to what Joyce called the 'Poolbeg flasher' (*FW* 215) – though it had a constant beam).

c) *When the Scotch House closed*: There was a variety of closing times in Dublin, some pubs operating under an Early Closing Licence.

d) *the parlour at the back*: A large room with large tables. It and the tables are still there.

e) *Funds were running low*: Originally 'getting low'. The amendment restores the theme of mechanisation.

f) *peacock-blue ... bright yellow ... dark brown*: In *Eclogue* VIII, the maidservant Amaryllis is told:

> Tie three colours Amaryllis in three knots
> Just tie them and repeat 'The Venus knot I tie'.

Farrington is similarly ensnared by three colours.

g) *Farrington gazed admiringly ...*: This passage is even more effective than the one Joyce was forced to delete as it was considered too lascivious:

> Farrington said he wouldn't mind having the far one and began to smile at her but when Weathers offered to introduce her he said 'No,' he was only chaffing because he knew he had not money enough. She continued to cast bold glances at him and changed the position of her legs often and when she was going out she brushed against his chair and said 'Pardon!' in a Cockney accent.

h) *She glanced at him once or twice*: The name Amaryllis (f) means 'casting glances'.

i) *a London accent*: The exotic (and no longer explicitly Cockney) opposite of his boss's Northern accent. Consider also (from *P* V.3) the 'kind gentlewomen in Covent Garden wooing from their balconies with sucking mouths'. The passage, however, runs on: 'and the poxfouled wenches of the taverns'. As Joyce well knew, Poolbeg Street was not even a stone's throw from the infamous Lock Hospital (on the corner of Luke Street and Townsend Street), which treated venereal conditions (though badly, as the Wassermann Test and modern antibiotics were still years away).

Looking down Grafton Street

stood he was being chaffed. Weathers made them all have just one little tincture at his expense and promised to meet them later on at Mulligan's in Poolbeg Street.

When the Scotch House closed they went round to Mulligan's. They went into the parlour at the back and O'Halloran ordered small hot specials all round. They were all beginning to feel mellow. Farrington was just standing another round when Weathers came back. Much to Farrington's relief he drank a glass of bitter this time. Funds were running low but they had enough to keep them going. Presently two young women with big hats and a young man in a check suit came in and sat at a table close by. Weathers saluted them and told the company that they were out of the Tivoli. Farrington's eyes wandered at every moment in the direction of one of the young women. There was something striking in her appearance. An immense scarf of peacock-blue muslin was wound round her hat and knotted in a great bow under her chin; and she wore bright yellow gloves, reaching to the elbow. Farrington gazed admiringly at the plump arm which she moved very often and with much grace; and when, after a little time, she answered his gaze he admired still more her large dark brown eyes. The oblique staring expression in them fascinated him. She glanced at him once or twice and, when the party was leaving the room, she brushed against his chair and said *O, pardon!* in a London accent. He watched her leave the room in the hope that she would look back at him, but he was disappointed. He cursed his want of money and cursed all the rounds he had stood, particularly all the whiskies and Apollinaris which he had stood to Weathers. If there was one thing that he hated it was a sponge. He was so angry that he lost count of the conversation of his friends.

When Paddy Leonard called him he found that they were talking about feats of strength. Weathers was showing his biceps muscle to the company and boasting so much that the other two had called on Farrington to uphold the national honour. Farrington pulled up his sleeve accordingly and showed his biceps muscle to the company. The two arms were examined and compared and finally it was agreed to have a trial of strength. The table was cleared and the two men rested their elbows on it, clasping hands. When Paddy Leonard said *Go!* each was to try to bring down the other's hand on to the

j) *the hope that she would look back*: In *Eclogue* VIII, Amaryllis is instructed by her mistress, 'Take out the ashes . . . don't look back.'

k) *a sponge*: A chronic 'borrower', or a drunk, and sometimes – as here – both. Lenehan in 'Two Gallants' is a prime example of such a cadger. Portia in *The Merchant of Venice* (I.ii) remarks:

I will do anything . . . ere I will be married to a sponge.

l) *uphold the national honour*: Farrington's failure is more than personal.

a) *such a stripling*: But Farrington forgets that his opponent is a professional acrobat and knockabout *artiste*, while he has a sedentary job (76k). Stanislaus reported that William Murray (76h) was proud of the strength of his arms.

b) *Play fair*: See 117k.

c) *peony*: Crimson, the colour of a wild rose. Robert Boyle (18i) observed:

> A physician had often tried the peony root unreasonably gathered without success; but having gathered it when the decreasing moon passes under Aries, and tied the slit root about the necks of his patients, he had freed more than one from epileptical fits.

d) *red head ... stupid familiarity*: Previously Joyce had 'loutish familiarity' – Bloom thinks of redheaded country curates on the make, in *U*, 'Calypso'.

e) *your gab*: Your speech. Technically the word means 'mouth', from the Irish.

f) *Pony up, boys*: Settle up (financially). The lads have been betting on the outcome of the tussle.

g) *one little smahan*: A 'nip' of whiskey – from the Irish *smeachán*, a 'little taste'.

h) *A ... man*: Farrington has lost his name again. His exhilaration is long spent.

i) *little Sandymount tram*: The 16 tram went every ten minutes from Westmoreland Street via College Green, Nassau Street and Merrion Square, to Lower Mount Street and Haddington Road. At the end of Shelbourne Road (opposite Beggar's Bush Barracks), it went under the main Dublin-Wexford railway line – hence the need for single-deckers, unique to this route. After Bath Avenue and London Bridge Road, it went on past Irishtown to its destination.

j) *he did not even feel drunk*: But Farrington has had fifteen drinks of various sizes that we are told about. Joyce originally had written 'A sullen partially-drunken man ...', but saw how to improve the sense of frustration.

k) *only twopence*: So he has spent 5/10d – over 97% of his six bob.

l) *He cursed everything*: Improved from 'He cursed himself and his luck'.

m) *Shelbourne Road*: Joyce lived there at No 60, from March to September 1904 (and from the evidence of *U*, 'Nestor', was badly behind with his rent). This was the home of the M'Kernans, parents of Susie, a model for Gerty MacDowell of 'Nausicaa'. Mrs M'Kernan was a family connection of William Murray's wife, née Josephine Giltrap. The Murrays at this time actually lived at North Strand Road (13s)

O'Connell Bridge by night: a 1903 postcard sent from the Wicklow Hotel

table. Farrington looked very serious and determined.

The trial began. After about thirty seconds Weathers brought his opponent's hand slowly down on to the table. Farrington's dark wine-coloured face flushed darker still with anger and humiliation at having been defeated by such a
a   stripling.

b   —You're not to put the weight of your body behind it. Play fair, he said—

—Who's not playing fair? said the other—

—Come on again. The two best out of three—

The trial began again. The veins stood out on Farrington's forehead, and the pallor of Weather's complexion changed to
c   peony. Their hands and arms trembled under the stress. After a long struggle Weathers again brought his opponent's hand slowly on to the table. There was a murmur of applause from the spectators. The curate, who was standing beside the table,
d   nodded his red head toward the victor and said with stupid familiarity:

—Ah! that's the knack!—

—What the hell do you know about it? said Farrington fiercely,
e   turning on the man. What do you put in your gab for?—

—Sh, sh! said O'Halloran, observing the violent expression
f   of Farrington's face. Pony up, boys. We'll have just one little
g   smahan more and then we'll be off—

.   .   .   .

h   A very sullen-faced man stood at the corner of O'Connell
i   Bridge waiting for the little Sandymount tram to take him home. He was full of smouldering anger and revengefulness.
j   He felt humiliated and discontented; he did not even feel drunk;
kl and he had only twopence in his pocket. He cursed everything. He had done for himself in the office, pawned his watch, spent all his money; and he had not even got drunk. He began to feel thirsty again and he longed to be back again in the hot reeking public-house. He had lost his reputation as a strong man, having been defeated twice by a mere boy. His heart swelled with fury and, when he thought of the woman in the big hat who had brushed against him and said *Pardon!* his fury nearly choked him.
m   His tram let him down at Shelbourne Road and he steered
n   his great body along in the shadows of the wall of the barracks.

but Joyce here transferred them to the M'Kernans' house, perhaps to improve the book's spread of the city. At one stage he planned another story for the collection, 'The Last Supper', which was to have been about Joe M'Kernan, apparently one of Susie's brothers.

n) *the barracks*: Beggar's Bush Infantry Barracks, founded in 1827, and a tacit reminder that Dublin was a garrison town. The expression 'Beggar's Bush' meant 'the road to ruin'. Robert Greene (81q) (the drunkard, debtor and rival of Shakespeare naturally thought of by Stephen in *U*, 'Scylla and Charybis') wrote in *Twelve Ingenious Characters*:

He throws away his wealth as heartily as young heirs, or old philosophers, and is so eager of a goal, or a mumper's wallet, that he will not wait fortune's leisure to undo him, but rides post to *beggar's-bush*, and takes more pains to spend money than day-labourers to get it.

The cap fits.

Beggar's Bush, at Shelbourne Road (84n)

a) *Ada!*: The description that follows is not that of William Murray's real wife, Joyce's Aunt Josephine, whom he admired and trusted (174a). The fictional woman is far from being someone who brings aid, as if at the end of 'An Encounter'. (Vladimir Nabokov's *Ada* had the foreign dignity of being a pun on ardour.) The contemporary novelist Ada Leverson was known as 'the Sphinx' and although remembered as a friend of Oscar Wilde was actually in love with Grant Richards, the once and future publisher of *D*.

b) *his son's flat accent*: The son is Bertie Murray, whose haplessness was recorded in Stanislaus' diary. The mimicry that follows is a strong counterpart of Alleyne's mimicry of Farrington with his 'what *Mr Shelley says, sir*' (76n).

c) At the chapel: Farrington too has been worshipping: his gods are alcohol and escape, whose communion is celebrated by secular curates. His pilgrimage even began at Temple Bar: the Irish *teach pobal* – literally 'public house' – likewise combines drink and religion in its name, meaning chapel or parish church.

d) *You let the fire out!*: In *P* (V.1), Stephen was to get a lesson on firelighting from the dean of studies, though later J. F. Byrne was to complain that the experience happened to him rather than Joyce.

e) *rolling up his sleeve*: For the second time that evening, though this time he will win the trial of strength – against a six year old. In *P* (I.4), Mr Gleeson's rolling-up of his sleeves is parodied by Athy.

f) *you little whelp!*: A pup or cub. The anger also recalls an epiphany written by Joyce in Mullingar, where a beggar takes a stick to two children, with the threat, 'I'll cut the livers and lights out o'ye'. The anger has been simmering throughout the story. Catiline, in Act 1 of Ben Jonson's play of that name (about a futile rebellion), says:

> Slave, I will strike your soul out with my foot,
> Let me but find you again with such a face:
> You whelp.

Joyce reviewed Ibsen's first play *Catilina* in a London magazine in 1903.

He loathed returning to his home. When he went in by the side-door he found the kitchen empty and the kitchen fire nearly out. He bawled upstairs:

a   —Ada! Ada!—

His wife was a little sharp-faced woman who bullied her husband when he was sober and was bullied by him when he was drunk. They had five children. A little boy came running down the stairs.

—Who is that? said the man, peering through the darkness—

—Me, pa—

—Who are you? Charlie?—

—No, pa. Tom—

—Where's your mother?—

—She's out at the chapel—

—That's right ... Did she think of leaving any dinner for me?—

—Yes, pa. I ...—

—Light the lamp. What do you mean by having the place in darkness? Are the other children in bed?—

The man sat down heavily on one of the chairs while the b little boy lit the lamp. He began to mimic his son's flat accent, c saying half to himself: *At the chapel. At the chapel, if you please!* When the lamp was lit he banged his fist on the table and shouted:

—What's for my dinner?—

—I'm going ... to cook it, pa, said the little boy—

The man jumped up furiously and pointed to the fire.

d   —On that fire! You let the fire out! By God, I'll teach you to do that again!—

He took a step to the door and seized the walking-stick which was standing behind it.

e   —I'll teach you to let the fire out! he said, rolling up his sleeve in order to give his arm free play—

The little boy cried O, *pa!* and ran whimpering round the table, but the man followed him and caught him by the coat. The little boy looked about him wildly but, seeing no way of escape, fell upon his knees.

—Now, you'll let the fire out the next time! said the man, f striking at him vigorously with the stick. Take that, you little whelp!—

The boy uttered a squeal of pain as the stick cut his thigh.

a) *a* Hail Mary: A standard Catholic prayer, out-rivalling the 'Our Father' in personal prayer, in penance for confession and of course in the Rosary. The text of the prayer is this:

Hail Mary, full of grace, the Lord is with thee. Blessèd art thou amongst women and blessèd is the fruit of thy womb, Jesus. Holy Mary, Mother of God, pray for us sinners now and at the hour of our death. Amen.

Stanislaus in his diary confirms that the detail of the story's climax is true. *Pace* hyperdulia (122a), the prayer was much parodied – e.g.:

Hail Mary full of grease, the lard is with thee ...

Protestant children sometimes mocked:

Hail Mary, Mother of God,
Send us down a couple of bob.

This was countered by:

Proddy, Proddy on the wall,
Half a loaf between yez all.
A farthing candle to show yez light,
To read the Bible on Saturday night.

The Irish idea that poverty among children was in itself a cause of shame was something that Joyce creditably did not endorse (but then neither did his father). At the end of O'Casey's *Juno and the Paycock* (1924) as Johnny Boyle is taken out to be shot for not being patriotic enough, he tries to recite the 'Hail Mary'. Though designated formally in the *Maynooth Catechism* as 'The Angelical Salutation', it is universally known as the 'Hail Mary'. Lesson XXIII has:

Q: Who made the Hail Mary?
A: The Angel Gabriel and Saint Elizabeth made the first part of the Hail Mary – and the Church made the second part.

The catechism goes on to explain that the prayer is so often repeated in order to honour the mystery of the Incarnation.

He clasped his hands together in the air and his voice shook with fright.

—O, pa! he cried. Don't beat me, pa! And I'll ... I'll say a *Hail Mary* for you ... I'll say a *Hail Mary* for you, pa, if you don't beat me ... I'll say a *Hail Mary* ...—

Opposite: Mary, full of grace, is told by Gabriel that she is to be the mother of the Saviour. (From a 1636 biography, The Life of the Glorious Bishop S. Patricke, Apostle and Primate of Ireland*)*

Afterword: 'Counterparts'

In general, Joyce's works became increasingly warm towards his native city, as if distance lent enchantment. In the bleakness of *Dubliners*, however, the most unpleasant character is surely Farrington. Against stiff competition – Corley, Mrs Kearney, the josser, Mrs Mooney, Mr Harford, Mr Henchy, *et al.* – Farrington takes the biscuit. He seems to commit all of the seven deadly sins, and yet the lingering impression of the story is not of indulgence or selfishness, but of sterility. Such sterility does not preclude begetting, and as in other stories there is a strong sense of a cycle of futility. No doubt Farrington when young said many a 'Hail Mary' (and similarly Bob Doran had been a keen altar-boy at Adam and Eve's and full of religious curiosity): the details are reminiscent of the narrator(s) of the first three stories. A developing interest in the ways of the world can lead – in the worst case – to a Farrington.

Joyce was also aware of the context of such brutishness. In a letter to Stanislaus in November 1906 he remarked that he was no friend of tyranny, but added about brutal husbands that

> the atmosphere in which they live (vide Counterparts) is brutal and few wives and homes can satisfy the desire for happiness.

One of the many ironies in the story is the detail that it is Mrs Farrington who bullies Farrington when he is sober, and *vice versa* when he is drunk. Thus they are counterparts, matching each other.

This story and the collection are full of such couplings and connections. The title-word of the story has the twin meanings of something complementary, and something parallel – rather as a mirror reflects something the same, yet also something opposite. For example, Mr Alleyne's evident enthusiasm for Miss Delacour is met by her open amusement at his embarrassment, but it is also matched by Farrington's attraction to the London woman. Again, Farrington's running out of time to do his copying can be paired with his abandonment of his watch to the pawnbroker. His use of his lower lip to wipe his moustache recalls Father Flynn's use of his to support his tongue. The London woman's eyes anticipate Mrs Sinico's though the outcome of each meeting is different. Furthermore, Farrington's possession of only a few pennies at the end of a deeply unsuccessful evening recalls the boy in 'Araby'. The man in 'Counterparts' enters a corrupt home by a side-door, as the penitent fivesome will do in 'Grace'. Also, the difficulties with his son form a reprise of 'A Little Cloud', while in 'Ivy Day' we learn of Old Jack suffering retaliation and being bullied by his son when the father is drunk. There is a dense and elaborate skein of such details, both in this story and in *Dubliners* as a whole: yet while details can be seen as symmetrical, Joyce's treatments are never identical.

A typically Joycean tension between naturalism and symbolism appears at the end of the story. Stanislaus' diary recorded little Bertie Murray trying to placate his drunken father by offering to say the

Hail Mary for him. Stanislaus added: 'such appalling cowardice on both sides nearly made me ill'. Little Tom Farrington offers to do the same thing, and tries to buy off his maleficent and sinful father by saying the same prayer. The detail of moral death is in the anecdote, and in the city, and in Joyce's story, and at the end of the prayer.

Throughout 'Counterparts' the theme of time is an intricately handled one. Again and again in the story, time is slipping away: Farrington's lunch-break habitually overruns. His copying deadline slips and slips, he takes his time in narrating his exchange with his superior, one pub closes and then another, and his defeat by the puny Weathers shows that it is later than he thinks: little wonder then that by c. 11.40 pm, when he gets home, the fire is out.

Mr Alleyne, by way of contrast, 'did not lose a moment'. Though that is an example of complementarity as counterpart, the story is dominated by the device of repetition as counterpart. Echolalia is a feature of Mr Alleyne's bullying: he repeats Farrington on Mr Shelley, and has his own verbal tic of saying 'Do you mind me?' Farrington makes the blunder of *Bernard Bernard* (a repetition that anticipates Maria's singing in the following story). In the pub, not only does Farrington mimic Alleyne, but Higgins (a man with 'two establishments') also mimics Farrington. Drinks are repeated, and so are the details of Farrington's heavy dirty eyes, and the arm-wrestling bout. Finally, at home, Farrington repeats his son's words about the chapel, and his own about the fire. Worst of all, in a domestic setting he emulates his own sadistic boss. His son meanwhile three times makes futile offers of prayer, as if all Dublin iteration were futile, or as mechanical as a rosary.

There is another, more hidden repetition: Joyce knew that Vergil was the first to use pastoral poetry as a device for the moral criticism of his own society. He wrote to Grant Richards in May 1906 about choosing Dublin for *Dubliners* because it seemed to him the centre of paralysis:

> My intention was to write a chapter of the moral history of my country.

This was the year after he had written 'Counterparts' which, as Joyce's text and the notes show, drew deliberately on the *Eclogues*. There are ten parts to Vergil's work, the original number of *epicleti* planned for *Dubliners*. Joyce's reworking in 'Counterparts' of Pope's reworking of Vergil is particularly telling. Vergil's pastoral blend of contemporary reality, recent history, myth and symbolic imagery all contributed to the rise of allegory. Though Dante's device of having Vergil as a guide also appealed to Joyce, so too did the Latin poet's self-acknowledged habit of inserting games and puzzles into his texts – a direct predecessor of Joyce's schemes to keep the commentators hard at it.

a) CLAY: The title is discussed in the Afterword.

b) *the women's tea*: In Ireland 'tea' is often the main evening meal.

c) *Maria*: The name and character came from a real Maria, part of a large and complex skein of relatives of Joyce's mother, who was particularly fond of her. Appropriately, 'Maria' is the Continental name for the Virgin Mary, and the character here is (or seems) as innocent (and virginal) as She. The name may also carry an ironic echo of the word 'marry'. Strangely, Maria was renamed Ursule in *Gens de Dublin*, the first French translation of the book, which was produced with Joyce's cooperation. St Ursula was famously martyred with 11,000 other virgins by the Huns. Her name is seen in the Ursuline order of nuns. Maria has been interpreted variously, but the evidence of the French translation suggests that she is a symbol of virginity, or sterility – and that in that sense she can be seen as incomplete, in common with so many of the cast of *D*. Her celibacy makes her a female counterpart of Mr Duffy in 'A Painful Case'.

d) *spick and span*: Clean and neat. Nautically, a 'spick' was a spike or nail, and a 'span' a chip. If the spicks and the spans are new, then the ship must be too.

e) *barmbracks*: A corruption of the Irish *báirín breac*, 'speckled loaf', and usually spelt as two words. Barm brack is a brown fruit loaf, still common in Ireland at Halloween. Typically it contains a ring and sometimes money and other trinkets of augury. Other things too, it seems: the *Irish Homestead* for Halloween 1904 accused bakers of using their 'sweepings' as flour for bracks, and the occasional 'beetle as a plump raisin'.

f) *a veritable peace-maker*: The expression naturally recalls the sermon on the Mount: 'Blessed are the peacemakers: for they shall be called the children of God' (Matthew V.9). Nevertheless, however inadvertently, Maria will be as much trouble-maker as peace-maker in the story.

g) *the Board ladies*: The Dublin by Lamplight Institution was managed by a voluntary committee of Protestant philanthropists.

h) *Ginger Mooney*: The Irish word *maonach* means 'dumb', and the word *monach* means 'guileful', or 'full of tricks', but the surname is so frequent in

Ireland (e.g. in 'The Boarding House') that no particular significance can reasonably be ascribed to it here.

i) *what she wouldn't do*: What she *would* do, in fact. The idiom is a hyperbole, implying that it would be easier to list the few things that wouldn't be done than those that would.

j) *the dummy*: Not an insult: someone who has no power of speech, probably because of deafness.

k) *Ballsbridge*: About two miles south-east of Nelson's Pillar, a prosperous suburb which is synonymous with the Royal Dublin Society (25j). Although her closest relatives lived nearer the river, the original Maria was not completely cut off here: Giltrap relations ran a shop around the corner from the laundry, while Mrs M'Kernan, another connection of the family, lived a short distance away in Shelbourne Road (84m).

l) *the pillar*: Nelson's Pillar was erected c. 1808 and blown up by Republicans in 1966. Nelson's head may still be viewed in the Dublin Civil Museum. The Pillar was paid for by Dublin's merchants and bankers. Its position and its height, 134 feet, made it the most important landmark of the city. It marked the centre of the centre of Dublin, and from the top the Wicklow (and sometimes the Mourne) Mountains could be seen. Trams in Dublin began and ended at the Pillar.

m) *Drumcondra*: An area, once a village, two miles north of the centre, where, according to Stephen in *P* (V.1), 'they speak the best English'. There, the following churchyard inscription was found:

> Nor tender youth nor hoary age
> Can shun the tyrant death's dark rage
> Yet truth and sense this lesson give:
> We live to die, and die, to live.

It is one theme of *D*.

n) A Present from Belfast: Though hardly exotic, the message is a constant proof to Maria of her popularity and of others' regard.

o) *Joe*: Joe Donnelly is based on Joyce's mother's brother, John Murray. He worked in accounts for the *Freeman's Journal*, and is the 'Red' Murray of *U*. John Joyce never had much affection for his in-

CLAY

^a

^{bc} THE MATRON HAD given her leave to go out as
soon as the women's tea was over and Maria looked
forward to her evening out. The kitchen was spick and
^d span: the cook said you could see yourself in the big copper
boilers. The fire was nice and bright and on one of the side-
^e tables were four very big barmbracks. These barmbracks
seemed uncut; but if you went closer you would see that they
had been cut into long thick even slices and were ready to be
handed round at tea. Maria had cut them herself.

Maria was a very, very small person indeed but she had a
very long nose and a very long chin. She talked a little through
her nose, always soothingly: *Yes, my dear*, and *No, my dear*. She
was always sent for when the women quarrelled over their
tubs and always succeeded in making peace. One day the
matron had said to her:

^f —Maria, you are a veritable peace-maker!—

^g And the sub-matron and two of the Board ladies had heard
^h the compliment. And Ginger Mooney was always saying what
^{ij} she wouldn't do to the dummy who had charge of the irons if
it wasn't for Maria. Every one was so fond of Maria.

The women would have their tea at six o'clock and she
^k would be able to get away before seven. From Ballsbridge to
^{lm} the Pillar, twenty minutes; from the Pillar to Drumcondra,
twenty minutes; and twenty minutes to buy the things. She
would be there before eight. She took out her purse with the
ⁿ silver clasps and read again the words *A Present from Belfast*.
^o She was very fond of that purse because Joe had brought it to
^p her five years before when he and Alphy had gone to Belfast
^q on a Whit-Monday trip. In the purse were two half-crowns
^r and some coppers. She would have five shillings clear after
^s paying tram fare. What a nice evening they would have, all
the children singing! Only she hoped that Joe wouldn't come
in drunk. He was so different when he took any drink.

Often he had wanted her to go and live with them; but she
would have felt herself in the way (though Joe's wife was ever
so nice with her) and she had become accustomed to the life

laws. Nor, accordingly, did
Simon Dedalus in *U*, 'Proteus':

O weeping God, the things
I married into! ...The
drunken little costdrawer
and his brother, the cornet
player. Highly respected
gondoliers!

p) *Alphy*: Alphy Donnelly
was based on William
Murray, John's brother, who
is Farrington in 'Coun-
terparts'. His name here is
perhaps suggested by St
Alphonsus Road, Fairview,
where Patrick and Charles,
John Murray's sons, lived at
Verbena House.

q) *Whit-Monday*: Irish superstitions related to Whitsuntide
abound. In particular it is bad
luck to travel on Whit-
Monday, or to give presents
at Whit. It is also said to be
unlucky to buy anything on a
Monday. Joyce is emphasising
Maria's willy-nilly capacity
for mischief-making.

r) *two half-crowns and some
coppers*: A half-crown was
worth two shillings and sixpence, and was silver-
coloured. Coppers (all brown)
were the small change —
pennies, halfpennies and far-
things. The amount is not
quite as much as Farrington
in 'Counterparts' spent on his
pubcrawl.

s) *after paying tram fare*: Maria
would have four fares to pay.
She probably had five shillings
and eightpence altogether.

a) *Mamma ... my proper mother*: Mamma is the Latin for 'breast'. Joyce chose this homonymic spelling rather than the more conventional 'Mama' or the standard Irish 'Mammy'. 'Proper mother' is precisely what Maria is not. There is an ironic echo also in the phrase 'She had nursed him', which when applied to babies usually refers to breastfeeding.

b) *the break-up at home*: The implication is that Maria's unmarried state puts her at the mercy of those who are married.

c) *Dublin by Lamplight* *laundry*: This was in fact a charitable institution, with a Church of Ireland chaplain. It was at 35 Ballsbridge Terrace, very close both to the premises of the Royal Dublin Society, where the Araby Bazaar was held, and to the River Dodder. The institution was founded in the 1850s, and had as object the 'rescue and reform of all the outcast women of society' – meaning prostitutes. Its prospectus (in *Dublin Charities* (1902)) continues:

> *Admission.* Inmates are received on their own application from all parts of the country, or when recommended by friends; others are gathered in after midnight meetings; they must conform to the rules of the house, and attend daily prayers ... *Further particulars* ... The laundry is the chief support of the institution; it is now one of the largest in the city, and has good drying grounds; friends will help by employing it. The conduct of the inmates is good, and not one per cent of those who leave return to their former evil life. Those who remain two years are placed in situations, or sent to America.

Thom's Directory (1902) (punningly) states that:

> Heads of families can materially help the Institution by employing the Laundry.

d) *Protestants*: Members of the Church of Ireland, Methodists, Presbyterians, *et al.* In Ireland Jews are often looked upon as honorary Protestants. In *P* (V.3) when Stephen is asked why he does not become a Protestant, he replies that he has lost his faith but not his self-respect:

> What kind of liberation would that be to forsake an absurdity which is logical and coherent and to embrace one which is illogical and incoherent?

e) *a little quiet and serious*: A Catholic stereotype about Protestants.

f) *ferns and wax-plants*: 'We have the receipt of fern seed, we walk invisible' (Shakespeare, *Henry IV,* Part I, II.i). The fern, the carrying of whose 'seed' traditionally bestows invisibility, has several roles in mythology and superstition, and in Christian iconography is a symbol of life after death and of humility. Of the 'wax-plants', *Monotropa uniflora* is sometimes known as the 'corpse-plant', as it feeds on other decaying plants and has white fleshy leaves, but it is more likely that Maria's wax-plant was *Hoya carnosa*, often grown as an ornamental. Maria's sterile and moribund life, dependent on the rotten undergrowth of Dublin, is analogous to her plants.

Not far from the laundry was the Trinity College Botanic Gardens. Its Curator at this time was the green-haired botanist Frederick W. Burbidge. (He had gone bald on an expedition to Borneo, and wore a wig that soon became infested with bright green mildew.) Burbidge had helped to found the short-lived Dublin Kyrle Society, one of whose aims was to decorate with flowers

> Workmen's Clubs, Schools, and other Rooms used for the gathering together of the Working Classes, without distinction of creed.

Maria may well have been given plants from Burbidge's gardens. Wild ferns were then widely collected and grown indoors, as part of the Victorian pteridomania (or fern-craze), and the steamy laundry atmosphere would have suited many indoor varieties.

g) *slips*: Cutting from the plants. Cuttings from ferns will not generally take, however.

h) *the tracts on the walls*: At this time, proselytising groups such as the Society for Irish Church Missions to the Roman Catholics and the Association Incorporated for Discountenancing Vice, and Promoting the Knowledge and Practice of the Christian Religion circulated 'carefully selected moral and religious books and tracts'. Maria is in an unusual position: a census within a few years of this time shows only one Roman Catholic on the staff of the laundry.

i) *the ring*: To find the ring in the brack meant marriage within a year.

j) *so many Hallow Eves*: Maria has been in the institution for quite a time. The occasion is now usually known as Halloween, the night of 31 October. It coincides with *Samhain*, the great feast of the dead at the end of the Celtic year. By tradition, this is when the fairies travel, or 'flit', moving from summer to winter quarters, and is an occasion of disruption. For mortal beings, travel is not advised, and feasting is indulged in at home, because the dead are out visiting

of the laundry. Joe was a good fellow. She had nursed him and Alphy too; and Joe used often say:

a —Mamma is mamma but Maria is my proper mother—

b After the break-up at home the boys had got her that position
c in the *Dublin by Lamplight* laundry, and she liked it. She used
d to have such a bad opinion of Protestants but now she thought
e they were very nice people, a little quiet and serious, but still very nice people to live with. Then she had her plants in the conservatory and she liked looking after them. She had lovely
f ferns and wax-plants and, whenever anyone came to visit
g her, she always gave the visitor one or two slips from her conservatory. There was one thing she didn't like and that was
h the tracts on the walls; but the matron was such a nice person to deal with, so genteel.

When the cook told her everything was ready she went into the women's room and began to pull the big bell. In a few minutes the women began to come in by twos and threes, wiping their steaming hands in their petticoats and pulling down the sleeves of their blouses over their red steaming arms. They settled down before their huge mugs which the cook and the dummy filled up with hot tea, already mixed with milk and sugar in huge tin cans. Maria superintended the distribution of the barmbrack and saw that every woman got her four slices. There was a great deal of laughing and joking during
i the meal. Lizzie Fleming said Maria was sure to get the ring
j and, though Fleming had said that for so many Hallow Eves, Maria had to laugh and say she didn't want any ring or man either; and when she laughed her grey-green eyes sparkled with disappointed shyness and the tip of her nose nearly met
k the tip of her chin. Then Ginger Mooney lifted up her mug of tea and proposed Maria's health, while all the other women clattered with their mugs on the table, and said she was sorry she hadn't a sup of porter to drink it in. And Maria laughed again till the tip of her nose nearly met the tip of her chin and till her minute body nearly shook itself asunder because she knew that Mooney meant well though of course she had the
l notions of a common women.

But wasn't Maria glad when the women had finished their tea and the cook and the dummy had begun to clear away the tea-things! She went into her little bedroom and, remembering
m that the next morning was a mass morning, changed the hand

their old haunts. Maria's journey can be seen as one of these visits – a 'dead' ancestor appearing at her old home.

k) *the tip of her nose nearly met the tip of her chin*: Maria's unfortunate physiognomy is mentioned three times in the story: in one of her manifestations Maria (who has no reported surname) is clearly a Halloween witch. Bloom, in *U*, 'Calypso', starts reading a short story: '*Matcham often thinks of the masterstroke by which he won the laughing witch who now*'.

l) *a common woman*: Maria's place on the social scale is ambiguous. She has probably been given a place in the Institution on the recommendation of Joe Donnelly – or more likely, of his wife. At the same time, it matters very much to Maria that she is not an inmate, but an employee, and that she has certain privileges, such as the small bedroom and her plants.

m) *a mass morning*: The day after Hallow Eve is 1 November – All Saints Day, a Holy Day of Obligation – and so attendance at Mass is compulsory.

a) *from seven to six*: Another omen: it is unpropitious to turn the hands of a clock backwards.

b) *she ... laid her best skirt out*: Joyce knew the Ben Jonson lyric:

Still to be neat, still to be drest,
As you were going to a feast;
Still to be powder'd, still perfum'd:
Lady, it is to be presumed,
Though art's hid causes are not found,
All is not sweet, all is not sound.

Yet another superstition is embedded here in the story: if a young girl's clothes are laid out on her bed, she will dream of her husband coming to turn them over.

c) *the mirror*: At moonrise on Halloween, it is said that a mirror will reflect the image of one's future husband. Maria, however, sees only herself.

d) *when she was a young girl*: Maria's age is never given, but she must at least be approaching sixty, and is perhaps older.

e) *quaint affection*: Of the undertone of the word 'quaint', Joyce was no less aware than was Edna O'Brien of 'country' in her novel *The Country Girls*, or than Shakespeare in Hamlet's mention (to Ophelia) of 'country matters'.

f) *her old brown waterproof*: Joyce by 1914 had amended this word from 1910's 'raincloak'. Flitting fairies at Halloween normally wear a magical cloak or mist which conveys invisibility. Maria is going to have difficulty being noticed in the cakeshops.

g) *The tram*: The Number 1 tram ran every five minutes from Ballsbridge to the Pillar, where Maria could change to the Number 8, from the Pillar to Drumcondra.

h) *facing all the people*: It is no good thing to travel north backwards as Maria is doing, particularly on this night of all nights! However, flowing water is a barrier against any pursuing evil spirits, so it is more auspicious that she will be crossing three – possibly four – bridges: Mount Street Bridge over the Grand Canal, O'Connell Bridge over the Liffey, Binns Bridge over the Royal Canal and first of all – depending where she boards her tram – Ball's Bridge over the Dodder.

i) *independent*: A strictly relative expression for an institutionalised spinster.

j) *nice evening*: Maria's overuse of the word 'nice' became a joke between James and Stanislaus. Just as Maria plays a variety of symbolic roles, so in its history 'nice' has had many different meanings. It comes from a Latin root (*nescio*: I do not know) and has at various times meant: foolish, flirtatious, wanton, trim (or extravagant) of dress, lazy, shy, uncommon, effeminate, luxurious, coy, fastidious, scrupulous, cultured, delicate, precise, subtle, full of danger or uncertainty, easily injured, pleasant, considerate, lucky and simply small. Many (though not all) of these meanings could be applied to Maria.

k) *Downes's cakeshop*: One of the shops owned by Sir Joseph Downes, JP, TC, of 25 Eccles Street, merchant, baker, confectioner, and restaurateur. This, his major outlet, was at 5 and 6 on the south side of North Earl Street, which runs from the Pillar east off O'Connell Street. Downes (1848–1925) was in 1900 High Sheriff of Dublin and was knighted in honour of Queen Victoria's visit to Ireland in that year. He became known to Dubliners as 'Lord Barmbrack'. Maria's low opinion of the plumcake may be inspired by Joyce's low opinion of the man (111g).

l) *it was a long time*: As was the case with Little Chandler in 'A Little Cloud', small (or passive) people have difficulty attracting attention.

m) *apples and nuts*: Traditional Halloween fare (and, incidentally, for those who seek ironic references to Maria's sterility, containers of fertile seeds).

n) *plumcake*: A dark cake of the sort used for Christmas and weddings, containing sultanas and other preserved fruit, though not plums. Originally prunes had probably been an ingredient, which would explain the name.

o) *Henry Street*: Like Earl and Moore Streets, this is named after Henry, First Earl of Drogheda. (Before it was Sackville Street, O'Connell Street was called Drogheda Street.) Maria crosses O'Connell Street and heads west down Henry Street, beside the General Post Office. Harrison and Co at No 17 specialised in 'Christmas Cakes, Plum Puddings & Shortbreads' and advertised 'A fully-matured stock of cake always on hand made only of the best materials'. When she catches the next tram to complete her northward journey, Maria will have made the sign of the cross at the very centre of Dublin.

p) *was it wedding-cake*: Maria does not notice that the young lady, in commenting on her unmarried and unmarriageable state, is being caustic. Given her stylishness and offhandedness, the shopgirl has a counterpart at the end of 'Araby'.

q) *Two-and-four*: Two shillings and fourpence. As ever, plumcake was expensive.

r) *an elderly gentleman*: A likely model is Joyce's own father, John Joyce. The description is accurate, and it seems that the 'elderly gentleman', who had been

of the alarm from seven to six. Then she took off her working
skirt and her house-boots and laid her best skirt out on the bed
and her tiny dress-boots beside the foot of the bed. She changed
her blouse too and, as she stood before the mirror, she thought
of how she used to dress for mass on Sunday morning when
she was a young girl; and she looked with quaint affection at
the diminutive body which she had so often adorned. In spite
of its years she found it a nice tidy little body.

When she got outside the streets were shining with rain and
she was glad of her old brown waterproof. The tram was full
and she had to sit on the little stool at the end of the car, facing
all the people, with her toes barely touching the floor. She
arranged in her mind all she was going to do and thought how
much better it was to be independent and to have your own
money in your pocket. She hoped they would have a nice
evening. She was sure they would but she could not help
thinking what a pity it was Alphy and Joe were not speaking.
They were always falling out now but when they were boys
together they used to be the best of friends: but such was life.

She got out of her tram at the Pillar and ferreted her way
quickly among the crowds. She went into Downes's cakeshop
but the shop was so full of people that it was a long time before
she could get herself attended to. She bought a dozen of mixed
penny cakes, and at last came out of the shop laden with a big
bag. Then she thought what else would she buy: she wanted
to buy something really nice. They would be sure to have
plenty of apples and nuts. It was hard to know what to buy
and all she could think of was cake. She decided to buy some
plumcake, but Downes's plumcake had not enough almond
icing on top of it so she went over to a shop in Henry Street.
Here she was a long time in suiting herself and the stylish
young lady behind the counter, who was evidently a little
annoyed by her, asked her was it wedding-cake she wanted to
buy. That made Maria blush and smile at the young lady; but
the young lady took it all very seriously and finally cut a thick
slice of plumcake, parcelled it up and said:

—Two-and-four, please—

She thought she would have to stand in the Drumcondra
tram because none of the young men seemed to notice her but
an elderly gentleman made room for her. He was a stout
gentleman and he wore a brown hard hat; he had a square red

drinking, did not actually give up his seat for Maria, but merely 'made room'. This seedy courtesy seems to fit John Joyce, whose presence and humour – despite his personal faults – fill his son's prose to an extent often underestimated.

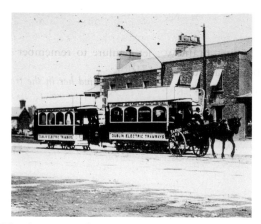

The change to mechanisation. This is not a long horse-drawn vehicle, but two electric trams being overtaken by an 'outsider'

An Irish-made 'porous rainproof' (90f)

a) *a colonel-looking gentleman*: He is not in uniform. There has never been a shortage of army officers from Ireland in the British army. Wellington is the most famous, but there were also Sir Garnet Wolseley, Commander-in-Chief (1895–1900), and many others.

b) *hems*: Nothing to do with her clothes – Maria is being nasally noncommittal.

c) *the Canal Bridge*: This is Binns Bridge over the Royal Canal, on the Drumcondra Road.

d) *along the terrace*: The house seems to be close to the Royal Canal, and Maria's destination was probably in Whitworth Terrace or Whitworth Road, right or left at the bridge, though Joyce may have had Verbena House (88p) in mind, as it was just around the corner at the end of a row of houses called Maria Villas.

e) *a drop taken*: Dublin synecdoche – a part for the whole.

f) *O, here's Maria!*: The first name heard on a Halloween journey is said to be that of one's future husband. Maria hears only her own. Joyce's careful punctuation suggests that her welcome is unenthusiastic, the exclamation mark being more than set off by the comma.

g) *games were going on*: Traditionally these might include ducking for apples, or trying to bite suspended apples without using one's hands.

h) *the bag of cakes*: It was a good omen to bring cakes and buns to a household on Halloween. Joyce was not himself averse to observing similar superstitions: Stanislaus describes his brother one New Year's Eve throwing a loaf of bread in through the front door of their house in Cabra.

i) *the eldest boy, Alphy*: This is not Joe's brother Alphy, but his son, so Joe named his son after his brother – a detail that emphasises the current rift.

j) *Mrs Donnelly*: Joe's wife. John Murray's wife's name was Lillie, whom the Joyces thought rather common.

k) *nowhere could she find it*: The favourable review of *Dubliners* in the *Times Literary Supplement* (Waterloo Day 1914) states that Maria

> – a capable washerwoman – falls an easy prey to a rogue on a tramcar and is cozened out of the little present she was taking to her family

but this interpretation seems unkind, particularly if we are to identify the rogue with John Joyce. She could have left it in the shop, or the plumcake could have been hidden or stolen from the hallstand by

face and a greyish moustache. Maria thought he was a colonel-

a looking gentleman and she reflected how much more polite he was than the young men who simply stared straight before them. The gentleman began to chat with her about Hallow Eve and the rainy weather. He supposed the bag was full of good things for the little ones and said it was only right that the youngsters should enjoy themselves while they were young. Maria agreed with him and favoured him with demure nods

b and hems. He was very nice with her and, when she was getting

c out at the Canal Bridge she thanked him and bowed, and he bowed to her and raised his hat and smiled agreeably; and

d while she was going up along the terrace, bending her tiny head under the rain, she thought how easy it was to know a

e gentleman even when he has a drop taken.

f Everybody said: O, here's Maria! when she came to Joe's house. Joe was there, having come home from business, and all the children had their Sunday dresses on. There were two

g big girls in from next door and games were going on. Maria

hi gave the bag of cakes to the eldest boy, Alphy, to divide and

j Mrs Donnelly said it was too good of her to bring such a big bag of cakes and made all the children say:

—Thanks, Maria—

But Maria said she had brought something special for papa and mamma, something they would be sure to like, and she began to look for her plumcake. She tried in Downes's bag and then in the pockets of her waterproof and then on the

k hallstand but nowhere could she find it. Then she asked all the children had any of them eaten it – by mistake, of course – but the children all said no and looked as if they did not like to eat cakes if they were to be accused of stealing. Everybody had a solution for the mystery and Mrs Donnelly said it was plain

l that Maria had left it behind her in the tram. Maria, remembering how confused the gentleman with the greyish moustache had made her, coloured with shame and vexation and

m disappointment. At the thought of the failure of her little surprise and of the two and fourpence she had thrown away for nothing she nearly cried outright.

But Joe said it didn't matter and made her sit down by the

n fire. He was very nice with her. He told her all that went on

o in his office, repeating for her a smart answer which he had made to the manager. Maria did not understand why Joe

one of the big next-door girls, who seem somewhat mischievous. The loss of this parcel parallels Little Chandler's failure to remember his (71j).

l) *left it behind her in the tram*: Unless Maria contrived to use the parcel as a footrest, there wasn't room for it to leave her lap. The mystery remains.

m) *shame and vexation and disappointment*: These emotions are also felt at the end of 'An Encounter', 'Araby' and 'A Little Cloud'.

n) *sit down by the fire*: Another witch-like pose.

o) *repeating for her a smart answer*: Farrington in 'Counterparts' has a similar habit (81(o)).

St Alphonsus Road, Fairview, looking towards Maria Villas and Verbena House (88p and 91d)

A contemporary stage-Irish representation of emigration

a) *rub him the wrong way*: Irritate him, as when stroking a cat from tail to head. Maria promptly rubs him the wrong way in the next paragraph.

b) *how did they expect Maria to crack nuts without a nutcracker*: Having already twice said that her nose almost touched her chin, it is unnecessary for Joyce to inform the reader that there were giggles when Joe makes this remark. Of Joyce in Dublin it was once said that 'that fella has a chin like a nutcracker'.

c) *port wine*: Port: a shabby-genteel expression still in use in rural Ireland.

d) *Joe insisted*: Maria has a dread of Joe's drinking. Both Murray brothers were heavy drinkers.

e) *a good word for Alphy*: Again Maria's well-intentioned efforts are about to go badly wrong. This is beginning to look like culpable carelessness.

f) *no brother of his*: Joe and Alphy are in a long tradition of fraternal strife that includes Cain and Abel, Jacob and Esau – and Jim and Stannie Joyce, with their fictional counterparts Shem the Penman and Shaun the Post in *FW*.

g) *there was nearly being a row*: Another of the many childish or colloquial usages in the story's narrative voice: this is Maria speaking.

h) *on the head of it*: As a result of the conversation.

i) *some saucers*: They are setting up a traditional Halloween divination game. Common elements in the saucers included a prayer-book, water, a ring, a coin and, frequently, clay. In this game no coin is mentioned, suggesting that there is to be no possibility of wealth for anyone.

j) *the prayer-book*: Touching this prophesies a life in the church, as a 'religious'.

k) *the water*: This signifies emigration, or sometimes a life at sea. For any family of children in Dublin at the time, this proportion (three out of four) of likely emigrants is no exaggeration.

l) *the ring*: For marriage, as at 89i.

m) *blindfolding Maria*: She is the only adult who joins in the play with the children, or is asked to.

n) *laughed and laughed again*: For the last time, the image of the cackling old witch. One is reminded of Shakespeare's three witches: 'Thrice to thine, and thrice to mine, and thrice again, to make up nine' (*Macbeth* I.iii). Several readers have commented on the possible role of numerology in 'Clay', some seeing everything in pairs, and some noticing threes. It is certainly true that Maria is the last of nine to arrive at the Donnelly's, and she is one of nine mentioned in the laundry. Nine was a number used by the Romans for exorcism, and there were nine rivers in Hell. There are even nine letters in

laughed so much over the answer he had made but she said that the manager must have been a very overbearing person to deal with. Joe said he wasn't so bad when you knew how to take him, that he was a decent sort so long as you didn't rub him the wrong way. Mrs Donnelly played the piano for the children and they danced and sang. Then the two next-door girls handed round the nuts. Nobody could find the nutcrackers and Joe was nearly getting cross over it and asked how did they expect Maria to crack nuts without a nutcracker. But Maria said she didn't like nuts and that they weren't to bother about her. Then Joe asked would she take a bottle of stout and Mrs Donnelly said there was port wine too in the house if she would prefer that. Maria said she would rather they didn't ask her to take anything: but Joe insisted.

So Maria let him have his way and they sat by the fire talking over old times and Maria thought she would put in a good word for Alphy. But Joe cried that God might strike him stone dead if ever he spoke a word to his brother again and Maria said she was sorry she had mentioned the matter. Mrs Donnelly told her husband it was a great shame for him to speak that way of his own flesh and blood but Joe said that Alphy was no brother of his and there was nearly being a row on the head of it. But Joe said he would not lose his temper on account of the night it was and asked his wife to open some more stout. The two next-door girls had arranged some Hallow Eve games and soon everything was merry again. Maria was delighted to see the children so merry and Joe and his wife in such good spirits. The next-door girls put some saucers on the table and then led the children up to the table, blindfold. One got the prayer-book and the other three got the water; and when one of the next-door girls got the ring Mrs Donnelly shook her finger at the blushing girl as much as to say: *O, I know all about it!* They insisted then on blindfolding Maria and leading her up to the table to see what she would get; and, while they were putting on the bandage, Maria laughed and laughed again till the tip of her nose nearly met the tip of her chin.

They led her up to the table amid laughing and joking and she put her hand out in the air as she was told to do. She moved her hand about here and there in the air and descended on one of the saucers. She felt a soft wet substance with her fingers and was surprised that nobody spoke or took off her bandage.

'Dubliners'. However, although such speculation may encourage the closer reading of the text, which is always valuable, it is doubtful that much encoding was intended by Joyce in these stories.

o) *a soft wet substance*: The clay of the title, which means death within a year. In the Victorian period the game was sanitised, and the clay was often omitted from the game.

Ball's Bridge over the Dodder, with perhaps the only known photograph of Maria's laundry, whose chimneys can be glimpsed over the right-hand arch

Miss McCloud's Reel (b)

a) *it was wrong*: Maria blithely evades the question as to who, if anyone, is to blame.

b) *Miss McCloud's Reel*: A traditional Irish tune. In November 1906 Joyce wrote from Rome to his Aunt Josephine Murray to find out how to spell 'Miss McCleod's (?) Reel'. His aunt helped him on many points of detail for this and subsequent books.

c) *before the year was out*: i.e. within twelve months, or the ancient Celtic Year which ran from that very midnight; alternatively, before the end of the modern calendar year, exactly two months away. The real Maria, upon whom Joyce based his character, died between Halloween and the New Year.

d) *I Dreamt that I Dwelt*: A famous song by Balfe from *The Bohemian Girl* (31h), recalling Eveline. It is bad luck not to finish any song, but this is worse. From an old encyclopaedia of superstitions comes the following:

> One of the most disturbing of superstitions is the playing of 'I Dreamt I Dwelt' in a musical show except in the light opera for which it is written. It is held that such playing will bring bad luck to the orchestra pit, and also to the musical show on stage at that time.

e) *she sang again*: That is, she sang the first verse twice. It is a matter for speculation whether Maria has forgotten the second verse, or whether she has realised how ironically inappropriate to her celibate and unwanted situation it is. Verse two:

> I dreamt that suitors sought my hand,
> That knights upon bended knee,
> And with vows no maiden heart could withstand,
> That they pledged their faith to me.
> And I dreamt that one of this noble host,
> Came forth my heart to claim;
> Yet I also dreamt, which charmed me most,
> That you lov'd me still the same.

f) *poor old Balfe*: Joe's remark is pure boozy maudlin indulgence. In fact Balfe was never very poor or very old. He died (1870) in his early sixties and tablets were put up to him in Westminster Abbey and Drury Lane Theatre. His greatest success, the opera *The Bohemian Girl*, was written for Drury Lane. The failure of Dublin to put up a statue to Balfe (as promised) led to a sardonic suggestion for its inscription: 'I dreamt that I dwelt in marble'.

There was a pause for a few seconds; and then a great deal of scuffling and whispering. Somebody said something about the garden, and at last Mrs Donnelly said something very cross to one of the next-door girls and told her to throw it out at once:

a that was no play. Maria understood that it was wrong that time and so she had to do it over again: and this time she got the prayer-book.

b After that Mrs Donnelly played Miss McCloud's Reel for the children and Joe made Maria take a glass of wine. Soon they were all quite merry again and Mrs Donnelly said Maria

c would enter a convent before the year was out because she had got the prayer-book. Maria had never seen Joe so nice to her as he was that night, so full of pleasant talk and reminiscences. She said they were all very good to her.

At last the children grew tired and sleepy and Joe asked Maria would she not sing some little song before she went, one of the old songs. Mrs Donnelly said *Do, please, Maria!* and so Maria had to get up and stand beside the piano. Mrs Donnelly bade the children be quiet and listen to Maria's song. Then she played the prelude and said *Now Maria!* and Maria, blushing very much, began to sing in a tiny quavering voice. She sang

d *I Dreamt that I Dwelt*, and when she came to the second verse

e she sang again:

> *I dreamt that I dwelt in marble halls*
> *With vassals and serfs at my side*
> *And of all who assembled within those walls*
> *That I was the hope and the pride.*
> *I had riches too great to count, could boast*
> *Of a high ancestral name,*
> *But I also dreamt, which pleased me most,*
> *That you loved me still the same.*

But no one tried to show her her mistake, and when she had ended her song Joe was very much moved. He said that there was no time like the long ago and no music for him like poor

f old Balfe, whatever other people might say; and his eyes filled up so much with tears that he could not find what he was looking for and in the end he had to ask his wife to tell him

g where the corkscrew was.

g) *where the corkscrew was*: Only at the end of this long twisting sentence do we learn of a third Halloween absence (after the lost plumcake and nutcracker). It could be suggested that the missing corkscrew is actually in the very centre of Dublin – the spiral staircase running to the top of Nelson's Pillar (symbol of the city), around which Maria bustles in her quest for cakes and the No 8 tram. But Joe is no longer sober, and his connection with Whitsuntide (88q) brings again to mind the Acts of the Apostles (II.12–13):

> And they were all amazed, and were in doubt, saying one to another, What meaneth this? Others mocking said, These men are full of new wine.

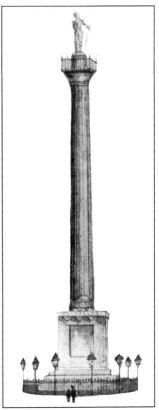

93

Afterword: 'CLAY'

'Clay' was the fourth story of the collection to be written, after 'The Sisters', 'Eveline' and 'After the Race'. It began life as 'Christmas Eve', in which the main characters were to include Mr Callanan, based on Joyce's uncle, William Murray, and his daughter – who bore the name Katsey both in real life and in the unfinished story. However, Joyce recast the narrative, telling the tale from Maria's point of view, and using John Murray, William's brother, as the basis for the main male character. This later version was originally called 'Hallow Eve'.

In January 1905, while Joyce was living in Pola (now Pula), then in Austria, the story was almost in its final form. He tried to have it published in the *Irish Homestead*, but it was turned down, probably by AE, and he was no more successful with other periodicals: by the following October, Joyce was fulminating in a letter to Stanislaus that 'the cursedly stupid ape' that ran the journal, '*The LITERARY World*' had neither acknowledged nor returned the manuscript. He revised the story again in 1906, adding among other things the name of the laundry, which, he wrote to his brother in November 1906, was 'such a gentle way of putting it'. Stanislaus was baffled, so Joyce patiently explained that the phrase *Dublin by Lamplight* meant that the city at night was a 'wicked place full of wicked and lost women whom a kindly committee gathers together for the good work of washing my dirty shirts'.

'Clay' is the most sustained example of several in *Dubliners* of what has been called the 'Free Indirect Style'. Although the story is not told by Maria, its tone and language are strongly affected by her, and reflect her own self-esteem and limitations. The words roll out in a blank, breathless, ill-punctuated stream, far from the Flaubertian cadences elsewhere in the book. The narrative appears to slip seamlessly in and out of Maria's mind without making any overt judgments, but in fact judgments are made and ironies abound. All the other characters are seen through the anodyne medium of Maria, who seems unwilling to face the fact that not everything is perfect. She hardly notices that the 'stylish young lady' in the cake-shop in Henry Street is unpleasant to her, or that she – the 'peace-maker' – is the cause of anger in Joe, Mrs Donnelly and the children.

Maria literally wears the blindfold during the Halloween game, and metaphorically it is in place throughout the story. Reliance is thus placed on the reader to work out what is really going on, a technique that would later be used in Molly Keane's novel, *Good Behaviour* (1981), and in many Modernist and post-Modernist works of fiction. It is significant, to take another simple example, that Maria in her invincible ignorance does not realise what her first choice in the divination game portends, nor even, it seems, what precisely the saucer contains. This information, the only substantive element of the story that is known to the reader but not necessarily to Maria, has to be given in the title.

As well as being the 'soft wet substance' which has something to do with the garden, clay has obvious connotations of the grave – recalling Byron's poem that was so admired by Little Chandler in 'A Little Cloud':

Within this narrow cell reclines her clay,
That clay where once . . .

Clay is also, of course, the material from which mankind is ultimately made. Various punning meanings have been discerned in the word (French *clef*, 'key'; German *Klee*, 'clover', 'shamrock'), but the most convincing echo is in the Irish *clé*, which is primarily a word of direction, meaning 'left'. It shares with the Latin word *sinister* a strong suggestion of evil or 'wrongness' – 'Maria understood that it was wrong that time'. Dinneen's *Irish-English Dictionary* in addition gives *ar clé* (literally, 'on the left') meaning 'neglected' – suitably, for Maria's fate is to be 'left' on the shelf. The opposite direction in Irish to *clé* is *deas*, meaning 'right'. This too has subsidiary meanings in Dinneen, including 'pretty', 'expert', 'proper' and Maria's favourite word, 'nice', which occurs eleven times in the story.

Lefthandedness and its significances are far from being the only superstitions in 'Clay'. All the paraphysical paraphernalia of Halloween (well described by the critic Cóilín Owens) have a thematic place in the story as well, as indicated in the notes. These folk traditions help bind Maria to the past, when things were much better – although, as we have seen, she hardly acknowledges that they are worse now. She is a creature of habit, 'accustomed to the life of the laundry'. Even her purse, which she must see every day, assumes a talismanic importance. As she reads 'again' the inscription '*A Present from Belfast*', it reminds her of a time when Joe and Alphy were 'the best of friends'. Now, Joe says that Alphy is 'no brother of his', where previously he had said 'Maria is my proper mother'. Truly there has been a 'break-up at home'.

Finally, the story is a study of incompleteness. The family is incomplete. The refreshments are incomplete. Even the story is incomplete. More importantly, the language and the lifestyle of Maria conspire to suggest that she has never completely grown up. Sexually unfulfilled, although surrounded in the laundry by the loose women of Dublin, Maria is not even bold enough to face the fact that there is no hope of her ever having 'any ring or man either'. Accordingly, the romantic and plaintive song she sings is also incomplete, and the verse – telling of gallant and imploring suitors – is evaded. In any case, even the first verse is no more than a dream. In Browning's vast poem, *The Ring and the Book*, Pompilia leaves a convent and soon meets her death. Maria, who will never get the ring, finally gets the prayer-book, indicative not only of her convent-like life in the institution, but also of the funeral service that will at last unite, for a time at least, the estranged brothers. Joe has said that 'God might strike him stone dead if he ever spoke a word to his brother again', but, if Joe does, it will be Maria, not he, who is dead.

a) A PAINFUL CASE: See 100c.

b) *Mr James Duffy*: As Joyce knew, this was also the name of J. C. Mangan's Dublin publisher, who died in 1871 (though the firm continued to flourish). According to Stanislaus, however, the name was taken from the less-distinguished Pisser Duffy. The surname is derived from the Irish *dubh*, 'black' (as in Dublin itself). The character was based on Stanislaus, and his visit to a concert provided the initial basis of the story. Flann O'Brien wrote a parody, 'John Duffy's Brother', in which John Duffy dies on the day of his birth. His unnamed brother wakes up one morning in his room in Chapelizod and, believing that he is a train, steams into his office.

c) *Chapelizod*: Even in Mr Duffy's day the old garrison village was distinct from Dublin, three miles east, further down the Liffey. Now it is one of its more historic suburbs. It is named after Izod (Isolde), the Celtic princess who died for love of Tristan. Residents of Chapelizod have included Lord Harmsworth (12c), and Parnell's enemy Tim Healy KC, MP (132a). The incumbent of the church behind Mr Duffy's house at this time was the Rev. Amyrald Dancer Purefoy MA – another indication (as with Henry Flower) that Joyce's imagination, however excellent, was not what it might seem when it came to writing about the world around him.

d) *an old sombre house*: In the MS, 'an old gawky house'. The house is still there, and is still both gawky and sombre. It is the eponymous house of the Gothic novel by Sheridan Le Fanu (187a), *The House by the Churchyard* (1863), much featured in *FW*.

e) *disused distillery*: This was once the Dublin and Chapelizod Distillery Company, of which John Joyce became Secretary. It was later known as the Phoenix Park Distillery. The property had previously housed a barracks and a silk mill. (Mulberry trees abounded in Chapelizod (167j).) Talking to Cranly (in *P* V.3), Stephen says of his father that he was ' ... somebody's secretary, something in a distillery ... '.

f) *cane chairs*: They are also stipulated in the second act of *Michael Kramer* (m). The whole passage has a similarity to contemporary stage directions.

g) *a double desk*: A box with a sloping hinged lid.

h) *white bed-clothes and a black and scarlet rug*: These, the only colours in this paragraph, are painted with a care that justifies a symbolic reading: purity, sexual passion, blood, death. 'The mirror and the lamp' were used to connote mimesis and inspiration respectively in M. H. Abrams' work of that name on Romanticism.

i) *during the day a white-shaded lamp*: Possibly something is put beside it at night. More likely, in combination with the mirror, there is a whiff of autoeroticism. In *FW* (21) Jarl van Hoother is described 'high up in his lamphouse, laying cold hands on himself' (96b).

j) *Wordsworth*: William Wordsworth (1770–1850), the epitome of the Romantic poet, who in his wild youth fathered an illegitimate child in Revolutionary Paris. Joyce ranked him with Shakespeare and Shelley (in May 1905) as the greatest of writers. Outstanding though his best work is, however, Wordsworth produced little of worth after he was thirty, and he came to represent dull respectability.

k) Maynooth Catechism: The pantheism of the poet contrasts with the hidden Catholicism of the catechism, kept literally under wraps.

l) *Hauptmann*: Gerhart Hauptmann (1862–1946), German writer. In the summer of 1901, Joyce translated his *Vor Sonnenaufgang* – the first version in English, though unpublished until 1978. He is mentioned in *P* (V.1), when Convent Avenue (where Joyce lived in 1899) evokes for Stephen memories of the playwright's female characters.

m) Michael Kramer: Joyce is said to have attempted a translation, though there remains some doubt about this. Michael Kramer is beset by philistines and achieves a degree of freedom only after his son kills himself. Duffy and Kramer are similar: isolated and aloof. To be an artist one must be a 'true hermit'. Both are incapable of love. Hauptmann's play (159l) is mentioned in 'The Day of the Rabblement'.

n) *purple ink*: The first colour in the story that is not scarlet, black, or white.

o) Bile Beans: Joyce's name for Stanislaus' diary. The reference is to the traditional theory of bodily humours: phlegm, choler, blood and black bile (which indicated a melancholy temperament

A PAINFUL CASE

MR JAMES DUFFY lived in Chapelizod because he wished to live as far as possible from the city of which he was a citizen and because he found all the other suburbs of Dublin mean, modern and pretentious. He lived in an old sombre house, and from his windows he could look into the disused distillery or upwards along the shallow river on which Dublin is built. The lofty walls of his uncarpeted room were free from pictures. He had himself bought every article of furniture in the room: a black iron bedstead, an iron washstand, four cane chairs, a clothes-rack, a coal-scuttle, a fender and irons and a square table on which lay a double desk. A bookcase had been made in an alcove by means of shelves of white wood. The bed was clothed with white bed-clothes and a black and scarlet rug covered the foot. A little hand-mirror hung above the washstand and during the day a white-shaded lamp stood as the sole ornament of the mantelpiece. The books on the white wooden shelves were arranged from below upwards according to bulk. A complete Wordsworth stood at one end of the lowest shelf and a copy of the *Maynooth Catechism*, sewn into the cloth cover of a notebook, stood at one end of the top shelf. Writing materials were always on the desk. In the desk lay a manuscript translation of Hauptmann's *Michael Kramer*, the stage directions of which were written in purple ink, and a little sheaf of papers held together by a brass pin. In these sheets a sentence was inscribed from time to time and, in an ironical moment, the headline of an advertisement for *Bile Beans* had been pasted on to the first sheet. On lifting the lid of the desk a faint fragrance escaped – the fragrance of new cedarwood pencils or of a bottle of gum or of an over-ripe apple which might have been left there and forgotten.

Mr Duffy abhorred anything which betokened physical or mental disorder. A mediæval doctor would have called him saturnine. His face, which carried the entire tale of his years, was of the brown tint of Dublin streets. On his long and rather large head grew dry black hair and a tawny moustache did not quite cover an unamiable mouth. His cheekbones also gave his

(62m)). Joyce used to parody the 'biliousness' of Stanislaus' writing, along the lines of:

> Sometimes I do be thinkin', goin' along the road, etc.

p) *a faint fragrance*: An ironic suggestion of the Song of Solomon, where cedars, myrrh, pomegranates, frankincense and apples provide an odoriferous background to an erotic hymn to love.

q) *an over-ripe apple*: Friedrich von Schiller, the German Romantic writer, liked to work at a table that was deeply impregnated with the smell of apples.

r) *saturnine*: Richard Burton, in *The Anatomy of Melancholy* (1621), defines the word:

> If Saturn be predominant in his Nativity and cause melancholy in his temperature then he shall be very austere, churlish, black of colour, profound in his cogitations, full of cares, miseries and discontents, sad and tearful, always silent, solitary, still delighting in ... Rivers ... dark Walks ...

Burton goes on to say that music (beloved by Duffy) is

> a Sovereign remedy against Despair and Melancholy.

Stanislaus in his diary claimed sympathy with Jonathan Swift on the grounds that he fully understood much in his sullen and saturnine character.

a) *a redeeming instinct in others*: Originally 'in the lives his soul spurned'.

b) *a little distance from his body . . . doubtful side-glances*: Possibly the signs of a deep alienation, or perhaps a hint of Mr Duffy's possible practices with rug, lamp and mirror – practices mentioned generally by Stephen to Madden in *SH*. There is also a hint of Dickens' Mr Pecksniff about Mr Duffy: in Chapter III of *Martin Chuzzlewit*, that hypocrite is described warming his hands at the fire 'as benevolently as if they were someone else's, not his'.

c) *a short sentence about himself*: Among Joyce's books was an 1893 copy of Jerome K. Jerome's *Novel Notes*, with the telling inscription 'Stolen from Stanislaus Joyce by the present owner'. Either brother might have written it.

d) *a subject in the third person*: The detail reflects the impersonality of Joyce in his own fiction. *SH*, for example, takes its title from *Turpin Hero*, an eighteenth-century ballad that begins in the first person and ends in the third. So too do *D, P* and *U* go in the opposite directions. The implication is that Mr Duffy has written this story. Giambattista Vico, who is the central structural influence on *FW*, wrote his autobiography in the third person.

e) *a stout hazel*: A walking-stick, one traditionally carried by Irish poets, and also a useful deterrent against ruffians.

f) *a private bank*: The Irish Industrial Benefit Building Society was at No 108 Lower Baggot Street, almost opposite Dan Burke's (i).

g) *Baggot Street*: See 43j.

h) *by tram*: See 14d.

i) *Dan Burke's*: Daniel Burke and Co., family grocers and wine merchants, 50 Lower Baggot Street.

j) *lager beer*: Then an exotic and fairly rare drink in Ireland, but not the only sign of a continental predilection in Edwardian Dublin.

k) *arrowroot biscuits*: Arrowroot is an edible starch, obtained from the plant Maranta. It gets its name from the use of the tubers to counter the effect of poisoned arrows. Duffy might be using it as a prophylactic against Cupid's dart. Joyce's interest in the Italian thinker Ferrero (52), meanwhile, extended to exploring the latter's recherché theory that biscuits could be works of art.

l) *an eating-house*: The likeliest venue for Mr Duffy's custom seems to be the modest 'Refreshment Rooms' of R. Ross & Co at No 49.

m) *George's Street*: i.e. South Great George's Street (49k). This street was named after Saint George (because of the church there since 1233). North Great George's Street was a good distance away, near Belvedere College.

n) *gilded youth*: Like 'dissipations' at the end of the paragraph, this is a strictly relative expression. But Mr Duffy is growing old, and has never been a member of any *jeunesse dorée*.

Stanislaus' Rotunda couple (s)

face a harsh character; but there was no harshness in the eyes which, looking at the world from under their tawny eyebrows, gave the impression of a man ever alert to greet a redeeming instinct in others but often disappointed. He lived at a little distance from his body, regarding his own acts with doubtful side-glances. He had an odd autobiographical habit which led him to compose in his mind from time to time a short sentence about himself containing a subject in the third person and a predicate in the past tense. He never gave alms to beggars and walked firmly, carrying a stout hazel.

He had been for many years cashier of a private bank in Baggot Street. Every morning he came in from Chapelizod by tram. At midday he went to Dan Burke's and took his lunch – a bottle of lager beer and a small trayful of arrowroot biscuits. At four o'clock he was set free. He dined in an eating-house in George's Street where he felt himself safe from the society of Dublin's gilded youth and where there was a certain plain honesty in the bill of fare. His evenings were spent either before his landlady's piano or roaming about the outskirts of the city. His liking for Mozart's music brought him sometimes to an opera or a concert: these were the only dissipations of his life.

He had neither companions nor friends, church nor creed. He lived his spiritual life without any communion with others, visiting his relatives at Christmas and escorting them to the cemetery when they died. He performed these two social duties for old dignity's sake but conceded nothing further to the conventions which regulate the civic life. He allowed himself to think that in certain circumstances he would rob his bank but, as these circumstances never arose, his life rolled out evenly – an adventureless tale.

One evening he found himself sitting beside two ladies in the Rotunda. The house, thinly peopled and silent, gave distressing prophecy of failure. The lady who sat next him looked round at the deserted house once or twice and then said:

—What a pity there is such a poor house to-night! It's so hard on people to have to sing to empty benches—

He took the remark as an invitation to talk. He was surprised that she seemed so little awkward. While they talked he tried to fix her permanently in his memory. When he learned that

member of any *jeunesse dorée*.

o) *roaming about the outskirts*: There is an intentionally chaste contrast with the urban meanderings of Little Chandler.

p) *Mozart's music*: Its reputation at the time was far less high than it is almost a century later.

q) *escorting them to the cemetery*: A relationship with Mr Duffy appears to presuppose death. The point will be borne out later.

r) *in certain circumstances*: They are never defined.

s) *the Rotunda*: A round concert hall and theatre (now occupied by the Ambassador cinema). It was part of the maternity hospital of the same name – the oldest in the British Isles, founded in 1745. Both Bloom and Stephen have memories of visiting it. The Master of the hospital for many years was Richard Dancer Purefoy (95c), who lived in Merrion Square. One starting point of this story is Stanislaus' 1901 recollection in *MBK*:

> I went alone to a concert in the Rotunda given by Clara Butt and her husband, Kennerley Rumford . . .

t) *What a pity . . .*: This is the only direct dialogue in the story. (The two lines from the inquest later are reported.) The next story, 'Ivy Day in the Committee Room', is in stark contrast.

u) *so little awkward*: Such casual conversation, without an introduction, was not socially unremarkable, but Mr Duffy seems not to meet many women.

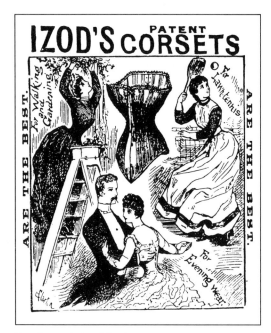

For the strait-laced (95c)

a) *which must have been handsome*: Note the tense. Josie Breen in *U*, 'Lestrygonians' is similarly appraised. It can be calculated that Mr Duffy and Mrs Sinico are just on opposite sides of forty.

b) *a deliberate swoon ...*: 'Swoon' was a favourite word of Joyce's. In the eighteenth century pupils had been enlarged by – perhaps appropriately – belladonna. The condition (artificial or not) was and is well-known as a symptom of attraction.

c) *Earlsfort Terrace*: The street meets the south-east corner of Stephen's Green. The concert room was in the Dublin International Exhibition Centre. It later became the Grand Hall of University College, and is now the National Concert Hall.

d) *Mrs Sinico*: Though frequently tortured for significance (*sine coitus, sine* communion, sin, cynical etc), the name was taken from Joyce's music teacher in Trieste. See also 104 for another musical Mrs Sinico in Dublin. Joyce excised from a draft the near-Triestine explanation:

> Her husband's great-great-grandfather had come from Udine.

e) *Leghorn*: In the eighteenth century it was the major port of Italy's west coast, and had several colonies of merchants – e.g. Jewish, Italian, English, Scottish. Shelley made his last voyage from here in 1822. Even the British now tend to know the town as Livorno.

f) *a mercantile boat plying between Dublin and Holland*: Steam communication between Rotterdam, Dublin and Belfast at this time was done by Palgrave, Murphy & Co, 17 Eden Quay, who had four boats and four captains.

g) *dismissed ... from his gallery of pleasures*: The elegant euphemism indicates the Sinicos' *mariage blanc*. It is typical of Joyce's quiet irony in these stories. A later example in 'A Mother' mentions Miss Devlin sitting 'amid the chilly circle of her accomplishments'.

h) *daughter out giving music lessons*: Mary Sinico is almost certainly a graduate of the Royal Irish Academy of Music (123c), as are some others in these stories.

i) *incongruity*: Mrs Sinico is in an incongruent triangle. Joyce possibly knew John Donne's lines from 'The First Anniversary':

> She, whom after what form soe'er we see,
> Is discord and rude incongruity:
> She, she is dead, she's dead.

j) *assisted at the meetings*: The verb is used in its French sense of 'attended'.

the young girl beside her was her daughter he judged her to be a year or so younger than himself. Her face, which must have been handsome, had remained intelligent. It was an oval face with strongly marked features. The eyes were very dark blue and steady. Their gaze began with a defiant note but was confused by what seemed a deliberate swoon of the pupil into the iris, revealing for an instant a temperament of great sensibility. The pupil reasserted itself quickly, this half-disclosed nature fell again under the reign of prudence, and her astrakhan jacket, moulding a bosom of a certain fulness, struck the note of defiance more definitely.

He met her again a few weeks afterwards at a concert in Earlsfort Terrace and seized the moments when her daughter's attention was diverted to become intimate. She alluded once or twice to her husband but her tone was not such as to make the allusion a warning. Her name was Mrs Sinico. Her husband's great-great-grandfather had come from Leghorn. Her husband was captain of a mercantile boat plying between Dublin and Holland; and they had one child.

Meeting her a third time by accident he found courage to make an appointment. She came. This was the first of many meetings; they met always in the evening and chose the most quiet quarters for their walks together. Mr Duffy, however, had a distaste for underhand ways and, finding that they were compelled to meet stealthily, he forced her to ask him to her house. Captain Sinico encouraged his visits, thinking that his daughter's hand was in question. He had dismissed his wife so sincerely from his gallery of pleasures that he did not suspect that anyone else would take an interest in her. As the husband was often away and the daughter out giving music lessons, Mr Duffy had many opportunities of enjoying the lady's society. Neither he nor she had had any such adventure before and neither was conscious of any incongruity. Little by little he entangled his thoughts with hers. He lent her books, provided her with ideas, shared his intellectual life with her. She listened to all.

Sometimes in return for his theories she gave out some fact of her own life. With almost maternal solicitude she urged him to let his nature open to the full: she became his confessor. He told her that for some time he had assisted at the meetings of an Irish Socialist Party where he had felt himself a unique figure

k) *an Irish Socialist Party*: Not necessarily the movement of James Connolly, therefore (37b). Connolly had first come to Ireland in 1882, in the uniform of a soldier of the King's Liverpool Regiment, and was shot at Kilmainham Gaol (35d) in 1916 by the British military authorities. Michael Davitt (mentioned on the first page of *P*) was another activist of the period. He abandoned Fenianism for open agitation, and founded the Land League in Irishtown in 1879. In 1890 he launched 'Labour World' and also wrote *The Fall of Feudalism in Ireland* (1904) (63c).

a) *an inefficient oil-lamp*: This is probably the darkest and most nocturnal of all the stories in *D*. Even Mr Duffy's political ideas have the smell of the lamp.

b) *the party had divided*: According to Brendan Behan, the first item on the agenda of any new political movement in Ireland was the split. 'The year of the split' is a long-running and versatile joke. Connolly (97k) had a split in his Social-Democratic Federation in 1903, as he objected to money he had raised for the cause being spent on drink bills.

c) *timorous*: An archaic meaning of the word is 'passionate', paradoxically.

d) *interest … in … wages was inordinate*: Class satire by Joyce (as at 102e). Wages were a serious matter for those who were poorly paid. In 1899, for example, the going rate for labouring in the Dublin docks was £1/4s per sixty-hour week. One of the shipping companies paid £1/7s, but made no provision for overtime. When the dockers went on strike (for 4s/6d a day and 7d an hour overtime), English scabs were brought in. The strike failed after two weeks and the men were forced to settle on the pre-existing terms. In 1900 much the same thing happened again and there were many other disputes. It was a consideration for any potential striker that, as unemployment was so widespread, often he could not be sure of getting his job back.

e) *To compete with phrasemongers*: The sentiment recalls Stephen's comments to Madden in *SH*:

> You can use these phrases of the platform but I can't … I am an artist.

f) *morality to policemen and its fine arts to impresarios*: The phrase is similar to Dr Johnson's famous remark on Lord Chesterfield teaching the morals of a whore and the manners of a dancing-master. Chesterfield was for a short time Viceroy of Ireland (180d). During the Jacobite rebellion of 1745, Chesterfield's policy of toleration helped to spare Ireland from the crisis that engulfed Great Britain. Despite historical obloquy, Chesterfield deserves to be remembered for his observation that the poor people in Ireland were worse used than negroes by their lords and masters. In his later years, Chesterfield said of a friend and himself: 'X and I have been dead these two years, but we do not choose to have it known', a comment that perhaps anticipates Mr Duffy.

g) *her little cottage outside Dublin*: Sydney Parade is no longer outside Dublin, being just south of Ballsbridge.

h) *an exotic*: An exotic plant not yet acclimatised to its environment. J. Baxter's *Library of Practical Agriculture*, published during the Irish Famine, stated that

> potatoes were first … cultivated as a rare exotic.

i) *music that still vibrated*: For the first time, Mr Duffy might be listening to what Wordsworth called 'the still, sad music of humanity'.

j) *caught up his hand passionately*: The earlier of the manuscript versions of the story has:

> …Mrs Sinico threw her arms ~~round~~ forward into his lap and seemed to faint.

k) *their ruined confessional*: Mr Duffy's displaced religiosity is emphasised. This is Mrs Sinico's home, and her distress recalls Father Flynn.

l) *cakeshop near the Parkgate*: William O'Connor at the Post Office on Parkgate Street also sold confectionery, near the main entrance to the Phoenix Park, the Upper Cavalry Gate.

amidst a score of sober workmen in a garret lit by an inefficient oil-lamp. When the party had divided into three sections, each under its own leader and in its own garret, he had discontinued his attendances. The workmen's discussions, he said, were too timorous; the interest they took in the question of wages was inordinate. He felt that they were hard-featured realists and that they resented an exactitude which was the product of a leisure not within their reach. No social revolution, he told her, would be likely to strike Dublin for some centuries.

She asked him why did he not write out his thoughts. For what? he asked her, with careful scorn. To compete with phrasemongers, incapable of thinking consecutively for sixty seconds? To submit himself to the criticisms of an obtuse middle class which entrusted its morality to policemen and its fine arts to impresarios?

He went often to her little cottage outside Dublin; often they spent their evenings alone. Little by little, as their thoughts entangled, they spoke of subjects less remote. Her companionship was like a warm soil about an exotic. Many times she allowed the dark to fall upon them, refraining from lighting the lamp. The dark discreet room, their isolation, the music that still vibrated in their ears united them. This union exalted him, wore away the rough edges of his character, emotionalized his mental life. Sometimes he caught himself listening to the sound of his own voice. He thought that in her eyes he would ascend to an angelical stature; and, as he attached the fervent nature of his companion more and more closely to him, he heard the strange impersonal voice which he recognized as his own, insisting on the soul's incurable loneliness. We cannot give ourselves, it said: we are our own. The end of these discourses was that one night, during which she had shown every sign of unusual excitement, Mrs Sinico caught up his hand passionately and pressed it to her cheek.

Mr Duffy was very much surprised. Her interpretation of his words disillusioned him. He did not visit her for a week; then he wrote to her asking her to meet him. As he did not wish their last interview to be troubled by the influence of their ruined confessional they met in a little cakeshop near the Parkgate. It was cold autumn weather but in spite of the cold they wandered up and down the roads of the park for nearly three hours. They agreed to break off their intercourse: every

a) *bond . . . a bond to sorrow*: The expression was lifted by Joyce from 'Bile Beans' by Stanislaus (95(o)).

b) *Nietzsche*: Friedrich Nietzsche (1844–1900) had an influence found not only here but also in Bob Doran of 'The Boarding House'. It can also be seen in Joyce's 1902 tract, 'The Day of the Rabblement'. Nietzsche affirmed the idea of the *Übermensch* or Superman, preached the doctrine of power and called for the revision of all values. George Bernard Shaw (1856–1950), native Dubliner, explored some of these themes in his *Man and Superman*. Joyce himself wrote at least one letter signed 'James Overman'. In *U*, 'Telemachus', Buck Mulligan derisively refers to Stephen and himself as 'Toothless Kinch and I, the supermen'. Joyce's associate Padraic Colum recalled discussing Nietzsche (and Ibsen) at George Roberts'

(76e) house during the Celtic Revival.

c) *Thus Spake Zarathustra and* The Gay Science: The many discourses of the first (published in 1883–4) are loosely connected musings on the holism of life. Buck Mulligan parodies this in *U*, 'Telemachus', intoning:

> He who stealeth from the poor lendeth to the Lord.

The second is one of the most explicitly anti-Christian of Nietzsche's writings, published in 1882.

d) *Love between . . . sexual intercourse*: Another apophthegm claimed by Stanislaus (a). In his *Human, All Too Human* (1878), Nietzsche observed:

> Women are perfectly able to make friends with a man; but to maintain the friendship perhaps requires the assistance of a slight physical antipathy.

The literary theorist Jacques Derrida, lecturing at Cornell University in 1988, said that

> true friendship is understood as possible between two men but never between a man and a woman or between two women.

e) *He kept away from concerts*: Music has been Mr Duffy's one connection with transcendence. This outlet is now destroyed. Even the music-stand is 'encumbered' with new pieces of music.

f) *corned beef and cabbage*: For a melancholic, he could hardly have chosen worse. According to Burton (95r), beef was condemned by Galen 'and all succeeding authors, to breed gross melancholy blood',

(*i*)

bond, he said, is a bond to sorrow. When they came out of the park they walked in silence towards the tram; but here she began to tremble so violently that, fearing another collapse on her part, he bade her goodbye quickly and left her. A few days later he received a parcel containing his books and music.

Four years passed. Mr Duffy returned to his even way of life. His room still bore witness of the orderliness of his mind. Some new pieces of music encumbered the music-stand in the lower room and on his shelves stood two volumes by Nietzsche: *Thus Spake Zarathustra* and *The Gay Science*. He wrote seldom in the sheaf of papers which lay in his desk. One of his sentences, written two months after his last interview with Mrs Sinico, read: Love between man and man is impossible because there must not be sexual intercourse, and friendship between man and women is impossible because there must be sexual inter-course. He kept away from concerts lest he should meet her. His father died; the junior partner of the bank retired. And still every morning he went into the city by tram and every evening walked home from the city after having dined moderately in George's Street and read the evening paper for dessert.

One evening as he was about to put a morsel of corned beef and cabbage into his mouth his hand stopped. His eyes fixed themselves on a paragraph in the evening paper which he had propped against the water-carafe. He replaced the morsel of food on his plate and read the paragraph attentively. Then he drank a glass of water, pushed his plate to one side, doubled the paper down before him between his elbows and read the paragraph over and over again. The cabbage began to deposit a cold white grease on his plate. The girl came over to him to ask was his dinner not properly cooked. He said it was very good and ate a few mouthfuls of it with difficulty. Then he paid his bill and went out.

He walked along quickly through the November twilight, his stout hazel stick striking the ground regularly, the fringe of the buff *Mail* peeping out of a side-pocket of his tight reefer overcoat. On the lonely road which leads from the Parkgate to Chapelizod he slackened his pace. His stick struck the ground less emphatically and his breath, issuing irregularly, almost with a sighing sound, condensed in the wintry air. When he reached his house he went up at once to his bedroom and,

and inadvisable for those 'any ways inclined to melancholy, or dry of complexion'. Cabbage was especially disallowed by Burton because it 'causeth troublesome dreams, and sends up black vapours to the brain. Galen of all herbs condemns cabbage ...'

g) *cold white grease*: Mr Duffy's reactions will be charted through images of food and eating, to climax with his realisation, near the end of the story, that 'he was outcast from life's feast'.

h) *the November twilight*: The accident on which Joyce based the report appeared in the *Freeman's Journal* of 14 July 1904. A few pages away, James A. Joyce BA is mentioned in the report of the funeral of Mathew Kane (140l). In *U*, 'Ithaca', the date of Mrs Sinico's fatal accident is given as 14 October 1903, with the funeral on the 17th.

i) *the buff* Mail: The *Dublin Evening Mail*, a traditionally unionist newspaper, the sister paper of the now long defunct *Daily Express*. The *Mail* lasted, however, until 1962, having been founded in 1821.

j) *reefer overcoat*: A coat made of stout cloth.

k) *On the lonely road*: Conyngham Road, leading onto Chapelizod Road. There are few buildings on the road, which is pressed between the Liffey and the Phoenix Park.

Carlo Goldoni (c)

The signal-box at Sydney Parade

a) Secreto: The secret, 'set apart' portion of the Mass is said just before the preface. The imagery reinforces the idea of Mr Duffy as a monk *manqué*.

b) *the paragraph*: Though the report seems like a parody, an actual account of the sad demise of Mrs Bishop will show that its tone is accurate.

c) A PAINFUL CASE: The story was originally to have been 'A Painful Incident', and its title is very likely derived from Goldoni's play *Un Curioso Incidente*, which Joyce studied for the second Italian pass examination in 1900 at University College. The story's final title refers of course both to the train accident and to Mr Duffy. Joyce re-used the expression in *U*, 'Cyclops' when he had Joe Hynes read out the hangman's letter:

> *Honoured sir i beg to offer my services in the above-mentioned painful case ...*

d) *City of Dublin Hospital*: In Upper Baggot Street, founded 1832, rebuilt and enlarged in 1893, as a result of fundraising at the Kosmos Bazaar in Ballsbridge. The hospital was non-sectarian.

e) *Sydney Parade*: The station was little more than a halt, but it had a station-master and Mrs Bishop was his wife. In 'Gas from a Burner', Joyce mocked the objectors to his use of the station's real name (172c).

f) *the deceased lady, while attempting to cross*: Previously 'the deceased lady travelled from Westland Row'.

g) *slow train*: i.e. a stopping train, not an express. The accident looks even less accidental.

h) *P. Dunne*: Originally written as 'Kilbride', but perhaps the pun was too excruciating. 'Kilbride the engine driver', however, gets a mention in *U*, 'Circe'. At one end of the suburban line, a Mr John Kilbride lived for several years at No 7 Martello Terrace, Bray, where the Joyces had lived at No 1.

i) *Constable 57E*: Policemen were commonly known by their numbers at this time, in order to emphasise their vocation, and to discourage favouritism based on kinship (143l). The 'E' denotes E-Division, in south-east Dublin. The drafts of the story had 'Constable 57D'. In *U*, 'Wandering Rocks' 2, Corny Kelleher has a chat with Constable 57C up on the North Strand Road. Despite the constabulary numbers, it is Corny Kelleher's familiarity with the Watch (and with Bloom) that gets Stephen out of trouble at the end of *U*, 'Circe':

CORNY KELLEHER: Leave it to me, sergeant, That'll be all right. (*He laughs, shaking his head*) We were often as bad ourselves, ay or worse. What? Eh, what?

taking the paper from his pocket, read the paragraph again by the failing light of the window. He read it not aloud, but moving his lips as a priest does when he reads the prayers *Secreto*. This was the paragraph:

DEATH OF A LADY AT SYDNEY PARADE

A PAINFUL CASE

To-day at the City of Dublin Hospital the Deputy Coroner (in the absence of Mr. Leverett) held an inquest on the body of Mrs. Emily Sinico, aged forty-three years, who was killed at Sydney Parade Station yesterday evening. The evidence showed that the deceased lady, while attempting to cross the line, was knocked down by the engine of the ten o'clock slow train from Kingstown, thereby sustaining injuries of the head and right side which led to her death.

James Lennon, driver of the engine, stated that he had been in the employment of the railway company for fifteen years. On hearing the guard's whistle he set the train in motion and a second or two afterwards brought it to rest in response to loud cries. The train was going slowly.

P. Dunne, railway porter, stated that as the train was about to start he observed a woman attempting to cross the lines. He ran towards her and shouted, but, before he could reach her, she was caught by the buffer of the engine and fell to the ground.

A juror – You saw the lady fall?

Witness – Yes.

Police Sergeant Croly deposed that when he arrived he found the deceased lying on the platform apparently dead. He had the body taken to the waiting-room pending the arrival of the ambulance.

Constable 57E corroborated.

Dr. Halpin, assistant house surgeon of the City of Dublin Hospital, stated that the deceased had two lower ribs fractured and had sustained severe contusions of the right shoulder. The right side of the head had been injured in the fall. The injuries were not sufficient to have caused

j) *Dr. Halpin ... City of Dublin Hospital*: Originally 'Dr Cosgrave ...Vincent's Hospital'. The amendment came after a relevant query to Stanislaus in a letter of September 1905 (6l).

SYDNEY PARADE FATALITY.

At the inquest held by Sir Henry L. Harty, Coroner, on the old lady, Mrs. Sarah Bishop, who died in St. Michael's Hospital on Wednesday afternoon from the injuries received while crossing the railway line at Sydney Parade Station, Signal-man James Byrne deposed he was on duty at the time of the accident, and saw the deceased crossing over the line from her house on the up-side of the line, as if she were going to catch the down train to Kingstown. The 3 p.m. train from Westland Row was then due, and immediately the engine-driver saw her he sounded his whistle, the woman being then about 20 yards from the front of the engine. The train was going about 17 or 18 miles an hour when the deceased was seen, and when she was struck it's speed would be about 7 or 8. She was drawn along the line about 12 or 15 yards before the train was drawn up. The driver did all in his power to pull up as soon as he saw the woman, but it was impossible for him to come to a standstill before he was down on her. During his time at the station witness had only known deceased to cross the ilne on two occasions. Dr. M'Dermott stated he examined the woman on being received in hospital, and found her in a state of collapse, and suffering from a scalp injury and contusions of the body, legs and arms. Death supervened about an hour after admission, and was due to shock, the result of the injuries. The jury found accordingly.

From the Illustrated Irish Weekly and Nation, *July 1904*

a) *sudden failure of the heart's action*: It is also Mr Duffy's heart that fails.

b) *Mr. H. B. Patterson Finlay*: Originally 'Higgins' (81b).

c) *Leoville*: Another link with the author's life: in 1892–3, the Joyce family were at Leoville, 23 Carysfort Avenue, Blackrock, where James began his writing.

d) *to join a League*: A Temperance (i.e. Abstinence) League (53f).

e) *No blame attached to anyone*: A standard formula of the time, though ironic in this context. In the *Mail* of 16 November 1903, a report on an inquest into the accidental death of an actress ends:

The jury also expressed the opinion that no blame could be attached to anyone.

f) *Mr Duffy ... gazed out of his window*: Like Eveline, and the narrator of 'Araby'.

g) *the Lucan road*: The village of Lucan lay four miles further to the west, but was nevertheless integrated into Dublin's modern transport system.

h) *The whole narrative ... revolted him*: Images of Mr Duffy's revulsion, which is physical, begin the moment he sees the newspaper report. But revulsion and intolerance will give way to resignation and paralysis.

From Reynolds's Newspaper (*57e*)

death in a normal person. Death, in his opinion, had been probably due to shock and sudden failure of the heart's action.

Mr. H. B. Patterson Finlay, on behalf of the railway company, expressed his deep regret at the accident. The company had always taken every precaution to prevent people crossing the lines except by the bridges, both by placing notices in every station and by the use of patent spring gates at level crossings. The deceased had been in the habit of crossing the lines late at night from platform to platform and, in view of certain other circumstances of the case, he did not think the railway officials were to blame.

Captain Sinico, of Leoville, Sydney Parade, husband of the deceased, also gave evidence. He stated that the deceased was his wife. He was not in Dublin at the time of the accident as he had arrived only that morning from Rotterdam. They had been married for twenty-two years and had lived happily until about two years ago, when his wife began to be rather intemperate in her habits.

Miss Mary Sinico said that of late her mother had been in the habit of going out at night to buy spirits. She, witness, had often tried to reason with her mother and had induced her to join a League. She was not at home until an hour after the accident.

The jury returned a verdict in accordance with the medical evidence and exonerated Lennon from all blame.

The Deputy Coroner said it was a most painful case, and expressed great sympathy with Captain Sinico and his daughter. He urged on the railway company to take strong measures to prevent the possibility of similar accidents in the future. No blame attached to anyone.

Mr Duffy raised his eyes from the paper and gazed out of his window on the cheerless evening landscape. The river lay quiet beside the empty distillery and from time to time a light appeared in some house on the Lucan road. What an end! The whole narrative of her death revolted him and it revolted him to think that he had ever spoken to her of what he held sacred. The threadbare phrases, the inane expressions of sympathy, the

The Lucan Tram (101g)

a) *one of the wrecks on which civilisation has been reared*: A sub-Nietzschean sentiment.

b) *her hand touched his*: A counterpart to the ghosts of the first and last stories.

c) *the public-house at Chapelizod Bridge*: This was and is the Bridge Inn, just across the river. Although the public bar would never have been suitable for Mrs Sinico, the inn incorporated a tea-room, which the couple might well have patronised during their walks. The bridge is now named Anna Livia Bridge, for Joycean reasons.

d) *hot punch*: See 79f.

e) *shop*: The word is no longer used to mean 'pub'.

f) *County Kildare*: A famously 'horsey' county, just west of County Dublin, dominated by big farmers and army officers. William Blake in his *Jerusalem: The Emanation of the Giant Albion* (1804) listed the counties of Ireland (in Chapter 3, Plate 72):

> Under Judah & Issachar & Zebulun are Lowth,
> Longford,
> Eastmeath, Westmeath, Dublin, Kildare, King's
> County,
> Queen's County, Wicklow, Catherloh, Wexford,
> Kilkenny . . .

g) Herald: The Dublin *Evening Herald*, a more popular and nationalist paper than the *Mail*.

h) *a tram*: The Lucan tram (101f).

i) *the two images*: The animated friend, and the sottish wreck.

j) *that she had become a memory*: The tenor of this paragraph will be parallelled near the end of 'The Dead'.

THE SECOND UNIVERSITY EXAMINATION IN ARTS

ITALIAN.*—*Pass.*

1. The following works : —
   Petrarca, . . Sonetti e Canzoni sopra varj argomenti.
   Machiavelli, . Istorie Fiorentine, Books I. to IV.
   Goldoni, . . Un Curioso Accidente.
   Alfieri, . . Oreste.
2. Italian Grammar.
3. A piece of English Prose for translation into Italian.
4. Elementary History of the Italian Language.
5. History of Italian Literature from 1260 to 1376.

(100c)

cautious words of a reporter won over to conceal the details of a commonplace vulgar death attacked his stomach. Not merely had she degraded herself; she had degraded him. He saw the squalid tract of her vice, miserable and malodorous. His soul's companion! He thought of the hobbling wretches whom he had seen carrying cans and bottles to be filled by the barman. Just God, what an end! Evidently she had been unfit to live, without any strength of purpose, an easy prey to habits, one of the wrecks on which civilisation has been reared. But that she could have sunk so low! Was it possible he had deceived himself so utterly about her? He remembered her outburst of that night and interpreted it in a harsher sense than he had ever done. He had no difficulty now in approving of the course he had taken.

As the light failed and his memory began to wander he thought her hand touched his. The shock which had first attacked his stomach was now attacking his nerves. He put on his overcoat and hat quickly and went out. The cold air met him on the threshold; it crept into the sleeves of his coat. When he came to the public-house at Chapelizod Bridge he went in and ordered a hot punch.

The proprietor served him obsequiously but did not venture to talk. There were five or six working-men in the shop discussing the value of a gentleman's estate in County Kildare. They drank at intervals from their huge pint tumblers and smoked, spitting often on the floor and sometimes dragging the sawdust over their spits with their heavy boots. Mr Duffy sat on his stool and gazed at them, without seeing or hearing them. After a while they went out and he called for another punch. He sat a long time over it. The shop was very quiet. The proprietor sprawled on the counter reading the *Herald* and yawning. Now and again a tram was heard swishing along the lonely road outside.

As he sat there, living over his life with her and evoking alternately the two images in which he now conceived her, he realized that she was dead, that she had ceased to exist, that she had become a memory. He began to feel ill at ease. He asked himself what else could he have done. He could not have carried on a comedy of deception with her; he could not have lived with her openly. He had done what seemed to him best. How was he to blame? Now that she was gone he understood

k) *he could not have lived with her openly*: In an earlier draft of the story, Mr Duffy concludes that he could not have gone abroad with Mrs Sinico, 'a ridiculous elopement'. To do this would have been as little in character as actually 'in certain circumstances' robbing his bank.

By Chapelizod Bridge (c)

The wicket-gate (a)

Magazine Hill and the Wellington Monument

fort there (from the Arabic *makhazin*, 'store-houses') was celebrated by a Dubliner no less alienated than Mr Duffy – Jonathan Swift:

Behold a proof of Irish Sense!
Here Irish wit is seen
When nothing's left that's worth defence
We build a magazine.

The Magazine Hill is also the site of Izod's Fount, another link (95c) with Tristan and Isolde (a legend re-embellished by Nietzsche's former friend, Wagner). In *FW* (44–5), the Magazine Wall is the scene of a bad accident:

Have you heard of one Humpty Dumpty
How he fell with a roll and a rumble
And curled up like Lord Olofa Crumple
By the butt of the Magazine Wall,
⠀⠀(Chorus) Of the Magazine Wall,
⠀⠀⠀⠀Hump, helmet and all?

d) *some human figures lying*: In *FW*, the park is again the scene of a sexual encounter.

e) *gnawed the rectitude of his life*: Mr Duffy is still starved of affection or approval. Though 'rectitude' connotes propriety, its literal meaning is also 'rigidity'. Rightness is uprightness.

f) *Kingsbridge Station*: At Islandbridge, on the south bank of the Liffey, now Heuston Station. Trains went to Limerick, Cork, etc, by the Great Southern and Western Railway.

g) *a worm with a fiery head*: Possibly a symbol of a penile urge, as in the description of Corley in 'Two Gallants' (43u). It is linked with Mr Duffy's revulsion at his food and at Mrs Sinico. The worm here suggests the physical or literal appetite for putrescence. It also recalls Blake's 1794 poem 'The Sick Rose' (from *Songs of Experience*).

h) *syllables of her name*: Joyce in a previous version of the story had spelt out these steamtrain dactyls: Èmily Sìnico, Èmily Sìnico, Èmily Sìnico (126a). Characteristically, he decided to make the reader do the work.

i) *He turned back*: the last eight sentences begin with 'He', emphasising Mr Duffy's isolation.

j) *alone*: But Mr Duffy – now aged c. forty-five – finally feels. It is potentially a sympton of a recovered humanity, and what he again has in common with Mrs Sinico. Consider *FW* (627):

It's something fails us. First we feel. Then we fall . . .

a) *He entered the park by the first gate*: Not Chapelizod Gate, beyond the outskirts of the village, but a closer wicket-gate on a lane leading up from the main road. Mr Duffy's route is almost the reverse of that of the Phoenix Park Murderers (62d). The coincidence has led some commentators to suggest that he has something in common with them.

b) *his moral nature*: Previously 'his morality'.

c) *Magazine Hill*: This landmark in the Phoenix Park is about a mile away from the bridge. The military

how lonely her life must have been, sitting night after night alone in that room. His life would be lonely too until he, too, died, ceased to exist, became a memory – if anyone remembered him.

a It was after nine o'clock when he left the shop. The night was cold and gloomy. He entered the park by the first gate and walked along under the gaunt trees. He walked through the bleak alleys where they had walked four years before. She seemed to be near him in the darkness. At moments he seemed to feel her voice touch his ear, her hand touch his. He stood still to listen. Why had he withheld life from her? Why had

b he sentenced her to death? He felt his moral nature falling to pieces.

c When he gained the crest of the Magazine Hill he halted and looked along the river towards Dublin, the lights of which burned redly and hospitably in the cold night. He looked down the slope and, at the base, in the shadow of the wall of the

d park, he saw some human figures lying. Those venal and furtive

e loves filled him with despair. He gnawed the rectitute of his life; he felt that he had been outcast from life's feast. One human being had seemed to love him and he had denied her life and happiness: he had sentenced her to ignominy, a death of shame. He knew that the prostrate creatures down by the wall were watching him and wished him gone. No one wanted him; he was outcast from life's feast. He turned his eyes to the grey gleaming river, winding along towards Dublin. Beyond

f the river he saw a goods train winding out of Kingsbridge

g Station, like a worm with a fiery head winding through the darkness, obstinately and laboriously. It passed slowly out of sight; but still he heard in his ears the laborious drone of the

h engine reiterating the syllables of her name.

i He turned back the way he had come, the rhythm of the engine pounding in his ears. He began to doubt the reality of what memory told him. He halted under a tree and allowed the rhythm to die away. He could not feel her near him in the darkness nor her voice touch his ear. He waited for some minutes, listening. He could hear nothing: the night was perfectly silent. He listened again: perfectly silent. He felt that he

j was alone.

In his volume of Wordsworth, Mr Duffy might also have read in *The Prelude* (VII) of

> the peace
> That comes with the night;
> the deep solemnity
> Of nature's intermediate
> hours of rest
> When the great tide of
> human life stands still;
> The business of the day to
> come unborn
> Of that gone by, locked up,
> as in the grave;
> The blended calmness of the
> heaven and earth,
> Moonlight and stars, and
> empty streets and sounds
> Unfrequent as in deserts; at
> late hours
> Of winter evenings, when
> unwholesome rains
> Are falling hard, with people
> yet astir,
> The feeble salutation from
> the voice
> Of some unhappy woman,
> now and then
> Heard as we pass, when no
> one looks about,
> Nothing is listened to.

One of J. C. Mangan's stanzas ended:

> ... all the philosophy, all
> faith,
> All earthly – all celestial
> love,
> Have but one voice, which
> only saith
> Endure – alone!

Afterword: 'A Painful Case'

Mr Duffy is one of the very few intellectual rivals of Gabriel Conroy in this collection. His failure is one that he is able to understand (perhaps like Father Flynn), but it is another Dublin failure nevertheless. Compared with Jimmy Doyle, Farrington, Lenehan, Bob Doran *et al*, Mr Duffy has few worries: he doesn't drink to excess, he has a satisfactory job and can afford not to give alms to beggars, he has artistic interests, and he believes he also knows his own mind. His library has a Romantic base and a religious superstructure. Only after the sundering with Mrs Sinico are we told that he has abandoned music and (by implication) read Nietzsche. 'A Painful Case' traces the destruction of Mr Duffy's certainties.

The story was one that gave Joyce great difficulty in writing, and he thought it one of the two worst stories in *Dubliners* – proving perhaps that he could be on occasion as good a critic as a poet.

Stanislaus Joyce was one model for Mr Duffy. He write in his autobiography that 'A Painful Case' was 'a portrait of what my brother imagined I should become in middle age', but any number of buttoned-up contemporaries would have served. Stanislaus, like his fictional part-self, rejected

> such adventures as one meets with by drinking and going the round of the town . . .

He added that he preferred

> rather to remain discontented and barren than to satisfy a false appetite.

In 'A Painful Case', however, the sterility (or perhaps potential sterility) of this attitude is explored. Mr Duffy's self-containment and self-satisfaction are incompatible with the realities of warm, full-blooded life exemplified by Mrs Sinico. The tensions between the couple's attitudes prove to be irreconcilable. Her Mediterranean spirit founders against his Chapelizod, hyperborean coldness. (Nietzsche in *The Antichrist* wrote of the Hyperboreans, a race of the cold North: the term was used of Stephen and Mulligan in *Ulysses*.) Significantly, where Mr Duffy lives is just outside the publicly unhealthy zone of Dublin. Living in Chapelizod also points up Mr Duffy's standing as a failed Tristan (as failed as Hauptmann's Michael Kramer, also isolated and incapable in love).

The identity of Mrs Sinico is also ripe with connotations. Richard Ellmann in his biography suggested that the name was derived from Joyce's music teacher in Trieste in 1905. There is another possibility: Joyce would have known from his musical relatives that there was a singer of that name: she sang in Dublin in every season from 1863 until 1879, and again in 1873 and 1876. A woman of many parts, she performed in September 1864 on consecutive evenings at the Theatre Royal in *La Traviata*, *Norma*, Gounod's *Mirella*, and *Il Trovatore*. The following week she did successively *Fidelio*, *Il Trovatore*, *Norma*, *Martha* and *Fidelio*. Her accomplishments extended to a much larger repertoire, and she sang and toured with Mdlles Titiens and Trebelli (who are mentioned in 'The Dead'). Thus even before Mr Duffy meets her at a Mozart concert, Mrs Sinico is a ghost, a musical spirit. But it is he who is the more dead.

During their repressed friendship, Mr Duffy had wanted to duplicate his thoughts in Mrs Sinico – rather than develop hers (or even theirs). His lack of engagement in the world is perilous, however. He has abandoned religion and politics, and disdains writing. (Like Little Chandler, Mr Duffy is a would-be writer though neither is ever described actually writing.) If at the end of the story, Mr Duffy feels 'an outcast from life's feast' (a point repeated), he forgets that feasting (like friendship and sexual intercourse) is a social activity, one that is more than eating, a matter of togetherness and some form of reciprocity. Behind his solipsistic posturing lies a selfish egotism, offset only by the timidity of his Nietzschean position as a would-be bank robber.

In a similar way, behind Mr Duffy's relentless superiority can be glimpsed a Pecksniff-like hypocrisy, as well as Steerforth-like arrogance that leads to the fall of Little Emily Sinico: he is vindictive even in death (though his secondary reaction can also be seen as futilely maudlin – about himself). Yet Joyce's treatment of the character has been careful enough to show that he is a victim too, another paralysed citizen. Mr Duffy's revulsion at his food, the unhealthiness of beef and cabbage is a deliberate detail – his indelicate stomach, the gnawing, her drinking, the tumblers and spits towards the end, have a cumulative effect akin to that of the 'Lestrygonians' chapter of *Ulysses*. Like Bloom's in 'Lestrygonians', Mr Duffy's gorge can rise at certain thoughts and feelings. Even at the end of 'A Painful Case', the 'goods train like a worm' suggests the food of the grave. Mr Duffy's intellectual detachment, the self-irony of his internal voice, must finally give way to a terrifying silence.

There has been a price to pay for Mr Duffy's rectitude. His concerns are not those of his fellow citizens. In rejecting their preoccupations, however – family, religion, adventure, politics, art, love, marriage, friendship, and the rest – he also rejects life itself. His remorse – when it finally comes – is a typically barren response, despite some signs of a lessened self-absorption. Although Mr Duffy is contrasted in just about every way with Maria in 'Clay', his superiority in the end counts for nothing.

Mrs Sinico's search for fulfilment is also an ugly failure. The story, in its delineation of bourgeois foibles, can also be seen as an ironic reprise of *Madame Bovary* (and there are also parallels with *Anna Karenina*): for Joyce's character, as for Flaubert's and Tolstoy's, the situation becomes too much to bear, and she retreats into self-destruction.

But life also imitates art. Joyce, in adapting the 'real' story of the accident at Sydney Parade, chose not to use the name of the engine-driver, as it has already been used in the first story: James Flynn.

THE PAPAL CONSISTORY—WHO WILL BE THE NEXT POPE?

Cardinal Rampolla — Cardinal Gotti — Cardinal Fischer — Cardinal Svampa — Cardinal Taliani — Cardinal Sarto

Cardinal Oreglia — Cardinal T. Vannutelli — Cardinal di Pietro — Cardinal Agliardi — Cardinal Nocella — Cardinal Cavicchioni

A CITY SLUM.

ONCE THE HOME OF PROSPERITY.

APPALLING CONDITIONS OF LIFE

MISERY AND SQUALOR

Clockwise from top left:

★ *Advertisements from* An Claidheamh Soluis *('The Sword of Light'), a newspaper supporting the Gaelic League (122c)*
★ *Note the 'flying inscriptions' (48g) behind this example of Irish street-life*
★ *Cardinals tipped to succeed Pope Leo XIII. Cardinal Sarto was to be victorious (150b)*
★ *Stories of corruption and hypocrisy were beginning to appear in the papers*
★ *The last sitting of the Irish House of Commons in 1800. By Ivy Day, 1900, it would still be more than twenty years before a recognised parliament would again be convened in Dublin*
★ *From Michael McCarthy's provocative* Priests and People in Ireland

Charles Stewart Parnell with 'Billy Walsh' behind (149a)

a) IVY DAY: By the time in which the story is set, eleven or so years after the death of Charles Stewart Parnell on 6 October 1891, the anniversary was celebrated by a diminishing band of followers. 'Ivy Day dying out,' Bloom thinks in 1904 (*U*, 'Hades'). The date was also the feast day of the third-century French martyr, St Faith.

b) THE COMMITTEE ROOM: The room is a centre of operations for the duration of the election. It was in Committee Room XV in Westminster that Parnell defended – and lost – his leadership of the Irish Party in early December 1890.

c) *Old Jack*: The old man can be seen as a representative of bygone times, still mechanically tending the Parnellite flame. The name 'Jack' is a teasing reference to John Joyce, often known by the name.

d) *the fire*: This is one of the most effective and obvious symbols in *D*. It is the fire of Parnellism (see Afterword).

e) *re-emerged into light*: The cinematic device allows the readers now properly to see Old Jack. This is the first of many services performed by the fire.

f) *Mr O'Connor*: The first of several rather unenthusiastic – and unprepossessing – canvassers.

g) *Mr Tierney*: The name is derived from the Irish *Tiarna*, 'Lord'. He is the Nationalist candidate in the forthcoming election.

h) *pasteboard*: Cheap card made from thin layers of paper.

i) *MUNICIPAL ELECTIONS*: Annual elections were held in each of the wards of Dublin, and the elected members served on the City Corporation.

j) *ROYAL EXCHANGE WARD*: One of twenty administrative areas in central Dublin, this was (loosely) between Dame Street and Stephen's Green. Stanislaus in a radio broadcast once quoted his brother saying to him:

> Do you really think that all Europe is waiting to hear the story of the municipal election in the Royal Exchange Ward in Dublin?

IVY DAY IN THE COMMITTEE ROOM

OLD JACK RAKED the cinders together with a piece of cardboard and spread them judiciously over the whitening dome of coals. When the dome was thinly covered his face lapsed into darkness but, as he set himself to fan the fire again, his crouching shadow ascended the opposite wall and his face slowly re-emerged into light. It was an old man's face, very bony and hairy. The moist blue eyes blinked at the fire and the moist mouth fell open at times, munching once or twice mechanically when it closed. When the cinders had caught he laid the piece of cardboard against the wall, sighed and said:

—That's better now, Mr O'Connor—

Mr O'Connor, a grey-haired young man, whose face was disfigured by many blotches and pimples, had just brought the tobacco for a cigarette into a shapely cylinder but when spoken to he undid his handiwork meditatively. Then he began to roll the tobacco again meditatively and after a moment's thought decided to lick the paper.

—Did Mr Tierney say when he'd be back? he asked in a husky falsetto—

—He didn't say—

Mr O'Connor put his cigarette into his mouth and began to search his pockets. He took out a pack of thin pasteboard cards.

—I'll get you a match, said the old man—

—Never mind, this'll do, said Mr O'Connor—

He selected one of the cards and read what was printed on it:

> ## MUNICIPAL ELECTIONS
>
> ### ROYAL EXCHANGE WARD
>
> Mr. Richard J. Tierney, P.L.G., respectfully solicits the favour of your vote and influence at the coming election in the Royal Exchange Ward

k) *P.L.G.*: Poor Law Guardian, one of two groups of elected officers (North and South Dublin) who oversaw the relief of the poor in the city, though they did not supplant the necessary work of Dublin's many charities.

An upstairs room in Central Chambers, Wicklow Street (107d)

106

a) *agent*: An election organiser on behalf of a particular candidate.

b) *to canvass*: To call from house to house, dropping in cards and seeking favourable promises – Leopold Bloom is a canvasser for advertisements for the *Freeman's Journal* in *U*. The word comes obscurely from the tough cloth, 'canvas', which itself is derived from 'cannabis', the hemp from which it was made.

c) *sitting by the fire*: Echoes of Maria and Old Cotter.

d) *Wicklow Street*: Wicklow means literally 'meadow of the Vikings'. The street shares its name with County Wicklow, where, at Avondale in 1846, Parnell was born. It is not certain exactly where the Committee Room is: possibly it has been rented or borrowed from a solicitor in Central Chambers, not far from the junction with St Andrew Street and William Street.

e) *the short day*: Sundown was just before half-past five.

f) *the sixth of October*: Municipal elections were in fact held in January each year, and Joyce overrode Stanislaus' advice that it was unlikely that an election could take place in October. Admittedly, it seems like January weather, but there are no rules about this in Ireland.

g) *ivy*: The evergreen shrub, said to grow profusely at Avondale (d), was a symbol of lasting remembrance. One Irish word for ivy is *íodha*, which also means 'yew' (a tree symbolic of death), and stands for the letter 'I' in the Irish alphabet. When his father died in 1931, Joyce sent an ivy wreath from Paris.

h) *continuing*: Continuing what? Irish pauses can be very long.

i) *children*: One of the recurring themes of 'Ivy Day' (and of much of the rest of Joyce's œuvre) is the mutually unsatisfactory nature of the father/son relationship. To an extent, all the characters in 'Ivy Day' are sons of Parnell, and they have almost all gone to the bad.

j) *the Christian Brothers*: See 21d.

k) *Only*: Except that . . .

l) *while I could stand over him*: In *U*, 'Circe', the Hon. Mrs Talboys cries: 'I'll scourge the pigeonlivered cur as long as I can stand over him'.

m) *as I done*: Though Polly Mooney (in 'The Boarding House') sometimes says 'I seen', the old man has perhaps the least refined speech of all in *D*.

n) *she cocks him up*: She gives him false notions.

o) *upper hand . . . a sup taken*: Old Jack is like an older Farrington – bullied when he has had a drink too many, though by a vengeful son.

p) *Sure*: In this usage the word is invariably unstressed

The Royal Victoria Hotel, Cork, at the turn of the century (t)

a　Mr O'Connor had been engaged by Mr Tierney's agent to
b　canvass one part of the ward but, as the weather was inclement
　　and his boots let in the wet, he spent a great part of the day
cd　sitting by the fire in the Committee Rooms in Wicklow Street
　　with Jack, the old caretaker. They had been sitting thus since
ef　the short day had grown dark. It was the sixth of October,
　　dismal and cold out of doors.

　　Mr O'Connor tore a strip off the card and, lighting it, lit his
g　cigarette. As he did so the flame lit up a leaf of dark glossy ivy
　　in the lapel of his coat. The old man watched him attentively
　　and then, taking up the piece of cardboard again, began to fan
　　the fire slowly while his companion smoked.

h　　—Ah, yes, he said, continuing, it's hard to know what way
i　to bring up children. Now who'd think he'd turn out like that!
j　I sent him to the Christian Brothers and I done what I could
　　for him, and there he goes boosing about. I tried to make him
　　someway decent—

　　He replaced the cardboard wearily.

k　　—Only I'm an old man now I'd change his tune for him.
　　I'd take the stick to his back and beat him while I could stand
lm　over him – as I done many a time before. The mother, you
n　know, she cocks him up with this and that . . .—

　　—That's what ruins children, said Mr O'Connor—

　　—To be sure it is, said the old man. And little thanks you
　　get for it, only impudence. He takes th'upper hand of me
o　whenever he sees I've a sup taken. What's the world coming
　　to when sons speaks that way to their fathers?—

　　—What age is he? said Mr O'Connor—

　　—Nineteen, said the old man—

　　—Why don't you put him to something?—

pq　　—Sure, amn't I never done at the drunken bowsy ever since
r　he left school? *I won't keep you*, I says. *You must get a job for
　　yourself*. But, sure, it's worse whenever he gets a job: he drinks
　　it all—

　　Mr O'Connor shook his head in sympathy, and the old man
　　fell silent, gazing into the fire. Some one opened the door to
　　the room and called out:

s　　—Hello! Is this a Freemasons' meeting?—

　　—Who's that? said the old man—

　　—What are you doing in the dark? asked a voice—

t　　—Is that you, Hynes? asked Mr O'Connor—

　　and pronounced 'shur', an intensive with a meaning similar to 'well'.

q) *amn't I*: Standard English is the seldom-used 'aren't I'. 'Ain't I' is frequent in English, but 'amn't I' is sensibly the construction still most usual in Ireland.

r) *bowsy*: Layabout, drunken lout. Derived from 'booze', it is still a much-needed word in Dublin.

s) *a Freemason's meeting*: i.e. a secret (male) ceremony. Freemasonry and Catholicism were deemed to be mutually exclusive (23h). Hynes' joke is not so wide of the mark in the sense that Masons have always been accused of peddling influence and mutual support.

t) *Hynes*: Joseph M'Carthy Hynes is a reporter on the *Freeman's Journal* and appears often in *U*. As perhaps the only Parnellite worthy of the name in the story, he heads straight for the fire, and stays close to it until he leaves the room. According to MacLysaght's *The Surnames of Ireland*, the name is from the Irish *eidhean*, another word for ivy (g). Some readers have heard an echo of the word 'hind' (118b) in the name: in Barry O'Brien's 1898 *Life* of Parnell, a Mr Horgan remembers Parnell's

visit to Cork after the fight in Committee Room 15. I saw him in the Victoria Hotel that night. He looked like a hunted hind . . .

The hotel is where Stephen and his father stay in *P* (II.4).

a) *a tall, slender young man*: Similar in appearance to James Joyce at this time.

b) *two candlesticks*: In 'The Sisters', two candlesticks are brought to the house, for they 'must be set at the head of the corpse' (2e).

c) *an election address*: As illustrated below.

d) *Has he paid you yet?*: They are sailing close to the wind. From *Eason's Almanac for Ireland* 1886–7:

> *Corrupt Practices Act 1883*: Treating is defined as ... giving or providing any meat, drink, entertainment to or for any person for the purpose of corruptly influencing that person or any other person to vote or refrain from voting at the election ... *Illegal Practices*: These include payment for the conveyance of voters, for exhibiting bills or notices by an elector, for committee rooms in excess of the number allowed by statute, of money except through election agent ...

e) *leave us in the lurch*: i.e. not pay us.

f) *It isn't but he has it*: It's not that he hasn't got it.

g) *tinker*: An itinerant tradesman or craftsman, without even the status of a gypsy. The word is used here as a general term of abuse, assuming poverty.

h) *Colgan*: The 'Labour' candidate. In the 1903 municipal elections, one of these was James Connolly. Colgan's name may have been suggested by the Nationalist winner of the 1904 election in this ward, J. Cogan, who beat the Unionist candidate, Andrew Beattie. In that election, no Labour candidate won in any Dublin ward.

i) *a working-man*: In Flann O'Brien's *At Swim-Two-Birds*, a parody of this story, and particularly its ending, is perpetrated with a come-all-you by Jem Casey, Poet of the Pick and Bard of Booterstown, which ends:

> Your Lords and ladies are fine to see
> And they do the best they can,
> But here's the slogan for you and me –
> THE GIFT OF GOD IS A WORKIN' MAN.
>
> A WORKIN' MAN, A WORKIN' MAN,
> Hurray Hurray for a Workin' Man,
> He'll navvy and sweat till he's nearly bet,
> THE GIFT OF GOD IS A WORKIN' MAN!

j) *a publican*: In January 1903, Arthur Griffith's paper, the *United Irishman*, discussed the election:

> A glance at the list of candidates at the forthcoming elections is an education in municipal politics. Thirteen are publicans or ex-publicans; ten are tenement-houseowners or jerry-builders; nine are loyal-address flunkeys or supporters of Dublin Castle detectives for Corporation jobs; and one is a music-hall singer ...
>
> In the Exchange Ward Mr. Cahill, of whom we know little, except that he is an Irish manufacturer, and we believe no flunkey, is being opposed by a

A RALLYING CALL
TO FIGHTING GAELIC LEAGUERS

Comrades,
I am going to fight the battle of Nationality in the Inns' Quay Ward. There is, as yet, no organisation there; but, with the men who won the St. Patrick's Day holiday, and have carried all before them up to this—with your help we should carry the seat, and send the Gaelic movement into the Corporation, a living force—and not have it used as a mere election catch-cry by politicians, publicans, and provincialists, who have never done a day's work for the Gaelic movement yet.

Will all among you who are willing to **work** for the Cause in this Fight, be good enough to communicate with me at Little Green Street?

u. l. mac cumaill.
(W. L. Cole).

(c)

—Yes. What are you doing in the dark? said Mr Hynes, advancing into the light of the fire—

He was a tall, slender young man with a light brown moustache. Imminent little drops of rain hung at the brim of his hat and the collar of his jacket-coat was turned up.

—Well, Mat, he said to Mr O'Connor, how goes it?—

Mr O'Connor shook his head. The old man left the hearth and, after stumbling about the room returned with two candlesticks which he thrust one after the other into the fire and carried to the table. A denuded room came into view and the fire lost all its cheerful colour. The walls of the room were bare except for a copy of an election address. In the middle of the room was a small table on which papers were heaped.

Mr Hynes leaned against the mantelpiece and asked:

—Has he paid you yet?—

—Not yet, said Mr O'Connor. I hope to God he'll not leave us in the lurch to-night—

Mr Hynes laughed.

—O, he'll pay you. Never fear, he said—

—I hope he'll look smart about it if he means business, said Mr O'Connor—

—What do you think, Jack? said Mr Hynes satirically to the old man—

The old man returned to his seat by the fire, saying:

—It isn't but he has it, anyway. Not like the other tinker—

—What other tinker? said Mr Hynes—

—Colgan, said the old man scornfully—

—Is it because Colgan's a working-man you say that? What's the difference between a good honest bricklayer and a publican – eh? Hasn't the working-man as good a right to be in the Corporation as anyone else – aye, and a better right than those shoneens that are always hat in hand before any fellow with a handle to his name? Isn't that so, Mat? said Mr Hynes, addressing Mr O'Connor—

—I think you're right, said Mr O'Connor—

—One man is a plain honest man with no hunker-sliding about him. He goes in to represent the labour classes. This fellow you're working for only wants to get some job or other—

—Of course, the working-classes should be represented, said the old man—

Queen's-address publican named Cummins who was kicked out of Arran-quay Ward last year. During Mr. Cummins' candidature for Arran-quay, free drink flowed among the free and independent. Now we find from the daily papers that this man is put forward by Father Staples of Aungier-street and Father Corbett of Clarendon-street. Father Corbett of Clarendon-street is a strong teetotal advocate. We are inclined to think his name has been used without his authority.

k) *the Corporation*: The local government of Dublin. It consisted of the eighty men elected to the wards, as well as the Lord Mayor, the High Sheriff and various more lowly officials.

l) *shoneens*: Collaborators with the British; mock English-men. John Bull was *Seán Buí* in Irish, whence the term of abuse, which means 'little Johns'.

m) *hat in hand*: Grovelling, wheedling, inveigling, but essentially begging.

n) *a handle to his name*: A title, such as Lord or Sir – or Doctor or Alderman. The phrase is still used.

o) *hunker-sliding*: This can mean either laziness or grovelling. 'On one's hunkers' means 'squatting', the word being related to 'haunches'.

Punch's *idealised view of the relationship between Ireland and Edward VII*

a) *all kicks and no halfpence*: Ill-treatment rather than kindness. The phrase is recorded as far back as 1785.

b) *a German monarch*: A frequent jibe in Ireland, alluding to the British Royal Family's German ancestry. (Queen Victoria was of the House of Saxe-Coburg-Gotha.) In *U*, 'Cyclops', Joe Hynes is scathing of 'the Prooshians and the Hanoverians' – 'those sausage eating bastards' (in contrast with the French, whom the Citizen calls a 'Set of dancing masters').

c) *kowtowing*: The word comes from the Chinese custom of touching the ground with the forehead to express respect or abasement.

d) *the Nationalist ticket*: After the fall of Parnell, the Irish Party split into various factions, two of which in this election would have been the Gaelic League and the United Irish League. 'The Nationalist ticket' covers all these aspirants for Home Rule. See also 'A Painful Case' (98b) for one split in the Labour camp.

e) *spondulics*: Money. The word is most likely derived from Greek *sp(h)ondylos*, a vertebra, after the resemblance between a pile of coins and the spine (demonstrated by Farrington's little cylinder (81)).

f) *address of welcome*: When King Edward VII arrived in Dublin in 1903, the Corporation had voted by forty to thirty-seven against an official welcoming speech, and none was given. However, a typical 'Irish solution' was found: a welcome was given outside the city boundary by officials from suburban Councils instead, particularly those of Kingstown and the Ballsbridge area. It is doubtful whether the King noticed the difference.

g) *Musha*: From the Irish *muise, má 'seadh*, meaning 'if so', 'nonetheless', 'indeed', 'ah well'.

h) *some life*: This implies that there is no life now, which is one of the messages of *D*. In 'Drama and Life', a paper he read to the University College Literary and Historical Society in 1900, Joyce declared: 'It is sinful foolishness to sigh back for the good old times'.

i) *Mr Henchy*: Stanislaus (who disliked John Joyce) in *MBK* writes that Henchy was 'my father toned down to his surroundings'. It seems an unkind assessment. John Henchy is as much the villain as Joe Hynes is the hero of the story. He has drifted far from the principles of Parnellism, is the most avid to be paid and the most scornful of those who are, and he jokes bitterly of his political ambitions.

j) *Did you serve*: i.e. canvass.

k) *Aungier Street*: It rhymes with manger or ranger, and leads north into South Great George's Street. Tom Moore was born here, and Peg Woffington (54g) played Ophelia at the Aungier Street Theatre.

—The working-man, said Mr Hynes, gets all kicks
and no halfpence. But it's labour produces everything. The
working-man is not looking for fat jobs for his sons and
nephews and cousins. The working-man is not going to
drag the honour of Dublin in the mud to please a German
monarch—

—How's that? said the old man—

—Don't you know they want to present an address of
welcome to Edward Rex if he comes here next year? What do
we want kowtowing to a foreign king?—

—Our man won't vote for the address, said Mr O'Connor.
He goes in on the Nationalist ticket—

—Won't he? said Mr Hynes. Wait till you see whether he
will or not. I know him. Is it Tricky Dicky Tierney?—

—By God! perhaps you're right, Joe, said Mr O'Connor.
Anyway, I wish he'd turn up with the spondulics—

The three men fell silent. The old man began to rake more
cinders together. Mr Hynes took off his hat, shook it and then
turned down the collar of his coat, displaying, as he did so, an
ivy leaf in the lapel.

—If this man was alive, he said, pointing to the leaf, we'd
have no talk of an address of welcome—

—That's true, said Mr O'Connor—

—Musha, God be with them times! said the old man. There
was some life in it then—

The room was silent again. Then a bustling little man with
a snuffling nose and very cold ears pushed in the door. He
walked over quickly to the fire, rubbing his hands as if he
intended to produce a spark from them.

—No money, boys, he said—

—Sit down here, Mr Henchy, said the old man, offering
him his chair—

—O, don't stir, Jack, don't stir, said Mr Henchy—

He nodded curtly to Mr Hynes and sat down on the chair
which the old man vacated.

—Did you serve Aungier Street? he asked Mr O'Connor—

—Yes, said Mr O'Connor, beginning to search his pockets
for memoranda—

—Did you call on Grimes?—

—I did—

—Well? How does he stand?—

l) *Grimes*: The first of three
people mentioned in *D* with
this name. Michael Grimes,
the pawnbroker, appears in
'Grace' (153l) and, in 'The
Dead' (164m), Mary Grimes
comes into the fragmented
anecdote told by Mr Browne.

m) *How does he stand?*: The
phrase is an echo of the street
ballad 'The Wearing of the
Green', which was popu-
larised by Dion Boucicault
and Madame Vestris, and
includes the lines:

> I met wid Napper Tandy,
> and he took me by the
> hand,
> And said he, 'How's poor
> ould Ireland, and how does
> she stand?'
> 'She's the most distressful
> country that iver yet was
> seen,
> For they're hangin' men
> and women there for the
> Wearin' o' the Green'.

Napper Tandy was a founder
of the 1790s revolutionary
organisation, the United Irishmen (112c).

a) **I won't tell anyone**: For some thirty years, elections had been conducted by secret ballot.

b) *nominators*: These usually 'solid' members of the community put forward the names of potential candidates for election. In a small constituency, the more friends these nominators have, the more likely their candidate's success. It is still wise, in the elections for University seats in the Irish Senate, for example, to have a priest among one's nominators. The 1903 election in the Royal Exchange Ward saw a delightful battle between the Prior of the Discalced (technically, 'barefoot') Carmelites in Clarendon Street and the Prior of the Calced Carmelites in Aungier Street who each nominated different candidates. Public letters were exchanged, in which priests were described as, among other things, 'unscrupulous wire-pullers'.

c) *Father Burke*: Like Grimes, at 109l, another one of the names that link the stories of *D* together. Father Burke can be seen as representative of the 'political' priesthood of Ireland, which used the pulpit to help topple Parnell. In 'Grace', 'Father Tom', the Catholic orator, is mentioned. Contemporary readers would have known that his surname was Burke, and should have picked up the echo.

d) *shoeboy*: Literally meaning 'shoeblack', a profession which involves kneeling at the feet of those who are paying you. The word has no connection with 'jewboy', as has been hazarded. In *U* there are shoeboys at the GPO – one of whom ('a bootblack') is a putative lover of Molly Bloom. The most notorious Dubliner to begin his career as a 'shoeboy' was the 'Sham Squire' Francis Higgins (1746–1802) who went on to work in the scullery of Mangan's maternal grandfather, and finally to own the *Freeman's Journal*. In D. L. Kelleher's *The Glamour of Dublin* (1928), Higgins' grave in Kilbarrack is celebrated thus:

> For to-day under his shattered headstone that indignant hands have broken up lies the dust of Francis Higgins, the type of all the Borgias of modern Dublin, the 'Sham Squire' who seduced and procured and informed from the days when a potboy in Fishamble Street, he progressed *via* shoeblack, waiter, and pimp to Castle spy in chief. Until, having sold Lord Edward Fitzgerald and

others of the rebels, he died and was buried here, by a bitter irony, in the circle of saints and seamen.

Higgins had betrayed Lord Edward Fitzgerald's whereabouts for the sum of £1,000, which led to Fitzgerald's capture. (See also 111h.)

e) **work going on properly**: It doesn't seem to be.

f) *'Usha*: A variant of 'musha' (109g).

g) *Mr Fanning*: This is Long John Fanning, modelled on 'Long' John Clancy, the Sub-Sheriff. He appears many times in *U*. Fanning is an appropriate name in a story in which fire has such an important role. The Sub-Sheriff is also alluded to in 'Grace' (141k).

h) *his little old father*: Knowing, or having known, or claiming to have known someone's father is a time-honoured putdown.

i) *hand-me-down shop in Mary's Lane*: In Partridge's *Slang*, such a shop means two things: 1) a shop for second-hand clothes and 2) an illegal pawnbroker's. Running behind the Four Courts north of the Liffey, Mary's Lane was an impoverished shopping street, then full of ruins and tenements.

j) *before the houses were open*: Before legal opening time in the public houses.

k) *a trousers*: One of Dublin's rare dual nouns (like 'a ballocks' – which Temple acknowledges being in *P* (V.3)). In *Cruiskeen Lawn*, Myles na Gopaleen featured 'a corduroys', meaning a man of artistic pretensions.

l) *moya!*: From the Irish *mar dheadh*, conveying 'as it were', 'hem hem', 'forsooth', 'my foot' (or even 'arse'), 'so to speak', 'I don't think'.

m) *little black bottle*: Presumably containing spirits, or even poteen, illegal because government duty has not been paid on it (rather than for any ill-effect is might have on the health).

n) *Do you mind now?*: Unlike Mr Alleyne's usage (77b), the question here means either 'Do you remember?' or simply 'Imagine that!'

o) *how-do-you-do*: A fine mess, bad business.

p) *stump up*: Pay up, pony up.

q) *bailiffs*: Tough men acting on behalf of landlords or other creditors. Mr Mooney of 'The Boarding House' (53l) is one of them. If Henchy is indeed modelled on John Joyce, this detail is accurate enough.

—He wouldn't promise. He said: *I won't tell anyone what way I'm going to vote.* But I think he'll be all right—

—Why so?—

—He asked me who the nominators were, and I told him. I mentioned Father Burke's name. I think it'll be all right—

Mr Henchy began to snuffle and to rub his hands over the fire at a terrific speed. Then he said:

—For the love of God, Jack, bring us in a bit of coal. There must be some left—

The old man went out of the room.

—It's no go, said Mr Henchy, shaking his head. I asked the little shoeboy, but he said: *O, now, Mr Henchy, when I see the work going on properly I won't forget you, you may be sure.* Mean little tinker! 'Usha, how could he be anything else?—

—What did I tell you, Mat? said Mr Hynes. Tricky Dicky Tierney—

—O, he's as tricky as they make 'em, said Mr Henchy. He hasn't got those little pigs' eyes for nothing. Blast his soul! Couldn't he pay up like a man instead of: *O, now Mr Henchy, I must speak to Mr Fanning first ... I've spent a lot of money ...* Mean bloody little shoeboy! I suppose he forgets the time his little old father kept the hand-me-down shop in Mary's Lane—

—But is that a fact? asked Mr O'Connor—

—God, yes, said Mr Henchy. Did you never hear that? And the men used to go in on Sunday morning before the houses were open to buy a waistcoat or a trousers – moya! But Tricky Dicky's little old father always had a tricky little black bottle up in a corner. Do you mind now? That's that. That's where he first saw the light—

The old man returned with a few lumps of coal which he placed here and there on the fire.

—That's a nice how-do-you-do, said Mr O'Connor. How does he expect us to work for him if he won't stump up?—

—I can't help it, said Mr Henchy. I expect to find the bailiffs in the hall when I go home—

Mr Hynes laughed and, shoving himself away from the mantelpiece with the aid of his shoulders, made ready to leave.

—It'll be all right when King Eddie comes, he said. Well, boys, I'm off for the present. See you later. 'Bye, 'bye—

He went out of the room slowly. Neither Mr Henchy nor the old man said anything but, just as the door was closing,

Eagerly awaited – Guinness! The bottles are of the old cork-stoppered sort

a) *Do you twig*: Do you understand? The slang verb 'twig' comes directly from the Irish *tuig*, 'to understand'.

b) *a decent skin*: Anglo-Irish slang, meaning 'a good sort', as in Brendan Behan's *Borstal Boy* (1958): 'He was known far and wide as a decent old skin'.

c) *nineteen carat*: Absolutely pure gold (twenty-four carat) is too soft to use for jewellery, the usual minimum for 'gold' being eighteen carat. But nineteen carat is not a recognised standard: the phrase 'He's nineteen carat' would mean, if anything, 'he's better than good quality'. The negative, as here, conveys, with dark irony, that he's not.

d) *sponging*: As does Weathers in 'The Boarding House', who is a 'sponge' (83k). No evidence is provided, but Henchy feels that he's hanging around in the hope of getting a drink.

e) *hillsiders and fenians*: 'The name "Hillside men" ... applied to the Fenians' (*Daily News* December 1890). Named after one of the ancient peoples of Ireland, the Fenians (founded in the mid-nineteenth century) were an organisation dedicated to the physical overthrow of British government in Ireland. A celebration of the old culture by P. J. McCall, *The Fenian Nights Entertainments* (1897), had this on the title-page:

> Michael O'Neill is my name
> Ireland is my nation
> Bargy is my dwelling-place
> And heaven my expectation ...

The 'cod' played by Fleming on Stephen in *P* (I.2) is related to this.

f) *Castle hacks*: Informers in the pay of Dublin Castle (44c). The phrase is on the model of the slang 'garrison-hacks', prostitutes who served the soldiery of a town's garrison.

g) *a certain little nobleman*: A photograph showing the far from popular Sir Joseph Downes (90k) with a squint of some sort would confirm a suspicion that this is he, though perhaps Sir Thomas Pile or any Lord Mayor is referred to. There is a parallel, as so often in this story, with 1798: Lord Cornwallis, appointed Lord Lieutenant in that year (and who presided over the implementation of the Union), also had eyes that did not match, one of them being smaller than the other and with a constant fluttering wink.

h) *Major Sirr*: Major Henry Charles Sirr (1764–1841), soldier and (like Tierney) Dublin wine-merchant, was the notoriously reactionary head of the Dublin police and therefore relied on a large network of

An affray in Dame Street a hundred years before. This one was crushed by Major Sirr (h)

Mr O'Connor who had been staring moodily into the fire, called out suddenly:

—'Bye, Joe—

Mr Henchy waited a few moments and then nodded in the direction of the door.

—Tell me, he said across the fire, what brings our friend in here? What does he want?—

—'Usha, poor Joe! said Mr O'Connor, throwing the end of his cigarette into the fire, he's hard up, like the rest of us—

Mr Henchy snuffled vigorously and spat so copiously that he nearly put out the fire, which uttered a hissing protest.

—To tell you my private and candid opinion, he said, I think he's a man from the other camp. He's a spy of Colgan's if you ask me. *Just go round and try and find out how they're getting on. They won't suspect you.* Do you twig?—

—Ah, poor Joe is a decent skin, said Mr O'Connor—

—His father was a decent respectable man, Mr Henchy admitted: Poor old Larry Hynes! Many a good turn he did in his day! But I'm greatly afraid our friend is not nineteen carat. Damn it, I can understand a fellow being hard up, but what I can't understand is a fellow sponging. Couldn't he have some spark of manhood about him?—

—He doesn't get a warm welcome from me when he comes, said the old man. Let him work for his own side and not come spying around here—

—I don't know, said Mr O'Connor dubiously, as he took out cigarette-papers and tobacco. I think Joe Hynes is a straight man. He's a clever chap, too, with the pen. Do you remember that thing he wrote . . . ?—

—Some of these hillsiders and fenians are a bit too clever if you ask me, said Mr Henchy. Do you know what my private and candid opinion is about some of those little jokers? I believe half of them are in the pay of the Castle—

There's no knowing, said the old man—

—O, but I know it for a fact, said Mr Henchy. They're Castle hacks . . . I don't say Hynes . . . No, damn it, I think he's a stroke above that . . . But there's a certain little nobleman with a cock-eye – you know the patriot I'm alluding to?—

Mr O'Connor nodded.

—There's a lineal descendant of Major Sirr for you if you like! O, the heart's blood of a patriot! That's a fellow now

informers. He was instrumental in the arrest of Robert Emmet and, thanks to the 'Sham Squire' (110d), in May 1798 he also captured Lord Edward Fitzgerald, leader of the United Irishmen. Nicholas Murphy, in whose house the arrest took place, later wrote that Major Sirr

> pushed by me quickly, and Lord Edward seeing him, sprung up instantly like a tiger, and drew a dagger . . . Major Sirr had a pistol in his waistcoat pocket which he fired . . .

In prison, Fitzgerald was to die from the results of the shoulder wound. Sirr lived on for many years in Dublin Castle.

Lord Edward Fitzgerald

a) *Father Keon*: An enigmatic character who, like Fr Flynn in 'The Sisters', no longer has an active role in the Church. He seems to be what is known in Ireland as a 'spoiled priest', and may act in the story as an embodiment of what Joyce saw as the simony of the Church. The only listed cleric of this name in Ireland at the time was the Very Rev. Canon William Keon, Parish Priest in Fairview, close to where the Joyces had lived.

b) *a discreet indulgent velvety voice*: These adjectives of priestly wheedling themselves suit the panoply of Roman Catholic practice: respectively, the circumspection of the confessional, the remissions given to sinners and the rich church-hangings. Originally the sentence continued: 'which is not often found except with the confessor or the sodomite'. The suppressed line makes explicit what might be inferred, and suggests further links with Fr Flynn.

c) *the* Black Eagle: A public house, owned by the Nationalist candidate, Tierney. The International Bar, a large establishment run by one M. O'Donohoe on the intersection of Wicklow Street and St Andrew's Street, is a nearby likely model. The fictional pub's name is possibly an allusion to a founding meeting in November 1791 of the Society of United Irishmen of Dublin which was held at the Eagle Tavern on Eustace Street (78f) near Cork Hill, with Napper Tandy in attendance as secretary. Some twelve years before, the Dublin Volunteers used to meet there, and there in 1735 the first Earl of Rosse founded the 'Hell-fire Club', whose rakish members dedicated themselves to toping, wenching and necromancy. The City Hall, to which Tierney hopes to be elected, stands near the site of the old Eagle Tavern.

d) *a little business matter*: What this might be is never specified.

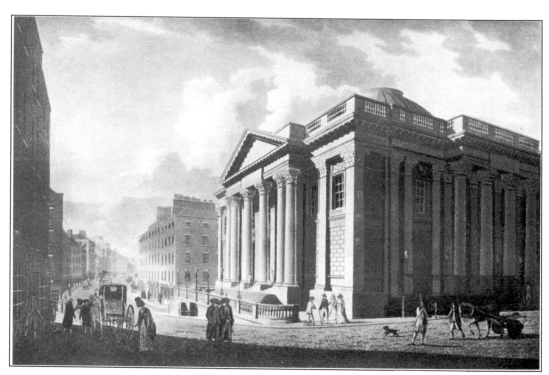

Malton's 1791 print of the City Hall – then the Royal Exchange

that'd sell his country for fourpence – aye – and go down on his bended knees and thank the Almighty Christ he had a country to sell—

There was a knock at the door.

—Come in! said Mr Henchy—

A person resembling a poor clergyman or a poor actor appeared in the doorway. His black clothes were tightly buttoned on his short body and it was impossible to say whether he wore a clergyman's collar or a layman's, because the collar of his shabby frock-coat, the uncovered buttons of which reflected the candlelight, was turned up about his neck. He wore a round hat of hard black felt. His face, shining with raindrops, had the appearance of damp yellow cheese save where two rosy spots indicated the cheekbones. He opened his very long mouth suddenly to express disappointment and at the same time opened wide his very bright blue eyes to express pleasure and surprise.

^a —O Father Keon! said Mr Henchy, jumping up from his chair. Is that you? Come in!—

—O, no, no, no! said Father Keon quickly, pursing his lips as if he were addressing a child—

—Won't you come in and sit down?—

—No, no, no! said Father Keon, speaking in a discreet ^b indulgent velvety voice. Don't let me disturb you now! I'm just looking for Mr Fanning . . .—

^c —He's round at the *Black Eagle*, said Mr Henchy. But won't you come in and sit down a minute?—

^d —No, no, thank you. It was just a little business matter, said Father Keon. Thank you, indeed—

He retreated from the doorway and Mr Henchy, seizing one of the candlesticks, went to the door to light him downstairs.

—O, don't trouble, I beg!—

—No, but the stairs is so dark—

—No, no, I can see . . . Thank you, indeed—

—Are you right now?—

—All right, thanks . . . Thanks—

Mr Henchy returned with the candlestick and put it on the table. He sat down again at the fire. There was silence for a few moments.

—Tell me, John, said Mr O'Connor, lighting his cigarette with another pasteboard card—

(c)

a) *Kavanagh's*: The Winerooms of James Kavanagh, Justice of the Peace, tea, wine and spirit merchant, were at 27 Parliament Street where the Parliament Inn is now, not far from the City Hall on Cork Hill. The establishment saw many a whispered political discussion. Long John Fanning is seen standing in a doorway of James Kavanagh's Winerooms in *U*, 'Wandering Rocks' 15 and 19.

b) *knock it out*: Earn his daily bread.

c) *shoeboy*: Again the word refers to Tierney (110d).

d) *goster*: Conversation, from the Irish *gasrán*.

e) *Alderman Cowley*: This character also appears in *U*, 'Wandering Rocks' 15, where he is sighted going into the City Hall with Councillor Abraham Lyon. There was one alderman to each ward, together with three councillors.

f) *I caught his eye*: Things had changed little since Swift's day. From one of his many political jibes, 'The Dog and the Thief':

The stock-jobber thus from Change Alley goes down
And tips you the freeman a wink:

Let me have your vote to serve for the town
And here is a guinea to drink.

g) *Yerra*: A contraction of the Irish *A Dhia ara* (hard to translate, but meaning something like 'in God's truth'), here used with a sense both dismissive and expostulatory.

h) *hop-o'-my-thumb*: Contemptuous synonym for dwarf. In 1748 Tobias Smollett used it in *Roderick Random*: 'You pitiful hop-o'-my-thumb coxcomb'.

i) *three of them hard at it*: Only by looking at the early manuscript of the story is it possible to know that Joyce had in mind Cowley, Tierney and Fanning rather than Cowley, Tierney and Keon.

j) *Suffolk Street corner*: The original site of the Viking Thingmote, the place of Dublin's first 'parliament', was here, at what is now the corner between Church Lane and Suffolk Street, which leads into Grafton Street.

k) *the City Fathers*: A somewhat inflated term for the Mayor and Corporation.

l) *Lord Mayor*: The outgoing Mayor was Timothy Charles Harrington (1851–1910), educated at both

'*Driving out of the Mansion House . . . in all me vermin . . .*' (m)

—Hm?—

—What is he exactly?—

—Ask me an easier one, said Mr Henchy—

—Fanning and himself seem to me very thick. They're often

a in Kavanagh's together. Is he a priest at all?—

—Mmmyes, I believe so ... I think he's what you call a black sheep. We haven't many of them, thank God! but we have a few ... He's an unfortunate man of some kind ...—

b —And how does he knock it out? asked Mr O'Connor—

—That's another mystery—

—Is he attached to any chapel or church or institution or ...?—

—No, said Mr Henchy, I think he's travelling on his own account ... God forgive me, he added, I thought he was the dozen of stout—

—Is there any chance of a drink itself? asked Mr O'Connor—

—I'm dry too, said the old man—

c —I asked that little shoeboy three times, said Mr Henchy, would he send up a dozen of stout. I asked him again now but he was leaning on the counter in his shirt-sleeves having a deep

de goster with Alderman Cowley—

—Why didn't you remind him? said Mr O'Connor—

—Well, I couldn't go over while he was talking to Alderman

f Cowley. I just waited till I caught his eye and said: *About that little matter I was speaking to you about ... That'll be all right, Mr*

gh *H,* he said. Yerra, sure the little hop-o'-my-thumb has forgotten all about it—

—There's some deal on in that quarter, said Mr O'Connor

i thoughtfully. I saw the three of them hard at it yesterday at

j Suffolk Street corner—

—I think I know the little game they're at, said Mr Henchy.

k You must owe the City Fathers money nowadays if you want

l to be made Lord Mayor. Then they'll make you Lord Mayor. By God! I'm thinking seriously of becoming a City Father myself. What do you think? Would I do for the job?—

Mr O'Connor laughed.

—So far as owing money goes ...—

m —Driving out of the Mansion House, said Mr Henchy, in

n all me vermin, with Jack here standing up behind me in a powdered wig – eh?—

the Catholic University and Trinity, MP for the Harbour Division of Dublin City, barrister and faithful Parnellite, who had been thrice elected Lord Mayor of Dublin for the years 1901–3. A man of some style, with two residences – one in Rutland Square – he was often accused of flunkeydom. He was a benevolent acquaintance of his fellow Corkman John Joyce, furnishing James with a glowing reference for his 1902 trip to Paris, a letter still being made use of in Rome in 1907 (47b).

m) *the Mansion House*: On Dawson Street, this Queen Anne building has been the official residence of the Lord Mayor of Dublin since 1715. Its Round Room and other chambers were and are used for public meetings and private functions (129d).

n) *vermin*: Henchy's ratty pun on 'ermine' refers to the Mayor's robes.

A taste of Dublin local politics, from the Evening Mail, *December 1903 (c)*

a) *a family party*: Mr Henchy as Lord Mayor with a corrupt chaplain and a hideous old footman makes for a grotesquerie worthy of Hogarth or Swift.

b) *Keegan*: Patrick Keegan presumably worked in the Mansion House. It was a common Dublin name.

c) your new master: As Harrington had been Mayor for three years, and had decided not to run in 1904, this would be his successor, Joseph Hutchinson of Drumcondra, General Secretary of the Irish National Foresters and a long-serving Nationalist councillor for Merchants' Quay Ward. His election was something of a surprise – the Unionist candidate, Alderman Cotton, was defeated by forty-one votes to thirty-seven. Hutchinson's first official act was to telegraph to Pope Pius X, feudally tendering 'on behalf of citizens and friends … his profound and dutiful homage' and wishing him 'a long and glorious reign'. The Pope sent his apostolic blessing.

d) the smell of an oil-rag: One of a large number of Dublin idioms connoting frugality or meanness: a current one is 'He wouldn't give you the steam off his piss'. By 1904, the salary of the Lord Mayoralty was, after London, the largest in the world: £3,650.

e) Wisha!: Musha (109g).

f) *tally*: The word can also mean 'a company or division of votes at an election'. It has its echo on the last page of 'Grace'.

g) *O'Farrell's*: A fictional name, but nearly opposite Central Chambers on Wicklow Street where the committee room may have been was Foley's Hotel, a good source for a corkscrew. 'The Rising of the Moon', another Fenian song of '98 (109m), begins: 'O then, tell me, Shawn O'Farrell …'

—And make me your private secretary, John—

—Yes. And I'll make Father Keon my private chaplain.
We'll have a family party—

—Faith, Mr Henchy, said the old man, you'd keep up better
style than some of them. I was talking one day to old Keegan,
the porter. *And how do you like your new master, Pat?* says I to
him. *You haven't much entertaining now,* says I. *Entertaining!* says
he. *He'd live on the smell of an oil-rag.* And do you know what
he told me? Now, I declare to God, I didn't believe him—

—What? said Mr Henchy and Mr O'Connor—

—He told me: *What do you think of a Lord Mayor of Dublin
sending out for a pound of chops for his dinner? How's that for high
living?* says he. *Wisha! wisha,* says I. *A pound of chops,* says he,
coming into the Mansion House. Wisha! says I, *what kind of people
is going at all now?*—

At this point there was a knock at the door, and a boy put
in his head.

—What is it? said the old man—

—From the *Black Eagle,* said the boy, walking in sideways
and depositing a basket on the floor with a noise of shaken
bottles—

The old man helped the boy to transfer the bottles from the
basket to the table and counted the full tally. After the transfer
the boy put his basket on his arm and asked:

—Any bottles?—

—What bottles? said the old man—

—Won't you let us drink them first? said Mr Henchy—

—I was told to ask for bottles—

—Come back to-morrow, said the old man—

—Here, boy! said Mr Henchy, will you run over to O'Farrell's and ask him to lend us a corkscrew – for Mr Henchy,
say. Tell him we won't keep it a minute. Leave the basket
there—

The boy went out and Mr Henchy began to rub his hands
cheerfully, saying:

—Ah, well, he's not so bad after all. He's as good as his
word, anyhow—

—There's no tumblers, said the old man—

—O, don't let that trouble you, Jack, said Mr Henchy.
Many's the good man before now drank out of the bottle—

—Anyway, it's better than nothing, said Mr O'Connor—

Mr. T. C. Harrington, M.P.

The Royal Exchange Hotel was almost opposite Kavanagh's Wine Rooms (113a)

—He's not a bad sort, said Mr Henchy, only Fanning has
a such a loan of him. He means well, you know, in his own
b tinpot way—

The boy came back with the corkscrew. The old man opened
three bottles and was handing back the corkscrew when Mr
Henchy said to the boy:

—Would you like a drink, boy?—

—If you please, sir, said the boy—

The old man opened another bottle grudgingly, and handed
it to the boy.

—What age are you? he asked—

c —Seventeen, said the boy—

As the old man said nothing further the boy took the bottle
and said: *Here's my best respects, sir,* to Mr Henchy, drank the
contents, put the bottle back on the table and wiped his mouth
with his sleeve. Then he took up the corkscrew and went out
of the door sideways, muttering some form of salutation.

—That's the way it begins, said the old man—

—The thin edge of the wedge, said Mr Henchy—

The old man distributed the three bottles which he had
opened and the men drank from them simultaneously. After
having drunk each placed his bottle on the mantelpiece within
hand's reach and drew in a long breath of satisfaction.

—Well, I did a good day's work to-day, said Mr Henchy
after a pause—

—That so, John?—

d —Yes. I got him one or two sure things in Dawson Street,
e Crofton and myself. Between ourselves, you know, Crofton
(he's a decent chap, of course), but he's not worth a damn as a
canvasser. He hasn't a word to throw to a dog. He stands and
looks at the people while I do the talking—

Here two men entered the room. One of them was a very
fat man, whose blue serge clothes seemed to be in danger of
falling from his sloping figure. He had a big face which
resembled a young ox's face in expression, staring blue eyes
and a grizzled moustache. The other man, who was much
younger and frailer, had a thin clean-shaven face. He wore a
very high double collar and a wide-brimmed bowler hat.

—Hello, Crofton! said Mr Henchy to the fat man. Talk of
the devil . . .—

—Where did the boose come from? asked the young man.

a) *has such a loan of him*: Has
such influence upon him, has
him under such an obligation.
b) *tinpot*: Inferior, shabby.
Rudyard Kipling, much-
admired by Joyce, used it in
The Light that Failed (1897):
'To the tin-pot music of a
Western waltz the naked Zan-
zibari girls danced furiously'.
c) *Seventeen*: Eighteen is now
the legal age for drinking
alcohol in an Irish pub,
although one can still be or
work in one under that age.
d) *Dawson Street*: Only the
western side of Dawson Street
is fully in the ward. It is named
after Joshua Dawson, who
sold the Mansion House to the
corporation for £3,500.
e) *Crofton*: J. T. A. Crofton
was a real person, who had
worked in the Rates Office at
the same time as John Joyce.
A Protestant, he is referred to
in *U*, 'Cyclops', as 'a pensioner
out of the Collector General's'. He was actually outside
Ireland from 1899 to 1907, and
was buried in Mount Jerome
Cemetery. Crofton is also
mentioned in 'Grace' (147f).

Victoria, regnant (117d)

a Did the cow calve?—

b —O, of course, Lyons spots the drink first thing! said Mr O'Connor, laughing—

—Is that the way you chaps can'vass, said Mr Lyons, and Crofton and I out in the cold and rain looking for votes?—

—Why, blast your soul, said Mr Henchy, I'd get more votes in five minutes than you two'd get in a week—

—Open two bottles of stout, Jack, said Mr O'Connor—

—How can I? said the old man, when there's no corkscrew?—

—Wait now, wait now! said Mr Henchy, getting up quickly. Did you ever see this little trick?—

c He took two bottles from the table and, carrying them to the fire, put them on the hob. Then he sat down again by the fire and took another drink from his bottle. Mr Lyons sat on the edge of the table, pushed his hat towards the nape of his neck and began to swing his legs.

—Which is my bottle? he asked—

d —This lad, said Mr Henchy—

Mr Crofton sat down on a box and looked fixedly at the other bottle on the hob. He was silent for two reasons. The e first reason, sufficient in itself, was that he had nothing to say; the second reason was that he considered his companions f beneath him. He had been a canvasser for Wilkins, the Conservative, but when the Conservatives had withdrawn their man and, choosing the less of two evils, given their support to the Nationalist candidate, he had been engaged to work for Mr Tierney.

g In a few minutes an apologetic *Pok!* was heard as the cork flew out of Mr Lyons' bottle. Mr Lyons jumped off the table, went to the fire, took his bottle and carried it back to the table.

—I was just telling them, Crofton, said Mr Henchy, that we got a good few votes to-day—

—Who did you get? asked Mr Lyons—

h —Well, I got Parkes for one, and I got Atkinson for two, and I got Ward of Dawson Street. Fine old chap he is, too – regular old toff, old Conservative! *But isn't your candidate a Nationalist?* said he. *He's a respectable man,* said I. *He's in favour of whatever will benefit this country. He's a big rate-payer,* I said. *He has extensive house property in the city and three places of business* i *and isn't it to his own advantage to keep down the rates? He's a*

a) *Did the cow calve?*: Has your ship come in?
b) *Lyons*: Identifiable from the manuscript of the story as Frederick M. (Bantam) Lyons, also in 'The Boarding House' (56c) and *U.*
c) *the hob*: The iron side of the grate. 'Hob' also means devil or goblin.
d) *This lad*: A very frequent Dublin idiom of personification, echoing the story's theme of fathers and sons.
e) *sufficient in itself*: The philosophical principle of Occam's Razor dictates that one apt explanation makes subsequent ones unnecessary. But Occam was not discussing fiction.
f) *Wilkins*: The Conservative candidate, although backing British rule in Ireland, is, significantly, closer to the Nationalist than to the Labour cause, the only one genuinely to challenge the status quo.
g) *Pok!*: Lyons' *Pok!* is 'apologetic', as Crofton's is to be 'tardy'. The adjectives can be seen as descriptive of the depth and duration of these canvassers' respect for Parnell.
h) *Parkes ... Atkinson ... Ward*: The first is a rare name in Dublin, and probably not a Catholic one. The implication is that Parkes was probably a natural Unionist voter. The second is most likely a Protestant name too. There were several Atkinsons in the ward at this time, including William Atkinson & Son, solicitors, in Molesworth Street. The only Ward of substance in the electoral district was the Rev. P. M. Ward, sub-prior of the Carmelite convent in Aungier Street (110b).
i) *rates*: See 143j.

a) Poor Law Guardian: See 106k.

b) *The King's coming here*: There was a good deal of controversy over the proposed visit of Edward VII, one of whose many titles was 'Earl of Dublin'. In April 1903, for example, the *Freeman's Journal* printed a letter from W. B. Yeats:

> ... Royal visits with their pageantry, their false rumours of concessions, their appeal to all that is superficial and trivial in society, are part of the hypnotic illusion by which England seeks to take captive the imagination of this country ...

c) *Didn't Parnell himself* ...: In 1885 Parnell had opposed the idea of an official welcome for Edward VII (then still Prince of Wales).

d) *his bloody old mother*: Queen Victoria, who died in 1901 aged eighty-two. Previous editions of this story omit the first adjective, which under pressure Joyce deleted from the manuscript.

e) *grey*: Edward VII was about sixty when he acceded to the throne. Joyce sent this passage to King George V when George Roberts objected to it, but the King, predictably, was noncommittal in his reply.

f) The old one: The device of putting Dublinese into the mouths of British royalty is one that was also used to good effect by Percy French (81(o)) and later by George D. Hodnett (in his song 'Monto').

g) never went to see: In fact, as Joyce, Edward VII, Mr. Henchy and Irish readers knew perfectly well, Queen Victoria had last visited Ireland in 1900 and had toured around the country for a considerable time. This reminder that what we are reading is fictional serves to highlight the contrast between the two kings in the story: Edward, crowned, and Parnell, uncrowned – a royal exchange in the Royal Exchange Ward.

h) *bloody Irish people*: Again under pressure, Joyce altered this to 'wild Irish', an epithet that Lady Morgan (66d) made famous with her 1806 novel, *The Wild Irish Girl*.

i) *knockabout*: A happy-go-lucky fellow. In the theatre, the word meant a slapstick actor (as used in 'Counterparts' (82m)).

THE KING AND QUEEN IN THE ROYAL CARRIAGE AT THE LANDING PLACE AT KINGSTOWN

At the jetty at the Victoria Wharf a detachment of marines and bluejackets was lined up as a guard of honour facing the pavilion, where the King and Queen were received and an address from the District Council of Kingstown presented. The pavilion was a dainty arrangement of delicate purple and yellow draping and choice plants. The furniture used in the pavilion was of the style of Louis XIV. The Earl of Meath, the Lord Lieutenant of the county of Dublin, took a leading part in directing the arrangements for the reception

Edward VII at Kingstown

117

a *prominent and respected citizen*, said I, *and a Poor Law Guardian, and he doesn't belong to any party, good, bad, or indifferent.* That's the way to talk to 'em—

—And what about the address to the King? said Mr Lyons, after drinking and smacking his lips—

—Listen to me, said Mr Henchy. What we want in this country, as I said to old Ward, is capital. The King's coming

b here will mean an influx of money into this country. The citizens of Dublin will benefit by it. Look at all the factories down by the quays there, idle! Look at all the money there is in the country if we only worked the old industries, the mills, the shipbuilding yards and factories. It's capital we want—

—But look here, John, said Mr O'Connor. Why should we

c welcome the King of England? Didn't Parnell himself . . .—

—Parnell, said Mr Henchy, is dead. Now, here's the way I look at it. Here's this chap come to the throne after his bloody

de old mother keeping him out of it till the man was grey. He's a man of the world, and he means well by us. He's a jolly fine decent fellow, if you ask me, and no damn nonsense about

fg him. He just says to himself: *The old one never went to see these*

h *bloody Irish people. By Christ, I'll go myself and see what they're like.* And are we going to insult the man when he comes over here on a friendly visit? Eh? Isn't that right, Crofton?—

Mr Crofton nodded his head.

—But after all now, said Mr Lyons argumentatively, King Edward's life, you know, is not the very . . . —

—Let bygones by bygones, said Mr Henchy. I admire the

i man personally. He's just an ordinary knockabout like you and

j me. He's fond of his glass of grog and he's a bit of a rake,

k perhaps, and he's a good sportsman. Damn it, can't we Irish play fair?—

—That's all very fine, said Mr Lyons. But look at the case of Parnell now—

—In the name of God, said Mr Henchy, where's the analogy between the two cases?—

—What I mean, said Mr Lyons, is we have our ideals. Why,

l now, would we welcome a man like that? Do you think now after what he did Parnell was a fit man to lead us? And why, then, would we do it for Edward the Seventh?—

—This is Parnell's anniversary, said Mr O'Connor, and don't let us stir up any bad blood. We all respect him now that he's

j) *grog . . . a bit of a rake*: Rum, or any 'hard stuff'. 'Rake' was originally an abbreviation of 'rakehell' (a despicable debauchee), and has come to mean a man of flamboyant and dissolute behaviour. Hogarth's series of pictures, 'The Rake's Progress', shows the decline of such a man, and R. B. Sheridan (54e), in *The Duenna* (1775), asks: 'Is he not a gay dissipated rake who has squandered his patrimony?' Scurrilous publications of the time described the king's rackety life: he was said to have made a nocturnal visit to Monto ('Nighttown') during at least one of his *Pax Britannica* visits to Dublin. As the Citizen says in *U*, 'Cyclops':

> There's a bloody sight more pox than pax about that fellow.

k) *a good sportsman*: Clearly, this implies that he was a huntsman and a gambling man, but the word also has an echo in the Dublin phrase 'sport king', one who goes out simply to enjoy himself.

l) *a man like that*: The phrase is also Cotter's in 'The Sisters'.

The King with his German cousin, Kaiser Bill

Route map

Driving from Kingstown Harbour

(b)

dead and gone – even the Conservatives, he added, turning to Mr Crofton—

Pok! The tardy cork flew out of Mr Crofton's bottle. Mr Crofton got up from his box and went to the fire. As he returned with his capture he said in a deep voice:

—Our side of the house respects him, because he was a gentleman—

—Right you are, Crofton! said Mr Henchy fiercely. He was the only man that could keep that bag of cats in order. *Down, ye dogs! Lie down, ye curs!* That's the way he treated them. Come in, Joe! Come in! he called out, catching sight of Mr Hynes in the doorway—

Mr Hynes came in slowly.

—Open another bottle of stout, Jack, said Mr Henchy. O, I forgot there's no corkscrew! Here, show me one here and I'll put it at the fire—

The old man handed him another bottle and he placed it on the hob.

—Sit down, Joe, said Mr O'Connor, we're just talking about the Chief—

—Aye, aye! said Mr Henchy—

Mr Hynes sat on the side of the table near Mr Lyons but said nothing.

—There's one of them, anyhow, said Mr Henchy, that didn't renege him. By God, I'll say for you, Joe! No, by God, you stuck to him like a man!—

—O, Joe, said Mr O'Connor suddenly. Give us that thing you wrote – do you remember? Have you got it on you?—

—O, aye! said Mr Henchy. Give us that. Did you ever hear that, Crofton? Listen to this now: splendid thing—

—Go on, said Mr O'Connor. Fire away, Joe—

Mr Hynes did not seem to remember at once the piece to which they were alluding but after reflecting a while, he said:

—O, that thing is it ... Sure, that's old now—

—Out with it, man! said Mr O'Connor—

—'Sh, 'sh, said Mr Henchy. Now, Joe!—

Mr Hynes hesitated a little longer. Then amid the silence he took off his hat, laid it on the table and stood up. He seemed to be rehearsing the piece in his mind. After a rather long pause he announced:

a) *bag of cats*: Kindred to the Anglo-Irish catchphrase, 'as cross as a bag of weasels'. A reportedly traditional swindle at country fairs was to sell cats (in place of piglets) in bags.

b) Down, ye dogs! Lie down, ye curs!: The image of Parnell as a hunted animal was frequently used. He was later seen by Yeats as a quarry which 'popular rage ... dragged down'. In a 1912 article in Italian, 'L'Ombra di Parnell', Joyce describes how the 'uncrowned king' begged his countrymen 'not to cast him as a sacrifice to the English wolves that howled around them'. The idea recurred in *FW* (479). Joyce's article went on to say of the Irish that they 'did not cast him to the English wolves: they ripped him to bits themselves'. And Joyce identified with the imagery himself: in *SH* Stephen invites the 'pack of enmities' to his 'highlands' where he would 'fling them disdain from flashing antlers'. This idea was also treated in 'The Holy Office'.

c) *show me one here*: 'Show here' is still often used for 'give' in Ireland.

d) *the Chief*: This honorific title for Parnell as leader of the Home Rule Party, and by extension, of Ireland, looks back to the ancient Irish chieftainships. More recently, Eamon de Valera enjoyed the title for a time, while Michael Collins was 'The Big Fellow'. Charles Haughey, however, became 'The Boss'.

e) *renege him*: Desert or deny him – hence 'renegade'. An unusual transitive use of the verb.

a) *THE DEATH OF PARNELL*: The poem is in the tradition of innumerable patriotic verses of the period, including one about Parnell, which was given the title 'Et Tu, Healy' (though Joyce in a letter of November 1916 referred to it as 'Parnell'). This was written by the precocious nine year old James, and was printed and distributed by John Joyce, the poet's proud father. What remains of it begins:

My cot alas that dear old shady home ...

In *FW* (231) Joyce parodies his own work:

– *My God, alas, that dear olt tumtum home*
Whereof in youthfood port I preyed
Amook the verdigrassy convict vallsall dazes.
And cloitered for amourmeant in thy boosome shede!

Parnell's Faithful Few, edited around this time by Mrs Leamy, printed poems similar to Mr Hynes'. The book included one by Katherine Tynan, and also the following:

He is not dead, he cannot die,
Remember it, brothers, early and late
Our king is buried, but not his heart ...
He leads us onward to slay the foe.
  His voice is the battle cry
  And our bugle call
From among the dead, where over all
  He standeth tall ...

(From 'A Lament, October 11th 1891' by U. Ashworth Taylor.) And from 'The Dead Chief' by Ethna Carbery:

We made of our heart's love a mantle
  That a monarch of men might have worn.
And we knew not the brave brows were bleeding
  'Neath the torture of men a thorn.
Woe to the stranger who prompted
  The sons of our land to disgrace –
Woe to the hypocrite whining
  That flaunted its creed in your face –
Woe to the false friend, the Judas,
  Who smote you to death in your place.

b) Erin: A frequent poetic name for Ireland.
c) the fell gang / Of modern hypocrites: No bad description of Mr Hynes' audience. Fell means cruel, or ruthless, as in *Hamlet* (V.ii): 'That fell sergeant, Death ...'
d) coward hounds / He raised to glory: Those of his parliamentary colleagues who did Parnell down had achieved their positions only because of his leadership. Their treachery was seen to be of a deep kind.
e) Erin's dreams / Perish upon her monarch's pyre: Probably true. Gladstone in old age said to Parnell's biographer, Barry O'Brien:

Ah! had Parnell lived, had there been no divorce proceedings, I do solemnly believe there would be a Parliament in Ireland now. Oh! it was a terrible tragedy.

f) cot: cottage. The archaism appears in 'Et Tu, Healy' (a).
g) where'er it be: In *SH*, reading some 'lines of excited patriotism', Stephen notices nothing but 'the frequency of such contracted forms' as 'e'en, ne'er and thro'.
h) The green flag: The traditional flag of Irish freedom. There is a Nationalist song of great sentimentality: 'Wrap the green flag round me, boys'. This attire would not have appealed to Parnell, who disliked the colour intensely.
i) World: A judicious spattering of capital letters is a *sine qua non* of this sort of verse.
j) Liberty ... that idol: Swift said of himself: 'Fair Liberty was all his cry', but in the eyes of Hynes, 'Liberty' is an idol to Parnell. He is inadvertently accusing the Chief of breaking the First Commandment (which is also broken, of course, through simony).
k) caitiff: Wretched, cowardly. By this time used only in historical novels and bad verse, the word originally meant 'captive', or 'subject'. The device of using two alliterative synonyms as an intensive is one frequently employed in poetry in the Irish language.
l) smote their Lord or with a kiss: The identification of Parnell with Christ is made nearly explicit with this allusion to Judas' kiss of betrayal. Mr Hynes is accusing them of vaticide.
m) rabble-rout: An obsolete form of 'rabble', a mindless mob (99b).
n) one who spurned them in his pride: In 'The Holy Office', Joyce wrote of his literary contemporaries:

And though they spurn me from their door
My soul shall spurn them evermore.

o) He fell as fall the mighty ones: As a tragic figure of Aristotelian proportions, Parnell's heroic stature, though not the question of his fatal flaw, is addressed in the poem.

THE DEATH OF PARNELL

6th October, 1891

He cleared his throat once or twice and then began to recite:

> *He is dead. Our Uncrowned King is dead.*
> *   O, Erin, mourn with grief and woe*
> *For he lies dead whom the fell gang*
> *   Of modern hypocrites laid low.*
>
> *He lies slain by the coward hounds*
> *   He raised to glory from the mire;*
> *And Erin's hopes and Erin's dreams*
> *   Perish upon her monarch's pyre.*
>
> *In palace, cabin or in cot*
> *   The Irish heart where'er it be*
> *Is bowed with woe – for he is gone*
> *   Who would have wrought her destiny.*
>
> *He would have had his Erin famed,*
> *   The green flag gloriously unfurled,*
> *Her statesmen, bards and warriors raised*
> *   Before the nations of the World.*
>
> *He dreamed (alas, 'twas but a dream!)*
> *   Of Liberty: but as he strove*
> *To clutch that idol, treachery*
> *   Sundered him from the thing he loved.*
>
> *Shame on the coward, caitiff hands*
> *   That smote their Lord or with a kiss*
> *Betrayed him to the rabble-rout*
> *   Of fawning priests – no friends of his.*
>
> *May everlasting shame consume*
> *   The memory of those who tried*
> *To befoul and smear th'exalted name*
> *   Of one who spurned them in his pride.*
>
> *He fell as fall the mighty ones,*
> *   Nobly undaunted to the last,*
> *And death has now united him*
> *   With Erin's heroes of the past.*

Parnell on his final campaign,
after the quicklime attack

Parnell, regnant

The Phoenix Pillar in the Phoenix Park

a) No sound of strife disturb his sleep!: But of course, it should – not only because of his unfulfilled aspiration for Home Rule, but also because of the calibre of his political successors.

b) list: Listen, hearken. In *Hamlet* (I.v), the Ghost cries of another tale of treachery: 'List, list, O list . . .'.

c) like the Phœnix from the flames: There was only ever one of these mythological birds, immolated and revived about every 500 years. Parnell and the phoenix are closely linked in *FW*. Indeed, Joyce wrote about the phoenix from first to last, and the image of the dead phoenix returning to affect the living is one which has its echoes in many of the stories in *D*. Gladstone, when Barry O'Brien asked him whether Parnell should have resigned, replied: 'From public life altogether. There ought to have been a death, but there would have been a resurrection.' But from the Parnellian flames in the corner of this room, there will be no resurrection today.

d) the dawning of the day: At the end of 'After the Race' Joyce uses this potent (and clichéd) image. Contemporaneously with the appearance of the 'Celtic Twilight', the 'dawnburst' became a symbol of Irish political and cultural revival. The 'device' of the *Freeman's Journal* was what Bloom, in *U*, 'Calypso', believes Arthur Griffith called 'a homerule sun rising up in the northwest from the laneway behind the bank of Ireland'. 'Ikey touch,' thinks Bloom. An early nineteenth-century poem, 'The Dawning of the Day', by Edward Walsh, describes the wooing of a personification of Ireland, ending thus:

> Beside me sat that maid divine
>   Where grassy banks outspread.
> 'Oh, let me call thee ever mine,
>   Dear maid,' I sportive said.
> 'False man, for shame, why bring me blame?'
>   She cried, and burst away –
> The sun's first light pursued her flight
>   At the dawning of the day.

e) Pledge in the cup: The drinkers in the Committee Room lift their bottles not to Joy, nor, even on this day, to the memory of Parnell, but merely to their mouths. The only real Parnellite in the story, Mr Hynes, will leave his bottle untouched.

f) Parnell: Parnell pronounced his name as a trochee, rhyming with 'carnal'. Hynes gets it wrong, but so do many Dubliners.

g) *even Mr Lyons clapped*: Lyons is the only one who has openly expressed support for the Anti-Parnellite position of the priests.

120

a
No sound of strife disturb his sleep!
  Calmly he rests: no human pain
Or high ambition spurs him now
  The peaks of glory to attain.

b
They had their way: they laid him low.
  But Erin, list, his spirit may
c
Rise, like the Phœnix from the flames,
  When breaks the dawning of the day,
d

The day that brings us Freedom's reign.
  And on that day may Erin well
e
Pledge in the cup she lifts to Joy
f
  One grief – the memory of Parnell.

Mr Hynes sat down again on the table. When he had finished his recitation there was a silence and then a burst of clapping:
g even Mr Lyons clapped. The applause continued for a little
h time. When it had ceased all the auditors drank from their bottles in silence.

i *Pok!* The cork flew out of Mr Hynes' bottle, but Mr Hynes remained sitting flushed and bareheaded on the table. He did not seem to have heard the invitation.

—Good man, Joe! said Mr O'Connor, taking out his cigarette papers and pouch the better to hide his emotion—

—What do you think of that, Crofton? cried Mr Henchy. Isn't that fine? What?—

j Mr Crofton said that it was a very fine piece of writing.

DUBLIN: THURSDAY, JUNE 16, 1904.

---

h) *auditors*: Listeners; but note that the financial theme of the story is underlined by this slightly pedantic term.

i) Pok!: The third utterance by a bottle. Frank O'Connor convincingly saw the three sudden reports as a three-gun salute over the grave of Parnell's memory. There is no hesitant adjective attached to this final report: Mr Hynes is a true mourner, selfless, silent and reverently bareheaded.

j) *a very fine piece of writing*: Mr Crofton adroitly addresses the style of the poem, not the message, which remains unheard by all.

Before Joyce had written 'The Dead', this was his favourite story. He wrote it in the summer of 1905, and it was first published with the rest of the collection. In its unity of place and time, it resembles a play, and indeed, of all the stories in the book, it has the largest proportion of dialogue. In 1916 Joyce wrote to W. B. Yeats that with his friend Nicolo Vidacovich he had attempted to translate it into Italian – 'a dismal failure', he said, perhaps because of the colloquiality of the conversations.

Joyce set the story in 1902, the year before King Edward VII's visit to Ireland, but it seems likely that he took details (including the old caretaker and the strange priest) from a letter that Stanislaus wrote to him in Paris. Stanislaus had helped his father who was engaged as election agent and canvasser in the 1903 municipal election to the Royal Exchange Ward. In *My Brother's Keeper* he comments: 'My brother was never in a committee-room in his life'. The story was further informed by Joyce's own observations of the 1904 municipal and mayoral elections, and by the everyday political finagling he had seen around him in Dublin.

In a letter to his brother sent in February 1907, Joyce mentioned that the work of Anatole France suggested 'Ivy Day' – 'and he has now suggested another story "The Dead"'. Joyce particularly admired France's *L'Affaire Crainquebille* (1901), but perhaps more influential here were *Thaïs* (1890), with its ironical narrator, as well as the four volumes of *Histoire Contemporaine* (1897–1901), where the disenchanted pedagogue M. Bergeret's wry obser-vations of the French social and political scene may have suggested to Joyce an approach to the 'stories of public life'.

'Ivy Day' has the only explicitly political subject of the collection. The years after the downfall of Parnell were gloomy ones for the Nationalists. The cause of Irish freedom, which had seemed so close to success, no longer possessed a leader who could unite the various factions behind moderate constitutional methods. Though most local politicians pretended to be – and called themselves – Nationalists, in reality many were flattered to have the entrée to Dublin Castle, and traded on their positions of influence to pursue various suspect financial activities. Discontent with this situation was growing among the enlightened, and socialism was beginning to organise in the cities. While John Redmond carried the increasingly limp Parnellite flag, Arthur Griffith promulgated his doctrine of passive resistance through the newspaper he capably edited, the *United Irishman*.

The initial split had been between those who supported Parnell and those who believed that the priests were right, that the immoral Protestant leader had betrayed Ireland through his lust. John Joyce was a fervent Parnellite – the Christmas dinner argument in *A Portrait* was no exaggeration. James was to inherit more than a sentimental attachment to the 'Lost Leader', and almost all his work, from 'Et Tu, Healy', via *Dubliners*, to *Finnegans Wake*, would testify to the important place that Parnell occupied in Joyce's personal mythology. 'Ivy Day' compares the genuine old Parnellite loyalty (still professed by a few) with what Joyce, with reason, saw as the opportunism of current Dublin life and of many of its politicians.

The story discusses directly an event that still has an effect on Irish politics today: Edward VII's visit. The Nationalist playwright Edward Martyn – who bore the ironic nickname of 'the Edward VII of the Kildare Street Club' – was with Maud Gonne MacBride one of the leaders of the 'People's Protection Committee', a movement founded in 1903 to protest against the King's proposed visit. At the Rotunda in May, the Committee met John Redmond and the Lord Mayor, Tim Harrington. A fracas followed, and though the King, as we know, arrived in July, the Committee by 1905 had become the basis of Sinn Féin, under the leadership of Arthur Griffith. Descended – through a series of splits – from the military wing of this organisation is an anachronistic remnant – the Provisional IRA.

While the memory of Parnell provided Joyce with one political template for Mr Henchy and friends to travesty, another was found in the rebellion of 1798, references to which are several times made in the story. The year that Joyce had entered University College was the centenary of '98, and the issue was the subject of much publication and a great deal of discussion during the next few years. 1901 was the anniversary of the Union and 1903 of the year of Robert Emmet's abortive insurrection and his execution. The betrayal and capture of the leaders of the United Irishmen meant that in Dublin the '98

rising failed before it began, though in other parts of the country it had some success – thanks in several instances to the leadership of individual Catholic priests – before being crushed. The theme of betrayal was one that obsessed Joyce, and his use of history in 'Ivy Day' allowed him to examine it from three perspectives, the betrayals of 1798, the betrayal of Parnell and the multiple betrayal of principle that he saw in contemporary Dublin politics.

In *A Portrait*, a 'great fire, banked high and red' blazes in the Dedalus grate at Christmas 1891. It contrasts starkly with the sickly pyre of eked-out coal and half-exhausted cinders in the Committee Room. Both are symbols of the fire of Parnell. The one witnesses to the true faith; the other is a simulacrum, shedding its dim light on men who, in the main, pay no more than an almost simoniacal lip-service to the memory of Parnell.

But if fire represents Parnell, so Parnell also represents fire. Symbols can work in more than one direction. In Joe Hynes' poem, the spirit of the 'Uncrowned King' is likened to the phoenix, the mythical bird which remakes its own life through fire – and which is itself a symbol of the Resurrection. The fire is the fire of enthusiasm, of action, of creation, and it is ignored and reviled – even spat upon – by the canvassers. 'Ivy Day' is more than a satirical story of various more or less corrupt and hopeless characters on a certain day in Dublin; it is also a universal depiction of the ultimate sin of mankind: the rejection of life.

a) A MOTHER: Irish society tends towards the matriarchal, and the status of 'the Mammy' is traditionally high. In the Roman Catholic Church there is much veneration (technically *hyperdulia*) of the Blessed Virgin Mary, conceived without original sin because she was to be the Mother of God. Joyce's robust mothers include Mrs Mooney of 'The Boarding House' and Bella Cohen of *U*, 'Circe'.

b) *Holohan*: He reappears in *U*. When Nora Barnacle was working at Finn's Hotel, a guest of this name ('a good Catholic, of course, who makes his Easter duty regularly', Joyce wrote in a letter of August 1909) made some basic suggestions involving the use of a french letter.

c) Eire Abu *Society*: The name means 'Ireland to Victory', 'Long Live Ireland'. No organisation of this name has been traced, but there were several nationalist/cultural groups at this time in Dublin.

d) *a game leg*: The word can be pronounced 'gammy'.

e) *arguing the point*: Hard at it, à la Alderman Cowley *et al.* (113i).

f) *a high-class convent*: Dublin continues not to be short of them, though alumnae differ about their merits. Such institutions include the Holy Child and the Loreto (near Stephen's Green).

g) *ivory manners*: The adjective neatly combines paleness, aloofness and piano-playing.

h) *a brilliant life*: Joyce's first play, written when he was eighteen, was modestly titled *A Brilliant Career*, and dedicated to his own Soul. No copy is known to survive.

i) *near the limit*: i.e. of (conventional) marriageable age. Mrs Mooney of 'The Boarding House' has had similar anxieties about Polly.

j) *a bootmaker*: Joyce knew that Coleridge in his youth had run away from college and asked to work for a bootmaker of great simplicity. Bootmakers were socially superior to cobblers, who did tinkers' work (108g).

k) *Ormond Quay*: On the north side, near the Four Courts. The quay is named after James Butler, Twelfth Earl and First Duke of Ormond, and Lord-Lieutenant (intermittently) under Charles I and II.

l) *he went ... every first Friday*: A Catholic practice derived from the twelfth promise given in the strange

A MOTHER

MR HOLOHAN, ASSISTANT secretary of the *Eire Abu* Society, had been walking up and down Dublin for nearly a month, with his hands and pockets full of dirty pieces of paper, arranging about the series of concerts. He had a game leg and for this his friends called him Hoppy Holohan. He walked up and down constantly, stood by the hour at street corners arguing the point and made notes; but in the end it was Mrs Kearney who arranged everything.

Miss Devlin had become Mrs Kearney out of spite. She had been educated in a high-class convent where she had learned French and music. As she was naturally pale and unbending in manner she made few friends at school. When she came to the age of marriage she was sent out to many houses, where her playing and ivory manners were much admired. She sat amid the chilly circle of her accomplishments, waiting for some suitor to brave it and offer her a brilliant life. But the young men whom she met were ordinary and she gave them no encouragement, trying to console her romantic desires by eating a great deal of Turkish Delight in secret. However, when she drew near the limit and her friends began to loosen their tongues about her, she silenced them by marrying Mr Kearney, who was a bootmaker on Ormond Quay.

He was much older than she. His conversation, which was serious, took place at intervals in his great brown beard. After the first year of married life Mrs Kearney perceived that such a man would wear better than a romantic person, but she never put her own romantic ideas away. He was sober, thrifty and pious: he went to the altar every first Friday, sometimes with her, oftener by himself. But she never weakened in her religion and was a good wife to him. At some party in a strange house when she lifted her eyebrow ever so slightly he stood up to take his leave and, when his cough troubled him, she put the eider-down quilt over his feet and made a strong rum punch. For his part he was a model father. By paying a small sum every week into a society he ensured for both his daughters a

vision of Margaret Mary Alacoque (29q). Mrs Kearney – unless she has done the Fridays already – is not a devotee.

m) *a society*: Almost certainly a 'friendly society', for the promotion of thrift.

Alias 'Marlborough Street' (55n)

Some amenities of Skerries

a) *one hundred pounds each*: A considerable sum, which in 1904 could, for example, buy one of several advertised cottages ('perfect order') on the Sorrento Road in Dalkey.

b) *French and music*: Kathleen is following precisely in her mother's footsteps. The implication is that neither mother nor daughter were taught anything else.

c) *the Academy*: The Royal Irish Academy of Music. It was founded in 1856 at 18 Stephen's Green, and its earliest fund-raising venture was a performance of *Maritana* (127d) at the Antient Concert Rooms. The Academy moved to 36 Westland Row in 1871 and the following year became 'Royal'. It was incorporated in 1889 and its qualifications were defined: above the 'grades', one could work for the diplomas of Fellow or Licentiate. It was also possible to pursue a Certificate of Proficiency in Teaching.

d) *Skerries . . . Howth . . . Greystones*: All seaside resorts near Dublin, with sizeable Protestant populations, and therefore strong connotations of gentility.

e) *Irish Revival*: A cultural movement to re-establish the general use of the Irish language. It developed in tandem with the growth in support for Home Rule. The Gaelic Athletic Association was founded in 1884 and the Gaelic League in 1893.

f) *her daughter's name*: Not simply her reputation, as the name itself is synonymous with Irishness. There is an Irish song, 'Kate Kearney', by Lady Morgan (66d), which begins:

> O did you not hear of Kate Kearney
> She lives on the banks of Killarney . . .

The famous attraction 'Kate Kearney's Cottage', in County Kerry, is the epitome of Celtic kitsch. In *U*, 'Penelope', Molly Bloom is contemptuous of the singing of various 'little chits of missies':

> Kathleen Kearney and her lot of squealers Miss This Miss That Miss Theother lot of sparrowfarts . . .

The daughter in this story is based on Eileen Reidy, whose mother gave Joyce whiskey at a morning rehearsal at her house. There was a contemporary bootmaker, Michael Kearney, in Wexford Street, whose name Joyce may have borrowed.

g) *Irish picture postcards*: Specifically, cards that were printed in the Irish languages. One of the firms that produced them was James Duffy on Wellington Quay (95b).

h) *special Sundays*: For example, Whit, Easter, Trinity Sunday etc.

i) *pro-cathedral*: See 55m. To this day, it remains an anomaly that Dublin has no (Roman) Catholic Cathedral, while there are two Church of Ireland ones.

j) *Cathedral Street*: Uneponymously at the corner of Marlborough Street, as the street is there and the cathedral is not. The name has been used for a very long time.

k) *Nationalist friends*: Supporters of Home Rule for Ireland – such as Molly Ivors of 'The Dead', or even (much previously) Mr Doyle (*père*) of 'After the Race'.

l) *grand concerts*: Their formal designation, and also Mr Holohan's homely Dublinese.

m) *Antient Concert Rooms*: In Great Brunswick Street (now Pearse Street). The building was occupied by the Oil Gas Company until taken over in 1843 by the Antient Concerts Society, forerunner of the Academy of Music (c). Joyce sang at the venue in both May and August 1904. The chaotic management of the latter concert (at which Joyce ended up accompanying himself) gave him the germ for

dowry of one hundred pounds each when they came to the age of twenty-four. He sent the elder daughter, Kathleen, to a good convent, where she learned French and music, and afterwards paid her fees at the Academy. Every year in the month of July Mrs Kearney found occasion to say to some friend:

—My good man is packing us off to Skerries for a few weeks—

If it was not Skerries it was Howth or Greystones.

When the Irish Revival began to be appreciable Mrs Kearney determined to take advantage of her daughter's name and brought an Irish teacher to the house. Kathleen and her sister sent Irish picture postcards to their friends and these friends sent back other Irish picture postcards. On special Sundays, when Mr Kearney went with his family to the pro-cathedral, a little crowd of people would assemble after mass at the corner of Cathedral Street. They were all friends of the Kearneys – musical friends or Nationalist friends; and, when they had played every little counter of gossip, they shook hands with one another all together, laughing at the crossing of so many hands, and said goodbye to one another in Irish. Soon the name of Miss Kathleen Kearney began to be heard often on people's lips. People said that she was very clever at music and a very nice girl and, moreover, that she was a believer in the language movement. Mrs Kearney was well content at this. Therefore she was not surprised when one day Mr Holohan came to her and proposed that her daughter should be the accompanist at a series of four grand concerts which his Society was going to give in the Antient Concert Rooms. She brought him into the drawing-room, made him sit down and brought out the decanter and the silver biscuit-barrel. She entered heart and soul into the details of the enterprise, advised and dissuaded: and finally a contract was drawn up by which Kathleen was to receive eight guineas for her services as accompanist at the four grand concerts.

As Mr Holohan was a novice in such delicate matters as the wording of bills and the disposing of items for a programme, Mrs Kearney helped him. She had tact. She knew what *artistes* should go into capitals and what *artistes* should go into small type. She knew that the first tenor would not like to come on after Mr Meade's comic turn. To keep the audience continually diverted she slipped the doubtful items in between the old

the story. Like the Rotunda (96s), the premises subsequently became a cinema.

n) *the decanter and the silver biscuit-barrel*: These are serious indicators of gentility and of Mrs Kearney's determination to be properly hospitable (f).

o) *guineas*: A guinea was a pound and a shilling, a favoured unit used for professional fees, by auctioneers, music teachers and others (127h).

p) *the disposing of items*: The arrangement of concert 'turns'. No vetoing is implied.

q) *Mr Meade*: Very likely to be the *artiste* from 'The Boarding House' (56b). The 'comic turn' was improved from 'funny recitation'. Gogarty mentions in *Mourning Becomes Mrs Spendlove* that he and Joyce had an associate called Cocky Meade.

a) *charmeuse*: A type of soft satin.

b) *Brown Thomas's*: Still in Grafton Street. The shop was described in the 1902 *Thom's* as 'Brown, Thomas and Co. silkmercers, milliners, costumiers, mantle makers and gen. drapers, 15 to 17 Grafton Street & 5, 6 & 7 Duke Street'. It had a rateable value of £600 (compared with – say – the Antient Concert Rooms' £150), which helps to explain the exclusivity of Grafton St (37i). Leopold Bloom window-shops lubriciously here in *U*, 'Lestrygonians' (78g).

c) *two-shilling tickets*: Given that Farrington's g.p. (78b) cost a penny, these tickets – costing twenty-four times that – were quite expensive. Alternatively, it is nearly a third of Eveline's weekly wage.

d) *bright blue badges*: Either simple stewards' badges, or perhaps similar to the one proudly worn by Miss Ivors in 'The Dead' (168d).

e) *a little man with a white vacant face*: Mr Fitzpatrick is noticeably similar to Mr Mooney of 'The Boarding House'.

f) *his accent was flat*: He has an ordinary Dublin accent. Given also his unfortunate manners (such as wearing a hat indoors), Mrs Kearney is quick to despise it. Joyce's Belvedere associate William Fallon (23b) said of him c. 1931:

> I noticed that he still spoke with a good class Dublin accent.

g) *rolled and unrolled their music*: A nervous mannerism found again in Mary Jane of 'The Dead'.

h) *his very flat final syllable*: A truly Dublin 'Baaaaalll' (in the international Phonetic Alphabet, bɑːɫ). In his diary Stanislaus comments on John Murray ('whose accent was bad') mentioning Dion Boucicault's *The Colleen Bawn* 'and coming down very flatly on the Bawn'. (In Murray's defence it can be argued that 'Bawn' is a homophone of the Irish *bán*, 'white' – which should be so pronounced.)

Kate Kearney's kitsch *cottage in Killarney*

favourites. Mr Holohan called to see her every day to have her advice on some point. She was invariably friendly and advising – homely, in fact. She pushed the decanter towards him, saying:

—Now, help yourself, Mr Holohan!—

And while he was helping himself she said:

—Don't be afraid! Don't be afraid of it!—

Everything went on smoothly. Mrs Kearney bought some lovely blush-pink charmeuse in Brown Thomas's to let into the front of Kathleen's dress. It cost a pretty penny; but there are occasions when a little expense is justifiable. She took a dozen of two-shilling tickets for the final concert and sent them to those friends who could not be trusted to come otherwise. She forgot nothing and, thanks to her, everything that was to be done was done.

The concerts were to be on Wednesday, Thursday, Friday and Saturday. When Mrs Kearney arrived with her daughter at the Antient Concert Rooms on Wednesday night she did not like the look of things. A few young men, wearing bright blue badges in their coats, stood idle in the vestibule: none of them wore evening dress. She passed by with her daughter and a quick glance through the open door of the hall showed her the cause of the stewards' idleness. At first she wondered had she mistaken the hour. No, it was twenty minutes to eight.

In the dressing-room behind the stage she was introduced to the secretary of the Society, Mr Fitzpatrick. She smiled and shook his hand. He was a little man with a white vacant face. She noticed that he wore his soft brown hat carelessly on the side of his head and that his accent was flat. He held a programme in his hand and, while he was talking to her, he chewed one end of it into a moist pulp. He seemed to bear disappointments lightly. Mr Holohan came into the dressing-room every few minutes with reports from the box-office. The *artistes* talked among themselves nervously, glanced from time to time at the mirror, and rolled and unrolled their music. When it was nearly half-past eight the few people in the hall began to express their desire to be entertained. Mr Fitzpatrick came in, smiled vacantly at the room, and said:

—Well now, ladies and gentlemen, I suppose we'd better open the ball—

Mrs Kearney rewarded his very flat final syllable with a quick

m.luntin ó ragallaig. ar gaillim.

beint de rinnceóiní luimnig.

pádraig mac donncada

Revival activities

Báṛṛ na maiḋne ḋuiṫ.

How sweet are thy Maidens
Oh, land of the Green!
The heart is entranced
By the charming Colleen.

a) *not good*: This is not quite the same as the 'no good' of Mr Holohan's reply. But Mrs Kearney has purported to know what *artistes* should go into capitals.

b) *go as they pleased*: An intentionally opaque expression.

c) *filled with paper*: The audience has been given free tickets. 'Papering the house' is a practice that con-tinues. Myles na Gopaleen once described the delights of diving from a theatre balcony into the soft and rustling paper sea of the stalls.

d) *the screen*: A theatrical device: there are no flies on Mr Fitzpatrick.

e) *the Friday concert was to be abandoned*: It was not always easy to fill the Antient Concert Rooms, however worthy the cause.

stare of contempt and then said to her daughter encouragingly:

—Are you ready, dear?—

When she had an opportunity she called Mr Holohan aside and asked him to tell her what it meant. Mr Holohan did not know what it meant. He said that the committee had made a mistake in arranging for four concerts: four was too many.

—And the *artistes*! said Mrs Kearney. Of course they are doing their best, but really they are not good—

Mr Holohan admitted that the *artistes* were no good but the committee, he said, had decided to let the first three concerts go as they pleased and reserve all the talent for Saturday night. Mrs Kearney said nothing but, as the mediocre items followed one another on the platform and the few people in the hall grew fewer and fewer, she began to regret that she had put herself to any expense for such a concert. There was something she didn't like in the look of things and Mr Fitzpatrick's vacant smile irritated her very much. However, she said nothing and waited to see how it would end. The concert expired shortly before ten and every one went home quickly.

The concert on Thursday night was better attended but Mrs Kearney saw at once that the house was filled with paper. The audience behaved indecorously, as if the concert were an informal dress rehearsal. Mr Fitzpatrick seemed to enjoy himself; he was quite unconscious that Mrs Kearney was taking angry note of his conduct. He stood at the edge of the screen, from time to time jutting out his head and exchanging a laugh with two friends in the corner of the balcony. In the course of the evening Mrs Kearney learned that the Friday concert was to be abandoned and that the committee was going to move heaven and earth to secure a bumper house on Saturday night. When she heard this she sought out Mr Holohan. She buttonholed him as he was limping out quickly with a glass of lemonade for a young lady and asked him was it true. Yes, it was true.

—But, of course, that doesn't alter the contract, she said. The contract was for four concerts—

Mr Holohan seemed to be in a hurry: he advised her to speak to Mr Fitzpatrick. Mrs Kearney was now beginning to be alarmed. She called Mr Fitzpatrick away from his screen and told him that her daughter had signed for four concerts and that, of course, according to the terms of the contract she

f) *move heaven and earth*: The committee seems incapable of even moving an orrery or putting on a successful concert.

g) *bumper*: Tip-top, full – from the sense of a glassful bumping the brim. Here, a capacity audience.

h) *buttonholed*: The verb was originally 'buttonhold'. Now Mr Holohan has Mrs Kearney (as well as her venal principles) on his lapel (124d).

i) *the terms of the contract*: In sticking so fiercely to the letter of the law, Mrs Kearney sets in train her downfall. Presumably some of the other *artistes* are in the same situation as Kathleen. As the Friday concert is being cancelled in order to save losing money, for someone of her status to insist on payment can be seen as both unprofessional and unreasonable.

A 'puff', little noticed since, from the Evening Mail

a) commetty: Mental derision for Mr Fitzpatrick's way of speaking. There are other significant dactyls in *D*, such as simony, Emily Sinico, and *Dubliners* itself (as well as Farrington, Araby, Counterparts, Boarding House, Lenehan, Mahoney, Gabriel 'Conneroy', Ivy Day etc). In Dublin even the greeting 'How are you?' is often dactylic.

b) *Special puffs*: 'Boosting' notices. Joyce himself was mentioned in one in the summer of 1904.

c) *General Post Office*: At the geographical centre of Dublin (beside Nelson's Pillar (88l)), from which all distances are traditionally measured. Its position halfway along O'Connell Street, and its imposing portico, made it an obvious choice for the headquarters of the insurrectionists at Easter 1916. Perhaps significantly for the Kearneys, the building is surmounted by statues of Hibernia, accompanied by Mercury (with rod and purse), and Fidelity. These seem like counterparts of Kathleen and her mother and father respectively.

d) *Beirne*: Pronounced like Byrne. This short sketch of her slightly recalls the bland disruptiveness of Maria, but she will show her teeth later.

Rival entertainments

should receive the sum originally stipulated for, whether the society gave the four concerts or not. Mr Fitzpatrick, who did not catch the point at issue very quickly, seemed unable to resolve the difficulty and said that he would bring the matter before the committee. Mrs Kearney's anger began to flutter in her cheek and she had all she could do to keep from asking:

_a   —And who is the *cometty*, pray?—

But she knew that it would not be ladylike to do that: so she was silent.

Little boys were sent out into the principal streets of Dublin early on Friday morning with bundles of handbills. Special

_b puffs appeared in all the evening papers reminding the music-loving public of the treat which was in store for it on the following evening. Mrs Kearney was somewhat reassured but she thought well to tell her husband part of her suspicions. He listened carefully and said that perhaps, it would be better if he went with her on Saturday night. She agreed. She respected her husband in the same way as she respected the General Post

_c Office, as something large, secure and fixed; and though she knew the small number of his talents she appreciated his abstract value as a male. She was glad that he had suggested coming with her. She thought her plans over.

The night of the grand concert came. Mrs Kearney, with her husband and daughter, arrived at the Antient Concert Rooms three-quarters of an hour before the time at which the concert was to begin. By ill luck it was a rainy evening. Mrs Kearney placed her daughter's clothes and music in charge of her husband and went all over the building looking for Mr Holohan or Mr Fitzpatrick. She could find neither. She asked the stewards was any member of the committee in the hall and, after a great deal of trouble, a steward brought out a little

_d woman named Miss Beirne to whom Mrs Kearney explained that she wanted to see one of the secretaries. Miss Beirne expected them any minute and asked could she do anything. Mrs Kearney looked searchingly at the oldish face which was screwed into an expression of trustfulness and enthusiasm and answered:

—No, thank you!—

The little woman hoped they would have a good house. She looked out at the rain until the melancholy of the wet street

a) *We did our best*: Anna Livia is more convincing (*FW* 627):

> I done me best when I was let. Thinking always if I go all goes ...

b) *the dear knows*: Lord knows. There is a rich semantic confusion in the Irish language origins of this phrase, *Fhiadha* ('Deer') and *Dhia* ('God') being pronounced identically. So it may in fact be 'the deer knows'.

c) *when an operatic* artiste *had fallen ill*: This is how the tenor Italo Campanini (1845/6–96) got his first break, aged twenty-six, singing with La Titiens. When John Joyce came to live in Dublin in the 1870s, his Italian music teacher declared of him (according to John Joyce):

> I have found the successor to Campanini.

d) Maritana: A popular opera (1845) by the Irish composer William Wallace, frequently performed in Dublin. It was bracketed with Balfe's *The Bohemian Girl*, and Sir Julius Benedict's *The Lily of Killarney*

as 'the Irish Ring'. Wallace and Balfe are buried contiguously in London (93f). In *U*, 'Penelope', Molly Bloom remembers making music with Simon Dedalus:

> he was always turning up half screwed singing the second verse first the old love is the new was one of his so sweetly sang the maiden on the hawthorn bough he was always on for flirtyfying too when I sang Maritana with him at Freddy Mayers private opera he had a delicious glorious voice ...

e) *Queen's Theatre*: On the other side of Great Brunswick Street, closer to the front of Trinity. At the other end of the century the site is very close to the Samuel Beckett Centre for the Performing Arts.

f) *wiping his nose in his gloved hand*: Presumably an ungloved hand would have been acceptable. Shakespeare's father (53c) was a glover.

g) yous: Like Polly Mooney's Dublinese (57h), a sure social indicator. It is simply the plural of 'you'. The expression is in Melbourne now, as well as in Dublin.

h) *Mr Bell*: Joyce's self-parody. On the day of the concert Joyce wrote to a Mr Bell, via their common

---

At the Feis competition for singing and piano, on Monday, we were glad to see Signor Denzu once more adjudicating Miss Marguerite Moriarty won first prize in the soprano solo singing, and Miss Kathleen Warwick second; Miss Fanny Vincent and Miss Francis Walsh being highly commended. Miss Mollie Byrne, who is a prime favourite, scored third in this competition, whilst her little niece, aged eight, Miss Lillie McNevin, surprised everybody by her playing of the Nocturne in G. Major (Field), and was afterwards surrounded by the many admirers who had warmly applauded her marvellous pianoforte performances. Miss Annie Treacy and Miss E. Kennedy, were bracketed for first prize, both getting silver medals. Miss Charlotte Graham and Miss E. Colohan were bracketed for second prize, and Miss Nora Ireland was commended. Mr. Joseph Walsh, from Belfast, carried off first prize for tenor solo singing, Mr. Rathborne having taken the silver medal at last Feis was disqualified from winning the second prize. Mr. Whiston R. Gage and James J. Joyce carried off second and third prizes respectively.

The Figaro *reports the Feis, April 1904*

effaced all the trustfulness and enthusiasm from her twisted features. Then she gave a little sigh and said:

ab   —Ah, well! We did our best, the dear knows—

Mrs Kearney had to go back to the dressing-room.

The *artistes* were arriving. The bass and the second tenor had already come. The bass, Mr Duggan, was a slender young man with a scattered black moustache. He was the son of a hall porter in an office in the city and, as a boy, he had sung prolonged bass notes in the resounding hall. From this humble state he had raised himself until he had become a first-rate *artiste*. He had appeared in grand opera. One night, when an

c operatic *artiste* had fallen ill, he had undertaken the part of the

de king in the opera of *Maritana* at the Queen's Theatre. He sang his music with great feeling and volume and was warmly welcomed by the gallery; but, unfortunately, he marred the

f good impression by wiping his nose in his gloved hand once or twice out of thoughtlessness. He was unassuming and spoke

g little. He said *yous* so softly that it passed unnoticed and he never drank anything stronger than milk for his voice's sake.

h Mr Bell, the second tenor, was a fair-haired little man who

i competed every year for prizes at the Feis Ceoil. On his fourth trial he had been awarded a bronze medal. He was extremely nervous and extremely jealous of other tenors and he covered his nervous jealousy with an ebullient friendliness. It was his humour to have people know what an ordeal a concert was to him. Therefore when he saw Mr Duggan he went over to him and asked:

   —Are you in it too?—

   —Yes, said Mr Duggan—

Mr Bell laughed at his fellow-sufferer, held out his hand and said:

   —Shake!—

Mrs Kearney passed by these two young men and went to the edge of the screen to view the house. The seats were being filled up rapidly and a pleasant noise circulated in the auditorium. She came back and spoke to her husband privately. Their conversation was evidently about Kathleen for they both glanced at her often as she stood chatting to one of her

j Nationalist friends, Miss Healy, the contralto. An unknown solitary woman with a pale face walked through the room.

k The women followed with keen eyes the faded blue dress

friend Gogarty, to cadge three guineas.

i) *Feis Ceoil*: An annual festival, established in 1897 as part of the Irish Revival (123e), with a view of promoting music (though not only Irish music). In May 1904, Joyce competed in it (at the Antient Concert Rooms) and won the bronze medal in the 'tenor solo' category.

j) *the contralto*: The lowest female musical voice. Stanislaus said that the voice of a contralto was the only one worth listening to.

k) *faded blue dress*: Again a hint of Josie Breen (18m) as seen by Bloom in Westmoreland Street in *U*, 'Lestrygonians':

> Same blue serge dress she had two years ago, the nap bleaching. Seen its best days.

A perennial Dublin favourite

An Claiдeaм Soluir

[An Claidheamh Soluis]
agur Fáinne an lae

[REGISTERED AS A NEWSPAPER.]

Leaban IV. Uimin 50. baile-áta-cliat, feabra 21, 1903. pinginn.
VOL. IV. No. 50. DUBLIN, FEBRUARY 21, 1903. ONE PENNY.

A newspaper founded in 1899

*John McCormack in 1903. In U, 'Hades', Bloom tells
Martin Cunningham of Molly's fellow* artistes:
    we'll have all the topnobbers. J. C. Doyle and
    John MacCormack I hope and. The best in fact.
*Bloom seems to be on the verge of mentioning James A.
Joyce*

128

which was stretched upon a meagre body. Some one said that she was Madam Glynn, the soprano.

—I wonder where did they dig her up, said Kathleen to Miss Healy. I'm sure I never heard of her—

Miss Healy had to smile. Mr Holohan limped into the dressing-room at that moment and the two young ladies asked him who was the unknown woman. Mr Holohan said that she was Madam Glynn from London. Madam Glynn took her stand in a corner of the room, holding a roll of music stiffly before her and from time to time changing the direction of her startled gaze. The shadow took her faded dress into shelter but fell revengefully into the little cup behind her collar-bone. The noise of the hall became more audible. The first tenor and the baritone arrived together. They were both well dressed, stout and complacent, and they brought a breath of opulence among the company.

Mrs Kearney brought her daughter over to them, and talked to them amiably. She wanted to be on good terms with them but, while she strove to be polite, her eyes followed Mr Holohan in his limping and devious courses. As soon as she could she excused herself and went out after him.

—Mr Holohan, I want to speak to you for a moment, she said—

They went down to a discreet part of the corridor. Mrs Kearney asked him when was her daughter going to be paid. Mr Holohan said that Mr Fitzpatrick had charge of that. Mrs Kearney said that she didn't know anything about Mr Fitzpatrick. Her daughter had signed a contract for eight guineas and she would have to be paid. Mr Holohan said that it wasn't his business.

—Why isn't it your business? asked Mrs Kearney. Didn't you yourself bring her the contract? Anyway, if it's not your business it's my business and I mean to see to it—

—You'd better speak to Mr Fitzpatrick, said Mr Holohan distantly—

—I don't know anything about Mr Fitzpatrick, repeated Mrs Kearney. I have my contract, and I intend to see that it is carried out—

When she came back to the dressing-room her cheeks were slightly suffused. The room was lively. Two men in outdoor dress had taken possession of the fireplace and were chatting

a) *Madam Glynn*: In life, Madame Halle, and another grim instance of 'The Madam' (53q), quite different from that much-admired soprano, Madame Marion Tweedy.

b) *where did they dig her up*: Miss Kearney's expression is less than refined. There is also a nudging restatement of one of the major themes of *D*.

c) *I never heard of her*: A pre-echo of Bartell D'Arcy on Parkinson (176g).

d) *from London*: She is in obvious contrast to the alluring woman that Farrington saw in Mulligan's of Poolbeg Street (83i).

e) *the little cup behind her collar-bone*: A grimly-noticed indicator of advancing years, and a contrast with how the Dublin lamplight caressed the white curve of Mangan's sister's neck (23e).

f) *it wasn't his business*: Like most of the inmates of Mrs Mooney's boarding house, he doesn't mean business. Whether or not the Eire Abu Society has a designated treasurer, Mr Holohan has a slight point, in that he is only assistant secretary to Mr Fitzpatrick's secretary.

g) *suffused*: John Dryden, sometime Poet Laureate, wrote in 'Palamon and Arcite' (Book II), his version of Chaucer's 'Knight's Tale':

Suspicions and fanatical Surmise
And Jealousy suffus'd with jaundice in her eyes.
Discolouring all she view'd ...

This is the second time Mrs Kearney's anger has shown in her face.

a) *the* Freeman *man*: The reporter from the *Freeman's Journal*, Mr Hendrick, who reappears briefly in 'Grace'. He was possibly based on Jack B. Hall, author of *Random Records of a Reporter* (1928). Hall reported favourably on Joyce's 1901 performance as Geoffrey Fortescue in Maggie and Hanna Sheehy's playlet *Cupid's Confidante*.

b) *O'Madden Burke*: A genial opportunist based on W. O'Leary Curtis, who is mentioned by name in 'Gas from a Burner' by a burlesqued printer-publisher who fulminates here about Joyce himself:

> But I draw the line at that bloody fellow,
> That was over here dressed in Austrian yellow,
> Spouting Italian by the hour
> To O'Leary Curtis and John Wyse Power
> And writing of Dublin, dirty and dear,
> In a manner no blackamoor printer could bear.

(The diatribe is continued at 172c). O'Madden Burke is seen again in *U*, 'Aeolus' and elsewhere. Like a sort of glorified Lenehan, O'Madden Burke is something of a sponge and an idler: he is going to write something about Saint Mary's Abbey 'one of these days'. O'Leary Curtis (whom Gogarty called 'the Japanese Jesus') did publish poems at least. He published verse in local periodicals such as the *United Irishman* and the *Irish Homestead*. 'Before and After' is from 1903:

> In the hush of the quiet dream-time,
> Ere the soul of the roses had fled,
> I kissed the ripe lips of my lady,
> Nor thought of the dead.
>
> Dark tresses fell o'er my bosom,
> When the soul of the roses had fled,
> And full of regret and remembrance
> I thought of the dead.

c) *an American priest*: Michael McCarthy regarded them more favourably than the indigenous kind. Among the many priestly American-Irish visitors at the turn of the century were Archbishop Ryan of Philadelphia, and 'Father O'Brien, P.P., of Ticonderoga in the State of New York', who joined a pilgrimage from Dublin to Rome, and through a ruse obtained the Pope's skullcap.

d) *Mansion House*: Another London parallel in Dublin (113m). Further examples (81i) included Smithfield, Pudding Lane, Constitution Hill, Pimlico, Watling Street, Chancery Lane, Holles Street, Marshalsea Debtors' Prison, the *cul-de-sac* Ely Place and even London Bridge.

e) *plausible voice*: The sly implication is that Mr Hendrick is not to be trusted. So too Rivière (38l).

f) *e held an extinguished cigar*: This is not the sign of careful manners.

g) *one reason for her politeness*: A mention in the *Freeman*, or respect for an elder, or perhaps even a little chaste flirtatiousness.

h) *rose and fell at that moment for him*: The expression recalls Bloom's compliment remembered by Molly in *U*, 'Penelope': 'the sun shines for you today'. It is unclear whether Hendrick is thinking something carnal or something benign.

i) *I'll see it in*: Mr Hendrick is not doing his job. The *Freeman* report was obviously written from the Programme, as Joyce did not sing 'The Croppy Boy', accompanying himself in 'In her Simplicity' instead, Miss Eileen Reidy having gone home.

j) *a little something*: drink – a smahan or two (84g) naturally, in return for the publicity.

k) *bottles for a few gentlemen*: As so often in *D*, the usage of the latter noun is subjective, or ironically respectful. The scene recalls 'Ivy Day'.

l) *magniloquent western name*: Redolent of the west of Ireland. In *U*, 'Sirens', he is referred to by Lenehan as 'that minstrel boy of the wild wet west'.

m) *the fine problem of his finances*: Mr O'Madden Burke is one of the Irish shabby-genteel. One classic account of financial improvisations is Sir Jonah Barrington's (81n) *Personal Sketches* (1827).

familiarly with Miss Healy and the baritone. They were the *Freeman* man and Mr O'Madden Burke. The *Freeman* man had come in to say that he could not wait for the concert as he had to report the lecture which an American priest was giving in the Mansion House. He said they were to leave the report for him at the *Freeman* office and he would see that it went in. He was a grey-haired man, with a plausible voice and careful manners. He held an extinguished cigar in his hand and the aroma of cigar smoke floated near him. He had not intended to stay a moment, because concerts and *artistes* bored him considerably, but he remained leaning against the mantelpiece. Miss Healy stood in front of him, talking and laughing. He was old enough to suspect one reason for her politeness but young enough in spirit to turn the moment to account. The warmth, fragrance and colour of her body appealed to his senses. He was pleasantly conscious that the bosom which he saw rise and fall slowly beneath him rose and fell at that moment for him, that the laughter and fragrance and wilful glances were his tribute. When he could stay no longer he took leave of her regretfully.

—O'Madden Burke will write the notice, he explained to Mr Holohan, and I'll see it in—

—Thank you very much, Mr Hendrick, said Mr Holohan. You'll see it in, I know. Now, won't you have a little something before you go?—

—I don't mind, said Mr Hendrick—

The two men went along some tortuous passages and up a dark staircase and came to a secluded room where one of the stewards was uncorking bottles for a few gentlemen. One of these gentlemen was Mr O'Madden Burke, who had found out the room by instinct. He was a suave elderly man who balanced his imposing body, when at rest, upon a large silk umbrella. His magniloquent western name was the moral umbrella upon which he balanced the fine problem of his finances. He was widely respected.

While Mr Holohan was entertaining the *Freeman* man Mrs Kearney was speaking so animatedly to her husband that he had to ask her to lower her voice. The conversation of the others in the dressing-room had become strained. Mr Bell, the first item, stood ready with his music but the accompanist made no sign. Evidently something was wrong. Mr Kearney

n) *The conversation ... had become strained*: Unlike the quality of mercy in *The Merchant of Venice* – another exploration of debts, contracts and doing the proper thing.

o) *the first item*: A Latin joke, as *item* means 'also' or 'likewise'. Shakespeare's will gives a correct instance of usage:

First ... Item ... Item ... Item ...

Like Mr Kearney, Shakespeare provided for both his daughters.

p) *made no sign*: A parallel with or parody of the end of 'Eveline' (33f).

'Mrs Pat' (d)

a) *stamping of feet*: A somewhat low expression of impatience.

b) *her new shoe*: In all unpublished versions of the story, it read 'her new boot' – a suppressed hint that Kathleen's thrifty father had been set to work.

c) *it was not her fault*: This incursion into Kathleen's mind does not reveal whose fault she thinks it is.

d) *Mrs Pat Campbell*: A famously lively actress (1876–1940) and friend of Bernard Shaw (99b). She frequently played in Dublin, including in 1899, 1900 and in July 1905, when she played in Maeterlinck's *Pelléas et Mélisande*, with Sarah Bernhardt. In 1908, she appeared in Yeats' *Deirdre* at the Abbey Theatre. This was a great success, and there was a supper afterwards at the Gresham (163c).

e) *random notes*: As random notes go, the word recalls the Bloomsday typology of Chapman's *Homer*:

> For, not to speak
> At needy random; but my breath to break
> In sacred oath, Ulysses shall return.

f) *This is four shillings short*: Mrs Kearney is holding Fitzpatrick to the letter of the contract. She has been promised guineas not pounds.

g) Now, Mr Bell: An echo of *'Now Maria!'* in 'Clay'.

h) *shaking like an aspen*: This type of poplar tree is proverbially famous for its quivering. By tradition this is because the aspen was nearly chosen for use in Christ's crucifixion. When the poet Thomas Parnell wrote in 1717, 'Thy aspens quiver in a breathing

The way to the Antient Concert Rooms and Westland Row Station

looked straight before him, stroking his beard, while Mrs Kearney spoke into Kathleen's ear with subdued emphasis. From the hall came sounds of encouragement, clapping and stamping of feet. The first tenor and the baritone and Miss Healy stood together, waiting tranquilly, but Mr Bell's nerves were greatly agitated because he was afraid the audience would think that he had come late.

Mr Holohan and Mr O'Madden Burke came into the room. In a moment Mr Holohan perceived the hush. He went over to Mrs Kearney and spoke with her earnestly. While they were speaking the noise in the hall grew louder. Mr Holohan became very red and excited. He spoke volubly, but Mrs Kearney said curtly at intervals:

—She won't go on. She must get her eight guineas—

Mr Holohan pointed desperately towards the hall where the audience was clapping and stamping. He appealed to Mr Kearney and to Kathleen. But Mr Kearney continued to stroke his beard and Kathleen looked down, moving the point of her new shoe: it was not her fault. Mrs Kearney repeated:

—She won't go on without her money—

After a swift struggle of tongues Mr Holohan hobbled out in haste. The room was silent. When the strain of the silence had become somewhat painful Miss Healy said to the baritone:

—Have you seen Mrs Pat Campbell this week?—

The baritone had not seen her but he had been told that she was very fine. The conversation went no further. The first tenor bent his head and began to count the links of the gold chain which was extended across his waist, smiling and humming random notes to observe the effect on the frontal sinus. From time to time every one glanced at Mrs Kearney.

The noise in the auditorium had risen to a clamour when Mr Fitzpatrick burst into the room, followed by Mr Holohan, who was panting. The clapping and stamping in the hall were punctuated by whistling. Mr Fitzpatrick held a few bank-notes in his hand. He counted out four into Mrs Kearney's hand and said she would get the other half at the interval. Mrs Kearney said:

—This is four shillings short—

But Kathleen gathered in her skirt and said: *Now, Mr Bell*, to the first item, who was shaking like an aspen. The singer and the accompanist went out together. The noise in the hall

breeze', it was already a cliché. Since the sixteenth century, the word has been particularly applied to a woman's tongue (one cause of the friction in this story). Sir Thomas More (the claimed forebear of George Moore) wrote in Book VIII of *The Confutation of Tyndale's Answer* (1532):

For if women myghte be suffered to begin ones in the congregacion to fal in disputing, those aspen leaves of theirs would never leave waggying.

a) Killarney: A song by Balfe (9f) from his *Innisfallen*, not related to Benedict's *Lily* (127d). The song is remembered by Stephen in *P* (V.2), being sung by the kitchengirl next door. The town in Kerry was part of the 'grand tour' in the nineteenth century, and had been visited by Queen Victoria and many others.

b) *old-fashioned mannerisms*: J. B. Hall for example referred to a Diva's handkerchief as a talisman

> without which no self-respecting soprano of the old school, à la Titiens, could possibly produce her effects.

c) *resurrected*: Madam Glynn is almost one of the dead, and her 'high wailing notes' are like the banshee (141d).

d) *a selection of Irish airs*: Irish airs are many and can be fitted to different songs. Yeats' poem 'Down by the Salley Gardens' is sometimes sung to the air 'Far beyond yon Mountains'. 'My Love She was Born in the North Countree' had the air 'Fair Maidens' Beauty will soon Fade away'. 'I'll Sing my Children's Death Song' has the air 'O Thou of the Beautiful Hair'.

e) *a stirring patriotic recitation*: The spoken equivalent of a come-all-you (22d). Pearse was one of many orators. During the First World War he declared:

> The last six months have been among the most glorious in the history of Europe . . . It is good for the world that such things could be done. The old heart of the earth needed to be warmed by the red wine of the battle fields. Such august homage was never offered to God as this, the homage of millions of lives given gladly for love of country.

f) *amateur theatricals*: A popular activity of the period. Maggie Sheehy's productions, such as *Cupid's Confidante*, are a case in point (176g).

g) *deservedly applauded*: Previously 'enthusiastically applauded'. The change prompts the question of whether Kathleen's applause was deserved, or merely accorded by the generosity of the audience.

h) *a hive of excitement*: The metaphor is comparable with the hornet's nest of 'Counterparts' (80g). For an extremely brief period in 1903, the sub-editor of the *Irish Bee-Keeper* was James Joyce.

i) *In one corner*: The detail cannot but recall a boxing match (and its participants – known in *U* as 'puckers').

j) *at peace with men*: Though 'men' meant mankind

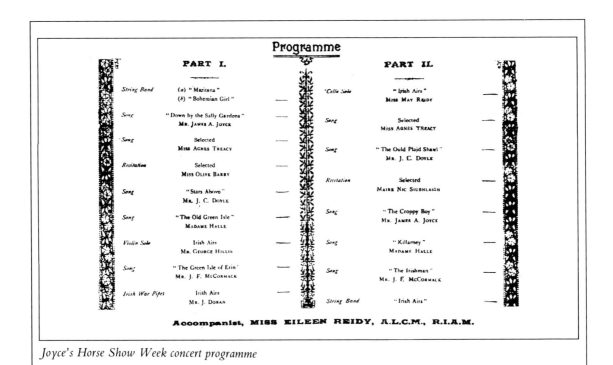

Joyce's Horse Show Week concert programme

died away. There was a pause of a few seconds: and then the piano was heard.

The first part of the concert was very successful except for Madam Glynn's item. The poor lady sang *Killarney* in a bodiless gasping voice, with all the old-fashioned mannerisms of intonation and pronunciation which she believed lent elegance to her singing. She looked as if she had been resurrected from an old stage-wardrobe and the cheaper parts of the hall made fun of her high wailing notes. The first tenor and the contralto, however, brought down the house. Kathleen played a selection of Irish airs which was generously applauded. The first part closed with a stirring patriotic recitation delivered by a young lady who arranged amateur theatricals. It was deservedly applauded; and, when it was ended, the men went out for the interval, content.

All this time the dressing-room was a hive of excitement. In one corner were Mr Holohan, Mr Fitzpatrick, Miss Beirne, two of the stewards, the baritone, the bass, and Mr O'Madden Burke. Mr O'Madden Burke said it was the most scandalous exhibition he had ever witnessed. Miss Kathleen Kearney's musical career was ended in Dublin after that, he said. The baritone was asked what did he think of Mrs Kearney's conduct. He did not like to say anything. He had been paid his money and wished to be at peace with men. However, he said that Mrs Kearney might have taken the *artistes* into consideration. The stewards and the secretaries debated hotly as to what should be done when the interval came.

—I agree with Miss Beirne, said Mr O'Madden Burke. Pay her nothing—

In another corner of the room were Mrs Kearney and her husband, Mr Bell, Miss Healy and the young lady who had to recite the patriotic piece. Mrs Kearney said that the committee had treated her scandalously. She had spared neither trouble nor expense and this was how she was repaid.

They thought they had only a girl to deal with and that, therefore, they could ride roughshod over her. But she would show them their mistake. They wouldn't have dared to have treated her like that if she had been a man. But she would see that her daughter got her rights: she wouldn't be fooled. If they didn't pay her to the last farthing she would make Dublin ring. Of course she was sorry for the sake of the *artistes*. But

('man embraces woman'), the sexual discrimination was not lost on Joyce.

k) *taken the* artistes *into consideration*: At this time in Dublin, with the rise of the labour movement the ethics of the strike (98d) became a contentious subject. There were many disputes between 1899 and 1914, the employers' Lockout of 1913 being only the most famous.

l) *ride roughshod*: Spoken like a bootmaker's wife.

m) *They wouldn't have dared*: She may have a point but she misplays her hand. Serious agitation for women's rights (notably the vote) grew during the reign of Edward VII, and the first woman to be elected to the House of Commons in Westminster in 1918 was a Dublin MP (41). Earlier writers such as Frances Power Cobbe (1822–1904) had been consistently critical of the treatment of women in nineteenth-century Ireland. Parnell had two activist sisters – combative, even against him.

n) *rights*: The rights of man, celebrated by Wordsworth (95j) *et al.* during the French Revolution, were interpreted differently by Edmund Burke, distinguished Dubliner and Westminster Demosthenes. But it was not until 1792 that his controverter Mary Wollstonecraft (180i) wrote of the rights of woman – an idea promptly derided and lampooned as *A Vindication of the Rights of Brutes*.

o) *the last farthing*: A quarter of an old penny ($\frac{1}{4}$d), i.e. 1/960th of a £.

a) *Miss Healy wanted to join the other group*: She too is a Nationalist but will betray Kathleen. Joyce knew intimately the story of how Tim Healy had betrayed Parnell: his first work was 'Et Tu, Healy'.

b) *four pounds eight*: As eight guineas is eight pounds and eight shillings, Mrs Kearney considers that her daughter is still owed £4/8s.

c) *inundated*: Literally flooded, from the Latin *unda*, 'wave'. The word recalls the 'waves of expression' on Lenehan's face.

d) *decency*: As so often, Alexander Pope hits a nerve here. From 'Of the Characters of Women: an Epistle to a Lady':

> She speaks, behaves, and acts just as she ought
> But never never reach'd one gen'rous Thought.
> Virtue she finds too painful an endeavour,
> Content to dwell in decencies for ever.

e) *a great fellow fol-the-diddle-I-do*: This is a verbal flourish taken from Irish balladry, here conveying Mrs Kearney's sarcastic emphasis along the lines of 'and three cheers for me'. Appropriately, it was Peadar Kearney (Joyce's contemporary and Brendan Behan's uncle) who composed the Irish national anthem, and also 'Whack Fol the Diddle', about England's relationship with Ireland:

> When we were savage, fierce and wild,
> Whack fol the diddle lol the di do day.
> She came as a mother to her child,
> Whack fol the diddle lol the di do day.
> Gently raised us from the slime,
> Kept our hands from hellish crime,
> And sent us to heaven in her own good time,
> Whack fol the diddle lol the di do day.

Mr Holohan's name is derived from the Irish *úallach*, which means both 'scatterbrained' and 'proud', or 'arrogant'.

f) *kindly consented to play*: Very much the hackneyed idiom of the concert stage.

A few Dublin gentlemen

what else could she do? She appealed to the second tenor, who said he thought she had not been well treated. Then she appealed to Miss Healy. Miss Healy wanted to join the other group but she did not like to do so because she was a great friend of Kathleen's and the Kearneys had often invited her to their house.

As soon as the first part was ended Mr Fitzpatrick and Mr Holohan went over to Mrs Kearney and told her that the other four guineas would be paid after the committee meeting on the following Tuesday and that, in case her daughter did not play for the second part, the committee would consider the contract broken and would pay nothing.

—I haven't seen any committee, said Mrs Kearney angrily. My daughter has her contract. She will get four pounds eight into her hand or a foot she won't put on that platform—

—I'm surprised at you, Mrs Kearney, said Mr Holohan. I never thought you would treat us this way—

—And what way did you treat me? asked Mrs Kearney—

Her face was inundated with an angry colour and she looked as if she would attack someone with her hands.

—I'm asking for my rights, she said—

—You might have some sense of decency, said Mr Holohan—

—Might I, indeed? . . . And when I ask when my daughter is going to be paid I can't get a civil answer—

She tossed her head and assumed a haughty voice:

—You must speak to the secretary. It's not my business. I'm a great fellow fol-the-diddle-I-do—

—I thought you were a lady, said Mr Holohan, walking away from her abruptly—

After that Mrs Kearney's conduct was condemned on all hands: everyone approved of what the committee had done. She stood at the door, haggard with rage, arguing with her husband and daughter, gesticulating with them. She waited until it was time for the second part to begin in the hope that the secretaries would approach her. But Miss Healy had kindly consented to play one or two accompaniments. Mrs Kearney had to stand aside to allow the baritone and his accompanist to pass up to the platform. She stood still for an instant like an angry stone image and, when the first notes of the song struck

g) *like an angry stone image*: The simile recalls Shakespeare's *Titus Andronicus* (III.i):

Even like a stony image . . .

The image also suggests a mediaeval gargoyle perhaps, rather than a victim of Medusa. There are other petrified people in *D*, and paralysis can take many forms.

An Popt ʒaeveaʟaċ—An ċeaʊ Ceim Súbaiʟce.
The Irish Jig - Leading off Double.

The jig is up – especially for Mrs Kearney

a) *wrapped the cloak around her daughter*: Irish Nationalist symbolism — a style of the Revival (119h).

b) *nice . . . nice*: Mr Holohan's usage is different from Maria's in 'Clay', but similar to Dante Riordan's in *P* (I.3). A discussion on the word and its versatility can be found in Chapter XIV of Jane Austen's *Northanger Abbey* (1803).

c) *umbrella*: The word means 'a little shadow' and recalls a little cloud. One critic has decribed it in this story as an 'unassigned symbol', so what it means' is almost a matter of personal choice. J. C. Mangan (21q) participated in Dublin eccentric tradition: sometimes, even in the most settled weather, he might be seen parading the streets with a very voluminous umbrella

her ear, she caught up her daughter's cloak and said to her husband:

—Get a cab!—

He went out at once. Mrs Kearney wrapped the cloak round her daughter and followed him. As she passed through the doorway she stopped and glared into Mr Holohan's face.

—I'm not done with you yet, she said—

—But I'm done with you, said Mr Holohan—

Kathleen followed her mother meekly. Mr Holohan began to pace up and down the room, in order to cool himself for he felt his skin on fire.

—That's a nice lady! he said. O, she's a nice lady!—

—You did the proper thing, Holohan, said Mr O'Madden Burke, poised upon his umbrella in approval—

under each arm. There is an echo in 'A Mother of 'The Sisters' (*Umbrellas recovered*) and of 'Two Gallants' (the slavey's umbrella). O'Madden Burke's use of the umbrella as a prop recalls Mrs Sairey Gamp from *Martin Chuzzlewit* (96b), who gave her name to the article. She, like O'Madden Burke, was noted for her opinionateness and her drinking:

'Don't ask me,' she said, 'whether I won't take none, or whether I will, but leave the bottle on the chimley-piece, and let me put my lips to it when I am so dis-poged.'

Afterword: 'A Mother'

As with 'An Encounter', the background is directly biographical, but the story is carefully balanced (like Mr O'Madden Burke and his umbrella) on the rights and wrongs of the situation, and is sprinkled with some very funny satire. Joyce sang at the Antient Concert Rooms in August 1904 and saw the attitudes close-up. The concert series in the story is a worthy one (in a vague, cultural-Nationalist sort of way), but the concerts are very badly managed by the *commetty*. (Joseph Holloway's diary confirms that Joyce needed to invent very little.) The ideals of 'the Revival' are far less substantial in practice than are the pettiness and back-biting found in 'A Mother'. Kate Kearney is a personification of Ireland, a veritable Kathleen ni Houlihan – whose name is mock-heroically echoed by Hoppy Holohan. She supports the cause but does what her mother tells her. It is a strange relationship. Given Mrs Kearney's own history of frustration, she is intensely ambitious on her daughter's behalf. The family and the society are also found wanting. Kate's only sister is unaccountably not there to give support. Mr Kearney wants a quiet life. So too do those *artistes* who have already been paid – and how were those decisions reached, one wonders? Joyce chose not to tell us. Mr Hendrick is professionally incompetent. Mr O'Madden Burke wants a drink.

From this *galère* (which includes the unfortunate Madam Glynn, and Mr Bell, who seems to shake with his own palsy), Joyce creates a problem of irreconcilable attitudes. The concert series is under-pinned by conflicting criteria – artistic, cultural-political, social, legal. The treatment of these areas is broadly evenhanded, and so each case to be argued is painfully inconclusive. But although the story is in the 'Public Life' section of the book, one of its many strengths is its rich anatomising of the personal foibles of Mrs Kearney, her Turkish Delight and all.

Biography brings its own ironies, however, and Joyce did not know that a decade after writing this story, he again would be involved in a similar unseemly backstage wrangle. When in Zürich during the First World War, he was instrumental in staging Wilde's *The Importance of Being Earnest* 'for the British war effort'. Friction with a diplomatic amateur actor concerning a pair of trousers (and some revenue from ticket sales) soon escalated into a lawsuit and much recrimination against officialdom. (Joyce even had the indignity of a visit by the Swiss bailiffs.) The situation had all the makings of a farce. (The farce became Tom Stoppard's *Travesties* in 1974.) Joyce (or the egregiously betrousered Henry Carr) cannot be said to have behaved any better in this *imbroglio* than Mrs Kearney or her opponents in 'A Mother'.

L'affaire Kearney is never going to set musical Dublin alight, but it affords Joyce the opportunity for some scrupulous derision about the rereregardant (backward-looking) nature of some aspects of 'the Revival'. In search of status – and perhaps a crock of gold – Miss Devlin (whose name means 'unlucky') married a large leprechaun (in his bootmaking, bearded taciturnity, Mr Kearney is precisely that), and she gives birth to Kate Kearney, Irish icon. The gestures and formulae outside the pro-Cathedral are a parody of Gaelic culture: in the Irish West, such posturing visitors are still known as lawbraws (from *lá breá*, 'fine day', which is virtually the only Irish they know). To Joyce, the kitsch of the Irish Revival was as bad as – or worse than – the flummery of the British Empire. In the end, Mrs Kearney is undone not by any principles of art or politics (or law or commerce) but by a shortcoming of etiquette. In social Dublin, niceness is all (or certainly more than the small print).

Patriotic recitations and suboptimal renditions of *Killarney* had little to do with the Irish life that Joyce saw around him. He attacked the high-minded activists in a letter to Stanislaus in November 1906:

I am nauseated by their lying drivel about pure men and pure women and pure love . . . : blatant lying in the face of the truth.

Even if the Kearney desire for pelf outweighs a Nationalist principle or two, still the show must go on, and the patriots should not be too surprised to find themselves betrayed by a Healy. The concert gets the audience it deserves, and *vice versa*. It is Mr Duffy in 'A Painful Case' who points out that Dublin entrusts its fine arts to impresarios: the impresarios here are Hoppy Holohan and his tight, gormless colleagues.

The shifting perspectives of 'A Mother' are to be relished. Hoppy Holohan visits Mrs Kearney and her decanter daily during the preparations for the concert. The baritone is friendly with the *Freeman* man and the well-connected Mr O'Madden Burke, and he has been paid. Mr Duggan's manners and grammar have not prevented him from appearing in grand opera. The organisers of the Nationalist concert have resorted to engaging Madam Glynn from London. When Messrs Fitzpatrick and Holohan confirm the offer of four guineas for the second half, Mrs Kearney is too self-righteous to have this witnessed, or to shake hands on the matter. Her distrust ensures her defeat.

So, unlike Mrs Mooney in 'The Boarding House', Mrs Kearney fails to achieve her end. Her assertiveness is certainly counter-productive, but she feels — perhaps with reason – that conceding is the worse option, and once locked into her course of action there is no going back. Her language slips from its base of 'ivory manners', and her last back-answer is her undoing. Her accomplishments are again ineffectual ones: even her moderately talented Kathleen, has clearly been 'talked-up', and is quite dispensable in the end. The devious Holohan and his feckless minions can hardly be said to have done the right thing, but that does not change the humiliation of Mrs Kearney on this particular occasion. She is A Mother: there are many others like her, scattered like confetti near the Kingstown and Dalkey line.

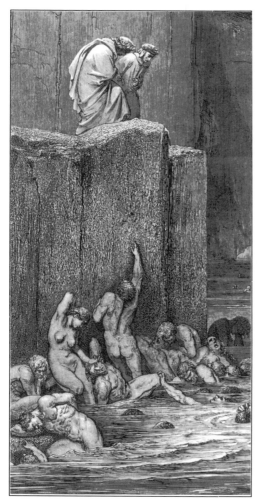

Vergil, Dante and the flatterers (e)

a) GRACE: The title is discussed in the Afterword. 'Grace' shares its structure with Dante's *Divine Comedy*.

Section One: *Inferno*

b) *Two gentlemen*: Perhaps even 'two gallants'. The word 'gentleman' has a variety of ironic nuances in 'Grace' – e.g. at the beginning of 137.

c) *lavatory*: 'what the great and good Lord Chesterfield calls the necessary house' – from the end of Beckett's *Murphy*.

d) *he had fallen*: The Fall of Man, Dante's descent into Hell and the fall of Milton's angels are all alluded to here, as they will be later in *FW* by the fall of Bygmester Finnegan from the ladder.

e) *smeared with the filth and ooze*: A prosaic instance of Joe Hynes' image: *To befoul and smear th'exalted name ...* (119). The fate of the flatterers in Dante's *Inferno* is similar, but Mr Kernan is also like one of the simoniacs, who are upside-down in holes in the ground.

f) *A thin stream of blood*: The only blood actually spilt in *D*. Of Father Flynn's broken chalice, Eliza said 'it contained nothing' (9a).

g) *curates*: See 48j.

h) *a ring of men*: Another image from Dante's *Inferno*. Simon Magus, corrupt Popes and other simoniacs are found together (in Canto XIX) at the same level of hell. Eliot's *The Waste Land* will associate a similar image with the Tarot pack.

i) *medal*: The word suggests both an award for gallantry in battle and also a badge of religious devotion. 'Grace' has a military theme marching through it, balancing the religious one.

j) *tessellated*: Tiled, mosaiced. A mock-heroic description of the pub floor.

k) *collar was unfastened*: Shirts of course had detachable collars at this time, to allow the same shirt to be reworn with a clean collar.

l) *dinged*: Not dingy, but with a bump in it. The hat has been seen as an important but unexplained symbol in this story, perhaps of grace itself, or merely of respectability. At the end of *U*, 'Hades', Bloom points out that John Henry Menton's hat is dinged, and he is proud of having once rescued Parnell's hat at a turbulent meeting.

GRACE

a

TWO GENTLEMEN WHO were in the lavatory at the time tried to lift him up: but he was quite helpless. He lay curled up at the foot of the stairs down which he had fallen. They succeeded in turning him over. His hat had rolled a few yards away and his clothes were smeared with the filth and ooze of the floor on which he had lain, face downwards. His eyes were closed and he breathed with a grunting noise. A thin stream of blood trickled from the corner of his mouth.

These two gentlemen and one of the curates carried him up the stairs and laid him down again on the floor of the bar. In two minutes he was surrounded by a ring of men. The manager of the bar asked everyone who he was and who was with him. No one knew who he was but one of the curates said he had served the gentleman with a small rum.

—Was he by himself? asked the manager—

—No, sir. There was two gentlemen with him—

—And where are they?—

No one knew; a voice said:

—Give him air. He's fainted—

The ring of onlookers distended and closed again elastically. A dark medal of blood had formed itself near the man's head on the tessellated floor. The manager, alarmed by the grey pallor of the man's face, sent for a policeman.

His collar was unfastened and his necktie undone. He opened his eyes for an instant, sighed and closed them again. One of the gentlemen who had carried him upstairs held a dinged silk hat in his hand. The manager asked repeatedly did no one know who the injured man was or where had his friends gone. The door of the bar opened and an immense constable entered. A crowd which had followed him down the laneway collected outside the door, struggling to look in through the glass panels.

The manager at once began to narrate what he knew. The constable, a young man with thick immobile features, listened. He moved his head slowly to right and left and from the manager to the person on the floor, as if he feared to be the

m) *or where had his friends gone*: The usage is Hiberno-English. Standard English would be 'or where his friends had gone (to)'.

n) *constable*: Like London, Dublin had its own metropolitan police, the 'DMP'.

o) *as if he feared …*: A knowing portrait of a ponderous policeman out of his urban depth.

A member of the Dublin Metropolitan Police. Note the 'thick immobile features' (n)

135

An 'outsider' (outside the National Library) (137e)

THE PUBLIC TASTE
IS RETURNING

to Brandy. The standard
of Purity, Flavour, and
Excellence in Brandy is
set by

HENNESSY'S
THREE
STAR.

INSIST UPON HAVING IT.

Mr Kernan does not need to insist: 'The brandy was forced down the man's throat'

a) *licked the lead*: This action, universal amongst fictional policemen of a certain calibre, is very rarely done in real life.

b) *indite*: Constabulary jargon. Like the more unusual 'indict', the word simply means 'inscribe, set down in writing'.

c) *provincial accent*: Provincials, or more rudely, 'culchies' or 'bogmen', were then (and are now) derided by many Dublin 'jackeens' – and their accent was a giveaway. Joyce planned a companion volume of short stories, to be called *Provincials*, but it was never written. The 'Mullingar fragment' of *SH* is virtually unique in Joyce's work, having a rural Irish setting.

d) *young man in a cycling-suit*: The identity of this good Samaritan is never stated. But as he is later referred to as 'that medical fellow' (143b), his origins might be among the Cecilia Street medical students with whom Joyce drank in 1900–1904. Later, one of these would boast of almost winning the Dublin University Mile Cycling Championship and would describe Joyce at this time as 'only a medical students' pal'. His name, inevitably, was Oliver St John Gogarty.

e) *Sha,'s nothing*: Sure, it's nothing. The sentiment has already been repeated by Little Chandler (74).

f) *hospital*: The nearest is Mercer's Hospital just around the corner in Stephen's Street. It was incorporated in 1730.

g) *without answering*: Mr Kernan is reluctant to risk prosecution for drunkenness.

h) *very thickly*: Not stupidly, but with slurred speech.

i) *ulster*: A long, loose, belted tweed overcoat, of the kind traditionally favoured by Sherlock Holmes. J. G. M'Gee & Co of Belfast launched their 'Ulster Overcoat' in 1867, whence the name.

j) *Mr Power*: Jack Power appears in *U*, where he is a friend of Martin Cunningham and Joe Hynes (of 'Ivy Day'). He works in Dublin Castle for the Royal Irish Constabulary, and has not only a wife, but also a mistress who is a barmaid. In *U*, 'Lestrygonians', Bloom sees some policemen and thinks: 'Jack Power could a tale unfold: father a G man'. He was based on a friend of the Joyce family, Tom Devan, of the Corporation Cleansing Department, who gets his own mention in *U*, 'Wandering Rocks' 19, as the viceregal procession goes by:

> From its sluice in Wood quay wall under Tom Devan's office Poddle river hung out in fealty a tongue of liquid sewage.

victim of some delusion. Then he drew off his glove, produced
a small book from his waist, licked the lead of his pencil and
made ready to indite. He asked in a suspicious provincial accent:

—Who is the man? What's his name and address?—

A young man in a cycling-suit cleared his way through the
ring of bystanders. He knelt down promptly beside the injured
man and called for water. The constable knelt down also to
help. The young man washed the blood from the injured man's
mouth and then called for some brandy. The constable repeated
the order in an authoritative voice until a curate came running
with the glass. The brandy was forced down the man's throat.
In a few seconds he opened his eyes and looked about him. He
looked at the circle of faces and then, understanding, strove to
rise to his feet.

—You're all right now? asked the young man in the cycling-
suit—

—Sha,'s nothing, said the injured man, trying to stand up—

He was helped to his feet. The manager said something
about a hospital and some of the bystanders gave advice. The
battered silk hat was placed on the man's head. The constable
asked:

—Where do you live?—

The man, without answering, began to twirl the ends of his
moustache. He made light of his accident. It was nothing, he
said: only a little accident. He spoke very thickly.

—Where do you live? repeated the constable—

The man said they were to get a cab for him. While the point
was being debated a tall agile gentleman of fair complexion,
wearing a long yellow ulster, came from the far end of the bar.
Seeing the spectacle he called out:

—Hallo, Tom, old man! What's the trouble?—

—Sha,'s nothing, said the man—

The new-comer surveyed the deplorable figure before him
and then turned to the constable, saying:

—It's all right, constable. I'll see him home—

The constable touched his helmet and answered:

—All right, Mr Power!—

—Come now, Tom, said Mr Power, taking his friend by
the arm. No bones broken. What? Can you walk?—

The young man in the cycling-suit took the man by the
other arm and the crowd divided.

*Oliver Gogarty (d), beneath a
'battered silk hat'*

136

a) *'an't we have a little ...?*: Tom Kernan is incorrigible: he wants another drink.

b) *the laneway*: This identifies the pub as John Nolan's, grocer, wine and spirit merchant, at No 3 Harry Street (near the top of Grafton Street). To the right of the building, Chatham Lane leads up to Chatham Street, where the B-Division police station was situated: the quickest route between the police station and Nolan's was down the lane. During the 1950s the pub, then McDaid's, but still with its basement lavatory, became a regular haunt of writers, including Patrick Kavanagh, Anthony Cronin, Brendan Behan, J. P. Donleavy, and Flann O'Brien, who might have commented that topographical inferences of this sort are likely to be fallacious, being based upon licensed premises.

c) *They agreed*: The manager is at pains to avoid the suspicion that he might have served someone who was already incapable. The country policeman has already deferred to the authority of Mr Power.

d) *Grafton Street*: See 37i.

e) *an outsider*: Known also as an Irish Jaunting Car. Although there was a small seat for the driver, he usually sat in one of the back-to-back passenger seats over the wheels, which meant that he was, in effect, driving the vehicle sideways. In *Highways and Horses* (1888) Athol Maudslay commented on its awkwardness and lack of balance, continuing:

> The Irish Car is inseparably connected in our minds with Ireland and the Irish; there is an eccentricity about it that appeals to our sense of the ludicrous.

f) *Kernan*: Tom Kernan, teataster and salesman, also appears frequently in *U*. Molly Bloom in her soliloquy alludes to his accident: 'that drunken little barrelly man that bit his tongue off falling down the mens W C drunk'. The initial accident in the pub actually happened to John Joyce, but the name may come from the M'Kernans, who were family connections (84m), while Joyce family memories suggest that Mr Kernan was based upon one Ned Thornton, a teataster, who at one time had been a neighbour (34). The character is very much a composite.

g) *Westmoreland Street*: On its short journey to the river, the outsider will pass Trinity College, Tom Moore's statue and the *Irish Times* office on the right and Hodges Figgis' bookshop, Kapp and Peterson (the tobacconist and pipemaker made more famous by Pozzo in *Waiting for Godot*), the Bank of Ireland,

The top of Grafton Street. Harry Street is first on the left (b)

—How did you get yourself into this mess? asked Mr Power—

—The gentleman fell down the stairs, said the young man—

—I' 'ery 'uch o'liged to you, sir, said the injured man—

—Not at all—

a   —'an't we have a little . . . ?—

—Not now. Not now—

The three men left the bar and the crowd sifted through the
b doors into the laneway. The manager brought the constable to
c the stairs to inspect the scene of the accident. They agreed that
the gentleman must have missed his footing. The customers
returned to the counter and a curate set about removing the
traces of blood from the floor.

d   When they came out into Grafton Street Mr Power whistled
e for an outsider. The injured man said again as well as he could:

—I' 'ery 'uch o'liged to you, sir. I hope we'll 'eet again. 'y
f na'e is Kernan—

The shock and the incipient pain had partly sobered him.

—Don't mention it, said the young man—

They shook hands. Mr Kernan was hoisted on to the car
and, while Mr Power was giving directions to the carman, he
expressed his gratitude to the young man and regretted that
they could not have a little drink together.

—Another time, said the young man—

g   The car drove off towards Westmoreland Street. As it passed
h the Ballast Office the clock showed half-past nine. A keen east
i wind hit them, blowing from the mouth of the river. Mr
Kernan was huddled together with cold. His friend asked him
to tell how the accident had happened.

j   —I 'an't, 'an, he answered, 'y 'ongue is hurt—

—Show—

k   The other leaned over the well of the car and peered into
Mr Kernan's mouth but he could not see. He struck a match
and, sheltering it in the shell of his hands, peered again into the
mouth which Mr Kernan opened obediently. The swaying
movement of the car brought the match to and from the
opened mouth. The lower teeth and gums were covered with
clotted blood and a minute piece of the tongue seemed to have
been bitten off. The match was blown out.

—That's ugly, said Mr Power—

and Bewley's Oriental Café
on the left.

h) *the Ballast Office*: See 82h.

i) *the mouth of the river*: They
are passing over O'Connell
Bridge, as later the Conroys
are to do.

j) *I 'an't 'an*: Mr Kernan's
attempt to articulate 'I can't,
man'. Oddly, the injury to his
tongue makes it difficult for
him to manage the consonants
'c' or 'm'.

k) *the well of the car*: This cavity
between the seats of an Irish
'outsider' was used for
luggage. Sir William Butler,
Irish homeruler and imperi-
alist soldier, who admired
both Parnell and Napoleon,
wrote in his *Autobiography*
(1911): 'He . . . took three or
four brace of grouse from the
bag, and . . . put the birds in
the well.'

The tessellated device of John
Nolan (b)

a) *a commercial traveller of the old school*: Note the return to the mock-heroic style. A similar alternation in tones is used in *U*, notably in the 'Cyclops' section.

b) *a silk hat of some decency*: Not the tautology it seems, given Mr Kernan's 'battered silk hat'. There is a likely reference here to the song 'The Hat My Father Wore' (related to the Orange anthem, 'The Sash'):

> It's old, but it's beautiful,
> The best was ever seen,
> 'Twas worn for more than ninety years
> In that little isle of green.
> From my father's great ancestors
> It's descended with galore,
> 'Tis the relic of old decency,
> The hat my father wore.

c) *gaiters*: Buttoned leggings which extend from the ankle to the knee. Save for the odd Anglican bishop they are now virtually extinct.

d) *grace*: One of three invocations of the title of the story.

e) *pass muster*: Another military metaphor. A 'muster' also means a 'commercial sample'.

f) *his Napoleon*: The man upon whom he modelled his campaigns. Father Flynn of 'The Sisters' tells the boy about Bonaparte.

g) *Blackwhite*: Is it cynical to suggest that the sign of a good commercial traveller is the ability convincingly to swear that black is white? The name or nickname may, however, be that of some mid-nineteenth-century tea salesman whom Joyce heard Mr Thornton (137f) reminiscing about, and may also be a hint of black and white photography (153a). Another theory connects the name with the Black and White factions in Dantean Florence.

h) *Crowe Street*: Then, and now, more usually spelt Crow Street, it was a street of agents, importers and accountants, off Dame Street. The Crow Street Theatre was in the eighteenth century the rival of Smock Alley. In *U*, 'Ithaca', Mr Kernan's office has moved to 5 Dame Street nearby, where he is agent for the London firm, Pulbrook Robertson and Co.

i) *London, E.C.*: East Central, loosely 'the City'. Pulbrook Robertson and Co were at 2 Mincing Lane, E.C. (again according to 'Ithaca'). London tea money helped to finance the foundation of Dublin's Abbey Theatre in 1904, thanks to Miss Annie Horniman's benevolence.

j) *spat it forth into the grate*: The action recalls Old Cotter and Mr Henchy.

k) *Royal Irish Constabulary*: The RIC was the police force for Ireland outside Dublin. In addition, it ran an armed intelligence force, charged with maintaining British hegemony over Ireland through the use of spies and by the discouragement of rebellion. Like the DMP (135n), it was disbanded when the British withdrew from the twenty-six counties of 'the South'.

l) *Dublin Castle*: The phrase was then often shorthand for British rule in Ireland (as in 'Ivy Day' (111f)). In December 1909, Joyce founded the Volta, the first permanent Irish cinema. Its opening programme featured a film entitled 'Bewitched Castle'. Today 'Dublin Castle' is more likely to evoke summit meetings of the European Community.

m) *arc . . . intersected*: The geometrical metaphor, in keeping with the Euclidian imagery of *D*, elegantly implies (without hyperbole) Mr Power's eventual decline.

n) *a character*: Virtually a Dublin career in itself. There have been hundreds, but admirable examples include 'Projecting' Pockrich, Zozimus, Bang-bang, Forty-coats, Alabaster, 'Pope' O'Mahony and Endymion (the Cashel Boyle O'Connor Fitzmaurice Tisdall Farrell of *U*).

o) *inexplicable debts*: These could be partly explicated by his maintaining a mistress (136j), and perhaps by his 'small loans' to the Kernans. Apart from the debt of gratitude that Mr Kernan owes Mr Power for his rescue from the pub – and even from possible imprisonment – this is the first mention of the network of debts and dishonesties that entangle all the main characters in the story.

p) *Glasnevin road*: North of the Royal Canal the road to Glasnevin (and the cemetery and the Botanic Gardens) was actually Prospect Road, and led into Botanic Road.

q) *what book they were in*: (Apart from *D*, of course.) How far they have progressed at school is indicated by what text they are studying.

r) *surprised at their manners and at their accents*: The Kernan arc of decline has been continuing since Mr Power was last in touch.

s) *Mrs Kernan*: See 139e.

t) *do for himself*: i.e. do himself in, kill himself through carelessness: the phrase (emphasised on the first word) is not a threat that she will leave her husband.

u) *the holy alls of it*: An Irish expression, meaning 'that's all there is to be said about it'.

v) *drinking since Friday*: Like Bob Doran in 'The Boarding House'. It is now likely to be well into the following week.

—Sha, 's nothing, said Mr Kernan, closing his mouth and pulling the collar of his filthy coat across his neck—

Mr Kernan was a commercial traveller of the old school which believed in the dignity of its calling. He had never been seen in the city without a silk hat of some decency and a pair of gaiters. By grace of these two articles of clothing, he said, a man could always pass muster. He carried on the tradition of his Napoleon, the great Blackwhite, whose memory he evoked at times by legend and mimicry. Modern business methods had spared him only so far as to allow him a little office in Crowe Street, on the window blind of which was written the name of his firm with the address – London, E.C. On the mantelpiece of this little office a little leaden battalion of canisters was drawn up and on the table before the window stood four or five china bowls which were usually half full of a black liquid. From these bowls Mr Kernan tasted tea. He took a mouthful, drew it up, saturated his palate with it and then spat it forth into the grate. Then he paused to judge.

Mr Power, a much younger man, was employed in the Royal Irish Constabulary Office in Dublin Castle. The arc of his social rise intersected the arc of his friend's decline, but Mr Kernan's decline was mitigated by the fact that certain of those friends who had known him at his highest point of success still esteemed him as a character. Mr Power was one of these friends. His inexplicable debts were a byword in his circle; he was a debonair young man.

The car halted before a small house on the Glasnevin road and Mr Kernan was helped into the house. His wife put him to bed while Mr Power sat downstairs in the kitchen asking the children where they went to school and what book they were in. The children, two girls and a boy, conscious of their father's helplessness and of their mother's absence, began some horseplay with him. He was surprised at their manners and at their accents, and his brow grew thoughtful. After a while Mrs Kernan entered the kitchen, exclaiming:

—Such a sight! Oh, he'll do for himself one day and that's the holy alls of it. He's been drinking since Friday—

Mr Power was careful to explain to her that he was not responsible, that he had come on the scene by the merest accident. Mrs Kernan, remembering Mr Power's good offices

Napoleon (f) and hats (b)

a) *money ... wife and family*: A clear definition of Farrington of 'Counterparts', down to the domestic quarrels and the opportune loans.

b) *Fogarty's*: A small grocer's shop, which also sells alcohol (148f).

c) *Mr Power stood up*: An admirably diplomatic way of declining Mrs Kernan's offer.

d) *Martin*: Martin Cunningham (140l).

Section Two: *Purgatorio*

e) *Mrs Kernan*: The plight of Dublin women is here described laconically but tellingly by Joyce. After twenty-five years of a marriage which she had found irksome after three weeks, it is a tribute to her that she is still 'active' and 'practical'. Joyce's mother survived only twenty-three years of marriage. The stoicism and common sense of Mrs Kernan recall Joyce's aunt, Josephine Murray.

f) *emptied her husband's pockets*: No revelations are at hand (and probably very little money). Molly Bloom finds out about Poldy's secret french letter this way.

g) *not ungallant*: The fact that this was so far in the past, the word 'seemed' and the grudging litotes together say a great deal about how gallant Mr Kernan is now. As a gallant, he matches Lenehan and Corley in their story.

h) *the chapel door*: The nearest 'chapel' was probably the Glasnevin parish church.

i) *Star of the Sea Church*: A handsome three-gabled family church, completed in 1858, where the parish priest is Father Conroy, brother of Gabriel in 'The Dead' (167r). It features in *U*, 'Nausicaa'. The church's name is from the Latin *Stella Maris*, one epithet for the Virgin Mary. Stephen during the traumatic Christmas dinner in *P* (I.3) thinks of others:

> the Protestants used to make fun of the litany of the Blessed Virgin. *Tower of Ivory* they used to say, *House of Gold!*

j) *a jovial well-fed man*: The indefinite article hints that Mr Kernan is not the man he was.

k) *carried a silk hat gracefully*: This was when grace was a possibility, at the other end of the 'social arc'.

The O'Connell Memorial in Glasnevin (138p)

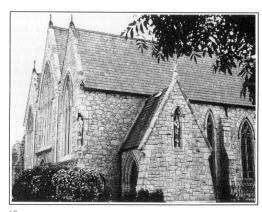

(i)

139

during domestic quarrels, as well as many small but opportune loans, said:

—O, you needn't tell me that, Mr Power. I know you're a friend of his, not like some of those others he does be with. They're all right so long as he has money in his pocket to keep him out from his wife and family. Nice friends! Who was he with to-night, I'd like to know?—

Mr Power shook his head but said nothing.

—I'm so sorry, she continued, that I've nothing in the house to offer you. But if you wait a minute I'll send round to Fogarty's at the corner—

Mr Power stood up.

—We were waiting for him to come home with the money. He never seems to think he has a home at all—

—O, now, Mrs Kernan, said Mr Power, we'll make him turn over a new leaf. I'll talk to Martin. He's the man. We'll come here one of these nights and talk it over—

She saw him to the door. The carman was stamping up and down the footpath and swinging his arms to warm himself.

—It's very kind of you to bring him home, she said—

—Not at all, said Mr Power—

He got up on the car. As it drove off he raised his hat to her gaily.

—We'll make a new man of him, he said. Good-night, Mrs Kernan—

. . . .

Mrs Kernan's puzzled eyes watched the car till it was out of sight. Then she withdrew them, went into the house and emptied her husband's pockets.

She was an active, practical woman of middle age. Not long before she had celebrated her silver wedding and renewed her intimacy with her husband by waltzing with him to Mr Power's accompaniment. In her days of courtship Mr Kernan had seemed to her a not ungallant figure: and she still hurried to the chapel door whenever a wedding was reported and, seeing the bridal pair, recalled with vivid pleasure how she had passed out of the Star of the Sea Church in Sandymount, leaning on the arm of a jovial well-fed man who was dressed smartly in a frock-coat and lavender trousers and carried a silk hat gracefully balanced upon his other arm. After three weeks

The 'mask of a capital' on O'Connell Bridge (137i)

A lamp on O'Connell Bridge, as damaged as Mr Kernan (137i)

a) *The part of mother*: Mrs Kernan is a mother of a different calibre from most mothers in *D*, and, as the next paragraph makes plain, her mothering extends to her husband.

b) *shrewdly*: Some have seen this adverb as hinting that Mrs Kernan is shrewish, but the story explicitly suggests otherwise.

The Freeman's Journal *report above (continued on 141) of mourners at the funeral of the original of Martin Cunningham included many characters who appear in Joyce's work (either under their own names or under pseudonyms) such as Alfred H Hunter (142h)*

c) *launched*: Whereas the upper classes were launched in 'society', these Dubliners were launched in 'trade'.

d) *The other children*: How many there are is unstated.

e) *sent a letter*: Which would arrive the same day.

f) *beef-tea*: In 'The Sisters', this was the ailing Father Flynn's concoction too. The laborious homemade recipe was gradually being ousted by proprietary brands.

g) *scolded him roundly*: The wife of Job also upbraids her sorry husband: 'Dost thou still retain thine integrity? curse God, and die' (Job II.90). However, Mrs Kernan does not speak 'as one of the foolish women speaketh', but hopes for a different solution to the problem.

h) *Thomas Street*: A mediaeval street between Christ Church Cathedral and Guinness's Brewery, on the original great road westwards out of Dublin, the *Slí Mhór*. Mr Kernan would have put in about half an hour's walking for the round trip from Crowe Street.

i) *his friends*: These are the counterparts of the wise Vergil (and Beatrice and St Bernard) who act as guides in *The Divine Comedy*. They can also be seen as Job's comforters.

j) *chairs at the fire*: The friends will not be breaking the law formulated in Laurence Sterne's *Tristram Shandy* (Slawkenbergius Tale): 'Heat is in proportion to the want of true knowledge'.

k) *veteran's pride*: Mr Kernan continues to suppose that he has been in the wars.

l) *Mr Cunningham, Mr M'Coy*: Martin Cunningham's name is borrowed from a Galway family connected to the Bodkins (194c). His looks and character come from an old family friend of the Joyces, Mathew F. Kane, accountant, who was Chief Clerk in the Crown Solicitor's Office in Dublin Castle. He died by drowning after a stroke on 13 July 1904: '... poor Merkin Cornyngwham, the official out of the castle on pension, when he was completely drowned off Erin Isles ...' (*FW* (387)). The funeral of Paddy Dignam in *U* is itself based on Kane's funeral which John Joyce attended with many friends and other Dublin personages, listed in the report that begins on this page. Though in a sense Mr Cunningham goes to his own funeral in 'Hades', Kane's death is also mentioned in 'Ithaca'. In *U* Mr Cunningham still has his alcoholic wife and is thought of by Father Conmee as a 'Good practical catholic: useful at mission time'.

M'Coy is one of several prototypes for Bloom, and is said to be based on John Joyce's friend Charles Chance. He is seen again in *U*, 'Lotus Eaters'.

m) *he had been converted*: Forcibly. In accordance with

140

she had found a wife's life irksome and, later on, when she was
beginning to find it unbearable, she had become a mother. The
part of mother presented to her no insuperable difficulties and
for twenty-five years she had kept house shrewdly for her
husband. Her two eldest sons were launched. One was in a
draper's shop in Glasgow and the other was clerk to a tea-
merchant in Belfast. They were good sons, wrote regularly
and sometimes sent home money. The other children were still
at school.

Mr Kernan sent a letter to his office next day and remained
in bed. She made beef-tea for him and scolded him roundly.
She accepted his frequent intemperance as part of the climate,
healed him dutifully whenever he was sick and always tried to
make him eat a breakfast. There were worse husbands. He had
never been violent since the boys had grown up, and she knew
that he would walk to the end of Thomas Street and back
again to book even a small order.

Two nights after, his friends came to see him. She brought
them up to his bedroom, the air of which was impregnated
with a personal odour, and gave them chairs at the fire. Mr
Kernan's tongue, the occasional stinging pain of which had
made him somewhat irritable during the day, became more
polite. He sat propped up in the bed by pillows and the little
colour in his puffy cheeks made them resemble warm cinders. He
apologized to his guests for the disorder of the room but at the
same time looked at them a little proudly, with a veteran's pride.

He was quite unconscious that he was the victim of a plot
which his friends, Mr Cunningham, Mr M'Coy and Mr Power
had disclosed to Mrs Kernan in the parlour. The idea had
been Mr Power's but its development was entrusted to Mr
Cunningham. Mr Kernan came of Protestant stock and, though
he had been converted to the Catholic faith at the time of his
marriage, he had not been in the pale of the Church for
twenty years. He was fond, moreover, of giving side-thrusts
at Catholicism.

Mr Cunningham was the very man for such a case. He was
an elder colleague of Mr Power. His own domestic life was
not very happy. People had great sympathy with him, for it
was known that he had married an unpresentable woman who
was an incurable drunkard. He had set up house for her six
times; and each time she had pawned the furniture on him.

the *Ne Temere* papal decree,
for a proposed marriage in
which only one partner was a
Roman Catholic, both had to
promise in writing to bring all
the children up as Catholics.
The Church's threat of refusing to marry the couple (and
thus to recognise the marriage) almost always caused
the couple to yield to priestly
pressure. Otherwise, the
entire family was effectively
excommunicated, and so
many Protestant fiancé(e)s
found it easier to 'be converted'. The promise has now
only to be made orally, and
the change insultingly pretends to be a relaxation of the
rule. There are very few Protestants now left in the south
of Ireland.

n) *in the pale*: The word is
related to 'paling' (fence). In
the fourteenth and fifteenth
centuries the (English) Pale
enclosed a variable area
around Dublin in which
English jurisdiction held
sway. At one time it ran
through the grounds of what
was to become Clongowes
Wood College. The use of the
term here is ironic, referring
as it does to the Irish (and pur-
portedly nationalistic) Roman
Catholic Church.

o) *unpresentable*: Like 'launched' (c), a socially sensitive
word.

p) *pawned*: Raised money by
leaving collateral with a
pawnbroker, as Farrington
does with his watch for the
same reason (81f). The theme
of debts, loans and bor-
rowings is taking substance.

F. Vance, T.C.; Edward P. Murray, J. F. C. Meyers, R.C.S.; J. J. Corry, P.L.G.; T. W. Little, M. Corry, Ed. O'Reilly, D.M.P.; John Gore, carrier; J. Dunne, P. Murphy, G Division; R. Rochford, V. Rochford, Wm. Sterling, C.E.; Martin Walsh, Thos. Balmer, John Tully, Thos. Williams, G. L. O'Connor, C.E.; J. J. Potter, W. G. Evans, J. Harvey, C. Wood, Denis P. Seery, John A. Egan, James Butler, Archibald Clarke, solicitor; Christopher Kelly, Henry J. Kelly, John Foley, E. P. M'Farland, William Buckley, solicitor; Alfred Grey, R.H.A.; Owen H. Dooley, D. Hishon, Henry Campbell, Town Clerk; F. F. Joyce, C. Rice, C. Burke Kennedy, W. J. Carroll, John J. Doherty, Dublin Castle; S. J. Hand, M. Lynam, John Parkinson, T.C., John J. Williams, John O'Sullivan, solicitor; H. Leonard, Thos P. Codd, LL.M., K.Q.C.P.I.; Dr O'Sullivan, T. R. Baillie-Gage, solicitor, Post Office; M. S. Bergin, solicitor; Jos. P. Swan, Ludlow M. Hamilton, J. M'Auley, James Thomas Cousins, John Behan, Joseph P. Behan, Edward Connolly, Joseph P. Lalor, John Magennis, Leo L. O'Connor, C.E.; P. M. Seales, solicitor; R. M. Hennessy, J. P. Doherty, Patk. O'Hanlon, J. O. Magennis, Robert Kelly, P. Kenny, M. Fitzpatrick, C. J. Hughes, C. A. Chance, Wm. M'Cune, solicitor; John Fernon, Patk. Kenny, late Staff Sergeant B Division; Timothy Lyons, Wm. Brophy, Richard Henderson, F. Kelly, C. O'Reilly, A. J. Charles, James Rickard, Professor T. H. Teegan, Patrick Nolan, John Curran, G. W. Hardy, Wm. Adrien, A. Keogh Nolan, L. O'Kelly, John F. O'Grady, James Crozier, J.P., T.C.; Jas. C. Mahon, M. Doyle, A. S. White, H. H. White, Adam S. Findlater, M.A.; N. Tarrant, Henry Egan, Capt. Fords, R.E., Francis Purcell, Martin Mortelle, P. L. Farrell, L. J. O'Neill, Paul Cox, John J. Reynolds, John Adams, Joseph L. Kelly, Ed. Taaffe, Edward Dwyer, New York, U.S.A.; Jas. Mortelle, C. O'Reilly, J. J. Gahan, M. C. Lough, Dr. Samuel A. Tucker, E. J Vaughan, Edward Gilligan, P.L.G.; P. Cahill, J. F. Mapleson, G. Kirkwood, jun.; A. Taaffe, F. Taaffe, G. A. Figgis, W. Butler, C.E., A. J. Morgan, C.E.; F. F. Joyce, Dr. Callinan, Jas. Adams, M. P. Clarke, F. Crowley, E. J. Charles, M. F. Fitzgibbons, Walter Butler, A. P. Lynch, F. F. Chance, J. Hurford, Daniel O'Connell, George H. Bogue, Alfred H. Hunter, John S. Joyce, James A. Joyce, B.A.; Charles P. Joyce, Matthew Tobias, solicitor; James Keogh, Wm. M'Dermott, John Gaffney, Dr. J. A. Whelan, P. Coll, jun.; D. R. Beckett, Jas. F. Egan, City Sword Bearer; W. Sherry, Alderman Hennessy, T. O'Reilly, T.C.; Geo. Washington, P. P. Hynes, U.D.C., Kingstown; Louis A. Byrne, E. W. O'Reilly, J. G. Cecil Webber, Thos. Grant, D.M.P., John Elliott, M.D.; C. H. Cullinan, W. J. Hughes, M.B.; R. W. MacNiece, solicitor; H. H. Booth, James M'Blaine, Jas. M'Blaine, jun.; W. E. Clancy, Alfred Bergin, Bruce Robinson, Samuel M. Figgis, M. O'Brien, G Division D.M.P.; John P. Collins, solicitor; T. J. Clegg, solicitor; Roger Greene, solicitor; Philip Smith solicitor; John O'Sullivan, solicitor; L. Monk, Philip O'Sullivan, solicitor; L. G. Waldron, Edward Carey, John Clancy, City Sub-Sheriff; Thomas O'Reilly, Christopher Dunne, John Murray, M. Lambert Kelly, Thos. Devin, Rev. P. Shiel, Thos. Dagg, John Adams, Alfred Bergin, P. L. Farrell, J. A. Dagg, Michael Nolan, L. O'Rourke, Wm. M'Grath, B.L.; J. Kane, Thos. Rowsome, James Kavanagh, J.P.; Thomas Figgis, P. Toomey, Christopher Devenish, Edward Gaynor, Timothy Keogh, P. Martin, John Donohoe, P.L.G.;

Mathew Kane's funeral, from 140, and concluded on 143. Note the Joyces, Stanislausless

a) *blade ... tempered by brief immersions*: A swordmaking metaphor for hardening, in keeping with the story's military (and Church Militant) tone.

b) *Religion for her was a habit*: As with many Irish nuns.

c) *the Sacred Heart*: As vouchsafed to the Blessed Margaret Mary Alacoque (29q).

d) *the banshee*: (Irish, *bean sí*, fairy woman.) A spirit who laments by keening the imminent death of a family member.

e) *the Holy Ghost*: Joyce derived much amusement from the idea of the 'Holy Ghost', and here, clearly, from coupling it with the banshee. In *U*, 'Telemachus', Mulligan's 'Ballad of Joking Jesus' is even more irreverent about the Holy Spirit: '*My mother's a jew, my father's a bird*'.

f) *had been a soprano*: Another mention of musical Dublin, and far from the last. In *U*, M'Coy's wife sings in Dublin concerts under the stage name of Madame Marie Tallon.

g) *the Midland Railway*: It went westward from the now defunct Broadstone Station just north-west of King's Inns.

h) *a canvasser for advertisements*: Leopold Bloom has the same job (for the *Freeman's Journal*) in *U*, and a similarly chequered commercial history (15f).

i) *the* Irish Times: Founded in 1859, it was then the main Conservative or Unionist newspaper, read by the Protestant establishment in Ireland.

j) *a coal firm*: There were dozens of coal firms in Dublin at the time, including Flower & M'Donald in Ringsend, and Tedcastle, M'Cormick & Co on Sir John Rogerson's Quay.

k) *the Sub-Sheriff*: This was then 'Long' John Clancy, MP, who had lived in North Richmond Street while the Joyces were there. He is Fanning of 'Ivy Day' (110g) and *U*. Though Clancy disliked that part of his job which involved organising the hanging of convicted murderers, his post was more permanent and practical than that of the High Sheriff, which was an annual and mainly ceremonial appointment.

The Irish Times.

VOL. XLVI.—NO. 14,509.   DUBLIN, SATURDAY, JANUARY 2, 1904.   PRICE ONE PENNY.

Every one had respect for poor Martin Cunningham. He was a thoroughly sensible man, influential and intelligent. His blade of human knowledge, natural astuteness particularized by long association with cases in the police-courts, had been tempered by brief immersions in the waters of general philosophy. He was well-informed. His friends bowed to his opinions and considered that his face was like Shakespeare's.

When the plot had been disclosed to her Mrs Kernan had said:

—I leave it all in your hands, Mr Cunningham—

After a quarter of a century of married life she had very few illusions left. Religion for her was a habit, and she suspected that a man of her husband's age would not change greatly before death. She was tempted to see a curious appropriateness in his accident and, but that she did not wish to seem bloody-minded, she would have told the gentlemen that Mr Kernan's tongue would not suffer by being shortened. However, Mr Cunningham was a capable man; and religion was religion. The scheme might do good and, at least, it could do no harm. Her beliefs were not extravagant. She believed steadily in the Sacred Heart as the most generally useful of all Catholic devotions and approved of the sacraments. Her faith was bounded by her kitchen but, if she was put to it, she could believe also in the banshee and in the Holy Ghost.

The gentlemen began to talk of the accident. Mr Cunningham said that he had once known a similar case. A man of seventy had bitten off a piece of his tongue during an epileptic fit and the tongue had filled in again, so that no one could see a trace of the bite.

—Well, I'm not seventy, said the invalid—

—God forbid, said Mr Cunningham—

—It doesn't pain you now? asked Mr M'Coy—

Mr M'Coy had been at one time a tenor of some reputation. His wife, who had been a soprano, still taught young children to play the piano at low terms. His line of life had not been the shortest distance between two points and for short periods he had been driven to live by his wits. He had been a clerk in the Midland Railway, a canvasser for advertisements for the *Irish Times* and for the *Freeman's Journal*, a town traveller for a coal firm on commission, a private inquiry agent, a clerk in the office of the Sub-Sheriff, and he had recently become

(c)

Martin Cunningham's 'face was like Shakespeare's'. His original, Mat Kane, was called by Stanislaus 'the Green Street Shakespeare'

a) *the City Corner*. At this time, according to *Thom's Directory*, 'Louis A. Byrne, F.R.C.S.I., LK.Q.C.P.I., L.M., F.R.I.A.M., city coroner, surgeon to Jervis street hospital'. M'Coy (who lacks letters) is clearly pleased to have dealings with such an important figure.

b) *retch off*: Either to vomit or to suffer from what in Dublin are known as the 'dry gawks'. *FW* (180) has a graphic description of a hangover.

c) *No*: Mr Kernan will not admit to the effects of the 'boose', just as the policeman and the bar manager do not address the question of why 'the gentleman must have missed his footing' (137c).

d) *Mucus . . . thorax*: M'Coy is showing off the expertise he has recently acquired at the Coroner's Office.

e) *all's well that ends well*: The proverb predates by three centuries the Shakespeare play (1602) of that name, where it appears at the end of the fourth scene of Act IV. The play, a love-tangle with a military background, is based on a story by Boccaccio.

f) *I'm very much obliged to you*: Kernan's favourite phrase. It continues the theme of this story, meaning, as it does, 'I'm indebted to you'. It is comforting that he can now enunciate it properly.

g) *Little chap with sandy hair*: Who this 'friend' who fled from the battlefield could be is uncertifiably suggested by the phrase used to describe him – '*Little cha(p)*'. Little Chandler is similarly timid, and with his similar ('fair silken') hair colour, he matches the particulars of the missing witness – a Silken Thomas (62g) who cut and ran, perhaps.

h) *Harford*: There is a kindly master of this name at Clongowes in *P* (I.4) during Stephen's time there, but the Harford here, who is scarcely even a presence in 'Grace', seems to be left over from a planned earlier version of the story, which was to tell of a cuckold's attendance at a funeral and later at a pub. 'Hades' in *U* is centred on this funeral (140l). Both Bloom and Harford as described share characteristics with the real-life city councillor, Reuben J. Dodd, who was not Jewish but an 'Irish Jew', being a Catholic moneylender. There also may be a connection with one Alfred H. Hunter (listed beside the Joyces at the Kane funeral), who was to be the protagonist in an intended story for *D*, to be called 'Ulysses'. From elements like these, some fictional and some historical, Leopold Bloom would be moulded.

i) *Hm*: In *U*, 'Hades', Martin Cunningham's anti-semitism is more explicit than this.

j) *secret sources of information*: The relationship between Corley and Dublin Castle has been mentioned in 'Two Gallants'. Dublin was a city of agents and informers.

k) *bona-fide travellers*: Until the middle of the twentieth century, Dublin was ringed by 'bona-fides', pubs on the outskirts that did a roaring trade by observing the letter of the law stating that anyone who had travelled a certain distance should be served with food (and, incidentally, drink), even when ordinary pubs had closed.

l) *usurious interest*: Such financial skulduggery helps to explain the workmen's attraction to socialism mentioned in 'Ivy Day' and 'A Painful Case'. Psalm XV ends:

> He that hath not given his money upon usury, nor taken reward against the innocent. Whoso doeth these things shall never fall.

Mr Kernan has already fallen, and prospects do not look good for others.

m) *Mr Goldberg*: A cartoon plutocrat, like those in 'After the Race'. The name recalls that of Bloom's boyhood friend, Owen Goldberg. In *U*, 'Lestrygonians', Bloom remembers that they used to climb trees together near 'Goose green'.

n) *Liffey Loan Bank*: Though this cannot be traced, there were many money brokers and semi-official moneylenders in Dublin, mostly in the streets around the Bank of Ireland on College Green, as for example the Irish Discount Company, at 9 Westmoreland Street. Joyce's father had recourse to such establishments from time to time.

o) *the Jewish ethical code*: In the Torah, Shammai is told by Hillel:

> Whatever is hateful to you, do not do to your neighbour. That is the whole Torah: the rest is commentary. Now go and study.

But while the satire in this story is mostly directed at the Roman Catholic Church, the Jewish references go towards establishing Joyce's thesis that simony, whether secular, clerical, masonic or whatever, was endemic in Dublin life.

p) *an Irish Jew*: In *U*, 'Nestor', Dominie Deasy explains jokingly to Stephen why the Irish never persecuted the Jews – because they never let them in. In fact Dublin had a thriving Jewish community. Chaim Herzog, President of Israel, was later to be educated there.

a secretary to the City Coroner. His new office made him professionally interested in Mr Kernan's case.

—Pain? Not much, answered Mr Kernan. But it's so sick-
b ening. I feel as if I wanted to retch off—

—That's the boose, said Mr Cunningham firmly—

c —No, said Mr Kernan. I think I caught a cold on the car. There's something keeps coming into my throat, phlegm or . . .—

d —Mucus, said Mr M'Coy—

—It keeps coming like from down in my throat, sickening thing—

—Yes, yes, said Mr M'Coy, that's the thorax—

He looked at Mr Cunningham and Mr Power at the same time with an air of challenge. Mr Cunningham nodded his head rapidly and Mr Power said:

e —Ah, well, all's well that ends well—

f —I'm very much obliged to you, old man, said the invalid—

Mr Power waved his hand.

—Those other two fellows I was with . . .—

—Who were you with? asked Mr Cunningham—

—A chap. I don't know his name. Damn it now, what's his
g name? Little chap with sandy hair . . .—

—And who else?—

h —Harford—

i —Hm, said Mr Cunningham—

When Mr Cunningham made that remark, people were silent. It was known that the speaker had secret sources of
j information. In this case the monosyllable had a moral intention. Mr Harford sometimes formed one of a little detachment which left the city shortly after noon on Sunday with the purpose of arriving as soon as possible at some public-house on the outskirts of the city where its members duly qualified
k themselves as *bona-fide* travellers. But his fellow-travellers had never consented to overlook his origin. He had begun life as an obscure financier by lending small sums of money to
l workmen at usurious interest. Later on he had become the
m partner of a very fat short gentleman, Mr Goldberg, in the
n Liffey Loan Bank. Though he had never embraced more than
o the Jewish ethical code, his fellow-Catholics, whenever they had smarted in person or by proxy under his exactions, spoke
p of him bitterly as an Irish Jew and an illiterate, and saw divine disapproval of usury made manifest through the person of his

*A 1903 advertisement for
another lending establishment (n)*

*Mathew Kane's funeral (continued from 141). The
listed mourners from a cross-section of Dublin life,
with many politicians, publicans and priests, though
few women are mentioned. This was a large part of
Joyce's early world*

a) *idiot son*: The son of Reuben J. Dodd (142h) is
described in *U* as trying to drown himself in the
Liffey: Dodd gave his rescuer (who had the equally
Irish name of Moses Goldin) two shillings. 'One
and eightpence too much,' said Mr Dedalus, the
implication being that the youth was not quite the
full shilling. A more accurate version of the episode,
from the *Irish Worker*, is reprinted in Richard
Ellmann's biography.

b) *that medical fellow*: See 136d.

c) *seven days without the option of a fine*: For being
drunk and disorderly, or breach of the peace, or
whatever charge the policeman was minded to bring.
In 1902–3 a new Licensing Act was being passed
which deemed the words 'and disorderly' or 'and
incapable' no long to be necessary addenda to a
charge of drunkenness.

d) *peloothered*: This portmanteau word, still current
in Dublin, is composed of 'polluted' and 'fluthered'.

e) *True bill*: A phrase used in preliminary court hear-
ings to signify that there are sufficient legal grounds
for holding a trial.

f) *squared*: Pressurised – or possibly bribed – not to
pursue the matter. The question is professionally
embarrassing, and made worse by the unwanted mat-
eyness of tone.

g) *a crusade . . .*: Mr Power had lent M'Coy a valise
'for his wife' which had not been returned: another
'unsettled account'.

h) *More than he resented . . .*: In *U*, 'Lotus Eaters',
Bloom meets M'Coy in Westland Row and worries
that he is going to try to extract another valise from
him. It's a 'true bill' – a case worth trying!

i) *playing of the game*: A late nineteenth-century
idiom, as in 'Ivy Day': 'can't we Irish play fair?' (117).
The concept is celebrated in Sir Henry Newbolt's old
warhorse 'Vitaï Lampada', a poem whose refrain is
'Play up! play up! and play the game!'

j) *rates*: The rates were a municipal tax on property.
They have now been abolished in Ireland for private
houses.

k) *bostooms*: Usually spelt 'bosthoon', the word comes
from the Irish *bastún*, 'bounder' or 'blockhead'. Mr
Kernan sees an unattended outsider in *U*, 'Wandering
Rocks' 12: 'Some Tipperary bosthoon endangering
the lives of the citizens'.

l) *65, catch your cabbage*: As in the report in 'A Painful
Case', the policeman's serial number is enough.

a idiot son. At other times they remembered his good points.

—I wonder where did he go to, said Mr Kernan—

He wished the details of the incident to remain vague. He wished his friends to think there had been some mistake, that Mr Harford and he had missed each other. His friends, who knew quite well Mr Harford's manners in drinking, were silent. Mr Power said again:

—All's well that ends well—

Mr Kernan changed the subject at once.

b —That was a decent young chap, that medical fellow, he said. Only for him . . .—

—O, only for him, said Mr Power, it might have been a

c case of seven days without the option of a fine—

—Yes, yes, said Mr Kernan, trying to remember. I remember now there was a policeman. Decent young fellow, he seemed. How did it happen at all?—

d —It happened that you were peloothered, Tom, said Mr Cunningham gravely—

e —True bill, said Mr Kernan, equally gravely—

f —I suppose you squared the constable, Jack, said Mr M'Coy—

Mr Power did not relish the use of his Christian name. He was not straight-laced, but he could not forget that Mr M'Coy

g had recently made a crusade in search of valises and portmanteaus to enable Mrs M'Coy to fulfil imaginary engage-

h ments in the country. More than he resented the fact that he

i had been victimized he resented such low playing of the game. He answered the question, therefore, as if Mr Kernan had asked it.

The narrative made Mr Kernan indignant. He was keenly conscious of his citizenship, wished to live with his city on terms mutually honourable and resented any affront put upon him by those whom he called country bumpkins.

j —Is this what we pay rates for? he asked. To feed and clothe

k these ignorant bostooms . . . and they're nothing else—

Mr Cunningham laughed. He was a Castle official only during office hours.

—How could they be anything else, Tom? he said—

He assumed a thick provincial accent and said in a tone of command:

l —65, catch your cabbage!—

a) *the depot*: At the eastern end of the Phoenix Park, the 'depot' was the headquarters of the Royal Irish Constabulary, and was called the 'Mecca' of the force. The main force quartered in the Depot was the Reserve, men who had been transferred there after service in the counties.

b) *omadhauns*: A phonetic spelling of the Irish word *amadán* meaning 'fool', still in currency.

c) *to drill*: i.e. to march and parade. Cabbages, appropriately, are planted in 'drills', though it was not just adeptness with cabbage that distinguished the physical prowess of the RIC: in August 1901 at the depot sports-day in Ballsbridge the world's first official long jump record was set by the policeman P. O'Connor. At almost twenty-five feet it was still the Irish record seventy-five years later.

d) *At dinner*: Meals had actually improved. In December 1904 the *Dublin Constabulary Gazette* looked back to 1890:

> The messing then was scandalous – consisting of quondam coffee and blackbread for breakfast and an eternal soup dinner for six days of the week, with a change on Friday to *bouquet* eggs, nothing for tea, and the same for supper ... [Now, however] messing is almost epicurean in its style ... [Reform has been] inspired by the administrative and organizing genius of Colonel Sir Neville Chamberlain.

Chamberlain was the Inspector-General. In 1938 his namesake was to organise things less well with Adolf Hitler.

e) *bloody*: One of the favourite local emphatics, and one of the instances which Joyce was asked to suppress for first general publication in 1914.

f) *yahoos*: A word invented by Swift in *Gulliver's Travels* for an imaginary race of man-like brutes; its antonym is 'houyhnhnms' – horse-like paragons of human nobility and reason.

g) *duckie ... hubby*: Mr Kernan's vainglorious indignation has been superseded by childishness, but there is still no glimmer of understanding. The tone behind these words is like that of Swift's affectionate teasing of his poppet in the *Journal to Stella*, though Tom Kernan's 'little language' is less complex.

The entrance to the depot (a)

Every one laughed. Mr M'Coy, who wanted to enter the conversation by any door, pretended that he had never heard the story. Mr Cunningham said:

—It is supposed – they say, you know – to take place in the depot where they get these thundering big country fellows, omadhauns, you know, to drill. The sergeant makes them stand in a row against the wall and hold up their plates—

He illustrated the story by grotesque gestures.

—At dinner, you know. Then he has a bloody big bowl of cabbage before him on the table and a bloody big spoon like a shovel. He takes up a wad of cabbage on the spoon and pegs it across the room and the poor devils have to try and catch it on their plates: *65, catch your cabbage*—

Every one laughed again: but Mr Kernan was somewhat indignant still. He talked of writing a letter to the papers.

—These yahoos coming up here, he said, think they can boss the people. I needn't tell you, Martin, what kind of men they are—

Mr Cunningham gave a qualified assent.

—It's like everything else in this world, he said. You get some bad ones and you get some good ones—

—O yes, you get some good ones, I admit, said Mr Kernan, satisfied—

—It's better to have nothing to say to them, said Mr M'Coy. That's my opinion!—

Mrs Kernan entered the room and, placing a tray on the table, said:

—Help yourselves, gentlemen—

Mr Power stood up to officiate, offering her his chair. She declined it, saying she was ironing downstairs, and, after having exchanged a nod with Mr Cunningham behind Mr Power's back, prepared to leave the room. Her husband called out to her:

—And have you nothing for me, duckie?—

—O, you! The back of my hand to you! said Mrs Kernan tartly.

Her husband called after her:

—Nothing for poor little hubby!—

He assumed such a comical face and voice that the distribution of the bottles of stout took place amid general merriment.

The recently knighted Colonel Sir Neville Chamberlain (d)

144

a) *Thursday night*: The retreat would be on Thursday night, Friday night, Saturday evening and night, and would come to a climax on Sunday morning.

b) *M'Auley's*: Thomas M'Auley's, grocer and wine merchant, 39 and 82 Lower Dorset Street, where there has been a tavern since 1453. His establishments were on both northern corners of the intersection of Lower Dorset Street and the North Circular Road. M'Auley himself was active in local political and cultural activities. From the pub it is a two-minute walk to St Francis Xavier's in Upper Gardiner Street (12h).

c) *be it*: An unusual usage, even for Dublin.

d) *wash the pot*: An unfortunate metaphor. As Mark VII makes plain, pot-washing is absolutely not what is necessary. When the Pharisees complained to Jesus that his disciples ate bread with unwashed hands:

> 6 But he answering, said to them: Well did Isaias prophesy of you hypocrites, as it is written: *This people honoureth me with their lips, but their heart is far from me.*
> 7 *And in vain do they worship me, teaching doctrines and precepts of men.*
> 8 For leaving the commandment of God, you hold the tradition of men, the washing of pots and cups: and many other things you do like to these.
> 9 And he said to them: Well do you make void the commandment of God, that you may keep your own tradition.

e) *a four-handed reel*: A square dance, previously seen (danced by five) in 'After the Race'.

The gentlemen drank from their glasses, set the glasses again on the table and paused. Then Mr Cunningham turned towards Mr Power and said casually:

a   —On Thursday night, you said, Jack?—

—Thursday, yes, said Mr Power—

—Righto! said Mr Cunningham promptly—

b   —We can meet in M'Auley's, said Mr M'Coy. That'll be the most convenient place—

—But we mustn't be late, said Mr Power earnestly, because it is sure to be crammed to the doors—

—We can meet at half-seven, said Mr M'Coy—

—Righto! said Mr Cunningham—

c   —Half-seven at M'Auley's be it!—

There was a short silence. Mr Kernan waited to see whether he would be taken into his friends' confidence. Then he asked:

—What's in the wind?—

—O, it's nothing, said Mr Cunningham. It's only a little matter that we're arranging about for Thursday—

—The opera is it? said Mr Kernan—

—No, no, said Mr Cunningham in an evasive tone, it's just a little . . . spiritual matter—

—O, said Mr Kernan—

There was silence again. Then Mr Power said, point-blank:

—To tell you the truth, Tom, we're going to make a retreat—

—Yes, that's it, said Mr Cunningham, Jack and I and M'Coy

d here – we're all going to wash the pot—

He uttered the metaphor with a certain homely energy and, encouraged by his own voice, proceeded:

—You see, we may as well all admit we're a nice collection of scoundrels, one and all. I say, one and all, he added with gruff charity and turning to Mr Power. Own up now!—

—I own up, said Mr Power—

—And I own up, said Mr M'Coy—

—So we're going to wash the pot together, said Mr Cunningham—

A thought seemed to strike him. He turned suddenly to the invalid and said:

—D'ye know what, Tom, has just occurred to me? You

e might join in and we'd have a four-handed reel—

—Good idea, said Mr Power. The four of us together—

The red-brick façade of one of Thomas M'Auley's establishments (b)

145

Mr Collopy discusses life and priests with Fr Kurt Fahrt,
S J, in Séan O'Sullivan's early draft for the cover of
Flann O'Brien's The Hard Life *(d)*

The Jesuits are expelled from France, 1880

Mr Kernan was silent. The proposal conveyed very little meaning to his mind but, understanding that some spiritual agencies were about to concern themselves on his behalf, he thought he owed it to his dignity to show a stiff neck. He took no part in the conversation for a long while, but listened, with an air of calm enmity, while his friends discussed the Jesuits.

—I haven't such a bad opinion of the Jesuits, he said, intervening at length. They're an educated order. I believe they mean well too—

—They're the grandest order in the Church, Tom, said Mr Cunningham, with enthusiasm. The General of the Jesuits stands next to the Pope—

—There's no mistake about it, said Mr M'Coy, if you want a thing well done and no flies about it, you go to a Jesuit. They're the boyos have influence. I'll tell you a case in point. . . .—

—The Jesuits are a fine body of men, said Mr Power—

—It's a curious thing, said Mr Cunningham, about the Jesuit Order. Every other order of the Church had to be reformed at some time or other but the Jesuit Order was never once reformed. It never fell away—

—Is that so? asked Mr M'Coy—

—That's a fact, said Mr Cunningham. That's history—

—Look at their church too, said Mr Power. Look at the congregation they have—

—The Jesuits cater for the upper classes, said Mr M'Coy—

—Of course, said Mr Power—

—Yes, said Mr Kernan. That's why I have a feeling for them. It's some of those secular priests, ignorant, bumptious . . .—

—They're all good men, said Mr Cunningham, each in his own way. The Irish priesthood is honoured all the world over—

—O yes, said Mr Power—

—Not like some of the other priesthoods on the continent, said Mr M'Coy, unworthy of the name—

—Perhaps you're right, said Mr Kernan, relenting—

—Of course I'm right, said Mr Cunningham. I haven't been in the world all this time and seen most sides of it without being a judge of character—

The gentlemen drank again, one following another's

a) *a stiff neck*: Shared with the Israelites when they were likewise faced with the concern of 'spiritual agencies' (Exodus XXXIII.5):

And the Lord said to Moses: Say to the children of Israel: Thou art a stiff-necked people: Once I shall come up in the midst of thee, and shall destroy thee . . .

b) *The General of the Jesuits*: The Head of the order, who is answerable only to the rules of the order and to the Pope. He is informally known as the Black Pope, but is in no sense a second-in-command.

c) *no flies about it*: No nonsense – but is there a smell of something rotten?

d) *They're the boyos have influence*: One of many examples in the book of the idiomatic Hiberno-English omission of 'that' or 'who' to introduce a relative clause. A more critical discussion of the Jesuits takes place in Flann O'Brien's novel *The Hard Life*, which culminates in the universal epithet for the archetypal boyo: 'Wily Willie, SJ'.

e) *It never fell away*: True, but it was expelled from several countries (including France in 1880), while in 1773 Pope Clement XIV signed 'Dominus ac Redemptor noster' to suppress the Jesuits in every part of the world. Pius VII reversed the decision in 1814 – just in time for the foundation of Clongowes Wood College.

f) *The Jesuits cater for the upper classes*: As Simon Dedalus points out in *P* (II.2), the Jesuits 'are the fellows that can get you a position'.

g) *priesthood on the continent*: Compare 'A Little Cloud' (68f).

(d)

a) *a retreat*: See 23c. This particular retreat was a mission to Dublin businessmen, and tailored to their busy lives. Michael McCarthy's *Priests and People in Ireland* (1902) describes a more rigorous timetable than this one:

> ...There will be masses each day at 6, 7, 8, 9, 10, and 11 o'clock, and sermons after 11 o'clock mass, and each evening after rosary at 8 P.M., except on Saturdays, which will be devoted entirely to confessions. Confessions will be held on the other days from 7 to 9 A.M., 11 A.M. to 4 P.M., and after evening devotions. The Mission will conclude with sermon, renewal of baptismal vows, plenary indulgence, papal benediction, and benediction of the Blessed Sacrament.

b) *Father Purdon*: The priest is named after Purdon Street, in Dublin's 'Nighttown', which was so notorious for prostitution that it had its name twice changed as even after the brothels were cleared nobody would admit to living there. It appears that Purdon is based on Fr Bernard Vaughan (1847–1922), an English evangelical Jesuit of such vulgarity that Archbishop Manning had barred him from his Catholic University lectures in Kensington. In October 1906 Joyce wrote that Vaughan was 'the most diverting public figure in England at present. I never see his name but I expect some enormity.'

c) *a man of the world*: Indeed. The concept is echoed in Fr Purdon's text (154d).

d) *Father Tom Burke*: Thomas Nicholas Burke (1830–1883), Dominican fund-raiser, orator and preacher, who was vastly successful both in Ireland and in America. His dissertations were often more nationalist than religious. His last sermon, on the parable of the loaves and fishes, was given to plead the cause of the starving children of Donegal, at St Francis Xavier's, Gardiner Street.

e) *he didn't preach what was quite orthodox*: Rather like Fr Flynn's teachings in 'The Sisters'.

f) *Crofton*: The same man as in 'Ivy Day' (115e).

g) *pit*: The ex-Protestant stumbles on a word more appropriate to the theatre – or to Hell, as in Psalm XXVIII which begins:

> Unto thee will I cry, O Lord, my rock ... if thou be silent to me, I become like them that go down into the pit.

h) *the late pope*: Pope Leo XIII (149a). This dates the story after July 1903 (as does 152c), but Joyce explicitly stated in a latter of November 1906 that it

example. Mr Kernan seemed to be weighing something in his mind. He was impressed. He had a high opinion of Mr Cunningham as a judge of character and as a reader of faces. He asked for particulars.

a   —O, it's just a retreat, you know, said Mr Cunningham.
b Father Purdon is giving it. It's for business men, you know—

—He won't be too hard on us, Tom, said Mr Power persuasively—

—Father Purdon? Father Purdon? said the invalid—

—O, you must know him, Tom, said Mr Cunningham,
c stoutly. Fine jolly fellow! He's a man of the world like ourselves—

—Ah . . . yes. I think I know him. Rather red face; tall—

—That's the man—

—And tell me, Martin . . . Is he a good preacher?—

—Mmmno . . . It's not exactly a sermon, you know. It's just a kind of a friendly talk, you know, in a common-sense way—

Mr Kernan deliberated. Mr M'Coy said:
d   —Father Tom Burke, that was the boy!—

—O, Father Tom Burke, said Mr Cunningham, that was a born orator. Did you ever hear him, Tom?—

—Did I ever hear him! said the invalid, nettled. Rather! I heard him . . .—

—And yet they say he wasn't much of a theologian, said Mr Cunningham—

—Is that so? said Mr M'Coy—

—O, of course, nothing wrong, you know. Only sometimes,
e they say, he didn't preach what was quite orthodox—

—Ah! . . . he was a splendid man, said Mr M'Coy—

—I heard him once, Mr Kernan continued. I forget the
f subject of his discourse now. Crofton and I were in the back
g of the . . . pit, you know . . . the . . .—

—The body, said Mr Cunningham—

—Yes, in the back near the door. I forget now what . . . O
h yes, it was on the pope, the late pope. I remember it well. Upon my word it was magnificent, the style of the oratory.
i And his voice! God! hadn't he a voice! *The Prisoner of the*
j *Vatican*, he called him. I remember Crofton saying to me when we came out—

k   —But he's an Orangeman, Crofton, isn't he? said Mr Power—

was set in 1901 or 1902. As has been seen, he juggled with facts and dates when it suited the story.

i) *hadn't he a voice!*: A theme returned to in 'The Dead'.

j) The Prisoner of the Vatican: The phrase came to be applied to the last two popes of the nineteenth century. After the papal lands in Italy were seized by Nationalists and Rome was made the Italian capital, the Pope's temporal jurisdiction, and his travel arrangements, were largely confined to the Vatican itself.

k) *an Orangeman*: A member of the Orange Order, which began in 1795 as a spin-off from Freemasonry, taking its name from King William III (William of Orange) (185g). It was dedicated to the defence of Protestantism in Ireland and the maintenance of British rule. In the early twentieth century, the headquarters of the Order were the Grand Orange Hall of Ireland in Rutland Square, next door to the Dublin County Council offices. By mid-century, however, there were few (or no) overt Orangemen in Dublin, though the Order still continues to thrive in Ulster.

a) *Butler's*: Patrick Butler, wine and spirit merchant, 1 and 2 Moore Street, off Great Britain Street, at the rere of Upper O'Connell Street. The religious platitudes of the pub are of no more moment than Bob Doran's free-thinking in 'The Boarding House'.

b) *we worship at different altars*: Dublin had long been a city of many faiths – the Plymouth Brethren, for example, had their origins in Aungier Street. The 'Ode to Donnybrook Fair', already quoted from in 'Two Gallants', names some others in attendance.

> Carmen, tinkers
> Blind free thinkers
> Grunting Quakers
> Kennel rakers
> Antiquarians
> Stubborn Arians
> Unitarians
> Presbyterians
> Destinarians
> Apollonians
> Antinomians
> Muggletonians
> Sandemonians
> Purgatorians
> Fam'd Chirurgeons
> Swedenbourgians
> Methodists
> With double fists . . .

c) *the Redeemer*: A frequent epithet for Christ, particularly apposite in a story where the theme of money and debt is predominant.

d) *they don't believe in . . .* : Of course, Protestants do 'believe' in the Pope and in the Mother of God. They simply do not accord them the degree of veneration that Catholics do.

e) *the old, original faith*: The lineage of the popes stretches unbroken back to St Peter, and Catholics would argue that Protestantism, because of the Reformation, is a new church. However, Anglicanism likewise has a continuous line of consecrated bishops back to the early Church, and Protestants would assert that theirs was the more authentic 'old religion', particularly because Catholicism over the centuries imposed a complex and artificial rule system (including Papal Infallibility) on the simple faith of the Bible, which made the Reformation justified and inevitable.

f) *Mr Fogarty . . . had failed in business*: Perhaps *Thom's Directory* throws some light on the declining Fogarty fortunes. In the 1897 edition there is listed a Patrick Fogarty, wine and spirit merchant, at No 133 North Strand Road. In the 1902 book the pub is under new ownership, but at 35 Glengariff Parade (where in that year the Joyces lived at No 32), P. Fogarty is now trading as grocer, tea, wine and spirit merchant. By 1906 the entry reads just 'Mrs M. Fogarty, grocer'.

Considered 'special' – at least by Dublin's Chief Medical Officer

'Passing-off' inferior beer, from the Dublin Daily Express *(f)*

—'Course he is, said Mr Kernan, and a damned decent
Orangeman too. We went into Butler's in Moore Street –
faith, I was genuinely moved, tell you the God's truth – and I
remember well his very words. *Kernan,* he said, *we worship at
different altars,* he said, *but our belief is the same.* Struck me as
very well put—

—There's a good deal in that, said Mr Power. There used
always be crowds of Protestants in the chapel when Father
Tom was preaching—

—There's not much difference between us, said Mr M'Coy.
We both believe in . . .—

He hesitated for a moment.

—. . . in the Redeemer. Only they don't believe in the pope
and in the mother of God—

—But, of course, said Mr Cunningham quietly and effectively, our religion is *the* religion, the old, original faith—

—Not a doubt of it, said Mr Kernan warmly—

Mrs Kernan came to the door of the bedroom and
announced:

—Here's a visitor for you!—

—Who is it?—

—Mr Fogarty—

—O, come in! come in!—

A pale oval face came forward into the light. The arch of
its fair trailing moustache was repeated in the fair eyebrows
looped above pleasantly astonished eyes. Mr Fogarty was a
modest grocer. He had failed in business in a licensed house in
the city because his financial condition had constrained him to
tie himself to second-class distillers and brewers. He had opened
a small shop on Glasnevin road where, he flattered himself, his
manners would ingratiate him with the housewives of the
district. He bore himself with a certain grace, complimented
little children and spoke with a neat enunciation. He was not
without culture.

Mr Fogarty brought a gift with him, a half-pint of special
whisky. He inquired politely for Mr Kernan, placed his gift on
the table and sat down with the company on equal terms. Mr
Kernan appreciated the gift all the more since he was aware
that there was a small account for groceries unsettled between
him and Mr Fogarty. He said:

—I wouldn't doubt you, old man. Open that, Jack, will
you?—

g) *ingratiate him with the housewives:* The approach seems
different from the behaviour
of that other shopkeeper, Mr
Mooney, in 'The Boarding
House' (53h), though the
result is much the same. But
Mr Fogarty flatters himself
more than his customers – he
may be in for a similar
Dantean fate to that which
Tom Kernan has suffered
(135e).

h) *a certain grace:* Far from the
'grace abounding' of John
Bunyan's early spiritual autobiography, *Grace Abounding to
the Chief of Sinners, or the brief
Relation of the exceeding Mercy
of God in Christ to his poor
servant John Bunyan* (1666).

i) *a small account for groceries
unsettled:* In *U,* 'Hades', Mr
Power asks:

> – I wonder how is our
> friend Fogarty getting on.
> – Better ask Tom Kernan,
> Mr Dedalus said.
> – How is that? Martin Cun-
> ningham said. Left him
> weeping, I suppose?
> – Though lost to sight, Mr
> Dedalus said, to memory
> dear.

What they are referring to is
that Mr Kernan still hasn't
settled his account with
Fogarty's shop, confirming in
U any suspicions that Fr Purdon's message at the end of
this story will have no earthly
effect. The passage in *U* can
only really be understood if
'Grace' has been read first.

a) *Pope Leo XIII*: Born Gioacchino Pecci in 1810, he was trained by the Jesuits and became Pope in 1878. Although he was a competent diplomat and administrator, he was by no means a great scholar or poet. His fatherly concern for the Irish people, even during the height of the 'plan of campaign' (the boycotting and other land agitation in the 1880s), led him to issue more than one decree or encyclical on the subject. There was one vice at least that he shared with Fr Flynn of 'The Sisters', as the *Evening Mail* reported after his death:

> The Pope's wardrobe budget was quite large for a man of his simple tastes, because he spoiled a good many of his white gowns by the snuff habit, to which he was addicted.

The report continues that still more gowns 'were ruined by the muse of poetry that visited him at all hours of the night and day': it seems that while he waited for her to get the right words in the right order, he waved his pen around agitatedly, spattering himself with ink. Pope Leo died in July 1903, while Edward VII was in Ireland, and official mourning was suppressed until the king had left the country. This unsurprisingly caused resentment: police repeatedly tore down a flag of mourning which Maud Gonne McBride flew over her house, and the *United Irishman* announced that

> within a few hours of the Pope's death the Archbishop [Walsh, of Dublin] was attending the King of England's levee.

b) *union of the Latin and Greek Churches*: A papal encyclical of 1897 called to all the eastern schismatic churches – the Copts, Ruthenians, Armenians, etc – to return to the true Universal Church.

c) *apart from his being pope*: The comic conversation that follows is a tissue of misunderstandings and half-truths. Here they assume that popes are intellectually gifted, *ex officio*.

d) Lux in Tenebris: The phrase comes from the Vulgate Gospel of John I.5: '*Et lux in tenebris lucet et tenebrae eam non comprehenderunt*', 'And the light shineth in the darkness; and the darkness did not comprehend it'. However, there is a double lack of comprehension here. As R. M. Adams has explained, the popes did not have mottoes, and it seems that the men are thinking of the 'Prophecies' of the twelfth-century Irish saint, Malachy of Armagh, which sum up the life of each future pope in a single phrase, each of which may be as obscure as any of Nostradamus' utterances. To compound matters, it is likely that these phrases were themselves later forgeries, as the popes are quite clearly described up to the sixteenth century, but thereafter the accuracy declines sharply. Malachy's phrase for Leo XIII was actually '*Lumen in Cælo*', 'A light in Heaven'.

e) *Pius IX*: Born in 1792, he was Pope from 1846 until 1878. His papacy was marked by political upheaval, but he found time to proclaim the dogma of the Immaculate Conception of the Blessed Virgin, and the dogma of Papal Infallibility (150e).

f) *Crux upon Crux*: Laughably, this is not even Latin, though, as always in this conversation, it is not utterly inaccurate. St Malachy's prophecy was '*Crux de Cruce*', 'A Cross from a Cross', or 'Agony from the Cross'.

g) *That's no joke*: Latin poetry is not noted for its jokes. Juvenal's urban satires are a case in point. The skill was not confined to popes, however, as John Milton and many others showed.

h) *penny-a-week school*: Descended from the hedge-schools of the Penal law period, penny-a-week schools no longed existed by the time this generation was born, though their humble standing was clear enough for the figurative name to be recycled.

i) *a sod of turf under his oxter*: The epitome of an impoverished rural upbringing: each pupil brought fuel under his arm to heat the school. The oxter is the armpit.

j) *plain honest education*: The idea that history and facts are interchangeable is still alive.

k) *trumpery*: Contemptuously applied since the sixteenth century to religious ceremonies – especially showy rituals – which are thought to be worthless. An obsolete technical use of the word means 'weeds that hinder the growth of other, more valuable plants'. From French *tromper*, to deceive. The redoubtable Michael McCarthy in his *Five Years in Ireland* (1901) quotes 'an old priest' on the subject:

> Education, pshaw! [Cardinal] Paul Cullen used always to say 'twas too much education the people had. 'They're attacking the Government now,' he used to say. 'If you give 'em any more education, they'll be attacking the Church.' . . . It is not for education the Bishops want the University, but for money and positions!

Mr Power again officiated. Glasses were rinsed and five small measures of whisky were poured out. This new influence enlivened the conversation. Mr Fogarty, sitting on a small area of the chair, was specially interested.

a —Pope Leo XIII., said Mr Cunningham, was one of the
b lights of the age. His great idea, you know, was the union of the Latin and Greek Churches. That was the aim of his life—

c —I often heard he was one of the most intellectual men in Europe, said Mr Power. I mean, apart from his being pope—

—So he was, said Mr Cunningham, if not *the* most so. His motto, you know, as pope, was *Lux upon Lux – Light upon Light*—

—No, no, said Mr Fogarty eagerly. I think you're wrong
d there. It was *Lux in Tenebris*, I think – *Light in Darkness*—

—O yes, said Mr M'Coy, *Tenebrae*—

—Allow me, said Mr Cunningham positively, it was *Lux*
e *upon Lux*. And Pius IX. his predecessor's motto was *Crux upon*
f *Crux* – that is, *Cross upon Cross* – to show the difference between their two pontificates—

The inference was allowed. Mr Cunningham continued.

—Pope Leo, you know, was a great scholar and a poet—

—He had a strong face, said Mr Kernan—

—Yes, said Mr Cunningham. He wrote Latin poetry—

—Is that so? said Mr Fogarty—

Mr M'Coy tasted his whisky contentedly and shook his head with a double intention, saying:

g —That's no joke, I can tell you—

—We didn't learn that, Tom, said Mr Power, following Mr M'Coy's example, when we went to the penny-a-week
h school—

—There was many a good man went to the penny-a-week
i school with a sod of turf under his oxter, said Mr Kernan
j sententiously. The old system was the best: plain honest
k education. None of your modern trumpery . . .—

—Quite right, said Mr Power—

—No superfluities, said Mr Fogarty—

He enunciated the word and then drank gravely.

—I remember reading, said Mr Cunningham, that one of
l Pope Leo's poems was on the invention of the photograph – in Latin, of course—

—On the photograph! exclaimed Mr Kernan—

l) *one of Pope Leo's poems was on the invention of the photograph*: An edition of *Poems, Charades, Inscriptions of Pope Leo XIII* was published in 1902, and would have been 'noticed' by the Catholic press in Dublin. Mr Cunningham is for once entirely correct. The poem runs:

Ars Photographia
(An. MDCCCLXVII)

Expressa solis spiculo
  Nitens imago, quam
    bene
  Frontis decus, vim
    luminum
Refers, et oris gratiam.

O mira virtus ingeni
  Novumque monstrum!
    Imaginem
Naturae Apelles aemulus
Non pulchriorem pin-
    geret.

It is not a good poem, and makes the dubious point that that modern invention, the photograph, surpasses even the paintings of the Ancient Greek artist Apelles (whose depiction of grapes fooled the birds). A modern translation (JWJ & BM) perhaps conveys some of its flavour:

The Photographer's Art
(1867)

Writing in the sun's script,
  The sparkling snap des-
    cries
A well-profiled face, eyes
Alight, and mouth full-
    lipped.

It's a miracle of ingenuity,
  A revelation! Tom
    Keating
(Old artificer) or any
    forger, cheating,
Can't match its fine con-
    gruity.

Pius IX (149e)

a) *Great minds are very near to madness*: Not quite correct. What Mr. Fogarty is groping for is from Dryden's *Absalom and Achitophel* (1681):

> Great Wits are sure to Madness near ally'd;
> And thin Partitions do their Bounds divide.

b) *our present man*: Pius X, elected in August 1903. Much of his episcopate was occupied with a struggle against Modernism in the Church, a struggle which he won.

c) *up to the knocker*: i.e. on a front door. They did not have the (moral) stature required for the job. Thus, for example, Pope Nicholas III and Clement V were consigned by Dante to the Eighth Circle of Hell. The poet was too early to include the simoniacal election of Cardinal Borgia (Alexander VI) and other less than satisfactory popes.

d) *not one of them ever preached* ex cathedra *a word of false doctrine*: If any had, it would be a far more astonishing thing. The Latin phrase, meaning 'from the throne', is used of statements (made in the Consistory) which bear full papal authority. These by definition cannot be false doctrine.

e) *the infallibility of the pope*: To augment the spiritual authority of the Holy See, Pope Pius IX in 1870, thanks in great part to the efforts of Cardinal Manning, succeeded in proclaiming the doctrine of Papal Infallibility as a dogma of faith, although it had had general tacit acceptance previously. Most of the controversy arose not from the rejection of the doctrine, but from the inadvisability of its proclamation at that time.

f) *sacred college*: The twentieth Ecumenical Council, or Council of the Vatican.

g) *conclave*: Technically, the room in which the electors of the Pope are bricked up, but also more loosely, as here, any gathering of ecclesiastics. (From the Latin, implying 'locked up together'.)

Pius X (b)

—Yes, said Mr Cunningham—

He also drank from his glass.

—Well, you know, said Mr M'Coy, isn't the photograph wonderful when you come to think of it?—

—O, of course, said Mr Power, great minds can see things—

a   —As the poet says: *Great minds are very near to madness*, said Mr Fogarty—

Mr Kernan seemed to be troubled in mind. He made an effort to recall the Protestant theology on some thorny points and in the end addressed Mr Cunningham.

—Tell me, Martin, he said. Weren't some of the popes – of

b course, not our present man, or his predecessor, but some of the old popes – not exactly . . . you know . . . up to the

c knocker?—

There was a silence. Mr Cunningham said:

—O, of course, there were some bad lots . . . But the astonishing thing is this. Not one of them, not the biggest drunkard, not the most . . . out-and-out ruffian, not one of them ever

d preached *ex cathedra* a word of false doctrine. Now isn't that an astonishing thing?—

—That is, said Mr Kernan—

—Yes, because when the pope speaks *ex cathedra*, Mr Fogarty explained, he is infallible—

—Yes, said Mr Cunningham—

e   —O, I know about the infallibility of the pope. I remember I was younger then . . . Or was it that . . . ?—

Mr Fogarty interrupted. He took up the bottle and helped the others to a little more. Mr M'Coy, seeing that there was not enough to go round, pleaded that he had not finished his first measure. The others accepted under protest. The light music of whisky falling into glasses made an agreeable interlude.

—What's that you were saying, Tom? asked Mr M'Coy—

—Papal infallibility, said Mr Cunningham, that was the greatest scene in the whole history of the Church—

—How was that, Martin? asked Mr Power—

Mr Cunningham held up two thick fingers.

f   —In the sacred college, you know, of cardinals and archbishops and bishops there were two men who held out against

g it while the others were all for it. The whole conclave except these two was unanimous. No! They wouldn't have it!—

Leo XIII (149a)

150

Archbishop John MacHale (c)

The statue of Sir John Gray in O'Connell Street (h)

a) *Dowling ...*: Dr Johannes Josef Ignaz von Döllinger (1799–1890) was never a cardinal, and did not attend the 1870 Council. However, he exerted considerable influence on the deliberations through his supporter Sir John Acton, an ally of Gladstone. In *Letters of Janus* (1869) Döllinger, who led a breakaway movement (which still exists) centered on Bavaria, wrote: 'I cannot accept these decrees'. His punishment was excommunication.

b) *a sure five*: A certainty. From billiards, where five points are scored by potting the red and cannoning onto (or potting) the opponent's ball. With skill, the pot-and-cannon manoeuvre can be repeated almost indefinitely. The importance of the number five in the story – there will be five penitents – suggests the five propositions of Jansenism, a dark and narrow creed involving the inevitable operation of God's grace and the impossibility of free will.

c) *John MacHale*: (1791–1881) Archbishop of Tuam, County Galway, 1835–76. He spoke out against English influence and rule in Ireland, and opposed (in vain) the plan for an Englishman (Cardinal Newman) to head the Catholic University. In 1850 he was instrumental in persuading the Vatican to break off diplomatic relations with England. As a boy, MacHale had attended a hedge-school (149h).

d) *some Italian or American*: Mr Fogarty is almost right – it was both. Two bishops, Edward Fitzgerald from Little Rock, Arkansas, and a Neapolitan called Riccio de Cajazzo, were the most stubborn objectors, but both accepted the decree in the end. Joyce, reading about this, was much amused. The Italian reminded him of the Triestine word for 'cabbage', he wrote in 1906 to Stanislaus, continuing:

> All the gents said 'Placet' but two said 'Non Placet'. But the Pope [said] 'You be damned! Kissmearse! I'm infallible!'

e) *declared infallibility a dogma of the Church* ex cathedra: But as Mr Fogarty has already stated (150d), 'when the pope speaks *ex cathedra*, he is infallible'. *Petitio principii*, it begs the question.

f) *shouted out with a voice of a lion*: John of Tuam's friend Daniel O'Connell called him 'The Lion of St Jarlath's'. But consider too Job IV.10:

> The roaring of the lion, and the voice of the lioness, and the teeth of the whelps of lions, are broken.

Mr Cunningham is correct that Archbishop MacHale with about 150 others at first opposed the doctrine of Papal Infallibility, and soon submitted – but he left Council and city before the vote, unobtrusively

—Ha! said Mr M'Coy—

—And they were a German cardinal by the name of Dolling

a ... or Dowling ... or ...—

b —Dowling was no German, and that's a sure five, said Mr Power, laughing—

—Well, this great German cardinal, whatever his name was,

c· was one; and the other was John MacHale—

—What? cried Mr Kernan. It is John of Tuam?—

—Are you sure of that now? asked Mr Fogarty dubiously.

d I thought it was some Italian or American—

—John of Tuam, repeated Mr Cunningham, was the man—

He drank and the other gentlemen followed his lead. Then he resumed:

—There they were at it, all the cardinals and bishops and archbishops from all the ends of the earth and these two fighting dog and devil until at last the Pope himself stood up and

e declared infallibility a dogma of the Church *ex cathedra*. On the very moment John MacHale, who had been arguing and arguing against it, stood up and shouted out with the voice of

f a lion: *Credo!*—

—*I believe!* said Mr Fogarty—

—*Credo!* said Mr Cunningham. That showed the faith he had. He submitted the moment the pope spoke—

—And what about Dowling? asked Mr M'Coy—

—The German cardinal wouldn't submit. He left the Church—

Mr Cunningham's words had built up the vast image of the Church in the minds of his hearers. His deep raucous voice had thrilled them as it uttered the word of belief and submission. When Mrs Kernan came into the room, drying her hands, she came into a solemn company. She did not disturb the silence, but leaned over the rail at the foot of the bed.

—I once saw John MacHale, said Mr Kernan, and I'll never forget it as long as I live—

g He turned towards his wife to be confirmed.

—I often told you that?—

Mrs Kernan nodded.

h —It was at the unveiling of Sir John Gray's statue. Edmund

i Dwyer Gray was speaking, blathering away, and here was this old fellow, crabbed-looking old chap, looking at him from under his bushy eyebrows—

and with no shouting. In fact the archbishop had kissed the Pope's hand, and murmured '*Modo credo, sancte Pater*'.

g) *to be confirmed*: A somewhat laboured pun – women still do not conduct religious confirmation.

h) *Sir John Gray*: (1816–1875). The marble statue by Thomas Farrell still stands in O'Connell Street. He was an MP, the owner of the *Freeman's Journal* and, like many a Protestant, an Irish patriot, being tried and sentenced with O'Connell at the state trials for conspiracy in 1844. The memorial celebrates his part in harnessing for the Dublin water supply the River Vartry, which word appears on his coat of arms. He appears in *FW* as Jean de Porteleau.

i) *Edmund Dwyer Gray*: Sir John's son, who also owned the *Freeman* and was a Nationalist, did not in fact speak at the unveiling in June 1879, but afterwards in the Antient Concert Rooms, by which time Archbishop MacHale had gone home.

St Francis Xavier's church portico

a) *I have you properly taped*: I have the measure of you.

b) *None of the Grays was any good*: The remark may reflect Mr Power's prejudice against these Protestant Nationalists: he upholds British rule in his work for Dublin Castle.

c) *to make a retreat together*: Stanislaus reports in his diary that Mathew Kane persuaded John Joyce to accompany him, Charles Chance and a Mr Boyd to a retreat at the Gardiner Street church in September 1904 led by Father Vernon. The occasion is also reported in *SH*, where Simon Daedalus goes on 'a little retreat' to this church.

d) *wiser to conceal her satisfaction*: Joyce's earliest extant prose is suitably titled 'Trust Not Appearances' (1896).

e) *do the other thing*: A catch-all euphemism for any number of insults. The complaint 'I don't like it!' may elicit the reply, 'Well, do the other thing!', meaning 'Lump it'.

f) *I'm not such a bad fellow*: Father Vernon told Joyce's father during his post-retreat confession that he was 'not such a bad fellow after all. Ha! ha! ha! ha!' (from Stanislaus' diary). Compare also Stephen's 'I have amended my life, have I not?' in *P* (IV.1).

g) *renounce the devil . . . works and pomps*: The phrases come from the sacrament of baptism.

h) *Get behind me, Satan!*: Mr Fogarty is again slightly misquoting. Matthew XVI.23 reads:

> But he turned, and said unto Peter, Get thee behind me, Satan: thou art an offence unto me: for thou savourest not the things that be of God, but those that be of men.

It will be the things 'that be of men' that Fr Purdon's sermon will discuss, taking a rather different point of view from that of Jesus Christ.

i) *out-generalled*: Although getting the renegade Mr Kernan to make a retreat was his initiative, Mr Power's military skills have been hardly been needed. The gentlemen's campaign has been a success.

j) *renew our baptismal vows*: The vows are made for a child by the godparents at baptism (g). 'As they were wounded by the sin of another,' says St Augustine, 'so they are healed by the word of another.' The vows can be personally remade in adulthood, and doing so at retreats was a usual occurrence.

k) *damn it all*: Not quite the most contrite of phrases.

l) *no candles*: Tom Kernan is neither the first nor the last in *D* to avoid candles. Father Keon in 'Ivy Day' and Gabriel in 'The Dead' both refuse offers of their

Mr Kernan knitted his brows and, lowering his head like an angry bull, glared at his wife.

a —God! he exclaimed, resuming his natural face, I never saw such an eye in a man's head. It was as much as to say: *I have you properly taped, my lad.* He had an eye like a hawk—

b —None of the Grays was any good, said Mr Power—

There was a pause again. Mr Power turned to Mrs Kernan and said with abrupt joviality:

—Well, Mrs Kernan, we're going to make your man here a good holy pious and God-fearing Roman Catholic—

He swept his arm round the company inclusively.

c —We're all going to make a retreat together and confess our sins – and God knows we want it badly—

—I don't mind, said Mr Kernan, smiling a little nervously—

d Mrs Kernan thought it would be wiser to conceal her satisfaction. So she said:

—I pity the poor priest that has to listen to your tale—

Mr Kernan's expression changed.

e —If he doesn't like it, he said bluntly, he can . . . do the other
f thing. I'll just tell him my little tale of woe. I'm not such a bad fellow . . .—

Mr Cunningham intervened promptly.

g —We'll all renounce the devil, he said, together, not forgetting his works and pomps—

h —Get behind me, Satan! said Mr Fogarty, laughing and looking at the others—

i Mr Power said nothing. He felt completely out-generalled. But a pleased expression flickered across his face.

—All we have to do, said Mr Cunningham, is to stand up
j with lighted candles in our hands and renew our baptismal vows—

—O, don't forget the candle, Tom, said Mr M'Coy, whatever you do—

—What? said Mr Kernan. Must I have a candle?—

—O yes, said Mr Cunningham—

k —No, damn it all, said Mr Kernan sensibly, I draw the line there. I'll do the job right enough. I'll do the retreat business
l and confession, and . . . all that business. But . . . no candles! No, damn it all, I bar the candles!—

He shook his head with farcical gravity.

—Listen to that! said his wife—

light. Like several of Joyce's symbols, the candles in the first paragraph of the book suggest two opposing interpretations, both of which can be valid. Candles signify death and also light (and life).

Stanislaus in his diary (September 1904) reports his father being told by Charlie Chance about the curriculum for the third day of the retreat. There would be Communion in the morning and the renewal of baptismal vows at half-past five, complete with candles. This was unwelcome:

Pappie (very drunk). Oh, I bar the candles, I bar the candles! I'll do the other job all right, but I bar the candles.

152

a) *magic-lantern business*: A magic lantern was an early type of slide-projector. Mr Kernan is railing against the symbolism of his adopted Church: he does not feel quite at home with the popish 'bells and smells'. In *SH* Stephen tells Cranly of three ancient lanterns, the lanterns of justice, revelation and tradition, which respectively once had investigated law, morality and art. However, Stephen continues,

> all these lanterns have magical properties: they transform, and disfigure.

But Mr Kernan means quite a different sort of magic lantern. His cynical reference (as David Berman and Terence Brown have shown) is to the famous apparition at Knock, Co Mayo, where in 1879 four images, including the Virgin Mary, were seen on the outer wall of the parish church. Archbishop MacHale (151c) instituted an inquiry, the results of which have never been made entirely public, but it is likely that a magic lantern had been obtained from Masons, the Dublin opticians, in order to emulate the recent success of Lourdes. There are other references to photography in 'Grace': Pope Leo's poem in particular, and perhaps also the obscure Blackwhite (138g) and the crowd outside the pub (135) 'struggling to look in through the glass panels' – early slides were square panels of glass.

Section Three: *Paradiso*

b) *transept*: The part of the church at right-angles to the nave, or body.

c) *lay-brother*: Although he has taken the vows and habit of an Order, a lay-brother is confined to broadly manual tasks, and is exempted from many of the studies and rituals of most members of the Order. Stephen notices a lay-brother in the same church in *SH*.

d) *green marble*: This in Ireland almost always means Connemara marble, from Galway. The detail links tidily with the end of 'The Dead', where many of the 'crooked crosses and headstones' would be made of the same material.

e) *lugubrious canvases*: In the nave and behind the high altar of the Ignatian Chapel, these paintings can still be seen, some by the artist Gagliardi. By no means lugubrious, they depict high points in the lives of the early Jesuit saints Francis Xavier, Ignatius Loyola and others.

f) *distant speck of red light*: This, another 'magic lantern', is the 'Sanctuary Lamp', kept lit to remind observers of the Real Presence in the tabernacle, and that the wafers there (through transubstantiation) are now the Body and Blood of Christ. Like Fr Purdon's name, however, this red light is also a reminder of the district of Dublin, not far away, where love is sold for money.

g) *quincunx*: An arrangement of four points equidistant from a central point, often (though not always) drawn with a circle linking the outer four. In Christian iconography it symbolises the five main wounds of the crucified Christ (see 151b). Seen as a cross within a circle drawn from the centre point, the quincunx is the grouping of the courageous in Dante's Fifth Heaven (*Paradiso* XIV.100–2).

h) *In a whisper*: Unlike in Italy (the culture in which 'Grace' was written) and other continental places, the Irish practice was to keep one's voice low, as a sign of reverence.

i) *some distance off*: Mr Harford (142h) is in the position of the prodigal son, who is seen by his father returning 'when he was yet a great way off' (Luke XV.20). This parable is followed in the Gospel by that of the unjust servant, from which Father Purdon's text is taken. Neither is likely to alter the philosophy of the moneylender.

j) *Mr Fanning*: Already discussed in 'Ivy Day' (110g). As one of the 'City Fathers', in charge of electoral listings, he is the most important of the 'business men' mentioned in the church. The fact that he is described as the 'mayor maker' calls to mind Mr Henchy's dictum (113k): 'You must owe the City Fathers money nowadays if you want to be made Lord Mayor'. Mr Fanning is not the least in need of spiritual guidance.

k) *one of the newly elected councillors of the ward*: As a protégé of Mr Fanning, he too is *ex officio* implicated in the network of minor corruption.

l) *Michael Grimes*: A successful pawnbroker, Grimes makes his living, like Mr Harford, from loans to the impoverished of the city. He may be the priest-loving voter mentioned in 'Ivy Day' (109l).

m) *Dan Hogan's nephew*: It is unknown whether Joyce intended either Dan or his nephew to be the Hogan mentioned in 'A Little Cloud' (66g). In any case the name is not the point, for the man here is nothing but a nephew. This word is a direct allusion to 'nepotism', the practice whose name began with the popes (particularly Pope Alexander VI (150c)) of unfairly favouring 'nephews' (often Cardinals' sons) and other relatives for lucrative jobs in their gift. In the case of Dan Hogan's nephew, strings are certainly being pulled.

n) *the Town Clerk's office*: The Town Clerk was the equivalent of Chief Executive of a modern local

—I bar the candles, said Mr Kernan, conscious of having created an effect on his audience and continuing to shake his head to and fro. I bar the magic-lantern business—

Everyone laughed heartily.

—There's a nice Catholic for you! said his wife—

—No candles! repeated Mr Kernan obdurately. That's off!—

.   .   .   .

The transept of the Jesuit Church in Gardiner Street was almost full; and still at every moment gentlemen entered from the side-door and, directed by the lay-brother, walked on tiptoe along the aisles until they found seating accommodation. The gentlemen were all well dressed and orderly. The light of the lamps of the church fell upon an assembly of black clothes and white collars, relieved here and there by tweeds, on dark mottled pillars of green marble and on lugubrious canvases. The gentleman sat in the benches, having hitched their trousers slightly above their knees and laid their hats in security. They sat well back and gazed formally at the distant speck of red light which was suspended before the high altar.

In one of the benches near the pulpit sat Mr Cunningham and Mr Kernan. In the bench behind sat Mr M'Coy alone: and in the bench behind him sat Mr Power and Mr Fogarty. Mr M'Coy had tried unsuccessfully to find a place in the bench with the others and, when the party had settled down in the form of a quincunx, he had tried unsuccessfully to make comic remarks. As these had not been well received he had desisted. Even he was sensible of the decorous atmosphere and even he began to respond to the religious stimulus. In a whisper Mr Cunningham drew Mr Kernan's attention to Mr Harford, the moneylender, who sat some distance off, and to Mr Fanning, the registration agent and mayor maker of the city, who was sitting immediately under the pulpit beside one of the newly elected councillors of the ward. To the right sat old Michael Grimes, the owner of three pawnbroker's shops, and Dan Hogan's nephew, who was up for the job in the Town Clerk's office. Farther in front sat Mr Hendrick, the chief reporter of the *Freeman's Journal*, and poor O'Carroll, an old friend of Mr Kernan's who had been at one time a considerable commercial figure. Gradually, as he recognized familiar faces, Mr Kernan began to feel more at home. His hat, which had been rehabili-

authority.

o) *Mr Hendrick*: The journalist in 'A Mother', who with his 'plausible voice and careful manners' left the concert before it began, having been there only for the offered drink. As a *quid pro quo* he promised without seeing it to get O'Madden Burke's report of the evening into his paper. He too is implicated in the mesh of obligations that involves everyone attending the retreat.

p) *poor O'Carroll*: Though his story is never told, it seems unlikely that he will be able to settle his accounts with any ease. There is perhaps a hint that he is not quite such a friend of Mr Kernan as he was in more prosperous days.

q) *His hat*: Men were required to be bareheaded in church, but for women it was the opposite.

One of the 'lugubrious canvases' in the church (e)

153

a) *struggling up*: Fr Purdon finds it as difficult to ascend the pulpit steps as Mr Kernan found it easy to fall down the lavatory ones. In fact, the steps up to the pulpit in St Francis Xavier's are not visible to the congregation, as they are ascended from behind a pillar on the left of the nave.

b) *unsettled*: The collective unease of the mildly penitent.

c) *the general example*: Mr Kernan is uncertain about the repertoire of sitting, kneeling and standing.

d) For the children . . . : The passage is the climax of a parable from St Luke's Gospel XVI:

1 There was a certain rich man, who had a steward: and the same was accused unto him, that he had wasted his goods.

2 And he called him, and said to him: How is it that I hear this of thee? give an account of thy stewardship: for now thou canst be steward no longer.

3 And then the steward said within himself: What shall I do, because my lord taketh away from me the stewardship? To dig I am not able; to beg I am ashamed.

4 I know what I will do, that when I shall be removed from the stewardship, they may receive me into their houses.

5 Therefore calling together every one of his lord's debtors, he said to the first: How much dost thou owe my lord?

6 But he said: An hundred barrels of oil. And he said to him: Take thy bill and sit down quickly, and write fifty.

7 Then said he to another: And how much dost thou owe? Who said: An hundred quarters of wheat. He said to him: Take thy bill, and write eighty.

8 And the lord commended the unjust steward, forasmuch as he had done wisely.

The Apparition at Knock (153a)

154

tated by his wife, rested upon his knees. Once or twice he pulled down his cuffs with one hand while he held the brim of his hat lightly, but firmly, with the other hand.

A powerful-looking figure, the upper part of which was draped with a white surplice, was observed to be struggling up into the pulpit. Simultaneously the congregation unsettled, produced handkerchiefs and knelt upon them with care. Mr Kernan followed the general example. The priest's figure now stood upright in the pulpit, two-thirds of its bulk, crowned by a massive red face, appearing above the balustrade.

Father Purdon knelt down, turned towards the red speck of light and, covering his face with his hands, prayed. After an interval he uncovered his face and rose. The congregation rose also and settled again on its benches. Mr Kernan restored his hat to its original position on his knee and presented an attentive face to the preacher. The preacher turned back each wide sleeve of his surplice with an elaborate large gesture and slowly surveyed the array of faces. Then he said:

For the children of this world are wiser in their generation than the children of light. Wherefore make into yourselves friends out of the mammon of iniquity so that when you die they may receive you into everlasting dwellings.

Father Purdon developed the text with resonant assurance. It was one of the most difficult texts in all the Scriptures, he said, to interpret properly. It was a text which might seem to the casual observer at variance with the lofty morality elsewhere preached by Jesus Christ. But, he told his hearers, the text had seemed to him specially adapted for the guidance of those whose lot it was to lead the life of the world and who yet wished to lead that life not in the manner of worldlings. It was a text for business men and professional men. Jesus Christ, with His divine understanding of every cranny of our human nature, understood that all men were not called to the religious life, that by far the vast majority were forced to live in the world and, to a certain extent, for the world: and in this sentence He designed to give them a word of counsel, setting before them as exemplars in the religious life those very worshippers of Mammon who were of all men the least solicitous in matters religious.

He told his hearers that he was there that evening for no

Fr Purdon's text follows at this point. Much casuistry has been expended in explaining the passage, which, in its confusion, is particularly suitable for 'Grace'. The steward, in danger of losing his job, offers his master's debtors large discounts on what they owe, in order to remain on good terms with them. This action, mysteriously, is not only commended by his master, but also by Jesus. Both the action and the exhortation in Fr Purdon's text appear to condone sharp (if not dishonest) financial practices, which will be rewarded finally by the 'everlasting dwellings' of heaven. In this reading, the unfortunate 'children of light', among whom Fr Purdon would presumably wish to number himself, seem to get no advantages whatever from their holy ways.

e) mammon: Milton in *Paradise Lost* (Book I) links Mammon, the god of this world, with Vulcan or Mulciber, evil gods of wealth and meanness. The root meaning of the word is 'riches'.

f) *exemplars in the religious life*: This is as close as Fr Purdon gets towards explaining his text. His argument appears to be that the children of this world, friends of the mammon of iniquity, are to be taken as metaphors for the holy children of light. If religious debts are paid, there is no need to bother about financial ones. As long as spiritual grace has been attained, one can take as much grace as one wishes in repaying one's creditors. The latter points at least would be appreciated by these particular penitents.

terrifying, no extravagant purpose; but as a man of the world speaking to his fellow-men. He came to speak to business men and he would speak to them in a business-like way. If he might use the metaphor, he said, he was their spiritual accountant; and he wished each and every one of his hearers to open his books, the books of his spiritual life, and see if they tallied accurately with conscience.

Jesus Christ was not a hard taskmaster. He understood our little failings, understood the weakness of our poor fallen nature, understood the temptations of this life. We might have had, we all had from time to time, our temptations: we might have, we all had, our failings. But one thing only, he said, he would ask of his hearers. And that was: to be straight and manly with God. If their accounts tallied in every point to say:

Well, I have verified my accounts. I find all well.

But if, as might happen, there were some discrepancies, to admit the truth, to be frank and say like a man:

Well, I have looked into my accounts. I find this wrong and this wrong. But, with God's grace, I will rectify this and this. I will set right my accounts.

a) *their spiritual accountant*: The expression recalls the Irish official euphemism 'turf accountant' for 'bookmaker'.

b) with God's grace: *The Divine Comedy* ends with St Bernard's prayer to the Virgin Mary for grace. She grants it, and finally Dante is enabled to behold the Trinity. However, he can no more describe it than he can square the circle. But grace has given him understanding. Fr Purdon's intercession for Tom Kernan is unlikely to be as efficacious.

c) I will set right my accounts: The final spurious knot is tied in the net of spiritual and financial indebtedness. It will not hold. The congregation would be well advised to remember that the phrase 'to be called to one's last account' means 'to die'.

Inside St Francis Xavier's

Because of its position in *Dubliners*, just before the comfortable felicities and the challenges of 'The Dead', 'Grace' tends to be overlooked. In fact it is a considerable story. Joyce intended it to be the finale of the book, and of the original scheme of 3–4–4–3 it was almost the last to be begun as well as being the last to be substantially revised. He put the finishing touches to it towards the end of 1906, after the previous stories had been given whatever final polishing they needed. Before Joyce had the afterthought of writing 'The Dead', the fourteen stories stood as a completed work, a book, crowned by the longest and most ambitious of the collection, 'Grace'.

Joyce began this story in October 1905, by which time his conception of *Dubliners* as a unity was well established. In most of his writings, to help achieve what in *A Portrait* Stephen calls '*consonantia*', Joyce used what might be called cyclism – the end returning to the beginning. It is seen in the morning-to-morning of *Ulysses*, and in the linking sentence at both ends of the *Wake*. Likewise, in *A Portrait*, Stephen Dedalus' parting invocation, 'Old father, old artificer', links with the storytelling father who had told baby tuckoo about the moocow. Although the echoes of 'The Sisters' in the last scene of 'The Dead' have long been recognised, it is rarely noticed that Joyce gave 'Grace' a similar role in his fourteen-story ur-*Dubliners*. Its position at the end of the book demanded that it should epitomise the concerns of the whole work and, in particular, it would need to illuminate the three themes set out in the first page of the first story: paralysis, the gnomon (incompleteness) and simony.

This it triumphantly achieves. 'Grace' and 'The Sisters' are the only stories whose subject-matter is primarily religious. The respective priests both seem in their different ways morally suspect, and while Father Flynn may be paralysed, Father Purdon has to 'struggle up into the pulpit'. The bedside group's ill-informed discussion of the popes – what Robert Browning called 'the raree show of Peter's successor' – balances the invalid priest's reminiscences of his days in the Irish College in Rome, and Tom Kernan's reaction in his bedroom to the prospect of candles in the chapel recalls the candlesticks brought from the chapel to the bedroom of the dead priest. The book begins with the boy who 'gazed up at the window', lighted 'faintly and evenly', and would have ended with the five penitents who 'gazed formally at the distant speck of red light' before the altar, little wiser than the boy.

As well as these and other correspondences between the first and last stories of *Dubliners* in its original form, two of the three words strange to the boy are slyly alluded to in the opening scene of 'Grace'. Tom Kernan is seen drunk (*paralytic*) on the floor of the lavatory. He has also bitten off a piece of his tongue, rendering the remainder incomplete, like a gnomon. The third word, simony, being the cause of both the paralysis and the 'unwholeness' depicted in *Dubliners*, is the theme of 'Grace'.

The title of the story has here two ironically opposing meanings that are important. The first is the most obvious: 'spiritual grace'. From one of the two Catechisms familiar to Joyce, the Deharbe Catechism of 1877, comes the following:

– What fatal consequences have, with original sin, passed to all mankind?

– 1, The privation of sanctifying grace, of the dignity of God's children, and of the right of inheriting the kingdom of Heaven; 2, ignorance, concupiscence and proneness to evil; 3, all sorts of hardships, pains, calamities, and, lastly, death.

Original sin is the direct consequence of the Fall of Man, parodied by Mr Kernan's fall into the Dantean Hell of the lavatory of John Nolan's public house. Mr Kernan's friends recognise how much he needs sanctifying grace, if only to retrieve the dignity he has lost – dignity being one of the things that he values most: he believes 'in the dignity of his calling', and owes 'it to his dignity to show a stiff neck'. The third section of the story, according to Joyce's admitted schema, is based on Dante's Paradise. Would Kernan go to the retreat? Would he reach *Paradiso*?

The second Deharbe consequence of the Fall in this story includes ignorance. A more ill-informed conversation than the Purgatorial bedroom one here would be hard to find. The third consequence of unabsolved original sin is more worrying – the fall down the stairs is itself part of it, but there are also strong hints of war, pain and death running through 'Grace'.

Tom Kernan, therefore, is in urgent need of grace. It is not, however, sanctifying grace that he gets. The second meaning of the word in the story is 'financial grace', or the time allowed before a debt need be repaid. All the men who appear in the story are, to use Mr Kernan's phrase, ' 'ery 'uch o'liged' to others. Mr Power has 'inexplicable debts', Mr Cunningham is implicated in his drunken wife's frequent transactions with the pawnbroker, Mr Fogarty has swindled his customers with second-rate drink, Mr M'Coy cadges valises on a false pretext – and hasn't returned them by the time he reappears in *Ulysses*, when it is also mentioned that Tom Kernan still owes Mr Fogarty for the groceries he had on tick in 'Grace'.

At St Francis Xavier's, things are no better: in the congregation are Harford the moneylender, Grimes the pawnbroker, Hogan's nepotistic nephew, and the penurious O'Carroll, come down in the commercial world. There are also old friends from earlier stories in the book: Hendrick the journalist who didn't do his job in 'A Mother', and the corrupt politician Fanning of 'Ivy Day' with his neophyte lackey. All have 'unsettled accounts'.

Finally, there is the vainglorious Father Purdon, 'powerful-looking' but half-immobile, whose bulk and 'massive red face' are outward and visible signs of his personal self-indulgence. With an 'elaborate large gesture' he introduces a dishonest interpretation of a corrupted text, and like a shady insurance man, he offers his auditors, 'with resonant assurance', a bribe. He, and, he implies, Jesus Christ, will (like Nelson at the dead centre of Dublin) turn a blind eye to their worldly – and manly – misdeeds in exchange for their spiritual souls. Father Purdon's is simony of the first order, and he is prepared to spread it around.

THE WREATH HOUSE,
MANSFIELD & CO.,

Largest   Natural

Selection   Wreaths

in   made to

Ireland.   Order.

Note Address: 76 Gt. Britain St.,

GLASGOW.—The second subscription concert of the season was given by the Tonic Sol-fa Choral Society, in the City Hall, on Wednesday, the 24th December, when, in accordance with a time-honoured custom, the Oratorio selected was Handel's *Messiah*. The members of the Society quite filled the large organ gallery, and were supported by a small orchestra, under the leadership of Mr. Sam. Smyth, and the organ, which was in the able hands of Mr. Charles Ferguson. The principal vocalists were Mdme. Otto-Aivsleben, Miss Jessie Blair, Mr. Parkinson, and Mr. Winn. The performance was conducted by Mr. W. M. Miller, under whose direction the Society has gradually assumed its present importance. Mdme. Alvsleben, who made her first appearance in Scotland, achieved a signal success; her singing of " Rejoice greatly " amply meriting the applause it elicited. Mr. Parkinson in " Thou shalt break them " was highly effective, and Mr. Winn in the music allotted him was careful and conscientious throughout.

PUBLIC HEALTH (IRELAND) ACT, 1878. (SECTION 209),

DEATH RATE IN DUBLIN CITY.

PUBLIC INQUIRY

FIRST DAY.—TUESDAY, FEBRUARY 13, 1900.

The First Public Sitting of the Committee appointed by the Local Government Board for Ireland, in pursuance of the provisions of Section 209 of the Public Health (Ireland) Act, 1878, to inquire and report to them as to (1), the cause of the high Death Rate in Dublin; and (2), the measures which in their opinion should be adopted with the view of improving the health of the city, was held in the Council Chamber, City Hall, Cork Hill, Dublin, on Tuesday, the 13th day of February, 1900

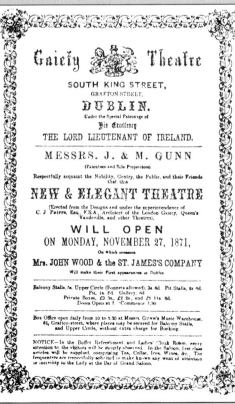

Clockwise from top left:

★ Note address
★ 'In the gloom of the hall', 15 Usher's Island (186)
★ From Moore's Melodies
★ Campanini (177l)
★ (177g)
★ Death Rate in Dublin City (82j)
★ The tenor Parkinson, in the Musical Times, in February 1874

a) THE DEAD: See Afterword.

b) *Lily*: She had her counterpart in real life but the name perhaps may come from the wife of John Murray whom the Joyces considered had married beneath him. The flower symbolises death, and accordingly it is placed on both altars and graves. The lily was the Archangel Gabriel's emblem (159e), and there is also a suggestion of Easter, and rebirth.

c) *literally*: The word here is the classic example of Joyce's ventriloquist style in *D*: the narrator has adopted Lily's solecism.

d) *bare hallway*: A very unVictorian detail, but it is a shared property.

e) *well for her*: i.e. 'just as well ...'

f) *Miss Kate and Miss Julia*: They were based on the Misses Flynn, the sisters who were actually widows, who ran for many years Flynn's Academy, an institution in Dublin musical life. Mrs Callanan, Joyce's godmother and great aunt, was the model for Aunt Kate. She appears in the 1902 *Thom's* as a music teacher, under her own name. The name Callanan was used in 'Christmas Eve', the abandoned story in *D*. The bestowing of the real name Flynn on the fictional priest in 'The Sisters' adds to the circularity of the book. Miss Julia was in life Mrs Lyons.

g) *the bathroom upstairs*: Automatically an indication of prosperity. Leopold Bloom and other contemporary Dubliners had to make do with the public wash-house. Joyce's son Giorgio in 1923 vetoed the offer of a flat for the family because it had no bathroom.

h) *the Misses Morkan's annual dance*: Joyce took Danish lessons in 1906 and would have known that *Mørke* in Danish means 'darkness'.

i) *pupils ... pupils*: Standards were maintained by a system of examinations introduced in 1894 at the suggestion of Professor Esposito (32e) at the Academy (123c).

j) *their brother Pat*: Patrick Flynn was Joyce's maternal grandfather (and himself the son of a Patrick Flynn).

k) *Stoney Batter*: By 1830, the family house of the Flynns was on Ellis Quay, visible across the Liffey from Usher's Island, in the area of the original rocky road (Irish *bóthar*) to Dublin, from Tara.

l) *Mary Jane*: This was also the name of Joyce's mother, who like her sisters was a good musician, familiar with the piano music of Chopin, Mendelssohn, Liszt, Schumann, Schubert *et al.* Joyce's main model here, however, was Mrs Callanan's daughter, Mary Ellen.

m) *the dark gaunt house on Usher's Island*: The house was at No. 15. Complete with its little pantry and other features, it is still standing. Usher's Island was not an island but an ordinary Liffeyside quay, on the south side, near the Phoenix Park. It is named after the noted Usher family, whose most distinguished member was Archbishop James Ussher, founder scholar of Trinity, whose dating of the Creation at 4004 BC was widely accepted until the age of Darwin. In the eighteenth century, Usher's Island was dominated by Moira House. John Wesley found here in 1775

> a far more elegant room than ever I found in England. It was an octagon, about twenty feet square and fifteen or sixteen high, having one window ... reaching from the top of the room to the bottom, the ceiling, sides, and furniture of the room equally elegant ... must *all* this pass away like a dream?

Unlike Arthur Wesley, later Wellesley (55b), John Wesley had a disappointed engagement in Dublin in 1749.

n) *Mr Fulham, the corn-factor*: Fulham is a fairly uncommon name in Ireland. In *SH*, Stephen's godfather in Mullingar is a Mr Fulham. The corn-factor's business is possibly the one where Polly Mooney used to work (54l). At 15 Usher's Island while the sisters were there was the corn firm of M. Smith and Son, 15 and 16 Usher's Island. The Flynns lived upstairs, as in the story.

o) *thirty years ago*: Nostalgia of the kind indulged in by the josser in 'An Encounter' and by the guests later in this story.

p) *she had the organ in Haddington Road*: Mary Jane plays at St Mary's (RC) Church, a short walk from Beggar's Bush Barracks (84n), near Balisbridge, in the prosperous south-east of the city. This elegant church (which had been enlarged in the 1890s) was celebrated for its music, so the youngest Miss Morkan

THE DEAD

LILY, THE CARETAKER'S daughter, was literally run off her feet. Hardly had she brought one gentleman into the little pantry behind the office on the ground floor and helped him off with his overcoat than the wheezy halldoor bell clanged again and she had to scamper along the bare hallway to let in another guest. It was well for her she had not to attend to the ladies also. But Miss Kate and Miss Julia had thought of that and had converted the bathroom upstairs into a ladies' dressing-room. Miss Kate and Miss Julia were there, gossiping and laughing and fussing, walking after each other to the head of the stairs, peering down over the banisters and calling down to Lily to ask her who had come.

It was always a great affair, the Misses Morkan's annual dance. Everybody who knew them came to it, members of the family, old friends of the family, the members of Julia's choir, any of Kate's pupils that were grown up enough, and even some of Mary Jane's pupils too. Never once had it fallen flat. For years and years it had gone off in splendid style as long as anyone could remember; ever since Kate and Julia, after the death of their brother Pat, had left the house in Stoney Batter and taken Mary Jane, their only niece, to live with them in the dark gaunt house on Usher's Island, the upper part of which they had rented from Mr Fulham, the corn-factor on the ground floor. That was a good thirty years ago if it was a day. Mary Jane, who was then a little girl in short clothes, was now the main prop of the household, for she had the organ in Haddington Road. She had been through the Academy and gave a pupils' concert every year in the upper room of the Antient Concert Rooms. Many of her pupils belonged to the better-class families on the Kingstown and Dalkey line. Old as they were, her aunts also did their share. Julia, though she was quite grey, was still the leading soprano in Adam and Eve's, and Kate, being too feeble to go about much, gave music lessons to beginners on the old square piano in the back room. Lily, the caretaker's daughter, did housemaid's work for them. Though their life was modest they believed in eating well; the

has some status. The organ was by Telford & Co, a famous Dublin company who also made harmoniums (29p).
q) *through the Academy*: Like Kathleen Kearney, Mary Jane has studied at the Royal Irish Academy of Music.
r) *Antient Concert Rooms*: See 123m.
s) *Kingstown and Dalkey line*: (39d). The line (which Mrs Sinico failed to cross) was extended from Kingstown to the town of Dalkey in 1843.
t) *Adam and Eve's*: A quayside Dublin Catholic church opposite the Four Courts, named after a tavern on the site. The Franciscan church achieves universality in the opening words of *FW*.
u) *music lessons to beginners*: A sign of Aunt Kate's frailty and decline. Mrs M'Coy (in 'Grace') is similarly reduced (141f).
v) *the old square piano*: The upright square piano was invented and patented by William Southwell, a Dubliner. Thirty years earlier, in 1768, Henry Walsh had played solo in Fishamble Street Music Hall 'a Lesson on that much-admired instrument called the Forte-piano': this was before the comparable public première in London.
w) *the caretaker's daughter, did housemaid's work*: See 160a.

a) *diamond-bone sirloins*: Such Dublin prosperity makes a mute reproach to the Lord Mayor's chops of 'Ivy Day' (114).

b) *three-shilling tea*: At this price for a pound, it was very expensive. Though Great Britain often claims to drink the most tea *per capita* in the world, Ireland outperforms it in that department. Tea is a major motif of *FW*.

c) *back answers*: 'Lip', such as that given to his employers by Farrington in 'Counterparts', or Joe in 'Clay'.

d) *long after ten o'clock*: It is noticeable how late this social evening is. In *U*, 'Wandering Rocks' 9, Lenehan tells M'Coy (140l) about a dinner at Glencree with Bartell D'Arcy and the lord mayor:

> We had a midnight lunch too after all the jollification and when we sallied forth it was blue o'clock in the morning after the night before …

e) *Gabriel*: The character is an amalgamation of Constantine Curran, John Joyce and Joyce himself. The choice of name suggests the archangel, sometimes regarded as the angel of death. Milton (in *Paradise Lost* IV) made him the chief of the angelic guards of paradise.

f) *Freddy Malins*: See 165g.

g) *screwed*: Saturated, squiffy, slewed, steamboats, stotious, soused, shot, sloshed, spifflicated, stoned, sodden, stewed, stitched, sozzled, etc.

h) *wish for worlds*: An Irish intensified form of 'wish for the world'.

i) *Good-night*: The expression served for greeting as well as bidding farewell. When Stephen first encounters a prostitute (*P* II.5), she says to him:

> —Good night, Willie dear!

j) *I'll engage*: Gabriel's assent establishes his inclination to pomposity, even before he has crossed the threshold.

k) *three mortal hours*: A casual thematic detail of death in life.

l) *goloshes*: Rubber overshoes. In *Michael Kramer* (95m), old Kramer's daughter arrives wearing them and they are discussed. In a letter to Stanislaus in March 1905, Joyce wrote from the continent

> you would smile to see me holding [out] for a lower price in goloshes.

m) *toddling*: Joyce knew of the chime with the German word *Tod*, 'death'. The word recurs in the story.

n) *she must be perished alive*: Yet another hint of death – a droll verb and a handsome oxymoron.

o) *as right as the mail*: The reliability of the postal service was proverbial. In Dublin at this time there were five collections a day, and five deliveries. Uncle Charles uses the expression to Simon Dedalus in the Christmas dinner scene in *P* (I.3).

p) *a cold fragrant air*: Some commentators have found this evidence of Gabriel as a Christmastide gift-bearing Magus.

q) *the three syllables*: Emerging as 'Conneroy'. Her rural accent also suggests King Conaire, mythical king of Tara, whose motto – 'To enquire of wise

Alias 'Haddington Road' (158p)

best of everything: diamond-bone sirloins, three-shilling tea and the best bottled stout. But Lily seldom made a mistake in the orders, so that she got on well with her three mistresses. They were fussy, that was all. But the only thing they would not stand was back answers.

Of course, they had good reason to be fussy on such a night. And then it was long after ten o'clock and yet there was no sign of Gabriel and his wife. Besides they were dreadfully afraid that Freddy Malins might turn up screwed. They would not wish for worlds that any of Mary Jane's pupils should see him under the influence: and when he was like that it was sometimes very hard to manage him. Freddy Malins always came late but they wondered what could be keeping Gabriel: and that was what brought them every two minutes to the banisters to ask Lily had Gabriel or Freddy come.

—O, Mr Conroy, said Lily to Gabriel when she opened the door for him, Miss Kate and Miss Julia thought you were never coming. Good-night, Mrs Conroy—

—I'll engage they did, said Gabriel, but they forget that my wife here takes three mortal hours to dress herself—

He stood on the mat, scraping the snow from his goloshes, while Lily led his wife to the foot of the stairs and called out:

—Miss Kate, here's Mrs Conroy—

Kate and Julia came toddling down the dark stairs at once. Both of them kissed Gabriel's wife, said she must be perished alive and asked was Gabriel with her.

—Here I am as right as the mail, Aunt Kate! Go on up, I'll follow, called out Gabriel from the dark—

He continued scraping his feet vigorously while the three women went upstairs, laughing, to the ladies' dressing-room. A light fringe of snow lay like a cape on the shoulders of his overcoat and like toecaps on the toes of his goloshes; and, as the buttons of his overcoat slipped with a squeaking noise through the snow-stiffened frieze, a cold fragrant air from out-of-doors escaped from crevices and folds.

—Is it snowing again, Mr Conroy? asked Lily—

She had preceded him into the pantry to help him off with his overcoat. Gabriel smiled at the three syllables she had given his surname and glanced at her. She was a slim growing girl, pale in complexion and with hay-coloured hair. The gas in the pantry made her look still paler. Gabriel had known her when

men that I myself may be wise' – is both seasonal and thematic. The March 1904 issue of AE's journal, the *International Theosophist*, mentions Andrew Lang on Conaire, whose father was a bird: the image recalls Stephen D, Aengus of the Birds, Joking Jesus *et al.* – as well as Mad Sweeney, 'Suibhne Gealt', the figure from Irish mythology treated by Flann O'Brien, Seamus Heaney and others.

a) *the lowest step*: The lowest step of Dublin's Georgian houses (including those on Usher's Island) meets the pavement. This picture of Lily recalls the children seen by Little Chandler in Henrietta Street. In life, the caretaker was named Mr Tallon, and his daughter was Elizabeth. The daily housemaid's grind might involve setting and lighting fires, cooking, cleaning, washing, shopping and the many other manual tasks of a 'slavey'.

b) *a night of it*: The expression refers to the bad weather rather than the snow.

c) *The men that is now ...*: Irish idiom. This use of a singular verb with a plural noun is quite common in Hiberno-English (as in Joxer's 'What is the stars?' in O'Casey's *Juno and the Paycock*). Here it manages to be damning. In Raymond Chandler's *The Big Sleep*, Marlowe inquires of Agnes if he has hurt her head. She answers: You and every other man I met.

d) *palaver*: Flattering talk. The word is related to the Latin *parabola*, 'parable'.

e) *flicked actively with his muffler*: Gabriel's displacement activity recalls the pretence of the schoolboys when Leo Dillon is caught out (13a). A muffler is a short woollen scarf. In *Henry V* (III.vi) the Welsh officer Fluellen observes:

> Fortune is painted blind with a muffler before her eyes, to signify to you that Fortune is blind: and she is painted also with a wheel, to signify to you, which is the moral of it, that she is turning and inconstant, and mutability and variation, and her foot, look you, is fixed upon a spherical stone, which rolls, and rolls, and rolls.

The passage sounds like a variation on the circular futility of Johnny the Horse (185h) and other Dubliners.

f) *a stout, tallish young man*: See 159e.

g) *colour ... scintillated ... lustre*: Gabriel is repeatedly described in terms of shining light, as befits an archangel.

h) *parted in the middle*: A contemporary hairstyle, though the facial hairlessness is quite twentieth century.

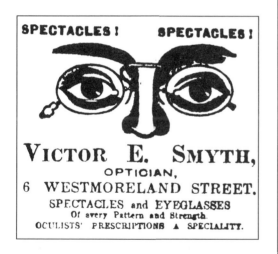

The Collection of our Surnames.

Conoo / Conway	¹Ó Connṁaıġ	C. Clare	—	—
Conrahy / Conroy	Ó Conṙaıċe	—	(D.C.)	—
Conree	Mac Conṙoı	—	—	—
Conroy / King	Ó Conṙoı	—	—	—
Conroy / Conry	Mac Conṙoı	Con'm'a	T.P.	D.C.
Conree / King	Ó Conṙoı	—	H.M.	L.C.
Conrahy	Ó Conṙaıċe	M'ns'r & Conna't	T.P.	—
Mulconry	Ó Maolċonaıṙe	M'ns'r & Conna't	T.P.	H.F.
		Stro'es'r & Cl'ah'e	H.M.	—
Considine	Mac Conṡaıḋín	Co.Clare	I.S.	—
Convey / MacConvey	Mac Conḃuıḋe		L.C.	
Conwell / MacConwell	Mac Conṁaoıl	Ulster	—	—
Convally	Ó Coınṙıaċla	C W'mth	Δ.	
	Ó Conḃuıḋe	—	H.F.	
	Ó Connṁaċáın	Co.Mayo	I.S.	L.C.
Conway	²Ó Connṁaıġ	C.Lımı'k	I.S.	Δ.
	Ó Connaıġ	—	L.C.	—
	Ó Connaċáın	N.Gal'ay	I.S.	T.P.
	Ó Coınneaċáın	W. Mayo	I.S.	—

Ƒeaḃṙa 21, 1903.   an claıḋeaṁ soluıs.
February 21, 1903.   [AN CLAIDHEAMH SOLUIS.]

Irish names and their roots

a she was a child and used to sit on the lowest step nursing a rag
doll.

—Yes, Lily, he answered, and I think we're in for a night
b of it—

He looked up at the pantry ceiling, which was shaking with
the stamping and shuffling of feet on the floor above, listened
for a moment to the piano and then glanced at the girl, who
was folding his overcoat carefully at the end of a shelf.

—Tell me, Lily, he said in a friendly tone, do you still go
to school?—

—O no, sir, she answered. I'm done schooling this year and
more—

—O, then, said Gabriel gaily, I suppose we'll be going to
your wedding one of these fine days with your young man –
eh?—

The girl glanced back at him over her shoulder and said
with great bitterness:

cd —The men that is now is only all palaver and what they can
get out of you—

Gabriel coloured, as if he felt he had made a mistake and,
without looking at her, kicked off his goloshes and flicked
e actively with his muffler at his patent-leather shoes.

fg He was a stout, tallish young man. The high colour of his
cheeks pushed upwards even to his forehead, where it scattered
itself in a few formless patches of pale red; and on his hairless
face there scintillated restlessly the polished lenses and the bright
gilt rims of the glasses which screened his delicate and restless
h eyes. His glossy black hair was parted in the middle and brushed
in a long curve behind his ears where it curled slightly beneath
the groove left by his hat.

When he had flicked lustre into his shoes he stood up and
pulled his waistcoat down more tightly on his plump body.
i Then he took a coin rapidly from his pocket.

—O Lily, he said, thrusting it into her hands, it's Christmas-
time, isn't it? Just . . . here's a little . . .—

He walked rapidly towards the door.

—O no, sir! cried the girl, following him. Really, sir, I
wouldn't take it—

—Christmas-time! Christmas-time! said Gabriel, almost
trotting to the stairs and waving his hand to her in de-
precation—

i) *he took a coin*: Money given
to a slavey, a mirror image of
the end of 'Two Gallants'. The
coin is almost certainly a sovereign (192f).

(b)

a) *a little paper*: Gabriel at this point unknowingly mimics Hoppy Holohan of 'A Mother'.

b) *Robert Browning*: Though English-born, the poet (1812–89) was drawn to the heart of Europe, a characteristic shared with Gabriel and his creator (and Synge, Ibsen and many others). Joyce in a review for the *Daily Express* in 1903 referred to Browning as 'the 'Master''. The proposed passage for the speech has been the subject of much inconclusive speculation. See also 195c.

c) *above the heads of his hearers*: In March 1904, Professor Dowden of Trinity (a biographer of Shelley) published a biography of Browning, which Joyce is likely to have sneered over in Hodges Figgis, or Browne & Nolan, or elsewhere. The epigraph of the book is from *Balaustion's Adventure*:

> If I, too, should try and speak at times
> Leading your love to where my love, perchance
> Climbed earlier, found a nest before you knew,
> Why, bear with the poor climber, for love's sake.

This might well have been above the heads of the hearers.

d) *the Melodies*: By Thomas Moore (34).

e) *clacking ... shuffling*: From the completed fragment, *Giacomo Joyce* (written c. 1914):

> High heels clack hollow on the resonant stone stairs ... Tapping, clacking, heels ...

f) *their grade of culture*: The assumed superiority suggests Mr Duffy and his isolation in 'A Painful Case'.

g) *They would think that he was airing his superior education*: They would be right. Gabriel is a graduate of the Royal University. This succeeded the Catholic University founded under Cardinal Newman in 1854. In 1909 it was superseded in turn by the National University of Ireland. One of the difficulties faced by the Royal was that it was an examining body only: the teaching was done separately, at institutions such as St Mary's University College, Merrion Square, where Hanna Sheehy (168b) went. Among those associated with the Royal in its brief existence were Gerard Manley Hopkins, Douglas Hyde, and Joyce and his generation.

h) *Her hair ...*: Note the cadences of this sentence.

i) *more vivacious*: Aunt Kate is more alive – or less dead. The word is derived from the Latin, *vivax*, *vivacis*, 'long-lasting', from *vivere*, 'to live'. Archaically, the word refers to tenacity of life, or longevity. In music *vivacissimo* means 'very lively'.

j) *like a shrivelled red apple*: An image of decay, as at 95q).

The girl, seeing that he had gained the stairs, called out after him:

—Well, thank you, sir—

He waited outside the drawing-room door until the waltz should finish, listening to the skirts that swept against it and to the shuffling of feet. He was still discomposed by the girl's bitter and sudden retort. It had cast a gloom over him which he tried to dispel by arranging his cuffs and the bows of his tie. He then took from his waistcoat pocket a little paper and glanced at the headings he had made for his speech. He was undecided about the lines from Robert Browning, for he feared they would be above the heads of his hearers. Some quotation that they would recognize from Shakespeare or from the Melodies would be better. The indelicate clacking of the men's heels and the shuffling of their soles reminded him that their grade of culture differed from his. He would only make himself ridiculous by quoting poetry to them which they could not understand. They would think that he was airing his superior education. He would fail with them just as he had failed with the girl in the pantry. He had taken up a wrong tone. His whole speech was a mistake from first to last, an utter failure.

Just then his aunts and his wife came out of the ladies' dressing-room. His aunts were two small, plainly dressed old women. Aunt Julia was an inch or so the taller. Her hair, drawn low over the tops of her ears, was grey; and grey also, with darker shadows, was her large flaccid face. Though she was stout in build and stood erect, her slow eyes and parted lips gave her the appearance of a woman who did not know where she was or where she was going. Aunt Kate was more vivacious. Her face, healthier than her sister's, was all puckers and creases like a shrivelled red apple, and her hair, braided in the same old-fashioned way, had not lost its ripe nut colour.

They both kissed Gabriel frankly. He was their favourite nephew, the son of their dead elder sister, Ellen, who had married T.J. Conroy of the Port and Docks.

—Gretta tells me you're not going to take a cab back to Monkstown to-night, Gabriel, said Aunt Kate—

—No, said Gabriel, turning to his wife, we had quite enough of that last year, hadn't we? Don't you remember, Aunt Kate, what a cold Gretta got out of it? Cab windows rattling all the

k) *their favourite nephew*: His only mentioned rival is his brother, the priest.

l) *the Port and Docks*: In all earlier unpublished versions, 'the Post Office' (126c). The Dublin Port and Docks Board had its headquarters in Westmoreland Street (81l). It was very important in Dublin's commercial life. Unlike its counterpart in Liverpool, it was not controlled by the municipal corporation (though J.P. Nannetti, William Field MP (35s) and other Dubliners were members of both the Corporation and the Port and Docks). The autonomous existence increased the standing of the P & D as well as its profile.

m) *Gretta*: To a very large extent Gabriel's wife is based on Nora Barnacle, but her name is taken from the wife of the poet James Cousins: Joyce stayed with the couple in June 1904.

n) *Monkstown*: Originally literally so, being named after the monastic settlement that used to be there. The lands once formed part of the estates of St Mary's Abbey, Dublin (129b). By the late nineteenth century it was a prosperous suburb on the Kingstown and Dalkey line, the hinterland of modern Dún Laoghaire. A nearby placename was Salt Hill, which might have helped Gretta to feel at home, as there was another one just outside Galway City.

way, and the east wind blowing in after we passed Merrion. Very jolly it was. Gretta caught a dreadful cold—

Aunt Kate frowned severely and nodded her head at every word.

—Quite right, Gabriel, quite right, she said. You can't be too careful—

—But as for Gretta there, said Gabriel, she'd walk home in the snow if she were let—

Mrs Conroy laughed.

—Don't mind him, Aunt Kate, she said. He's really an awful bother, what with green shades for Tom's eyes at night and making him do the dumbbells, and forcing Eva to eat the stirabout. The poor child! And she simply hates the sight of it! ... O, but you'll never guess what he makes me wear now!—

She broke out into a peal of laughter and glanced at her husband, whose admiring and happy eyes had been wandering from her dress to her face and hair. The two aunts laughed heartily too, for Gabriel's solicitude was a standing joke with them.

—Goloshes! said Mrs Conroy. That's the latest. Whenever it's wet underfoot I must put on my goloshes. To-night even he wanted me to put them on but I wouldn't. The next thing he'll buy me will be a diving suit—

Gabriel laughed nervously and patted his tie reassuringly, while Aunt Kate nearly doubled herself, so heartily did she enjoy the joke. The smile soon faded from Aunt Julia's face and her mirthless eyes were directed towards her nephew's face. After a pause she asked:

—And what are goloshes, Gabriel?—

—Goloshes, Julia! exclaimed her sister. Goodness me, don't you know what goloshes are? You wear them over your ... over your boots, Gretta, isn't it?—

—Yes, said Mrs Conroy. Guttapercha things. We both have a pair now. Gabriel says everyone wears them on the continent—

—O, on the continent, murmured Aunt Julia, nodding her head slowly—

Gabriel knitted his brows and said, as if he were slightly angered:

—It's nothing very wonderful, but Gretta thinks it very

a) *after we passed Merrion*: Near Sandymount. The detail is accurate, as the road out of Dublin becomes the coast road here (at the end of Sandymount Strand). When it blows, the sea-wind from the east can often be biting. Richard Rowan's house in *Exiles* is in Merrion.

b) *if she were let*: The expression recalls Anna Livia (*FW* 627):

> Anyway let her rain for my time is come. I done me best when I was let.

c) *Tom ... Eva*: Like the Joyces, the Conroys have a son and a daughter. The names, however, recall two other immature characters – Little Chandler and Eveline.

d) *stirabout*: As detested here as it seems to be in the first story, where it is strongly associated with unhappiness.

e) *Guttapercha*: A substance similar to rubber (from the Malay *getah percha*, 'gumtree').

f) *O, on the continent*: Like most people in the United Kingdom between 1815 and 1914 (e.g. Little Chandler), Aunt Julia seems never to have been there.

a) *the word reminds her of Christy Minstrels*: Gretta's dactylic Galway pronunciation is close to 'golly shoes'. The word 'gollywog' first appeared in 1895, and rapidly became popular. The minstrels were famous vaudeville entertainers who 'blacked up'. Consider also Samuel Beckett's unlikely associations:

> The conception of Philosophy and Philology as a pair of nigger minstrels out of the Teatro dei Piccoli is soothing, like the contemplation of a carefully folded ham-sandwich.

> (in 'Dante ... Bruno. Vico .. Joyce', from *Our Exagmination* ... (1929).)

b) *brisk tact*: Nobody seems to have got the joke, but perhaps Aunt Kate is being polite about Gretta's country accent.

c) *the Gresham*: Still one of Dublin's top hotels, in Upper O'Connell Street. As Aunt Kate says, 'by far the best thing to do'. Joyce visited the hotel in September 1909 (after the writing of 'The Dead'), when he attended the wedding reception of his friends Tom Kettle and Mary Sheehy. (She had been the inspiration for *Chamber Music* XII and XXV.)

d) *She's not the girl she was*: Lily seems to be a victim of the sexual cynicism shown in 'Two Gallants' and elsewhere. At the very least, Joyce is implying she is no longer a virgin. (It may be significant that her name is a variant of Lilith, who is mentioned in *U*, 'Oxen of the Sun' and referred to as 'the patron of abortions'.) In *U*, 'Telemachus', Mulligan and Haines discuss a different Lily, and wonder whether she is 'up the pole'. Consider too Shakespeare's Sonnet 94, which begins 'They that have the power to hurt ...'. It ends:

> For sweetest things turn sourest by their deeds;
> Lillies that fester smell far worse than weeds.

Joyce, at the end of his 1912 essay on the Aran Islands, associated Galway with the growing lily.

e) *some questions*: Gabriel's natural curiosity is possibly compounded by a deeper interest in Lily.

f) *two persons ... laugh*: The inept Freddy seems to be having more success flirting with Lily than Gabriel has had.

g) *It made lovely time*: Whosesoever pupil Miss Daly may be, Aunt Kate has not lost her professional instincts.

h) *wizen-faced*: Dried up and shrivelled. The symptoms seem fatal.

i) *swarthy skin, who was passing out*: Mr Browne is a 'black Protestant' (14q). 'Swarthy' was 'dark yellow' in earlier versions of the story. It has been suggested that Mr Browne, being everywhere, is a symbol of death (183f).

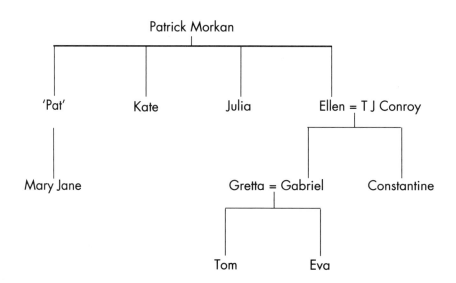

The Morkan Family Tree

funny because she says the word reminds her of Christy Minstrels—

—But tell me, Gabriel, said Aunt Kate with brisk tact. Of course, you've seen about the room. Gretta was saying . . .—

—O, the room is all right, replied Gabriel. I've taken one in the Gresham—

—To be sure, said Aunt Kate, by far the best thing to do. And the children, Gretta, you're not anxious about them?—

—O, for one night, said Mrs Conroy. Besides, Bessie will look after them—

—To be sure, said Aunt Kate again. What a comfort it is to have a girl like that, one you can depend on! There's that Lily, I'm sure I don't know what has come over her lately. She's not the girl she was at all—

Gabriel was about to ask his aunt some questions on this point, but she broke off suddenly to gaze after her sister, who had wandered down the stairs and was craning her neck over the banisters.

—Now, I ask you, she said almost testily, where is Julia going? Julia! Julia! Where are you going?—

Julia, who had gone halfway down one flight, came back and announced blandly:

—Here's Freddy—

At the same moment a clapping of hands and a final flourish of the pianist told that the waltz had ended. The drawing-room door was opened from within and some couples came out. Aunt Kate drew Gabriel aside hurriedly and whispered into her ear:

—Slip down, Gabriel, like a good fellow and see if he's all right, and don't let him up if he's screwed. I'm sure he's screwed. I'm sure he is—

Gabriel went to the stairs and listened over the banisters. He could hear two persons talking in the pantry. Then he recognized Freddy Malins' laugh. He went down the stairs noisily.

—It's such a relief, said Aunt Kate to Mrs Conroy, that Gabriel is here. I always feel easier in my mind when he's here . . . Julia, there's Miss Daly and Miss Power will take some refreshments. Thanks for your beautiful waltz, Miss Daly. It made lovely time—

A tall wizen-faced man, with a stiff grizzled moustache and swarthy skin, who was passing out with his partner, said:

Juliet: *Although I joy in thee, I have no joy in this contact tonight* . . .

a) *Mr Browne*: Based on Mervyn Archdall Browne, a Protestant who for a time lived in Great Denmark Street, near Belvedere College. He was a 'professor of music, organist, dance pianist', as well as a commercial man. A forebear, Mervyn Archdall, in 1786 published *Monasticon Hibernicum; or An History of the Abbies, Priories, and other Religious Houses in Ireland*. Clongowes Wood College (13c) was formerly known as Castle Browne, and was famous for its ghost (an Austrian Jacobite Count, named Ulysses). The Catholic family based there until 1814 also provided a general for Napoleon, Lieutenant-General Michael Browne.

b) *Furlong* . . . : What contemporary Dublin would have deemed a 'Protestant' name, though Joyce had a schoolfriend called Furlong, with whom he stole apples, and was punished (21g). The three young ladies suggest length, duration and strength – perhaps even space, time and energy.

c) *the reason . . . is*: Presumably that he's brown all over.

d) *the caretaker*: Strangely, the only appearance of this nameless figure in the story (158w).

e) *viands*: The obsolescent word might be an allusion from Milton's *Areopagitica* (1644). (The attack on censorship was cited (archly) by Joyce in his years-long wrangle with publishers over *D*.)

> To the pure, all things are pure, not only meats and drinks, but all kinde of knowledge whether of good or evil; the knowledge cannot defile, nor consequently the books, if the will and conscience be not defil'd. For books are as meats and viands are; some of good, some of evil substance . . .

f) *hop-bitters*: An unfermented drink, like the ginger beer of 'Two Gallants' (48h).

g) *thither*: An old-fashioned word for Mr Browne, one that recalls Anna Livia (*FW* 216):

> Beside the rivering waters of, hitherandthithering waters of.

h) *ladies' punch*: There is no such drink: this is another of Mr Browne's obscure, weak and off-colour jokes.

i) *filled out*: The term derives from the pre-plumbing days of pitchers and bowls. It was much-used in the Dedalus household (*P* V.1):

> – Fill out the place for me to wash, said Stephen.
> – Katey, fill out the place for Stephen to wash.
> – Boody, fill out the place for Stephen to wash.
> – I can't, I'm going for blue. Fill it out you, Maggie.

Romeo: *Let me stand here till thou remember it* . . .

—And may we have some refreshment, too, Miss Morkan?—

a —Julia, said Aunt Kate summarily, and here's Mr Browne
b and Miss Furlong. Take them in, Julia, with Miss Daly and Miss Power—

—I'm the man for the ladies, said Mr Browne, pursing his lips until his moustache bristled and smiling in all his wrinkles.
c You know, Miss Morkan, the reason they are so fond of me is . . .—

He did not finish his sentence but, seeing that Aunt Kate was out of earshot, at once led the three young ladies into the back room. The middle of the room was occupied by two square tables placed end to end, and on these Aunt Julia and the
d caretaker were straightening and smoothing a large cloth. On the sideboard were arrayed dishes and plates, and glasses and bundles of knives and forks and spoons. The top of the closed
e square piano served also as a sideboard for viands and sweets. At a smaller sideboard in one corner two young men were
f standing, drinking hop-bitters.

g Mr Browne led his charges thither and invited them all, in
h jest, to some ladies' punch, hot, strong and sweet. As they said they never took anything strong, he opened three bottles of lemonade for them. Then he asked one of the young men to
i move aside, and, taking hold of the decanter, filled out for
j himself a goodly measure of whisky. The young men eyed him respectfully while he took a trial sip.

k —God help me, he said, smiling, it's the doctor's orders—

His wizened face broke into a broader smile, and the three young ladies laughed in musical echo to his pleasantry, swaying their bodies to and fro, with nervous jerks of their shoulders. The boldest said:

—O, now, Mr Browne, I'm sure the doctor never ordered anything of the kind—

Mr Browne took another sip of his whisky and said, with sidling mimicry:

l —Well, you see, I'm like the famous Mrs Cassidy, who is
m reported to have said: *Now, Mary Grimes, if I don't take it, make me take it, for I feel I want it*—

His hot face had leaned forward a little too confidentially
n and he had assumed a very low Dublin accent, so that the young ladies, with one instinct, received his speech in silence.

j) *a goodly measure of whisky*: Orotund idiolect from a performing Mr Browne. The Lord Bishop of Cork and Rosse, Peter Browne (a schoolfriend of Swift and a former Provost of Trinity), published several tracts c. 1713, *Against the Custom of Drinking to the Memory of the Dead*. These Brownes are certainly not against drinking in itself. A Joycean joke can be divined.

k) *the doctor's orders*: In respectable Dublin society, the chemist dispensed alcohol in the form of tonic wine and other medicinal potions, which could be bought (particularly by women) without incurring gossip. Respectable women did not go to public houses (83g).

l) *the famous Mrs Cassidy*: Possibly she was related to James Cassidy, owner of the popular Dorset House pub in Upper Dorset Street. In *U*, 'Calypso', Bloom sees a 'bent hag' crossing from Cassidy's 'clutching a noggin bottle by the neck'.

m) Now, Mary Grimes . . .: A parody of Dublin low women, akin to Buck Mulligan's Mrs Cahill jape in *U*, 'Telemachus'. There are other Grimeses in 'Ivy Day in the Committee Room' and 'Grace'.

n) *a very low Dublin accent . . . silence*: He has gone too far. Yet again Joyce is commenting on the importance of accent.

a) *pansy*: Bluish-purple, or violet. The colour would go badly with Mary Jane's red face. John Locke observed:

> The real essence of gold is as impossible for us to know, as for a blind man to tell in what flower the colour of a pansy is, or is not, to be found, whilst he has no idea of the colour of a pansy.

b) *Quadrilles!*: A type of square dance (39l) involving five separate 'figures' (or 'set pieces') and four couples. (The fourth pairing here is not identified.) The dance, a complex one, was most famously celebrated by Lewis Carroll in the Lobster Quadrille in Chapter X of *Alice's Adventures in Wonderland*.

c) *Mr Bergin*: The name was very likely borrowed by Joyce from the family friends (father and son), Alf Bergan. In *U*, Alf Bergan is the prime suspect for sending an insulting postcard to Denis Breen (181).

d) *so short of ladies to-night*: An echo of 'After the Race' (39k). There are about a dozen of both men and women mentioned as present in the house, but it is likely that the party has perhaps forty guests. At least three of the women are of no age for dancing, and another is the slavey.

e) *Mr Bartell D'Arcy*: The name is another of the tribes of Galway (76m). This young man is in part based on a contemporary tenor, P. J. D'Arcy, who performed as Bartholomew D'Arcy. Richard Ellmann's suggestion (derived from a perhaps spur-ious late interview with John Joyce, later attributed to Brian O'Nolan) that the character was largely Barton M'Guckin seems unlikely, as M'Guckin was a well-established performer by then. He was born in 1853 and had made his London début in the month of Joyce's birth. He had also sung in Italy and travelled widely with the Carl Rosa Company. On the night of the Phoenix Park Murders, he was singing in Dublin in the Carl Rosa production of *Maritana* (127d) at the Gaiety. He and his sister were both very well known in the Dublin music circles of the time, so his renown would not need to be explained to the musical Miss Daly. A further indication that M'Guckin was not D'Arcy in Joyce's mind is that both are mentioned in *U*, D'Arcy as one of Molly Bloom's putative lovers.

f) *the first figure*: Of the quadrille.

g) *a young man of about forty*: Freddy is obviously well into middle age. The point is that emotionally he is immature, being a drunkard dominated by his mother, whose speech pattern he has inherited. See 193a.

h) *a convex and receding brow*: A somewhat ungainly zeugma, as Joyce means that Freddy's forehead is convex and his hairline is receding – as in a domed forehead.

i) *tumid*: Swollen.

j) *protruded*: Not 'protruding', which would be a natural condition. It is a symptom of Freddy's drunkenness.

Miss Furlong, who was one of Mary Jane's pupils, asked Miss Daly what was the name of the pretty waltz she had played; and Mr Browne, seeing that he was ignored, turned promptly to the two young men, who were more appreciative.

A red-faced young woman, dressed in pansy, came into the room, excitedly clapping her hands and crying:

—Quadrilles! Quadrilles!—

Close on her heels came Aunt Kate, crying:

—Two gentlemen and three ladies, Mary Jane!—

—O, here's Mr Bergin and Mr Kerrigan, said Mary Jane. Mr Kerrigan, will you take Miss Power? Miss Furlong, may I get you a partner, Mr Bergin. O, that'll just do now—

—Three ladies, Mary Jane, said Aunt Kate—

The two young gentlemen asked the ladies if they might have the pleasure, and Mary Jane turned to Miss Daly.

—O, Miss Daly, you're really awfully good, after playing for the last two dances, but really we're so short of ladies to-night—

—I don't mind in the least, Miss Morkan—

—But I've a nice partner for you, Mr Bartell D'Arcy, the tenor. I'll get him to sing later on. All Dublin is raving about him—

—Lovely voice, lovely voice! said Aunt Kate—

As the piano had twice begun the prelude to the first figure Mary Jane led her recruits quickly from the room. They had hardly gone when Aunt Julia wandered slowly into the room, looking behind her at something.

—What is the matter, Julia? asked Aunt Kate anxiously. Who is it?—

Julia, who was carrying in a column of table-napkins, turned to her sister and said, simply, as if the question had surprised her:

—It's only Freddy, Kate, and Gabriel with him—

In fact right behind her Gabriel could be seen piloting Freddy Malins across the landing. The latter, a young man of about forty, was of Gabriel's size and build, with very round shoulders. His face was fleshy and pallid, touched with colour only at the thick hanging lobes of his ears and at the wide wings of his nose. He had coarse features, a blunt nose, a convex and receding brow, tumid and protruded lips. His heavy-lidded eyes and the disorder of his scanty hair made him look sleepy.

a) *left eye*: Like Joyce himself, Freddy seems to have eye trouble. After the second iridectomy to his left eye, Joyce dictated and Nora wrote in a notebook (now at Buffalo):

> to day 16 of June 1924 twenty years after. Will anybody remember this date

b) *an undertone*: Freddy does not want to be overheard, especially by his mother.

c) *he raised them quickly*: Wide-eyed lying by Gabriel.

d) *the pledge on New Year's Eve*: i.e. less than a week previously (53f). The date is perhaps 6 January – the Feast of the Epiphany, the last day of Christmas.

e) *buck you up*: Give you a boost.

f) *a disarray in his dress*: Freddy must have his flies open, a condition for which there have been many coded warnings. They include: showing your charms, flying the flag of distress, gazelles in the garden, Johnnie's out of gaol, one o'clock at the waterworks, a star in the East.

g) *Academy piece*: One chosen for its technical demands on the player (in a proficiency examination at the RIAM) rather than for the pleasure of the listener. Gabriel's attitude is patronising, as it is in the matter of the Browning quotation (161c).

(*167d*), *as illustrated in* The Leopold Shakspere

15 *Usher's Island*

He was laughing heartily in a high key at a story which he had been telling Gabriel on the stairs and at the same time rubbing the knuckles of his left fist backwards and forwards into his left eye.

—Good evening, Freddy, said Aunt Julia—

Freddy Malins bade the Misses Morkan good-evening in what seemed an offhand fashion by reason of the habitual catch in his voice and then, seeing that Mr Browne was grinning at him from the sideboard, crossed the room on rather shaky legs and began to repeat in an undertone the story he had just told to Gabriel.

—He's not so bad, is he? said Aunt Kate to Gabriel—

Gabriel's brows were dark but he raised them quickly and answered:

—O no, hardly noticeable—

—Now, isn't he a terrible fellow! she said. And his poor mother made him take the pledge on New Year's Eve. But come on, Gabriel, into the drawing-room—

Before leaving the room with Gabriel she signalled to Mr Browne by frowning and shaking her forefinger in warning to and fro. Mr Browne nodded in answer and, when she had gone, said to Freddy Malins:

—Now, then, Teddy, I'm going to fill you out a good glass of lemonade just to buck you up—

Freddy Malins, who was nearing the climax of his story, waved the offer aside impatiently but Mr Browne, having first called Freddy Malins' attention to a disarray in his dress, filled out and handed him a full glass of lemonade. Freddy Malins' left hand accepted the glass mechanically, his right hand being engaged in the mechanical readjustment of his dress. Mr Browne, whose face was once more wrinkling with mirth, poured out for himself a glass of whisky while Freddy Malins exploded, before he had well reached the climax of his story, in a kink of high-pitched bronchitic laughter and, setting down his untasted and overflowing glass, began to rub the knuckles of his left fist backwards and forwards into his left eye, repeating words of his last phrase as well as his fit of laughter would allow him.

. . . .

Gabriel could not listen while Mary Jane was playing her Academy piece, full of runs and difficult passages, to the hushed

a) *a priestess in momentary imprecation*: A slight contradiction, as what is invoked by any imprecation is traditionally evil. The image adds to the sense of unease.

b) *standing at her elbow to turn the page*: William Southwell (158v) also invented a machine known as the Volto Subito, a page-turner worked by levers at the pianist's knees. It was part of his 'piano-sloping-backwards' of 1828.

c) *the balcony scene in* Romeo and Juliet: This is an important detail: Romeo comes to Juliet's window to declare his love, just as young Michael Furey comes to Gretta's to do the same in saying goodbye (and Sonny Bodkin had done to Nora (194(c)). In each case it is a presage of death, through the device of death-in-life. Juliet says to Romeo (II.i):

> The orchard walls are high and hard to climb,
> And the place death.

There is a different usage of the names in *U*, 'Cyclops', when the Citizen sneers at Bloom:

> Love, moya! He's a fine pattern of a Romeo and Juliet.

d) *two murdered princes in the* Tower: The two young sons of Edward IV, *viz*. Edward V and Richard, Duke of York. The brothers were deemed by Tudor propaganda to have been killed in the Tower of London (c. 1483) by their uncle, the future Richard III. The detail fits the theme of doomed youth. Lambert Simnel was passed off as the son of George, Duke of Clarence (himself a native of Dublin), and crowned as Edward VI in Christ Church Cathedral, Dublin in 1486. Dublin was a Yorkist centre, an influence and an interest that lingered – see *P* (I.2).

e) *worked ... work ... worked*: An old-fashioned usage, related to 'workbox'.

f) *red, blue and brown wools*: This is embroidering history as well as embroidering Shakespeare, though the playwright did the former too, in *Richard III* (d). A Homeric detail could also be seen, with Gabriel playing Telemachus to his weaving mother's Penelope.

g) *Probably*: Gabriel's stream of consciousness has perhaps been brought on by the glare, or by his boredom with the music.

h) *taught for one year his mother had*: A comma after 'for' might have clarified this seemingly incoherent sentence.

i) *a waistcoat of purple tabinet with little foxes' heads*: This , or one like it, is a Joycean heirloom, preserved at the Martello Tower, Sandycove. The heads are of dogs and stags rather than foxes. Tabinet is a damask-like material, similar to poplin and particularly popular in nineteenth-century Ireland. By the late 1880s tabinet-weaving was dying out, though in January 1866 the *London Review* could report:

> The Lord Lieutenant of Ireland ... holds ... levées which serve to demoralise the middle-class into dire extravagance and a tabinet gentility.

Joyce changed the detail from little dogs perhaps because of the Song of Solomon (II.15):

> Take us the foxes, the little foxes, that spoil the vines, for our vines have tender grapes.

j) *mulberry*: Rather neatly, the leaves of the mulberry tree are the food of silkworms.

k) *brains carrier*: A much-used expression of John Joyce's. The point about being a carrier is that one does not participate oneself.

l) *pier-glass*: See 56h.

m) *Constantine*: The name was very likely inspired by Joyce's friend C.P. Curran, who became an authority on the interiors and architecture of Georgian Dublin.

n) *man-o'-war suit*: The description fits the well-known photograph of '6½', at which age young Joyce set out for Clongowes. Here, however, the wrong brother is described. Possibly (as in 'A Painful Case' and *FW*'s 'Tales Told of Shem and Shaun'), Stanislaus is being anatomised or plagiarised again, and there exists or existed a separate photograph of him. One detail in favour of Sailor Stannie is the beginning of *U*, 'Nausicaa', where the little Caffrey boys are

dressed in sailor suits with caps to match and the name *H.M.S. Belleisle* printed on both.

o) *the names of her sons*: The weighty influences of an archangel and the first Christian emperor respectively.

p) *Thanks to her*: The theme of *amor matris* is a major one for Joyce, as shown in Cranly's observation to Stephen in *P* (V.3.):

> —Whatever else is unsure in this stinking dunghill of a world a mother's love is not.

q) *senior curate*: Gabriel's brother is the chief assistant to the parish priest. It was a Father Conroy who baptised John of Tuam (151c) in Mayo in 1791: a few years later the priest was hanged for treason relating to the French invasion.

r) *Balbriggan*: A seaside resort to the north of Dublin.

drawing-room. He liked music but the piece she was playing had no melody for him and he doubted whether it had any melody for the other listeners, though they had begged Mary Jane to play something. Four young men, who had come from the refreshment-room to stand in the doorway at the sound of the piano, had gone away quietly in couples after a few minutes. The only persons who seemed to follow the music were Mary Jane herself, her hands racing along the keyboard or lifted from it at the pauses like those of a priestess in momentary a imprecation, and Aunt Kate standing at her elbow to turn the b page.

Gabriel's eyes, irritated by the floor, which glittered with beeswax under the heavy chandelier, wandered to the wall c above the piano. A picture of the balcony scene in *Romeo and* d *Juliet* hung there and beside it was a picture of the two murdered e princes in the Tower which Aunt Julia had worked in red, blue f and brown wools when she was a girl. Probably in the school g they had gone to as girls that kind of work had been taught h for one year his mother had worked for him as a birthday i present a waistcoat of purple tabinet, with little foxes' heads j upon it, lined with brown satin and having round mulberry buttons. It was strange that his mother had had no musical k talent though Aunt Kate used to call her the brains carrier of the Morkan family. Both she and Julia had always seemed a little proud of their serious and matronly sister. Her photograph l stood before the pier-glass. She held an open book on her knees m and was pointing out something in it to Constantine who, n dressed in a man-o'-war suit, lay at her feet. It was she who o had chosen the names of her sons, for she was very sensible of p the dignity of family life. Thanks to her, Constantine was now qr senior curate in Balbriggan and, thanks to her, Gabriel himself s had taken his degree in the Royal University. A shadow passed over his face as he remembered her sullen opposition to his t marriage. Some slighting phrases she had used still rankled in his memory; she had once spoken of Gretta as being country u cute and that was not true of Gretta at all. It was Gretta who v had nursed her during all her last long illness in their house at Monkstown.

He knew that Mary Jane must be near the end of her piece w for she was playing again the opening melody with runs of scales after every bar and while he waited for the end the

By Bloomsday, in *U*, 'Nausicaa', Father Conroy is based on the other side of Dublin Bay, at the Star of the Sea Church in Sandymount (139i), where his duties will include hearing Paddy Dignam's last confession. The Dublin church really did have a Father Conroy from July 1903 onwards (who was in fact transferred from Wicklow).

s) *Royal University*: See 161g.

t) *her sullen opposition to his marriage*: Gabriel has this in common with Bob Doran of 'The Boarding House', and with Eveline (and also with John Joyce, who was looked down on by the Murrays – a feeling he reciprocated with interest).

u) *country cute*: An urban sneer. The rest of the saying is 'and city clever'. 'Cute' is meant not in the American sense but as a pejorative abbreviation of 'acute'. In *U*, 'Cyclops', the Citizen derides Bloom:

> There's a jew for you. All for number one. Cute as a shithouse rat.

v) *nursed her during all her last long illness*: The model here is not Nora Barnacle, who never knew Mrs Joyce, but Joyce's sister Poppie (34). Possibly Joyce is also looking back a generation for the detail: it was his mother who nursed his paternal grandmother in Dublin (in the mid-1880s) before the elder woman returned to Cork to die.

w) *playing again*: Gabriel's musical knowledge is much inferior to Joyce's.

a) *Lancers*: A type of quadrille (165b) popular since the 1830s, which could be danced by more than four couples.

b) *Miss Ivors*: The character is a composite of Joyce's 'Emma Clery' (in *SH* and *P*) and the Sheehy sisters (13c). 'E—C—' has been rediscovered by Peter Costello, and she did not appreciate nose-picking geniuses. Kathleen Sheehy dressed like Miss Ivors, but it was Hanna Sheehy BA who in 1903 wrote an essay on 'Women and the University Question' (169c) in the *New Ireland Review*. The former became the mother of that noted Irishman of parts, Conor Cruise O'Brien (among whose achievements is a biography of Edmund Burke (1992)). The latter married Joyce's associate Francis Skeffington (169f). On Mary Sheehy, see 163c. The fourth sister, Maggie (131f) married Frank Culhane, once a Belvedere classmate of Joyce and later the Taxing Master in Dublin City.

c) *She did not wear a low-cut bodice*: Miss Ivors is serious and sensible. The Gaelic League deplored any décolleté style – one Irish description of which is 'Low and behold!'

d) *fixed in the front of her collar*: More than the casual young stewards in 'A Mother', Miss Ivors is making a prominent advertisement for her cause, and the language badge is at her larynx.

e) *an Irish device and motto*: This may have been a de luxe version of the badge of *Cumann na Gaedheal*, which came in several grades. In August 1903, the *United Irishman* published this deathless prose:

THE LIFE OF A GAELIC LEAGUE BADGE

... I am a small tin person; my face is enamelled, and all round me are little sham-rocks. On my surface there are five Irish words. Three of these words have a special meaning, which I am sorry to say some of my possessors take no heed of whatsoever, and they are *Tír agus Teanga* (country and language). At my back there is a pin, by means of which I can be attached to a coat, or in fact wherever my owner wishes to have me.

Alternatively, the brooch might be a Tara brooch or some other Celtic jewellery of the Revival.

f) *I have a crow to pluck with you*: Irish variant of 'a bone to pick'. The bird is obviously dead. In *The Comedy of Errors* (III.i), one of the Dromios says:

If a crow help us in sirrah, we'll pluck a crow together.

g) *innocent Amy!*: A catchphrase of the time, mocking naïvety.

h) Daily Express: As the name is shared with a UK national newspaper, it is often overlooked that the reference is to a Dublin publication. Regardless of its vigorously Unionist political tone, its Irish and other coverage was commendably thorough. Joyce wrote book reviews for the paper between 1902 and 1904. Bernard Shaw in his Preface to *Androcles and the Lion* referred to

a most respectable newspaper in my native town, the Dublin *Daily Express* . . .

i) *paper*: At one stage the word was 'rag' – the latter expression is still current as an insult for a worthless newspaper.

j) *West Briton*: An Irishman whose perceived loyalty is to the English. 'West British' was the favourite vituperation of Arthur Griffith's *United Irishman*. The term remains seriously offensive.

k) *fifteen shillings*: 15/-. For each column, Gabriel receives more than twice Eveline's weekly wage, the equivalent of a week's board at Mrs Mooney's (beer or stout excluded). Such a sum would buy an Acme Melodeon from Kearney's in Capel Street (the rate-payer who is Bloom's library guarantor in *U*). Alter-natively, it would buy three-quarters of a ton of Best Orrell Coal from one of Dublin's many coalyards.

l) *paltry cheque*: Dr Johnson defined the adjective as being derived from the Italian *paltrocca*, a low whore. Joyce's articles were usually not signed, though once the *Express* appended his initials after his honest review of Lady Gregory's *Poets and Dreamers*, in order to distance itself. The occasion is recalled by Mulligan to Stephen in *U*, 'Scylla and Charybdis':

... after what you wrote about that old hake Gregory. O you inquisitional drunken jew jesuit! She gets you a job on the paper and then you go and slate her drivel to Jaysus.

m) *the quays*: As in Paris, an area of the riverside was a mecca for book-browsers.

n) *Hickey's* [etc]: Hickey's was at 8 Bachelor's Walk, just off the north side of O'Connell Bridge. Michael Hickey, the blackbearded and aggressive proprietor,

168

resentment died down in his heart. The piece ended with a trill of octaves in the treble and a final deep octave in the bass. Great applause greeted Mary Jane as, blushing and rolling up her music nervously, she escaped from the room. The most vigorous clapping came from the four young men in the doorway who had gone away to the refreshment-room at the beginning of the piece but had come back when the piano had stopped.

Lancers were arranged. Gabriel found himself partnered with Miss Ivors. She was a frank-mannered talkative young lady, with a freckled face and prominent brown eyes. She did not wear a low-cut bodice and the large brooch which was fixed in the front of her collar bore on it an Irish device and motto.

When they had taken their places she said abruptly:

—I have a crow to pluck with you—

—With me? said Gabriel—

She nodded her head gravely.

—What is it? asked Gabriel, smiling at her solemn manner—

—Who is G. C.? answered Miss Ivors, turning her eyes upon him—

Gabriel coloured and was about to knit his brows, as if he did not understand, when she said bluntly:

—O, innocent Amy! I have found out that you write for the *Daily Express*. Now, aren't you ashamed of yourself?—

—Why should I be ashamed of myself? asked Gabriel, blinking his eyes and trying to smile—

—Well, I'm ashamed of you, said Miss Ivors frankly. To say you'd write for a paper like that. I didn't think you were a West Briton—

A look of perplexity appeared on Gabriel's face. It was true that he wrote a literary column every Wednesday in the *Daily Express*, for which he was paid fifteen shillings. But that did not make him a West Briton surely. The books he received for review were almost more welcome than the paltry cheque. He loved to feel the covers and turn over the pages of newly printed books. Nearly every day when his teaching in the college was ended he used to wander down the quays to the second-hand booksellers, to Hickey's on Bachelor's Walk, to Webb's or Massey's on Aston's Quay, or to O'Clohissey's in the by-street. He did not know how to meet her charge. He wanted to say that literature was above politics. But they were

was quite unlike Webb on the opposite bank. *Webb's* belonged to George Webb at 5 Crampton Quay. Padraic Colum called him 'that most knowing of all booksellers'. *Massey's* was Edward Massey's, at 6 Aston's (now Aston) Quay, facing Hickey's across the Liffey. *O'Clohissey's* was at 10 and 11 Bedford Row, a by-street between Aston's Quay and Temple Bar.

o) *literature was above politics*: A foolish thought by Gabriel, when his creator has written the stories of Public Life in Dublin. The description of paralysis and corruption in *D* constituted, Joyce said (in a letter to Grant Richards of April 1906),

the first step towards the spiritual liberation of my country.

The spiritual and the political are conjoined in all these stories, and the artist is a part of society.

a) *teachers*: Teaching was one of the few professions open to middle-class women at this time. A contemporary booklet on the subject (issued by the Central Bureau for the Employment of Women, Molesworth Street, Dublin) lists eight sub-categories of teaching, not including music, which has its own entry.

b) *turn to cross*: One of the dance steps.

c) *the University question*: There was a current controversy to do with the representation of 'Irish values' in higher learning. The issue convulsed the Parliament at Westminster, where fiscal reform was jeopardised by a threatened split over the issue. The proposal of a National University of Ireland, incorporating Trinity, Queen's (Belfast), and University College Dublin, led to Protestant fears of 'a Jesuit university' paid for from public money (149k). The failure of Newman's Catholic University and the growth of Gaelic Nationalism, as well as social and economic change, made these Irish values difficult to define. In 1909, the National University was set up on a different basis. (*Exiles* is ostensibly concerned with Richard Rowan's candidature for the chair of romance literature there.) Trinity had managed to retain its separate standing as the University of Dublin, as it was to do again in 1967, thanks in part to the efforts of the University senator, Owen Sheehy Skeffington. His father was Joyce's friend Francis Skeffington (f), who gave the issue a spin concerning the 'woman question' (170i), also topical. In 1901 he and Joyce pooled resources in order independently to share a pamphlet, *Two Essays*. Skeffington's piece was 'A Forgotten Aspect of the University Question' (while Joyce published 'The Day of the Rabblement'). Dublin University decided in 1903 to open its degrees to women. At Jimmy Doyle's other university, Cambridge, this reform waited until 1948.

d) *Browning*: See 161b. There is no record of Joyce's having reviewed any of Browning's work. The Everyman edition of his *Poems and Plays* appeared in 1906 shortly before Joyce wrote the story.

e) *the Aran Isles*: Off the coast of County Galway (and not to be confused with Aran Island off the coast of County Donegal). J.M. Synge made the islands famous beyond Ireland in his book on them (with a little help from Jack B. Yeats), and in his play *Riders to the Sea* (despite Joyce's Aristotelian flaying of the latter, as 'dwarf-drama', in Paris in 1902). In *SH* Stephen learns 'Emma had gone away to the Isles of Aran with a Gaelic party'. The islands were for a long time regarded as a Gaelic social ideal. This mythmaking was to receive a significant boost in 1934, when Robert Flaherty made his famous film, *Man of Aran*, which celebrated the islanders' noble savagery. Flaherty was a friend of that other Irish-American film-maker John Huston, whose last work was *The Dead*. Perhaps the Aran Islands' most notable native was the writer Liam O'Flaherty, whose best known novel *The Informer* (1925) is a scrupulous exploration of the forms of Irish betrayal.

f) *Mr Clancy*: Joyce's college friend George Clancy contributed to the characters of Madden in *SH* and Davin in *P*. This seems to be him under his own name. At UCD he was noted for his involvement in founding a branch of the Gaelic League. He became the Mayor of Limerick, and was shot in 1921 by the British forces, during the War of Independence. Sheehy-Skeffington, though a pacifist, as *P* (V.1) testifies (concerning 'MacCann'), met a similar fate.

g) *Kilkelly*: The name of an eminent Irish family. One member was a sometime Grenadier Guardsman, whose father had been a Surgeon-General and Justice of the Peace of Galway. Another was the model for the heroine of *Evelyn Innes* (33c). Quite a number of establishment families came to support independence (e.g. the Gore-Booths and the Childers), though many remained Southern Unionist in outlook.

h) *Kathleen Kearney*: The Nationalist accompanist seen but little-heard in 'A Mother'.

i) *She's from Connacht . . .*: Previously this read, 'She's half-Connacht . . .' The westernmost and bleakest of Ireland's four provinces (the others are Ulster, Munster and Leinster) comprises the counties of Galway, Mayo, Sligo, Roscommon and Leitrim. Bernard Shaw wrote in his Preface to *John Bull's Other Island* (1904) that the name rhymed with 'bonnet', whereas its anglicised version, Connaught, rhymed with 'untaught'. With Gabriel's evasiveness the east-west tensions in the story are beginning to develop.

j) *already arranged*: Previously 'just arranged'.

k) *France or Belgium*: Arguably something of a wild-goose chase, as French and Belgian history are full of Irish soldiers, artists, scholars, ecclesiastics and others. In the Battle of Fontenoy (1745), fought in Belgium during the War of the Spanish Succession, there was an Irish regiment on each side. Richard Stanyhurst, son of the Speaker of the Irish House of Commons and uncle of Archbishop Ussher (158m), died in Belgium in 1618. Two of his sons became Jesuits there. Oliver Goldsmith survived at Louvaine (where Daniel O'Connell (190p) was later to study) by busking on his flute and giving English lessons. Indirect instances of the continental connection (35i)

friends of many years' standing and their careers had been
a parallel, first at the University and then as teachers: he could not risk a grandiose phrase with her. He continued blinking his eyes and trying to smile and murmured lamely that he saw nothing political in writing reviews of books.

b When their turn to cross had come he was still perplexed and inattentive. Miss Ivors promptly took his hand in a warm grasp and said in a soft friendly tone:

—Of course, I was only joking. Come, we cross now—

When they were together again she spoke of the University
c question and Gabriel felt more at ease. A friend of hers had
d shown her his review of Browning's poems. That was how she had found out the secret: but she liked the review immensely. Then she said suddenly:

—O, Mr Conroy, will you come for an excursion to the
e Aran Isles this summer? We're going to stay there a whole month. It will be splendid out in the Atlantic. You ought to
fg come. Mr Clancy is coming, and Mr Kilkelly and Kathleen
h Kearney. It would be splendid for Gretta too if she'd come.
i She's from Connacht, isn't she?—

—Her people are, said Gabriel shortly—

—But you will come, won't you? said Miss Ivors, laying her warm hand eagerly on his arm—

j —The fact is, said Gabriel, I have already arranged to go . . .—

—Go where? asked Miss Ivors—

—Well, you know, every year I go for a cycling tour with some fellows and so . . .—

—But where? asked Miss Ivors—

k —Well, we usually go to France or Belgium or perhaps
l Germany, said Gabriel awkwardly—

—And why do you go to France and Belgium, said Miss Ivors, instead of visiting your own land?—

—Well, said Gabriel, it's partly to keep in touch with the languages and partly for a change—

—And haven't you your own language to keep in touch
m with – Irish? asked Miss Ivors—

n —Well, said Gabriel, if it comes to that, you know, Irish is not my language—

Their neighbours had turned to listen to the cross-examination. Gabriel glanced right and left nervously and tried to

are Patrick MacMahon, who was President of the French Republic in the 1870s, and Hennessy Brandy celebrated in 'Circe' and around the world.

l) *perhaps Germany*: Germany was also traditionally regarded as an ally of Ireland, notably in 1916. Later, the Galway-born William Joyce (the one with the first-class degree in English) was fanatically pro-Nazi and went to Germany at the outbreak of war in 1939. Samuel Beckett, travelling in a hurry at this time, took a different view, observing that France at war was better than Ireland at peace. Lord Haw-Haw (Joyce) was eventually hanged for treason (still a matter of legal controversy), while the other was awarded the Croix de Guerre for his work in the French Resistance.

m) *Irish*: Irish is not an easy language to learn. Apart from its three distinct dialects, and a large number of irregular verbs and nouns, it not only has case endings to many nouns (as in Latin), but inflects the beginning (and often the middle) of words as well. Excursions to Irish-speaking districts were frequent, as the best way to become proficient was (and is) through conversation. Recently a degree of simplification has taken place and the distinctive Irish lettering has been virtually abandoned – causes of regret to many.

n) *Irish is not my language*: Only a small and diminishing proportion of the population were native speakers.

THE SOUL OF IRELAND

"Poets and Dreamers: Studies and Translations from the Irish." By Lady Gregory. Hodges, Figgis, and Co., Dublin: John Murray, London.

Aristotle finds at the beginning of all speculation the feeling of wonder, a feeling proper to childhood, and if speculation be proper to the middle period of life it is natural that one should look to the crowning period of life for the fruit of speculation, wisdom itself. But nowadays people have greatly confused childhood and middle life and old age; those who succeed in spite of civilisation in reaching old age seem to have less and less wisdom, and children who are usually put to some business as soon as they can walk and talk, seem to have more and more "common sense;" and, perhaps, in the future little boys with long beards will stand aside and applaud, while old men in short trousers play handball against the side of a house. This may even happen in Ireland, if Lady Gregory has truly set forth the old age of her country. In her new book she has left legends and heroic youth far behind, and has explored in a land almost fabulous in its sorrow and senility. Half of her book is an account of old men and old women in the West of Ireland. These old people are full of stories about giants and witches, and dogs and black-handled knives, and they tell their stories one after another at great length and with many repetitions (for they are people of leisure) by the fire or in the yard of a workhouse. It is difficult to judge well of their charms and herb-healing, for that is the province of those who are learned in these matters and can compare the customs of countries, and, indeed, it is well not to know these magical sciences, for if the wind changes while you are cutting wild camomile you will lose your mind. But one can judge more easily of their stories. These stories appeal to some feeling which is certainly not that feeling of wonder which is the beginning of all speculation. The story-tellers are old, and their imagination is not the imagination of childhood. The story-teller preserves the strange machinery of fairy-land, but his mind is feeble and sleepy. He begins one story and wanders from it into another story, and none of the stories has any satisfying imaginative wholeness, none of them is like Sir John Daw's poem that cried tink in the close. Lady Gregory is conscious of this, for she often tries to lead the speaker back to his story by questions, and when the story has become hopelessly involved, she tries to establish some wholeness by keeping only

the less involved part; sometimes she listens "half interested and half impatient." In fine, her book, wherever it treats of the "folk," sets forth in the fulness of its senility a class of mind which Mr. Yeats has set forth with such delicate scepticism in his happiest book, "The Celtic Twilight." Something of health and naturalness, however, enters with Raftery, the poet. He had a terrible tongue, it seems, and would make a satirical poem for a very small offence. He could make love-poems, too (though Lady Gregory finds a certain falseness in the western love-poems), and repentant poems. Raftery, though he be the last of the great bardic procession, has much of the bardic tradition about him. He took shelter one day from the rain under a bush: at first the bush kept out the rain, and he made verses praising it, but after a while it let the rain through, and he made verses dispraising it. Lady Gregory translates some of his verses, and she also translates some West Irish ballads and some poems by Dr. Douglas Hyde. She completes her book with translations of four one-act plays by Dr. Douglas Hyde, three of which have for their central figure that legendary person, who is vagabond and poet, and even saint at times, while the fourth play is called a "nativity" play. The dwarf-drama (if one may use that term) is a form of art which is improper and ineffectual, but it is easy to understand why it finds favour with an age which has pictures that are "nocturnes," and writers like Mallarme and the composer of "Recapitulation." The dwarf-drama is accordingly to be judged as an entertainment, and Dr. Douglas Hyde is certainly entertaining in the "Twisting of the Rope," and Lady Gregory has succeeded better with her verse-translations here than elsewhere, as these four lines may show:—

I have heard the melodious harp
On the streets of Cork playing to us;
More melodious by far I thought your voice,
More melodious by far your mouth than that.

This book, like so many other books of our time, is in part picturesque and in part an indirect or direct utterance of the central belief of Ireland. Out of the material and spiritual battle which has gone so hardly with her Ireland has emerged, with many memories of beliefs, and with one belief—a belief in the incurable ignobility of the forces that have overcome her—and Lady Gregory, whose old men and women seem to be almost their own judges when they tell their wandering stories, might well add to the passage from Whitman which forms her dedication, Whitman's ambiguous word for the vanquished—"Battles are lost in the spirit in which they are won."

—J.J.

(168l)

---

a) *invade*: A curious and loaded usage repeated from 'Eveline'. Gabriel is a victim of his own involuntary emotions.

b) *your own land ... people ... country*: The difference between land, people and country is the stuff of which theses are made. It is sufficient to say that Miss Ivors is verbalising the Gaelic League button (168e). Joyce had (or grew to have) some sympathy with Miss Ivors' viewpoint, though he never became reconciled with the language movement. In his 1912 essay on Galway (written after he had finally been to the west), he began by complaining of

The lazy Dubliner, who travels little and knows his own country only by hearsay ...

c) *go visiting together ... the long chain*: The phrases describe details of the dance, the former where the partners cross the floor to liaise with another couple.

d) *tiptoe*: A detail in 'The Sisters' to be found again at the end of this story.

e) *a good crossing*: Joyce's first journey beyond Ireland was similarly to Glasgow, made with his father (a friend of the ship's captain) in 1896. A family funeral has been suspected as the reason for the journey.

170

keep his good humour under the ordeal which was making a
a blush invade his forehead.

b —And haven't you your own land to visit, continued Miss
Ivors, that you know nothing of, your own people, and your
own country?—

—O, to tell you the truth, retorted Gabriel suddenly, I'm
sick of my own country, sick of it!—

—Why? asked Miss Ivors—

Gabriel did not answer for his retort had heated him.

—Why? repeated Miss Ivors—

c They had to go visiting together and, as he had not answered
her, Miss Ivors said warmly:

—Of course, you've no answer—

Gabriel tried to cover his agitation by taking part in the
dance with great energy. He avoided her eyes for he had seen
a sour expression on her face. But when they met in the long
chain he was surprised to feel his hand firmly pressed. She
looked at him from under her brows for a moment quizzically
until he smiled. Then, just as the chain was about to start again,
d she stood on tiptoe and whispered into his ear:

—West Briton!—

When the lancers were over Gabriel went away to a remote
corner of the room where Freddy Malins' mother was sitting.
She was a stout feeble old woman with white hair. Her voice
had a catch in it like her son's and she stuttered slightly. She
had been told that Freddy had come and that he was nearly all
e right. Gabriel asked her whether she had had a good crossing.
f She lived with her married daughter in Glasgow and came to
Dublin on a visit once a year. She answered placidly that she
g had had a beautiful crossing and that the captain had been most
attentive to her. She spoke also of the beautiful house her
h daughter kept in Glasgow and of all the friends they had there.
While her tongue rambled on Gabriel tried to banish from his
mind all memory of the unpleasant incident with Miss Ivors.
i Of course the girl or woman, or whatever she was, was an
enthusiast, but there was a time for all things. Perhaps he ought
not to have answered her like that. But she had no right to call
him a West Briton before people, even in joke. She had tried
j to make him ridiculous before people, heckling him and staring
at him with her rabbit's eyes.

He saw his wife making her way towards him through the

f) *Glasgow*: A commercial improvement on the original 'Galway' (which would have clashed with the end of the story). Glasgow at this time was one of the most important cities in the Empire. Its industrial population included a large number of Irish immigrants – particularly from Donegal. Glasgow put up its column to Nelson before Dublin did (though the latter in turn was ahead of London). Similarly, Glasgow was quick to put up a memorial to Sir Walter Scott (16m), much to the annoyance of the novelist's native Edinburgh.

g) *a beautiful crossing*: Certainly not what Gabriel has had with Miss Ivors. 'Beautiful' is as much a part of Mrs Malins' idiolect as 'nice' is of Maria's in 'Clay'.

h) *all the friends*: In the 1910 proofs, 'nice friends'. The amendment is a nice instance of character subjectivity, and is a reminder that Joyce did some work on the 1914 proofs.

i) *the girl or woman*: A contemporary problem was the Woman Question – explored in works such as Bernard Shaw's *Candida* (1894) and H.G. Wells' *Ann Veronica* (1909). Much later, one of Beckett's *Krapp* reveries was:

Hard to think of her as a girl. Wonderful woman though. Connaught I fancy.

j) *heckling him*: But she whispered to him too and seems rather fond of him. Gabriel's subjectivity and timidity are marked.

a) *into his ear*: Gretta's action repeats Miss Ivors'.

b) *All right*: An echo of the green-eyed sailor of 'An Encounter' (151).

c) *What words . . . words*: Originally 'row', though these words were by definition cross ones, and their cause was more words in the *Express*.

d) *conceit*: The word had a variety of meanings, and this one is not complimentary. Consider Proverbs XXVI.12:

> Seest thou a man wise in his own conceit?
> There is more hope of a fool than of him.

e) *There were no words*: Originally 'There was no row'.

f) *she cried*: Improved from 'she said'.

g) *I'd love to see Galway again*: The voice of Nora Barnacle.

h) *a nice husband*: The best ones in *D* are Mr Kearney and Joe Donnelly – hardly exalted company.

i) *threading her way back*: A suggestion of Ariadne in the labyrinth, and that Gabriel has not a clue.

j) *beautiful places there were in Scotland*: The Romantics had a particular appreciation of the grandeur of Scottish scenery. Mendelssohn, for example, wrote his *Fingal's Cave* overture after a visit to the isle of Staffa, in the Hebrides. Keats set some of 'Hyperion' there, after his visit. Sir Walter Scott also drew on Scotland's natural grandeur in a number of his novels.

k) *fisher*: The word was even then archaic, and recalls Matthew (IV.18–19):

> And Jesus, walking by the sea of Galilee, saw two brethren, Simon called Peter, and Andrew his brother, casting a net into the sea: for they were fishers.
> And he saith unto them, Follow me, and I will make you fishers of men.

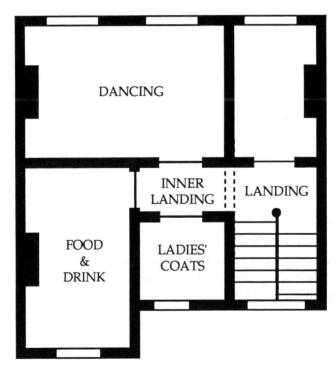

The party rooms (not to scale)

a waltzing couples. When she reached him she said into his ear:

—Gabriel, Aunt Kate wants to know won't you carve the goose as usual. Miss Daly will carve the ham and I'll do the pudding—

b —All right, said Gabriel—

—She's sending in the younger ones first as soon as this waltz is over so that we'll have the table to ourselves—

—Were you dancing? asked Gabriel—

c —Of course I was. Didn't you see me? What words had you with Molly Ivors?—

—No words. Why? Did she say so?—

—Something like that. I'm trying to get that Mr D'Arcy to

d sing. He's full of conceit, I think—

e —There were no words, said Gabriel moodily, only she wanted me to go for a trip to the west of Ireland and I said I wouldn't—

His wife clasped her hands excitedly and gave a little jump.

fg —O, do go, Gabriel, she cried. I'd love to see Galway again—

—You can go if you like, said Gabriel coldly—

She looked at him for a moment, then turned to Mrs Malins and said:

h —There's a nice husband for you, Mrs Malins—

i While she was threading her way back across the room Mrs Malins, without adverting to the interruption, went on to

j tell Gabriel what beautiful places there were in Scotland and beautiful scenery. Her son-in-law brought them every year to the lakes and they used to go fishing. Her son-in-law was a

kl splendid fisher. One day he caught a fish, a beautiful big big fish, and the man in the hotel boiled it for their dinner.

Gabriel hardly heard what she said. Now that supper was coming near he began to think again about his speech and about the quotation. When he saw Freddy Malins coming across the room to visit his mother Gabriel left the chair free

m for him and retired into the embrasure of the window. The room had already cleared and from the back room came the clatter of plates and knives. Those who still remained in the drawing-room seemed tired of dancing and were conversing quietly in little groups. Gabriel's warm trembling fingers

n tapped the cold pane of the window. How cool it must be

o outside! How pleasant it would be to walk out alone, first

l) *a fish … boiled it*: Previously Joyce wrote 'a beautiful big fish and the man in the hotel cooked it'.

m) *the embrasure of the window*: The narrow side of the window recess. In Shakespeare's *Troilus and Cressida*, the word means 'an embrace', however. To avoid a family celebration by preferring the embrace of Dublin's cold night air is perhaps a hint of Gabriel's alienation.

n) *tapped the cold pane*: Originally 'tipped', through several revisions (198a).

o) *How pleasant*: Gabriel is preparing a speech in praise of hospitality, yet he longs to be alone in the park. There is something of Mr Duffy (of 'A Painful Case') in him.

a) *alone … along by the river*: A brief anticipation of the loop of the line between the end and the start of *FW* (628/3):

A way a lone a last a loved a long the / riverrun

b) *the park*: The Phoenix Park (180d).

c) *Wellington Monument*: The 'Testimonial' was erected in 1817 and at 205 feet was acclaimed as the highest obelisk in the world. It is clearly visible above Kingsbridge Station from outside No 15 Usher's Island. In 'Gas from a Burner', Joyce had his printer-publisher reflect on his verisimilitude:

The Wellington 'Testimonial', more than half as high again as Nelson's Pillar

Shite and onions, d'ye think I'll print
The name of the Wellington Monument,
Sydney Parade and the Sandymount tram,
Downes's Cakeshop and Williams's jam?
I'm damned if I do – I'm damned to blazes!
Talk about *Irish Names of Places*!

(But there is no Williams's jam in *D*.)

d) *the Three Graces*: In Greek mythology, named Aglaia, Thalia and Euphrosyne, the daughters of Zeus and Eurynome. They bestowed beauty and charm, and were its embodiment.

e) *Paris*: Gabriel (as it transpires) will not be speaking of the continental city but of a brave prince with an upbringing among the liberal shepherds. Paris was appointed by the gods to award a golden apple to the fairest of three candidates. These were Hera, Athene and Aphrodite (in Roman mythology Juno, Minerva and Venus) – not the Three Graces. Either Gabriel or Joyce knew that the Graces were nothing to do with Paris, or the same author did not care.

f) *. . . a thought-tormented music*: Later, Gabriel will see and hear precisely this, but fail to recognise it (187a).

g) *What did he care that his aunts were only two ignorant old women?*: A reprise of an implied theme of 'The Sisters'.

h) *gallantly*: Browne is flattering and embarrassing Aunt Julia.

i) *hanging her head*: Aunt Julia's modesty also suggests 'hanging on the bough' – remaining unmarried. Similarly, someone whose wedding was deferred was said to 'hang in the bellropes'.

j) *irregular musketry*: The report of a smattering of applause recalls the idiom of Uncle Toby in Sterne's *Tristram Shandy*. Even the adjective here is suggestive of a part-time soldier.

k) *gradually ceased*: Like the end of what, for Joyce, is a singularly awkward sentence.

l) *Arrayed for the Bridal*: From Bellini's *I Puritani di Scozia* (1835), words by George Linley, based on Sir Walter Scott's *Old Mortality*:

Arrayed for the bridal, in beauty behold her
A white wreath entwineth a forehead more fair
I envy the zephyrs that softly enfold her
              enfold her
And play with the locks of her beautiful hair
May life to her prove full of sunshine and love
              full of love yes! yes! yes!
Who would not love her
Sweet star of the morning! shining so bright!
Earth's circle adorning, fair creature of light
              fair creature of light.

along by the river and then through the park! The snow would be lying on the branches of the trees and forming a bright cap on the top of the Wellington Monument. How much more pleasant it would be there than at the supper-table!

He ran over the headings of his speech: Irish hospitality, sad memories, the Three Graces, Paris, the quotation from Browning. He repeated to himself a phrase he had written in his review: *One feels that one is listening to a thought-tormented music.* Miss Ivors had praised the review. Was she sincere? Had she really any life of her own behind all her propagandism? There had never been any ill-feeling between them until that night. It unnerved him to think that she would be at the supper-table, looking up at him while he spoke with her critical quizzing eyes. Perhaps she would not be sorry to see him fail in his speech. An idea came into his mind and gave him courage. He would say, alluding to Aunt Kate and Aunt Julia: *Ladies and Gentlemen, the generation which is now on the wane among us may have had its faults but for my part I think it had certain qualities of hospitality, of humour, of humanity, which the new and very serious and hypereducated generation that is growing up around us seems to me to lack.* Very good: that was one for Miss Ivors. What did he care that his aunts were only two ignorant old women?

A murmur in the room attracted his attention. Mr Browne was advancing from the door, gallantly escorting Aunt Julia, who leaned upon his arm, smiling and hanging her head. An irregular musketry of applause escorted her also as far as the piano and then, as Mary Jane seated herself on the stool, and Aunt Julia, no longer smiling, half turned so as to pitch her voice fairly into the room, gradually ceased. Gabriel recognized the prelude. It was that of an old song of Aunt Julia's – *Arrayed for the Bridal.* Her voice, strong and clear in tone, attacked with great spirit the runs which embellish the air and though she sang very rapidly she did not miss even the smallest of the grace notes. To follow the voice, without looking at the singer's face, was to feel and share the excitement of swift and secure flight. Gabriel applauded loudly with all the others at the close of the song and loud applause was borne in from the invisible supper-table. It sounded so genuine that a little colour struggled into Aunt Julia's face as she bent to replace in the music-stand the old leather-bound song-book that had her initials on the

The opera was first performed in Dublin in 1837, in the reign of William IV, and became a standard part of the repertory there. Aunt Julia's skilled but inappropriate performance parallels that of Maria in 'Clay' (93e).

m) *grace notes*: Skilled decorative insertions into a musical piece.

n) *swift and secure flight*: This concept of music was repeated in *U*, 'Sirens':

> It soared, a bird, it held its flight, a swift pure cry, soar silver orb, it leaped serene, speeding, sustained, to come, don't spin it out too long long breath ...

172

Edward Martyn, no Ignatius Gallaher (174a)

cover. Freddy Malins, who had listened with his head perched sideways to hear her better, was still applauding when every one else had ceased and talking animatedly to his mother, who nodded her head gravely and slowly in acquiescence. At last, when he could clap no more, he stood up suddenly and hurried across the room to Aunt Julia, whose hand he seized and held in both his hands, shaking it when words failed him or the catch in his voice proved too much for him.

—I was just telling my mother, he said, I never heard you sing so well, never. No, I never heard your voice so good as it is to-night. Now! Would you believe that now? That's the truth. Upon my word and honour that's the truth. I never heard your voice sound so fresh and so ... so clear and fresh, never—

Aunt Julia smiled broadly and murmured something about compliments as she released her hand from his grasp. Mr Browne extended his open hand towards her and said to those who were near him in the manner of a showman introducing a prodigy to an audience:

—Miss Julia Morkan, my latest discovery!—

He was laughing very heartily at this himself when Freddy Malins turned to him and said:

—Well, Browne, if you're serious you might make a worse discovery. All I can say is I never heard her sing half so well as long as I am coming here. And that's the honest truth—

—Neither did I, said Mr Browne. I think her voice has greatly improved—

Aunt Julia shrugged her shoulders and said with meek pride;

—Thirty years ago I hadn't a bad voice as voices go—

—I often told Julia, said Aunt Kate emphatically, that she was simply thrown away in that choir. But she never would be said by me—

She turned as if to appeal to the good sense of the others against a refractory child while Aunt Julia gazed in front of her, a vague smile of reminiscence playing on her face.

—No, continued Aunt Kate, she wouldn't be said or led by anyone, slaving there in that choir night and day, night and day. Six o'clock on Christmas morning! And all for what?—

—Well, isn't it for the honour of God, Aunt Kate? asked Mary Jane, twisting round on the piano-stool and smiling—

Aunt Kate turned fiercely on her niece and said:

a) *the honest truth*: A frequent Dublin pleonasm, often 'the God's honest truth'.

b) *shrugged her shoulders*: A 'successful' Gallicism.

c) *Thirty years ago*: i.e. in the early 1870s. See 178c. Joyce in time made the same claim (177q).

d) *never would be said by me*: A dialect or archaic use of the verb, meaning to submit to advice or orders. By 1900 the usage was rare, but Aunt Kate is not young.

e) *refractory*: Unruly, but with the underlying meaning of stubborn or unmanageable. The word also means 'resistant to disease or fire', as the Phoenix (120c) is said to be.

f) *Six o'clock on Christmas morning!*: Aunt Julia would very likely also have been working hard at Midnight Mass, and so have had virtually no sleep.

a) *the pope to turn out the women*: Pope Pius X's decree *Tra le sollecitudini* (*motu proprio*) of November 1903 was a topical controversy. It was an informal document, drawn up on the Pope's own initiative, and was followed in December by another: *Circa choros mixtos in missi cantatis*. The Dublin *Daily Express* reported that Pius had issued yet another decree in late December, in which he clarified his position by prescribing Gregorian chant, and condemning the transformation of church services into concerts. The *Figaro and Irish Gentlewoman* crisply observed:

> Thus a number of women musicians have suddenly lost a valuable means of livelihood without any compensation. The deprivation is felt severely in Ireland as well as on the continent ... the Pope himself might easily devote at least one year's 'Peter's Pence' to repairing some of the havoc he has wrought.

Pius had recently assumed office in 1903, succeeding the late Leo 'Lux Upon Lux' XIII. Earlier that year, Edward Martyn (46b) had approached the archbishop and offered to endow the choir of the Pro-Cathedral (for £10,000), provided that it became all-male. This was duly done and was later found to conform in every way with the papal instructions. In a letter to Aunt Josephine on the last day of 1904, Joyce wrote, 'I spit upon the image of the Tenth Pius'. He has since been canonised.

b) *whippersnappers*: Jumped-up, insignificant young fellows. William Makepeace Thackeray in his *Paris Notebook* described the local menfolk:

> Not that he feared such fellows as these – little whippersnappers – our men would eat them.

It is certainly a contrast with the Paris women described by Ignatius Gallaher (67f). When Winston Churchill was a little whippersnapper living in the Viceregal Lodge in the Phoenix Park, he took the term literally by attacking the equally young future Earl of Iveagh with a whip, damaging his forehead severely. A doctor prescribed caustic soda, and the Guinness eyebrows never regrew.

c) *the other persuasion*: A cliché nearly as grinding as Crofton's in 'Grace': '*we worship at different altars, but our belief is the same*' (148f).

d) *I don't question the pope's being right*: Neither did John of Tuam in 'Grace' (151f).

e) *that Father Healey*: The common name of a common occupation. He is possibly the much-travelled brother of Mrs Daniel in *SH* (she being based on Mrs Sheehy).

f) *hungry ... quarrelsome ... thirsty ... quarrelsome*: Echoes of the Irish Famine, and of its aftermath of political unrest.

g) *cloak*: See 133a. As well as attempting to revive the Irish language, some revivalists adopted traditional Gaelic dress, or stylised versions thereof.

h) *Molly*: Miss Ivors' first name is shared with that epitome of Dublin death (and life-in-death), Molly Malone:

> And her ghost wheels her barrow
> Through streets broad and narrow
> Crying cockles and mussels
> Alive alive – o.

The name was quite a common one, usually a diminutive of Mary, or Máire. Marion Tweedy was transmogrified into Molly Bloom. Synge's fiancée had the splendid offstage name of Molly Allgood (and was the first Pegeen Mike of *Playboy of the Western World*). Bernard Shaw's final fling was to be with another actress, Molly Tompkins, who had 'eyes like muscatel grapes'.

i) *To take a pick itself*: i.e. (as in 'The Sisters') to take even a little to eat.

j) *two steps up the quay*: Irish meiosis. She means a short distance away.

—I know all about the honour of God, Mary Jane, but I think it's not at all honourable for the pope to turn out the women out of the choirs that have slaved there all their lives and put little whippersnappers of boys over their heads. I suppose it is for the good of the Church if the pope does it. But it's not just, Mary Jane, and it's not right—

She had worked herself into a passion and would have continued in defence of her sister for it was a sore subject with her but Mary Jane, seeing that all the dancers had come back, intervened pacifically:

—Now, Aunt Kate, you're giving scandal to Mr Browne, who is of the other persuasion—

Aunt Kate turned to Mr Browne, who was grinning at this allusion to his religion, and said hastily:

—O, I don't question the pope's being right. I'm only a stupid old woman and I wouldn't presume to do such a thing. But there's such a thing as common everyday politeness and gratitude. And if I were in Julia's place I'd tell that Father Healey straight up to his face . . .—

—And besides, Aunt Kate, said Mary Jane, we really are all hungry and when we are hungry we are all very quarrelsome—

—And when we are thirsty we are also quarrelsome, added Mr Browne—

—So that we had better go to supper, said Mary Jane, and finish the discussion afterwards—

On the landing outside the drawing-room Gabriel found his wife and Mary Jane trying to persuade Miss Ivors to stay for supper. But Miss Ivors, who had put on her hat and was buttoning her cloak, would not stay. She did not feel in the least hungry and she had already overstayed her time.

—But only for ten minutes, Molly, said Mrs Conroy. That won't delay you—

—To take a pick itself, said Mary Jane, after all your dancing—

—I really couldn't, said Miss Ivors—

—I am afraid you didn't enjoy yourself at all, said Mary Jane hopelessly—

—Ever so much, I assure you, said Miss Ivors, but you really must let me run off now—

—But how can you get home? asked Mrs Conroy—

—O, it's only two steps up the quay—

Edward VII and his subjects in Connemara

a) *I'll see you home*: This is doubly improper, as Gabriel is needed to carve the goose, and because he must be aware of a certain frisson between them.

b) *you're the comical girl*: Irish idiom, but Gretta's 'Molly' is in friendly contrast to Gabriel's 'Miss Ivors'.

c) Beannacht libh: Goodbye, literally 'blessing to ye'. In *SH*, when Stephen walks Emma home after she has spent the evening studying Old Irish, she says goodnight to him with an '*Au revoir*'.

d) *blankly*: The word anticipates Cochrane at the beginning of *U*, 'Nestor':

> The boy's blank face asked the blank window.

e) *Where on earth is Gabriel?*: A good question to ask of an archangel (and Gabriel has already been asked, by Miss Ivors, who he is). Stanislaus Joyce wrote to Herbert Gorman telling how in July 1909 Jim had taken his ticket from him (96c) and gone back to Dublin from Trieste:

> He was met at the station of Westland Row in Dublin by a family group who asked him 'Where's Stannie?' It's a question I have often asked myself. Yours very truly . . .

f) *stage to let*: There is as yet no performance.

g) *a flock of geese*: A goose was much more common as a Christmas dish than it is today. Although Gabriel says he would carve a 'flock' of them, the correct word for a living collectivity is 'skein' or 'gaggle'.

h) *crust crumbs*: In *U*, 'Calypso', Bloom's fondness for crustcrumbs on his liverslices is mentioned.

i) *spiced beef*: A particularly Irish Christmas dish, being beef long marinaded in a mixture of saltpetre and spices.

j) *side-dishes*: This spread is reminiscent of that in Keats' 'The Eve of Saint Agnes' (XXX) (whose feast-day pends on 21 January):

> a heap
> Of candied apple, quince, and plum, and gourd
> With jellies soother than the creamy curd,
> And lucent syrups, tinct with cinnamon;
> Manna and dates, in argosy, transferr'd
> From Fez; and spiced dainties, every one,
> From silken Samarkand to cedar'd Lebanon.

Joyce wrote 'The Dead' in 1907 in Rome, near where Keats had died of tuberculosis at the Spanish Steps. He had a 1903 edition of Keats' *Poems*, but little to eat.

k) *minsters of jelly*: Not containers of any kind, but cathedrals of confectionery.

l) *Smyrna figs*: Still the attraction of the east, and a

Gabriel hesitated a moment and said:

a —If you will allow me, Miss Ivors, I'll see you home if you really are obliged to go—

But Miss Ivors broke away from them.

—I won't hear of it, she cried. For goodness' sake go in to your suppers and don't mind me. I'm quite well able to take care of myself—

b —Well, you're the comical girl, Molly, said Mrs Conroy frankly—

c —*Beannacht libh*, cried Miss Ivors, with a laugh, as she ran down the staircase—

Mary Jane gazed after her, a moody puzzled expression on her face, while Mrs Conroy leaned over the banisters to listen for the halldoor. Gabriel asked himself was he the cause of her abrupt departure. But she did not seem to be in ill humour:

d she had gone away laughing. He stared blankly down the staircase.

At that moment Aunt Kate came toddling out of the supper-room, almost wringing her hands in despair.

e —Where is Gabriel? she cried. Where on earth is Gabriel?

f There's everyone waiting in there, stage to let, and nobody to carve the goose!—

—Here I am, Aunt Kate! cried Gabriel, with sudden

g animation, ready to carve a flock of geese, if necessary—

A fat brown goose lay at one end of the table and at the other end, on a bed of creased paper strewn with sprigs of parsley, lay a great ham, stripped of its outer skin and peppered

h over with crust crumbs, a neat paper frill round its shin and

i beside this was a round of spiced beef. Between these rival ends

jk ran parallel lines of side-dishes: two little minsters of jelly, red and yellow; a shallow dish full of blocks of blancmange and red jam, a large green leaf-shaped dish with a stalk-shaped handle, on which lay bunches of purple raisins and peeled almonds, a companion dish on which lay a solid rectangle of

l Smyrna figs, a dish of custard topped with grated nutmeg, a small bowl full of chocolates and sweets wrapped in gold and silver papers, and a glass vase in which stood some tall celery stalks. In the centre of the table there stood, as sentries to a fruit-stand which upheld a pyramid of oranges and American apples, two squat old-fashioned decanters of cut glass, one

m containing port and the other dark sherry. On the closed square

hint of Mr Eugenides in T.S. Eliot's *The Waste Land*.
m) *port*: It is no longer port-wine (92c). We are a step up the social ladder.

175

a) *lay in waiting*: The words suggest an ambush about to happen.

b) *squads*: Where the decanters are sentries, the lesser drinks are merely squaddies.

c) *stout and ale and minerals*: The first is the classic Dublin beverage and diphthong, which Dr Johnson defined as 'A cant name for strong beer'. Swift, however, could write of a hack (in 'To Stella, Who Collected and Transcribed his Poems'):

> Should but his muse descending drop
> A slice of bread and mutton-chop,
> Or kindly, when his credit's out,
> Surprise him with a pint of stout.

The second word is one that Stephen realises sounds so different between his English dean of studies and himself (*P* V.1), and the third is often pronounced in Ireland with a Lilylike three syllables.

d) *brown and red labels*: Descriptions of (e.g.) Guinness and Bass (58k) respectively. An old Dublin joke has it that the best biblical text for Guinness should be from Hebrews XXX.

e) *transverse green sashes*: Political or military interpretations are secondary to the point that the sizes, colours and labels of the bottles are all accurate.

f) *he was an expert carver*: As the narrator is not omniscient (158c), this might be Gabriel's opinion. But a carver in Shakespearean terms was a bad actor, one given to affected gestures and amorous advances.

g) *Miss Higgins*: See 81b.

h) *This was Mary Jane's idea*: The conservatism of the sisters at their annual event is marked.

i) *walking on each other's heels*: See 6h.

j) *everyone had been well served*: A faint echo of Tiny Tim's 'God bless us every one' in *A Christmas Carol* (with Oliver Twist salivating in the background). Of all those known to be at the meal, only Gretta neither speaks nor – until she serves out the pudding – is she even mentioned (and then only as 'Gabriel's wife').

Stout flowing by on the Liffey

a piano a pudding in a huge yellow dish lay in waiting
b and behind it were three squads of bottles of stout and
c ale and minerals, drawn up according to the colours of their
d uniforms, the first two black, with brown and red labels,
e the third and smallest squad white, with transverse green
sashes.

Gabriel took his seat boldly at the head of the table and, having looked to the edge of the carver, plunged his fork firmly into the goose. He felt quite at ease now, for he was an
f expert carver and liked nothing better than to find himself at the head of a well-laden table.

—Miss Furlong, what shall I send you? he asked. A wing or a slice of the breast?—

g —Just a small slice of the breast—

—Miss Higgins, what for you?—

—O, anything at all, Mr Conroy—

While Gabriel and Miss Daly exchanged plates of goose and plates of ham and spiced beef, Lily went from guest to guest
h with a dish of hot floury potatoes wrapped in a white napkin. This was Mary Jane's idea and she had also suggested apple sauce for the goose but Aunt Kate had said that plain roast goose without any apple sauce had always been good enough for her and she hoped she might never eat worse. Mary Jane waited on her pupils and saw that they got the best slices, and Aunt Kate and Aunt Julia opened and carried across from the piano bottles of stout and ale for the gentlemen and bottles of minerals for the ladies. There was a great deal of confusion and laughter and noise, the noise of orders and counterorders, of knives and forks, of corks and glass-stoppers. Gabriel began to carve second helpings as soon as he had finished the first round without serving himself. Every one protested loudly so that he compromised by taking a long draught of stout, for he had found the carving hot work. Mary Jane settled down quietly to her supper but Aunt Kate and Aunt Julia were still toddling
i round the table, walking on each other's heels, getting in each other's way and giving each other unheeded orders. Mr Browne begged of them to sit down and eat their suppers and so did Gabriel but they said there was time enough so that, at last, Freddy Malins stood up and capturing Aunt Kate, plumped her down on her chair amid general laughter.

j When everyone had been well served Gabriel said, smiling:

a) *what vulgar people call stuffing*: More properly, forcemeat, or more jocularly, stopping.

b) *let him or her speak*: Gabriel is invoking the marriage service, concerning impediments.

c) *Lily came forward with three potatoes*: This is the last mention of her, and she is as busy as ever.

d) *the opera company*: J.F. Byrne mentioned (in his *Silent Years*(56d)) how he and Joyce would go to the Carl Rosa Company and the Rouseby whenever they came to Dublin. At Christmas 1903, however, the visiting company was the Moody-Manners Opera Company.

e) *Theatre Royal*: The patent for a theatre royal in Dublin went back to the 1630s, when Sir William Davenant (reputedly the illegitimate son of William Shakespeare) was granted a licence as Master of the Revels there. A new building opened in 1821 (16g) in Hawkins Street, near Burgh Quay, with *The Comedy of Errors*. Until its destruction by fire in 1880, it was Dublin's prime venue. Among its performers were Edmund Kean, the majestic Siddons, Henry Irving, Titiens, Jenny Lind and Adelina Patti. The theatre reopened in 1897.

f) *a negro chieftain*: The pantomime at the Gaiety at Christmas 1903 was *The Babes in the Wood*, a tale of doomed innocence, like the Princes in the Tower. A review (178h) explains that Freddy's 'negro chieftain' was actually the 'Chocolate Coloured Coon': evidently Freddy was drunk at the pantomime too. As pantomime was far below opera or *bel canto* in esteem, he is lowering the tone of the discussion. Contemporary blacks included the Bohea Brothers, 'Banjoists to the Royal Family', who are the 'coloured coons in white duck suits' in *U*, 'Circe'.

'Only a black'

g) *the Gaiety*: Still in South King Street, off Stephen's Green. It opened in 1871 with a production of Goldsmith's *She Stoops to Conquer*. Sarah Bernhardt played *La Dame aux Camellias* (the source of *La Traviata*) at the Gaiety in 1881. Joyce went there often, as his father knew the Gunns, who ran it.

h) *Teddy*: Mr Browne is suffering from memory loss consistent with his age and his toping.

i) *only a black*: The word has been full circle and more. In July 1829 there was established in South Frederick Street the Dublin Negro's Friend Society, to strive for the 'utter abolition' of slavery and promote related ameliorations. The board of managers included such redoubtable Dublin names as Major Sirr, Dr Orpen and Mr Bewley, with subscriptions to be handled by Mr La Touche.

j) Mignon: A very popular nineteenth-century opera by Ambroise Thomas (1866), based on the priceless pages of Goethe's *Wilhelm Meister*.

k) *Georgina Burns*: A celebrated soprano of the 1880s, she made her Dublin debut in 1878 with *The Bohemian Girl* at the Theatre Royal. She sometimes sang with Barton M'Guckin (165e). In his diary, Stanislaus mentions her singing *Mignon*, describing how Uncle Willie (Murray) commented on the 'extraordinary flexibility' of Georgina Burns' singing of Philine's polonaise 'I am Titania' from that opera.

l) *Tietjens* [etc]: 'Mdlle' Theresa Titiens (1831–77), German dramatic soprano, and a major figure. Her first Dublin performance was in 1859 (in *Les Huguenots*) and her last (in *Il Trovatore*) in 1876. She was exceptionally popular in Dublin. *Ilma di Murzka*, or Murska (1836–89), was a Croatian soprano, who sang widely in Europe and North America. She made her Dublin debut in 1869, appearing with a Madame Sinico (104). Among her acclaimed roles was Ophelia in Ambroise Thomas' *Hamlet*. She died by suicide. For *Campanini*, see 127c.

m) *the great Trebelli* [etc]: Zelia Trebelli (1838–92), French mezzo-soprano. She appeared first in Dublin in 1863 in *Martha*, and often subsequently with Titiens. Her 'Oh! Araby' was a great favourite. Antonio *Giuglini* (1827–65) was an Italian tenor, who is remembered by Bloom in *U*, 'Nausicaa'. J.B. Hall (129a) called him 'the greatest tenor in the world'. He made his Dublin debut in 1857 (in *Il Trovatore*) and appeared as Guialtiero in the first Italian production of *The Bohemian Girl*. In the early 1860s he and Titiens sang much in Dublin. He had a meteoric career and was extremely talented, but he died of madness. In a letter in July 1937, Joyce recalled how 'R.J. Thornton ('Tom Kernan')' (137f) used to tell

—Now, if anyone wants a little more of what vulgar people call stuffing let him or her speak—

A chorus of voices invited him to begin his own supper and Lily came forward with three potatoes which she had reserved for him.

—Very well, said Gabriel amiably, as he took another preparatory draught, kindly forget my existence, ladies and gentlemen, for a few minutes—

He set to his supper and took no part in the conversation with which the table covered Lily's removal of the plates. The subject of talk was the opera company which was then at the Theatre Royal. Mr Bartell D'Arcy, the tenor, a dark-complexioned young man with a smart moustache, praised very highly the leading contralto of the company but Miss Furlong thought she had a rather vulgar style of production. Freddy Malins said there was a negro chieftain singing in the second part of the Gaiety pantomime who had one of the finest tenor voices he had ever heard.

—Have you heard him? he asked Mr Bartell D'Arcy across the table—

—No, answered Mr Bartell D'Arcy carelessly—

—Because, Freddy Malins explained, now I'd be curious to hear your opinion of him. I think he has a grand voice—

—It takes Teddy to find out the really good things, said Mr Browne familiarly to the table—

—And why couldn't he have a voice too? asked Freddy Malins sharply. Is it because he's only a black?—

Nobody answered this question and Mary Jane led the table back to the legitimate opera. One of her pupils had given her a pass for *Mignon*. Of course it was very fine, she said, but it made her think of poor Georgina Burns. Mr Browne could go back farther still, to the old Italian companies that used to come to Dublin – Tietjens, Ilma de Murzka, Campanini, the great Trebelli, Giuglini, Ravelli, Aramburo. Those were the days, he said, when there was something like singing to be heard in Dublin. He told too of how the top gallery of the old Royal used to be packed night after night, of how one night an Italian tenor had sung five encores to *Let me like a Soldier fall*, introducing a high C every time, and of how the gallery boys would sometimes in their enthusiasm unyoke the horses from the carriage of some great *prima donna* and pull her themselves

him about Giuglini flying his big kite on Sandymount Strand. Luigi *Ravelli* (b.1848) was prominent in the 1880s with the Naples Opera Company and was best known for his singing in *Maritana*. Antonio *Aramburo* (1838–1912) was a Spanish tenor with a European reputation, also successful in South America. He and Campanini were rivals.

n) *the old Royal*: See e.

o) *night after night*: A recollection of the opening lines of these stories.

p) *Let me like a Soldier fall*: Don Caesare's song from *Maritana*. When Joyce was being caricatured in 1934 for the magazine *transition*, he stipulated that the picture show him with the sheet music of this song sticking out of his pocket. The song is a stock fantasy of dying an honourable death. The second verse ends:

> Tho' o'er my clay no
> banner wave
> Nor trumpet requiem
> swell,
> Enough they murmur o'er
> my grave
> He like a soldier fell
> Enough they murmur o'er
> my grave
> He like a soldier fell.

q) *a high C every time*: In his promotional campaign for the opera singer John Sullivan in the early 1930s, Joyce continued to show a keen interest in the pattern of notes sung. His puff for that tenor mentions his

456 Gs, 93 A flats, 54 B flats, 15 Bs, 19 Cs, and 2 C sharps. Nobody else can do it.

a) *through the streets to her hotel*: In early October 1868, Mlle Titiens appeared in Dublin in Weber's *Oberon*, where she sang Tom Moore's 'The Last Rose of Summer', literally (and actually) to the sound of a pin dropping. Afterwards the gallery boys, including the medical students there, took the Queen of Song back to her hotel. They fastened ropes (obtained from a convenient chandler's) to her carriage and set off. Others on the roof were letting off fireworks. On arriving at Dawson Street, one strand of the procession went up it, while the other one went along Nassau Street 'the result being a violent collision against Morrison's Hotel'. But La Titiens was staying at the Shelbourne. There was difficulty and delay and confusion, and police concern for the safety of the *diva*, but a multilingual student reassured her. Finally she got back to the right hotel. Despite the wet night, a passage had to be cleared for her, and the enthusiasts laid down a carpet of their own coats. She went inside the Shelbourne but the crowd stayed on for more than an hour, disregarding the coy message of her low-lighted window. Eventually the police had a word with her and she reappeared to tell the crowd that she would sing if they then dispersed. This was agreed to, and so she sang again 'The Last Rose of Summer'.

b) Dinorah, Lucrezia Borgia: The first was by Giacomo Meyerbeer (1859). Mlle di Murska played in it many times. The fair copy of the story mentioned Bellini's *Norma* instead of this. The second opera was by Gaetano Donizetti (1833). Titiens was famous for (among many other substantial things) nearly dying in the role. She and Campanini and Trebelli all sang in the same production in 1872.

c) *Because they could not get the voices*: One contemporary international connoisseur, Hermann Klein, wrote in 1903:

> In 1872 the patrons of opera were complaining that they no longer possessed an Italian tenor of front rank.

d) *Milan*: The third city in Bartell D'Arcy's list was changed by Joyce from Berlin to Vienna to Berlin again, before Milan was adopted.

e) *Caruso*: Enrico Caruso (1873–1921), world-famous tenor, just beginning to become well known at the time of the story. In 1901, after a controversial performance in his native Naples, he vowed never to perform there again – and never did. (So Joyce felt about Dublin.) The following year he appeared at Covent Garden, and he flourished thereafter. Joyce's sketch 'From a Banned Writer to a Banned Singer', was published in the *New Stateman* in 1932, and describes 'Enrico' and two others:

> ... three dulcetest of our singers, in liontamers overcoats, holy communion ties, and clique-claquehats.

f) *picking a bone*: For one whose life has revolved around musical Dublin, Aunt Kate has been very silent. Like Gretta later, she is thinking of a person long ago who used to sing. Nobody suspects any more of the matter, but everyone around the table has a private past. Of hers we learn no more.

g) *Parkinson*: Speculation about his identity has been surprisingly muted. It has been suspected that he did not exist, or that he was named after the 1890s Wagnerophile, or perhaps the disease, or the biographer of Cardinal Vaughan, or various Americans.

Alternatively, the name was possibly derived thus: Robert Parkinson MP was the High Sheriff of County Louth, Ireland, in 1770. His nephew and heir was Thomas Fortescue, also an MP and High Sheriff of the county in turn, who married the daughter of the Town Clerk of Dublin (153n). Eventually a descendant, Chichester Samuel Parkinson (1823–98), assumed the additional name of Fortescue by Royal Warrant. He was Chief Secretary for Ireland during the Prime Ministership of Earl Russell in 1865–60.

In 1900 in the XL Café in Grafton Street, the Sheehy sisters' *Cupid's Confidante* was performed. In 1901 at the Antient Concert Rooms, Joyce acted in the revival. His performance as the prize cad, Geoffrey Fortescue, was widely praised by J.B. Hall amongst others. So: if the political Parkinson was Fortescue, and the dramatic Fortescue was Joyce, then Aunt Kate's tenor with the sweetest voice was algebraically the young artificer, Sunny Jim himself.

But, there was in fact a real Parkinson: he was born in Scorton, Lancashire, and developed his musical skills by playing the organ in the local Catholic church. Like Barton M'Guckin, he joined the well-known Carl Rosa Opera Company (177d), and he enjoyed a good reputation. Later he retired from singing to pursue theatre management. His obscurity among the diners is in inverse proportion to how important he is to Aunt Kate. On the standing of the company, consider Corley's remark to Stephen in *U*, 'Eumaeus':

> God, you've to book ahead, man, you'd think it was for the Carl Rosa.

a through the streets to her hotel. Why did they never play the
b grand old operas now, he asked, *Dinorah, Lucrezia Borgia*?
c Because they could not get the voices to sing them: that was
why.

—O, well, said Mr Bartell D'Arcy, I presume there are as
good singers to-day as there were then—

Where are they? asked Mr Browne defiantly—

d —In London, Paris, Milan, said Mr Bartell D'Arcy warmly.
e I suppose Caruso, for example, is quite as good, if not better
than any of the men you have mentioned—

—Maybe so, said Mr Browne. But I may tell you I doubt
it strongly—

—O, I'd give anything to hear Caruso sing, said Mary Jane—

f —For me, said Aunt Kate, who had been picking a bone,
there was only one tenor. To please me, I mean. But I suppose
none of you ever heard of him—

—Who was he, Miss Morkan? asked Mr Bartell D'Arcy
politely—

g —His name, said Aunt Kate, was Parkinson. I heard him
when he was in his prime and I think he had then the purest
tenor voice that was ever put into a man's throat—

—Strange, said Mr Bartell D'Arcy. I never even heard of
him—

—Yes, yes, Miss Morkan is right, said Mr Browne. I remember hearing of old Parkinson, but he's too far back for me—

—A beautiful, pure, sweet, mellow English tenor, said Aunt
Kate with enthusiasm—

Gabriel having finished, the huge pudding was transferred
to the table. The clatter of forks and spoons began again.
Gabriel's wife served out spoonfuls of the pudding and passed
the plates down the table. Midway down they were held up
by Mary Jane, who replenished them with raspberry or orange
jelly or with blancmange and jam. The pudding was of Aunt
Julia's making and she received praises for it from all quarters.
She herself said that it was not quite brown enough.

—Well, I hope, Miss Morkan, said Mr Browne, that I'm
h brown enough for you because, you know, I'm all brown—

All the gentlemen, except Gabriel, ate some of the pudding
out of compliment to Aunt Julia. As Gabriel never ate sweets
the celery had been left for him. Freddy Malins also took a
stalk of celery and ate it with his pudding. He had been told

h) *I'm brown enough*: The sentiments also of Freddy's chieftain (177f). The *Daily Express*
reviewed the Gaiety show
thus:

> The outlook of Mr E.H.
> Elliott, the 'Chocolate Col-
> oured Coon', is one of the
> best and most pleasing
> artists in the Company, and
> will, no doubt, become
> very Popular.

Elliott (actually G.H.) performed until the 1940s, the
heir of one of the earliest
blackface acts, Eugene Stratton (who was at the Theatre
Royal on the night of
Bloomsday). The younger
corked-man blithely per-
formed Stratton's material,
including 'All Coons Look
Alike To Me'. In Freddy's
condition, that is true, and Mr
Brown isn't too clear about
who he's talking to either.

Caruso's self-caricature (e)

a) *her son was going down to Mount Melleray*: This was no casual jaunt, as Freddy is off to be 'dried out'. The name is the colloquial one for the Abbey of St Bernard de Trappe, in County Waterford. It was founded in 1831, by the Cistercian monks of La Trappe after they were obliged to leave France (though the Trappists were founded in 1140). They settled on the side of the Knockmealdown Mountains, on the borders of Tipperary.

b) *like that*: There are indeed Anglican monasteries where the spiritually weary may rest for a few days of prayer and contemplation, but not in Ireland. Mr Browne is not as expert on monastic matters as his putative forebear (164a).

c) *the monks never spoke*: The Trappist branch of the Cistercians was silent.

d) *slept in their coffins*: Other such practitioners included Sarah Bernhardt and John Donne. The Trappists themselves were not required to sleep in their coffins: the story is a lay exaggeration of their already rigorous devotion. The detail nonetheless explicitly links the first story of the collection with this, the last. In 'The Sisters', the anonymous young narrator thinks of Father Flynn smiling in his coffin: in 'The Dead', Gabriel and the rest of the grown-ups hear of other religious men sleeping in their coffins, in a building thought of by Joyce as 'Flynn's Academy'.

e) *make up for the sins*: Expiation.

f) *all the sinners in the outside world*: Though some on the inside were not quite up to the knocker either (150c).

g) *their last end*: (198k). From the Book of Numbers (XXIII.10), Jacob is referred to:

> Let me die the death of the righteous, and let my last end be like his!

h) *the subject ... was buried*: A logical thing to do with a discussion of coffins.

i) *whispered something*: Presumably that he was going to have to drink a toast to the Misses Morkan.

Mount Melleray (a)

that celery was a capital thing for the blood and he was just then under doctor's care. Mrs Malins, who had been silent all through the supper, said that her son was going down to Mount Melleray in a week or so. The table then spoke of Mount Melleray, how bracing the air was down there, how hospitable the monks were and how they never asked for a penny-piece from their guests.

—And do you mean to say, asked Mr Browne incredulously, that a chap can go down there and put up there as if it were a hotel and live on the fat of the land and then come away without paying a farthing?—

—O, most people give some donation to the monastery when they leave, said Mary Jane—

—I wish we had an institution like that in our Church, said Mr Browne candidly—

He was astonished to hear that the monks never spoke, got up at two in the morning and slept in their coffins. He asked what they did it for.

—That's the rule of the order, said Aunt Kate firmly—

—Yes, but why? asked Mr Browne—

Aunt Kate repeated that it was the rule, that was all. Mr Browne still seemed not to understand. Freddy Malins explained to him, as best he could, that the monks were trying to make up for the sins committed by all the sinners in the outside world. The explanation was not very clear for Mr Browne grinned and said:

—I like that idea very much but wouldn't a comfortable spring bed do them as well as a coffin?—

—The coffin, said Mary Jane, is to remind them of their last end—

As the subject had grown lugubrious it was buried in a silence of the table during which Mrs Malins could be heard saying to her neighbour in an indistinct undertone:

—They are very good men, the monks, very pious men—

The raisins and almonds and figs and apples and oranges and chocolates and sweets were now passed about the table and Aunt Julia invited all the guests to have either port or sherry. At first Mr Bartell D'Arcy refused to take either but one of his neighbours nudged him and whispered something to him, upon which he allowed his glass to be filled. Gradually as the last glasses were being filled the conversation ceased. A pause

Diversions of Christmas 1903

a) *gazing up at the lighted windows*: This almost 1890s image is an obvious invocation of the opening of the collection. Yeats' friend Arthur Symons had published in 1892 a volume of poems called *Silhouettes*, a title which Joyce recycled for his own early prose sketches. The closest echo with this passage, however, is found in Oscar Wilde's 'The Harlot's House':

We caught the tread of dancing feet,
We loitered down the moonlit street,
And stopped beneath the harlot's house.

Inside, above the din and fray,
We heard the loud musicians play
The 'Treues Liebes Herz' of Strauss.

Like strange mechanical grotesques,
Making fantastic arabesques,
The shadows raced across the blind.

We watched the ghostly dancers spin
To sound of horn and violin,
Like black leaves wheeling in the wind.

Like wire-pulled automatons,
Slim-silhouetted skeletons
Went sidling through the slow quadrille.

They took each other by the hand,
And danced a stately saraband;
Their laughter echoed thin and shrill.

Sometimes a clockwork puppet pressed
A phantom lover to her breast,
Sometimes they seemed to try to sing.

Sometimes a horrible marionette
Came out and smoked its cigarette
Upon the steps like a live thing.

Then, turning to my love, I said,
'The dead are dancing with the dead,
The dust is whirling with the dust.'

But she – she heard the violin,
And left my side, and entered in:
Love passed into the house of lust.

The suddenly the tune went false,
The dancers wearied of the waltz,
The shadows ceased to wheel and whirl.

And down the long and silent street,
The dawn, with silver-sandalled feet,
Crept like a frightened girl.

b) *The Wellington Monument*: See 172c.

c) *westward*: Gabriel's imagination anticipates the end of the story (198b). The word also recalls Berkeley's famous prediction (in 'On the Prospect of Planting Arts and Learning in America') of a new golden age:

Not such as Europe breeds in her decay;
  Such as she bred when fresh and young,
When heavenly Flame did animate her Clay,
  By future poets shall be sung.
Westward the Course of Empire takes its Way …

d) *Fifteen Acres*: Far more substantial than might be supposed (and a symbol of the fifteen stories of *D* perhaps). It comprises about 200 acres of the 1760 of the Phoenix Park, and was used for military reviews and parades. It was formerly a duelling ground. The park, formerly the demesne of the Knights Hospitallers, was opened to the citizens of Dublin by Lord Chesterfield in 1747. The Phoenix, though excellently redolent of Joyce's themes of rebirth and universality (so too Eden Quay, Adam and Eve's, the King's Inns etc), gets its name from a spring called Fionn-uisge ('White-water'), later Feenisk. As the waters were 'a chalybeate spa', famous for health-giving and restorative properties, the anglicisation is quite appropriate.

e) *my poor powers as a speaker*: Stanislaus said that Gabriel's speech was an exact pastiche of the orations of John Joyce.

f) *take the will for the deed*: Attention-seeking modesty, along the lines of 'the spirit is willing but the flesh is weak'. In *U*, 'Aeolus', Myles Crawford tells J. J. O'Molloy:

Sorry Jack. You must take the will for the deed.

g) *the victims*: *Victima* is a beast for sacrifice.

h) *a circle in the air*: As in several of the other stories, the image of the circle conveys the immobility of Dublin life, as if virtually everyone had one foot nailed to the floor, or was constrained by the city's elegant curving roads and canals. Various Dubliners are being tortured (often by themselves) on various parts of the wheel. What 'The Dead' commodiously adds to the image is the cycle of birth, life, death and rebirth.

i) *no tradition which does it so much honour*: Joyce was making sincere amends for the 'scrupulous meanness' of the other stories. Mary Wollstonecraft, who had the same relationship to Shelley as Mrs Mooney will to Bob Doran, wrote of Dublin that it was 'the most hospitable city I ever passed through'.

followed, broken only by the noise of the wine and by unsett-
lings of chairs. The Misses Morkan, all three, looked down at
the tablecloth. Some one coughed once or twice and then a
few gentlemen patted the table gently as a signal for silence.
The silence came and Gabriel pushed back his chair and stood
up.

The patting at once grew louder in encouragement and then
ceased altogether. Gabriel leaned his ten trembling fingers on
the tablecloth and smiled nervously at the company. Meeting
a row of upturned faces he raised his eyes to the chandelier.
The piano was playing a waltz tune and he could hear the skirts
sweeping against the drawing-room door. People, perhaps,
were standing in the snow on the quay outside, gazing up at
the lighted windows and listening to the waltz music. The air
was pure there. In the distance lay the park where the trees
were weighted with snow. The Wellington Monument wore
a gleaming cap of snow that flashed westward over the white
field of Fifteen Acres.

He began:

—Ladies and Gentlemen—

—It has fallen to my lot this evening, as in years past, to
perform a very pleasing task but a task for which I am afraid
my poor powers as a speaker are all too inadequate—

—No, no! said Mr Browne—

—But, however that may be, I can only ask you to-night
to take the will for the deed and to lend me your attention for
a few moments while I endeavour to express to you in words
what my feelings are on this occasion—

—Ladies and Gentlemen, it is not the first time that we
have gathered together under this hospitable roof, around this
hospitable board. It is not the first time that we have been the
recipients – or perhaps, I had better say, the victims – of the
hospitality of certain good ladies—

He made a circle in the air with his arm and paused. Everyone
laughed or smiled at Aunt Kate and Aunt Julia and Mary Jane
who all turned crimson with pleasure. Gabriel went on more
boldly:

—I feel more strongly with every recurring year that our
country has no tradition which does it so much honour and
which it should guard so jealously as that of its hospitality. It
is a tradition that is unique as far as my experience goes (and I

*Like celery, a capital thing for
the blood (179)*

Titiens as Lucrezia Borgia (1771)

The voices of seasons past: from the Musical Times *of February 1874*

a) *not a few places abroad*: Pompous litotes, and Gabriel has visited precious few at home (170b).

b) *a princely failing*: A suggestion of *Hamlet*, further ventilated in *U*, 'Scylla and Charybdis'. In general terms, it is a *felix culpa*, a happy fault – a theme of *FW*, as in the denunciation (23) of Earwicker: 'O foenix culprit!'.

c) *forefathers*: Almost an invocation of another celebration of the dead, Gray's 'Elegy Written in a Country Church-Yard' (1751):

> Each in his narrow Cell for ever laid,
> The rude Forefathers of the Hamlet sleep.

d) *actuated*: Stirred into activity, energised.

e) *in the main*: A private swipe at Miss Ivors for her abruptness. Gabriel's sequence of topics is the same as his mental rehearsal (172d), except that he omits the Browning.

f) *spacious age*: The Wide Streets Commission was set up in Dublin in 1757, and has been widely praised for its achievements in laying out the city. O'Connell Street is (or was) the most spacious example. Though the streets still exist, Gabriel means more than physical space. The word 'spacious' can be used to refer to time. Milton did it in *An Apology for Smectymnuus* (1642):

> Neglecting the main bulk of all that spacious antiquity, which might stunne children but not men.

g) *beyond recall*: A hint of the opening bars of Molly Bloom's evergreen favourite, 'Love's Old Sweet Song' ('Just a Song at Twilight'):

> Once in the dear dead days beyond recall,
> When on the world the mists began to fall,
> Out of the dreams that rose in happy throng
> Low to our hearts, Love sang an old sweet song;
> And in the dusk where fell a firelight gleam,
> Softly it wove itself into our dream …

(Joyce himself was still performing the song in the 1920s in Paris.)

h) *cherish … the memory of those dead*: The phrase recalls the famous poem by the Trinity Fellow, John Kells Ingram, though 'The Memory of the Dead' is better known by its opening line, 'Who fears to speak of Ninety-Eight?'

i) *the world will not willingly let die*: The phrase was recorded by Joyce in an early notebook, 'For "Dubliners"'. The expression comes from the Second Book of Milton's *The Reason of Church Government Urg'd Against Prelaty* (1641), in

a have visited not a few places abroad) among the modern nations. Some would say, perhaps, that with us it is rather a failing than anything to be boasted of. But granted even that,

b it is, to my mind, a princely failing, and one that I trust will long be cultivated among us. Of one thing, at least, I am sure. As long as this one roof shelters the good ladies aforesaid – and I wish from my heart it may do so for many and many a long year to come – the tradition of genuine warm-hearted

c courteous Irish hospitality, which our forefathers have handed down to us and which we in turn must hand down to our descendants, is still alive among us—

A hearty murmur of assent ran round the table. It shot through Gabriel's mind that Miss Ivors was not there and that she had gone away discourteously: and he said with confidence in himself:

—Ladies and Gentlemen—

—A new generation is growing up in our midst, a generation

d actuated by new ideas and new principles. It is serious and enthusiastic for these new ideas and its enthusiasm, even when

e it is misdirected, is, I believe, in the main sincere. But we are living in a sceptical and, if I may use the phrase, a thought-tormented age: and sometimes I fear that this new generation, educated or hypereducated as it is, will lack those qualities of humanity, of hospitality, of kindly humour which belonged to an older day. Listening to-night to the names of all those great singers of the past it seemed to me, I must confess, that

f we were living in a less spacious age. Those days might, without exaggeration, be called spacious days: and if they are

g gone beyond recall let us hope, at least, that in gatherings such as this we shall still speak of them with pride and affec-

h tion, still cherish in our hearts the memory of those dead and

i gone great ones whose fame the world will not willingly let die—

j —Hear, hear! said Mr Browne loudly—

—But yet, continued Gabriel, his voice falling into a softer inflection, there are always in gatherings such as this sadder thoughts that will recur to our minds: thoughts of the past, of

k youth, of changes, of absent faces that we miss here tonight. Our path through life is strewn with many such sad memories: and were we to brood upon them always we could not find the heart to go on bravely with our work among the living.

which Milton wished to confer on posterity something

> written to aftertimes, as they [the world] should not willingly let it die.

j) *absent faces*: There are many: Father Conroy (Constantine) is among the missing. So too are Gabriel's parents, Patrick Morkan and Mr Malins. Poor old Balfe, and Parkinson, and the other composers and singers, are also not physically present. Neither is Michael Furey.

The Wellington Monument

The unerected statue of Balfe (93f)

a) *... living ... living ...*: Gabriel is protesting too much.

b) *bustle and rush*: There is a suggestion of the lush seventeenth-century verse of Richard Crashaw, written after his continental sojourn:

> Him while fresh and fragrant time
> Cherisht in his golden prime,
> The rush of death's unruly wave
> Swept him off into his grave.

c) *good-fellowship*: A good-fellow once meant a mischievous thief (as in Shakespeare's Robin Goodfellow). Good-fellowship then came to mean conviviality (as in the American 'Good Ol' Boys'), and finally, as here, the spirit of true companionship.

d) camaraderie: A casual reminder of the French Revolution, and that death superseded the *jeunesse dorée* (96n).

e) *the Three Graces*: See 172d.

f) *this sally*: Previously 'this allusion', but perhaps Joyce did not wish to put in more allusions (65d).

g) *Paris*: See 172e.

h) *chief hostess*: Aunt Kate. As in 'The Sisters', there is an imbalance in the relationship of the siblings.

i) *perennial youth*: As so often in the speech, Gabriel is not saying what he really feels. Note for example his imminent description of Aunt Julia's singing as 'a surprise and a revelation'. As she has not lost her gifts, what does he really mean? Later he will imagine Aunt Julia's death: she is soon to be 'a shade with the shade of Patrick Morkan and his horse' (197f).

j) *award the prize*: The prize of Paris was a golden apple, on which the words 'For the fairest' were inscribed. (Ignatius Gallaher speaks of awarding the palm, but that is a gladiatorial award.)

k) *hastened to his close*: This is where the Browning quotation was to have been used. Gabriel decides against it.

l) *self-won*: The affection and respect that the Misses Morkan enjoy was achieved not conferred.

a We have all of us living duties and living affections which claim, and rightly claim, our strenuous endeavours—

—Therefore, I will not linger on the past. I will not let any gloomy moralizing intrude upon us here to-night. Here we b are gathered together for a brief moment from the bustle and rush of our everyday routine. We are met here as friends, in c the spirit of good-fellowship, as colleagues also to a certain d extent, in the true spirit of *camaraderie*, and as the guest of e – what shall I call them? – the Three Graces of the Dublin musical world—

f The table burst into applause and laughter at this sally. Aunt Julia vainly asked each of her neighbours in turn to tell her what Gabriel had said.

—He says we are the Three Graces, Aunt Julia, said Mary Jane—

Aunt Julia did not understand but she looked up, smiling, at Gabriel, who continued in the same vein:

—Ladies and Gentlemen—

g —I will not attempt to play to-night the part that Paris played on another occasion. I will not attempt to choose between them. The task would be an invidious one and one beyond my poor powers. For when I view them in turn, h whether it be our chief hostess herself, whose good heart, whose too good heart, has become a byword with all who know her; or her sister, who seems to be gifted with perennial i youth and whose singing must have been a surprise and a revelation to us all to-night; or, last but not least, when I consider our youngest hostess, talented, cheerful, hard-working and the best of nieces, I confess, Ladies and Gentlemen, that I j do not know to which of them I should award the prize—

Gabriel glanced down at his aunts and, seeing the large smile on Aunt Julia's face and the tears which had risen to Aunt k Kate's eyes, hastened to his close. He raised his glass of port gallantly, while every member of the company fingered a glass expectantly, and said loudly:

—Let us toast them all three together. Let us drink to their health, wealth, long life, happiness and prosperity, and may l they long continue to hold the proud and self-won position which they hold in their profession and the position of honour and affection which they hold in our hearts—

All the guests stood up, glass in hand, and, turning towards

a) For they are jolly gay fellows: A drinking song and still a popular refrain, usually sung as 'jolly good' and in the singular.

b) Unless he tells a lie: But this is a trait of many of these Dubliners. Nowadays these lines are usually rendered 'And so say all of us'. Joyce rewrote the song in a letter of January 1927 to his patron, Miss Weaver.

c) *The piercing morning air . . .* : It contrasts with that in the second sentence of *U*. This marks the beginning of the third part of the story. It is unstated how much time has elapsed, or what has happened since the meal. Most of the guests have left.

d) *get her death*: A thematic detail. The phrase is a translation from the Irish, where 'to die' is rendered 'to get death' (*bás a fháil*). French constructions such as '*J'ai faim*' are closely related.

e) *Browne is everywhere*: His ubiquity is trying.

f) *laid on here like the gas*: A relatively recent Dublin utility. Mr Browne is similarly 'on tap'.

The Great Trebelli (177m)

the three seated ladies, sang in unison, with Mr Browne as leader:

a

> *For they are jolly gay fellows,*
> *For they are jolly gay fellows,*
> *For they are jolly gay fellows,*
> *Which nobody can deny.*

Aunt Kate was making frank use of her handkerchief and even Aunt Julia seemed moved. Freddy Malins beat time with his pudding-fork and the singers turned towards one another, as if in melodious conference, while they sang with emphasis:

b

> *Unless he tells a lie,*
> *Unless he tells a lie,*

Then, turning once more towards their hostesses, they sang:

> *For they are jolly gay fellows,*
> *For they are jolly gay fellows,*
> *For they are jolly gay fellows,*
> *Which nobody can deny.*

The acclamation which followed was taken up beyond the door of the supper-room by many of the other guests and renewed time after time, Freddy Malins acting as officer with his fork on high.

.   .   .   .

c The piercing morning air came into the hall where they were standing so that Aunt Kate said:

d —Close the door, somebody. Mrs Malins will get her death of cold—

—Browne is out there, Aunt Kate, said Mary Jane—

e —Browne is everywhere, said Aunt Kate, lowering her voice—

Mary Jane laughed at her tone.

—Really, she said archly, he is very attentive—

f —He has been laid on here like the gas, said Aunt Kate in the same tone, all during the Christmas—

She laughed herself this time good-humouredly and then added quickly:

—But tell him to come in, Mary Jane, and close the door. I hope to goodness he didn't hear me—

At that moment the halldoor was opened and Mr Browne

1 N.—Denmark-street, Gt.
From Gardiner's-row to Temple-street.
P. St. George.—Rotunda W.

1 and 2 Barry, Mrs. private hotel, 58l., 58l.
3 Kennedy, Hugh Vincent, solicitor, commissioner of oaths, 55l.
4 Dwyer, F. Conway, M.D. surgeon to Jervis-street hospital, 60l. rere—M'Donnell, 5l.
5 & 6 *College of Saint Francis Xavier,* 220l.
  Henry, Rev. William, s.j. rector
  Campbell, Rev. Richard, s.j.
  Ryan, Rev. F. X. s.j.
  Farley, Rev. Charles, s.j.
  Cullen, Rev. James A. s.j.
  Tunney, Rev. Hugh, s.j.
  M'Donnell, Rev. Joseph, s.j.
  Kirwan, Rev. James, s.j.
  Doyle, Rev. Charles, s.j.
  Egan, Rev. Michael, s.j.
  O'Brien, Rev. John, s.j.
  Sillery, Rev. George, s.j.
7 Ellis, Mrs. 60l.
8 Kennedy, Hugh B. L.R.C.S.I. 52l.
9 Bodkin, Math. M'Donnell, Q.C. 40l.
10 M'Cluskey, Miss, Northern private hotel, 48l.
11 *Eblana Private Hotel*—Mrs. Nora Hishon, proprietress, 48l.
  „ Hishon, D. J. insurance agent
12 Kearney, Mrs., 30l.
13 Hughes, Henry, tea & wine mercht. 42l.
  „ TOWN SUB-POST OFFICE, MONEY ORDER AND SAVINGS BANK OFFICE —Henry Hughes, sub-postmaster
....*here Temple-street, Upper, intersects*...
14 Kennedy, Mrs. E. hosiery and drapery house, 27l.
14* Beggs, N. G., C.E., and architect.
15 Earner, Thomas, fruiterer, 27l.
16 Howse, A. M. stationer, 27l.
17 Smyth, Miss Henrietta, fruiterer, 19l.
18 Lynch, Mrs. M. Woodville dairy, 19l.
19 Miller, Fredk. J. L.P.S.I. chemist, qualified dispenser, A.H.D.—res. 13 Belgrave-sq. Rathmines, 23l.
19 *Glennon, Patrick, house painter and decorator
20 Short, Patrick J. boot and shoe warehouse, & May-mount, Howth, 12l.
21 Browne, Mervyn Archdale, prof. of music, organist, mus. dir. 40l.
North City Academy of Music—Mervyn A. Browne, principal.

4 S.—Denzille-lane.
From Hamilton-row to Holles-street.
P. St. Peter.—Trinity W.

6 to 9 Lynch, P. marine stores, 13l.
11 Vacant
13 Murphy, John, car owner

4 S.—Denzille-street.
From Holles-street to Hamilton-row.

From the 1897 Thom's: *Mr Browne and some of his recognisable neighbours*

Henrik Ibsen (1828–1906): a lingering presence

a) *laughing as if his heart would break*: An opaque oxymoron. Joyce used the expression again in *FW* (159):

> But the river tripped on her by and by, lapping as though her heart was brook: *Why, why, why! Weh, O weh! I'se so silly to be flowing but I no canna stay!*

b) *Miss O'Callaghan*: This is the first mention of her: presumably she is the last remaining guest of those who did not attend the family meal. Bartell D'Arcy, whose amorous nature is commented on in *U*, seems to have made a dead set at her.

c) *fooling at the piano*: Originally 'strumming', i.e. vamping.

d) *at home*: Despite her thirty-year residence at Usher's Island, Aunt Julia still feels an exile from the old place on the north side, ten minutes' walk across the nearest bridge.

e) *old gentleman ... a glue-boiler*: Quite possibly, though being both would take much contriving. At Clongowes Wood College (*P* I.2), young Stephen is asked by Nasty Roche what his father is. His answer, 'A gentleman', is quickly followed up: 'Is he a magistrate?' Joyce's own criterion was given in 'Gas from a Burner', in a swipe at George Moore,

a genuine gent
That lives on his property's ten per cent.

As for glue, it was traditionally derived from dead horses. There were many knackers in the Back Lane area (though that word's connections with sex and death are post-Joycean). That tanners so abounded recalls the grave-digging scene in *Hamlet*, and the Clown's observation that Adam was a gentleman.

f) *starch*: A passing reminder of the working world of 'Clay'.

came in from the doorstep, laughing as if his heart would
a break. He was dressed in a long green overcoat with mock
astrakhan cuffs and collar and wore on his head an oval fur
cap. He pointed down the snow-covered quay from where the
sound of shrill prolonged whistling was borne in.

—Teddy will have all the cabs in Dublin out, he said—

Gabriel advanced from the little pantry behind the office,
struggling into his overcoat and, looking round the hall,
said:

—Gretta not down yet?—

—She's getting on her things, Gabriel, said Aunt Kate—

—Who's playing up there? asked Gabriel—

—Nobody. They're all gone—

—O no, Aunt Kate, said Mary Jane. Bartell D'Arcy and
b Miss O'Callaghan aren't gone yet—

c —Someone is fooling at the piano, anyhow, said Gabriel—

Mary Jane glanced at Gabriel and Mr Browne and said with
a shiver:

—It makes me feel cold to look at you two gentlemen
muffled up like that. I wouldn't like to face your journey home
at this hour—

—I'd like nothing better this minute, said Mr Browne
stoutly, than a rattling fine walk in the country or a fast drive
with a good spanking goer between the shafts—

d —We used to have a very good horse and trap at home, said
Aunt Julia sadly—

—The never-to-be-forgotten Johnny, said Mary Jane, laughing—

Aunt Kate and Gabriel laughed too.

—Why, what was wonderful about Johnny? asked Mr
Browne—

—The late lamented Patrick Morkan, our grandfather that
is, explained Gabriel, commonly known in his later years as
e the old gentleman, was a glue-boiler—

f —O, now, Gabriel, said Aunt Kate, laughing, he had a starch
mill—

—Well, glue or starch, said Gabriel, the old gentleman had
a horse by the name of Johnny. And Johnny used to work in
the old gentleman's mill, walking round and round in order
to drive the mill. That was all very well; but now comes the
tragic part about Johnny. One fine day the old gentleman

The statue of King William III, on College Green (f)

a) *drive out with the quality*: In order to drive out with Dublin's 'top people', Mr Morkan must first drive in to where they set off from. Stonybatter is quite close to the Parkgate, so he has to go directly away from it, riding east to College Green (and perhaps even to Merrion Square or Ballsbridge), before turning back westward for the park. On 'the quality', see 37i.

b) *stock collar*: The old-fashioned accompaniment to gaiters (138c).

c) *ancestral mansion*: Only the 'glue factory' was in this area. Gabriel is teasing his aunts about the shabbiness and smelliness of Back Lane.

d) *Back Lane*: Near Christ Church Cathedral. It was once the site of an illicit (unchartered) church and Jesuit teaching institution (referred to at *FW* (287)), suppressed in 1630. Later there was a Back Lane Parliament, a short-lived movement of the United Irishmen (112c). In 1850 one M. Murray (perhaps a relation of Joyce's mother's family) ran a leather warehouse at No 2. At No 49, Mary Murray was a provision dealer.

e) *the mansion of his forefathers*: A hint of John's gospel (XIV.2):

> In my Father's house are many mansions.
> In this mansion there were many forefathers.

f) *the horse King Billy sits on*: Irish Nationalists celebrated the horse for throwing the supremacist king to his death. The statue of it and King Billy stood in College Green, outside both Trinity and the Irish Parliament. It was by the sculptor Grinling Gibbons, and was erected in 1701 (in the king's own lifetime). In the next two centuries, however, it was much vandalised. Even the Trinity 'bloods', Unionist in sympathy, traditionally defined it as an insult to be constantly faced with a horse's arse.

g) *King Billy*: The colloquial name for William III (of Orange), who vanquished King James II and VII at the Battle of the Boyne (4g) in 1690, and brought about the Protestant Ascendancy in Ireland. His victory was celebrated at the Vatican with a *Te Deum*.

h) *paced in a circle*: The endless grind recalls Dante's sinners and Shakespeare's Fortune (160e). Gabriel's story, however, suggests that Johnny may once have been a 'Protestant horse': in Chapter 25 of George Borrow's *Wild Wales* (1862), an Irish fiddler describes

> the glorious first of July when with my whole body covered with Orange ribbons I fiddled

thought he'd like to drive out with the quality to a military review in the park—

—The Lord have mercy on his soul, said Aunt Kate compassionately—

—Amen, said Gabriel. So the old gentleman, as I said, harnessed Johnny and put on his very best tall hat and his very best stock collar and drove out in grand style from his ancestral mansion somewhere near Back Lane, I think—

Every one laughed, even Mrs Malins, at Gabriel's manner and Aunt Kate said:

—O now, Gabriel, he didn't live in Back Lane, really. Only the mill was there—

—Out from the mansion of his forefathers, continued Gabriel, he drove with Johnny. And everything went on beautifully until Johnny came in sight of King Billy's statue: and whether he fell in love with the horse King Billy sits on or whether he thought he was back again in the mill, anyhow he began to walk round the statue—

Gabriel paced in a circle round the hall in his goloshes amid the laughter of the others.

—Round and round he went, said Gabriel, and the old gentleman, who was a very pompous old gentleman, was highly indignant. *Go on, sir! What do you mean, sir? Johnny! Johnny! Most extraordinary conduct! Can't understand the horse!*—

The peals of laughter which followed Gabriel's imitation of the incident were interrupted by a resounding knock at the halldoor. Mary Jane ran to open it and let in Freddy Malins. Freddy Malins, with his hat well back on his head and his shoulders humped with cold, was puffing and steaming after his exertions.

—I could only get one cab, he said—

—O, we'll find another along the quay, said Gabriel—

—Yes, said Aunt Kate. Better not keep Mrs Malins standing in the draught—

Mrs Malins was helped down the front steps by her son and Mr Browne and, after many manœuvres, hoisted into the cab. Freddy Malins clambered in after her and spent a long time settling her on the seat, Mr Browne helping him with advice. At last she was settled comfortably and Freddy Malins invited Mr Browne into the cab. There was a good deal of confused talk, and then Mr Browne got into the cab. The cabman settled

Croppies Lie Down, Boyne Water, and the Protestant Boys before the procession which walked round Willie's figure on horseback in College Green, the man and horse all ablaze with Orange colours. But nothing lasts under the sun ...

The fiddler goes on to excoriate the other side, complaining that 'Daniel O'Connell never gave me the sovereign he promised me for Croppies Get Up', which he had promised to play 'under the nose of the Lord-Lieutenant himself', and goes into exile denouncing repealers and 'emancipators'.

i) *his hat well back on his head*: So too Lenehan (42e), another wastrel – and also Eveline's Frank.

The ghosts of Trinity Library (a)

186

his rug over his knees, and bent down for the address. The confusion grew greater and the cabman was directed differently by Freddy Malins and Mr Browne, each of whom had his head out through a window of the cab. The difficulty was to know where to drop Mr Browne along the route and Aunt Kate, Aunt Julia and Mary Jane helped the discussion from the doorstep with cross-directions and contradictions and abundance of laughter. As for Freddy Malins he was speechless with laughter. He popped his head in and out of the window every moment, to the great danger of his hat, and told his mother how the discussion was progressing, till at last Mr Browne shouted to the bewildered cabman above the din of everybody's laughter:

—Do you know Trinity College?—

—Yes, sir, said the cabman—

—Well, drive bang up against Trinity College gates, said Mr Browne, and then we'll tell you where to go. You understand now?—

—Yes, sir, said the cabman—

a —Make like a bird for Trinity College—

b —Right, sir, said the cabman—

The horse was whipped up and the cab rattled off along the c quay amid a chorus of laughter and adieus.

Gabriel had not gone to the door with the others. He was d in a dark part of the hall gazing up the staircase. A woman was standing near the top of the first flight, in the shadow also. He could not see her face but he could see the terracotta and e salmon-pink panels of her skirt which the shadow made appear black and white. It was his wife. She was leaning on the banisters, listening to something. Gabriel was surprised at her stillness and strained his ear to listen also. But he could hear little save the noise of laughter and dispute on the front steps, a few chords struck on the piano and a few notes of a man's voice singing.

He stood still in the gloom of the hall, trying to catch the air that the voice was singing and gazing up at his wife. There was grace and mystery in her attitude as if she were a symbol f of something. He asked himself what is a woman standing on the stairs in the shadow, listening to distant music, a symbol g of. If he were a painter he would paint her in that attitude. Her h blue felt hat would show off the bronze of her hair against the

a) *Make like a bird for Trinity College*: But there is no direct route from Usher's Island. Perhaps speed rather than direction is implied.

b) *said the cabman*: The third 'said' is a dry improvement on 'cried', when the jarvey is so much put upon.

c) *adieus*: Until publication, Joyce had 'adieux'.

d) *A woman . . .*: It seems that Gabriel may not at first recognise Gretta.

e) *terracotta and salmon-pink panels*: Gretta's clothing indicates the Conroys' prosperity, and is a sight more Grafton Street than Galway. In *U*, 'Calypso', Bloom remembers Molly asking, 'What had Gretta Conroy on?'

f) *a symbol of*: As in the previous sentence, Gabriel wonders what Gretta's revery might mean, but has no answer. Answers will come later. In her profound regret, the music she hears is not the music Gabriel hears. It is significant that Joyce advertises his symbolism thus, and that Gabriel reflects on 'grace and mystery'.

g) *If he were a painter*: Joyce, in his 1899 essay 'Ecce Homo' described a pale and emotional woman on a staircase, her hair blown over her arms:

Her expression is reverential, her eyes are straining up through her tears . . .

h) *the bronze of her hair*: Nora Barnacle's most striking feature was her magnificent hair. In *U*, 'Sirens', Miss Lydia Douce ('Aren't men frightful idiots?') has something of the same quality, bronze to Miss Mina Kennedy's gold.

a) Distant Music: Paintings with such titles were a sentimental staple of Victorian genre painting. There is here an invocation of Sheridan Le Fanu's *All in the Dark* (1866):

> She had quite vanished up the stairs, and he still held the door handle in his fingers, and stood looking up the distant steps, and, as it were, listening to distant music.

b) *the old Irish tonality*: The plangent tones of indigenous Irish balladry have similarities with the music of the Near East. Moore's *Melodies* (with the help of Sir John Stevenson) westernised Europe's westernmost music and made it fit for the parlour.

c) O, the rain falls . . .: Originally Scottish, the song travelled and developed over many years, and was long known as 'The Lass of Roch Royall'. Child's *Ballads*, the standard work, gives eleven versions of the song, so Bartell D'Arcy has good reason for being uncertain of the words. The song has a strong affinity with the *Romeo and Juliet* theme of importunate death. It tells of two lovers, high- and low-born, who are separated by the machinations of Lord Gregory's mother. In one version, 'the lass' kills herself, believing wrongly that she and her child have been rejected: when Lord Gregory finds her body, he too commits suicide. This Irish version was noted in County Westmeath c. 1830. (The setting is a false conversation through a closed door.):

> If you'll be the lass of Aughrim,
> As I am taking you mean to be,
> Tell me the first token
> That passed between you and me.
>
> O don't you remember
> That night on yon lean hill,
> When we both met together,
> Which I am sorry now to tell.
>
> The rain falls on my yellow locks
> And the dew it wets my skin;
> My babe lies cold within my arms:
> Lord Gregory let me in.

It was from Nora that Joyce first heard the song, and later her mother sang it to him in Galway. In August 1909 he wrote from Dublin to his beloved:

> The tears come into my eyes and my voice trembles with emotion when I sing that lovely air.

d) *hoarse as a crow*: The crow, a symbol of discord and strife, makes its second appearance in the story. The 'roughly' economically describes both Mr D'Arcy's manner and his voice.

One version of Bartell D'Arcy's song (c)

darkness and the dark panels of her skirt would show off the

a light ones. *Distant Music* he would call the picture if he were a painter.

The halldoor was closed; and Aunt Kate, Aunt Julia and Mary Jane came down the hall, still laughing.

—Well, isn't Freddy terrible? said Mary Jane. He's really terrible—

Gabriel said nothing but pointed up the stairs towards where his wife was standing. Now that the halldoor was closed the voice and the piano could be heard more clearly. Gabriel held up his hand for them to be silent. The song seemed to be in

b the old Irish tonality and the singer seemed uncertain both of his words and of his voice. The voice, made plaintive by distance and by the singer's hoarseness, faintly illuminated the cadence of the air with words expressing grief:

c
> *O, the rain falls on my heavy locks*
> *And the dew wets my skin,*
> *My babe lies cold …*

—O, exclaimed Mary Jane. It's Bartell D'Arcy singing, and he wouldn't sing all the night. O, I'll get him to sing a song before he goes—

—O, do, Mary Jane, said Aunt Kate—

Mary Jane brushed past the others and ran to the staircase, but before she reached it the singing stopped and the piano was closed abruptly.

—O, what a pity! she cried. Is he coming down, Gretta?—

Gabriel heard his wife answer yes and saw her come down towards them. A few steps behind her were Mr Bartell D'Arcy and Miss O'Callaghan.

—O, Mr D'Arcy, cried Mary Jane, it's downright mean of you to break off like that when we were all in raptures listening to you—

—I have been at him all the evening, said Miss O'Callaghan, and Mrs Conroy, too, and he told us he had a dreadful cold and couldn't sing—

—O, Mr D'Arcy, said Aunt Kate, now that was a great fib to tell—

d —Can't you see that I'm as hoarse as a crow? said Mr D'Arcy roughly—

He went into the pantry hastily and put on his overcoat.

a) *It's the weather*: Predictably, Aunt Julia does not drop the subject. The weather remains a never-failing topic of conversation in Ireland and Great Britain.

b) *snow like it for thirty years*: The Misses Morkan have an easy way of remembering, as that was when they moved from the family home in Stonybatter. Such weather both affirms and denies the josser's comment (16k) that the weather has changed since his day. Presumably he would feel at home in this – if still alive.

c) *in the newspapers that the snow is general*: Read in the *Freeman's General* (7k) perhaps. The phrase recurs to Gabriel later. The significance of the snow has been interpreted in many ways (including life-in-death, Ibsen, Ireland, a shroud, history, Benediction, etc). The actual weather of early January 1904 had no snow.

d) *the dusty fanlight*: Virtually a symbol of Joyce's Dublin, though Gogarty himself (after reading Tolstoy) could also be lyrical about such a detail, as in 'Ringsend':

> I will live in Ringsend
> With a red-headed whore,
> And the fanlight gone in
> Where it lights the hall-door …

e) *the flame of the gas*: 15 Usher's Island had a gaslight incorporated in the fanlight over the front door, to shine both into the hall and onto the steps outside the house.

f) *the rich bronze of her hair*: see 186h.

g) *the same attitude*: An attitude, as has been said, of 'grace and mystery' (186f).

h) *colour on her cheeks and that her eyes were shining*: These are pointers that Gabriel grossly misinterprets. There are tears in her eyes.

i) *A sudden tide of joy*: Gabriel has a moment of spontaneous and unselfish love, quite different from Eveline's spasm when 'All the seas of the world tumbled about her heart' (33b).

j) The Lass of Aughrim: The title for the Irish version of 'The Lass of Roch Royall'. Aughrim is a small town in County Galway, about halfway between Galway City and Athlone. Irish history being what it is, there was a battle here in July 1691, when an Irish army, led by Patrick Sarsfield and the French general Marshall St Ruth (fighting for James II and VII), was defeated by the forces of William III, after St Ruth was killed by a cannonball. 41 Aughrim Street, off the North Circular Road, was the Dublin address of Mary Ellen Callanan (158l).

k) *she shepherded them*: The famous Christmas carol, 'While shepherds watched their flocks by night', was written by Nahum Tate, Dubliner and Poet Laureate (in 1692). He unfortunately features in Pope's *Dunciad* (79g).

The fanlight (e)

The others, taken aback by his rude speech, could find nothing to say. Aunt Kate wrinkled her brows and made signs to the others to drop the subject. Mr D'Arcy stood swathing his neck carefully and frowning.

_a —It's the weather, said Aunt Julia, after a pause—

—Yes, everybody has colds, said Aunt Kate readily, everybody—

—They say, said Mary Jane, we haven't had snow like it for

_b thirty years; and I read this morning in the newspapers that the

_c snow is general all over Ireland—

—I love the look of snow, said Aunt Julia sadly—

—So do I, said Miss O'Callaghan. I think Christmas is never really Christmas unless we have the snow on the ground—

—But poor Mr D'Arcy doesn't like the snow, said Aunt Kate, smiling—

Mr D'Arcy came from the pantry, fully swathed and buttoned, and in a repentant tone told them the history of his cold. Every one gave him advice and said it was a great pity and urged him to be very careful of his throat in the night air. Gabriel watched his wife, who did not join in the conversation.

_d She was standing right under the dusty fanlight and the flame

_e of the gas lit up the rich bronze of her hair, which he had seen

_f her drying at the fire a few days before. She was in the same

_g attitude and seemed unaware of the talk about her. At last she turned towards them and Gabriel saw that there was colour on

_h her cheeks and that her eyes were shining. A sudden tide of

_i joy went leaping out of his heart.

—Mr D'Arcy, she said, what is the name of that song you were singing?—

_j —It's called *The Lass of Aughrim*, said Mr D'Arcy, but I couldn't remember it properly. Why? Do you know it?—

—*The Lass of Aughrim*, she repeated. I couldn't think of the name—

—It's a very nice air, said Mary Jane. I'm sorry you were not in voice to-night—

—Now, Mary Jane, said Aunt Kate, don't annoy Mr D'Arcy. I won't have him annoyed—

_k Seeing that all were ready to start she shepherded them to the door, where good-night was said:

—Well, good-night, Aunt Kate, and thanks for the pleasant evening—

The Four Courts

a) *Good-night ... Good-night ...*: There are thirteen good-nights. The passage caps Ophelia's penultimate exit (*Hamlet* IV.v):

> Come my coach. Good night ladies, good night, sweet ladies, good night, good night.

Gretta, like Ophelia, is perturbed. Nearly fifteen years after 'The Dead' was written, Eliot recycled a variation of the idea in Part II of *The Waste Land*.

b) *The morning was still dark*: The time must be well after 2 am (159d).

c) *area railings*: A fleeting reminder of the love of 'Araby' (21(o)), and an anticipation of the little spears of the final passage.

d) *the palace of the Four Courts*: Ireland's foremost legal building, on the north bank of the Liffey. Its construction was begun in 1786. Stanislaus thought it 'a snobbish, utterly stupid, noisy hole'.

e) *holding her skirt up*: The detail recalls the alarmed Atalantas (63j). Stephen remembers his youthful erotic fantasies in *U*, 'Proteus':

> You prayed to the devil in Serpentine avenue that the fubsy widow in front might lift her clothes still more from the wet street. *O si, certo*! Sell your soul for that, do, dyed rags pinned round a squaw.

f) *grace of attitude*: One of three graces in the story.

g) *valorous*: Bold and worthy. Gabriel is thinking himself into a very 'gallant' state of mind. 'Proud', taking its cue from his bounding blood and 'rioting' brain, has the secondary connotation of 'erect' – a word repeated in the next sentence.

h) *secret life*: There was a notorious Victorian pornographic novel called *My Secret Life* by 'Walter'.

i) *burst like stars upon his memory*: Gabriel has memories parallel to Joyce's own. Three scenes follow: the breakfast scene, the platform scene, the furnace scene.

j) *A heliotrope envelope*: Of a purplish colour, like the flower that turns to the sun – hence the name. One of Nora's earliest letters to Joyce was on such stationery.

k) *he could not eat for happiness*: Though Gabriel is 'well-fed', Joyce ostensibly was not. (When Dr Gogarty saw him in 1909 after five years, he remarked 'Jaysus man, you're in phthisis'.) There is a comparison of Gabriel with Mr Duffy of 'A Painful Case', who could not eat for shock and disgust (99f).

l) *platform ... warm palm of her glove*: The first known presents from Nora to Joyce (and *vice versa*) were gloves. He wrote in July 1904 telling her how it had slept beside him ...

a   —Good-night, Gabriel. Good-night, Gretta!—

—Good-night, Aunt Kate, and thanks ever so much. Good-night, Aunt Julia—

—O, good-night, Gretta, I didn't see you—

—Good-night, Mr D'Arcy. Good-night, Miss O'Callaghan—

—Good-night, Miss Morkan—

—Good-night, again—

—Good-night, all. Safe home—

—Good-night. Good-night—

b   The morning was still dark. A dull yellow light brooded over the houses and the river; and the sky seemed to be descending. It was slushy underfoot, and only streaks and patches of snow lay on the roofs, on the parapets of the quay
c   and on the area railings. The lamps were still burning redly in the murky air and, across the river, the palace of the Four
d   Courts stood out menacingly against the heavy sky.

She was walking on before him with Mr Bartell D'Arcy, her shoes in a brown parcel tucked under one arm and her
e   hands holding her skirt up from the slush. She had no longer
f   any grace of attitude, but Gabriel's eyes were still bright with happiness. The blood went bounding along his veins; and the thoughts went rioting through his brain, proud, joyful, tender,
g   valorous.

She was walking on before him so lightly and so erect that he longed to run after her noiselessly, catch her by the shoulders and say something foolish and affectionate into her ear. She seemed to him so frail that he longed to defend her against something and then to be alone with her. Moments of their
hi   secret life together burst like stars upon his memory. A helio-
j   trope envelope was lying beside his breakfast-cup and he was caressing it with his hand. Birds were twittering in the ivy and the sunny web of the curtains was shimmering along the floor:
k   he could not eat for happiness. They were standing on the
l   crowded platform and he was placing a ticket inside the warm palm of her glove. He was standing with her in the cold,
m   looking in through a grated window at a man making bottles
n   in a roaring furnace. It was very cold. Her face, fragant in the
o   cold air, was quite close to his; and suddenly he called out to the man at the furnace:

—Is the fire hot, sir?—

unbuttoned – but otherwise conducted itself very well – like Nora.

In the story, the ticket is perhaps going inside Gretta's glove for safety. There may have been a scene like this on the platform at the North Wall station in 1904. Nora and Joyce boarded the boat separately, lest either family found out and sought to prevent them escaping Dublin.

m) *making bottles*: The bottle-making factories were nearly all in Ringsend (15a), both for ease of export and because it was downwind of most residential districts (even poor old Irishtown). It was in this area that Nora and Joyce first 'walked out', on 16 June 1904. This appears to be a distorted memory of the occasion.

n) *fragrant in the cold air*: An echo of the 'cold fragrant air' which Gabriel brought on his arrival at Usher's Island.

o) *he called out*: Previously 'she'. Gabriel's question is also addressed to Gretta: he is asking about her 'fire' too.

a) *could not hear with*: Previously 'could not hear her with', because of 189(o).

b) *wave of yet more tender joy*: The erotic tone of the passage is similar to that of Stephen's awakening in *P* (V.2):

> what sweet music! His soul was all dewy wet.

c) *fires of stars*: An allusion to Hamlet's letter to Ophelia (II.ii):

> Doubt that the stars are fire;
> Doubt that the sun doth move;
> Doubt truth to be a liar;
> But never doubt I love.

d) *illumined*: *Lux in Tenebris* (149d). Valentine muses in *The Two Gentlemen of Verona* (III.i):

> If I be not by her fair influence
> Fostered, illuminated, cherished, kept alive,
> I fly not death, to fly his deadly doom;
> Tarry I here, I but attend on death
> But fly I hence, I fly away from life.

e) *their souls' tender fire*: As he has elsewhere, Joyce is using repetition to build up a hypnotic effect. 'Tender', for example, appears four times in this paragraph.

f) *no word tender enough to be your name*: Onomastics (2f). The idea is adapted from a letter of Joyce to Nora of September 1904, another link with the Joyces' courtship.

g) *Like distant music*: See 187a.

h) *borne towards him from the past*: A theme of *D* and of 'The Dead' is the influence and weight of the past on the present, and the question of the interpretative role of the artist.

i) *Winetavern Street*: The fair copy of this story had 'Bridgefoot Street', which is at the first bridge towards central Dublin from Usher's Island. Winetavern Street runs north from Christ Church to the Liffey. The ancient street took its name from its many hostelries, now gone. The party has walked past Adam and Eve's (158t) close by.

j) *looking out of the window and seemed tired*: A casual reprise of 'Eveline'.

k) *galloped ... galloping ... galloping*: Romantic adventurism, as in the early stories. There is also a sugges-

tion of the atypical poem by Robert Browning (161b), 'How They Brought the Good News from Ghent to Aix':

> I sprang to the stirrup, and Joris, and he;
> I galloped, Dirck galloped, we galloped all
>
> > three ...

The theme of the poem is joy and sadness (including some deaths) in Gabriel's favoured Low Countries.

l) *old rattling box*: The description brings to mind the Dignam funeral procession in *U*, 'Hades', where the excessive speed of the cortège is noted. Indeed, it is a good description of a coffin itself.

m) *O'Connell Bridge*: From the end of Merchant's Quay, the party has travelled in the cab along Wood Quay, Essex Quay, Wellington Quay and Aston's Quay. O'Connell Bridge is so spacious that it is as broad as it is long. It replaced in 1880 the previous structure, Carlisle Bridge.

n) *white horse*: There is a proverb, 'He that has a white horse and a fair wife never lacks trouble'. Revelation (XIX.11) has:

> And I saw heaven opened, and behold a white horse; and he that sat upon him was called Faithful and True ...

Furthermore, there is a tradition that the Angel Gabriel on a White Horse fought with the prophet Mohammed in the Battle of Badr. Also, Ibsen's *Rosmersholm* also has the recurring imagery of a white horse for death. Joyce's allusion is getting to be hydra-headed.

o) *the statue*: The O'Connell Memorial is no ordinary statue. He stands, 'hugecloaked', many feet above the roadway, on a plinth supported by four allegorical figures – often erroneously supposed to be 'angels'. It was unveiled in 1882, the year of Joyce's birth. The 'patches of snow' on the statue recall Gabriel's caped arrival at his aunts' house.

p) *he nodded familiarly*: As well he might: Joyce (through his Cork father) was a kinsman of the Liberator, who undoubtedly had many descendants. In his diary, Stanislaus opined:

> I have O'Connell blood in me, and an O'Connell face. I would prefer I hadn't. The Joyce blood is better.

a   But the man could not hear with the noise of the furnace.
It was just as well. He might have answered rudely.

b   A wave of yet more tender joy escaped from his heart and
went coursing in warm flood along his arteries. Like the tender
c fires of stars moments of their life together, that no one knew
d of or would ever know of, broke upon and illumined his
memory. He longed to recall to her those moments, to make
her forget the years of their dull existence together and remember only their moments of ecstasy. For the years, he felt, had
not quenched his soul or hers. Their children, his writing, her
e household cares had not quenched all their souls' tender fire.
In one letter that he had written to her then he had said: *Why
is it that words like these seem to me so dull and cold? Is it because*
f *there is no word tender enough to be your name?*

g   Like distant music these words that he had written years
h before were borne towards him from the past. He longed to
be alone with her. When the others had gone away, when he
and she were in the room in the hotel, then they would be
alone together. He would call her softly:

—Gretta!—

Perhaps she would not hear at once: she would be undressing.
Then something in his voice would strike her. She would turn
and look at him . . .

i   At the corner of Winetavern Street they met a cab. He was
glad of its rattling noise as it saved him from conversation. She
j was looking out of the window and seemed tired. The others
spoke only a few words, pointing out some building or street.
k The horse galloped along wearily under the murky morning
l sky, dragging his old rattling box after his heels, and Gabriel
was again in a cab with her, galloping to catch the boat,
galloping to their honeymoon.

m   As the cab drove across O'Connell Bridge Miss O'Callaghan
said:

—They say you never cross O'Connell Bridge without
n seeing a white horse—

—I see a white man this time, said Gabriel—

—Where? asked Mr Bartell D'Arcy—

o   Gabriel pointed to the statue, on which lay patches of snow.
p Then he nodded familiarly to it and waved his hand.

—Good-night, Dan, he said gaily—

When the cab drew up before the hotel Gabriel jumped out

Winetavern Street, looking to Christ Church Cathedral in the old heart of Dublin: where the cab journey began

a) *kerbstone*: The manuscript had 'kerbstone', and so did the 1914 proofs. The 1910 proofs and the 1914 published version had 'curbstone'.

b) *musical and strange and perfumed*: The first and third adjectives have had their place already in the story. 'Strange', however, recalls the letters from Joyce to Nora in August 1909, in which he tells of singing 'The Lass of Aughrim' (187c). He finishes one by saying that there is a place where he would like to kiss Nora now, 'a *strange* place, not on the lips'. That November, Joyce visited Finn's Hotel, where Nora had worked in Dublin, and wrote to Trieste that he missed her terribly, seeing

> a strange land, a strange house, strange eyes and the shadow of a strange strange girl standing silently by the fire ...

c) *run away together ... a new adventure*: Joyce and Nora actually did this, though they did not escape 'from their lives and duties'. Gabriel is not alone in *D* in wishing to seek adventure abroad, but his ambitions do not go far beyond daydreaming.

d) *a great hooded chair*: Thus, as nineteenth-century hotels could be notoriously high-ceilinged and draughty.

e) *head bowed*: A reworking of Nannie ascending the stairs in 'The Sisters'. The description is also reminiscent of the penitent crowds in Dante's *Purgatorio*.

f) *stress of his nails*: Gabriel is stigmatising himself. The crucifixion imagery recurs at the very end of the story.

g) *guttering candle*: Candles are mentioned in the first paragraph of the collection, and in six stories altogether.

h) *a toilet-table*: i.e. at which one grooms oneself.

i) *the tap of the electric-light*: i.e. the switch. When electricity was first introduced, it was often thought of as flowing, and even leaking, like gas or water.

j) *a muttered apology*: It is unclear whether or not the power failure is the responsibility of the hotel. In any case, the power generated at the Pigeon House (13n) has failed to reach Gabriel.

k) *you might remove that handsome article*: A refined variant of 'I bar the candles' (152l), and yet another shunning of the light in these stories.

191

and, in spite of Mr Bartell D'Arcy's protest, paid the driver. He gave the man a shilling over his fare. The man saluted and said:

—A prosperous New Year to you, sir—

—The same to you, said Gabriel cordially—

She leaned for a moment on his arm in getting out of the cab and while standing at the kerbstone, bidding the others good-night. She leaned lightly on his arm, as lightly as when she had danced with him a few hours before. He had felt proud and happy then, happy that she was his, proud of her grace and wifely carriage. But now, after the kindling again of so many memories, the first touch of her body, musical and strange and perfumed, sent through him a keen pang of lust. Under cover of her silence he pressed her arm closely to his side; and, as they stood at the hotel door, he felt that they had escaped from their lives and duties, escaped from home and friends and run away together with wild and radiant hearts to a new adventure.

An old man was dozing in a great hooded chair in the hall. He lit a candle in the office and went before them to the stairs. They followed him in silence, their feet falling in soft thuds on the thickly carpeted stairs. She mounted the stairs behind the porter, her head bowed in the ascent, her frail shoulders curved as with a burden, her skirt girt tightly about her. He could have flung his arms about her hips and held her still, for his arms were trembling with desire to seize her and only the stress of his nails against the palms of his hands held the wild impulse of his body in check. The porter halted on the stairs to settle his guttering candle. They halted too on the steps below him. In the silence Gabriel could hear the falling of the molten wax into the tray and the thumping of his own heart against his ribs.

The porter led them along a corridor and opened a door. Then he set his unstable candle down on a toilet-table and asked at what hour they were to be called in the morning.

—Eight, said Gabriel—

The porter pointed to the tap of the electric-light and began a muttered apology but Gabriel cut him short.

—We don't want any light. We have light enough from the street. And I say, he added, pointing to the candle, you might remove that handsome article, like a good man—

Sackville Street monuments to O'Connell and Nelson: the nationalist perspective is perhaps intended

a) *ghostly*: Not 'ghastly', as has been printed in many editions. The adverb is crucial for the 'ghost' scene that follows.

b) *a large swinging mirror*: Pivoted about its central axis. This is almost the last reflection of the collection.

c) *unhooking her waist*: Loosening the waistband of her 'girt skirt'. There is a parallel with the distraction of the hooked skirt in 'The Sisters'.

d) *diffidence*: The word anticipates a personal dedication of *At Swim-Two-Birds* (1939) by Flann O'Brien. He inscribed a copy:

To James Joyce from the author, Brian O'Nolan, with plenty of what's on page 305.

On page 305 the phrase 'diffidence of the author' was underlined.

e) *Gabriel in a false voice*: Could he be lying? Gabriel at any rate is making small-talk as his romantic stratagem has failed. Gretta is the third woman to rebuff him in the story.

f) *sovereign*: If the loan was returned, it happened offstage (183c). Gabriel is financially even (except for his payment to the cab-driver). It is even possible that Freddy wheedled the coin from Lily (163f) – or that she gave it to him out of revulsion. Money, like men, can go in circles (even though Bloom's marked florin (in *U*, 'Ithaca') never ascertainably did).

g) *really*: Previously 'at heart'.

h) *her strange mood*: It is not long since Gabriel was celebrating her strangeness (191b).

192

The porter took up his candle again, but slowly, for he was surprised by such a novel idea. Then he mumbled good-night and went out. Gabriel shot the lock to.

a   A ghostly light from the street lamp lay in a long shaft from one window to the door. Gabriel threw his overcoat and hat on a couch and crossed the room towards the window. He looked down into the street in order that his emotion might calm a little. Then he turned and leaned against a chest of drawers with his back to the light. She had taken off her hat

b and cloak and was standing before a large swinging mirror,

c unhooking her waist. Gabriel paused for a few moments, watching her, and then said:

—Gretta!—

She turned away from the mirror slowly and walked along the shaft of light towards him. Her face looked so serious and weary that the words would not pass Gabriel's lips. No, it was not the moment yet.

—You looked tired, he said—

—I am a little, she answered—

—You don't feel ill or weak?—

—No, tired: that's all—

She went on to the window and stood there, looking out.

d Gabriel waited again and then, fearing that diffidence was about to conquer him, he said abruptly:

—By the way, Gretta!—

—What is it?—

—You know that poor fellow Malins? he said quickly—

—Yes. What about him?—

—Well, poor fellow, he's a decent sort of chap, after all,

e continued Gabriel in a false voice. He gave me back that

f sovereign I lent him, and I didn't expect it really. It's a pity he wouldn't keep away from that Browne, because he's not a bad

g fellow, really—

He was trembling now with annoyance. Why did she seem so abstracted? He did not know how he could begin. Was she annoyed, too, about something? If she would only turn to him or come to him of her own accord! To take her as she was would be brutal. No, he must see some ardour in her eyes first.

h He longed to be master of her strange mood.

—When did you lend him the pound? she asked, after a pause—

a) *sottish*: Not just drunken, but habitually so. One of the models for Freddy, Edward Malins, had been sottish, and was sent for a cure to Mount Melleray (179a). He died young.

b) *to overmaster*: Hamlet says of his strange actions concerning the ghost (I.v):

> ∙By Saint Patrick but there is Horatio,
> And much offence too. Touching this vision here –
> It is an honest ghost, that let me tell you –
> For your desire to know what is between us,
> Overmaster it as you may.

The word also has a Nietzschean touch, invoking the Übermensch, and recalling Joyce's pseudonym when he wrote to George Roberts (99b) in July 1904 and asked him for a pound.

c) *Christmas-card shop*: Commercial Christmas cards dated from 1862, and such shops rapidly became a feature of a Victorian Christmas. Another model (a) for Freddy was Mrs Lyons' (158f) son, also Freddy, who kept a Christmas-card shop.

d) *tiptoe*: So too Miss Ivors, and also the boy in 'The Sisters' on approaching the dead man.

e) *quaintness*: Also a Chaucerian vulgarity, as Joyce well knew (90e).

f) *impetuous desire*: The adjective means 'vehement' rather than (say) 'whimsical' or 'random'.

g) *yielding*: Joyce's 1924 'pome', 'A Prayer', opens:

> Again!
> *Come, give, yield all your strength to me!*
> From far a low word breathes on the breaking
> > brain
> Its cruel calm, submission's misery,
> Gentling her awe as to a soul predestined.

Pomes Penyeach was published in 1927 mainly to forestall critical and patronal opinion that Joyce – after the manifest strain of writing *U* and the early fragments of *Work in Progress* (later *FW*) – was a brick short of a hod.

h) *bedrail*: Gretta is leaning over the end of the bed, as Polly Mooney and Mrs Kernan have done previously.

i) *stock-still*: Wholly immobile. One of the meanings of 'stock' (found in Spenser and Shakespeare) is 'a man proverbially stupid'.

j) *cheval-glass*: A full-length adjustable mirror, hung in a frame (192b).

Gabriel strove to restrain himself from breaking out into
brutal language about the sottish Malins and his pound. He
longed to cry to her from his soul, to crush her body against
his, to overmaster her. But he said:

—O, at Christmas, when he opened that little Christmas-
card shop in Henry Street—

He was in such a fever of rage and desire that he did not
hear her come from the window. She stood before him for an
instant, looking at him strangely. Then, suddenly raising herself
on tiptoe and resting her hands lightly on his shoulders, she
kissed him.

—You are a very generous person, Gabriel, she said—

Gabriel, trembling with delight at her sudden kiss and at the
quaintness of her phrase, put his hands on her hair and began
smoothing it back, scarcely touching it with his fingers. The
washing had made it fine and brilliant. His heart was brimming
over with happiness. Just when he was wishing for it she had
come to him of her own accord. Perhaps her thoughts had
been running with his. Perhaps she had felt the impetuous
desire that was in him, and then the yielding mood had come
upon her. Now that she had fallen to him so easily, he wondered
why he had been so diffident.

He stood, holding her head between his hands. Then, slipping one arm swiftly about her body and drawing her towards
him, he said softly:

—Gretta dear, what are you thinking about?—

She did not answer nor yield wholly to his arm. He said
again, softly:

—Tell me what it is, Gretta. I think I know what is the
matter. Do I know?—

She did not answer at once. Then she said in an outburst of
tears:

—O, I am thinking about that song, *The Lass of Aughrim*—

She broke loose from him and ran to the bed and, throwing
her arms across the bed-rail, hid her face. Gabriel stood stock-
still for a moment in astonishment and then followed her. As
he passed in the way of the cheval-glass he caught sight of
himself in full length, his broad, well-filled shirtfront, the face
whose expression always puzzled him when he saw it in a
mirror and his glimmering gilt-rimmed eyeglasses. He halted
a few paces from her and said:

193

a) *Galway when I was living with my grandmother*: Nora virtually *verbatim* (196a).

b) *dull . . . dull*: The repetition suggests Pope's denunciaton of 'Dulness', in *The Dunciad* (80b). The original ending of Book III (in 1728) was:

> Then, when these signs declare the mighty Year,
> When the dull stars roll round and reappear;
> *Let there be darkness!* (the dread pow'r shall say)
> All shall be darkness, as it ne'er were Day;
> To their first Chaos Wit's vain works shall fall,
> And universal Dulness covers all!

c) *Michael Furey*: He is an amalgam of two of Nora Barnacle's early admirers: Michael Feeny, who died when he was sixteen, and later, Michael 'Sonny' Bodkin, who died when he was twenty, after leaving his sickbed to sing to Nora in the rain. Joyce reworked these biographical experiences again in *Exiles*, as his notes to the play partly explain.

d) *He was very delicate*: i.e. liable to sickness and disease. His emaciated, tubercular appearance is in strong contract to Gabriel's healthy stoutness.

e) *to go out walking*: Courting, nothing more or less.

f) *that Ivors girl*: Whom Gretta knows as 'Molly'.

g) *the shaft of light*: This, mentioned for the third time, is affecting the identities of those present.

h) *at length*: The meaning is 'eventually' rather than 'slowly' or 'portentously'.

i) *seventeen*: In the manuscript copy of the story, 'nineteen'. Because of Joyce's eye-trouble, Stanislaus acted as amanuensis.

j) *He was in the gasworks*: The occupation is as lowly and honest as it sounds, and contrasts with Gabriel's literary pretentions.

'Who is G. C.?'

—What about the song? Why does that make you cry?—

She raised her head from her arms and dried her eyes with the back of her hand like a child. A kinder note than he had intended went into his voice.

—Why, Gretta? he asked—

—I am thinking about a person long ago who used to sing that song—

—And who was the person long ago? asked Gabriel, smiling—

a —It was a person I used to know in Galway when I was living with my grandmother, she said—

b The smile passed away from Gabriel's face. A dull anger began to gather again at the back of his mind and the dull fires of his lust began to glow angrily in his veins.

—Someone you were in love with? he asked ironically—

—It was a young boy I used to know, she answered, named

c Michael Furey. He used to sing that song, *The Lass of Aughrim*.

d He was very delicate—

Gabriel was silent. He did not wish her to think that he was interested in this delicate boy.

—I can see him so plainly, she said after a moment. Such eyes as he had: big dark eyes! And such an expression in them – an expression!—

—O, then you are in love with him? said Gabriel—

e —I used to go out walking with him, she said, when I was in Galway—

A thought flew across Gabriel's mind.

—Perhaps that was why you wanted to go to Galway with

f that Ivors girl? he said coldly—

She looked at him and asked in surprise:

—What for?—

Her eyes made Gabriel feel awkward. He shrugged his shoulders and said:

—How do I know? To see him perhaps—

g She looked away from him along the shaft of light towards the window in silence.

h —He is dead, she said at length. He died when he was only

i seventeen. Isn't it a terrible thing to die so young as that?—

—What was he? asked Gabriel, still ironically—

j —He was in the gasworks, she said—

Gabriel felt humiliated by the failure of his irony and by the

a) *gasworks. While he had been*: Joyce deleted the previously interpolated sentence 'The irony of his mood soured into sarcasm'.

b) *a pennyboy for his aunts*: A cheap entertainer at family feasts. Gabriel, rejected, feels very foolish.

c) *sentimentalist*: Stephen defines a sentimentalist in his telegram, read out in *U*, 'Scylla and Charybdis' and repeated in 'Oxen of the Sun':

> The sentimentalist is he who would enjoy without incurring the immense debtorship for a thing done.

The definition is plagiarised from *The Ordeal of Richard Feverel*, by George Meredith, of whom Oscar Wilde said (in *The Critic as Artist*) 'Meredith is a prose Browning, and so is Browning'.

The second and last stanza of *Chamber Music* XII (163c) is:

> Believe me rather that am wise
>   In disregard of the divine,
> A glory kindles in those eyes
>   Trembles to starlight. Mine, O Mine!
> No more be tears in moon or mist
> For thee, sweet sentimentalist.

d) *shame ... forehead*: A suggestion perhaps of the mark of Cain (from Genesis IV). Gabriel's creator subsequently became the subject of Stanislaus' striking memoir, *My Brother's Keeper*, whose title was inspired by the same biblical chapter.

e) *I was great with him*: Not pregnant, but from the Irish *mór le* – 'friendly with'. (Compare with 'great wish' in 'The Sisters' (3b).) In the fair copy of the story, the expression here was 'very fond'.

f) *whither he had purposed*: Gabriel's internal pomposity.

g) *Consumption*: At this time in Ireland and Great Britain, the disease (also called tuberculosis) was a big killer. To the extent that it had one, its romantic reputation was derived from the profusion of good-looking young corpses (such as John Keats'). Close up, it was a far from elegant condition.

k) *I think he died for me*: Gretta's guilelessness. There is a clear allusion to Christianity, and also to Yeats' *Cathleen ni Houlihan*, where the old woman (symbol of Ireland) in answer to a similar question replies 'He died for love of me'.

i) *as if, at that hour when he had hoped to triumph*: There is many an 'as if' in 'The Dead'. This clause has the unwieldiness of a translation from Latin (12g).

j) *some impalpable and vindictive being*: The attitude recalls the comment on paralysis in 'The Sisters' – 'some maleficent and sinful being'.

k) *vague world*: The realm of the dead.

l) *come up here to the convent*: Although Gretta's story is wholly based on Nora's, Joyce changed a few details. Nora was associated with both the Convent of Mercy and the Presentation Convent in Galway, but with none in Dublin. Among the convents of Dublin was the Lakelands Convent near the Star of the Sea church, not many miles from the Conroys' home in Monkstown.

m) *his people*: An old joke alleges an Irish marriage proposal: Would you like to be buried with my people?

n) *Oughterard*: In the Joyce Country, in County Galway, about twenty miles from Galway City. In a letter of August 1912 Joyce wrote:

> Today I went to Oughterard and visited the grave-yard of 'The Dead'.

The actual grave of Sonny Bodkin (194c) is at Rahoon on the way back from Oughterard, nearer Galway.

o) *was in decline*: The manuscript version was 'had consumption'.

p) *was such a gentle boy*: Originally 'had such a gentle manner'.

evocation of this figure from the dead, a boy in the gasworks. While he had been full of memories of their secret life together, full of tenderness and joy and desire, she had been comparing him in her mind with another. A shameful consciousness of his own person assailed him. He saw himself as a ludicrous figure, acting as a pennyboy for his aunts, a nervous well-meaning sentimentalist, orating to vulgarians and idealizing his own clownish lusts, the pitiable fatuous fellow he had caught a glimpse of in the mirror. Instinctively he turned his back more to the light lest she might see the shame that burned upon his forehead.

He tried to keep up his tone of cold interrogation but his voice when he spoke was humble and indifferent.

—I suppose you were in love with this Michael Furey, Gretta, he said—

—I was great with him at that time, she said—

Her voice was veiled and sad. Gabriel, feeling now how vain it would be to try to lead her whither he had purposed, caressed one of her hands and said, also sadly:

—And what did he die of so young, Gretta? Consumption, was it?—

—I think he died for me, she answered—

A vague terror seized Gabriel at this answer as if, at that hour when he had hoped to triumph, some impalpable and vindictive being was coming against him, gathering forces against him in its vague world. But he shook himself free of it with an effort of reason and continued to caress her hand. He did not question her again, for he felt that she would tell him of herself. Her hand was warm and moist: it did not respond to his touch, but he continued to caress it just as he had caressed her first letter to him that spring morning.

—It was in the winter, she said, about the beginning of the winter when I was going to leave my grandmother's and come up here to the convent. And he was ill at the time in his lodgings in Galway and wouldn't be let out, and his people in Oughterard were written to. He was in decline, they said, or something like that. I never knew rightly—

She paused for a moment and sighed.

—Poor fellow, she said. He was very fond of me and he was such a gentle boy. We used to go out together, walking, you know, Gabriel, like the way they do in the country. He was

a) *I was in my grandmother's house*: Nora grew up mostly with her maternal grandmother, Catherine Mortimer Healy, in Whitehall, Galway City, rather than in Bowling Green, which is where her mother lived. (In fact the last meeting between Nora and Sonny Bodkin took place in the garden of the Presentation Convent when Nora was living and working there, and not yet sixteen.) In Joyce's notes to *Exiles*, Bodkin is linked with 'convent garden'.

b) *Nuns' Island*: Like Usher's Island (158m), no longer one in any meaningful sense, but where Nora Barnacle used to live in Galway. In the manuscript, the detail read 'Bowling Green', but it was changed.

c) *gravel thrown up against the window*: The detail echoes Gabriel's tapping of the window as he looked out from the party (171n).

d) *as well as well!*: Gretta is being emphatic, using her mind's eye. The expression is short for 'as well as well can be'.

e) *buried in Oughterard*: The inscription on Sonny Bodkin's grave reads:

Michael Marion Bodkin, son of Patrick and Winifred Bodkin died on 11 February 1900 at [the] age of 20.

f) *that he was dead!*: The admirer of Joyce and friend of Beckett, B.S. Johnson, wrote a piece called 'Everybody Knows Somebody Who's Dead' (1972).

g) *It hardly pained him now*: After the outrush of emotion.

WHEN WE DEAD
AWAKEN

A DRAMATIC EPILOGUE
In Three Acts

By *HENRIK IBSEN*

Translated by
WILLIAM ARCHER

LONDON: WILLIAM HEINEMANN
MCM

Ibsen's swan-song, written about by Joyce in 1900

going to study singing only for his health. He had a very good voice, poor Michael Furey—

—Well, and then? asked Gabriel—

—And then when it came to the time for me to leave Galway and come up to the convent he was much worse and I wouldn't be let see him so I wrote him a letter saying I was going up to Dublin and would be back in the summer and hoping he would be better then—

She paused for a moment to get her voice under control and then went on:

—Then the night before I left I was in my grandmother's house in Nuns' Island, packing up, and I heard gravel thrown up against the window. The window was so wet I couldn't see so I ran downstairs as I was and slipped out the back into the garden and there was the poor fellow at the end of the garden, shivering—

—And did you not tell him to go back? asked Gabriel—

—I implored of him to go home at once and told him he would get his death in the rain. But he said he did not want to live. I can see his eyes as well as well! He was standing at the end of the wall where there was a tree—

—And did he go home? asked Gabriel—

—Yes, he went home. And when I was only a week in the convent he died and he was buried in Oughterard, where his people came from. O, the day I heard that, that he was dead!—

She stopped, choking with sobs, and, overcome by emotion, flung herself face downward on the bed, sobbing in the quilt. Gabriel held her hand for a moment longer, irresolutely, and then, shy of intruding on her grief, let it fall gently and walked quietly to the window.

She was fast asleep.

Gabriel, leaning on his elbow, looked for a few moments unresentfully on her tangled hair and half-open mouth, listening to her deep-drawn breath. So she had had that romance in her life: a man had died for her sake. It hardly pained him now to think how poor a part he, her husband, had played in her life. He watched her while she slept, as though he and she had never lived together as man and wife. His curious eyes rested long upon her face and on her hair: and, as he thought

a) *petticoat*: As the book nears its end, there are flurries of evocations of the previous stories. This detail recalls 'Araby'. See 23f.

b) *One boot . . . the fellow of it*: In their positions, these may be symbols of Gabriel and of Michael Furey respectively

c) *riot of emotions*: An echo of Farrington.

d) *silk hat on his knees*: A position of piety last seen in 'Grace' (153q).

e) *The blinds would be drawn down*: As at the beginning of 'The Sisters'.

f) *how Julia had died*: In *U*, 'Ithaca', Stephen thinks of her as still dying. In a letter to Nora in the autumn of 1904, Joyce wrote 'my grand-aunt is dying of stupidity'.

g) *under the sheets*: Shrouds were also known as winding-sheets. Blake wrote a 'Song' (from *Poetical Sketches* (1783)) which ends:

> Bring me an axe and spade,
>   Bring me a winding sheet;
> When I my grave have made,
>   Let winds and tempests beat:
> Then down I'll lie, as cold as clay,
>   True love doth pass away!

h) *all becoming shades*: Ghosts of a kind. One of Yeats' poems on Parnell was called 'To a Shade'.

i) *Better pass boldly*: Michael Furey's very name suggests this.

j) *such a feeling must be love*: In his 1902 essay on Mangan, Joyce wrote:

> Novalis said of love that it was the Amen of the universe.

Novalis was Friedrich Leopold von Hardenburg, a mainstay of the German Romantic movement, whose grief at the death of his fiancée led to his writing prose poems on death and life. His view of Christianity as cyclical has some affinities with Vico's theories. Novalis had the classic Romantic death – from tuberculosis.

Bloom's definition of love (in *U*, 'Cyclops') is also worth considering:

> – But it's no use, says he. Force, hatred, history, all that. That's not life for men and women, insult and hatred. And everybody knows that it's the very opposite of that that is really life.
> – What? says Alf.
> – Love, says Bloom. I mean the opposite of hatred.

k) *the vast hosts of the dead*: The hosts are the dead of history and mythology. The Battle of Aughrim took place near Ballinasloe, which means 'the ford mouth of the hosts', and the epic Irish poem, the *Táin*, has great battles and crowds of dying men. The past weighs heavily on the present.

l) *their wayward and flickering existence*: This is as close in the story as Joyce ever comes to the ectoplasmic ghosts of spiritualism, for which there had recently been a vogue. Joyce's ghosts are less defined, being also projections of the minds of living people as well as the lost spirits of the dead.

m) *His own identity was fading out*: Compare this with what Shelley wrote in 'Adonais':

> The One remains, the many change and pass;
> Heaven's light forever shines, Earth's shadows fly,
> Life, like a dome of many-coloured glass,
> Stains the white radiance of Eternity
> Until Death tramples it to fragments – Die,
> If thou wouldst be with that which thou dost seek!

The spirit of the English poet haunted Joyce. In a note on Nora (for *Exiles*) he wrote:

> Moon. Shelley's grave in Rome. He is rising from it: blond she weeps for him. He has fought in vain for an ideal and died killed by the world. Yet he rises. Graveyard at Rahoon by moonlight where Bodkin's grave is …

of what she must have been then, in that time of her first girlish beauty, a strange friendly pity for her entered his soul. He did not like to say even to himself that her face was no longer beautiful, but he knew that it was no longer the face for which Michael Furey had braved death.

Perhaps she had not told him all the story. His eyes moved to the chair over which she had thrown some of her clothes. A petticoat string dangled to the floor. One boot stood upright, its limp upper fallen down: the fellow of it lay upon its side. He wondered at his riot of emotions of an hour before. From what had it proceeded? From his aunts' supper, from his own foolish speech, from the wine and dancing, the merrymaking when saying good-night in the hall, the pleasure of the walk along the river in the snow. Poor Aunt Julia! She too would soon be a shade with the shade of Patrick Morkan and his horse. He had caught that haggard look upon her face for a moment when she was singing *Arrayed for the Bridal*. Soon perhaps he would be sitting in that same drawing-room, dressed in black, his silk hat on his knees. The blinds would be drawn down and Aunt Kate would be siting beside him, crying and blowing her nose and telling him how Julia had died. He would cast about in his mind for some words that might console her, and would find only lame and useless ones. Yes, yes: that would happen very soon.

The air of the room chilled his shoulders. He stretched himself cautiously along under the sheets and lay down beside his wife. One by one they were all becoming shades. Better pass boldly into that other world, in the full glory of some passion, than fade and wither dismally with age. He thought of how she who lay beside him had locked in her heart for so many years that image of her lover's eyes when he had told her that he did not wish to live.

Generous tears filled Gabriel's eyes. He had never felt like that himself towards any woman but he knew that such a feeling must be love. The tears gathered more thickly in his eyes and in the partial darkness he imagined he saw the form of a young man standing under a dripping tree. Other forms were near. His soul had approached that region where dwell the vast hosts of the dead. He was conscious of, but could not apprehend, their wayward and flickering existence. His own identity was fading out into a grey impalpable world: the solid

a) *taps*: Also the ghost of Michael Furey's tapping at the window. It is a detail of passion which also invokes Emily Brontë's *Wuthering Heights*, which Joyce admired.

b) *his journey westward*: Going west is famously an expression for death, but here the word is ambiguous. (Unsurprisingly, it also has an ecclesiastical significance: 'Westward', in the early church, was the position of the celebrant of the Eucharist until about the ninth century, facing the people.) 'Westward' also suggests that Gabriel might well follow Miss Ivors' advice and explore Ireland. He has earlier thought of the snow flashing westward across the Phoenix Park (180c), and now his imagination goes further. *D* contains many tensions between east and west, city and country, the Europe of the future and the Ireland of the past. Stephen's diary entry for 14 April (*P* V.4, on John Alphonsus Mulrennan and the old Irishman) is somewhat oracular in this matter.

Joyce himself, in a letter to Nora of December 1909, wrote that he was going to Cork, but

> would prefer to be going westward, toward those strange places whose names thrill me on your lips, Oughterard, Clare-Galway, Coleraine, Oranmore, towards those wild fields of Connacht ...

c) *snow was general*: See 188c. The opening of Bret Harte's interestingly-named novel, *Gabriel Conroy* (1875), has a meteorological hint:

> Snow. Everywhere. As far as the eye could reach – fifty miles, looking southward from the highest white peak – filling ravines and gulches, and dropping from the walls of the cañons in white shroud-like drifts, fashioning the dividing ridge into the likeness of a monstrous grave, hiding the bases of giant pines, and completely covering young trees and larches, rimming with porcelain the bowl-like edges of still, cold lakes, and undulating in motionless white billows to the edge of the distant horizons. Snow lying everywhere over the Californian Sierras on the 15th of March 1848, and still falling ...

d) *falling softly ... softly falling*: After visiting Galway in 1912, Joyce wrote 'She Weeps Over Rahoon' (197m) on the same subject, which later appeared in *Pomes Penyeach*:

> Rain on Rahoon falls softly, softly falling ...

In *P* (III.2) Stephen's imagination similarly addresses the rain:

> Rain was falling on the chapel, on the garden, on the college. It would rain for ever, noiselessly.

There is a burlesque of (or tribute to) Joyce's ending of 'The Dead' at the end of Beckett's 'A Wet Night' (in *More Pricks than Kicks*) and also in Edna O'Brien's *The Country Girls*.

e) *Bog of Allen*: To the west of Clongowes Wood College, south of the Grand Canal, in counties Offaly and Kildare. It is therefore directly between Dublin and Galway.

f) *dark mutinous Shannon waves*: The River Shannon curves through Ireland, and for much of its length is regarded as the boundary between the West and the rest of the country. 'Waves' implies the Shannon estuary. Though derivation from a Vergilian simile has been suggested here, Joyce took the detail from Thomas Moore's 'O Ye Dead', having had his attention drawn to it by Stanislaus:

> Oh, ye Dead! oh, ye Dead! whom we know by
> the light you give
> From your cold gleaming eyes, though you move
> like men who live—
> Why leave you thus your graves,
> In far-off fields and waves,
> Where the worm and the sea-bird only know your
> bed,
> To haunt this spot, where all
> Those eyes that wept your fall,
> And the hearts that bewailed you, like your own,
> lie dead?

In 1935 he was recommending that his son Giorgio sing it.

g) *thickly drifted ... the snow falling*: Like the *Inferno*, the book ends with a view of a desolate frozen landscape. Dublin, like Dante's Cocytus, is an emotional and moral territory too.

h) *crosses ... spears ... thorns*: Three of the physical agents of Christ's crucifixion.

i) *swooned*: 'swoon' is a partial reversal of 'snow', adding to the assonance.

j) *last end*: see 179g.

k) *the living and the dead*: The Apostle's Creed has the telling detail:

> Hence He shall come to judge the living and the dead.

Gabriel, drifting out, realises that, like his unknown rival, he will soon face his maker. Even virtue is not proof against mortality. Time always passes. Change and decay happen anew.

world itself, which these dead had one time reared and lived in, was dissolving and dwindling.

a   A few light taps upon the pane made him turn to the window. It had begun to snow again. He watched sleepily the flakes, silver and dark, falling obliquely against the lamplight.
b   The time had come for him to set out on his journey westward.
c   Yes, the newspapers were right: snow was general all over Ireland. It was falling on every part of the dark central plain,
de   on the treeless hills, falling softly upon the Bog of Allen and, farther westward, softly falling into the dark mutinous Shannon waves. It was falling, too, upon every part of the
f   lonely churchyard on the hill where Michael Furey lay buried.
gh   It lay thickly drifted on the crooked crosses and headstones, on the spears of the little gate, on the barren thorns. His soul
i   swooned slowly as he heard the snow falling faintly through
j   the universe and faintly falling, like the descent of their last
k   end, upon all the living and the dead.

The cartoonist Thomas Rowlandson drew a cartoon (c. 1812) entitled 'The Dance of Death'. The caption (by William Combe) was quite inexorable.

*The Careful and the Careless led
To join the living and the dead (k)*

'The Dead' is a turning-point in Joyce's personal and artistic development. The shift of attitude towards Dublin is noticeable – warmer, more indulgent. Though he would later write 'Gas from a Burner' and the bleaker passages of the novels, the sardonic hostility to Dublin life that characterises much of *Dubliners* is softened here. Hungry in Rome, he found aspects of his own city to celebrate, in a way that he had not when he was hungry in Paris or anywhere else.

The story moves (like *Ulysses* and *Finnegans Wake*) from the general to the particular, from a lively social scene to the mind of a contemplative, drowsy spouse. The party is as much a success as ever, and yet Gabriel is troubled by the developments of the evening. There is unease too among the other characters.

The *bonhomie* of the occasion is often overlooked, however. Though Gretta's joke about gollyshoes has always gone unappreciated, there is much good humour throughout the evening. Mr Browne goes too far, but many of the other guests show lots of Christmas spirit: it is an evening of much laughter. Even Gabriel somewhat ponderously participates with his antics over Johnny the Horse: and yet Gabriel's shortcomings are made cumulatively more obvious by the successive rebuffs he receives from strong-minded women (who are the true Three Graces of his platitudinous speech). His well-filled shirtfront makes for a deliberate contrast with the thin, loving intensity of Michael Furey. 'The Dead' explores the turning-points of at least three lives.

As the story moves towards its end, Gabriel's mind, instead of thinking of the continent, the home of civilisation and goloshes, stretches westward, to Connacht, the heartland of honest Irish primitivism. ('Going west' was also an early Christian belief about how souls went to heaven – in an Irish context, to the Isles of the Blest.) The drift south and east of the first three stories has been reversed. Gabriel, a would-be cosmopolitan, finally begins to realise that there is something to be said for his home land after all.

At the hotel, Gabriel's persistent emotional dishonesty and emotional ignorance are answered by the shocking intimacy of Gretta's telling him what she is thinking of, a young man who had loved her, and died. Mortality is a hard act to follow. Gabriel at last addresses his own after having felt superseded – even cuckolded – by a ghost. The living Gabriel is less alive than (the no-less-fictional) Michael Furey, buried many years before. Both Conroys feel it. There even exists for the Milton-quoting protagonist of 'The Dead' a Miltonic reminder of his second-best status: in Book VI of *Paradise Lost*, God says:

> Go, Michael of celestial armies prince,
> And thou, in military prowess next
> Gabriel . . .

Religion and literature continue their uneven symbiosis. Joyce's use of the device of the epiphany has often provoked the suggestion that readers are to understand that the Misses Morkan's party (or Gabriel's revelation) takes place on the Feast of the Epiphany, 6 January. The boy(s) of 'An Encounter' and 'Araby' gained some understanding, some 'epiphany' or 'showing forth'. But although they and others (e.g. Mr Duffy and Lenehan) may have dimly recognised manifestations of their own individual spiritual paralysis, it is only Gabriel Conroy who realises that his own death is now pending. He is becoming a shade.

In the library episode of *Ulysses*, the situation of Gabriel (and other Dubliners and Galwegians and Danemen – hyperboreans all, and spirits of Ireland past) is expertly summed up:

– What is a ghost? Stephen said with tingling energy. One who has faded into impalpability, through death, through absence, through change of manners ... Who is the ghost from the *limbo patrum* returning to the world that has forgotten him?

The world will forget Gabriel, and he has already nearly forgotten himself and his purpose in existence. Michael Furey's passion lives on.

The question of the 'meaning' of the story is finally a meaningless one, ineffably so. 'The Dead' is rooted in Joycean autobiography and biography, distilled from a fine mash of ambiguity and deliberate obliquity. Joyce noted the propensity of Celtic philosophers towards 'incertitude or scepticism', and cited Hume, Berkeley, Balfour and Bergson. A similar approach to genial nihilism can also be found in the work of Samuel Beckett (e.g. in *Malone Dies*). Joyce's many devices in the stories of *Dubliners* – including narrative ambiguity, an exploitation of gullibility, shifting repetition, unknowingness, lethal etymology, dry juxtaposition, deft allusion, and a sense of omission – help to suggest that the mystery of life and death must always remain just that. 'Restless living wounding doubt' was preferable for Joyce (as it is for Richard Rowan at the end of *Exiles*) to 'the darkness of belief', the dull certitude of religion. In *Stephen Hero*, Irish dogma likewise is declared to be absurd drivel by Stephen Daedalus, notably in the matter of Jesus Christ:

He comes into the world God knows how, walks on the water, gets out of his grave and goes up off the Hill of Howth.

The casualness of death was sardonically shown at Joyce's own minimalist funeral, in wartime Zurich.

Decades later, it was Nora who was got out of the grave in order to be reburied with her husband. In the *Portrait*, Stephen's diary entry for 21 March, *night* (also Nora's birthday), had already addressed the pressures of mortality.

The weight of the past is especially heavy in Ireland. The country's population is a fraction of what it was in the early nineteenth century. Dublin, (for all the changes of recent decades), still often seems to live on its past glories, on the sanitised myth of one of its Golden Ages, when giants walked in Stephen's Green. Leopold Bloom too, on his quintessential ordinary day, feels the pull of the dead:

How many! All these here once walked round Dublin. Faithful departed. As you are now so once were we.

Very few citizens of Dublin today were alive when Joyce was last there, in 1912. A cityful has passed away, and another cityful has passed away too. Though 'Joyce's Dublin' tends to mean 'everyone's Dublin', the city that Joyce wrote of will remain recognisable for as long as human nature survives. In any individual case, however, there will be an end. Processes such as Gabriel Conroy's transition from a form of self-deception to a form of self-knowledge are not much reducible. Behind a window in O'Connell Street, he is little wiser than the boy (in 'The Sisters') who used to look up to a window just around the corner. Death is a fact, and victorious Michael Furey has experienced it. The details and tone of 'The Dead', given the cumulative effects of *Dubliners*, make it the justified development of the earlier stories, moral paralysis *in excelsis*. As his identity fades, in a frozen, moribund city, Gabriel may draw the blankets over his head and try to think of Christmas; but it is always far too late.

Acknowledgements

We wish to thank many Dubliners, actual and honorary, living and dead. In particular, the book would have been a lesser thing without the wise suggestions of Peter Costello, the painstaking editing of James Woodall and the photographs of Patrick Wyse Jackson.

For their help and encouragement in many other directions, we also thank Bernard and Shari Benstock, Elfi Bettinger, Declan Burke, Mary Costello, Tom Durham, Richard Ellmann, Lorraine Estelle, Andrew Gibson, Vivien Igoe, Rüdiger Imhof, the 3rd Earl of Iveagh, Maria Jolas, Peter van de Kamp, Lucie Léon-Noël, Stephen Lalor, Aibhistin Mac Amhlaidh, Brenda Maddox, John Murray, Robert Nicholson, David Norris, Edna O'Brien, Peggy O'Brien, Seán Ó Mórdha, John Ryan, Maura Scannell, W. B. Stanford, Stephen Stokes, Philip Stolzfus, Brian Tipping, Vicki Traino, Eileen Veale, Katie Wales, D. A. Webb, and many kind and, we hope, forgiving people whom we have accidentally omitted.

For keeping us going during the preparation of this book we thank Lois, Peter, Diane, Vanessa and Michael Wyse Jackson, Margery and Larry Stapleton, Eoghan Mitchell and Biddy Mitchell, Lucy, Julie and Ruth Moller, Johnny, Stewart, Rubio and Perina of John Sandoe (Books) Ltd, David Barry and Isolde Victory, Caroline Bullen, Mike McLaughlin, Judy Dempsey, Margaret McGinley and many other McGinleys – especially Bill.

Thanks are also due to the staffs of the Gilbert Library, Pearse Street, Dublin; the National Library of Ireland; Trinity College Library, Dublin; the Catholic Library, Dublin; the British Library; the Senate House library, London; the London Library; the Manuscripts Room, University College, London; John Thornton Booksellers, London; Cornell University Library; the *James Joyce Broadsheet*; the *James Joyce Literary Supplement*; the *James Joyce Quarterly*; the Society of Authors; the James Joyce Society of London.

Very many sources were consulted in the preparation of this book, and the work of many others facilitated the project. The great majority of the pictures are from the private collections of the authors, who would be glad to hear from any people whom they have inadvertently omitted to thank. The list is necessarily incomplete, but should include Robert Adams, Chester G. Anderson, Bruce Arnold, J. S. Atherton, Derek Attridge, Deborah M. Averill, James R. Baker, Joseph E. Baker, Messrs

BT Batsford & Co., Ruth Bauerle, Samuel Beckett, Morris Beja, Douglas Bennett, David Berman, Bruce Bidwell, Zack Bowen, Brian Boydell, Henry Boylan, Robert Boyle sj, Bruce Bradley sj, Anne M. Brady, Edward Brandabur, Richard Brown, Terence Brown, Frank Budgen, Anthony Burgess, J. F. Byrne, Herbert Cahoon, Joseph Campbell, D. A. Chart, Hélène Cixous, Brian Cleeve, Alan Cohn, Padraic and Mary Colum, Thomas E. Connolly, E. Mac-Dowel Cosgrave, Anthony Cronin, C. P. Curran, Mary E. Daly, Stan Gébler Davies, Leonard de Vries, Frank Delaney, Robert H. Deming, Margaret Drabble, T. S. Eliot, William G. Fallon, Sidney Feshbach, Gerard Flaherty, John Freimarck, Marilyn French, P. K. Garrett, John Garvin, Robert A. Gates, Bernard Gheerbrandt, T. H. Gibbons, Denis Gifford, Don Gifford, Stuart Gilbert, Brewster Ghiselin, Oliver St John Gogarty, Maurice Gorham, Herbert Gorman, Michael Groden, Stephen Gwynn, Nathan Halper, Clive Hart, John Harvey, Johannes Hedberg, Linda Heffer, Suzette Henke, Cheryl Herr, Phillip Herring, Kieran Hickey, Joseph Hone (*père*), Patricia Hutchins, William A. Johnsen, John Jordan, P. W. Joyce, Weston St John Joyce, Richard Kain, Thomas Keating, Sister Eileen Kennedy, Hugh Kenner, R. B. Kershner, Harry Levin, A. Walton Litz, F. S. L. Lyons, J. B. Lyons, Robert McAlmon, Colin MacCabe, Michael McCarthy, Alistair McCleery, Donagh MacDonagh, Roland McHugh, Edward MacLysaght, Marvin Magalaner, Jerome Mandel, Dominic Manganiello, Augustine Martin, Ellsworth Mason, Virginia Moseley, Joseph V. O'Brien, Frank O'Connor, Laurence O'Connor, Ulick O'Connor, Patrick O'Farrell, Brian O'Higgins, Colm O'Lochlainn, Brian O'Nolan, Mary O'Toole, Cóilín Owens, C. H. Peake, Mary Power, Jean-Michel Rabaté, Patrick Rafroidi, Mary T. Reynolds, Thomas J. Rice, J. P. Riquelme, Robert Scholes, Fritz Senn, Patrick W. Shakespeare, Eugene Sheehy, John J. Slocum, Thomas F. Smith, Peter Spielberg, Robert E. Spoo, Thomas F. Staley, Hugh B. Staples, W. D. Stein, Weldon Thornton, W. Y. Tindall, Donald T. Torchiana, Arland Ussher, Florence Walzl, David Weir, Terence de Vere White, Craig Werner, Charles D. Wright, David G. Wright, Robert Wyse Jackson and the brothers Yeats.

Finally, this book is dedicated to
Professor Stanislaus Joyce and to his memory.